San Francisco
Turn-of-the-Century

▨▨▨ AREA NOT DAMAGED BY FIRE, (APRIL 18-20, 1906)

Don Pitcher

Old San Francisco

THE BIOGRAPHY OF A CITY

from Early Days to the Earthquake

Other Books by Doris Muscatine

A COOK'S TOUR OF SAN FRANCISCO
A COOK'S TOUR OF ROME

Old San Francisco

THE BIOGRAPHY OF A CITY

from Early Days to the Earthquake

by DORIS MUSCATINE

G. P. Putnam's Sons, New York

SBN: 399-11594-3

Library of Congress Cataloging in Publication Data

Muscatine, Doris.
  Old San Francisco: the biography of a city from early days to the
earthquake.

  Bibliography.
  Includes index.
  1. San Francisco—History.   I. Title.
F869.S3M88   979.4′61   75-16409

To Jeff and Lissa

ACKNOWLEDGMENTS

I owe thanks to the following friends, colleagues, helpers, staffs, and institutions for their generous assistance and support:

The Bancroft Library: Robert H. Becker, Cecil Lee Chase, Alma Compton, Suzanne H. Gallup, George P. Hammond, Peter Hanff, James D. Hart, Phillip Hoehn, J. R. K. Kantor, Irene Moran, William Roberts, and J. Barr Tompkins;

The California State Library: Ethel S. Crockett; and Kenneth I. Pettitt and the staff of the California Collection;

The Oakland Museum: Dayton Lummis, Lon Rabe, and Gretchen Snyder;

The San Francisco Negro and Cultural Society: Elena Albert and Roy Thomas;

The Silverado Museum: Norman Strouse;

The California Historical Society: Lee Burtis, M. K. Swingle, and Jay Williar;

The Chinese Historical Society: Thomas W. Chinn; the Chinese Cultural Center: Dr. William Wu; and from the Chinese community: the late Johnny Kan, Ching Wah Lee, and Charles Leong for generous advice and assistance;

The Wells Fargo History Room;

The San Francisco Public Library: Kevin Starr; and Gladys Hansen of the Special Collections;

The San Francisco Maritime Museum: Albert Harmon and Karl Kortum;

The Judah L. Magnes Memorial Museum;

The Society of California Pioneers: Irene Lichens;

The Mechanics' Institute;

The Musée National de Céramique de Sèvres: Jean-Paul Fourest and L. B. Nobele; and the Musée de l'Île de France de Sceaux: M. Aries;

Marianne von Adelmann, Wayne Andrews, Rhoda Asnien, Harriet Berg, Carlo Cipolla, Linda Ellinwood, Marlene Griffith, Frances Hailman, Eva Hance, Robert B. Honeyman, Joyce Jansen, Helen Josephine, Anita Lynn, Grace O'Connell, Anthony Pels, James Rawles, Ann Saltzman, Neil Shumsky, Catherine Stearns, Warrington Stokes, Marina Than, Franklin Walker, and L. T. Wallace variously for information, good cheer, and other assistance;

Carl D. Brandt for his friendship and encouragement; Harvey Ginsberg for his constructive editing; Hugh Howard; George Stewart, who most generously turned over his uncompleted manuscript on the Churching of California; Lissa and Jeff Muscatine for many hours of help; and Charles Muscatine for his invaluable criticism.

CONTENTS

Illustrations will be found
following page 224

INTRODUCTION

APART from its physical beauty, San Francisco is unique for its tolerance and for a vivacity that captures resident and visitor alike. Within a century it grew out of a fog-swept wilderness inhabited by a handful of natives into a metropolis as sophisticated and lively as any in the world. Its differences from other cities result in large part from the character of its history.

Its heritage was Spanish-Mexican—that is, Continental and Catholic. When the Gold Rush started, Orientals, South Americans, Australians, and Europeans of every nationality joined hordes of new arrivals from the United States, the latter largely Protestant Anglo-Saxons. Besides being mixed, the resulting population was transient, almost entirely male, and given to discarding past careers with impunity. Thrown into an agglomeration of races, creeds, and religious differences, everyone, the American in particular, was forced into a more liberal environment than might normally have been his choice. The isolation of San Francisco made it easier to suspend old values. Necessity created a tolerance for difference, a habit of accepting an individual for himself. Experience taught that today's millionaire could be tomorrow's pauper and vice versa and that the most successful financial entrepreneur could in an instant be robbed of his life by an enemy or a swift bout of cholera. This atmosphere of variety and change enriched the emerging culture and early established San Francisco as the cosmopolitan community it remains.

Further, an evolution that elsewhere spread over centuries took a fraction of the time in San Francisco. The city withstood in only a few decades a series of monumental bonanzas and disasters of a sort that most communities have never experienced at all: the Gold Rush, the discovery of silver, the development of the transcontinental railroad, two sieges of vigilantism, recurring fires and earthquakes, culminating in the catastrophe of 1906. The city's capacity to adapt, to deal with the unexpected, followed naturally. The people and the events which first shaped San Francisco are the focus of this work.

SECTION ONE
Before Gold

No history . . . of the city, could be complete, unless it included some account of the circumstances which preceded and immediately accompanied its rise, and which have made it what it almost already is, but which it will more plainly soon become, the greatest and most magnificent, wealthy and powerful maritime city in the Pacific—a city which is destined, one day, to be, in riches, grandeur and influence, like Tyre or Carthage of the olden time, or like Liverpool or New York of modern days.

—FRANK SOULÉ, JOHN H. GIHON,
and JAMES NISBET in
The Annals of San Francisco (1885)[1]

I

The Beginnings

THE first San Franciscans were dark-skinned and usually naked. If it was cold, before the sun came up, they coated themselves in mud to keep warm. Sometimes they wore fiber sandals and made mantles out of their rabbitskin bedding. The woman, like so many females in other times and other places, wore an apron, hers of bark or tule or deerskin; but she sported little else except a tattoo, and that was on her face. The tribes whose habitat lay along the coast between the southern portion of San Francisco Bay and Point Sur below Monterey were Costanoans, their name derived from the Spanish word *costano* for coast dweller. In the San Francisco area they included five roughly associated tribal or language groups: the Ahwastes, Olhones or Costanos, Romonans, Tulomos, and Altatmos. The early San Francisco Costanoans used redwood in their houses, chunks and slabs of the bark, but more often wooden poles with brush or tule matting or an earth covering. They didn't expend much on dwellings since they moved so often. The men loved a good sweat and built temescals—sweathouses—where, amid a profusion of perspiration, a great deal of male socializing took place. After that daily ritual they bathed in the nearest water and dried off by rolling in the dirt like a dervish. No doubt this custom helped brand them as "filthy" in the eyes of the white men who were later to observe them, but this view wasn't universal. The ethnologist Stephen Powers found the aboriginal sweet of breath and white of teeth, and reported that "there is no nation, unless it was the ancient Romans, who bathed oftener than they."[2]

Their life was relatively peaceful, unmarked by barbarous puberty rites or bloody battles with neighbors. Their arsenal was meager: no shields, few weapons of war, no infernal devices beyond simple hunting tools. When disagreements reached the point of physical violence, they were as likely settled by an exchange of gifts from one chief to another as by bloodshed and terror. If there were occasional captives, they were never tortured.

17

The people were merrymakers, fond of dancing and singing (their songs were reported as "unusually pleasing to civilized people"[3]), of athletics for the sheer physical enjoyment, of gambling, guessing and number games, religious rituals with all the elaborate costuming and accouterments, of storytelling (a whole oral literature was passed on in the sweathouses), of eating and feasting, and of having a good time generally. Like fashionable Romans or Victorians, they had their favorite out-of-town watering places, warm mineral springs, where they repaired from time to time to take the cure. Marriage was an easy arrangement, usually an exchange of shell money for the bride. Divorce was just as casual. Children, well loved by their elders, went with the mother. Death prompted the removal of every trace of the individual. His body was generally buried although sometimes cremated, his memory never evoked, his possessions demolished to leave no wayward reminders. Even his name was avoided forevermore, and any reference to the deceased was the most horrible affront to his family still living. In fact, such an oath as "Your dead mother!" was to the Costanoan the equivalent of a four-letter word.

As for vices besides swearing and gambling, the Indians smoked tobacco, usually for ritual purposes, and drank a bit of manzanita cider and a kind of beer, but not enough even to be thought of as tippling. They took sexual freedom as a matter of course. They had no word for prostitute, because they had no prostitutes, and they had no venereal diseases, "those appalling maladies which destroyed so many thousands on their first acquaintance with Americans."[4]

They believed that the earth was originally covered with water, from which rose a mountain. On the mountain, Eagle was chief; Humming Bird and Coyote were early inhabitants; Coyote created humans according to Eagle's directions, to inhabit the land when the waters receded. Coyote also had other credits: he married the first woman, brought culture, devised languages, and grouped the humans into tribes, instructing them in obtaining food, houses, and implements. In some accounts he was also a glutton, a lecher, and a tricky customer generally.

Like most California tribes, Costanoans were small, loosely knit groups, moving about to search for food or to escape disease or bad luck. In spite of a great deal of trading back and forth, there was little real influence from one to the other. Throughout California hundreds of different languages and dialects managed to exist side by side, unchanged and often not even understood by neighbors. Government, concerned mostly with such matters as game and fishing rights, consisted of a few well-established rules with rare innovations. Family units generally had a leader, who could settle disputes arising over personal rights. The tribal chief had very limited authority. His function was more philosophical and ceremonial than governmental: he presided over festivities, entertained visitors, and was a generally eloquent orator, delivering long, morally persuasive dissertations peppered with good advice. Indian society offered roles for many different personalities. There were storytellers, song captains, fishermen, hunters, artisans, midwives, and several kinds of doctors. There were herbalists for everyday aches and pains, dispensing angelica for headaches and balm for neuralgia; there were shamans for more serious disorders, who cured by trances, singing, dancing, and witchcraft and who even had some influence over the weather and crops; and there were Indian specialists for the treatment of psychic disorders—which in those days arose from breaking taboos.

The San Francisco Costanoan was an omnivorous fellow, but no glutton—no gorging or Bacchanalian feasting as in some other tribes. He nibbled the lily bulb, along with all the usual berries, seeds, fruits, and grasses, dosed and seasoned with the pepperwood, and replaced salt with seaweed. The acorn was less abundant on the coast than inland, but the early cook, often burning the land to make gathering easier, collected it when he could and made acorn flour for bread and gruel. It wasn't easy. Before he could get rid of the bitter tannic acid, he had to go through six grinding, leaching, drying, and roasting operations. He hunted the deer, raccoon, and bear. He took rabbits with hunting sticks and paddled a tule boat after sea lions and salmon. If a whale was grounded, he ate that, too. In later years, one member of a Russian expedition of 1816 reported the belief that the diet of the California natives also included prisoners taken from shipwrecks.[5] But no subsequent anthropological reportage bears this out.

What he ate most of were clams, mussels, and oysters, the accumulated shells of which made up the kitchen middens or refuse dumps of some 425 Indian campsites along the shores of the Bay. The shellmounds, oval in shape with gently sloping sides, sometimes extended 500 or 600 feet in diameter and as much as 20 or 30 feet in depth. Based on the excavated evidence yielded by strata of mollusk shells, ashes, skeletal remains, broken cooking rocks, charcoal, burned debris, charmstones, and remnants of tools, weapons, and ornaments, archaeologists date the aboriginal habitations back 3,000 and 4,000 years. Since the shellmounds' discovery in the eighteenth century, we know the Californian's life was more than a mere savage struggle for existence, enabling him to enjoy fire and such froufrous as pipes, musical devices, and decorative objects.[6]

The shellmounds also disclose that the native San Franciscan culture remained remarkably consistent over the centuries. The materials traded among the different Bay groups were the same over several thousand years, the identical religious fetishes seemed to retain their charms, and the earliest coiled basketry, reed mats, and stitched animal skins were much the same as the most recent ones.

> In a word, the basis of culture remained identical during the whole of the shellmound period. . . . It means that at the time when Troy was besieged and Solomon was building the temple, at a period when even Greek civilization had not yet taken on the traits that we regard as characteristic, when only a few scattering foundations of specific modern culture were being laid and our own northern ancestors dwelled in unmitigated barbarism, the native Californian already lived in all essentials like his descendant of today.[7]

The white men who at first discovered the Indians during their explorations and later attempted to save their souls in the Spanish missions became the unwitting agents of change in the aboriginal culture. The most "obvious and impressive result" of the white settlement in California was the decimation of the natives.[8]

The downfall of the Indians had its beginnings in the European and English forays into the New World in the late sixteenth century. The Spaniards were shipping home, as fast as they could jam their holds, a fabulous store of looted treasures uncovered during their explorations of the West. Their galleons, in fair turn, were the prey of the English, whose government, not averse to a little vicarious buccaneering of its own, licensed its pirates officially. In 1577 Sir Francis Drake, blessed by his queen and outfitted by his friends, set sail from England bent on just such a privateering expedition. He made his way to the Pacific, attacked and robbed ships and towns, always keeping a weather eye out for the supreme prize, Spain's Philippine galleon. By 1579, swollen with plunder, his ship was heading home. The usual vicissitudes of weather and the vagaries of sixteenth-century sailing forced Drake's company to seek shelter in an inlet just north of San Francisco. Here, besides relief from the weather, they found a small settlement of natives, who were very much in deportment and appearance like their brothers in San Francisco and like the Indians described in 1709 by a still later privateer along that coast, Captain Woodes Rogers: naked men, women skirted in fronds, villagers who dwelled in conical huts weather-stripped with earth and warmed by open fire. Francis Fletcher, the chaplain of the Drake expedition, made copious notes. He recounts faithfully each shriek and feather, although in the opinion of later critics he woefully misinterprets the Indians' intentions.

According to Fletcher, a day after the *Golden Hind* anchored in the bay, an Indian emissary approached in a canoe. This Indian harangued the Englishmen with a long speech, then returned to shore. He repeated his performance several times, on the last occasion bearing as gifts a feathered headdress and an herb-filled reed basket typical of those woven by the California Indians, so tightly constructed they were waterproof. He would take none of the gifts offered in exchange, save for a fancy hat which he couldn't resist. His peaceful signs and behavior did not dissuade Drake, however, from taking several precautions when he landed his party the following day. The Indians, perceiving the English walling in their tents, descended to the beach prudently bearing bows and arrows. Drake quickly persuaded the Indians to lay down their weapons, and there followed an elaborate exchange of gifts: linens, shirts, and such from the English, and "feathers, cawles of networke, the quiuers of their arrowes, made of fawne skins, and the very skins of beasts that their women wore vpon their bodies," from the Indians. The English queen's company took the occasion to demonstrate to the Indians the usefulness of the gifts "to couer their nakednesse; withall signifying vnto them we were no Gods, but men, and had neede of such things to couer our owne shame; teaching them to vse them to the same ends. . . ."

In 1770, two centuries after Drake's visit, when the white man began to count native Californian heads, he tallied roughly 135,000; by 1848, the beginning of the real foreign invasion, there were 88,000; one-third that number survived into the sixties; by the last decade of the century there were 16,000 natives remaining. The total Costanoan group, including about 1,000 San Franciscans, originally numbered around 7,000, although some authorities put the total closer to 10,000. They supplied the population of several missions until the early 1800's, by which time their number was so depleted that the missionaries were depending on expeditions to bring in fresh recruits from tribes farther afield. Except for a few groups like the Costanoans, the annihilation was never quite complete, never quite reached that point of the old chant "and then there were none."

The latest state figures, in fact, show a deceptive reversal: the

Indian population (swelled, one should note, by thousands of people relocated from outside the state) doubled from 20,000 to 40,000 in the decade between 1950 and 1960 and reached 90,000 by the 1970 census, increasing with the rest of the state's population. At the same time the Indian's status has declined proportionately until he has been reduced to a position inferior to that of all other minorities. According to the California Advisory Commission on Indian Affairs, which after a five-year study issued a report in February, 1966, the modern (*i.e.*, reservation) Indian is widely unemployed (seven or eight times the national average), badly educated and untrained, and lives in shockingly unsanitary conditions. Often he lacks proper sewage disposal (in 60 to 70 percent of the cases); if he has any domestic water supply at all (in 40 to 50 percent of the cases, he has to haul in his own), it is often contaminated. His health is further blighted by inadequate nutrition, and what medical attention comes his way is so insufficient that, for example, he dies from tuberculosis with six times the frequency of the rest of the population. The final insult is rampant racial persecution.

After 4,000 tranquil years the reign of the California Indians has thus succumbed ingloriously in a few hundred, victim of the course of empire, the white man's materialism, philosophy, and religion, and, not least of all, his civilized diseases.

It has been the melancholy fate of the California Indians to be more vilified and less understood than any other of the American aborigines. They were once probably the most contented and happy race on the continent, in proportion to their capacities for enjoyment, and they have been more miserably corrupted and destroyed than any other tribes within the Union. They were certainly the most populous, and dwelt beneath the most genial heavens, and amidst the most abundant natural productions, and they were swept away with the most swift and cruel extermination.[9]

Spanish exploration and colonialism beginning in the fifteenth and sixteenth centuries sounded the death knell; American frontier expansion finished off what was left.

II

The Whale, the Otter,
and the Empire

EUROPE was on the search for trade routes to the East by the fifteenth century, and the next 200 years were an era of wide geographical inquiry. Explorers led the way; plunderers, missionaries, whalers, fur trappers, and woodsmen followed.

The Spanish were the first to stake a claim to California. They thrust out from their Mexican empire into the wilds and uncertainties of the north to explore for a network of defensive settlements against foreign encroachment. They needed northern harbors, ports that could provide fresh supplies to combat one of their crews' worst enemies, scurvy; they needed shelter against an even more formidable enemy, the English privateer; and they needed a northern barrier against the Russians, who had been hunting otters in the Aleutians for a good many years and were to occupy Alaska by the end of the eighteenth century.

Fifty years after Columbus, Juan Rodríguez Cabrillo was exploring California territories and may even have penetrated as far north as San Francisco. By the earliest days of the seventeenth century Sebastián Vizcaíno had laid claims to parts of California in the name of Spain. Gaspar de Portolá discovered San Francisco Bay in 1769, although he was actually looking for Monterey. In the same year the first mission was established in San Diego. Antonio María de Bucareli, the farsighted Spanish viceroy who governed the Mexican empire during the seventies, was instrumental in sponsoring intensified explorations by land and boat, expeditions which resulted in the founding of a permanent settlement at San Francisco. Other Spanish explorers, including Pedro Fages, Fernando Rivera, Francisco Palóu, Juan Bautista de Anza, Pedro Font, José Moraga, and Juan Manuel de Ayala—the first to sail through the Golden Gate—mapped, charted, and recorded their further searches through San Francisco.

Anza had, by 1776, selected sites for a Catholic mission, a Spanish device for the extension of control over the frontier by the conversion of the Indians into Christian colonists, and for an

23

armed fortress, or presidio, whose function was the military protection and assistance of the mission, on whose good graces it was largely dependent for support. The Spanish government supplied funds to the missions in recompense for their services to the rest of the community. During the selection of the appropriate sites, Font, the Anza expedition's official diarist, exclaimed that San Francisco Bay was the "most pleasing" he had yet seen. He could envisage it, well populated like a European city, as beautiful as any in the world. On June 29, 1776, Spain officially founded its most northerly outpost at Mission Dolores.

At the same time that the Spanish were establishing themselves in San Francisco, interest in the Northwest had begun to take on an international character, attracting English, French, Russian, and American explorers. Diaries and journals of the increasing number of foreign callers provided the best accounts of the commercial possibilities in the Pacific and of life in California.

By the middle of the eighteenth century the Hudson's Bay Company had begun extensive searches for a Northwest Passage. In the late 1770's Captain James Cook, as an agent of the English government, had switched his explorations from the South to the North Pacific, likewise seeking a northern waterway. During his searches his company incidentally bought a large allotment of otter skins, which they later sold at fantastic profits in China. The word of their successes spread like village gossip, speeded by the posthumous publication in 1784 of Cook's four volumes on his adventures. Heavily underscoring the possibilities of a Northwest fur trade with China, the book immediately awakened the interest of Boston traders. The first New England ship joined the Pacific trade in the same year, marking the beginning of Yankee contact with California.

Other chroniclers, from George Heinrich von Langsdorff to F. W. Beechy, provided firsthand accounts of California. One of the earliest records of San Francisco came from a Frenchman, Comte Jean François Galup de La Pérouse, who visited the area in 1786. He found the Spanish development of California slow, the mission system largely unsuccessful, but, like Cook before him, the fur trade promising.

More important was the account of the journey of Captain George Vancouver, who seven years later sailed into the Pacific to look after British treaty interests and incidentally to press the search for a Northwest Passage to the Atlantic. On Wednesday, November 14, 1792, he entered the Bay of San Francisco, the first Englishman to set foot there.

Vancouver described the Presidio, set in a verdant plain, as "the only object of human industry which presented itself." It took the form of a large square, walled in on three sides by mud and on the fourth by some indifferent bush fencing. To Vancouver it had a great similarity to "a pound for cattle." Its inhabitants consisted of thirty-five Spanish soldiers, their wives and families, and a few Indian servants, housed in small thatch-roofed dwellings with earthen floors, no glass or other "defence" in the windows, and the rudest of furnishings. Besides these houses, lined up like sentinels against the wall, there were the house of the commandant and the church, whitewashed with lime extracted from the local cache of seashells. The whole establishment "ill accorded with the ideas we had conceived of the sumptuous manner in which the Spaniards live on this side of the globe."

Vancouver appraised the Mission's accommodations as cleaner and somewhat larger than the Presidio's, despite the scanty and ill-kept kitchen gardens, the small quantity of grain, the barren hillsides, and the crudity of even the carts in use—"by no means so well calculated as the [Indians'] miserable straw canoes."

Although the missionaries reported about 600 Indians living in the little hut village attached to the Mission, Vancouver thought that count too high. Besides those in the village, a number of unmarried Indian women lived under strict surveillance in the Mission, guarded from contact with the rest of the tribe except by special permission as insurance of good behavior on the part of the remaining natives. Vancouver observed that the missionaries had no trouble converting these docile people to Catholicism and subjecting them to Spanish ways, yet the benefits were almost negligible. "They seemed," he recounts, "to have treated with the most perfect indifference the precepts, and laborious example, of their truly worthy and benevolent pastors . . . they still remained in the most abject state of uncivilization." However, this is no wonder, he continues, for "they are certainly a race of the most miserable beings, possessing the faculty of human reason, I ever saw. Their persons, generally speaking, were under the middle size, and very ill made; their faces ugly, presenting a dull, heavy, and stupid countenance, devoid of sensibility or the least expression. One of their greatest aversions is cleanliness, both in their persons and habitations; which, after the fashion of their forefathers, were still without the most trivial improvement."

The most important of Vancouver's observations pertained to the Spanish government's apparent lack of interest in its San Francisco settlement. Maintained in such a rude and unprotected state, it could hardly serve as protection for more valuable establishments farther south. It was a clue to the shaky hold the Spanish Empire held on its northern territories and an augury of the limit of its days there.

In spite of its meager aspect and an officially conservative position toward foreigners, Spanish San Francisco displayed generous hospitality to its English guests. The English vessels took on enough meat and supplies to eradicate all signs of scurvy within a few days; further, the Spanish hosts would accept no payment, nor would their chief commander when Vancouver reached him in Monterey.[10] This cordial reception came out of a tradition that extended to guests generally such civilities as good eating and a readiness for entertainment that could produce a barbecue or a fiesta at the least excuse possible. Beyond these amenities, it was standard Spanish practice to furnish travelers with free horses and free lodgings and to leave a bit of money in a guest's room before his departure to assure him necessities during the rest of his journey. It was in this spirit that the Spanish in California provided so handsomely for Vancouver without accepting any recompense. Hospitality was, in fact, one of the traits of Spanish culture that left an everlasting influence on the West: as a group, Californians today are known as friendly, outgoing, and hospitable people. Their easy welcome, as much as the California scenery or its sunshine, accounts for the area's popularity with visitors.

The Russians, who had been in Siberia since the sixteenth century, were constantly pushing their frontier forward. They crossed to Alaska and the Aleutians, and by the mid-eighteenth century they were engaged in a brisk business of otter and seal hunting there. By the beginning of the nineteenth century Alexander Baranov had established headquarters for the Russian American Fur Company in Sitka, and his expeditions were penetrating southward into California.

Unfortunately for the Sitkan Russians, supplies were not as easy to obtain as pelts. In 1805 Nikolai Petrovich Rezanov, an emissary of the czar and agent of the fur company, arrived in Sitka to improve the conditions of the colony. He was shocked by the distress in which he found his countrymen. Their trade had been depleted by competition of the Bostonians; far worse, they were close to starvation. Of the three Russian supply ships which had embarked for Sitka, one had been wrecked, a second had never arrived, and the third was nearly exhausted. Famine and scurvy had overwhelmed the outpost. When an American vessel, the *Juno*, put in to the harbor, Rezanov negotiated with its commandant to buy both ship and cargo. At best, this was makeshift relief, and further remedies were essential. He set off in the *Juno* for California ports, to convince the Spanish to trade foodstuffs for some of his less necessary acquisitions. Before his voyage was over, he was to become one of the most romantic figures in California history.

The commandant of the port of San Francisco was away when Rezanov sailed through the Golden Gateway, but his family and officers extended their hospitality, marred somewhat by a shadow of suspicion. However, one member of the family, Concepción, fell immediately under Rezanov's sway; in the end she was instrumental in convincing her father, Commandante José Argüello, to provide the Russians with ample supplies and to engage in discussions for the renewal of trade. Concepción was only fifteen, but already the most noted beauty of the province. In spite of the obstacles of age and religion, Rezanov wooed and won her and gained the consent of her father and the Catholic mission fathers to their marriage. When Rezanov departed, to return to Russia to report to the czar and conclude his mission—and incidentally to obtain the Pope's official permission for the marriage—his ship was well stocked with supplies for Sitka. As has been told in many a romantic novel and poem by such authors as Gertrude Atherton and Bret Harte, Rezanov was tragically stricken ill during his homeward journey and died en route. It took thirty-six years before Sir George Simpson of the Hudson's Bay Company arrived in San Francisco to bring the first news and details of Rezanov's death. He found that Concepción, having waited faithfully for many years, had finally entered a Dominican convent to devote her life to teaching and to charity.

But Russian exploration did not end with Rezanov. He had felt the urgency of establishing headquarters in positions south of Sitka, and had strongly recommended two locations on his return there. By 1808 Baranov had commissioned two ships to carry out the mission. One was lost, but the second reached Bodega Bay, just north of San Francisco, where the company engaged in hunting and trading furs for almost a year. The skipper returned several years later, hunted surreptitiously and highly successfully under the noses of the distracted Spanish in San Francisco Bay, and laid the groundwork for a Russian settlement thirty miles to the north. He bought the acreage from the Indians at the site of what was to become, in 1812, the Russian outpost Fort Ross. Agriculture was introduced there. But it was never much of a success, and the small company struggled along for years. The fur supply declined alarmingly; the Spanish, the Mexicans after 1822, and the Americans blocked attempts at reasonable trade; in 1823, with the Monroe Doctrine, the American government officially gave notice to the Russians of its firm stand against foreign colonization on this continent. Finally, the Russian settlers gave up: in 1841, they sold all their livestock and properties to John Sutter.

Some of the best accounts of early nineteenth-century San Francisco come from the reports of a Russian ship, the *Rurik,* which visited the city from October 2 through November 1, 1816.

Several of the ship's diaries provide generous scientific observations, as well as detailed accounts of the Presidio, the Mission, and the declining state of the Indians. One was the record of the captain of the ship, Otto von Kotzebue; another, supplemented with many illustrations, was written by a young painter aboard, Louis Choris; the third consisted of the expert findings of Adelbert von Chamisso, naturalist and botanist.

The *Rurik*'s reports are filled with details of the destitute and forlorn circumstances in which the Russians found the Spanish in San Francisco. Several of Spain's colonies were in the throes of revolutionary upheavals, and Napoleon had deposed the Spanish king in favor of Joseph Bonaparte. The Spanish-Americans, refusing to recognize the deposition, were rewarded with complete neglect. Chamisso writes:

> Spain . . . maintains her Presidios at a great expence, and tries, by the prohibition of all trade, to force ready money back to its source. . . . Yet California lies without industry, trade, and navigation, desert and unpeopled. It has remained neglected, without any importations from Mexico, during the six or seven years of the war between Spain and its colonies. . . . Strangers catch otter-skins even in the Spanish harbours; and only a smuggling trade, which the new governor of California, since his appointment (fourteen months ago) has tried to suppress, furnishes this province with the most indispensable articles.[11]

The Spanish soldiers were the worst off. They had received no pay for seven years and barely scraped by with the most elementary necessities. The missionaries, not being much better provided, still reaped the agricultural benefits of the colony. Kotzebue reports that at a dinner at the Mission the Russians dined on an abundance of dishes and drank well of the Mission-produced wines. However, the Spanish military did not fare half so well as the guests. The soldiers got nothing from the Mission without an official requisition and then obtained only the barest essentials. Furthermore, the Spanish had closed their ports to foreign vessels; no legal trade with Europe or the United States existed in any form, depriving the colonials of even such relief as they might have secured through commerce. Choris reports that at least half the Boston ships made enormous profits from the illegal traffic with the Spanish at every point along the coast from Chile to California. What Spanish warships were still in the Pacific attempting to rout them were no match for the stronger, well-armed American vessels. But one still wonders how much trading the penniless San Franciscans could afford.

By the 1820's the otter and seal populations were nearly exhausted. The Yankee fur ships soon became as extinct as the otters but were replaced by the whalers and the hide and tallow merchants. The whalers, whose voyages lasted for years, developed the necessary trading of goods for foodstuffs into a legal and thriving sideline. And Spanish cattle stocks adequately supplied New England hide and tallow dealers.

This heightened Yankee-California traffic provided the East Coast with information about and interest in the unknown land. Crews and their captains brought back descriptions of everything, aboriginal to geographical. Beyond the word-of-mouth accounts, two authors had a tremendous influence: Richard Henry Dana, who dropped out of Harvard in his junior year because of an illness which badly affected his eyesight and sailed west as an ordinary seaman, bound on recovering his health,* and Alfred Robinson, who sailed west as a hide and tallow agent, subsequently married a Spanish senorita, became a Californian, and wrote at length about it in *Life in California*.

Dana thrived on the hardships of the voyage, returned in excellent condition to graduate and subsequently to obtain his law degree. In between his studies he began to set down the details of his travels in what was to become his *Two Years Before the Mast*, the best-seller of its day. It has never been out of print since its publication in 1840, and the number of copies sold must at this date number well over half a million.[12] The fact that a well-educated and well-bred professional man could participate in an adventure generally reserved for the more robust and less learned members of society had marked influence in later years in persuading all classes and callings to seek their fortunes in the West.

Also something of a classic, Robinson's book was full of sound prophecies: "It [San Francisco] is the grand region for colonization; and if peopled by our industrious backwoodsmen, who are gradually emigrating from the Western States, it must hold, in a very few years, a conspicuous station among the nations of the earth."

*It was common practice to send people suffering from even the most severe illnesses on rigorous sea journeys on the theory that such voyages might prove beneficial to their health. Many a forty-niner joined the Gold Rush under such conditions. Too often it proved to be a fatal error of judgment.

He announced that the only thing lacking to the success of upper California gold and silver mines—and this before the Gold Rush—was the employ of skilled miners; he predicted the rise of steam navigation in the West, aided by the recently rumored discoveries of coal;* he further imagined the overwhelming commercial success of the West Coast should a canal ever be built through the Isthmus of Panama—and he felt that such an event was not improbable. There was no doubt in his mind that the West should become a thriving chain of harbor-metropolises, supported by European trade with the Indies and peopled by hordes of immigrants from the United States and abroad. If the United States should ever annex the province, he felt, the waterways would soon be bobbing with maritime traffic, the coast would be mushrooming with towns, the riverbanks would be fenced with factories and mills, and the whole country would undergo such an increase of population, consumption, and industry that the new sign of wealth would be the possession of only a fraction of the landholdings that now signified affluence. "All this," he concludes, "may come to pass; and indeed, it must come to pass, for the march of emigration is to the West, and naught will arrest its advance but the mighty ocean."[13]

---

*Probably the stone coal from nearby Bellingham Bay, which by 1854 supplied a good part of the city's needs. Before that the town burned mostly local oak and brush gathered on the sand hills and sold by vendors who also dealt in charcoal. In 1880 the discovery and mining of coal on Mount Diablo turned its slopes into the site of a successful local industry.

III

The Spanish and the
Anglo-Saxons

TWO diverse political and ethical systems left their marks on California culture: Spanish Catholic and Yankee Protestant.

The first San Franciscans of European origin were part of a contingent that set forth from the Mexican state of Sinaloa in October, 1775. They numbered 240 persons when they left; including births en route, a death by childbirth, and a few dropouts who settled farther south, 244 settlers arrived. The roster listed 3 officers and a purveyor, 3 Fathers, 18 veteran soldiers and 20 recruits, 29 soldiers' wives plus the rest of their families, 40 families of colonists—some of whom retraced their steps southward to settle in San José—20 muleteers, 3 men to herd the beef cattle, 4 servants for the Fathers, and 3 Indian interpreters.

The government had induced the colonists to emigrate by providing them with over 1,000 animals, a quantity of substantial equipment, and all manner of clothing from hair ribbons and petticoats to heavy boots. The outlay for food reflects the class-consciousness of the Spanish society which the expedition represented. Not including the provisions carried for the two principal leaders, Captain Juan Bautista de Anza and Lieutenant José Moraga, the whole assembly was fed at a cost of $1,957. Anza and Moraga, however, dined on comparative delicacies—sausages, chocolate, spices, cheeses, oil and vinegar, wine and such—at a cost of $2,232.40. Anza, to his credit, protested this inequality, but the spirit of the times prevailed.[14]

At the most, a total of 3,000 people migrated from Mexico to California, and for the first several years the whole province was held down by only a few hundred. Considering the sparse population that Spain supported there, even at the peak of its colonizing efforts, the impact of Spanish culture on the land is impressive.

Three primary forces shaped the country during that early period: the missions, the presidios, and the pueblos and ranches. Although the missions were conceived as a temporary institution, the early viceroys had granted almost unlimited authority to the

31

mission fathers, whose power lasted until 1836; then a program of secularization transformed the last of the missions into regular parish churches for the pueblos surrounding them and released the Indian neophytes and the adjacent land from their control. The ranches, a rather feudal setup of large estates, increased immensely in importance as the missions declined. They were the basis of a generous system of land division and what was then the principal foundation of the state's economy, the cattle industry. The Spanish and later the Mexican governments had casually begun to grant enormous tracts of land to their California settlers, who needed vast acreage to support their flocks of cattle and horses. Political connivance diverted the secularized mission lands and livestock, destined for division among the Indians, to private ownership, often adding to the power of the already-dominant Spanish gentry. Although later the American Land Act of 1851 forced any owner to prove his title or forfeit his property, "nevertheless, a substantial fraction of present land titles in California rests upon the 'Spanish land grants,' most of which were really Mexican."[15]

In San Francisco the Mission and its surrounding pueblo remained, in effect, a separate entity through the 1840's. The present close-knit Spanish-Mexican character of the Mission District has survived from these early foundations.

The mission system failed because it proved more of a responsibility than a help to the paternal government which created it. For much the same reason, Mexico did not prosper under Spanish protection. During the nineteenth century the Spanish Empire had its troubles, and its rebellious colonies were among them. Because upper California, which had no inclination to rebel from the homeland, was a most distant outpost of the beleaguered empire and communication was tedious and costly, there was a minimum of help from—or interference by—the official hand of government. The state in which the Russians found the San Franciscans in 1816 clearly indicated how little commitment Spain had to its northern colonies.

In 1821 Mexico, which had been under Spanish domination for over two centuries, won its independence. It took some time for upper California to shift its loyalties, but in any case, under the imperial Mexican regime there was very little immediate effect on the life and laws of the province. The Spanish patterns of life that were brought to California had come from Mexico and had already weathered for a long time.

The period of Mexican domination over California was marked likewise by political turmoil at home. As is often the case with governments spawned of political upheavals, the secessionist Agustín de Iturbide empire was short-lived. By 1824 Mexico had forsaken the imperial patterns of its Spanish past and uneasily established itself as a constitutional federal republic.

The colonial system had provided little training ground for a citizenry now faced with self-determination. In spite of the number of well-phrased slogans revering democracy, Mexican politics were characterized by "particularism, personalism, and militarism." However, government by revolution set an example, and for growing numbers of Californians, desire became conviction. Mexican independence carried California a step closer to its own emergence from foreign domination.[16]

The days under the Mexican republic were transitional, serving to ease the colony away from its largely agricultural origins toward a more commercial orientation, and away from Spanish ecclesiasticism and authoritarianism toward a more liberal ideal. Reflecting the 1824 constitution, the Mexican reign began to bring to California changes in the direction of democratization: one was the secularization of the missions, already discussed; another was the election of local representative governments; a third allowed freer trade with foreigners; and perhaps most important, the new policy greatly increased the number of land grants, extending the rights of ownership to naturalized foreigners of Catholic faith. During their time the Spanish had issued about two dozen grants; the Mexicans legalized more than 500. By 1846 grantees had claimed 8,000,000 acres. But "to the very end, Mexico's grip on the province was insecure and her voice in its affairs slight." Separation became the dominant theme. The increase of trade and of settlers from the United States, auguries of California's impending acquisition, was perhaps the most "momentous development of the quarter century."[17]

By the time the Americans took over the ground had been prepared. The dominant theme of Spanish life, the mission system, had crumbled, and the Indians were in large part annihilated. There is no doubt that the principal aim of the mission system had been to save the infidel population of California—for God, for themselves, and incidentally for church and country. However, Christianity had surrounded and slowly inundated the native population of its Western outposts; the Indian, intended to be saved, was in practice no better off than a drowning man tangled in a lifeline.

The journals and diaries of the voyagers to the Pacific brim with accounts of the unintentional mistreatment of the Indians and the alarming statistics of their illnesses and deaths. Although many writers described the natives as less civilized than their Eastern brethren, there was general agreement that the mission system was not the one to save them. The early conversions on a spiritual basis gave way to the expedience of subjugation, and the church claimed its converts forever after. With few exceptions the fathers learned none of the dialects, nor accepted any of the customs of the subjugated; in their turn, the Indians, not being conversant with Latin, found the daily religious rituals tedious as soon as the noisy music stopped. Further, the living conditions imposed such an unbearable confinement on a people used to the utmost freedom that many escaped and returned to their mountains, and others gazed into the distance pining longingly after them. Toward the end the missionaries were granting yearly two-week leaves in an attempt to forestall permanent desertion. The penalties for running away were generally severe. The work at the mission was considerably more demanding than the Indian would grow accustomed to, and the pay reverted to the mission for "upkeep." Syphilis, dysentery, tuberculosis, and the measles swept through the settlements like scythes through a hayfield. The white man's medicine was primitive; according to one account, it consisted mainly of bloodletting, taught to one of the missionaries by a passing ship's surgeon. The *Rurik* journals tell us that out of 1,000 Indians at San Francisco, 300 died yearly. Dietary changes weakened them physically and psychologically; one hardly wonders that they sought release through alcohol.

When control of the decaying missions was secularized, thrusting the Indians back onto the land, they found their natural hunting and gathering grounds invaded or diminished by the herds of the white settlers. A large part of the Indian population was left destitute, unprepared for their former primitive life, and in a complete state of dejection.

Although the missions brought about the decline of the Indians, they also left California a positive heritage more important than a style of architecture and a design of furniture. One can trace the extent of Spanish influence by the boundaries of the areas where its emissaries made wine: throughout California the mission fathers planted wine grapes, to start one of the state's noblest industries. It was the Spaniards who introduced irrigation to California. The agricultural basis of their society established a lasting pattern for the character of the state, and their cattle industry gave us the whole era of the Western cowboy.

Fortunately some of the more callous aspects of the Spanish commitment to entertainment carried over in spirit more than in specifics. Several of the early California sports are reminiscent in their barbarism of the days of the Roman arenas and certainly of the Spanish bullring. Wild bears and bulls, first goaded to increase their ferocity, were pitted against each other in fights to the death. Gertrude Atherton describes a racetrack on the Argüello ranch where one of the favorite amusements of the vaqueros was to bury roosters and wrench off their heads as they galloped by. Greased pigs on the run lost their tails in similar fashion.[18]

More congenial to modern tastes are the fiestas, rodeos, and barbecues of early California. Accepting a gentleman farmer's invitation to dinner, Alfred Robinson reports that "we found him rather a lover of good eating," a remark that applies "to all Californians, for the lowest personage must have his three or four different dishes. Their *olla, azados, quisados,* and *frijoles,* are found at every board."[19]

The English dispatched colonists to America who were imbued with a spirit of individualism and independence and a heritage of free assembly. By the time they reached California they also had formulated some pretty certain ideas about Indians, evolved from European philosophical analyses of man and society coupled with personal observations that were largely altered by selecting what best bolstered these theories. Beyond his opinions about the natives, the Easterner had a twofold image of the West. There was the West of a steady, agrarian nature, hardworking and dull, based on a strong class prejudice against the farmer, who represented the solid lower class. The other side of the coin was romantic: the woodsman and pathfinder symbolized courage, independence, adventure and a rugged glamor that altogether spelled exciting release from the humdrum problems of ordinary civilization.[20] The English emigrants' intention in America was to re-create the Protestant society they had left behind them. It was, in their experience, the only means to life's fulfillment, and everything must be fitted to that end. So the savage would be elevated from his lowliness to fulfill his greatest civilized potential. He was, to the Englishman, a challenge and an obligation. It was the white man's duty to save him, and Christianity was the means to his civilization. A notable lack of success, however, soon began to produce a more pragmatic line of reasoning. Contrary to first impressions, it must be that the Indian was basically different from the white man, after all, a primitive who stood in the way of civilization and progress. Alas, it was God's will and nature's way that he be destroyed. The English colonial's ideas of property rights shifted accordingly. Whereas he first purchased his lands from the Indians—ownership was a "natural right"—he came soon to believe that it was in fact unchristian to allow lands to remain fallow in the hands of barbarians; it must be God's design that Christians take them over and use them to the good agrarian purposes for which they were intended. "God is to be glorified as His rich and abundant Virginia is properly used."[21]

Thus eventually the American philosophy of righteous self-determination reached the West and was superimposed on the Spanish-Mexican heritage that had slowly lost its potency.

IV

The Emigrants

BEFORE technology transformed America's agrarian society, the farm family best expressed the country's republican orientation. Its advance westward ensured the expansion of republican values. By the last quarter of the eighteenth century westward movement was steadily increasing. After 1845 the doctrine of Manifest Destiny provided the United States with philosophical reasons for westward expansion; the European powers inching in from the Pacific supplied political reasons; the profits in land speculation provided entrepreneurs with practical reasons. Official American policy encouraged independent farmers and trappers to move overland, pushing the frontier and the forms of democracy before them.

Thomas Jefferson, a Western advocate long before he became President, was preoccupied with domestic plans for United States territorial exploration at a time when his official duties were exclusively diplomatic and furthermore in Paris. His proposals drew interest and support from Americans in the profitable Oriental trade who had to use the strenuous sea route around Cape Horn. As President he launched Lewis and Clark on their memorable scientific expedition of 1804 to 1806; their incidental discovery of British trappers throughout the Missouri Territory was the incentive for an American advance into the same area.

The Lewis and Clark exploration did not immediately prevent British domination. Its importance "lay on the level of imagination: it was drama, it was the enactment of a myth that embodied the future. It gave tangible substance to what had been merely an idea, and established the image of a highway across the continent so firmly in the minds of Americans that repeated failures could not shake it."[22]

Fur-trading explorers learned the intricacies of the geography and blazed the trails on which others would follow west. By the 1820's Jedediah Smith and William Ashley had pushed an overland route from the Platte Valley across the Rockies at South Pass. Smith further pioneered a route from the Great Salt Lake into

37

southern California. One of the most expert of the beaver trappers, Joseph Walker, etched out a trail down the Humboldt Valley, through the Sierras, and into California's San Joaquin Valley. Crossing through the central Sierras, Walker Pass was to become the most frequently traveled route for settlers and miners and the earliest course for the railroads. During their original exploration the Walker party incidentally discovered Yosemite Valley.

Throughout the 1840's many of the trappers and explorers led parties of migrating settlers over the Western trails that they had hewn. The attorney Lansford Hastings typified another type of guide; he was interested in the profits he might obtain through land sales and the possibility of political leadership in a burgeoning new territory. To these ends he published the *Emigrants' Guide*, crammed with worthless and misleading information. Also with an eye on potential real estate profits, Dr. John Marsh, an early settler, and Thomas O. Larkin, merchant and consul at Monterey, encouraged Western migration through favorable personal accounts and official correspondence.

Two types of settlers came to California before the discovery of gold: those on business who either through accident or design stayed on; and, somewhat later, Southerners and Easterners who came overland specifically to farm and settle down. In the first case, the settlers generally married the Spanish residents, the "native" Californians, and adopted the colonial life, Spanish style. In the latter group, encouraged by a government anxious to beat out the English in the Asian trade by installing a tangible force toward United States territorial acquisition, families generally emigrated together and thereby retained more of their own customs. They formed a vanguard of permanent American inhabitants.

The Southerner had been among the first settlers to advance beyond colonial borders. A roster of Southern names connotes Western exploration: Boone, Lewis and Clark, James Clyman, and John Charles Frémont among them.[23] It is not altogether coincidence that some of these emigrants from the American South found the structure of California life familiar. When, after the 1830's, the missionary management of land and society was transformed into the ranchero system of a large, landed upper class, Indians and peasants became to this structure what the black slaves were to the Southern plantation system, ensuring the perpetuation of leisure for the *gente de razón*. Frémont, French-born and Old-South bred, writing his memoirs in the 1880's, showed much compassion for the gentlemen rancheros and a marked admiration for the charms of their aristocratic style of existence—which forty years earlier he had helped overthrow in a premature American revolt against Mexico, the Bear Flag Rebellion.

More characteristic of the Southern émigré's past was the back-woodsman. His emerging social patterns, which often reflected the aggression, crudeness, and impulsivity of life on the frontier, also demonstrated the most rudimentary democracy. In the long run, this exerted a more fundamental influence on Western social patterns than an elaborate set of manners based on artificial aristocratic premises. The enforced equality, stamina, and practicality of frontier life made telling contributions. Hardships and opportunities confronted all alike. Family illnesses and difficult labors had to be conquered by community efforts, out of the joint necessity for survival, just as, conversely, festivities and ceremonies were occasions for sharing individual joys. When a frontier marriage or housewarming took place, the community assembled for an appropriate celebration, including a rousing good "bran" or "barn" dance.* By the mid-1850's the process of equalization on the frontier had turned the yeoman, Southern or otherwise by origin, into the fulfillment of Jefferson's political ideal, the free man.

The mountain men, most of whom hailed from Virginia, Kentucky, and other Southern states, were a different breed, although they shared many characteristics with the farmers. In the seventeenth century the French, Dutch, and English had been dominant in the North American fur trade; by the beginning of the eighteenth the Americans had joined in. Whereas the English and French had been primarily traders—the English in established outposts, the French seeking out the Indians on the trails—the American fur men started at the source and caught the beaver themselves. By the nature of their work, these men were loners. With the exception of those who had created common-law Indian families, they were only occasionally associated in loose-knit organizations. Their life was very hard, literally dependent on an intelligence alert enough to survive physically and adequate enough to nourish the soul during long periods of immobility and isolation. Most of the trappers were readers, many acquainted with some formal education before embarking on more rigorous adventures. Winter seasons were devoted to books, and the literary trade among the men was as brisk as snow and sleet would allow. Bibles, worn out by constant use, and a whole variety of printed materials, from scientific discourses to the highly popular works of William Shakespeare, were exchanged season after season.

*The custom of first seeding the new floorboards with bran or corn siftings served the practical function of applying a fine oil finish to the timber with no more exertion than it took to make merry. It is from a corruption of "bran" dance that the term "barn" dance evolved; the connection to "barn" is purely typographical. See Thomas D. Clark, *Frontier America* (New York: Scribner's, 1959), p. 209.

Illiterate hunters such as Joe Meek sometimes paid another trapper to teach them to read; less ambitious men such as Jim Bridger satisfied themselves with listening whenever they could persuade someone else to read aloud. William Hamilton, who wrote at length about his experiences in the Western wilds, noted that fellow trappers always kept an abundance of reading matter with them, since "old mountain men were all great readers."[24]

Annual trade fairs, two-week-long centralized markets for buying and selling furs and supplies, made up for the tedium and loneliness of the rest of the year. Individual dealers, along with such firms as the Hudson's Bay Company, organized the assemblies at Pierre's Hole, Ogden, Green River, and other mutually accessible outposts.[25] White men and Indians of both sexes gallivanted and gambled, stoking up on whiskey and sex along with firearms, reading matter, and pots and pans. In the face of the heavy trade in Bibles, these annual explosions ran the gamut of vices with the same abandon characteristic later of the miners' camps and early San Francisco society.

In contrast, the first American seaborne contact with California, largely based on New England commerce, transmitted the strict Calvinist and Puritanical doctrines peculiar to the Yankee. The Latin-Catholic culture of Spanish California was alien to the New England comprehension. The Mexican natives, like the Indians, seemed dirty, wasteful, and indolent. The easygoing pace and enjoyment of leisure appeared sinful—although it was often described with a tone of admiration bordering on envy. The New Englanders were aghast at such brutality as they witnessed at the cockfights and the bear-against-bull matches—although, judging from the prevalence of accounts, a great many managed to force themselves to the arena. Paradoxically, the Yankees were charmed by the grace and elegance of the gentry and overwhelmed by their hospitality. But taken altogether, the apparent immorality and lack of enterprise outweighed the overt Spanish charm. Backed by undertones of racial intolerance and religious antipathy, these traits seemed unmistakable signs to the New England conscience that the Spanish and Mexicans were aliens on God's lands. Later they provided ideological support for the Mexican-American War and the subsequent American takeover of California.

Besides transmitting their stricter guidelines, the New Englanders made more positive contributions to California culture. They passed on a sense of thriftiness and enjoyed order. The original scale of New England village life had taught the Yankee cooperation and a respect for domestic institutions. The severity of Northeastern winter climate had made small, closely knit communities more practical than large ones. The resulting system of landownership was based on careful surveys and small individual grants, in contrast with the more grandiose Southern and Spanish systems, both of which resulted in inequities followed by interminable litigations. The Yankees were often men of good education. They seasoned industriousness with ingenuity and a generous dash of contrariness. In spite of their Puritanical background, a good number married early into the Spanish culture, became bilingual, converted to Catholicism, and even took out full-fledged citizenship. Compared to that of the backwoodsmen, the New England style was conformist, moralistic, and at the same time intellectual and sophisticated. California life molded the Yankee's New England habits in much the same way that the frontier leveled the social patterns of the Southern immigrants. Both groups and the many diverse groups which followed contributed a rich variety of cultural traits to their new communities; Western life absorbed them and at the same time contributed an equalizing effect on all of them.

San Francisco's first Anglo-Saxon settler arrived in 1822, when the English whaler *Orion* touched port and the mate, William Richardson, deserted. The governor at that time, Vicente de Solá, granted the twenty-six-year-old sailor permission to remain in exchange for services to the colony. Within the year he was baptized "Antonio" by the Mission, was acting as pilot on the Bay, and was busily teaching the populace carpentry, calking, and navigation. Two years later he had married María Antonia Martínez, whose father was the commandante, and within a short time was a naturalized citizen. His career was not all smooth sailing: he was troubled by frequent debts, suspicions of smuggling (in league with his father-in-law) and irregularities in collecting taxes as captain of the port of San Francisco. However, he was "given a good name" by all and performed such worthwhile services to the colony as vaccinating the mission Indians, which earned him the honorific title of Doctor. He was responsible for San Francisco's first civilian dwelling, after the official buildings of the Mission and Presidio: a commodious tent of redwood posts and ship's foresail erected near the waterfront in June, 1835.[26]

San Francisco's first election, in December, 1834, had put Don Francisco de Haro in the alcalde's (mayor's) chair. One of his earliest orders was to mark out an official street, La Calle de la Fundación, which followed the shore northwestward toward the fort, along what is now Grant Avenue. With a mayor and a main street, San Francisco was on its way.

By early October the home government sent Haro orders for

the development of the port: he was to reserve 200 varas (about 560 feet) along the beachfront for official buildings, to measure off the rest of the area for a small town and make a plan of it, to direct Richardson to assist him in these matters, and to grant to him, the first settler, a lot of 100 varas. Richardson's property was on Grant Avenue, from about the present numbers 827 to 843, between Clay and Washington streets—one of the busiest sections of modern Chinatown. It was there that he erected the tent which Dana (whose ship, the *Alert*, touched the cove the following December) later described as the port's only habitation. By 1836 the canvas and wood had been replaced by a one-story adobe, and "Dr." Richardson, making use of a launch service that he had also established, was trading grain, hides, and country vegetables with arriving vessels and neighboring Indians.

The town acquired its second house and its first retail firm when Jacob P. Leese built on a land grant just adjacent. Leese sailed to what was until 1847 still called Yerba Buena with $12,000 worth of merchandise, a considerable quantity of lumber, and an orchestra of six musicians. The lumber quickly took the shape of a house on the grand scale of 60 by 25 feet, in time for the orchestra to fiddle away at a Fourth of July gala that lasted two full days and a night. All the leading Mexican citizens attended. Several years and as many occupants later, the house was removed to make way for the first St. Francis Hotel.

Leese, along with his partners Nathan Spear and William Hinckley, enlarged his fortunes by boating up the rivers and around the Bay exchanging merchandise for fresh foodstuffs. After 1838, when they had a falling out over the equitable division of the profits, each continued with his separate interests.

As was typical of life in those days, these interests proved diverse. The versatility of men like Leese, the ups and downs of their fortunes, the interweaving of enormous differences of personality among the population already foretold of the color and complexity that were to make later San Francisco society unique.

Leese, for example, subsequently made an excursion to China, transferred to Sonoma, became its mayor, was imprisoned during the Frémont rebellion, and profited from mining during the Gold Rush. By the 1880's his fortunes had diminished; he turned up finally in Texas, poverty-stricken. The Society of California Pioneers, of which he had been vice-president thirty years earlier, circularized its membership for help in his behalf.

Hinckley, a practical joker whose tongue waggled recklessly when he was drunk, first landed in California in 1830. Before entering into partnership with Leese and Spear, he was twice arrested by the revenue authorities for smuggling. A widower, he married Susana Martínez, and by 1844 became the mayor of the town—the first American-born alcalde. The year following, he was the captain of the port, all this before he reached thirty-nine, at which age he died in 1846.

Spear, like Hinckley, was a New Englander. After the dissolution of the partnership, he continued running the original firm on Clay and Montgomery and, in addition to operating two schooners, he set up the area's first flour mill. In 1841, when San Francisco's population had swelled to thirty families, Nathan Spear's house was considered the most impressive in town. However, like many of the early settlers, he did not stay put permanently, shifting to Napa in 1846. After his wife's death there, he returned to live in San Francisco until his own untimely death a few years later at the age of forty-seven. Unlike so many of his peers, he had married not a Californian, but a half-breed Hawaiian, and had perhaps therefore lacked their incentive to become a Mexican citizen. In any case, because he never took out citizenship, he could hold no land grants. Much more than his partners, he displayed the demeanor and practices of a gentleman and the curiosity of a scholar; like them, he had the initiative of a good businessman.

Another early arrival, Jean Jacques Vioget, a former Swiss sea captain, had made the first survey of Yerba Buena in the fall of 1839 under a commission from Mayor Haro, and later performed the same service for his countryman Sutter's New Helvetia properties. Vioget, a cheerful, capable man, excelled in languages and music. In San Francisco since 1837, he had built a house by '39 and become naturalized by '40. He followed the pattern of diversity by opening a tavern and billiard parlor on Montgomery Street between Clay and Sacramento next door to the Hudson's Bay Company, later became an innkeeper, and returned for several years to the sea before finally settling down in San Francisco.

Although Americanization of California was indirectly abetted by such Mexican reforms as the secularization of the missions, the major force was immigration. By 1840 there were almost 400 "foreigners." By 1841 trains of pioneers headed overland to seek the attractions of the Far West. One of the first to organize, the Western Emigration Society, never did set off for California. However, one of its members, John Bidwell, joined forces with Talbot Green and John Bartleson to form the first major party of Western settlers. Like most groups in the next few years, it started from the Midwest. Scores of followers dropped by the wayside, suffering severe hardships; some trains aimed northward for Oregon, but large numbers also managed to reach California.

The United States had had a protective, if also acquisitive, eye on California even earlier. Andrew Jackson had instigated an offer to buy San Francisco Bay as well as the adjacent northern territory from Mexico for $500,000; the offer ended in failure but announced without a doubt America's interest in that harbor. There were various other abortive efforts at acquiring the territory, which finally fell into American hands at the conclusion of the Mexican-American War. The changeover to American rule was peaceful, but important; it signaled the end of autocratic rule and the beginning of the American-English system of self-determination.

After the American takeover in 1846, when the village consisted of fewer than fifty buildings and a population of only a few hundred inhabitants, a great number of immigrants arrived. Over the years accounts by word of mouth and in writing had been disseminating information and arousing interest in the West.* The freshest and most comprehensive reports of California came from the New Englanders engaged in trade with the coast. Like Dana, they were often educated men capable of effective observations. They wrote accounts such as Robinson's which encouraged a newly emerging tolerance for West Coast customs. His orthodox New England views of the Californians were tempered by genuine sympathies for a society in which he was personally involved. When his book was published, American possession of California was already a fact, and the danger of foreign domination had diminished. Those native characteristics that had previously seemed troubling and immoral became less so and even managed in some cases to take on a color of exoticism.

All during the 1840's a flood of panegyrics appeared, lauding California as a paradise of healthful climate, agricultural fertility, and hospitable, easygoing inhabitants. The early accounts, which had prophetically described a government so weak that it was about to collapse altogether, enticed adventurers. In general, the written praises of the West gave inspiration and provided a rationale for the hundreds who were seeking relief from Southern poverty, the still-lingering effects of the 1837 depression, and such political upheavals as the 1848 Revolutions in Europe. The election of James Polk to the Presidency in 1844 on an expansionist ticket had been an accurate reflection of the climate of the times. The total effect of this burgeoning volume of eyewitness accounts, literature, and growing legend was to turn the attention of

*In *American Images of Spanish California*, James D. Hart catalogues the early writings—from William Shaler, the otter trader, to Washington Irving, the novelist—that helped establish and finally influence the popular concepts of life in the West.

the world westward: it established the perfect context for annexation and then for the Gold Rush.

Americans who had settled permanently in Mexican California were at first no grave cause of alarm to the authorities, in spite of the official suspicion of all foreigners and the government's unenforceable attempts to limit immigration.

The agriculturally oriented overland migrants offered little competition to the more commercially oriented town population, although they may have occasioned some unrest in the Mexican ranchers. Unlike the male populace that arrived by sea, intermarried, became naturalized, and readily converted to Catholicism, however, the family groups of overlanders represented unassimilable units, a fact which made the authorities increasingly uneasy. As tension mounted, the Mexican Congress, which now permitted foreign trade, passed ordinances endorsing restrictively high tariffs and ordering the expulsion of more than forty foreigners, largely British and American troublemakers. But in spite of such acts by the Mexicans, the settlers were far too numerous to fear the weak fist of the emaciated government, most of whose proclamations remained unenforced. In 1841 the provincial governor, Juan Alvarado, issued decrees limiting foreign trade. Many vessels, finding the Pacific islands more congenial, began to avoid San Francisco, and for a time the port declined. Such signs of nervousness on the part of the Mexican authorities, plus internal political intrigue among that government's representatives in California, further awakened feelings of discontent and encouraged the Americanization of the province.

Thomas O. Larkin, who first arrived in Monterey in 1832 and became the most prominent California merchant, was in 1844 appointed the first and only U.S. consul. During his days as an official, his most important function was secret: as agent responsible to President Polk, he was to wage a campaign of suasion aimed at the acquisition of California by his government. His efforts were noble, but they failed.

Texas established a precedent for California's change of allegiance by declaring its independence from Mexico in 1836. Its revolt, the subsequent war, and its final admission by the Congress in 1845 as a state of the Union produced some tension among the Mexican people regarding the United States. Likewise, Americans were unhappy about the seizure of their ships and goods over tne years and the lack of compensation for damages.

The mood was ripe for open hostilities. Before the actual eruption of the war between Mexico and the United States in 1846, there were a number of preliminary skirmishes tipping the American hand. A U.S. naval officer, Commodore Thomas ap Catesby Jones, acting on misinformation that led him to assume that war had already begun, had seized Monterey in 1842, but on learning his error, he readily gave it up again and apologized. In June, 1846, under the Bear Flag banner, Captain John C. Frémont and his band had captured Sonoma—most probably with Polk's blessing—and had taken General Mariano Guadalupe Vallejo prisoner. But when the Mexicans and Americans came to a full-scale conflict, much of it was far to the South below the Rio Grande. The northern Californians, well removed and primed for a changeover, offered little resistance.

At eight o'clock on the morning of July 9, 1846, a band of seventy sailors and marines disembarked from the USS *Portsmouth*, anchored in San Francisco Bay. To the beat of drums and the piping of fifes, they filed up Clay Street to Yerba Buena Plaza, where they unfurled the American banner. As it caught the breeze atop the adobe customhouse, Captain John Montgomery read to the assembled villagers the official proclamation of Commander John D. Sloat, taking possession of California in the name of the United States. The sloop of war fired off a proper twenty-one-gun salute, aides posted copies of the proclamation in both Spanish and English, and California came under United States dominion. It was not until February 2, 1848, however, with the signing of the Treaty of Guadalupe Hidalgo that the war officially ended, and all Mexican territory west of the Rockies was ceded to the United States. The motives behind expansionism—unfettered trade with Asia and territory free from foreign encroachment—were now actualities: American interest began to shift to the care and feeding of the new acquisition.

On August 26, 1846, Captain Montgomery appointed Washington Allen Bartlett the first American mayor of American Yerba Buena, a temporary selection confirmed by popular vote a few weeks later. The official election, offering the voters a choice between two candidates—Bartlett and Robert T. Ridley—took place in a room behind the black pioneer William Leidesdorff's store; the ballot box had formerly contained bottles of lemon syrup.

The new Mayor Bartlett was a lieutenant from the *Portsmouth* who spoke Spanish well. One of his first orders of business, after a hard look at Vioget's early San Francisco survey, was to revise it. He selected as chief mapmaker an Irish civil engineer, Jasper O'Farrell, who had come to California in 1843 by way of South America and Mazatlán. O'Farrell was soon at work correcting the angles of street intersections, which Vioget had recorded at two and a half degrees off a right angle; although now accurate, the new lines could not accommodate all the projecting building fronts and land divisions that had already been established, making it necessary to appoint a committee for the "removal of fences to their proper boundaries." More important, O'Farrell's survey set the basic pattern of the city's development, marking out the wide main thoroughfare of Market Street, from which subordinate avenues take off on the diagonal.

John Henry Brown, a former English sailor, cast the first vote in the election. Although he later spent thirty years in Santa Cruz, he returned to San Francisco, where one of the last local records of him states that at age seventy-five he was busy keeping a grocery store. At that time he also started to write his reminiscences, which though set down some forty years after most of the facts, show a surprising accuracy, if also charmingly inaccurate spelling. Defying the actuarial odds of his day, he died in Santa Cruz, to which he returned for his final days, in 1905 at the age of ninety-four.

Before he became a hotel proprietor, Brown had worked as a barkeep and accountant in a saloon. One of the two owners, Mr. Finch, was a man of poor education and, until Brown turned up, kept his records largely by illustration: each person entered in the accounts was identified by a drawing emphasizing one of his main characteristics. Brown left Finch and Thompson's to become manager of Robert Ridley's billiard parlor and liquor saloon at $50 a month. The bar and billiard room was a natural gathering place for townspeople and newcomers and thereby a natural headquarters for the promotion of real estate, which Ridley promptly took up. The barroom contained a large map on which the saloonkeeper charted each owner's holdings.

Brown's written reminiscences gave the details of Ridley's barroom and real estate business, as well as other aspects of the still primitive life of Yerba Buena in the mid-forties. There were a few stores, billiard rooms, and saloons. There were no paved streets, and the town was peopled by a vividly conglomerate bunch. The city officials derived their pay largely from fines exacted from curfew-breaking sailors off of whaling vessels that had put in for supplies.

Among Brown's recollections, two events point up the serious fear still lurking that the Mexicans might attempt to regain the city by surprise attack. In the first instance a steam coffeepot in Brown's hotel kitchen exploded with such a bang that Captain Hull at the military post ordered the long roll beat, alerted the ships and their crews to stand by for action, and sent forth a reconnoitering party to ascertain the strength of the enemy. Matters were not put in their proper perspective until Brown dashed into the post to obtain the services of a doctor for his scalded cook.

The other incident involved one Captain Watson, whose wont it was to take a full flask with him when he went on guard duty. He and Brown worked out a password to signal that the flask needed replenishing: two raps on the hotel door, followed by the words "The Spanish are in the brush!" Inevitably Brown slept too soundly one night, and an already tipsy Watson, getting no response to his tapping, fired off his pistol, instead, and in clarion tones shouted the key words. The shot and the shouting aroused the barracks, and the military leaped into action: the men on the *Portsmouth* received orders to stand ready to come ashore, the long roll was beat again, and the town's armed population fired off several shots, mostly into the scrub oaks, which by now loomed large as "Spaniards in the brush."

On July 31, 1846, a few weeks after the American occupation, the good ship *Brooklyn* put into San Francisco Harbor. The voyage had begun in New York in early February with a company of 238, mostly farmers and mechanics from various states of the northern and central seaboard. The party included a hundred youngsters and an almost even complement of men and women. The whole shipload, with but few exceptions, were Mormons. They were to rendezvous on the coast with an overland party led by Brigham Young, whose imminent arrival they anticipated. Although they did not know it, Young had decided to settle at Salt Lake City instead.

The sea journey had been rough; such severe storms had battered the ship that the captain once gave it up for lost. Ten people perished en route, and two babies were born, named appropriately Atlantic and Pacific. Physical hardships were only a part of the difficulties that tried the faith of the sect. During the passage, Elder E. Ward Pell, Green Smith, A. T. Moses, and Mrs. Lucy Eager were excommunicated from the church for "licentious and wicked conduct." In fact, their leader, Samuel Brannan, particularly singled out as "conduct of the most disgraceful character" the behavior of the two elders among the four, Moses and Pell, who had been his own counselor. It did not seem to be a permanent blemish; Pell was serving as sheriff by spring.

After the company's arrival in San Francisco three more souls had strayed: Elisha Hyate, James Scott, and Isaac Addison now numbered among the excommunicated. Beyond this, twenty more men had, in Brannan's words, "gone astray after strange gods, serving their bellies and their own lusts, and refuse to assist in providing for the reception of their brethren by land." This more likely meant that the twenty refused to knuckle under to Brannan's orders. On arrival, some of the company had already registered complaints against him, specifying bad treatment during the journey, but a legal investigation by Captain Montgomery cleared his name. As Brannan himself put it, "the truth was mighty and prevailed."

The arrival of the ship more than doubled Yerba Buena's population and just about turned it into a Mormon community, at least until the discovery of gold in '48, when most of the company took off for the mines along with the rest of the population. Although they were a strange clan, the Saints displayed conduct and industry that brought praise and respect. But it was Brannan himself who had the largest influence on the growing community.

The *Brooklyn* arrived on a Friday. On Sunday, Brannan was preaching the first sermon in English. He performed the first American wedding, uniting Lizzie Winner and Basil Hall, both Mormons, in a ceremony in the former Mexican jailhouse. He published the first San Francisco newspaper, the *California Star*. He figured in the first trial by jury and threw his weight behind the campaign for public education. He set off for Sutter's Fort in the autumn of '47 and from there reportedly helped with the building of a sawmill on the American River, at the very millrace where, on January 24, 1848, James Marshall discovered gold. It was Sam Brannan who later hurtled into town with a quinine bottle full of gold flakes, bellowing the news to all who could hear. With a flash the town was deserted, and it as he who headed the first stampede back to the diggings.

The first issue of the *Star* on January 9 featured a lead article on the progress of the war. A second dispatch reported that Mexican captors treated American prisoners so gently as to lodge them in the general's hotel and feed them at his table. Another column questioned by which laws California was presently being governed. Concluding that no one really knew and, further, that decisions of the alcalde's office were rumored to be influenced by the highest bidder, the *Star* advocated considering the proclamations of the chief territorial officer, Commodore Stockton, as paramount. The publisher then stated his intent to produce a paper of quality and interest, to pursue a policy of truth, fairness, and independence, and to print all articles in Spanish as well as English—as soon as a suitable translator could be found.

The second issue editorialized on the freedom of the press; reprinted a New York *Sun* proposal that Mexico, by joining the Union, would better fulfill the liberal goals of its revolution; reported on a lecture in New York by a geologist, Dr. Smith, who pointed out that the centrifugal force of the earth caused the Mississippi River to run uphill, putting its mouth four miles higher than its source; printed a "hint" to young ladies that to waste their time in trivial amusements between the ages of sixteen and twenty would be a loss that they would later bitterly regret; and issued notice that after January 24 all hogs must be securely penned up, any strays to be confiscated and their owners fined $5. There was also this brief insertion reporting on a party of emigrants that were trapped in the mountains:

> It is probably not generally known to the people, that there is now in the California mountains in a most distressing situation, a party of emigrants from the United States, who were prevented from crossing the mountains by an early heavy fall of snow. The party consists of about sixty persons, men, women and children. They were, almost entirely out of provisions, when they reached the foot of the mountain, and but for the timely succor afforded them by Capt. J. A. Sutter, one of the most humane and liberal men in California, they must have all perished in a few days. Captain Sutter, as soon as he ascertained their situation, sent five mules loaded with provisions to them. A second party was dispatched with provisions for them, but they found the mountain impassable, in consequence of the snow. We hope that our citizens will do something for the relief of these unfortunate people.

The unfortunate people were the ill-fated members of the Donner Party.

The third issue on January 23 indicated that all was not rosy with the local government. A letter from Alcalde Bartlett to the Navy's commanding officer of the Northern California District, Commander Joseph B. Hull, Esq., requests a thorough investigation of charges leveled against Bartlett by the *Star,* accusing him of misappropriating city funds. Two letters from Hull follow, the first announcing the appointment of a committee of leading citizens to hold an inquiry, the second reporting that the examination had exonerated the alcalde. Two unrelated notices appeared in both Spanish and English. The first announced to all persons that Jno. Fuller would no longer be responsible for the debts of his wife; the second, a proclamation signed by Bartlett, ordered that hereafter the name San Francisco should be used in all official communications and documents pertaining to the town. However, it took the reluctant *Star* until March 20 to change the town's name in its masthead.

By the fourteenth issue the paper could already afford space for some of the heavy jocularity that California journalism was never to give up:

GRAND NATIONAL WIFE AGENCY ASSURANCE COMPANY —The object of this society is purely philanthropic being to relieve the frightful amount of matrimonial destitution now so alarmingly prevalent. Perhaps the united classes are not aware that there are at this moment many, very many individuals, of one- and-twenty to thirty years, and upwards, now dragging on their existence in a state of cheerless celibacy; the female portion of them without a protector, the male without nobody to look after their things—The wife Assurance Society will place within reach of almost every man, a partner of his joys and a soother of his sorrows; as well as a decided ornament to his establishment. For the accommodation of persons anxious for immediate felicity, a large number of hands will be continually ready for disposal on the following scale of fees:—

A good serviceable wife	£10 10
Do. with accomplishments	15 15
Do. handsome	23 00
Do. intellectual	26 5
Do. of superior beauty and fascinating manners	27 16
Do. extra superfine in every respect, all that the imagination can conceive, etc.	31 10

Monied wives at one per cent, each on their capital. Ladies are respectfully invited to register their names gratis, for the present at Punch's office; but to prevent obstruction in the street, he intends to open a new office shortly in some more commodious situation.

N.B. The amiability of all wives guaranteed, if required, on payment of one shilling extra.—

A year later on April 1, 1848, Brannan put out a special extra edition of 2,000 copies designed to promote Eastern interest in California. Carried to the Mississippi Valley by an overland mule team—which through typical Brannan foresight also carried letters contracted for delivery at fifty cents an ounce—the paper had an immense and unforeseen impact. Its main feature was Dr. Victor Fourgeaud's article "Prospects of California," more than a page of favorable impressions based on his own experiences.

Fourgeaud, a native of Charleston, South Carolina, attended school in France on through the university. He returned to South Carolina for medical training, and three years later settled in St. Louis, Missouri, where he became an associate of the hospital and university and a coeditor of the *St. Louis Medical and Surgical Journal*. Missouri was crowded with fur traders, whose stories of the Far West continuously intrigued him. Somewhat later, by publication of the Mary Dugan case, a controversial medicolegal tempest, he became an innocent victim of fierce attack and cruel invective. The resultant disillusion gave him the final impetus to push on for California. He left with his wife and son in April,

1847, and by mid-November advertised the opening of offices in Jones' Hotel.

An instant advocate of California's life and climate, he extolled its resources, lovingly explored its hills and valleys, and thoroughly involved himself in the town's social and political activities. He gave the first masked ball, inviting leaders from all the surrounding areas. He served the board of education as its chairman. He bought a ranch on the Bear River for use as a summer place. It was small wonder that Brannan sought him out to write a panegyric. The express extra was intended to counteract unfavorable references to California in the East, particularly in Missouri, where business had slackened considerably because of the large-scale migration westward. Fourgeaud's article began, "Our now flourishing little town is destined ere long to become the manufacturing metropolis and the commercial emporium of Western America. . . ." But this optimism held small sway against his report of California's mineral wealth:

> It would be utterly impossible at present to make a correct estimate of the immense mineral wealth of California. . . . The discoveries that have already been made will warrant us in the assertion, that California is one of the richest mineral countries in the world. . . . We saw a few days ago, a beautiful specimen of gold from the mine newly discovered on the American Fork. From all accounts the mine is immensely rich—and already, we learn the gold from it, collected at random and without any trouble, has become an article of trade at the upper settlements. This precious metal abounds in this country.

Buried in another article under the heading "The Great Sacramento Valley" appeared a brief factual account of the discovery. These articles gave the first printed notice beyond California that gold had been discovered at Sutter's Mill. By August 19 the New York *Herald* had picked up the news.

The Gold Rush that followed meant for Fourgeaud a total loss of practice; there was nothing to do but follow his patients to the mines. However, a severe attack of valley fever forced him back to San Francisco by the fall of '49. With such a transient population, the city was still no place to practice medicine, so the doctor set himself up as a merchant and made a fortune. After a visit east, he returned to find that San Francisco, only eight months later, had become a thriving metropolis. That was August, 1850. The doctor eventually returned to medicine, a profession he followed until his death in 1875, but only by removing his family to Paris for a few years. This proved to be a lucky coincidence for California: Fourgeaud brought back with him a highly successful cure for diphtheria, which saved many a victim during the 1856 epidemic. He further served his adopted state in the legislature and as editor of the *Pacific Medical and Surgical Journal.*

In May, 1847, the *Californian,* a "dim, dirty little paper printed at Monterey," transferred operations to San Francisco. (By preceding the *Star* into print in August, 1846, it held the distinction of having been the first newspaper printed in California.) Dr. Robert B. Semple, the *Californian's* editor and publisher, sold it within a few months to a watchmaker named B. R. Buckelew, from whom it passed successively to Robert Gordon and H. L. Sheldon. When news of the gold discovery hit San Francisco, neither the *Californian* nor the *Star* paid it much attention, and what facts they did report were mostly inaccurate. When rumors persisted, the *Star's* young editor, Edward Cleveland Kemble, being a thorough journalist, got together with Sutter and made an on-the-spot investigation; finding nothing to support the hints of a bonanza, he dismissed the claims as extravagant. As the stories grew, the press succumbed to the excitement. Both the *Star* and the *Californian* suspended publication in June, 1848, because there was neither staff nor reader who had not galloped off to the goldfields. After a few months, the *Star's* editor, Kemble, had had his fill of mining and returned to the city. During the summer each journal published a sporadic issue or two in acknowledgment of some important event. By November, with Kemble as editor and publisher, the two rivals merged as the *Star and Californian.* By the first of the new year, 1849, Kemble joined forces with Edward Gilbert and G. C. Hubbard, both of whom had come to California in 1847 with Colonel Jonathan D. Stevenson's disbanded New York regiment of Mexican War volunteers. They discarded the old format and title and enlarged the staff; the first issue of the new *Alta California* appeared on January 4, 1849.

The *Star* in March, 1847, had prophesied that if lumber and men could be obtained, 300 to 500 houses would go up in a year. The April 1 total came to 79 buildings: 31 frame, 26 adobe, and 22 "shanties." By mid-April the newspaper recorded that 50 more houses had been constructed during the last month. By the end of summer, the total reached 157. The *Star* reported in late August and early September on the makeup of the population, a total, by their count in June, of 459 souls. There were 34 Indians, 40 Sandwich Islanders, 10 blacks; of the whites, 128 were females and 247 males. There were 228 natives of the United States, 38 of them from California; 27 were Germans, 22 English, 14 Irish, 14

Scotch, 6 Swiss, and 5 Canadian; and 21 others hailed from various and sundry places not specified. The *Star* estimated four-fifths of the citizenry to be under forty and counted 273 who could read and write. Among the white males, there were 10 professional men, 12 farmers, 16 traders, 13 clerks, 7 navigators, 20 laborers, 3 hotelkeepers, 26 carpenters, and 62 "other mechanics." The town offered 41 places of business: 1 apothecary's shop, 3 bakeries, 2 blacksmith shops, 3 butcher shops, 1 cabinetmaker's shop, 2 carpenter's shops, 1 cigarmaker's shop, 2 cooper's shops, 7 groceries, 1 gunsmith's, 2 hotels, 2 mills (one horse-driven, the other wind-generated), 2 printing offices, 1 shoe shop, 8 general stores, 2 tailor shops, and 1 watchmaker's shop. There were also a number of saloons and bowling alleys, a slaughterhouse on Broadway, a shanty hospital, and a cemetery which was moved from the corner of Sloat and Vallejo to North Beach in 1847. Fort Montgomery, a protective battery on the waterfront, rose between the cove and Battery Street, to which it gave its name. By the end of 1847 the school census showed 473 men, 117 women, 60 children, and others, not officially recorded, making a total population of more than 800. Shortly before Sam Brannan sounded the gold alarm, the *Star* reported 1,000 inhabitants and 192 buildings for the town.

At that point, San Francisco consisted physically of about fifty square blocks mostly clustered around the waterfront. The architecture blended adobe, wood, and an occasional converted ship's caboose. An enterprising merchant named Holbrook had brought out a prefabricated store on the ship *Sabine* and in March, 1848, was busy acquiring a site on which to put it together. In 1848 Henry Mellus and William D. M. Howard, the town's leading businessmen, built a one-story brick structure on the southwest corner of Clay and Montgomery. They offered for sale such items as nails, axes, yardage, Guayaquil hats, Spanish cards, turpentine, brooms, crockery, buckets, tobacco, tea, gin, brandy, rum, letter paper, friction matches, shoes, American soap, pots and pans, flour, wheat, and aniseed. The brick building adjoined a store and warehouse that the firm had purchased from the Hudson's Bay Company.

Howard, originally a New Englander, was the more aggressive of the two business partners. As a civic leader he was instrumental in the construction of the Central Wharf and, after the discovery of gold, one of Brannan's chief backers in an enterprise at Mormon Diggings on the North Fork of the American River. The venture made Brannan and Howard prosperous. Mellus, also a New Englander, had come as a cabin boy on the *Pilgrim* with Richard Henry Dana. He early sold his interest in the store to Howard, afterward claiming that he had been tricked, which prompted his

former partner to see to it that Mellus Street was suddenly renamed Natoma Street, which it remains today.

Exports from California in the mid-forties were largely hides,
tallow, wheat, soap, and furs, along with lumber and some barreled brandy and wine. By 1847 and '48 San Francisco had clearly
emerged as the principal port on the coast, even nudging Honolulu's leadership in Pacific commerce. For the last quarter of 1847,
San Francisco exported goods worth $49,598, more than $30,000
of which originated in California; imported merchandise totaled
$53,590, a large part of it from the Sandwich Islands. For the year
ending in April, 1848, just at the point when the exodus to the
mines began, eighty-five merchant ships had dropped anchor in
San Francisco Harbor.

Town lots at first sold for between $12 and $25 for parcels of
approximately 150 to 300 feet. Later prices—even in advance of
the gold discovery—had climbed to about $600. Before the end of
the year of the gold strike choice corner real estate was going for
$10,000. Forty years after the Gold Rush many properties un-
desirable in '48 had a reported market value of more than
$1,000,000 each.

In January, 1847, the *Star* editorialized on the need for educat-
ing the community's forty children, many of whom were running
aimlessly about the streets. By February the town had elected its
first school board: Dr. Fourgeaud, Dr. John Townsend, Charles
L. Ross, John Sirrine, and William Heath Davis. Townsend was a
practicing physician, a native Virginian, an overland immigrant,
and eventually a San Francisco mayor. He joined the Gold Rush
miners in the Sierras and also did some local digging in the hills of
Marin. Like many early settlers, he and his wife succumbed to
cholera in the winter of '50–'51 in San Jose. Ross was the proprietor of the New York Store at Montgomery and Washington
streets, where in February, 1849, the first regular mail shipment,
landed from the steamer *Oregon,* was sorted and dispersed. Sirrine was an elder of the Mormon establishment. Davis, Nathan
Spear's nephew and successor in the Montgomery and Clay Street
trading post, later wrote *Seventy-Five Years in California,* an autobiographical account of life in the West.

By April, 1847, J. D. Marston had opened a private school. In
December, culminating a year of editorial crusades and citizens'
debates, a newly completed community schoolhouse stood on the
square. Thomas Douglas, a Yale graduate, became the first public
schoolteacher on April 3, 1848, with a $1,000 stipend appropriat-
ed by the trustees. Students paid a fee of $5 to $12 a quarter. The
scholars did not complete their first term: by June everyone, from
the school board to the teacher, had left for the mines, and educa-

tion, like almost everything else expendable, temporarily ceased.

In the fall of 1849 John C. Pelton, a Baptist, sailed around the Horn with assorted school equipment and a bell inscribed "Presented to First Free Grammar School of San Francisco by the Henry Hooper Co. of Boston, Mass." By December Pelton had set up a public, tuition-free school in the church basement, financed at first by voluntary citizens' subscriptions and in the spring following by a municipal subsidy.

T. D. Hunt, San Francisco's first salaried clergyman, began his official duties on November 1, 1848. His church was the schoolhouse on Portsmouth Square, his salary $2,500 a year. The Mormons had held weekly services, but otherwise, until the appointment of the Presbyterian minister, the Reverend Mr. Hunt, as official chaplain, the town's religious observances had been confined to infrequent sermons by transient practitioners. On a Sunday in June, 1847, about a year after the first English sermon by Sam Brannan, the Reverend Mr. Roberts had conducted the first Methodist service. He was a ship's passenger en route to Oregon and took advantage of a stopover on the Sabbath. John Henry Brown recalls that it was a well-attended event and that most of the congregation had not worshiped formally in ten or fifteen years. They took up a collection that amounted to more than $50 and one old salt appreciatively invited the minister and his family to dinner with him the next day. The dining room was in the hotel, contiguous to the billiard room and saloon and two gambling rooms for cardplayers.

A week later Thaddeus M. Leavenworth, a Connecticut Episcopalian, preached the sermon. He had arrived as chaplain of Colonel Stevenson's Regiment of Volunteers from New York. Three ships, the *Perkins,* the *Drew,* and the *Loo Choo,* had carried the large contingent of fighting men and their assigned chaplain to California. Many of them had brought along their families. Although the entire group hardly lived up to the expectations for them, they had been chosen to provide the expansionist government with a select company of good habits and a variety of interests: in short, a stable group likely to stay on at the conclusion of hostilities, as did many, such as Gilbert and Hubbard, Kemble's partners in the *Alta California.* Chaplain Leavenworth was also a physician and a druggist; his pharmacy on Washington Street was the city's first. He owned several lots, and served as alcalde from '47 to '49.

Early San Francisco politics were chaotic. Constant charges and countercharges riddled the city air, a practice that has not much abated. On the occasion of the first municipal election, the official clerk, Joe Downey, reportedly carried out his duties while heavily drunk, tampered with the ballots, and announced himself mayor. His glory was short-lived, however; he was speedily arrested and confined aboard the *Portsmouth*; the ballots were put in order, and Bartlett then assumed office.

The second mayor, Edwin Bryant, a native of Massachusetts, had pursued a career of journalism in Kentucky and headed the party with which he migrated overland. He followed a military career before his election as mayor, a position he held briefly from February to May, before he returned to the East.

His successor was George Hyde, whose qualifications included service as alcalde at San Jose, and as second-in-command under Bartlett in San Francisco. In spite of his previous experience in the role, he had a troubled regime, marked by acrimony on all sides. In September a six-man council was elected to aide him: William Glover, W. D. M. Howard, William S. Clark, Robert A. Parker, William Leidesdorff, and E. P. Jones. Like many of their fellow citizens, they were soon bringing charges against Hyde, unproved charges which were often personal or had to do with rivalries in the business community. However, even after John Townsend succeeded him in office in March, Hyde retained a prominent voice in city matters and, along with his law practice, engaged in the real estate business.

After a similarly short term by Townsend, Thaddeus M. Leavenworth took over in September. And again in October. The second election was necessary after the first one was declared invalid. Although his administration suffered numerous criticisms, history honored him by naming a street after him.*

In those pre-gold days, the small community was frequently enlivened by celebrations: a feast and ball in honor of Thanksgiving; a grand illumination in honor of General Taylor's military successes south of the border; a splendid July Fourth observance; a

---

*San Francisco counts its mayors officially from 1850, the year that California was admitted to the Union. Under this system, the first mayor was John White Geary, who assumed office on May 1. His successors through the 1906 earthquake were: Charles James Brenham, 1851; Steven Randall Harris, 1852; Charles James Brenham, 1852; Cornelius Kingsland Garrison, 1853; Stephen Palfrey Webb, 1854; James Van Ness, 1855; George J. Whelan, July–November, 1856; Ephraim Willard Burr, from November 15, 1856; Henry Frederick Teschemacher, 1859; Henry Perrin Coon, 1863; Frank McCoppin, 1867; Thomas Henry Selby, 1869; William Alvord, 1871; James Otis, 1873; George Hewston, 1875; Andrew Johnson Bryant, 1875; Isaac Smith Kalloch, 1879; Maurice Carey Blake, 1881; Washington Bartlett, 1883; Edward B. Pond, 1887; George Henry Sanderson, 1891; Levi Richard Ellert, 1893; Adolph Sutro, 1895; James Duval Phelan, 1897; and Eugene Edwards Schmitz, 1902.

great dinner honoring the anniversary of the flag raising in Yerba Buena; fancy balls on the visits of dignitaries.

A good deal of activity centered on the hotels and groggeries. One of the most popular spots was Brown's Hotel, a low adobe with a wide veranda across the front. Many of its rooms fronting on the square were used for offices and business premises. After the beginning of the Gold Rush, it returned more profit than many a mine in the Sierra.

On June 8, 1847, a fire in the brush growing at the back of the town had caused some consternation, and well it should have. Most of the early construction consisted of wood framing lined with cotton and paper. The dangers of fire were to become more serious and more frequent. As the town grew and prosperity increased, so did the damage. Not until the fall of 1850—after a third fire had consumed the flimsy structures with the ferocity of a starving man after a fast—did the builders begin to replace wooden buildings with brick. By then arson, followed by looting, had become a silent partner of the Gold Rush; incendiaries took a large and unearned share of the new affluence.

SECTION TWO
The Gold Era

V

Gold

THE discovery of vast treasures by Hernando Cortez and Francisco Pizarro early in the sixteenth century led to European speculations about New World riches. In 1546, in Zacatecas, Mexico, some friendly Indians had shown Juan de Tolosa silver deposits so rich that their future production amounted to well over a billion dollars. Tolosa and three friends who joined him as partners became millionaires. The Zacatecas mines were only the beginning; rich silver deposits abounded everywhere. There was a tumultuous rush to the mines. Whole areas were sheared of their populations; whole new towns mushroomed near the mining districts. "The excitement and hectic conditions that prevailed were the prototype for the whole series of mining rushes in western North America; indeed, the 'days of '48' at Zacatecas, though three centuries removed, are often compared with the 'days of '49' in California."[1]

Spain, enriched by its New World treasures, became a dominant sixteenth-century power. European speculation on Spanish wealth assumed California to be just as rich a source as Mexico and Peru. Reports abroad even extended to tales of enormous pearls and of silver studding the beaches and countryside like jewels in the royal crown. The discovery of gold in California came as no surprise to those acquainted with the history of Spanish treasures, whether real or legendary. It was furthermore the call to a splendid new adventure for all those Americans whose perpetual restlessness originated in pioneering and was bolstered by the war with Mexico.

One of the first gold nuggets found in California, the "Wimmer" nugget (which, according to affidavits, was the actual mass of mineral that started the Gold Rush) presently reposes in a glass case in Berkeley inside the entry to the University of California's Bancroft Library. Youngsters on field trips from the elementary schools, shushed and herded by their teachers, jostle and poke each other past the exhibit case. The nugget is about the size of a lumpy five-cent piece pushed into roughly elliptical shape and weighs six pennyweights eleven grains. It was among several pieces first retrieved from the tailrace of John Sutter's mill in the foothills of the Sierra Nevada. Most of the samples found by James Marshall on that fateful morning of January 24, 1848, were slightly smaller, ranging from tiny specks to pieces the size of a pea. After Marshall retrieved them from the shallows, he beat them between rocks, pounded them thin with a hammer, compared them to a $5 gold piece, bit them, threw them into a hot wood fire, and finally gave one of the baubles, presumably the nugget now in Bancroft Library, to Mrs. Wimmer, the camp cook and laundress, to plunge into her boiling soap kettle. After trial by heat, beating, and chemistry, the unscathed samples seemed fairly certain to be genuine gold.

Marshall rushed to Sutter, the specimens tied loosely in a white cotton rag stuffed into his pants pocket. A torrential rain was falling, and Marshall, a singular individual under the driest of circumstances, arrived sloshing, dripping, and paranoiacally secretive. Late in his life Sutter reminisced about Marshall: "He was a very curious man, quarreled with nearly everybody though I could get along with him very well. He was a spiritualist. He used to dress in buckskin, and wear a serape, I thought him half crazy." He was, however, a good mechanic and had turned out excellent looms, sloughs, and spinning wheels for Sutter. On the basis of these skills, Sutter had provided the laborers, materials, and an interest in the Coloma sawmill in exchange for Marshall's constructing it. Now this half-drowned apparition stood before Sutter, demanding to see him in the utmost secrecy, insisting on locked doors, and startled almost witless by the innocent passage of a serving man. Finally secured within the confines of Sutter's private apartments, Marshall produced the flakes of gold for Sutter's perusal. With the help of the *Encyclopedia Americana*, a set of balances, and some nitric acid, Sutter put them to further tests, after which he pronounced them definitely "auriferous" and probably of very high quality to boot. He shortly sent a package of gold flakes to San Francisco for more deliberate scientific analysis. Dr. Fourgeaud, after suitable testing, also certified them to be the real thing. California's first commercial transaction using gold took place over the counters of C. C. Smith and Co. of New Helvetia, one of the many enterprises launched by Brannan and an advertiser in his *Express Extra*. The firm, which offered a general assortment of clothing and other requisite articles for crossing the mountains from victuals to pack mules, accepted a few specks of gold in exchange for a bottle of *aguardiente* from a teamster named Jacob Wittmer, who himself had obtained them from some of the men at the tailrace in Coloma.

On July 1, 1848, Thomas O. Larkin wrote from Monterey to his three young sons in Boston about the discovery of gold in California,

> My DEAR SONS
>   . . . The greatest excitement I have ever seen is now in our midst. In February some Mormons and others discovered gold on the banks of a branch of the Sacramento River, called the Rio de los Americanos. . . . In San Francisco I found the gold diggers arriving every day by land and water with the gold to shew for itself. . . . There was such a demand for picks, crowbars, tin pans & turned wooden bowls that the two weeks I was there the makers were earning twenty or thirty dollars per day. Some of these have since broke up and gone to the "placer" which as you are aware means a place where gold is found in sand or loose dirt and not in mines—rather a republican working ground where one workman is equal to another, where no one can be hired and each man must do his own work even to cooking—wash out gold six days in the week and his clothes on Sunday, where strenght [sic] and hands are an over match for head and knowledge. . . . It is the opinion generally that the gold regions extend over many rivers and can not be exhausted in a hundred years. . . . I believe there is now being taken from the sand daily ten thousand dollars, and as the workmen increase the quantity of gold taken will likewise increase. When this will end we can not at present imagine. We only know that in the mean time all the other business is almost entirely broken up.
>
>   YOUR AFFECTIONATE FATHER[2]

Ironically, the gold which was found on his land spelled disaster for Sutter. Until the time of its discovery, he had cut a swashbuckling path through life, no matter how dreary the reality of his circumstances, leaving his subsequent biographers in rich disagreement over his merits and his faults. But on one point there is accord: he was a born loser. His native village was Kandern, Baden, a few miles from Basel. By the age of twenty-three he was married. The day after the wedding his first son was born. He was a total failure at business and was cheated by his partner besides. His marriage was an unhappy match. At thirty-one, now father of five, doomed to debtor's prison and the probability of a life of nagging, he fled to America, allowing sixteen lean years to pass before finally sending for his wife and children.

In America he headed west. With stopovers in Indiana and Missouri, he journeyed overland by the Santa Fe Trail. At one point he joined a force of trappers, although he declined to take up company with a bunch of roughnecks who promised to rob the mission churches and steal livestock for him in exchange for being staked to the overland journey. His final route led him by way of Oregon, Hawaii, and Alaska. Once in California, he secured permission from the Mexican government to settle in the Sacramento Valley and a year later obtained a grant for the land from Governor Alvarado. He also purchased Fort Ross from the Russians and spent the next two years removing furnishings, cattle, and armament up the Sacramento on a launch which was part of his purchase.

His aim was to create a feudal domain based on agriculture and commerce and thereby make his fortune. His fortified settlement of New Helvetia expanded until he had under cultivation acres of wheat, owned enormous herds of livestock, operated a distillery whose product, pisco brandy, was always in demand, dealt in furs, ran a tannery, employed carpenters, blacksmiths, and a full-time physician, conducted a launch service up the river from San Francisco, built a grist mill and an irrigation system, and—the occasion which stirred up the river bottom and uncovered gold—had under construction a sawmill to facilitate his lumber business. All these accomplishments, however, were realized through the most elaborate series of economic flirtations, grandiose fantasies, and inflated promises that had ever constructed a house of cards. He made a fine presentation. He was a man of good manners and splendid dress, well read, fluent in several languages, and proud of a brilliant military career, largely imaginary. Men of prominence wrote letters for him; these introductions produced more. From such a stock of goodwill, credit followed like the floods after the spring rains. Yet, in spite of sincere efforts to pay off his creditors, he was always heavily in debt. He managed, whatever the ups and downs of his finances, to maintain a standard of hospitality that made him a hero of the frontier. Every traveler was welcomed, fed handsomely, and stocked with provisions.

His greatest preoccupation was with military matters. During his childhood, when Austrian troops marched on Switzerland, Sutter was an enthralled spectator; but soldiering remained only an ambition until he reached twenty-five. He then volunteered for the Swiss reserve corps, was trained and commissioned second underlieutenant, with a later advancement to first underlieutenant. However, by the time he traveled the Santa Fe Trail his military adventures had grown in his imagination, and he successfully played the role of Captain Sutter, a dashing ex-Swiss Guard, who under Charles X during the July, 1830, Revolution, had chummed about, militarily speaking, with Napoleon II himself.

During his transcontinental journey westward the fortress which he would build on the Sacramento began to take shape in his mind. At each stop along the way—Fort Laramie, the Hudson's Bay Company's Fort Hall, Fort Boise, Fort Walla Walla, Fort Vancouver—new detail heaped upon new detail in his vision of a fortified community with himself as feudal lord and commander in chief. With his excellent references and abundant credit, he established himself quickly as the great land baron of the frontier, on holdings which spread over 49,000 acres. The Mexican government supplied its new citizen with a title, Alcalde of the Northern District—a combination justice of the peace and government agent. His community housed assorted foreigners, immigrants and mountain men, Indians, and nearly a dozen loyal Kanakas, two of them women, whom he had picked up on the Hawaiian leg of his westward journey. With the help of several ships' cannons, plus the forty he got from Fort Ross, he equipped a fortress that could protect itself from any adversaries, be they unfriendly Indians or, as it later became clear to an increasingly suspicious faction, the Mexican government itself. Within its barricaded walls, Sutter drilled his company of Indians. Dressed in secondhand Russian uniforms that came with the Fort Ross package and keeping step to snare drums and fife, the toy soldiers marched up and down the parade ground in response to commands barked by the captain variously in German, English, Spanish, or native Mokelumne.

In 1844, when the worsening relations between Mexico and the United States caused Governor Manuel Micheltorena to initiate conscription and establish nine companies of militia, he put Sutter in charge of the Sacramento group. Shortly after, the Mexicans themselves had become so divided on the issue of independence that they erupted into a halfhearted civil war, Juan Alvarado and José Castro playing the rebels. Sutter's loyalties lay with the loyalist Governor Micheltorena, although he was much more committed to actual battle than the former, whose forces consisted largely of about 250 ex-jailbirds. In exchange for military aid, the governor granted Sutter additional lands and powers, although through a technicality—the absence of the secretary of state—no written document was issued at that time. (In later years, the courts decided that Sutter's claim to the El Sobrante Grant was thereby technically illegal.) Sutter assembled his battalions, a motley assortment of Indians, Hawaiians, mountain men, and anyone else who either sought revenge, mustered sufficient loyalty, or fell to Sutter's coercive powers. It was the strongest force assembled in California in more than 300 years. To add to the confusion, the rebels and a great many others, particularly in the southern part of the state, feared that Sutter had raised an army to take over California on his own behalf.

There followed one of the most delicious military campaigns in the history of warfare: a concerted effort to avoid bloodshed at all costs. Sutter's schooner, fitted out with heavy armament, became Micheltorena's navy. When it approached Yerba Buena, the officials there immediately captured it, disarmed it, and turned over all the military equipment to the rebel Castro faction, which in turn promptly turned it all back again. Armies fled before the Sutter-Micheltorena advance, not through cowardice but to prevent injuries to either side. When confrontation could not be avoided, most of the contestants managed to fire well over each others' heads. Soon Micheltorena promoted Sutter to colonel. Now heralded by a trumpeter and a cavalry escort, he could stalk the rebels in style, the splendor of the campaign marred somewhat, unfortunately, by Micheltorena's appearance: the governor, suffering miserably from hemorrhoids, could not mount his horse and had to be borne horizontally in a carriage. Slipping and sloshing through torrential rains and hampered by the conveyance of Micheltorena's carriage over steep mountain passes, the demoralized band of loyalists began thinking of desertion, which seemed even more attractive when the governor was deposed by a southern junta.

Sutter himself was finally defeated and captured, but in return for sworn allegiance to the new government, he was made military commander and magistrate of the northern domain, with more executive powers than he had had to begin with. Eventually, Sutter was caught between the faltering Mexican government, to whom he owed allegiance, and the increasing numbers of American immigrants, with whom his future and his sympathies lay. Captain Frémont, however, became an enemy and was largely responsible for Sutter's eventual loss of power. When roughneck Bear Flaggers, with a push from Frémont, set up the California Republic, Sutter found his fort taken over, his command pushed aside, and his jail used for housing General Vallejo and other Mexican functionaries. At first he tried to maintain a position of neutrality, but he rejoiced with the announcement of the American annexation of California. For the remainder of the Mexican-American War, he found his fort and his authority preempted. In the final stages of the war, he volunteered for the U.S. Army, was commissioned lieutenant, placed second-in-command at his own headquarters (by now humiliatingly renamed Fort Sacramento), and restored to his function of justice of the territory. Not until the cessation of hostilities, however, did Sutter again become master of New Helvetia. Although at that point he received another title, he was never reimbursed in any way for the use of his property or for his losses. Based on his dealings with the Indians—half pacification, half punitive campaigning—which had maintained order on the frontier (and had incidentally provided him with a continuous supply of orphaned Indians, whom he generously supplied to his friends and creditors to earn their favor), Sutter now received the appointment of official Indian agent for his new government.

The rest of Sutter's career was downhill, brightened only by an occasional gesture of honor. His efforts to sell his properties, first to Mexico, then to the United States—final attempts at financial salvation—ended in naught. He began to drink more and more heavily. With the discovery of gold, he was overrun by a reckless mob whose greed far outweighed any respect for law or property. His fort was left a shambles. What was not stolen outright lay wrecked or pillaged. Even his cattle were slaughtered, and his wheat fields trampled. His own attempts at mining, although close to spots where quantities of gold were taken, were a dismal failure. In 1848 his eldest son, now twenty-one, arrived to find his father's affairs in complete disarray. Sutter's spirits lifted briefly when he was made a delegate to the Monterey constitutional convention, where he was revered as the "grand old figurehead of the group."[3] However, when he then ran for governor, he came in a very laggard third.

When the rest of the family arrived, they settled in at Hock Farm, which Sutter had been developing simultaneously with the fort and to which his attentions had now completely turned. Here, among the peach and pear trees, the nagging took up where it had left off sixteen years before. Sutter became alienated from his son, and as his prospects for survival looked increasingly gloomy, he depended more and more on the relief of the bottle. In 1853 he had another moment of glory: the state legislature appointed him major general in command of the California militia, a ceremonial position ideally suited to him. His faltering ego bolstered by appointed aides, splendid uniforms, dress balls, military reviews, and colorful parades, he magnanimously issued a call for a military convention.

However, by 1864, after several empty years, he found himself on the brink of impoverishment. The legislature voted him a five-year monthly allowance of $250, totaling $15,000, which Sutter accepted on the grounds that it was a return of the taxes he had wrongly paid. He could thus probably have lived out his days on Hock Farm, always one step ahead of the rabble that still roamed his territories, but for another disaster. An ex-soldier whom Sutter had taken in with his usual kindness to vagrants, responded by robbing him. The thief had the misfortune to be caught and whipped; his revenge was to burn Hock Farm to the ground. Sutter was left with his wife, who in spite of her nagging remained loyal, a few military mementos, and his five-year allowance from the state of California. In despair, he moved east to the Moravian town of Lititz, Pennsylvania and devoted the rest of his days to petitioning Washington for reimbursement of his losses. The roster of prominent citizens who addressed the Congress supporting his claims of injury and loss of property included Governor Frederick Low of California, Adolph Sutro of San Francisco, Mark Twain, J. Ross Browne, and General William T. Sherman. The *Alta California* published editorials backing him. The Association of Pioneers of the Territorial Days of California elected him its president and honored him with flowery words and a gold-headed cane. But Congress, year after year, postponed action. On June 16, 1880, it finally seemed that success was at hand; the Congress had before it a bill introduced by Senator Daniel W. Voorhees for a settlement of $50,000. But in a last-minute scramble for adjournment, the bill never reached consideration. On June 18 Sutter died of despair. The July 10 *Harper's Weekly* ran an obituary which read in part:

> His claim to remembrance proved to be his great calamity, and he died, it is said, from the effect of his efforts and anxiety in importuning Congress to vote him a national indemnity because of the misfortunes he had suffered through the very discovery which has done so much toward enriching the country of his adoption.

By May, 1848, the news of the January gold discovery was common knowledge, and San Franciscans were heading for the area in droves. By June 2,000 Californians were at the diggings; by the first of July the number had doubled. In August the word spread in the East when the New York *Herald* reprinted the facts from Brannan's *Express Extra* of April. At about the same time Colonel Richard B. Mason, California's military governor, dispatched a messenger to Washington bearing a report on the gold mines and $3,000 worth of nuggets by way of illustration. The messenger's route took him through Peru, the Isthmus of Panama, the island of Jamaica, and New Orleans. In each place he prattled the news like a proud mother announcing her daughter's engagement to a millionaire. When the retiring President Polk delivered his farewell message to Congress on December 5, Mason's report was an integral part of it. That was as good as an official signal: the Gold Rush began in earnest.

Companies formed, advertised for members, bought their own ships, and bound their organizations by signed articles. Frémont's reports on his explorations went into frequent reprintings. Edwin Bryant's *What I Saw in California,* a literate and accurate account by San Francisco's second alcalde of an overland journey and conditions in California just prior to the Gold Rush, became an instant best-seller. The publishers hurriedly appended maps and mining information and came out with an up-to-date second edition by 1849. By 1850 it had gone into half a dozen American editions. Meanwhile, other guidebooks, often containing as much nonsense as fact, were multiplying on the market with the alacrity of drosophilas on a fruit bowl.

In Europe, still shaky economically as an aftermath of the 1848 Revolutions, the gold news seemed a panacea. Almost immediately, native language guidebooks to the goldfields began to appear: *Californiens Gegenwart und Zukunft* in Berlin; *Neuer Praktischer Wegweiser für Auswanderer nach Nord-Amerika* in Mainz; the *Emigrant's Guide to California* (a pirated copy of the Mainz book, hurriedly translated into English) in London; *Gids Naar California* in Amsterdam; *The Digger's Hand-Book, and Truth About California* in Sydney; *California, Texas and the Gold Rush,* in England, a pocket book shamelessly incorporating large sections of Bryant without the slightest nod of acknowledgment; and several pages, including maps and illustrations, in *Le Magasin pittoresque* in Paris— all in 1849.

In the same year in France, the decorative drawings on a set of Sèvres porcelain dishes illustrated the surprises in store for various frock-coated, spatted, top-hatted gentlemen, some even carrying walking sticks, as they confronted the facts of life at the California mines. There are bears to startle the arriving miner; Indians, brandishing spears and knives, to accost the sleeping miner (*"Agréable rencontre pour des sauvages affamés,"* reads the caption, whose author has confused not only the costumes of the California natives, but their dietary habits as well); armed ruffians to intercept the miner lucky enough to be laden with bags of gold; and open-jawed crocodiles to snatch the bathing miner from the Sacramento River (*"Plaisirs du bain dans le Sacramento,"* a river here surrounded by lush tropical foliage and coconut palms, a geographical notion which the illustrator has no doubt borrowed, along with the misplaced crocodiles, from the Isthmus of Panama). The final statement turns to the city, deserted by its gold-seeking inhabitants: in a kitchen at the stove, forlornly tending a steaming pot, stands the governor, stoutly booted, shoulders squared by epaulets, sword hung at his side, a forest of plumes adorning his tricornered hat, an apron, with a butcher knife thrust through his belt, draped around him. (Alas, *"tous ses domes-tiques étant partis aux mines. Le gouverneur est réduit à se servir lui-même."*) The fact that all the servants had left for the mines, re-ducing the governor to serving himself, was hardly an exaggera-tion of the state in which Gold Rush San Francisco found itself.

Perhaps 1849's most curious document came from Henry Vize-telly, a London printer and later well-known author, who in ten days, without leaving England, wrote *Four Months Among the Gold-Finders in Alta California; Being the Diary of an Expedition from San Francisco to the Gold Districts,* by "J. Tyrwhitt Brooks, M.D." The book received enthusiastic English reviews, from the *Athenaeum* to the London *Times,* and was referred to by scholars even after it was revealed to be a hoax in 1893.

By 1850 the list had been augmented by *California* in Edin-burgh; *Le Courrier de la Californie,* which printed a verbatim trans-lation of Colonel Mason's official report and a rundown of the var-ious French mining companies, in Paris; several guidebooks in Polish, Russian, and Swedish; and Bryant again, in English, Tas-manian, Swedish and French editions. The French put out flyers to advertise various *compagnies des mines d'or de la Californie* (some-what later to be followed by less optimistic titles such as *Misères ou-bliées, Californie 1850-1853, Aventures et souvenirs d'un chercheur d'or*). The Italians produced *Ragguagli geografici statistici e minera-logici intorno alla California ed a quanto riguardo l'oro che vi si ritrova.* The British issued *A Stroll Through the Diggings of California, Three Years in California,* and *The New Supplies of Gold,* as well as a pamphlet, "The Impolicy of Providing for a Family by Life Assur-ance, since the recent discoveries in California and Australia; with a proposal for the establishment of a new office, upon a plan which would secure the assured from the effects of a fall in the value of gold." In Brussels in 1852, no less a literary figure than Alexandre Dumas published *Californie—Un An sur les bords du San Joaquin et du Sacramento,* the story of some young Frenchmen in the goldfields of California. A German translation appeared al-most immediately in Leipzig, *Reiseerinnerungen aus Californien oder Ein Jahr an den Ufern des San Joaquin und des Sacramento.* The French version, its title mercifully shortened to *Un Gil Blas en Cal-ifornie,* came out in a second edition as late as 1861. This in turn gave inspiration to a rather second-rate Spanish novelist, Julio Nombela y Tabares, who almost ten years later produced *La fiebre de riquezas; siete años en California,* 1,100 pages in two volumes (which appeared in Madrid, as was the custom of the time, in seri-al form over a two-year period). Its huge readership included the intelligentsia and all social levels, who read about the discovery at

Sutter's Mill with the rapt attention common to all followers of soap opera.[4]

In America, East Coast churches devoted their Sunday services to the departing miners, frequently sending them on their way with brand-new Bibles. Thousands of dollars in bonuses were offered skippers who could get their ships to San Francisco in particularly speedy fashion. Pitched propaganda figured largely in the competition for business along the various overland routes: this way had easier passage through the mountains, that way fewer hostile Indians; this route provided better water and more abundant grazing, that road led to supply posts where goods were better and cheaper. Poor "Pikes" from Missouri and Arkansas joined affluent Northern men of affairs in a headlong rush to instant riches.

On February 28, 1849, the first steamship sailed through the Golden Gate. She was the *California,* jammed to the scuppers with treasure hunters from New Orleans taken aboard at Panama and with Mexicans, Peruvians, and Chileans, who had heard via vessels shipping from California that $250,000 worth of gold dust had found its way down the Sacramento River in June and July. Passengers and crew alike spilled from the steamer's decks in a frenzy to reach the mines and abandoned the *California* to the tides.

The resident Mormons were just as anxious to try mining as the strangers arriving from everywhere. At Mormon Diggings Sam Brannan assumed authority and began collecting the "Lord's tithes" from his mining brethren.

At the end of 1848 there were some 20,000 residents in California; one year later gold had changed that figure to 100,000; by the end of 1852 there were 225,000 people in the state. They had made their way by ship around the Horn; by ship, and canoe, native bearer, and their own two feet across the Isthmus of Panama; or by pack train and caravan cross country on the overland trails.

VI

The Voyagers

ON Sunday, February 11, 1849, the rector of St. John's Church, Brooklyn, Samuel Roosevelt Johnson, DD, preached a sermon to his congregation dedicated to the welfare of the barque *St. Mary* and all her company—which included his own son. The reverend's purpose was to provide to large groups of emigrants to California, such as this one, a proper spiritual context before, during, and after their travels. To the last end, the extension of the church in California, a collection was taken up. Dr. Johnson asked for a just and charitable interpretation of the rush to the goldfields; in order that families be well provided for, God had made the desire for property a part of the human constitution; this was not avarice, but a natural and lawful thing, and certainly much preferred to being poor, worthless, and lazy like the Southerners and the contented Californians; besides, would God have concealed gold so long from the peoples who possessed the land if He intended any injury or woe to its discoverers? Since the event was "so strange, so momentous, so romantic, well nigh bordering on the miraculous," the reverend prayed that those in attendance be blessed with such "sympathies, exertions, and benefactions" as were appropriate to the nobility and grandness of the occasion.[5]

Amen.

The Panama Route
The greatest imposition that the public ever saw,
Are the California steamships that run to Panama;
They're a perfect set of robbers, and accomplish their designs
By a gen'ral invitation of the people to the mines. . . .
—From "Humbug
Steamship Companies,"
an original Gold Rush
song by J. A. Stone

Late in 1848, Alfred Robinson booked passage to California on the barque *John Benson* to Chagres in Panama, thence across the Isthmus to meet the steamer *California,* out of New York October 6 and bound for San Francisco. When he arrived at the first port, he was amazed to find what seemed like more than 1,000 gold seekers already disembarked from the *Falcon* out of New Orleans; they were likewise hoping to find berths on the *California.* Canoes, the sole means of conveyance across the Isthmus, had all been pressed into service, necessitating waits of several days. En route the weather was miserable. Many persons, unable to stand the prolonged exposure to the rains, fell ill. Rumors circulated that cholera had struck. Panic followed. Travelers abandoned their possessions everywhere in an effort to move on to the port of Panama as quickly as possible. It was another month, however, before the *California* arrived; each day of waiting added new arrivals also headed for the goldfields. The steamship, when it finally departed, was crammed well beyond its capacity.

Robinson reports that San Francisco, in a great flurry of preparations, looked more like a battleground than a village, with lean-tos and tents hurriedly pitched on its sandhills. Many people set off immediately up the Sacramento in open launches; others stayed to look for better transportation or to wait for merchandise being shipped from the East. Cargo was eventually dumped all over the place, there being no facilities to accommodate it properly, but Robinson states that it suffered less from thievery, the early comers being a reasonably honest bunch, than from wet weather later in the fall.

Many others traveling the Isthmus route recorded its miseries in letters and diaries. One of the early accounts was written by Heinrich Schliemann, a man more famous for his later archaeological excavations of Troy and Mycenae than for his Gold Rush adventures. A self-made man with an extraordinary gift for languages—he was fluent in twenty-one*—Schliemann had traveled widely in Europe. In 1851, at age twenty-eight, he made his first trip to America to settle the affairs of a brother who had died in Sacramento and to lay claim to his fortune for the family. It was not an uneventful voyage: his steamship out of Liverpool became disabled in midocean but made it safely back to Dublin; the company started afresh on a second boat and this time made the crossing without incident. This was his second near disaster at sea. When he was still a youth of nineteen, he had been shipwrecked

---

*George R. Stewart in *Good Lives* (New York: Houghton Mifflin, 1967) says that Schliemann knew Greek, both ancient and modern, Plattdeutsch, German, French, English, Dutch, Spanish, Italian, Portuguese, Russian, Latin, Polish, Swedish, Slovenian, Danish, Norwegian, Arabic, Turkish, Persian, and Hindustani, plus some Chinese that he picked up during his California sojourn.

on a trip to South America but had clung to the wreckage and was finally washed ashore barely alive.

Once safely arrived in the eastern United States, Schliemann paid a social call on President Fillmore and his family, or so his records show, before leaving for Chagres on the *Crescent City* from Philadelphia. Of the 180 cabin and 80 steerage passengers, 60 were only going as far as Panama, where they had been taken on to build the railroad at $35 per month plus food. Thus they hoped to earn enough in half a year to pay their passage on to California.

Schliemann kept extensive diaries. He records the oppressive heat of Panama which made the dirty lavatories and poor accommodations seem even worse. Chagres, he notes, was among the most miserable places he had ever seen anywhere in the world. With much relief he finally watched his captain drop anchor among the 800 other ships already in San Francisco Harbor. He gladly paid $1.50 to be put ashore and another $2.50 to get his luggage over the planked streets to the Union Hotel, where his six-by-five fourth-floor room, the best in the house, cost him $7 a day with board.

A year later, on his return trip East with 1,300 other passengers of the steamer *Golden Gate*, he paid $600 for a single stateroom. En route to Panama the company suffered a terrible typhoon. Native stealing made giant inroads in their baggage. When they reached the Atlantic port of Aspinwall for the final leg home, there was no steamer. There was no housing either, and in spite of the torrents of rain, many found themselves bedded down in blankets under the nearest tree. Food was scarce, and fire impossible. They were often reduced to eating raw meat: turtle, lizard, mule, monkey, or crocodile. Plagued by painful mosquitoes, they shared their miseries with an increasing population of waterlogged travelers that finally numbered 2,600. This woebegone group waited fourteen soggy days for rescue. Finally, four steamers spirited them out of the place. Many had not survived the wait.

Not until 1855, when the Panama Railroad reached completion, did the route become relatively secure to travelers. The builders were not so lucky: among the 1,000 Chinese laborers, for example, who helped in its construction, 800 were dead of disease before the first several weeks had passed. The native population also suffered devastations from abroad. Cholera, epidemic in Asia and Europe, accompanied German political refugees to New York and New Orleans and thence to Panama when the Gold Rush migrations started in earnest. The very first epidemic felled one-quarter of the resident Panamanian population.

An alternate route developed across Nicaragua, often a favorite of people who had done with the Gold Rush and were on their way home. The same difficulties held however, coming or going. One passenger described his journey on the *Cortes* as one of 150 with staterooms in cabin class—everybody else was herded together in steerage. When the ship reached the coast of Nicaragua, they found no docking facilities. They anchored offshore, and small boats got them to within 25 or 30 yards of land. They had to choose between wading the rest of the way or riding astride the backs of nearly naked natives. The author was much upset to find that women were carried the same way. He also reported that a number of passengers who proved too heavy or too squirmy toppled headlong into the sea. Before the country was finally traversed, the passengers rode muleback, slept in a hotel which provided hammocks strung up in groups of forty or fifty, and shifted about on three different schooners, one for crossing the lake, one for the river, and one for the shallows. Their only food was what they could buy along the wayside. The heat was intense. The only distinction made between cabin and steerage was price. Sometimes the passengers even had to get off and walk to prevent the boat from miring in the shoals.

Jacob Davis Babcock Stillman's *Seeking the Golden Fleece* describes the author's homeward journey from California in 1850. Stillman, a physician by training, preferred the Nicaragua route because the "ravages of the cholera are so serious on the Isthmus."[6] He was rudely reminded of those perils on the way out of San Francisco harbor by the ship *Montague,* which lay in quarantine: more than half of the forty men who had left New Haven with her had died, the captain and second mate, as well as six passengers, having succumbed most recently to the cholera. The Nicaragua run, several years later, earned the dubious distinction of being chosen by 113 persons who succumbed on a single voyage: in 1855, the ship *Uncle Sam* debarked from the Nicaraguan coast with 750 passengers aboard, of whom 104 perished en route and 9 more on arrival in San Francisco.

Stillman's voyage to the coast of Nicaragua was smooth and well run, thanks to an intelligent captain. Once landed, the company made its way by canoes, or bungos, upriver, then by foot to the town of El Realejo. This place lay in filthy ruins, although there existed some evidence of former wealth and glory before its destruction by seventeenth-century buccaneers. Its present accommodations turned out to be the Hotel American, run by one Mr. Mulhado, arrived here by way of San Francisco and Sacramento. The hammocks he provided were comfortable enough, though mosquitoes and disorderly travelers managed to prevent sleep almost entirely. Mr. Mulhado sold tickets for his dinners, and Stillman observed ruefully: " . . . we regretted that we had not eaten our tickets and left the dinner. . . ." Furthermore, the charges were "extortionate."

The next trek onward was accomplished by oxcart, with passengers in a jumble with the baggage, or by horseback with the baggage dispatched separately. The author found the local forwarding business run by conspirators and swindlers, again ex-California men, but there was no alternative to their services. Finally, the party reached Granada on the borders of Lake Nicaragua, their destination San Carlos on the other side. The only boat, a small schooner, took on two of the party; they died on board two days later of the fever. The rest engaged to have a boat built. When it was finished, they loaded it with their possessions, and slept the night on shore ready for an early takeoff. The boat, however, was swamped during the night, completely soaking all the baggage and making it necessary to have a second and, it was hoped, more watertight conveyance hammered together. There was further delay for lack of a pilot and a crew, but finally, all necessary hands assembled, the voyage began. The lake was choppy, the provisions drenched, the sail could not be hoisted for want of a cleat to attach it to. There was nothing to do but head back for port, a lucky decision: when the boat went down, which it did almost immediately, they were close enough to shore to prevent drownings.

The company decided to await passage on a bona fide steamer, and three days later found themselves part of a complement of fifty on a craft designed to accommodate thirty. They slept on the cabin roof or on an 18-inch-wide gangway perch, some with their feet dangling in the water. The entire group locked themselves together to prevent someone's rolling overboard should he be lucky enough to get to sleep. The lake voyage completed, the bedraggled travelers faced a thirty-six-hour journey by trail, with sleeping accommodations varying from hammocks to floors to bare ground. The next portion, another water journey, was by large bungo. They had to sit crammed precisely on the floor; otherwise the unbalanced vessel careened so wildly that it might capsize. Thus they remained for four days and four nights. An all-night drenching, with recurrent rainstorms during the remainder of the trip, kept them wet as well as cramped. When patience was near an end, the master and his crew had a severe disagreement, and the voyage halted until tempers cooled. At last the exhausted company reached San Juan, the port from which they could embark for the United States. The author booked passage on an American brig, the *Mechanic*, one of two small ships in the harbor, and "home, with all its comforts, of the smallest of which we had been deprived so long, seemed almost at hand."[7]

Stillman reflected on this journey across Central America. It caused him pain and humiliation to think of the "brutal conduct of many of my countrymen . . . with less claims as individuals to a character for refinement, they perpetrate the most indecent outrages upon a people whom they call unenlightened, but who are greatly their superiors in every virtue that gives value to civilization."[8] They were not, however, the only breed of ugly Americans Dr. Stillman was to meet.

As the *Mechanic* made ready to embark, its passengers learned that its captain, Mr. Lawrence, had made an agreement with a Captain Hutchinson to engage first in rescuing a shipload of men, now ensconced on a small island of the Serrana Keys. Hutchinson, the master of the ship *Union*, had been en route from Chagres to New Orleans with forty-five passengers on their way home from California. Three weeks previously, owing to a faulty chart, they had struck a reef. All hands fortunately made it to the island, where they managed to transport a comfortable stock of provisions from the vessel. After two weeks without rescue, however, the captain took two men and set off in the long boat for a larger island in a more frequented zone. Unfortunately, he also took his faulty chart, missed the island, was finally picked up after long suffering in the open boat, and carried to San Juan. The passengers of the *Mechanic*, none of whom wished to hinder the rescue operation, nonetheless did not care to risk further adventures or to postpone their own return. They therefore proposed to find themselves other transportation, but their captain refused to refund their money, and so eighty unwilling souls took off for the Serrana Keys.

It soon became clear that the *Mechanic* was not altogether seaworthy and, to make matters worse, already running short of provisions. Further, a number of the crew came down with the fever, and no medicine had been put aboard. The author then learned from the first mate that the ship had been wrecked at Chagres and condemned. Several gamblers there had bought it cheap, refitted it, and sent it to engage passengers in a port where its identity would not be known.

It became imperative to put in to a port for provisions, a highly dangerous operation because most of the islands were ringed with treacherous coral reefs. Disaster nearly struck when the cable parted from the anchor in rough seas, but finally, provisions stowed away, they set out again for Serrana. En route they sighted an unexpected wreck. The *Martha Sanger*, out of Chagres for New

Orleans with ninety passengers from California, had hung up on
the Quita Sueno Reef and was in great distress. The captain decided to come to its aid. Three small boats, one manned by the
mate and two men from the stricken vessel, spent the day in rescue operations. The *Martha Sanger*'s captain, Mr. Robinson, was
rescued before the others. He, his own chest, a keg of whiskey, all
his valuables, and everybody else's gold dust (obtained on the pretext of safekeeping) were all that came off the first day. The passengers had to risk another night on board.

There followed several days and nights of ferrying back and
forth, with the near loss of a number of men engaged in the rescue, including the author. Most of the saved were suffering from
exposure and fever; many were already dead or dying. They were
assigned a filthy space on the main deck, where they lay without
even blankets. The gold and money was divided between Captain
Robinson and his mate as "salvage." Provisions again became a
problem. Although there were still men left aboard the wreck, the
Mechanic pushed off for Old Providence Island and fresh supplies. Fortunately the *Polly Hinds*, a trading ship there, discharged
some of her cargo and set forth to complete the rescue operation.
Meanwhile, the *Mechanic* put ashore its contingent of survivors,
no matter their condition, while Captain Lawrence confessed that
his intentions to proceed on to the stricken ship *Union* were not to
rescue it, but to wreck it and claim the salvage. Nine passengers,
including the author and four former shipmasters, demanded to
be put ashore with their baggage, "determined to trust ourselves
to the uncertainties of the climate and the chance of an opportunity to get home, rather than be witnesses of such barbarity any
longer, or trust our lives in the keeping of such drunken pirates."[9]
On this remote shore, one month and 200 miles from San Juan,
the nine men now found themselves with a dying band of survivors and a few natives. The *Polly Hinds*, however, came to their
rescue: having taken the remaining passengers off the *Martha
Sanger*, she returned to Old Providence to complete her cargo operations. The discharged cargo left room aboard for Dr. Stillman
and his companions, who arrived with her in Baltimore 113 days
after he had left San Francisco.

The Nicaraguan route became more popular after Cornelius
Vanderbilt's involvement as operator of a line of steamships in
1851. With foresighted control of the transport rights across the
strait, he later could provide continuous shipping service in both
oceans. There was so much subsequent traffic that when Mark
Twain made the journey some ten years later, he "complained
that the natural beauty of the jungle had been altogether spoiled
by the billboards of the Yankee merchants."[10]

The Cape Horn Route

> Now miners, if you'll listen, I'll tell you quite a tale,
> About the voyage around Cape Horn, they call a pleasant sail;
> We bought a ship, and had her stowed with houses, tools and grub,
> But cursed the day we ever sailed in the poor old rotten tub.

> *Chorus*:
> Oh, I remember well the lies they used to tell,
> Of gold so bright, it hurt the sight, and made the miners yell.
>
> —From "Coming Around the Horn,"
> an original Gold Rush song by
> J. A. Stone

In Hartford, Connecticut, on December 16, 1848, a group of men met to form an association for mining and trading in California. They purchased and fitted out the *Henry Lee*, circulated a handbill, "California Ho!" and quickly counted up 122 members. In January they met in Gilman's Saloon to adopt official articles for the Hartford Union Mining and Trading Company, and on February 17 they set sail for San Francisco by way of Cape Horn, a journey of some 15,000 miles. On board ship John Linville Hall wrote and printed a journal of the trip.

Hall records that the average age of the company was twenty-seven, there were forty-six married men, and the largest number in any vocation was twenty-three farmers. The rest of the company represented three dozen assorted professions, including joiners, machinists, blacksmiths, silversmiths, upholsterers, potters, pewterers, tanners and curers, coopers, harnessmakers, brickmakers, molders, tinners, stonecutters, masons, papermakers, shoemakers, painters, cabinetmakers, tailors, dyers, wool sorters, watchmakers, carriagemakers, sawyers, printers, millers, butchers, stagedrivers, barbers, lawyers, physicians, merchants, manufacturers, clerks, navigators, seamen, and one minister—who came along for his health. There were five crew members.

Besides two years' provisions, they stowed on board all the equipment to be used for mining, complete sets of mechanics' tools, and a good amount of merchandise—$1,200 worth of boots and shoes and $1,000 worth of other apparel, for example. They took along stoneware, hatchets, hardware, clocks, groceries, garden seeds, and miscellaneous clothing, totaling more than $3,000, on consignment. The capital stock of the company amounted to $37,025.

Among the rules for shipboard conduct, the members were admonished to keep "clean and wholesome." No guns could be fired without permission, and all lights were to be out by 10 P.M. So organized, this exemplary company set forth.

First off, they were beset by seasickness. The weather was not just rough. It was cold and wet; the seas ran so heavy they washed out the fires. In spite of the constant drenching, the galley managed to catch fire accidentally. Lightning struck the main mast, which fell, together with the yards and rigging, into an incredible tangle on the deck. Six dogs were swept overboard. The weather at Cape Horn was fearful. Chilblains swelled hands and feet. In spite of such rigors, Hall, as a good diarist, also reports on the beauties of nature, the interest shown in the ports of call, the fish and fowl sighted along the way, and the festive celebration in honor of Independence Day. They arrived in San Francisco on September 13 after seven months at sea.

> We lived like hogs penned up to fat, our vessel was so small,
> We had a "duff" but once a month, and twice a day a squall;
> A meeting now and then was held, which kicked up quite a stink
> The captain damned us fore and aft, and wished the box
>   would sink.
>
> We sobered off, set sail again, on short allowance, of course,
> With water thick as castor oil, and stinking beef much worse;
> We had the scurvy and the itch, and any amount of lice,
> The medicine chest went overboard, with bluemass, cards
>   and dice.
>
> *Chorus:*
> Oh, I remember well the lies they used to tell,
> Of gold so bright, it hurt the sight, and made
>   the miners yell.

Samuel Upham, a twenty-nine-year-old Philadelphian, married with one child, holder of a good position in the countinghouse of a mercantile firm, greeted the first news of the gold strike with skepticism. He and his friends thought it was just another Washington scheme to encourage Western migration. After President Polk's message to Congress, however, the skeptics found themselves hurriedly making plans to share in the California bonanza. Upham at first opted to go by the Isthmus route, but after reading an account of the trip in the December 23, 1848, New York *Herald,* he hastily booked passage on the *Osceola,* which sailed via Cape Horn. The *Herald* warned its readers that the Isthmus climate was "the most pestiferous for whites in the whole world." The region, furthermore, abounded with poisonous snakes and alligators, and "bilious, remittant, and congestive fevers, in their most malignant forms, hover over Chagres." However, Upham's own trip by way of Cape Horn was so bad that when he returned a year and a half later, the Panama route seemed preferable.

Since he planned to be in California a year, Upham supplied himself accordingly: flannels, "California-style" hats, a rifle and a six-shooter with ammunition for both, a knife, a chestful of medicine, a medical primer, a pick, a spade, a crowbar, a nest of sieves, a large tin pan, three different types of patented gold washers, an India-rubber waterproof suit ("coat, cap, long boots, and gauntlets"), and a tent of the same material. Everybody else was similarly outfitted; besides being a constant burden, it turned out that most of the fancy equipment didn't work.

Before booking, Upham inspected the steerage accommodations on the ship *Osceola* and found them in good order, with adequate skylights and a comfortable table fitted out for thirty diners. He was much taken aback when he boarded to find that the owners had ordered the dining-room furniture removed and the space utilized for cabin-class baggage, assorted pigpens, chicken coops, and water casks. He further discovered that he now shared the steerage with forty-four companions, including mates, stewards, and cooks, twelve more than the law allowed. Later he learned that the deck above was so leaky that the upper berths would become completely waterlogged. The morning of departure was a bleak day in January. The ship took off so early that half the passengers had not yet boarded. Farewells were lost among cries from those who ran screaming after, and finally caught up with the aid of small boats. The final party consisted of sixty-five passengers, all but three of whom were hopelessly seasick within two or three days.

The weather was ferocious with squalls and gales that split the jib; severe cold, hail, and furious storms that battered them for weeks off the Cape; and tropical heat so unbearable that the author pined, "If I could truly divest myself of flesh and sit in my bones for an hour or so, wouldn't it be altogether lovely?"[11]

At one point the brig was on the verge of breaking up. The captain ordered most of the deck cargo jettisoned over the sides to relieve the strain: it consisted mainly of the passengers' own provisions, from brandy and house frames to trunks and mining equipment. Some passengers were left entirely destitute. Upham, reading Edwin Bryant's *What I Saw in California*, regretted not having made his journey overland. Other passengers had even debated leaving the ship at Rio, crossing the mountains, and meeting her again at Valparaiso, to avoid the most severe trials at the Cape.

Mess in the steerage proved to be disgracefully inadequate. On one occasion a codfish and two dozen potatoes served for thirty-six people. Some took to eating the flying fish that floundered on deck. It soon developed that the water casks had been improperly secured, in the haste of the owners to speed their ship's departure, and several of them had leaked all or part empty. After this, the travelers greeted new storms with mixed emotions—at least rain bolstered the freshwater supply. At Cape Horn the thrashing about was so violent that it broke up the steerage galley—built by two carpenters among the passengers—and all the stoves. They now had to suffer not only the cold—Mr. Upham met the situation by staying in his bunk—but a diet of raw salt pork and hard tack. There were improvements whenever a port was reached. At Rio they obtained butter, pickles, and vinegar for the first time. The water, by then unpalatable and covered with a green scum, was replaced by fresh stores, enough to last to San Francisco. And the passengers bought fresh fruits and some jellies from an enterprising French lady. The Rio provisions, except for the water, didn't last a month, and the diet returned to a steady round of salt beef, salt pork, hard tack, and an occasional pudding. At Talcahuana, Chile, the passengers were elated because the cook promised them a batch of dumplings from the apples put on board. They were no more palatable, boiled in salt water, than the infrequent plum puddings had been.

The captain, who had the respect neither of his passengers nor of his crew, found himself in constant altercations with one or the other. He flogged a sailor to enforce discipline, shocking the passengers. He forbade gambling on board, denying them one of the few pastimes on such a long voyage. He employed untrained passengers, on one occasion even a boy, to stand watch when he was short a first mate. Fifty-one signed a petition protesting this peril to their lives, but it did not restore the first mate to his duties. About one-third had feet so badly swollen from scurvy or chilblains that they could hardly pull their boots on. The cabin passengers held a meeting to express their indignation and to formulate a statement of their grievances to present to the American consul at Rio. Those in steerage struck a bargain with the captain, who promised them a new galley and cook at Rio, under their threat of a report to the authorities there.

After a journey of 201 days—176 of them at sea—and 19,308 miles, the *Osceola* dropped anchor in San Francisco Bay on Sunday, August 5.

Not all travelers via the Cape had it so bad. In 1852 Hinton Helper booked space on the *Stag-Hound*, a clipper ship from New York, as one of seven passengers. He reported that the new ship was fitted out with the best of furnishings, that the accommodations were spacious, and that the trip was both speedy (113 days) and enjoyable. Had it not been for the inconvenience of a hurricane (of such severity that it caused the masts and their appendages to come crashing down, necessitating a delay of about two weeks while the extra masts aboard were hoisted in their place) the trip might have come closer to the eighty-nine-day record of the clipper ship *Flying Cloud*. The author managed to conquer his seasickness in a mere three weeks' time. Monotony was broken by such interludes as rescuing a boatload of Swedes from a wrecked ship off Brazil and visiting Valparaiso during an earthquake. In addition to the hurricane, there was one other admittedly frightening episode: during seven days and nights of continuous buffeting by the usual tempest off Cape Horn, the ship nearly sank.

Even in the early days, the passengers were a cosmopolitan group. E. I. Barra, who made the trip to San Francisco from Philadelphia via the Horn in 1849, reports that on his ship, the *Samson*, there were several French families. Refugees from the French upheavals, they had settled briefly in Philadelphia and now were among the first to try their fortunes in the goldfields. He also notes that in those days only a man of substance to begin with could make the trip to California. He would have to have adequate funds to cover his own expenses and simultaneously support his family left behind. Barra concludes: "Therefore, it may be safely said that a finer, more enterprising or determined body of men never collected before, than those that came to California from the year 1849 to 1852."[12] However, there were differences of opinion.

Between 1851 and 1853, eleven passenger steamers went down on trips around Cape Horn. The Panama route, though it involved less time at sea and less prolonged turbulence of weather, was by no means without danger. Many early sailings by that route ended as shipwrecks, and three later disasters stand out: the wreck of the *Yankee Blade* with a loss of 30 lives and $153,000 in the fall of 1854; the burning at sea of the *Golden Gate* in 1862 with a loss of 223 lives and $1,500,000; and, the greatest catastrophe of them all, the sinking of the *Central America* in 1857 with 423 persons and $8,000,000 worth of gold from California.

It is no wonder that some immigrants preferred the overland trails.

The Overland Routes

Oh don't you remember sweet Betsey from Pike,
Who crossed the big mountains with her lover Ike,
With two yoke of cattle, a large yellow dog,
A tall shanghai rooster and one spotted hog.
— From "Sweet Betsey
from Pike," an original
Gold Rush song by J. A.
Stone

The overlanders were a heterogeneous gaggle that included those who preferred land travel to sea, those who wanted their families and possessions with them, those who already lived inland, and those who couldn't afford the high costs of a sea voyage. Sweet Betsey and Ike were among many goldseekers from places like Pike County, whose typical character was described in a book by an early overlander, William F. Swasey. Southern Missouri, he found, was the "wildest, most lawless country I have ever seen"; its residents, "rough, ignorant people," lived mostly by hunting and "were a law unto themselves." Their habits were so primitive that Swasey considered them nearly savages. Nothing much happened even for killing a man—and there were deadly feuds in abundance.[13]

More law-abiding were the "military" contingents, such as that of J. Goldsborough Bruff, organized in Washington, D. C. His men paraded smartly in their new gray uniforms, up and down in front of the White House, before taking off for California. Once onto the trails, they fared so badly that they barely missed sharing the fate of the Donner Party in the mountain snowstorms.

They were representative of the great wave of patriotic militarism in the wake of the Mexican War, now bolstered by imagined foreign threats to the newly discovered goldfields. Men actually petitioned the War Department, official records show, to go to California as military units in exchange for clothes, food, equipment, and a guaranteed chance to mine for gold in between carrying out protective duties. Some prospective millionaires even offered to split their take with the government. But segregation, racism, intolerance, and antiforeign sentiments often accompanied the patriotic-military pose. Fed by greed and the lack of law prevalent at the mines, these attitudes influenced the behavior of the mining communities and, in turn, the structure of San Francisco itself.

At the outset, the overland companies were generally well organized, and whether or not with official military recognition, often along military lines. Duties and rules were meticulously spelled out, sometimes by formal contract. One such, executed between E. Butler and the Joseph Dana Company on March 2, 1852, in Cincinnati, describes a typical set of arrangements. The company agreed to secure for Butler a cabin accommodation on a steamboat to Council Bluffs on the Missouri River; from there to provide a substantial wagon pulled by a minimum of three yoke of oxen, to Sacramento City; and during the journey to supply the following provisions, in quantities of not less than three pounds (per man) per day, their quality first to be attested to by a representative five-man committee: bacon, flour, meal, sea biscuit, hominy, beans, sugar, coffee, pepper, salt, etc. In his turn, Butler agreed to pay $25 on signing and to be the driver of a team of oxen, thereby reducing his total fees by $45. The normal schedule was $100 down payment, an additional $50 when landing at Council Bluffs, and $200 for each family member accompanying the subscriber. Family units received individual light spring wagons, but the joining member had to perform the same duties as all single males, such as standing sentry duty and preparing the mess. Each traveler had to furnish his own gun, ammunition, knife, two blankets, and sack for clothing. The baggage allowance, excluding blankets and gun, was 25 pounds. The Dana Company, besides taking the responsibility for the direction of the march, supplied each man a tent and each mess of five with its cooking equipment. In case of disagreements among members, a majority vote could oust an individual, who would then be allotted his share of the provisions. He could not be taken back without a unanimous amnesty.

Many companies formed around harebrained schemes which appealed to people in too much of a hurry. One such was the New York Mutual Protection California Company, whose originator, John Gildersleeve, envisioned a flatboat propelled by twenty-four paddle wheels, capable of landing the company within 800 miles of the gold fields in record time and for only $50. The remaining distance would be by horse- or muleback, the cost to be equal to the first half of the journey. The only uneventful part of the trip was to Cincinnati by rail, canal, and river. Once there, the construction of the flatboat began. The craft, 120 feet long and 8 feet wide, immediately proved too much for its 8-horsepower engine, and the paddle wheels too much for hand operation. Taking the flatboat in payment, a steamship towed the company as far as Wittsburg, where they set forth on land by ox-drawn wagons. They were soon mired in the Arkansas swamps and ravaged by illness, including cholera; were it not for the stamina provided by another party which they joined, they might not have finally dragged their way overland.

Parodying the competition for speed, Nathaniel Currier invented timely cartoon schemes for air travel to California. The "Grand Patent India-Rubber Air Line Railway to California" was in effect a giant rubber band. Strung taut between two high poles on the Atlantic side of the continent, it carried its passengers seated astride it well above the city rooftops, picks and shovels prominently projecting from their baggage. "One, two, three, four and five, off they go all alive," chants a young man who has shinnied up the pole to hack away at the rubber band with an ax: in one slingshot spasm, the company will be hurtled to California.[14]

Another 1849 Currier lithograph depicts a skinny spindle-legged gentleman, cape, tailcoat and long hair streaming behind his aquiline profile, straddling a rocket headed west. It bears the legend "ROCKET LINE" and spews exhaust convincingly behind it. The sole passenger has lost his hat and, with the distress of a newly coiffed lady, shouts, "My hair!! how the wind blows." The caption beneath announces: "through in advance of the Telegraph. Passengers not found, (if lost.)." Sharing the skies with the rocket is a large cigar-shaped balloon, its exhaust pipe puffing, the Stars and Stripes unfurled over its rudder, the lettering on its side proclaiming "Air Line, through by daylight Passage $50. Each passenger must provide a boy to hold his hair on." One of the passengers in the crammed gondola beneath asks, "Augustus, don't you wish we were down and not up?" to which he replies, "Yes—for I begin to feel air sick—Oh dear! Oh dear!" Far below, a man grasping shovel in one hand and pickax in the other floats gently downward, thanks to a parachute for landing passengers, to which he is connected by a large hook through the seat of his pants. He admonishes those on a ship's deck below, "Stand from under."[15] At least two inventors, Rufus Porter, a New Englander, and Fred Marriott, a Western immigrant, designed actual (but unsuccessful) machines for use in flying west.

Because of the inherent commercial advantages to those along the route, pressures for the development of the Northern versus the Southern overland passages resulted in a Congressional bill in March, 1849, to provide some answers by exploration and surveying and some protection by a military escort for large bands of emigrants. At the same time the government gave its blessing to 479 people in a seventy-five-wagon convoy that extended over three miles of roadway. Captain Randolph Marcy of the United States Army accompanied them and ten years later drew on his experiences to write a travelers' handbook.

To cross the plains and mountains successfully, the overland traveler needed luck, endurance, and a lot of reliable advice: on the availability of water and grass, the distances between stops, where to find firewood, how to ford rivers, where the mountain passes lay, and how to prevent the livestock from being injured or stolen. Long before Captain Marcy's work, a plethora of guidebooks attempted to provide the answers. One of the best was Joseph E. Ware's 1849 *The Emigrants' Guide to California*, dedicated to Senator Thomas Hart Benton for his championship of Western expansion. Besides maps and surveys, Ware offers his readers invaluable advice: they must be on the frontier no later than April 20 or risk being marooned in the snows in the mountains; there should be no more than fifty men to a party for the best management of resources; teams should be oxen, no more than six years old, and of not too great a size—or appetite; mules were a second choice; travel on the Sabbath was a false economy—that day of rest would assure a speedier arrival in the long run; sentinels must be posted at all stops without fail, or the animals would be stolen by the Indians; cows brought along for their milk became unfit in certain areas where the poisonous water infected them; shortcuts might lead to such disasters as the Donner Party needlessly experienced. Each person's provisions should include a barrel of flour or 180 pounds of kiln-dried ship biscuit, 150 to 180 pounds of bacon, 25 pounds of coffee, 40 pounds of sugar, 25 pounds of rice, 60 pounds of beans and peas, one keg of clear beef suet, one keg of lard, 30 to 40 pounds of dried fruit, and molasses and vinegar. There follows a description of the various stopping places en route, with notations about their facilities: Little Blue was 50 feet wide, with plentiful timber and good grass and water; Castle Bluffs had scarce firewood for some distance onward—the main fuel was bois de vache, buffalo chips; at Sweet Water the current was swift, the fuel wild sage and willows; the 400-foot vertical granite walls of Devil's Gate, a fissure through which the Sweet Water River surged, could best be avoided by leaving the trail previously and fording the river; Naphtha Springs provided a tar good for healing the galls on horses and cattle; Ash Hollow onward was so sandy that wagon wheels sank 6 to 10 inches in the road; Thomas Fork was unsurpassed in beauty and blanketed with an abundance of wild flax that made excellent fodder for the animals. Just in case the reader made it to the mines, an appendix gave tests for the detection of gold and new methods for the reduction of silver.

Captain Marcy's book, *The Prairie Traveler, A Handbook for Overland Expeditions*, was published by the authority of the War Department. The captain, a West Point graduate, had served on the frontier beyond his 1849 expedition, duty which included extensive Western explorations into 1854. He passed on to his readers such detailed advice as the best type of wagon, how to repair broken wheels, which supplies to purchase, and how best to load them. He warned of the Indians' tricks of stampeding herds into their own corrals and advised having a herdsman always saddled up ready to turn them back. He also advised that the spittle obtained by chewing plantain leaves would reduce the irritation of mosquito and gnat bites and that when people forded a stream, a good way to avoid being swept away by swift currents was to place strong swimmers with lariats in "expeditious" positions.

Such counsel did not save thousands of overlanders from disaster. Animals died, stranding their passengers in zones of desert heat or mountain cold. Hostile Indians accounted for lives as well as livestock. Scurvy crippled to the point that its victims had to be lifted on and off their horses. Cholera and dysentery were epidemic. In his daybook Major Osborne Cross mentioned coming on a party of fourteen travelers: in one day six were dead of cholera, another near death, and the others so sick that they could not bury their companions. Poor swimmers, in spite of the warnings, were lost in large numbers attempting to ford the rivers. A few strategic ferries grew up to profit from the traffic, but their rates were exorbitant. The settlements en route sold provisions at equally outrageous prices; in any case, the going was so rough that what at one instant had been dearly sought after became a burden the next.

The main trails became depositories for cast-off supplies and remains both animal and human. On bleached skulls and weathered planks, messages multiplied for those who followed. For 1,000 miles this macabre bulletin board stretched, giving news of the passing caravans and issuing warnings against such perils as the bad water which "poisoned six of our cattle." The John Wolf party recounted the unbelievable devastation that littered the trail as they crossed the Nevada desert. They picked their way through a junkyard—iron stoves, wagons, utensils, trunks, clothes, beds, coffee, bacon, books. A stench of decaying flesh permeated the vast open spaces. There was no possibility of losing the trail.

The main stopping points were early grazed out. Each new party had to forage a wider circle to find food for its animals. In some cases there were even "individuals who fired the grass as a deliberate hindrance to those who followed, apparently on the theory that they were thereby reducing competition in the diggings."[16] Others poured turpentine on abandoned food supplies and shredded discarded clothing to tatters to prevent their use by any who came behind them. The dying were sometimes left by the wayside, but compassionate strangers as often stopped to minister to them, more often to bury them. Not unlike the milestones of the Roman legions, the headstones of the forty-niners marked the California trail.

In 1850 a broadside appeared in France, whose humorous-sarcastic view of the Gold Rush came uncomfortably near the truth. It addressed itself to all who were avaricious, all who were down-and-out, to improve their fortunes and remedy their misfortunes at the mines: girls without dowries and consequently without husbands; smugglers; entertainers and vaudevillians; those in terror of the Paris police; usurers; Jews; lawyers; bailiffs; notaries; men of affairs; pirate journalists; poor artists; poor husbands; unpaid landlords; assassins; bankrupts; "humanity's lepers." "All aboard for the California gold mines! Go!" it cried. But don't expect beefsteaks dressed with anchovy butter, well-baked French rolls, or truffled turkeys, it warned, for food and chefs were scarce at the mines, but roots there were in abundance. Further, since the rest of the world was also on its way to California, one could not be choosy about companions: there would be Chinese, Tatars, Basques, Germans, Arabs, Englishmen, Russians, Spaniards, Portuguese, Swedes, Italians, and—*Sacre bleu!* worst of all, Americans! One must not regret the museums, the *grands boulevards*, the omnibuses, and all the comforts and amusements of Parisian civilization, nor must one fear the perilous five-month trip at sea or the seasickness, colic, and fever; gold would make it all worthwhile! It would not even matter whether in dying one should turn black or yellow—after all, for the rest of eternity one would be enclosed in a golden shroud.[17]

One phrase, "seeing the elephant," best incorporated the sense of combined hardship and experience common to the forty-niner. Although the phrase originated in the East, its meaning changed with Western circumstances. Gold Rush songs and journals filled with allusions to the elephant, and San Francisco lithographers did a thriving business illustrating letter sheets with "a view of the elephant"—usually vignettes of mining life surrounding the ubiquitous pachyderm. The circus, when it had started traveling beyond New York in 1830, became a tremendously popular attraction, and it was everyone's ambition to see the show. The elephant, introduced to this country in 1796, was the highpoint and generally its closing feature. To have seen the elephant was to have seen everything, to be a worldly sophisticate, an experienced person. In the context of the Gold Rush, the meaning expanded and was commonly used to imply also surfeit, disappointment, suffering, and frequently failure. When a miner wrote home to his loved ones that he had "seen the elephant," he meant that he had experienced the worst rigors of travel, the hardships of mining life, the temptations of drink and the risks of gambling, and he was not often pleased with the results.

The trip to California, whether by sea, by land, or by combination of both, was a grueling journey under the best of circumstances. The weakest travelers did not survive. Many men returned home disillusioned. Many by choice and others by the necessity of recouping their losses turned from the mines to San Francisco and to an entirely different mode of life. The most aggressive often shed their morals and their manners to ensure self-preservation. The surviving forty-niners by circumstance became formidably self-reliant, and some turned out to be veritable blackguards. For many, the journey west was only the first of several dehumanizing experiences of the Gold Rush, with far-reaching effects on later California society. Those who stayed on, either through success or through failure, the majority of the burgeoning populace, the founders of the city's institutions, the stylists of its ways, all these men had had a most rigorous training for citizenship. They could deal with city problems as men accustomed to hardships, reversals, strong disappointments, outrageous successes, and uninhibited pleasures. They could take in their stride the fluctuations of the economy, the boom and panic of business, the destruction of fire, and later earthquake, they could face with perseverance changing circumstances and shed one career for another, and they knew how to live it up. They had seen the elephant.

For all it was a great leveling device: social background, position, training, and wealth finally meant nothing. People had to be valued for what they really were, which often meant a reversal of their previous roles in society. Within the next decade they created a unique metropolis.

VII

The Mines

In a cavern, in a canyon,
Excavating for a mine,
Dwelt a miner, forty-niner,
And his daughter Clementine.

A mine is a hole in the ground and owned by a liar.
—MARK TWAIN

THE majority of gold seekers who arrived in San Francisco remained only briefly, no longer than it took to secure passage to the mines. The few who stayed and the many who returned later—including a large contingent of overlanders—formed a population whose lives, forever changed, reflected the disruption of their customary patterns of living. No wonder that the city which emerged was unique. Exigencies of the moment remolded traditions that had been formed in diverse corners of the world. San Francisco's culture evolved through a reexamination—however involuntary—of the moral convictions, religious beliefs, financial philosophies, likes and dislikes, folkways, languages, and governmental patterns of a heterogeneous assembly, in the light of the extraordinary events following the discovery of gold.

In spite of some of the stories to the contrary, nuggets did not lie scattered about for the taking. The process for the extraction of gold required backbreaking labor, patience, a stamina and industry altogether absent in the stories that the gold fever conjured up. Gold and gold-bearing materials generally deposit in dry veins or in rivers and their tributaries, upstream of gravel bars, behind boulders, in pockets and crevices of bedrock. Over the centuries man has developed various techniques for its extraction. Panning, an old process and the one first used by the California miners, requires shoveling mixtures of gravel and mud from the watercourse into shallow slope-sided pans. Large rocks and stones, roots and clinging plant material must be carefully washed over the rim and discarded. Because gold is about seven times as heavy as the other particles with which it is mixed, when encouraged by the proper series of motions it will sink to the bottom and eventually separate out. First, it is necessary to submerge the pan to twice its depth in a hollow of the stream where the water runs clear and the current is swift—swift enough to carry off the lighter products without taking the gold along with them. A firm, semirotating, to-and-fro motion sloughs off the first debris. A dipping motion, with the pan angled away from the miner, spills off additional unwanted particles. After about twenty minutes of alternate dippings and shakings, the pan finally holds about two tablespoons of material. A quick swirl reveals small pieces of gravel and minerals, largely iron pyrite—a heavy black sand, which, like gold, sinks to the bottom—and, cleanly washed apart, whatever nuggets, gold flakes and dust the material had originally entrapped. Unfortunately, metallic flecks of mica and crystalline pyrite, or fool's gold, among the black grains of sand have caused unbounded flashes of excitement, but the early miner learned quickly enough to distinguish the real thing.

However, no matter which way his luck ran, he had to cope with the same extraordinarily trying conditions: the weather was almost always extreme—a harsh sun beating down, torrential rainstorms, spring floods, winter snows. The streams and rivers in which he worked, no matter what the temperature of the air, were always ice, having melted directly off the snow packs and mountain glaciers. Harassed by rheumatism, afever with ague, shivering with pneumonia, swollen from scurvy or chilblains, he still might wash as many as fifty pans on a favorable day. Unless he was working a rich field, this was often too slow a process to reward him with even a day's expenses. And although income was erratic, expenses remained constant. It followed that miners did not delay in working out improvements.

The first innovation was the rocker, or cradle, a small slanted rectangular box of wood, mounted on a rocking base and fitted out with two filters, a sieve across the top and ridges across the bottom. The miner shoveled in gravel and stones, poured in a bucket of water, and rocked the contraption. The large materials caught on the sieve, the waste flushed out the low end along with the water, and the heavy gold particles fell through and lodged on the riffled bottom for extraction by the primitive panning process. Unfortunately, the fine gold often escaped with the waste products, a defect which the miners soon corrected by first mixing in mercury to hold the gold and later vaporizing the mercury to release it. The rocker substantially increased the daily output. Further, because it needed only a small amount of water for each operation, water which could be transported easily by bucket, it could be used in dry diggings. With the next improvement, the 10- to 20-foot Long Tom, a much enlarged version worked by several men at once, the miners had to dig courses to obtain an adequate water supply. When mining reached this stage of development, the lone miner was an anachronism.

The next evolution was the sluice box, an even longer Long Tom, often several of them strung together. Individual panning was still necessary for refining, but teams of men cooperated in the initial operations. In 1853 hydraulic mining took over. Jets of water under great pressure melted down banks of gravel as if they were slush. The loosened rubble rushed downward into waiting sluice boxes, where the separation took place, leaving huge mountains of waste at the end of the process. Networks of flumes and channels slashed the foothills, supplying enormous volumes of water to the hydraulic nozzles—totaling more than 5,000 miles of man-made waterways before the decade was over.

Today the entire perimeter of California State Highway 49 bears testimony to the industry of the miner and to his brutal abuse of the land. The highway winds through a slow-paced network of settlements, marred by a litter of bashed cars and rusted machinery. There are ghost towns and modernized ones. Supermarkets stand next to dried adobes and old Pony Express offices. Corrugated aluminum rooftops flash blindingly along the road. Everywhere there are ruins and reminiscences: abandoned buildings, restored buildings, old buildings in use, carefully designated with historical plaques; viaducts and canals carrying crystal glacier water; white orchard blossoms gone wild among the pines and manzanitas; mountain slopes shaved in half by hydraulic devastations; poison oak and rattlesnakes; slouching old-timers with a twang to their speech; and everywhere, relentless piles of mining waste, gravel mounds pimpling the face of the land with a massive acne.

It seems improbable that these lazy, ramshackle foothill communities could have been basically instrumental, either financially or culturally, in the establishment of San Francisco. Originally, they were more cosmopolitan places. Mrs. Louise Clappe,* a literate New Englander, wrote in a series of letters from the mines:

*The young Mrs. Clappe accompanied her physician husband to San Francisco in 1849 and two years later to the mines on the North Fork of the Feather River. Her lengthy letters to her sister in the East contained outstanding insights into Gold Rush California, combined with such wit and charm that the *Pioneer*, the first of the West's literary journals, serialized them in 1854–55 under the pseudonym Dame Shirley.

You will hear in the same day, almost at the same time, the lofty melody of the Spanish language, the piquant polish of the French, (which, though not a *musical* tongue, is the most *useful* of them all,) the silver, changing clearness of the Italian, the harsh gangle of the German, the hissing precision of the English, the liquid sweetness of the Kanaka, and the sleep-inspiring languor of the East Indian.To complete the catalogue, there is the *native* Indian, with his guttural vocabulary of twenty words! When I hear these sounds so strangely different, and look at the speakers, I fancy them a living polyglot of the languages, a perambulating picture gallery, illustrative of national variety in form and feature.[18]

The mining settlements reflected this diversity in their names: Dutch Flat, Chinese Camp, French Corral, Malakoff Diggings, Nigger Hill, Hornitos, Mokelumne Hill, Kanaka Creek, Murphys, attested to the international character of the men who came to the Gold Rush.

Ships from every nation sailed through the passageway between the sea and the Bay, which only a short time before, John Charles Frémont had so prophetically named *Chrysopylae*, or Golden Gate, after the Byzantine harbor *Chrysoceras*, or Golden Horn—a port he had never laid eyes on.

William Shaw, an English midshipman, sailed on June 8, 1849, on one of the first of forty-eight ships to reach the California gold regions that year from Australia. By the time he reached San Francisco the harbor was bobbing with deserted vessels flying colors of every nation. Shaw's ship, the *Mazeppa*, joined the ranks, the crew indecorously debarking in small boats or on floating planks, leaving the passengers to fend for themselves. Once ashore, the voyagers found a frantic community. Happy Valley, the most prominent settlement, was crammed with tents, although still lacking sanitation. Because some of the crowded occupants tended to become scrappy, and because there were now several untrustworthy characters on the prowl, the tent dwellers existed in a general state of jitters, which had not been true of the earlier inhabitants. Shaw reports that few people dared to sleep without a firearm next to them. Tents and houses scattered toward the central plaza, presently Portsmouth Square, pushing from every conceivable crevice. Gambling and drinking arenas ringed the square. There was a constant babble of foreign tongues. Signs and notices were multilingual. The whole area had become a makeshift marketplace, a chaos of discards and merchandise imported for sale. Storage facilities were open to the air and to the honesty of the transient population. The laws against thievery were sufficiently severe to ensure a generally upright climate.

On the very first day, Shaw, like many of his fellow campers, finding that he had too many possessions, emptied his trunks onto some rough planks under a baldacchino made from a sheet and in short order had exchanged his excess gear for $70 cash. He then went into partnership with a shipmate who had brought along several barrels of spirits, which they put up for sale in a ramshackle shelter—public groggery by day and private bedroom by night. The whole thing went up in flames the first night, however, when the shipmate,who had sampled heavily of the merchandise, fell asleep with his pipe still going.

Dr. John Middleton, a Gold Rush physician, described the community as "one vast garbage heap. Spoiled food and the intestines of slaughtered animals were tossed into streets and yards." Rotting debris littered the wharves and polluted the Bay, and the encampments of tents he found filthier still. "This," he proclaimed, "is the most abhorrent place that man ever lived in."[19]

The heavy traffic turned the unpaved streets into dangerous quagmires, from which carts and animals and an occasional human who had missed his footing were dragged with difficulty. Pedestrian passage was normally erratic, over pathways of stepping-stones made of discarded cases, tree trunks, empty barrels, anything that projected one clean side above the mud—mud which sometimes measured as much as four feet in depth.

There was a general shortage of sleeping places, and all sorts of makeshift lodging houses crowded the scene. They were often mere sheds, as much as 60 feet long and one-third as wide. Windowless, they got their air through the chinks and gaps in the plank construction. If the weather was bad, they also got the rain. Two rows of bare wooden shelving along the sides served as bunks, the sleepers supplying their own blankets. When the shelves were filled, latecomers bedded down on the floor. In wet weather, Shaw reported, there were often as many as eighty men jammed together, sleeping in their wet clothes and muddy boots.

Food was another matter, and boardinghouses and taverns offered a wide variety of cooking. Stands provided pastry, coffee, and other short orders. Except in the fancier restaurants—where there were separate tables, menus, and bills triple those of the table d'hôte eating houses—food was generally served family-style. Down the middle of a double row of plank tables, all the dishes appeared simultaneously, from fish and stews to rice and frijoles. Although many national tastes were acknowledged, the meals were nutritionally unbalanced. Beef, grizzly bear, and venison were plentiful, but green vegetables were totally lacking. The boardinghouses summoned their patrons with gongs and bells, and each sitting generally lasted ten minutes. No wonder that some diners ate with only a knife. Most eating places made some attempt at sprucing up the decor. Often sides of beef or venison hung by way of a sign at the entries. Calico papered the interiors, and prints adorned the walls. There was always a bar, usually set at one end. Shaw found the Chinese eating places best, their small dishes of curries, hashes, and fricassees "exceedingly palatable."

The gambling houses were among the most sizable structures in the community; certainly they were the most frequented. They provided music, cards, wine and liquor, and, in some cases, elaborately costumed women. A good deal of gold dust exchanged hands within their mirrored walls.

Passage to the mines offered a whole new set of discomforts. Shaw's experience was typical. He traveled to the diggings on the 12-ton cutter *Diana*, crammed in among thirty other deck passengers. They had neither shade to protect them from the intensely strong sun nor shelter to shield them from the heavy night fog. At least they fared better than some: Upham's brig, for example, went aground several times on sandbars and mud flats and had to be towed out by the combined efforts of all hands manning a rope on shore. Each traveler provided his own food; Shaw managed on brandy, biscuits, and a bit of ham. The passengers debarked at Stockton, where they joined forces with a party of twenty Americans, Chileans, Frenchmen, Germans, Cornish miners, Chinese, a Malay boy, and two guides. A train of five pack mules accompanied them, bearing provisions for storekeepers in remote areas of the mines and a week's supplies for each of the party. All sported pistols, Bowie knives, or shotguns. Soon after they got under way, they experienced a shocking encounter with a bedraggled group of overlanders, what was left of a party of backwoodsmen from Illinois, emaciated, haggard, shriveled figures. As they pushed on, they found the trail studded with abandoned debris, broken equipment, burial mounds, and skeletons.

Through sand sometimes ankle deep and under a noon sun that brought the temperature up to 120 degrees, Shaw's group trudged on to the mines. Their eyes and throats were parched, but they found no water the first night and a dried-up hole the second. Two men were so desperate they licked the sweat off the mules' bodies. There was no firewood and consequently no cooking, but everyone was exhausted beyond caring. Howling wolves prevented sleep, and it was a weary crew that struggled on in the morning. Four men finally dropped behind. The rest strapped their water bags more closely to them and, when night fell, slept with their pistols in their hands. When they reached the river, some of them jumped in, clothes and all. Although they were now assured of water and wood, they made no attempt to turn back to rescue their four weakened colleagues.

The mountain ascent was equally rugged. Another traveler, Leonard Kip, wrote in his recollections that one road was so bad—sand-covered and pitched at what seemed to be 45 degrees—that his wagon slipped and capsized. His party then had to backpack all the provisions a steep half mile uphill.

When the diggings finally came into view, they were a wondrous sight. For miles along the river, miners worked at their tasks like ants bustling in a colony, their picks and shovels tearing at the earth. The final washing process often employed the same pan used for bathing, eating, feeding the animals, and doing the weekly laundry every Sunday. After Shaw's party had joined the activities, he reflected on the monotony of such hard labor from dawn to nightfall, with such poor returns for the effort. The most they obtained in a single day, and that only once, was about $25 worth of gold. More usually, the take was closer to $15, and so with most of the others. Real fortunes were rare; some men never had a strike or even saw anyone else get one. The only sure income was from selling provisions or providing amusements, and a number of people thus made their fortunes.

Some argonauts were just not lucky at all. One of them, who was also among the most literate of the Gold Rush diarists, Elisha Douglass Perkins, journeyed overland in the spring and summer of 1849. He recorded the trip and the life at the mines in considerable detail: the illnesses and deaths, the extremes of weather, and the exhausting labors, even to the hourly bailing out of the flooded diggings. For his group, as for so many, the financial returns were negligible. Perkins concluded that to mine a fortune in California, with occasional exceptions, was not much different from making a fortune elsewhere, taking the same enormous expenditure of time and effort. Such a miserable life he was not about to continue, for any fortune; he would simply return home. Before heading back to Ohio, however, he took on employment locally as a steamboat captain. In 1852, still without a fortune, he succumbed to a severe case of dysentery on a wharfboat in the Sacramento.[20]

Around Auburn, however, which was then named Rich Dry Diggings, the early yield was several hundred dollars a day per miner, and there is a record of as much as a $15,000 daily take by one man. The mines there ran out early, but more sophisticated methods, such as the construction of flumes, produced a second Auburn bonanza in 1852.

Another pioneer, C. W. Haskins, remarked in his reminiscences of early mining days that although it would be natural to imagine that the men who mined the gold should retain at least the major part of it, such was not the case. The miners, in short order, were the poorest, not the richest, members of the community. Barring the few who did amass, and manage to retain, real fortunes, even men with excellent claims usually failed after a period of time. Haskins felt that the continuously heavy expenses of mining were responsible since income, although sometimes stupendous, was also unpredictable. Besides, miners had learned to treat gold with extreme casualness and had forgotten whatever habits of economy they may once have known.[21]

In his chronicle of events, Samuel Upham reported that his first day's efforts yielded one-quarter ounce or $4 worth of dust, but that he improved and made $10 on the second day. Changing his position to a new digging, he then made nothing for two days; several boulders had to be removed before work could progress. However, he finally met with good results: in two hours he obtained nuggets worth $45 and in several days had amassed $400. Some miners, he observed, however, did not average as much as $1 a day, and many considered themselves lucky to clear their expenses. Upham's intention to remain through fall and winter was short-lived. By early October, only three weeks after his arrival, he suffered a severe attack of rheumatism, had to sell all his possessions, and ended up in the hospital in Stockton. Like many another who gave up mining by choice or necessity, he eventually turned to business: he sold to greenhorns on their way to the mines equipment which he purchased in Stockton from disillusioned miners on their way back.

Kip, on his way to the goldfields, met many returning miners whose efforts had proved uniformly unsuccessful. They commented that although dissuasion of others should now be their proper course, it would be useless, for no one would believe how bad things were until he tried mining for himself. Kip's party dismissed these remarks as cynicism, attributing poor success to laziness and lack of proper work habits. Clearly, no fortune would come unsolicited. When they themselves set to work, however, the daily average did not reach $3 per man, no matter how diligent their labors. The luckiest miners in their area, perhaps one out of a hundred, might get $10. Several men in the vicinity were in debt for food and clothing. The perversity of gold was such that even the trained geologists among Kip's party had no luck. Kip was convinced that the exaggerated reports bandied about in town were based on the actions of a few lucky individuals who spent their fortunes with wild abandon and on the claims of braggarts and liars whose successes were more imaginary than real.

In any case, there was a steady trek away from the gold areas, not just to them. The group that stayed on, hopeful that their luck

would change, were those who enjoyed the rough life, the drinking, the unrestrained gambling. The group that left formed the
nucleus of permanent urban settlers in San Francisco. They established businesses and molded the government to accommodate
the problems which the Gold Rush thrust upon them. The life-
style of San Francisco was conditioned by the life-style at the
mines, which, in many instances, set a rugged example.

Ethnic groups tended to band together, then as now, and to
guard their own prejudices. The largest group of migrants, from
the summer of 1849 on, were Americans from the East. Intoler-
ant of all Indians and all foreign born, emboldened by greed, and
encouraged by the impermanence of their society, many of these
men expressed their attitudes through actions that ranged from
verbal bigotry to actual violence. Native Americans suffered the
most severely at their hands, but the Chinese, Mexicans, and
Spanish-Americans were not far behind. Racial or ethnic prejudice was often the source of injustice in the mining community.[22]

Mrs. Clappe remarked that there was nothing more amusing
than to observe the way the Americans, bolstered by the knowledge of a few ill-pronounced Spanish words, talked in broken English, as she puts it, *at* the Spaniards; some relied on shouting,
others on grotesque gesturing; in every case, they assumed that
the Spaniards' inability to understand was due to Spanish contrariness and certainly no reflection on their own agility with the
language.[23]

Such intolerance ran deeper than mere impatience. Mrs.
Clappe reported on the case of a Spaniard who asked an American, one evening, for the return of several dollars he had lent him
some time before. The American's response was to stab his bene-
factor in the chest, wounding him severely. "Nothing was done,
and very little was said about this atrocious affair," Mrs. Clappe
commented in dismay. At Rich Bar, the antiforeign feeling ran so
high that the American miners passed a resolution excluding all
foreigners from work at that site. Residence in the mines, of
which Mrs. Clappe designated Rich Bar the nucleus, was so devastating that it debased the most excellent of men. Often forced by
bad weather to remain endlessly in their glum mountain communities, unable to work the mines, with no entertainments or
means of diversion, "even the most moral [became] somewhat
reckless."[24]

Violence flared on other counts as well. For example, in Shaw's
area, at a bend in the river, a large group had turned their ener-
gies toward digging a diversion channel in order to expose the river bottom. The new course completed, they turned the waters
into it and consequently also over all the other diggings. When the
offenders refused to concede damages, the flooded miners took

matters into their own hands, appropriating shares in the newly uncovered riverbed. The inevitable result was a battle and a massacre. Every implement and weapon on hand came into play, leaving men crushed, slashed, shot, even disemboweled.

Most men did not countenance such behavior, and as a deterrent many communities elected alcaldes, who also served as sheriffs. Larger districts eventually incorporated lesser mining areas in the hope that justice could follow a more familiar pattern. However, as often as not, the elected official turned out to be the worst ruffian of all, eager to take bribes and to find innocent parties guilty for the fines he could then demand. In most cases his word was final, juries and courts of appeal being scarce. When there was a jury, it usually consisted of the first people to arrive on the scene of the crime. Men learned to deal out and to receive "justice" with savage immediacy. Penalties were harsh, punishment swift, decisions irreversible. Petty larceny called for cutting off a man's ears; hanging was not an uncommon sentence for burglary. The most ordinary articles were so difficult to replace that the miners instinctively imposed cruel punishments; not many a sinner got off with fifty lashes or a shaved head. Even though it was difficult to prove that one man's gold dust really belonged to another, no one could be sure that his itchy fingers might not prove the end of him.

Upham's party, when they debarked at Stockton, confronted a crude gallows that had just served to execute two thieves. Kip reported on the case of a man who was caught trying to take money, was given a jury trial on the spot, sentenced to a flogging, had his head shaved and his ears cut off, and was then drummed out of camp without a thing to his name. Since his appearance gave clear evidence of his criminal character, his only chance of survival lay in a quick getaway. So he stole a horse. A posse pursued him and gunned him down.

Such rudimentary laws as existed evolved largely from the articles of incorporation that the organized companies had signed in the East. The original rules had spelled out a strict division of labor and profits and in many instances a rigid code of behavior as well. But neither travel conditions nor mining camp life nor a virtually masculine society encouraged adherence to Puritan morals. Beyond this, such real difficulties as widespread illness made it impossible for many men to work, let alone to fulfill the simplest community obligations. Since many came west independent of organized groups, on-the-spot regulations were often more expedient. One such spontaneous rule, universally accepted, allowed any man in an area to lay claim to a certain number of feet by placing his equipment on it. It was his until he removed his implements.

Or until one of the rough bunch of overlanders from Missouri or one of the ex-convicts from Australia—or anyone else of similarly forceful persuasion—decided to take it over.

Many of the patterns of justice which San Francisco adopted came from the mining-camp society which named Hangtown, Chicken Thief Flat, Murderers' Bar, Garrotte and Second Garrotte, Cut Throat Bar, and Gouge Eye. Poker Flat, Euchre Bar, Seven-Up Ravine, Brandy Gulch, Milk Punch, Port Wine, Whiskey Bar, and the inevitably logical conclusion Delirium Tremens give further evidence of its temper. These outrageous names "primarily gave vent to the lusty high spirit which was the distinguishing mark of that amazing time. No censorship restrained it; society was of men only. Most of them looked upon their sojourn in California, particularly in the mining-camps, as a temporary and riotous adventure."[25]

SECTION THREE
From Village to Metropolis

VIII

Transformation

THE Gold Rush, whose impact historically was as great, perhaps, as a political revolution or a catastrophic war, converted San Francisco almost instantly from a village of a few hundred inhabitants to an urban and commercial center. Although there was money on an unprecedented scale, enough for the population to obtain anything it wanted, no matter the extravagance, at first neither goods nor accommodations were available. Such was the speed of change that by 1852 San Francisco had already passed the first great peak of its development and started sliding gently into an economic decline, the scale of which, within three years, attained the proportions of a panic.

At first, the extraordinary demand for goods and services, coupled with the ready abundance of gold, caused inflation. During the summer of 1849, eggs sold for $12 a dozen, wages started at $12 to $16 a day, houses of the cheapest construction rented for $800 a month.[1] By the winter of 1849 the disparity of wages between San Francisco and the even more economically inflated mining communities triggered the city's first strike. Among the thirty San Francisco "carpenters" participating, fourteen had come to California as lawyers, doctors, bookkeepers, and ministers.

In response to the demand for goods, there was an immediate influx of merchandise, everyone became an instant businessman, cargoes piled up on the beaches and in the streets, and there was a frantic call for wharves and warehouses. Daniel Wadsworth Coit, a financier and agent for the Rothschilds, sent home to his wife several bales of black twilled worsted, of which the supply far exceeded the demand and which, consequently, he could buy at auction for one-fourth their value in New York. He also ordered iron warehouses from England, which he set up on shoreside hills where he hoped they would be out of the range of fire. The federal government rented most of the space. Unfortunately, the terrain gradually eroded and finally gave way. The warehouses slid down the collapsing cliffs, and they and the merchandise they contained were a total disaster.

Jacques Antoine Moerenhout, who took up the duties of French consul in San Francisco during the winter of 1849, wrote immediately to the French Minister of Foreign Affairs suggesting that prefabricated houses of wood or iron, manufactured in France and shipped to San Francisco, would yield considerable profits. In April he was respectfully but insistently repeating a previous observation that his expenses were still far in excess of his salary. In June he reported that there was such an increase in the arrival of vessels and cargo—at his writing, 200 to 300 merchant ships were reportedly on their way from the United States alone—that he did not believe the high level of prices and profits could possibly hold up. Speculation in land "being carried to an extreme approaching madness," it pushed values up as much as 1,000 percent. The lack of bonded warehouses, the cash duties, and the exorbitant charges for private storage furthered Moerenhout's economic pessimism. He had, moreover, another serious concern. Since bricks were $1 apiece, early building was largely of wood, and some 3,000 people were still living in tents. In a locale where dry weather prevailed for all but a few months of the year and where there was a "furious northwest wind," Moerenhout was one of several observers who anticipated, rightly, a frightful destruction of property through a phenomenon that was increasingly becoming one of the major influences on the city's development: fire.[2]

Physically the city spread out from a shorefront scattering of canvas, wooden, and adobe structures that clambered inland over chaparral-studded hills. At about Stockton Street the hills rose high enough to be virtually impassable, imposing a western barricade on Washington, Clay, California, and parallel streets. Expansion in that direction was difficult, if not impossible. In the seventies the installation of two cable car lines made the area one of the city's most desirable; there, on Fern Hill, which came to be known as Nob Hill (possibly from the Cockney for "snob"), the wealthiest citizens built enormous mansions.

Montgomery Street in the earliest days ran along the shoreline. Its busiest section extended from California Street north to Broadway. The recent much-debated practice of filling the Bay actually started in 1847. As the community grew, Yerba Buena Cove appeared to the townspeople more valuable as real estate than as lagoon, and gradually several square blocks of North Beach—a large segment of Market Street, a part of what is now Fisherman's Wharf, almost a dozen blocks along Sansome and Battery streets from Bush to Broadway, and an area in between

running from the Embarcadero inland almost to Kearny—stood
where the Bay had been before. Before bay fill created the several
blocks that now separate Montgomery Street from the water,
some early firms had used the address "Montgomery Street on the
Beach" in their newspaper advertising.

The city, with the aid of private citizens and business firms, constructed wharves set on pilings in the cove extending from Broadway, Clay, and California streets and later from numerous other
points; the result facilitated shipping, increased accommodations
by several hundred wooden buildings, and spurred trade generally. The idea to reclaim the mud flats by filling in the Bay had
originated early partly because of the hilly barriers to western expansion. Besides converting Yerba Buena Cove and the northern
inlet from harbor to prime commercial real estate, it had changed
the character of Happy Valley, whose sand dunes provided the
ideal material. A steam excavator leveled the hills, and a freight
car delivered the fill to its destination. Parker's City Directory for
1852–53 noted that the water trapped in the docks above the newly formed streets grew more offensive by the day, its stagnation re-
leasing sulfuretted hydrogen in such quantities that the painted
signs along Sansome and Battery streets were blackened nearly to
illegibility.

The quarter that is still called North Beach, although it seems
incongruously far removed from the water, was in original fact
just what its name describes, extending up to the shoreline above
Broadway. At Mason near Francisco Street, Henry Meiggs set up
a sawmill, making use of a racing stream that traveled there. The
area became a focal point for the lumber trade, which was expanding rapidly with significant imports from Oregon. A cove at
the present Aquatic Park near Black Point and the Marina was
then known as Washerwomen's Lagoon, a good place for doing
laundry. Professional launderers set up enormous three-legged
boiling kettles and brought washboards for heavy-duty scrubbing.
Tents housed the ironing facilities. The washerwomen were mostly Indians and occasionally Mexicans and Chileans. When a Chinese established a rudimentary laundry business there, the price
of washing shirts came down from $8 to $5 a dozen. A. T. Easton
soon was running the largest laundry in the city from this site.
The Bergins, Thomas and his four sons, established the only
soapmaking firm, supplying the laundry industry with soap and
the rest of the city with soap and candles. Local laundry prices,
however, were still relatively so high that it was common practice
to send dirty linen overseas for washing or to buy new clothing
altogether.

In 1848, when the city lifted the regulations on the sale of land lots, real estate speculation increased. The first survey which Jasper O'Farrell had done under Bartlett had described the central area, as well as corrected the two-and-a-half-degree error that had occurred in Vioget's original survey of San Francisco. In 1847 O'Farrell made a second survey, taking in a larger compass, including some 450 beach and water lots, which the city then offered up in a widely advertised sale. In spite of the fact that most of them were completely inundated at flood tide and often quite soggy otherwise, about half of them sold at from $50 to $600. In 1853 less desirable lots, half the size, and completely water-covered, sold for between $8,000 and $16,000.

The terrain beyond Yerba Buena Cove was hilly, windswept, sandy, marked by occasional tortured oaks and stands of shrubs. The city remained largely barren of trees well into the 1860's. Beyond Mason Street a long trail led out to the original Presidio. Inland through the fields to the south, the Mission Dolores now stood decaying, but the area was a favorite outing place especially on Sundays. The much-frequented path was difficult, much easier for horsemen than pedestrians. A private firm, headed by Colonel Charles L. Wilson, constructed a plank road and charged tolls, with the legal blessings of the legislature and city council but the opposition of the mayor. By 1851 the area around the Mission sported racetracks, roadhouses, and other such secular amusements. In 1850 A. A. Greene built the first regulation racetrack between Twentieth and Twenty-fourth streets. By 1852 the sport was so popular that race horses were imported from Australia. A reminder of the area's Spanish heritage, the two early rings for bullfights, located out by the Mission, proved insufficient for the community; in 1850 two additional arenas were constructed closer in, one next to the Catholic church on Vallejo (now the site of the church of St. Francis of Assisi), the other near Washington Square, in the heart of the present Italian community. Bullfighting continued to thrive in San Francisco for another decade.

One of the reflections of the city's rapid expansion and changing composition was its graveyards, the earliest of which was the Catholic burial ground at the Mission. When the non-Catholic gold-seeking population began to arrive in hordes, burial practices became haphazard. During the worst periods of epidemics, unburied corpses littered the beach at Miller's Point until the tides and sands claimed them. Usually, however, there was some attempt at interring the dead in at least rudimentary graves, which clustered in different areas of the city. By far the largest portion was in a plot of land in North Beach, which gradually took on the dimensions of an unofficial public cemetery. When the land became more valuable for commercial purposes, the bodies were exhumed and moved to new sites. Several other graves joined the Russians interred on the summit of Russian Hill (the exact site is now a ramp and staircase on the corner of Jones and Vallejo; during its construction, the work crews unearthed several skeletons), a good number of burials took place in the Happy Valley area, and still another congregation developed on the rise of Telegraph Hill above Clark's Point. By 1854 fifty people of Jewish faith were buried together in Presidio Cemetery, located beyond Van Ness, within the boundaries of Franklin, Gough, Broadway, and Vallejo, on property owned jointly by congregations Emanu-El and Sherith Israel. In 1859 Emanu-El joined the Eureka Benevolent Society, a Gold Rush philanthropic group now called the Jewish Family Service Agency, to obtain a plot of land near the Mission Dolores for the Home of Peace Cemetery.

In 1850 the city council had designated a large acreage west from Market and McAllister streets on the outskirts of town as the official burial ground, Yerba Buena Cemetery. (In the seventies the city chose this site for the new city hall; the present Civic Center, constructed after 1906, is on approximately the same spot, although very slightly to the west.) In 1854, 160 acres lying between the Mission and the Presidio, a few miles west of Portsmouth Square, became the new public resting place, Lone Mountain Cemetery. By this time the haste, the despair, and the loneliness that characterized the burials of a transient and disparate population had given way to a more standard attitude toward death. The new cemetery, unlike any of the previous public sites, was enclosed, set in an area of some natural beauty, enhanced by shrubs and flowering plants, its lanes named reverently after hometown Eastern graveyards.

By late fall of 1849 more than 600 ships had anchored in the cove. By 1851 there were 774, most of them abandoned, many with cargoes still aboard. Several deserted vessels served as housing for people who were willing to pay the $2 charge to be rowed back and forth. Some were scuttled or sank where they anchored, some became basements for buildings rising from their decks, some were made over into stores, saloons, and boardinghouses, and later some were dismantled for their lumber, in a supreme effort to acquire building materials and clear the harbor at the same time. Several served as storeships, among them the *Apollo* at Sacramento and Battery streets, and the *General Harrison* at Clay and Battery streets. The *Georgean* may be the hull which is incorporated into the building at 716–720 Montgomery Street, known as the Ship Building. Unfortunately, modernization conceals much of the original construction. The *Euphemia* became the city's first jail; the *Niantic* a storehouse and later a hotel built over the burned-out superstructure; the sailing ship *Panama* a church. A vessel abandoned at what is now the intersection of Davis and Pacific became the city's first Italian waterfront restaurant under the direction of Signor Giuseppe Bazzuro from Genova. Among Signor Bazzuro's dishes was a succulent fish stew, very likely the original *cioppino*, San Francisco's version of bouillabaisse.* Signor Bazzuro had to give up his sailing ship when the city began to reclaim the Bay, but he built nearby and continued to serve his pastas and stews until his restaurant burned in the disastrous earthquake of 1906.

In spite of diligent efforts, starting in 1850, to clear the harbor, the hulks of hundreds of ships remained, some of these later consumed by the frequent city fires. By October, 1850, eleven wharves extended two miles of boardwalks into the Bay at a cost of $1,500,000. With such rapid expansion, the wharves simply surrounded and incorporated many vessels, while sand fill completely covered others. As the city spread out over the water, the wharves became streets, and new extensions served the harbor. During the recent excavations for the subway line, workmen on Market Street uncovered the remains of several Gold Rush vessels, among them the *Callao,* the *Byron,* the *Galen,* the *Autumn,* and the *Roma,* all abandoned ships which had burned in the San Francisco fire of May 4, 1851. The San Francisco Maritime Museum records that hundreds of other ship skeletons lie under the whole area from the Bay and from Market Street back to Sansome Street as far north as Pacific—roughly the area of Yerba Buena Cove that was so soon filled in and built over.

As the city expanded, distinct neighborhood patterns began to emerge. On the beach and inland from the southern flank of the cove for about two miles west, transient miners still encamped in a city of 1,000 tents. The Market Street ridge and surrounding dunes sheltered them from the buffeting winds, and at some seasons a bit of greenery was in evidence, but that was scarce compensation for the indignities imposed by armies of fleas, battalions of lice, and regiments of rats. Although there were one or two good springs, the camp obtained almost its entire water supply from hundreds of shallow wells, whose brackish contents infected nearly the entire population with dysentery. When it was dry, sand was a major problem. When it was wet, water tended to seep

---

*In Genoa the great fish market was called the Chiappa, and in Genoese dialect the word *cioppin* means fish stew.

into and sometimes flood the lower-lying areas, imposing on them a permanently dank character. There was yet no system of sanitation, a circumstance which drew the fire of some of the early physicians. This fetid spot was known as Happy Valley, one of whose earliest inhabitants was Samuel Upham. When he disembarked in the summer of 1849, he found hotel accommodations limited and costly and consequently set up housekeeping among the tents. His abode was a ship's galley, purchased for $100, which he furnished with an empty flour barrel for a table, a nail keg for a chair, and assorted secondhand untensils for kitchenware. His bed consisted of a pair of blankets with a block of wood for a pillow, but because Mr. Upham's four-by-five-foot cabin was eight inches shorter than he was, he had to sleep on the bias. A year later he was astonished, on returning to the city after a four-month absence, to find that the most populated neighborhoods, having twice burned down, were now resplendent with brick buildings and planked sidewalks and that Happy Valley itself boasted hundreds of frame structures. Only a few years later the Palace Hotel, constructed (and, once rebuilt, still standing) on the very spot, drew worldwide acclamation for its breathtaking elegance.

Slightly east and south of Happy Valley, Pleasant Valley adjoined the government reservation at Rincon Point, where, after 1853, the quarter-million-dollar all-brick United States Marine Hospital housed between 500 and 700 patients. From an early date the surrounding area was busy with light manufacturing; shipbuilding; dockyards, including a dry dock; lumberyards; foundries that made use of the iron ore that came in as ballast in ships carrying wheat; gristmills for grinding the wheat; and similar enterprises. The promontory of land curved around to form the lower end of Yerba Buena Cove. The residues from the First and Howard Streets Gas Works gave that area the name of Tar Flat. Rincon Annex Post Office, below Mission between Spear and Steuart, stands on land that was once part of the cove.

Because, from its 100-foot height, Rincon Hill provided a good view and a certain remoteness from the rest of the city, it developed early as one of the most desirable places to live. Seventeen elegant brick houses, in an uncompleted, stylish, London-type mews at the foot of Rincon Hill, made South Park the first socially elite neighborhood in 1854. George Gordon, an Englishman, designed the residential blocks to center on a floral park, the whole area to be enclosed by locked iron fencing to which only residents had a key, a custom still observed in Gramercy Park in New York City. The Second Street area around Market Street became an elegant shopping mall to serve the Park and Hill dwellers, and Third Street, handsomely planked, provided its main access. By

1854, thanks to public horse-drawn cars, Park residents could ride into town and home again every half hour.

In the same area the Potrero Hill neighborhood south of Market became a settlement for workers and owners of the nearby industries. Many Irish, who liked to live in close proximity to the church, established themselves around St. Patrick's and later churches in the area.

About one mile north was Clark's Point, named for William Squire Clark, an overland immigrant of 1846, whose grandfather was a signer of the Declaration of Independence. It marked the end of the cove, the site of the first wharf where Broadway ran into the bay. Inland toward Montgomery Street, confined by Telegraph Hill, a cluster of shoddy structures housed the Sydney Ducks, English convicts from Australia, rowdies who caused the city some of its blackest moments. From Sydney Town, as the section came to be known, arsonists, looters, and robbers made their sweeps on the rest of the city.

By April, 1850, a semaphore station crowned Telegraph Hill, and at the approach of a vessel, it would signal below to the anxious populace. There was a haphazard development of hill dwellers then, in spite of such fierce winds as those in December, 1870, which flattened the two-story building housing the semaphore. The random character of the neighborhood persists. Swank glass-walled apartments that turn up as movie settings stand side by side with little frame cottages, some of which date back to the Gold Rush: the wooden house at 31 Alta Street, for example, was built in 1852; the two residences on Union Street at numbers 287 and 291 and the house at 9 Calhoun Terrace, in the 1860's. The inhabitants were largely Latin Americans, joined to the south and west by Italians and around Jackson Street by the French, most of whom dwelled in makeshift cottages and tents. Two hotels at Clark's Point were also frequented mainly by a French clientele. The section from the southern slopes of the hill down to Washington was known as Little Chile.

Germans congregated in large numbers at the end of Montgomery Street. Lütgen's Hotel, on Montgomery between Pine and Bush, one of their most popular resorts, remained in high favor for more than twenty-five years. Christian Russ, a neighborhood businessman, jeweler, and later owner of the Russ House, converted his country property at Harrison and Sixth near the road to the Mission, into a pleasure garden. There the German population in particular repaired for songfests and outings, perhaps the most notable of which was the May Day celebration. Dominated by the Turner Gesang Verein (the Gymnastic Musical Union), decked out in loose coats and pantaloons of brown linen, the assembled crew marched out from town in a massive parade. Once arrived, they participated in a series of exhibitions and contests, performances of acrobatics, singing, dancing, prize giving, and general carousing. Flags fluttered, the band played the requisite accompaniment of oomphas, and everyone was a hail fellow and had a jolly good time. *"Das deutsche Vaterland"* was "chanted in the most rapturous manner," reflecting a spirit of German brotherhood. In spite of the fierce love of fatherland, most of the Germans meant to stay in San Francisco and consequently shared their loyalty with their new homeland, participating actively in its affairs. By 1854 there were between 5,000 and 6,000 Germans resident, providing the major portion of the city's professional musicians, beer parlor owners, and cigar-stand proprietors. In these and other enterprises the early German immigrants made up about half the entire merchant community. They meanwhile maintained their ethnic identity by supporting a paper printed in the native tongue, a German school, from time to time a theatre, and a number of benevolent and social organizations such as the Deutsches Club.[3]

The Chinese immigrants were, albeit unknowingly, laying the roots of what is now the largest Chinese settlement outside the Orient. The San Francisco *Star* mentioned a few Chinese in the city early in 1848, but until the Gold Rush their numbers were negligible. By the beginning of 1850 there were just under 800 Chinese in San Francisco. They clustered on Sacramento Street, which they called *Tong Yan Gai*, Chinese Street, at first in the area of Grand and Kearny, later branching out into adjacent streets. In the first few years, however, Chinese merchants also established businesses at other points throughout the city, and there was even a small habitation of fishermen at Rincon Point. But the center of the Chinese community, certainly from the beginning, was Chinatown, which soon counted thirty-three retail stores, half as many pharmacies, and five bustling restaurants, strange to, but highly touted by, their non-Asian clientele. By 1854 there was a semiweekly community newspaper, the *Golden Hills News*. A bilingual journal, the *Oriental*, followed within a year. A Chinese Theatre, which shortly performed in its own building imported from China, existed well before that.

In 1851 Wah Lee, who is generally credited with opening the first full-scale Chinese laundry, set up his washtubs in a building at the corner of Washington and Grant. Withint twenty years almost 2,000 Chinese engaged in the laundry business. In several instances, by changing crews and signs, two firms could alternate around the clock, using the same premises. Until the seventies they made their deliveries by balancing across their shoulders bamboo poles from the ends of which hung baskets containing the linens. The Chinese quarter was bustling and noisy, ornamented with handsome calligraphy, bright-hued decorations, fluttering ribbons, and shops crammed with exotic foods and an endless variety of Oriental trappings.[4]

Early black immigration was intimately tied to the national dilemma over slavery and racism. Whereas the Chinese immigrant aroused feelings largely of curiosity, at least at first, the black man called forth all the American attitudes that were pushing the country irrevocably toward armed conflict. Such Africans as the Spanish brought to Mexico had merged into the general Mexican population by the early nineteenth century. By then slavery was illegal in Mexico, and hence in California, under the Republic. A scattering of American blacks settled in California before the Gold Rush, mostly escapees from ships that touched Western ports; other Afro-Americans made their way west as trappers and trailblazers, but few of these men got as far as San Francisco.

The first acknowledged San Franciscan of color, a man of mixed parentage, was William Alexander Leidesdorff, a multilingual civic leader, born in the Virgin Islands. After his arrival in 1841, he continued as a successful ship's master and prospered in a lucrative trading venture. He bought considerable lands, owned a large warehouse at California and Leidesdorff streets, erected one of the first two hotels in the city in 1846 on a corner of the Plaza and a good-sized home for himself on the waterfront at Montgomery and California streets. In 1847 he bought a 37-foot steamship, a side-wheeler, from the holdings of the Russian American Fur Company and launched her into service on San Francisco Bay and the rivers up to Sacramento. That same year he also sponsored the first organized horse race in the state. His political career encompassed a term as vice-consul to Mexico during Consul Larkin's tenure, membership on San Francisco's first municipal council and its first school board, and a stint as city treasurer. In 1848 Leidesdorff succumbed to brain fever. In spite of the enormous achievements of his short thirty-eight years, his estate owed $50,000 at the time of his death. Ironically, the Gold Rush, of which he died unaware, inflated San Francisco interests to such an extent that not only were his debts erased, but his properties appreciated to a value of $1,000,000. Most ironic of all, the repressive measures instituted in the late 1840's and 1850's against black people in California would have severely limited Leidesdorff's distinguished career and prevented his important contributions to San Francisco and the country.

Although measures proposed by the legislature to bar blacks entirely were defeated and the state constitution prohibited slavery, a black in the 1850's could not vote, could not homestead, could not hold public office, could not serve on a jury, could not give testimony in court, could not attend a school with white children, and, until 1864, could not ride a San Francisco streetcar. Early in the Gold Rush, when minorities posed no threat to the Anglo-American, there was a general spirit of tolerance. Most foreigners, for instance, had no prejudices against color, and several nonplussed American accounts depict scenes which could not have taken place previously in the United States—slavery South or Jim Crow North: a black man having his shoes shined by a French bootblack; black men carousing with white men in mining camp saloons, lodging in the same hotels, or entering into mixed marriages, generally to foreign-born partners. The 1860 census reported Chinese servants in some San Francisco black homes.

As the Anglo-American began to dominate the Gold Rush, he tried to secure his claim to the major part of the profits; racism was one of his most powerful weapons, embracing all non-Anglo peoples. At the mines there was an unwritten rule designed to prevent any one miner from gaining an advantage over any other: one man could not employ another to help work his claim. The Southern slaveholder thwarted the rule by setting up all-Southern camps or by working his slaves under the pretense that they were free men on their own claims.

Among the Gold Rush migrants, many blacks, perhaps the majority, were free men, but the new land also attracted fugitive slaves. The slave accompanying his master often had the opportunity to earn his own freedom as well as that of his family back home in the South. By 1850, 1,000 black people were in California; within the decade, 4,000, about half of whom were in San Francisco.

The black city population lived largely in the area west of Montgomery Street and north of Jackson, expanding over the years west toward Larkin and north to the Bay. Life centered on the church and the community's efforts to fight rampant discrimination. The 1860 census listed the occupation of 20 percent of the San Francisco black working population as cooks, with others employed as laborers, mechanics, waiters, porters, barbers, and businessmen. The women, besides working as cooks, did sewing, and the census mentions one prostitute. About one-half of the community was married, and by 1860, eighty-four black children in the state could claim to be native Californians. A black cultural organization, the San Francisco Athenaeum, supported its own library, and the community had its own newspaper, the *Mirror of the Times*. A later journal, the *Elevator*, came out weekly between 1865 and 1898. The community also had a formal political group, the Franchise League of San Francisco, founded in 1852, which began lobbying to gain the right to give testimony and to vote.

Central Stockton Street was perhaps the city's most presentable early residential neighborhood; close by several churches converged near Powell Street. In 1850 congregations worshiped on Sundays, usually at eleven in the morning, some at four in the afternoon, and again at half past seven in the evening. There was citywide confusion in the call of the bell, since the same pealing was summons to both church and fire. Worshipers met in the Reverend T. D. Hunt's First Congregational Church on the corner of Jackson and Virginia; the First Baptist Church on Washington Street; the Methodist Episcopal Church on Powell; Grace Church on the corner of Jackson and Powell; the First Presbyterian Church in a tent on Dupont between Pacific and Broadway, as well as in the City Hall in the Superior Court Room, until a prefabricated Gothic building arrived from New York (which burned in June, 1851); and in the Roman Catholic church, where the morning service was given in French and Spanish as well as English, on Vallejo between Stockton and Dupont (now Grant Avenue). The Unitarians met in Robinson and Evrard's Dramatic Museum on California Street. There was, besides, open-air preaching by the Methodist minister, the Reverend William Taylor, on Sundays at half past two in Portsmouth Square. The Asian community worshiped in Confucian, Taoist, and Buddhist temples called joss houses, in its own neighborhood. In 1854, however, the white citizens raised funds for a chapel for the Chinese on the corner of Stockton and Sacramento streets.

In the fall of 1849 two groups of Jewish pioneers celebrated the high holidays, fifty people in a hired second-story room on Montgomery Street and another dozen in a tent on Jackson Street near the square. As the Jewish community expanded, it maintained differences based on national origins, the preference for Orthodox or Reformed rituals, social affinities, and educational accomplishment. Two distinct congregations emerged, although a few people were charter members of both. The Polish and English Jews and originally a few northern Germans founded Sherith Israel in April, 1850, the first official congregation. Within a few months the less conservative German Jews established Temple Emanu-El, and although it was organized after Sherith Israel, it was incorporated officially a month before it, in the spring of 1851. The Sherith Israel congregation dedicated its first synagogue on Stockton Street, between Broadway and Vallejo, early in September, 1854. The Emanu-El synagogue opened its doors a few weeks later on Broadway, between Powell and Mason streets, and the rabbi delivered his address in German. From the beginning, disagreement over adhering to the Orthodox ritual divided the Emanu-El group. In 1855 the dispute came to a head. The Reform faction prevailed, and the congregation was among the first to endorse the liberal resolutions of the Cleveland Reform Conference of Rabbis. In 1863 the contingent which preferred stricter adherence to Orthodox procedures separated to establish Congregation Ohabai Shalom, which met in its own synagogue on Mason Street by 1865.

The First Colored Baptist Church of San Francisco (later changed to the Third Baptist Church) held its meetings on Kearny Street in 1852 in a private home. The congregation soon bought a building on Washington Street, then moved it to Dupont between Greenwich and Filbert. Another black congregation established the Wesleyan Episcopal Zion Church; a third, the African Methodist Episcopal Church, met in each other's homes in 1852 but had relocated at the corner of Jackson and Virginia streets by 1854.* By 1856, now know as the St. Cyprian African Methodist Episcopal Church, they moved to a converted carpenter's shop on Scott Street; by the beginning of the next decade, renamed the Union Bethel African Methodist Church, they purchased the Powell Street building vacated by the Grace Episcopal Church. By the mid-1850's thirty-two churches were meeting in San Francisco.

The import firms, warehouses, and auction rooms centered on Montgomery Street. Thought of today as the Wall Street of the West, it got its business start because of its early proximity to the harbor. The Montgomery Street firms continued to do business on their original sites, even as the wharves and storage facilities pushed eastward past them onto the land reclaimed from the Bay. The core of the imaginatively restored brick and cast-iron offices of Melvin Belli at 722 Montgomery Street probably predates the devastating blazes of 1851. The building next door, whose restoration is truer to the real-life 1850's style, was built a year or two later for a chinaware concern. Both buildings stand on the original sand beach by means of flexible foundations of cross-hatched timbers. The buildings at 287, 289, and 732 Montgomery also date from the early 1850's, although the latter owes its cast-iron pillars to a later remodeling. It housed the most popular of all San Francisco journals, the *Golden Era*, which thrived from its incep-

---

*Because California law prohibited children of any color from attending public schools with white children, the black community organized the first black San Francisco public school in 1854; 23 students met in the basement of the Jackson Street church. By the end of the fifties, there were 100.

tion in 1852 until the turn of the century. Emphasizing literary pieces over news reports, it served as a training ground for a whole gamut of California writers from Bret Harte and Ina Coolbrith to Mark Twain and Joaquin Miller.

Several early importing businesses and the customhouse to serve them were neighbors on California Street. The customhouse, an imposing four-story brick building, stood at the corner of California and Montgomery until it was consumed in the fire of May, 1851. Work then started on designs for a combined customhouse and post office on Battery Street between Washington and Jackson. Although the post office has since moved, the modern customs building makes use of the same location. By the time of completion in October, 1855, three years after the cornerstone was set, the three-story Boston-designed building had cost more than $850,000. It contained elaborations on a basically Greek Revival theme, numerous Corinthian columns, a respectable granite portico, mahogany furnishings, and two sweeping interior stairways. Granite, brick, and cast iron combined in the construction, "the first example of the monumental federal office building on the Pacific Coast."[5] Resting on bay fill, it was locked to its site by pilings and granite foundations and was considered fireproof. Best of all, its stately proportions could accommodate as many as 1,000 people simultaneously in front of the first-floor postal delivery windows. It was considered the most refined building of its day.

Nearby on Battery near Clay, a three-story brick building dating from 1851, housed the Merchants' Exchange which supplied ship and cargo information, foreign newspapers, a library, and a meeting place for the burgeoning business community. Clay Street became the dry goods center, and Kearny bustled with a large number of retail shops. Domingo Ghirardelli, whose later enterprises have been so handsomely restored as Ghirardelli Square, moved into the bustling Jackson Street area in the mid-fifties. Taking up the increasingly frequent practice of combining home and business site, he used the upper floor of number 415 as his family residence and the lower for his thriving chocolate factory. A business neighbor, the Lucas, Turner and Company Bank, was directed by a partnership which from 1853 to 1857 included William Tecumseh Sherman who had come to California with the New York Regiment before the discovery of gold and later became famous as a Civil War general. On the west side of Montgomery, almost at the corner of Washington, C. Jansen and Co. dealt in dry goods; it later became prominent as the victims of the robbery which led to the first trial conducted by the Vigilance Committee of 1851. William T. Coleman, one of the participants and the president of the Committee of 1856, then had offices on the east side of Sansome Street in the block bounded by Jackson and Washington.

On the corner of Commercial and Montgomery, Rowe's Olympic Circus, which had opened in the fall of 1849, entertained the city with "Ethiopian serenaders" (actually white minstrels in black face) and numerous other attractions. Crossing Montgomery, Commercial Street ran between Clay and Sacramento, pushing out into the cove as Long or Central Wharf. Here a small complex of hawkers did business, and many Jewish merchants took up residence in the quarter. One of them, the Englishman Joshua Abraham Norton, a prosperous shipper on Montgomery Street, later suffered severe losses in the rice market. His reverses affected his sanity, and he wandered the streets, proclaiming himself Emperor of the United States and Protector of Mexico. The city readily accepted his masquerade, from plumed hat and gold braid to epauletted frock coat, which they provided him by proclamation of the town council. They always addressed him as Emperor, they treated his presence in the saloons and restaurants as an honor, and they never allowed him to pay. They pungled up his modest taxes, purchased the "official" bonds he issued, and cashed the small checks he wrote on the Royal Treasury without batting a sentimental eye. In the conduct of his Empire's business, he became one of San Francisco's most beloved characters. After a reign of twenty years he collapsed on the sidewalk in the winter of 1880. The entire city turned out for his funeral.

Early San Francisco architecture generally was a hodgepodge of iron, adobe and canvas, wood and brick, and assorted ship's parts. There stands today at 825 Francisco Street, now considerably remodeled, a house constructed originally of salvaged lumber from abandoned vessels. Each time that fire forced the disorderly city to rebuild there was a lessening of confusion architecturally and an improvement in terms of solidity. The state of transition, including the leveling of hills, the reclamation of the bay and mud flats, the new building and the rebuilding, was so rapid that just about every commentator of the period remarks on the enormousness of the change from one week to the next. A lawyer, writing home in the early fifties to the editor of the *Southern Literary Messenger* on the subject of bay fill, speculated that it was going so rapidly that after a few weeks there would likely be no "sea" to fill.

Perhaps the most dramatic changes took place around Portsmouth Plaza. It quickly lost the barren character of its animal-grazing days, when it was justly described as a cowpen, and of its subsequent period as a campsite of shanties and tents, to flourish as the city's main square. Booths set up with merchandise of many nations lent the quality of a bazaar. Surrounding the Plaza were thriving gambling establishments, hostelries, and saloons: most notably the El Dorado, which started in a tent on the southeast corner of Washington Street and by the summer of 1851, still on the square, occupied one of the earliest fireproof buildings of the city; the Parker House; Dennison's Exchange; the Crescent City; and the Empire; and on the southwest corner of Clay, Brown's City Hotel. Generally the more common gambling resorts stood to the north of the El Dorado, the more soigné to the south.

Also ringing the Plaza were doctors', dentists', and business offices, attorneys, the public schoolhouse, various shops, a high-class house of prostitution with a New Orleans flavor, auction facilities, the offices of the *Alta California*, banks and brokerages, the old adobe City Hall, courthouse and customhouse, engineering and surveying offices, and even the first gristmill, which Spear and Hinckley originally imported on the *Corsair* and set up near the north edge of the square. Washington Street, which bordered the north side of the square and now runs from the Embarcadero through modern Chinatown, was the site of Sam Brannan's *California Star*, the pioneer San Francisco newspaper. In later years the building, at number 743, housed the pagoda-peaked Chinese Telephone Exchange, unique in the Western world; it is now part of the Bank of Canton.

After the official 1848 flag raising had pronounced its public character, the square became increasingly the scene of mass meetings, celebrations, public whippings, and, in the days of the Vigilance Committees, public hangings. As early as 1849 San Franciscans were beginning to show the same public concern about maintaining the attractions of the city that still militates against abandoning the cable cars, erecting high-rise buildings, or destroying the waterfront. In its earliest manifestation, a protest to the city council, sixty prominent businessmen argued strongly against construction of a particularly unesthetic building, as well as for the removal of others which detracted from the square, the only ornament, they wrote, of which the city could yet boast.

The early Post Office at Clay and Pike streets was the scene of incredible excitement whenever a shipment of mail arrived. In August, 1849, some 200 people were already in line at daybreak for the 7 A.M. opening, and it took each person easily over two hours to reach the window. The first postmaster, Colonel John W. Geary, arrived on March 31, 1849, on the *Oregon*. Whenever the mails came in, he, his sons, and the hired clerks needed two solid days and nights to sort the thousands of items received. They worked behind barred doors, to discourage any overenthusiastic assistance from the impatient throngs. Things got worse instead of better, but to some people with an enterprising cast of mind, such as Alexander Todd, the difficulties suggested profitable business enterprises. Suffering ill health, he gave up mining in favor of running a mail delivery service for individual miners. By paying 25 cents a letter to the San Francisco postmaster, he bought the privilege of entering the office directly and sorting out the mail for his subscribers, of whom there were at first about 100 and eventually 2,000. He charged them an ounce of gold a letter, on delivery to the mines, but competition soon brought the price down to $1. Since the lines sometimes stretched all the way to the square, some particularly anxious recipients stood all night, no matter the weather, to be in an advantageous position in the morning. Some people paid stand-ins as much as $20 to hold their places, while others purposely queued up early, then sold their choice locations for handsome sums.

It was natural for the facilities for mail delivery to merge with the facilities for dealing with gold: its remittance, its safekeeping, and its conversion into currency. Such firms as Wells, Fargo, which was organized to transport mail in July, 1852, ended up in the banking business. Its original office occupied what was then 114 Montgomery Street, between Sacramento and California. Wells, Fargo also used the clipper ships and the Pacific Mail Line steamers as carriers. Twice a month shipments left for Panama and the East. It became the custom, followed until this century, to settle accounts on Steamer Day. Although stagecoach service reached impressive quality by the mid-fifties, thanks largely to the use of the Concord coach, it was considerably more limited than steamer service. Not until 1858 did Butterfield's overland stage line improve the situation, covering a 2,800-mile run from Missouri to San Francisco and making eight deliveries a month.

Because of the hazards of transporting valuable cargoes, the early San Francisco banking and express companies made use of what were called Firsts, Seconds, and Thirds of exchange: for each money transaction, the company issued three documents, the First sent via Cape Horn, the Second via Panama, and the Third via stage. The named recipient honored whichever arrived first, the two remaining becoming automatically void.

Spurred on by the business of the Gold Rush, express and banking companies grew tremendously prosperous. Wells, Fargo had moved its headquarters in 1856 to the Parrott Building on California and Montgomery streets, where it remained for twenty years. By 1880 the company had opened 573 Western offices.

Other efforts at moving the mail were bizarre, some spectacular and most of them unsuccessful. Perhaps the most farfetched scheme was the Army-run camel express. On the theory that camels could endure long periods without water and bear heavy loads, the Army imported seventy-five unhappy and very seasick camels from Arabia. Unfortunately they neglected to bring along even one experienced camel driver. The finicky beasts knew no English commands, and the muleteers who were hired to drive them knew less Arabic. The camels proved handily the predictions that they could cover a great deal of ground in a very short time, often scattering tons of baggage in their wake. The Army conceded defeat and gave up the experiment after only a few trial runs. The animals were auctioned off, some ending up in the silver mines of Missouri.

Dog teams proved more successful than camels in pulling heavily loaded sleighs across snowy passes; horses, using a special snowshoe, looked promising, but both turned out to have limited capacities. Perhaps the most admirable effort was made by a single individual, John "Snowshoe" Thompson, who delivered the post by skiing through the Sierras with a rough staff in one hand and a 100-pound sack of mail strapped to his back.

The Pony Express, launched under Russell, Majors, and Waddell in April, 1860, lasted a heroic eighteen months. It was probably the most dramatic and surely the most famous of all the schemes, although the actual quantity of mail handled was small. The initial charge for a letter was $5 a half ounce, but mail handled by the Wells, Fargo Company finally came down to about one-fourth that amount. A bronze plaque at the southwest corner of Montgomery and Merchant streets, just off Portsmouth Square, commemorates the first Pony Express relay to San Francisco. Inauguration of the Western telegraph in 1861, which spelled the end of the Pony Express, meant some improvement in major communications, although lines often went down and delays were common.

Such romantic, if rudimentary, systems for getting mail and news to the West, the daring of the express rider, the drollery of the camel caravan, caught the public imagination and so helped focus the country's attention on the need for better coast-to-coast communication. The demand for a transcontinental railroad was satisfied by 1869. Until then, in spite of surges of prosperity and steady cultural improvement, California remained in effect a Western colony, still heavily influenced by the sea and by the frontier, by the continuing scale of migration (600,000 people by 1869), by its isolation from the East, and by the fact that its population, including a very large mixture of foreign born, was at least still 70 percent male. The long freedom from any national pattern compelled San Francisco to develop its own standards, which allowed it to be a highly spirited, innovative, cosmopolitan, and unorthodox community.

In early California architecture, where the primary concern was shelter, improvisation was the rule. When the thatched roofs of California missions proved to be a dangerous fire hazard, tiles to replace them were molded over the thighs of Indian women. Early attempts to pretty things up turned to "papering" with calico, more readily available than wallpaper. When fifty inches of rain turned San Francisco into a quagmire in the winter of 1849–50, a unique sidewalk appeared along the west side of Montgomery Street, constructed of surplus provisions: 100 sacks of Chilean flour, unopened boxes of tobacco, cooking stoves, a piano, and numerous cartons filled with boots and shoes (which had been imported in such quantity that every individual could have had fifty pairs of them). Boxes of tobacco served also as the foundations of a house built on the mud flats of Jackson Street; during the course of construction the price of tobacco rocketed to such a high that the underpinnings became worth more than the house.[6]

Several animals and at least four known human bodies were exhumed from the mud of Montgomery Street, presumably of persons who had become intoxicated, lost their footings, and sunk unwitnessed into the ooze. To convert the main walkways from disastrous quicksand to passable thoroughfares before the advent of the next rainy season, the city, at considerable expense, graded the main streets and covered them with planking. The 1850 winter was unseasonably dry; by spring the parched boardwalks made perfect tinder for the two fires that broke out during May and June. Estimated damage amounted to almost $4,000,000, with 300 houses and most of the business establishments in the area of the square destroyed. The destruction of the planking was particularly disastrous for the city treasury, which was still heavily in debt for its original construction. By imposing a heavy tax and issuing bonds, the city restored its credit balance, the first of many occasions where both physical and financial structures were in jeopardy and only quick response could save them. The handling of repeated municipal crises was energetic training for such later full-scale disasters as the 1906 earthquake and fire. Determination in the face of adversity, a built-in San Francisco characteristic, was one of the unifying factors for its diverse population.

In San Francisco, as in all California, the adobe was the most common architectural form during the Spanish-Mexican period. An extension of the European Spaniard's use of mud bricks, which followed naturally in Mexico and then in Colonial California, it provided a rude and serviceable architecture relying on local materials and needing little skill in construction. Yankee immigrants introduced more elaborate details and refinements, such as flooring and brick chimneys. Much "Spanish-Mexican" architecture was actually heavily influenced by New England. The romantic combination of wood and adobe, an unintentional result of substitutions, was soon replaced by all-frame, 100 percent flammable structures.

Signs of permanence were sorely lacking in the early city: by the end of the 1840's the only house with a garden belonged to the old-time resident Leidesdorff. The Gold Rush called forth a dramatic demand for quick personal shelters, commercial buildings, and government facilities. A tremendous business in prefabs grew out of the urgency to fill the building needs, while skirting the lack of materials and skilled labor.

The Chinese made only a minor impact architecturally, in spite of their large numbers. They simply adapted basic Western patterns, adding decorative motifs, banners, ribbons, and signs in Chinese lettering. The more Oriental architecture of modern Chinatown was created during the tremendous reconstruction following the 1906 earthquake and fire.

When affluence set in following the Gold Rush and the silver bonanza, the trend in the city's architecture generally was to recreate the style associated at home with wealth and prestige. However, not until late in the century, when the regional character began to merge with the imitative, traditional styles imported from abroad, did San Francisco architecture really begin to mature on its own.

The significant factor in California history is the interaction of successive immigrant waves upon its life and culture. And nowhere is this so evident as in architecture. . . . In 1869 . . . California's population and architecture were truly international. The positive cultural achievements resulting from this heterogeneous immigration are too often obscured by the racial and national animosities that accompanied them. The talent, training, and experience that the alien architects in the great immigration contributed to California's architectural frontier are, with the exception of Federalist Washington, historically and regionally unique. The discipline of the École des Beaux-Arts, the precepts of the English masters, the competence of the German academies, together with the American classic tradition, merged in California after 1850 to produce a remarkable architectural renaissance.[7]

The early frame buildings came in sections from New England and often ended up with a coat of Colonial white paint and green trim, although a good many were left unfinished. Maine and New York shipped thousands of sectional wooden houses, as well as churches, bowling alleys, hospitals, and even the makings of the Astor House, a 100-room, three-and-a-half-story hotel. Philadelphia and Baltimore were soon sending prefabricated sectionals to San Francisco, and the accounts of many an ocean traveler described the various portable buildings aboard ship. There were houses arriving from Europe and Asia: from Hamburg and London and Belgium and Le Havre, Hong Kong, Australia, and Canton, and even a few from Tasmania. Some of the Chinese houses used mortised joints for nailless construction, whereas others came complete with a custom crew of Cantonese carpenters. The Chinese granite used in the fifties was imported because practically no one was mining or shipping the local inland stone. Work crews sometimes also came along with it. However, stone was not commonly used; only 6 of the more than 20,000 buildings standing in 1869 were of that construction. The local quarry on Goat Island (now Yerba Buena), established in 1851, yielded a blue rubblestone, which was used, together with cement, in the foundations of the Parrott Building. The upper levels were made of enormous blocks of granite custom-cut in China, then shipped to San Francisco, where a crew of imported Chinese laborers neatly put them together. They worked from dawn to dusk, at a daily wage of one dollar, one-quarter pound of fish, one-half pound of rice, and one hour off to eat them in. When completed in 1852, it had cost $117,000, and architect Stephen Williams received the credit for the first commercial building of importance in California.[8]

For prefabricated buildings, wood was only one material used during the Gold Rush. At least as popular initially, and certainly more adaptable to architectural variety, corrugated iron and galvanized sheet-metal houses, warehouses, churches, and other buildings arrived from all over Asia and Europe. Advertisements appeared in East Coast journals and abroad, extolling their economy, the ease of freighting, and the speed of assembly, or disassembly if that should become necessary—less than a day for a small house. Two widely advertised claims, the relative comfort of an iron house and the security deriving from the fireproof quality of metal, proved to be overstated. Conductivity, another of metal's characteristics, when combined with the strong Western sunshine, produced ungodly hot interiors, which no amount of ventilating equipment, movable sash, or wooden insulation—offered by one Liverpool firm as an optional extra—seemed able to counteract. Resistance to fire was not, unfortunately, resistance to heat. The temperature of a roaring blaze curled the molten structures like so many twists of confetti. The *Alta California* of May 29,

1851, chronicled one such fiery disaster: when the misshapen remains of Howard and Green's warehouse obstructed the corner of Clay and Leidesdorff streets, it took several weeks to cut it up and cart it away, at a cost of $9,000.[9]

In spite of such packaged refinements as plate glass, wallpaper, carpeting, furniture, and "fireproof" paint, the use of prefabs, particularly the iron ones, diminished considerably. Discomfort was certainly one factor; a glutted market another. Building materials were becoming increasingly available from local sources, and prices were coming down. Both Brannan's Mormons and the military regiment of Colonel Stevenson, two major migrations in the forties with intentions to settle permanently in the region, had crews of carpenters, joiners, masons, and other construction workers. From their ranks, and other professionals like them, came a labor force to build San Francisco, once they had had their fling at mining. They replaced such men as George Dornin, a New Yorker who came out in '49 and found work during the fall and winter putting together imported zinc and corrugated iron houses, a job that needed little mechanical aptitude. But he was no builder, and when the peak of the prefab housing was over, the builders took over the building and he opened a restaurant.

By 1853, when a large number of miners returned to other forms of living, the considerable group of skilled young architects among them began to create the California Renaissance in architecture. They had arrived adept at the art of frontier improvisation, thanks to the rigors of the westward journey. They were equipped by education with a broad sense of Western civilization. The Northeasterners, who made up the early majority, brought a style based on New England architecture. The Europeans, who matched the Americans in number by the time of the railroad, were responsible for the emergence of an international architecture, generally reflective of Western culture and certainly far beyond the expectations of a frontier city.

It was inevitable that in a new, rich, progressive, and international society important architectural advances would take place. That California anticipated by three decades the American Classic Renaissance was one of the cultural compensations for the turbulence, disappointment, and waste of the Gold Rush.[10]

The European architects began to add embellishments to the Yankee models that predominated: mansard roofs and cast-iron grillwork, Gothic spires and detailings, English town houses, Italianate villas, country estates, and, perhaps most unusual of all, several octagonal structures. Two of these still stand in San Francisco, an 1857 Russian Hill residence at 1067 Green Street and one from 1861—now the California headquarters of the National Society of Colonial Dames of America—at 2645 Gough Street. Both were based on plans for the book *A Home for All*, whose author, Orson S. Fowler, believed that the shape of one's life and the shape of one's house were intimately connected. Both have seen some remodeling—in fact, the Gough Street house was moved from its original site across the street—but they retain the basic construction and concrete walls prescribed by Fowler.

On the civic side, the architecture relied heavily on classic Greek and Roman forms, while church buildings began to emulate the Gothic. Commercial buildings took on elegance with the use of elaborate stuccowork and incorporated innovative designs to foil damage by earthquakes. Several relics of fifties' architecture, domestic and other, stand today. Probably the oldest house which has not been remodeled, although it has twice been moved from its original site, is 329 Divisadero Street, nestled mid-block but visible from an Oak Street vantage point. Built in 1850 or '51, it came in sections around the Horn, probably from New Orleans, which had been the home of the owner's wife. Its earliest setting, of 160 acres, resembled a country estate and is now the Panhandle of Golden Gate Park. An older house, probably from 1847, is at 765 Bay Street, having also been moved twice. Its façade, imported from the East Coast, was installed during an early renovation. An 1854 remodeled house stands at 1032 Broadway, and an 1852 house at 2006 Bush Street. Intelligent rebuilding of 2626 Hyde Street has retained the decorative hand carvings that were so stylish at the time. For reasons of economy, carpenters' stock productions soon replaced such handwork. One of the early occupants of 11 Blackstone Court gave his name to the street. His frame house was built in 1851, as was the remodeled building at 604 Commercial Street. The building at 2475 Pacific was a farmhouse in Gold Rush times, surrounded by a 25-acre dairy. Several of the warehouses in the waterfront area date back to the fifties, as do some of the still-functioning churches. Old St. Patrick's on Eddy Street stood on Market Street in 1854 until its removal to make way for the Palace Hotel. Old St. Mary's Church, on Grant Avenue and California Street since 1854, preserves the original brick walls and bell tower, both of which withstood the 1906 fire.[11]

After 1854 the city required all downtown commercial buildings to be of brick or stone. Fifteen hundred new buildings rose, some of them fireproofed with walls two or three feet thick. Within two years, to fill the demand, a local factory was machining 60,000 bricks a day. Stone appeared usually in foundations. Iron shutters and doors protected against theft as well as fire, the former becoming increasingly as much of a menace as the latter. Cast-iron buildings began to appear by the mid-fifties, and gained in popularity throughout the sixties. Adorned with stamped ornamental motifs—everything from caryatids to floral friezes—innumerable columns, balustrades, porticoes, and balconies of painted iron formed the supports and separations for vast areas of glass. A building of moderate scale might have used 200 tons of cast iron.

At the end of the Mexican period in California the Treaty of Guadalupe Hidalgo had assured titleholders that all land grants would be respected. In fact, however, the government followed the opposite course, and the Land Act of 1851 resulted in almost all of the colonials' land ending up in the hands of the newcomers. Landowners found their claims suddenly considered worthless unless they could prove otherwise. Compounded by an endless series of hearings and litigations, the legal costs, including reprinting all briefs and records, grew astronomical. A case might last fifteen or more years, going through as many as six defenses. Legal fees from land cases paid the entire costs of construction for the 1853 Montgomery Block in San Francisco, a complex of offices and shopping arcades that was a model for Western commercial building throughout the 1850's.* The enormous numbers of Gold Rush immigrants thrust into the middle of this unsettled real estate added to the complications by squatting indiscriminately on any convenient property. In the end, most claimants lost their properties either to squatters who refused to abide by legal decisions against them or through financial depletion and finally default.

Early in 1853 an enterprising Frenchman, José Yves Limantour, claimed about one-half of all San Francisco real estate, both civic and private, encompassing the most valuable property of the community. The claimant backed up his case with official ten-year-old deeds and legal documents, all of which, along with the depositions of witnesses, seemed to be perfectly in order. After a substantial three-year investigation, the Board of Land Commissioners had no alternative but to approve the claim, immediately throwing a good number of citizens into understandable panic. All was set to rights two years later, when the claim proved to have been counterfeited, falsely witnessed, with forged signatures and fraudulent date. Limantour, still one jump ahead of the hoodwinked courts and irate citizenry, disappeared from the country.

---

*Transamerica Corporation's Pyramid, an 800-foot building that comes to a point, now occupies the site.

There were two effects of land problems on the Gold Rush immigration. Some prospective residents, who could not count on any security of title, were reluctant to bring out their families, and some conservative businessmen hesitated to risk financial involvement in unsteady properties. The breaking up of the enormous holdings, on the other hand, opened up for many newcomers the opportunity to obtain land with the hopes that the titles would remain constant. In southern California, where the land policy favored the Mexican system and preserved the enormous original estates, the opposite prevailed: very few people settled, hardly any land came under cultivation, and the area around Los Angeles remained undeveloped for years. This lag fortunately allowed the area to be used as one vast ranchero, where enough cattle could graze to supply meat for the hordes involved in the Gold Rush. San Francisco, besides benefiting from the supply of beef, developed tanneries to handle the hides and turned a nice profit.

George Dornin's restaurant was one of the many early eating places in a city soon crammed with hotels, restaurants, boardinghouses, and refreshment stands of all descriptions. Such facilities were increasingly necessary with a swelling population that included so many transients and so few women and families. Because the earliest lodgings were at best rudimentary, business and professional men often bedded down in their shops and offices. Since the living room did not exist and the common dining room was noted for the speed with which it discharged its patrons, it was not surprising that a large number of gambling halls and drinking establishments took over as the city's living rooms.

Only at the end of the decade did respectability and elegance, hand in hand, set the style for the great saloons. By 1850, there were, according to Kimball's City Directory, 39 restaurants, 28 hotels, 16 refreshment stands and vendors, 53 boardinghouses, and 66 saloons, many of which offered multiple services, although listed only under one category. Supplies—their scarcity at first and their variety when imports flooded the market—determined the richness of the menus. A passion for eating and drinking, still one of the trademarks of the city, was bolstered from the earliest days by such gourmands as Dr. Charles Parke, a young physician, who on one occasion, while making his way through a mountain blizzard, seasoned the milk of two cows with oil of peppermint, then stashed it away in the back of his wagon until it churned into ice cream.

Dame Shirley, writing in September, 1851, from the mines, also reflected the taste for good eating: When she and her husband arrived exhausted at midnight at the hotel in Marysville, the good

Dr. Clappe "went to a restaurant and ordered a *petit souper* to be sent to our room. Hot oysters, toast, tomatoes and coffee. . . ." In October she and her husband moved into a new cabin òn Indian Bar. In honor of the occasion, the recently hired mulatto cook, delighted to have an appreciative woman to taste the refinements of his cooking, presented the family with a six-course dinner of oyster soup, fried salmon (freshly caught in the adjacent river), roast beef and boiled ham, fried oysters, potatoes and onions, a pastry course of both mince pie and pudding (made by necessity without eggs or milk), a dessert of nuts and raisins with Madeira, and finally coffee. Claret and champagne flowed throughout the meal. Later that winter, again writing from Indian Bar, Dame Shirley described another dinner, this one notable for its setting, claimed to be the best cabin on the river, among whose features was a large window made entirely of glass jars, "brought here in enormous quantities containing brandied fruits; for there is no possible luxury connected with drinking, which is procurable in California, that cannot be found in the mines; and the very men, who fancy it a piece of wicked extravagance to *buy* bread, because they can save a few dimes by *making* it themselves, are often those who think nothing of spending from fifteen to twenty dollars a night in the bar-rooms." Bread was included in that evening's repast, a splendid freshly baked loaf which one of the gentlemen residents of the house had turned out. [12]

Howard Gardiner, in his reminiscences of San Francisco and the mines, recalled the difficulties of baking a good batch of bread before one finally got the hang of it. After mixing the ingredients carefully, the miner had to knead the dough to a velvety-smooth texture, set it aside until it had risen to well more than twice its bulk, then bake it over hot coals in a kind of Dutch oven, the lid of which was covered with the same glowing embers. In the cold weather the miner often took the dough pot to bed with him to preserve the precious sourdough starter. It was used continuously, a part of the previous batch always being left in the pot to help start the new. Happily Gardiner could report that after a short initial period of failure, he always turned out an excellent loaf.[13] San Francisco is still widely noted for its sourdough bread, and it is a continuing matter of serious local concern whether it retains its proper sourness.

Supplying the expanding Western population with oysters soon took on the dimensions of a major San Francisco industry. Easterners and foreigners alike loved oysters and had eaten them at home by the bushel. During the Gold Rush their taste created an instant local demand. By 1849 the *Alta California* ran advertisements for Eastern oysters, mostly shipped to San Francisco from canneries in Baltimore. Since the oyster can seal in its own oxygen supply for several days at a time by clamping closed its adductor muscle when its valves are filled with water, it can survive healthily dry for a substantial period of time. This adds to ease of handling as well as to its attractive presentation at market in a wicker basket; more important, it makes the oyster ideal for short-term shipping. However, such extremes as the long sea voyage from Boston or Baltimore, the heat of the Isthmus, or the lack of ice in transit from Mazatlán, all were difficulties far beyond the oyster's natural ability to survive. The successful Eastern shipments, therefore, came canned or preserved, which still left a large unsatisfied market for the fresh mollusk. Oysters from Shoalwater (now Willapa) Bay, Washington, filled the need, although the population preferred the flavor of the Eastern oyster. Washington imports to San Francisco started in 1850 and on a year-round basis supplied 90 percent of the demand for fresh oysters, a market large enough to support its own fleet of sailing vessels transporting nothing but oysters in the shell. Holding beds in San Francisco Bay provided fresh oysters continuously to the market, storing as many as 5,000 baskets at a time. By the end of the 1850's three San Francisco firms were importing yearly 35,000 baskets of fresh Washington oysters. John S. Morgan, a forty-niner and owner of the most prominent firm, had been an unsuccessful miner before he turned to oystering.

While the mining communities made up an extensive part of the market, they inadvertently created one of the major problems for fresh oyster storage in San Francisco waters: hydraulic mining techniques produced silt in the Sierras, which the coursing rivers deposited in the Bay at the end of their race, making it necessary to relocate the storage grounds. However, with the completion of the transcontinental railroad in 1869, fresh Eastern oysters became readily accessible and soon outsold the Washington supply. Some San Francisco firms succeeded in growing, though not reproducing, seed oysters in the Bay; spat then made up the major portion of imports. At its peak in 1899 the industry produced more than 2,500,000 pounds of oyster meat. At this point extensive pollution in the Bay began to take its toll and oystering settled into a complete decline by the first decade of the new century.[14]

At the height of the oyster business, several firms had their own counters, retail stalls, and restaurants in the California Market. One old-timer, Maye's Oyster House, in business since 1867 and now on Polk Street, still produces a Gold Rush favorite, Hangtown Fry. A scramble of oysters, eggs, and bacon, it originated in Placerville, then Hangtown, supposedly as the last dinner for a condemned prisoner, whose request was designed to delay his execution as long as possible. For years it has been assumed that the difficulty of obtaining oysters at the mines was the delaying tactic; now it is clear that the oyster was plentiful and that the uncommon ingredient was actually the egg, a luxury item that sometimes sold for more than the choicest meat.

Gold Rush San Francisco contained restaurants of all possible descriptions, operating in abandoned omnibuses, tents, shacks, and a substantial number of regulation buildings. The Commercial, one of the typical early restaurants of 1850 stood on the waterfront at the foot of Broadway on a leased lot at Clark's Point. A few unoccupied friends assisted the owners, Bruce and Will Huntting, in constructing a one-and-a-half-story 20- by 40-foot building, which offered food and lodging to an assortment of tenants, including a large horde of rats. Waiting table, Will Huntting, arms laden with steaming platters for the diners above, entered the first-floor dining room through a trapdoor from the basement kitchen below, opening it with his head. The upper level contained sparse accommodations for a limited number of lodgers.

There were "the American *dining rooms*, the English *lunch houses*, the French *cabarets*, the Spanish *fondas*, the German *wirtschafts*, the Italian *osterie*, the Chinese *chow-chows*, and so on to the end of a very long chapter. There were cooks, too, from every country: American, English, French, German, Dutch, Chinese, Chileno, Kanaka, Italian, Peruvian, Mexican, Negro, and what not."[15] In very short order dining accommodations ranged from the most ordinary to the most elegant. The commonest boardinghouses charged $8 to $10 a week, $10 to $15 with lodging, although hotel rooms were much higher, reaching $250 for the most elegant. Single meals ran between $1 and $3, $1 at the Chinese places (which were easy to distinguish by their fluttering triangular yellow silk flags) and at some of the simpler tables, as the one at the City Hotel. Meals in less modest establishments came to double or more. In the most fashionable resorts such as Delmonico's, a man could run up a bill of $15 to $20. Such worthy but far from deluxe establishments as the Sutter, the Graham House, the Lafayette, and the Empire offered their guests many-coursed dinners—soups, fish, a boiled course, entrées, roasts and game, vegetables, pastries, and desserts of nuts and raisins—at comparatively moderate prices.

In 1850 typical restaurant entrees might include baked hog's head with cranberry sauce, calf's head, dressed heart, mutton pie, and fricasseed oxtail. There was an abundance of game: venison, hare, antelope, elk, bear, curlew, goose, partridge, snipe, plover, quail, duck—a good assortment of which appeared on every menu. Champagne at the Empire House was listed at $5 a bottle;

sherry, Madeira, and port at $3; chateau clarets at $2; and hock at $5. Since fresh vegetables, eggs, and potatoes were scarce in the beginning, it as not uncommon for a restaurant to advertise when they had them on the menu. On the front page of the July 1, 1852, *Daily Alta California,* an insertion typical of the day announced that Wilson's Exchange Hotel and Restaurant was in a fireproof brick building; that the price of board, covering three meals a day, had been reduced to $12 a week, payable in advance ($20 to $22 with lodgings); that it was contemplating adding one or two stories to accommodate 200 guests; that it was open for meals from 6 and ½ o'clock in the morning until 9 in the evening; and that its menu included beefsteak and potatoes, mutton chops, boiled tripe, salmon steak, ham, fried sausage, and mackerel at 37 ½ cents a portion; hash, pork and beans, etc., at 25 cents; and for the extravagant gourmet, venison steak with potatoes at 50 cents.

Wilson's Exchange was also the scene of a testimonial dinner on October 12, 1853, tendered by the citizens of San Francisco to General Hiram Walbridge, member elect of the Third Congressional District of the City of New York. After a first course of soups, there was a choice of fish and seafood, including lobster; a choice of a half dozen boiled dishes; two dozen entrées such as broiled plover, hare chops in salmi, brains, veal tartare, venison steak, teal duck, turkey giblets, braised chicken with oyster sauce, quail on toast, tame duck with olives, calves' heads, bear steak and spareribs; roasts; a game course, including five varieties of duck, brant, English snipe, wild goose, quail, plover, *non*-English snipe, venison, elk; dessert of ice cream, nuts, raisins, oranges, grapes; and fancy cake. At a similar testimonial on October 25 the public honored John Mitchell, an Irish leader who had just escaped his political enemies and five years' captivity, with an equally abundant spread. The Hotel du Commerce catered the banquet for 400, going Wilson's Exchange one better, however, by printing the menu entirely in French.

Although many banquets were as sumptuous, they did not all end up as well as they started. At the end of November, 1855, a group of 10,000 people celebrated the Allied victories in the Crimean War. Their committee erected a 230-foot, flower-bedecked tent for the festivities in South Park, enclosing ten enormous tables abundantly set for the feast. There was a great deal of champagne, a bottle of claret at each setting, and, for anyone who might still be thirsty, an endless supply of beer in kegs. The participants, starting at ten in the morning, paraded from Market Street to the accompaniment of a marching band and salutes fired from land and sea. Faget's Clay Street Market roasted an entire ox as the centerpiece for the occasion and mounted him, horns and all, in a standing posture for all to admire. After a good deal of celebration, the long series of speeches proved deadly dull. A small contingent of listeners relieved their boredom by tossing bread at one of the desserts, a twelve-foot-high tower of cake. From the few rowdies, a general multilingual brawl spread through the assembly, rivalries developed, American, French, English and Sardinian flags rose and fell, tables collapsed, and the party broke up finally when a section of the pavilion roof caved through.[16]

By the time that the author Amelia Ransome Neville arrived in 1854 the city had already acquired a reputation for its cooking, and California agriculture was producing most of the state's food. In her memoirs Mrs. Neville remarked that such restaurants as Clayton's in Commercial Street and Martin's, just beyond, were better than most in New York. One of her favorites, Captain Cropper's on Second Street, grew famous for its terrapin and oyster suppers and later, under a caterer named Harkness, for its take-out orders for many of the city's social functions.[17]

To meet the early demand for sleeping as well as eating accommodations, the number of hotels increased quickly. Several of the early groggeries expanded their facilities to take in lodgers, sometimes bedding them down in the bowling alleys which a number of them featured. Hangouts for sailors and the rougher elements in town, many of these places evolved naturally as the early headquarters for crimping and shanghaiing. The Hounds, the city's earliest organized band of ruffians, added to the notoriety of a tavern called the Shades. Fortunately the hasty and shoddy construction of such establishments made them particularly vulnerable to fire; in the first few years they disappeared almost as rapidly as they were built.

A converted tavern became the city's first real hotel, Vioget House, in August, 1846. Its former bartender and first proprietor, John Henry Brown, providentially opened the hotel just before the arrival in August of eight or ten whaling vessels for a four-month stay. He almost immediately changed its name to the Portsmouth House after Captain Montgomery's sloop of war, then anchored in the Bay; its sailmaker and carpenter agreed to supply the hotel's sign if the premises were named for his ship.

The hotel's first registrant was a Captain Simmonds, one of the officers from the whaling fleet. His lodgings were furnished with articles made by various ship's carpenters who had previously touched port; his bed, covered with thick flannel blanketing and calico quilts, may have been mattressed with moss from the Sand-

wich Islands, or perhaps it was one of four feather beds bought
from a party of Mormons who had arrived in July.

After a short time, Brown sold the Portsmouth House to Dr.
Elbert Jones. He then briefly operated the more elaborate City
Hotel, known familiarly as Brown's Hotel, across the street on the
corner of Clay and Kearny in the large adobe building owned by
William Leidesdorff. When the landlord upped the annual rent to
$3,000, Brown sold out. With Robert Parker, he started a new ho-
tel which was still under construction in May, 1848, when Leidesdorff died. Brown and Parker, though continuing the work on
their own new building, re-leased the City Hotel from Leidesdorff's estate. With the discovery of gold, their daily profits, including the cut from the hotel's gambling tables, the bar, and the
rent from the stores and offices on the premises, produced an
enormous income.

The two-story Parker House was put together of materials imported in sections. During the construction, when some glass arrived cut too small for the windows, the proprietors ordered a
new batch shipped posthaste from Hawaii, rather than alter the
size of the openings. By the fall of 1848 the new hotel had opened
for limited business and marked its completion the following summer with a grand ball and supper, free to all comers. It prospered
briefly as the town's most elite hostelry but turned its real profit as
a gaming house. Dealers took tables at $10,000 a month in the
main rooms, a sum which, together with the rentals from the rest
of the premises, brought the total yearly income to well into six
figures.[18] In spite of such profits, Parker's overwhelming generosity coupled with bad management left him personally in heavy
debt. Brown bought his share but found the leftover incum-
brances still so entangling that he sold out. Four days later the
property burned to the ground.

The original four-story St. Francis Hotel, built in 1849 on the
southwest corner of Clay and Dupont, achieved its grand proportions by joining a dozen small imported houses one to the other. It
did not allow gambling and was the first really fashionable hotel, a
social gathering place, and the site of the first state election poll,
held in the basement. The huge tent adjoining it housed a restaurant. It burned in October, 1853. The all-brick quarter-of-a-mil-
lion-dollar Union Hotel on Kearny Street offered early competition, but it, too, burned in the spring of 1851. During its brief existence, it also offered luxurious accommodations to discriminating lodgers. The Tehama House, formerly called Jones', and the
affiliated Alden's Branch Restaurant occupied one corner at California and Sansome streets. Circled by verandas and colonnades,
it lent a gracious Southern appearance in keeping with the aristo-

cratic character of such a genteel establishment. Among its clientele was a large contingent of military officers. The Colonnade House near the square also affected a Southern appearance but was more famous for its temperance and ban on gambling. Fashionable people, including several of the city's scarce number of ladies, patronized the deluxe Oriental Hotel on Market at Bush and Battery. Porticoes embellished its four-story façade and formed a shaded gallery on the entrance level, and it had a ballroom where stylish dances were given. It also had paper-thin walls, affording no greater degree of privacy than any of the less elegant hotels in town. Another of the better hotels, the five-story Rassette House on Bush and Sansome, was rebuilt in brick after burning down in 1853. The Garrett House on Pike and Clay, Wilson's Exchange on Sansome, and the Brannan House, a glorified boardinghouse run by a Mrs. Yates, added first-class facilities to the expanding number of accommodations. The elegant five-story fireproof International Hotel on Jackson Street between Montgomery and Kearny, was the elite place to stay by 1854. The Portsmouth House, the Franklin House, the Mansion House, the Crescent, and the Niantic were considered among the early-day hotels of more ordinary character.[19] Outnumbering the hotels were the large number of lodging houses, many of which took in nonresident boarders.

Robert Lamotte, in a letter dated February 25, 1851, had written to his mother in Pennsgrove, Pennsylvania, that San Francisco living standards had already very much improved during his short residence there:

Beef, veal, pork, mutton, and venison are plenty as are ducks, geese, fish and vegetables—I board at a small restaurant where there are about 25 regular customers, paying $10 a week. It is very neat, quiet and comfortable,—everything that is in market we get well cooked. For instance, our breakfast this morning was tea, coffee, chocolate, beef and venison steaks, veal cutlets, pork chops, fried trout, hot rolls, toast and brown bread, and this slightly varied is our general bill of fare. Not so very bad for California, is it? Those who board at the best Hotels (of which there are five) and pay $25 or $30 live very little better than we do, who pay the lowest board that can be got in town.[20]

In contrast with the upright proprietors of the better houses, the most unscrupulous hotelkeepers employed the system of "calling." In anticipation of each newly arriving vessel they unleashed teams of city-licensed runners. Swarming over the decks, attaching themselves to the passengers and their baggage, they inundated their victims with hyperbole extolling the nonexistent glories of their employers' accommodations and the equally exaggerated extravagances of their cuisines. Thus many an innocent traveler ended up in scrubby quarters, supplied by indifferent kitchens, at outrageously princely prices.

The growing trends to the gambling resort and to the fashionable saloon were influenced by the Gold Rush women. In several fancy places, artful female employees and occasionally proprietors employed their charms to part their clientele as expeditiously as possible from the contents of their pocketbooks. There were establishments of the utmost respectability, on the other hand, designed to attract the patronage of women of gentility. Clayton's, the earliest of these family-oriented places, was augmented in the summer of 1851 by W. L. Winn's Fountain Head of Luxuries and early in 1853 by his Branch. Neither of Winn's handsomely decorated resorts offered alcoholic beverages, concentrating instead on confectioneries, ices, and other such refreshments. Winn had arrived by ship in 1849 already in debt for travel; he borrowed further and invested his talents in making homemade candies. He hawked his wares through the San Francisco streets on a tray made of an old trunk lid hung on his person by a pair of suspenders. At night he sold his sweetmeats to the distinguished gentlemen visiting the Countess, the city's leading courtesan, whose two-story house of prostitution was conveniently located on Washington Street across from the square. The volume of business allowed him to cancel his debts and open the shops, where he once estimated his average daily number of local customers at 3,000. On occasion he even sent orders abroad. Caterer Peter Job's on Washington Street was also much in favor for its ice cream and baked treats. The French Monsieur Job was a skilled confectioner, and his classically adorned compositions graced early bridal tables.

Other ventures into respectability flourished as many of the ordinary resorts became more disreputable. Barry and Patten's Montgomery Street saloon, which opened in March, 1852, was one of the forerunners of the stylish drinking houses. Although customers could play billiards on the second-floor English slate tables, they could not engage in any forms of gambling on the premises. Huge gilt-framed paintings decorated the walls in established saloon fashion, but the subjects were chaste. A bountiful free lunch under the glittering chandeliers heralded a long and splendid San Francisco tradition. Inspired by the success of Barry and Patten's, saloons competed in extravagance. By the seventies the most ordinary saloons offered excellent free lunches, and even the inexpensive beer parlors set out platters of cheese and cold cuts. Bars tucked into the rear of corner groceries, which abounded in the city, served as neighborhood gathering places much in the manner of English pubs, although many of them were of an extremely rough character. B. E. Lloyd wrote in the mid-seventies that drinking was such a fact of city life that it was certainly considered no disgrace to frequent a saloon, which the entire male populace did without embarrassment. Since everybody acknowledged that everybody drank, large-scale social drinking became taken for granted, and there was consequently little stigma attached.[21] San Francisco has never lost its enthusiasm for alcohol.

In response to the heavy traffic, a veteran bartender named Charles Campbell issued in 1867 a small booklet of recipes for the edification of his less practiced confreres. *The American Barkeeper,* "Containing Experimental Knowledge and the Elements of Success, Acquired in the Management of the Most Popular Bars Throughout the United States," gave detailed instructions for serving every popular drink from brandy straight ("Two small bar tumblers; one should contain iced-water. Place both before your customer, with bottle of brandy") to sours, fizzes, hot and cold punches, smashes, juleps, cocktails, toddies, cobblers, slings, sangarees, shrubs, and even lemonades and other temperance beverages. Absinthe and wormwood appeared among the ingredients, and the manual provided directions for a number of exotic combinations such as the Dog Days Drink (one pound of loaf sugar, one-quarter pound of ground nutmeg, one wineglass of ginger extract, two quarts of port and one each of brandy and blackberry brandy, all well shaken together); the Pop Goes the Weasel (sugar, gin, ice, and lemon soda); and the famous Blue Blazer, an invention which Mr. Campbell proudly claimed as his own although the credit is generally bestowed on the El Dorado's Professor Jerry Thomas, who also invented the Tom and Jerry (one teaspoon of sugar, one wineglass of scotch and Irish whiskey mixed, placed in one of a pair of handled glass-bottomed silver mugs to which the practitioner adds one wineglass of boiling water and then touches a lighted match, pouring the blazing liquid from one tumbler to the other, finally finishing it off with a twist of lemon peel when the flames have subsided).

In the final section, "The Art of Manufacturing Liquors," Mr. Campbell offered recipes that "will enable every dealer to manufacture his own liquors, instead of paying from 50 to 75 per cent. for making them for him." He recommended only non-poisonous products, all readily obtainable in any large drugstore and estimated an average cost of 75 cents a gallon for liquor and $2 for the finest imitation French brandy, for which real article the uninitiated were currently paying $7. To obtain Irish whiskey, Mr.

Campbell added sugar, creosote, and burnt sugar, for color, to pure spirit. Rye whiskey called for green tea, oil of wintergreen, and extract of bitter almonds; sherry for cider, extract of bitter almonds, sugar, mustard, essence of cinnamon, and a small part of Jamaica rum. Cochineal or a deep tincture of logwood gave grapeless port wine an authentic color, while good hop yeast fermented for two days gave to an equally grapeless champagne the requisite bubbles. To add a heavy body to the liquors, Mr.Campbell recommended an authoritative decoction of slippery elm, made by boiling the tree bark in water.

Since physical life itself was a gamble for the forty-niner, he was naturally receptive to risks as a way of life. Games of chance were his principal entertainment; speculation in everything from imports to mining shares was his standard mode of business. Although the city council had outlawed gambling at the start of 1848, even going so far as to confiscate for city use all money found on the table, it hastily repealed its ruling at the next meeting, and from then on gambling establishments thrived, especially around Portsmouth Square. Constantly jammed with the hard-drinking clientele that preferred the convivial atmosphere around the nugget-laden tables to the cheerless comfort of rented quarters, the gambling resorts were one of the most democratic institutions in the early community. Although the places soon took on airs of elegance and within a short time were vying over the splendors of their cut crystal chandeliers, antiqued mirrors, European paintings, the quality of their musicians, the abundance and variety of their refreshments, and the richness of their appointments generally, they still welcomed indiscriminately anyone who had the stakes. This included cheats and con men who employed everything from sleight of hand to marked cards and established a tradition for dishonesty which, within a few decades, reached the proportions of an industry.

Will and Finck Company, a Market Street dealer in and manufacturer of sporting goods—"The Only Sporting Emporium on the Pacific Coast"—issued an undated (but probably from the early 1880's) printed catalogue advertising its wares, delivery by mail or express on a strictly cash and strictly confidential basis. It offered standard Faro tools, including endless varieties of dealing boxes; shuffling boards; cards; layouts; billiard cloth by the yard; trimming shears; dealing equipment for games from Red and Black and High for Luck to High Ball and Diana; tables for Faro, Poker, and Dice, and the latter two combined; and the Grand Hazard Dice Table, electric, complete, "our own invention," with electric half-inch dice ($175 for the table and $2.50 each for the dice). The listings under dice games were far more interesting: equipment for Mustang, Over and Under Seven, Blue Jay, and Chuck Luck included an ivory dice top "to throw high or low as required," a rolling log "to come red or black, high or low," and, for a mere $75, a "New Hyronemus Tub" to control the dice.

Dozens of spindles, belts, and wheels included many that could serve equally for street work or indoor use, as well as portable units for traveling. Along with the complete outfits for Keno, Rondo, and short games, the buyer could ensure his success with the vest holdout, "our own pattern" for $25; the sleeve holdout, ranging from $25 to $100; the table holdout, to work with the knee, at $15; the bug, to hold out extra cards from the table, at $1; various reflectors for table use, some already installed in dollars, half dollars or pipes, or available to work on any finger ring, to fasten to greenbacks, or "to attach to machine, where it can be brought to palm of hand at will," for $25. Nail pricks at 25 cents were a real bargain. A floor telegraph listed for $5, and acid fluid for shading cards came in three colors, complete with directions. Singly or by the dozen, decks of marked cards for Monte, Poker, and other games included glazed backs with rounded corners, strippers cut to order for any short game ("in ordering these cards state what kind of card preferred, and be particular to give full directions—just what you want them for, and what cards you want stripped"). Dice came in nine basic varieties, any one of which could be furnished in celluloid, in ivory, or in bone, some shaped to come craps or seven, and, at $6 the pair, the most expensive of the lot, "Eastern" dice, guaranteed to come up three high, three low, and three fair. "In ordering dice," the catalogue advised, "please state which side you want to come up; also state if you want a square set to match."[22]

Although in 1850 less than 8 percent of the people in California were female—and most of them of dubious character—the number of respectable women was slowly increasing, and with it a slight domestication of the frisky male society. Under this mildly taming influence, San Francisco outlawed gambling on Sundays in the fall of 1850, but with little effect; along with lotteries, it remained one of the preferred Sabbath pastimes until legally restricted again in 1855. Women still made up only one-third of the population by the 1880's and were not a full half of it until the century ended.

Another major influence on Gold Rush living was its youth: more than half the participants were in their twenties; two decades later the large majority were still under fifty. The youthful San Franciscans found diversion in dances—male often paired with male by necessity—country outings, parades, balls, banquets, illuminations, horse races, songfests, athletic contests, regattas, circuses, concerts, theatrical performances, cockfights, bullfights and other animal contests, and vaudeville. The dominantly male spirit of adventure, coupled with the youthful vigor that prevailed throughout the early years, demanded of even the least hell-raising entertainments a degree of excitement far beyond the normal—enough to arouse an audience that was already at a high pitch of stimulation. There was little early demand for finesse or for esthetics, but the obvious, the gory, the boisterous, the slapstick, the maudlin, and the sentimental found a ready acceptance. On Sundays, after they had to forgo gambling, the population frolicked nonetheless, preferring the Spanish tradition to the Puritanical.

IX

Entertainment and the Arts

BEFORE the Gold Rush a new few amateur theatrical performers, including members of Stevenson's Regiment, entertained limited audiences; after the Gold Rush the professional theater flourished until the depression of the middle fifties. The glint of gold lured a steady stream of actors, the talented, the famous, and a fair share of the inferior. The viewers responded to each with ebullience, in the former case showering them with gold, and in the latter with catcalls, hisses, and boos. The largely male audience demanded less talent from women, whose presence alone occasioned unrestrained adulation. Within a few years, when they were not such a novelty and the theatrical market became crowded with performers of both sexes jostling for a share of the bounty, the audiences became bolder, more discriminating, demanding, sometimes even fickle, lavishing their affections on a new star to the dismay of a recent favorite who could still hear the applause in her ears. A group of admirers might bid at auction for a choice seat at one performance of a special favorite. The Empire Engine Company, for example, once honored singer Catherine Hayes by paying $1,150 for a single seat for her concert. Money, gold nuggets, and jewelry littered the stage. On at least one occasion an admirer threaded a valuable diamond ring to a bouquet tossed to the ravishing leading lady, and at the height of her career, Lotta Crabtree, one of the West Coast's favorite actresses, received a gold and diamond tiara.

If the earliest theater was of poor to mixed quality, it rose very quickly before the depression to a high level. The foreign language productions kept the scene international and well nourished. The frequency of English-speaking performances and the emphasis on English playwrights and classical dramas, however, had, besides the entertainment value, the more important quality of unifying the motley community around good language and proved standard-bearers of civilization. The sophistication of the Gold Rush audience was a surprise that inspired many acting companies. From the beginning, Shakespeare was a favorite; in the first decade, San Francisco saw twenty-two of his plays. *Othello,* the city's first Shakespearean production, was coupled with a comic piece and a circus performance. The Gold Rush audience could not complain that it did not get its money's worth.

A somewhat bohemian Englishman, Stephen C. Massett, was the city's first professional entertainer, opening on June 22, 1849, in the courthouse on the square. To the accompaniment of a borrowed piano, the only one in California at that moment,* he presented a concert of songs—some of his own composition—imitations, dramatic skits, and recitations. The audience, including four women for whom front-row seats were reserved, paid $3 a ticket; Mr. Massett made a profit of $500. Under the name of Jeems Pipes of Pipesville, he also wrote engaging commentary for one of the early literary journals, the *Pioneer.*

In October, 1849, Joseph Rowe's Olympic Circus arrived by way of Panama, pitched a tent on Kearny Street big enough to accommodate almost 1,500 people, and gave their first performance by the end of the month. The crowd happily paid $2 to $3 to get in, whereas the going rate elsewhere was well under $1. It was at Rowe's that the city's first production of Shakespeare took place. By January a theatrical troupe, the Eagle Theatre Company, which had been flooded out of Sacramento, played the first professional dramatic entertainment. It performed Sheridan Knowles' *The Wife,* followed by *Charles the Second* for an audience assembled in Washington Hall above Foley's Saloon. It was the beginning of a rich theatrical outpouring.

Rowe engaged an Australian Company to give dramatic performances in his refurbished amphitheater. The National Theatre presented a French troupe. The city soon housed the Italian Theatre; the Phoenix Theatre; the Adelphi, which hosted Italian, French, Chinese, and English companies and for a time employed a Chinese orchestra; the Varieties; Elleard's Hall; Foley's Circus, started by one of Rowe's former clowns; the American Theatre, incorporating circus acts, which was torn down and rebuilt as the American Theatre II; the Lyric Casino, later called the Verandah; the Metropolitan, sumptuous and gaslit; Armory Hall; the Olympic; the Gaieties, an inexpensive waterfront theater; the Bella Union, noted for its minstrels and later for its variety, which made it the most popular melodeon of the Barbary Coast; Meiggs' Musical Hall; the Lyceum Music Hall; the Union, which also presented foreign companies; and the Athenaeum, whose propri-

*A widely accepted statistic challenged by other reports of as many as four pianos in San Francisco at that time.

etor, Dr. Collyer, tried to entice the local audience by posing live female models. Draped in filmy veilings over flesh-colored under-pinnings, they depicted scenes from the Bible and famous paint-ings. Another genre, the Panorama, generally unremarked al-though it prophesied the motion picture, presented the first travelogue and the first newsreel; in the former, thousands of yards of painted landscape unrolled slowly to music; in the latter, the moving painting chronicled timely events, sometimes embel-lished by live scenes. On the slopes of Telegraph Hill, a Chinese theater added a mysterious cacophony of clashing Oriental gongs and unfamiliar Eastern instruments.

The first Jenny Lind Theatre, named to honor the great Swed-ish Nightingale, who never sang a note in San Francisco, flour-ished briefly in the fall of 1850 above the Parker House Saloon. When fire consumed the building only a few months later, the un-daunted proprietor, Tom Maguire, an uneducated New York hack driver turned bartender, opened a second Jenny Lind. It also burned within days of its June opening. When he went on to build a third, the audience hailed it after the first performance in October, 1851, as the most extravagant theater on the coast. In the summer of 1853, the city bought the building from him, re-portedly for $200,000, and made it over into City Hall. Maguire's thirty-year career in the theater was an important influence on the early development of the San Francisco stage: by the late fifties he owned virtually all the important halls in San Francisco and the mining communities, was a talent scout of considerable ability, and the manager of many of the foremost players, and later was instrumental in producing grand opera.

Another of the early theatrical figures—entrepreneur, compos-er, performer, and intermittently city councilman—was his rival, Dr. D. G. Robinson, from Maine, so titled because he had at first run a drugstore on Portsmouth Square. Together with James Ev-rard, whose versatility included playing female roles and who be-came a San Francisco police sergeant when he gave up the stage, he opened the Dramatic Museum on California Street on July 4, 1850. The company, employing some amateur talent, presented skits and musical satires, including on opening night "Seeing the Elephant." A collection of Robinson's satirical verse came out in 1853, probably the first songbook in the state. During the heyday of Lola Montez, he wrote and produced a full-length satire on the actress' flamboyant life. It was a huge success, in spite of heated criticisms aimed at its bad manners and its lack of generosity to-ward a humane, if somewhat eccentric, figure. Robinson's Cal-houn Street house on Telegraph Hill was the center of a lively co-lony of actors. Among their other exploits, they liked to water their jointly owned horse on champagne out of a silver server. During the early fifties Robinson had a hand in building several theaters, among them the Adelphi, the American, the New Dramatic Museum, and the Bryant Minstrels. By the mid-fifties Tom Maguire's monopolistic hand acquired the Minstrels, combined them with the rival Christy's Minstrels, and presented the amalgamated troupe in San Francisco Hall, which in an even later refurbishing and renaming, became Maguire's Opera House.

Theaters were quick to overcome their early makeshift qualities and the discomforts that accompanied them. Fires forced them to be rebuilt frequently, almost always with improvement. It was common practice to build theaters in connection with existing saloons to which the audiences could repair for entr'acte refreshments. In many instances drinking halls and gambling resorts offered the theaters direct competition, providing, instead of stars of renown, suggestive variety acts, dramatic and musical entertainments, "freak" shows, animal fights pitting customers' dogs against resident rats, and similar titillations, without any charge whatsoever. In the flush times of the early fifties, however, there was always an audience for the expensive paid seats in the legitimate houses. Theater benefits quickly caught on as an established form of fund raising for clubs and charities and later for the performers themselves. Within a few years the star of a benefit might often be its own financial beneficiary as well. Many a contract featured the special self-benefit performance as one of its provisions, and soon such terms became established tradition.

Besides playing San Francisco, the actors who flocked west toured the gold communities and usually Australia. As a whole, they were a well-traveled, sophisticated bunch, wrapped in a colorful cloak of bohemianism, if not outright eccentricity. Their private doings and flamboyant life-styles intrigued the community as much as the city's uniqueness intrigued them, and several theatrical families settled down, at least for a number of years, in San Francisco. The Booths, the Bakers, Mrs. Judah, and the Chapmans, among others who stayed on, leased and managed theaters as well as acted in them, providing the San Francisco stage with the nucleus of a resident company through its formative years. The melodeons, although not noted for their consummate good taste, still afforded training for a number of aspirants, from Lotta Crabtree to the vaudevillian Eddie Foy, who later rose to the top of their profession.

As the San Francisco stage flourished, the list of favorites grew: Stephen Massett, James E. Murdoch, the minstrels Bryant and Christy, Dr. Robinson, Alexina Baker, the numerous Chapmans, and Junius Brutus Booth, Sr., and his sons Junius, Jr., young Edwin, and one who was later to upstage them all, John Wilkes. San Franciscans acclaimed the appearances of the tragedian James Stark; Edwin Forrest and his divorced wife, Catherine Sinclair; Matilda Heron for her role of Camille and her natural style. Another favorite, the much-married Adah Isaacs Menken, was during her thirty-three years an acknowledged poetess, a favorite of the foremost literary figures of the day (including the elder Dumas, with whom she had an affair), and a practitioner of the sensationalist dramatic school, as well as style of life. Her most famous performance, in cropped hair and flesh-colored leotards, was in the male role of Mazeppa, the Tartar prince. Mrs. W. C. Forbes, another male interpreter, numbered among her roles Hamlet, anticipating the controversial Judith Anderson performance by more than 100 years. The city accorded Julia Dean a brilliant reception and warmly applauded Laura Keene, an English import, who later became one of the city's outstanding theatrical managers.

Lola Montez, onetime mistress of Liszt, later the Countess of Lansfeldt, mistress of King Ludwig I of Bavaria, noted for her exotic Spanish looks (although she was born in Ireland), her fiery Spider Dance—a derivative of the tarantella—for her mediocre acting ability, and for forgetting her lines, was nonetheless a ravishing success. Walter Leman's acting career spanned several decades in San Francisco, where he was also a playwright and historian of the theater. Mrs. John Wood, a wildly popular actress, was remembered for the white japonica blossom an admiring judge always tossed onstage, which she wore entwined in her hair in the next scene (much to the community's surprise, the judge ruled against her when she brought divorce proceedings in his court against her husband).

The darling of them all was Lotta Crabtree, a curly-haired red-headed eight-year-old gamine with tremendous charm, a great deal of talent, and an extremely enterprising mother. Her father, a former New York book dealer, brought the family west during the Gold Rush; within two years, Lotta had given her first theatrical performance at the mines. She was an immediate favorite, certainly because of her spirited presentations, but in some part because of the strong wave of sentiment among the homesick miners which embraced both women and children. There were innumerable child actors, and even one whole troupe of thirty, the Marsh Juvenile Comedians, aged five to fifteen, who successfully trod the boards in the middle and late fifties. The Bateman children performed *Hamlet* to local applause. When the critic Frank Soulé panned a later play, *The Mother's Trust* (the grand winner of a contest sponsored by the Batemans' father, and incidentally written by their mother, who had largely plagiarized it) the outraged father, Hezekiah Linthicum Bateman, stalked him to the square and gunned him down, fortunately without fatal consequences.

Lotta won the affections of the miners and, more significantly, the admiration of the many professionals who saw her perform. In particular she impressed Lola Montez, who briefly made her a companion and protégée. From her various teachers the apt pupil learned a whole range of theatrical specialties, from playing the banjo, singing, and dancing jigs and ballet, to mimicry, blackface repartee, and recitations. Under her mother's strict chaperonage, she made her way through the mining camps, the variety halls of San Francisco, and the Eastern theater circuit and returned to San Francisco with a national reputation as an innovative comedienne. Later in her life she left two monuments: Lotta's Fountain at Market and Kearny streets, her gift to the city (there Tetrazzini sang to thousands on Christmas Eve of 1910, in thanks for the city's hospitality), and $4,000,000, in a heavily contested will, bequeathed mostly to charities and other worthy causes.

When the fortunes of the theater fell with the economy of the mid-fifties, and ticket prices and serious presentations declined, the minstrel, the vaudevillian, and the reed organ took over. By the summer of 1855 five troupes of minstrels were giving regular performances. The melodeons, many of which were of questionable character, the music halls, and the cheap "one-bit" theaters dominated the scene. The late fifties and early sixties marked an era of unrestrained diversity and experimentation. The stage featured live elephants, horses, and even a crocodile; Chinese jugglers were a curiosity; a Chinese acting troupe, on its way to Paris to play before the emperor, inspired more laughter than appreciation. Other showplaces relied on electrobiological exploits, magic tricks, tightrope dancing, and the contortions of an India rubber man.[23]

A number of people in the early sixties found themselves facing jury trials for presenting indecent performances. (Some were found guilty, others acquitted, perhaps aided inadvertently by the respectability of the witnesses called up by the prosecution, gentlemen whose sterling character would certainly never have allowed them to be present at an improper performance.) The stage shows became more dependent on sensationalism, the producers more on local writers and current events than on repertory. Pantomimes, tableaux, burlesques of the classics, ballets, leg shows, and spectaculars flourished until the middle of the decade, when, the trials of adolescence mainly behind, the San Francisco theater settled down temporarily into a more balanced period.

The theater district began to move over to the Bush Street

neighborhood by the end of the decade. The seventies was a time of change in San Francisco, and the theaters reflected the fluctuating fortunes of the community. The railroad and the silver mines created vast fortunes, powerful families, and the acquisition of instant culture. The completion of the railroad meant also the easy transportation of complete Eastern companies, and the importance of local casts began to diminish, although both Maguire and John McCullough held their excellent stock companies together through the decade. While old stars continued to return for San Francisco performances, many new voices declaimed from behind the footlights. Tastes remained catholic, reflecting the equal needs for entertainment and for culture. *Nan-the-Good-for-Nothing* and *Bertha the Sewing Machine Girl* shared popularity with the tragedies of Shakespeare and Bulwer-Lytton.

In spite of the new splendors, melodeons still outnumbered legitimate houses, while the enormousness of the new theaters was no guarantee of the continued size of the audience. Legislation repealing the 1864 law against Sunday performances gave the theater something of a boost at the beginning of the decade. In January, 1869, the opening of the first of several showy new houses, the California Theatre, attracted the whole corps of local celebrities: James Flood, Leland Stanford, James Fair, John Mackay, and even Joshua Norton, dressed to the hilt for the occasion. They marveled at its elaborate construction, its advanced equipment, and its generally plush ambience, all befitting emerging society in America's most extravagantly new metropolis. The wealthy William Ralston's backing made the venture possible, while Bret Harte composed a special verse to launch the enterprise properly. Shiel's Opera House—known later by a number of other names, Gray's, the Standard, and Emerson's among them—epitomized the trend of the early seventies, the quick creation of symbols of cultural magnificence. But even Shiel's brilliance was eclipsed in 1876 by Dr. Thomas Wade's glorious, if elephantine, Opera House, shortly after called the Grand Opera House, and by Lucky Baldwin's plush Academy of Music. Under Maguire's management, the latter theater, constructed as part of Baldwin's tony Market Street Hotel, opened on March 6 with a performance of *Richard III*. Wade's Opera House had fascinated its resplendent opening-night audience two months earlier with the Grand Spectacular and Dramatic Romance, *Snowflake! And the Seven Pigmies* in five acts, preceded by the Fabbri Opera Troupe's rendition of "The Star-Spangled Banner." Borrowed from the Snow-White saga, the new play named its heroine, played by Miss Annie Pixley, Snowflake, and its dwarfs, now pygmies, Blick, Pick, Dick, Klick, Knick, Slick, and Strick.

The financial boom based on Nevada silver and speculation in mining stocks had begun to wane by the mid-seventies. In 1875, when Ralston's Bank of California failed and he drowned in the Pacific surf, a possible suicide, San Francisco was momentarily shaken. By 1877 the city had followed the rest of the country into a full-scale depression which lasted into the early eighties. The financial disasters went hand in hand with a growing social awareness. The Workingmen's Party thrived, and its anger at the profit takers was as vociferous as its retributions against the Chinese laborer. In this context, the theater, too, made changes and retrenchments. Financing and accordingly names and owners changed with amazing frequency. As packaged troupes commuted from the East, local stock companies became more flexible, supplying whatever number of players was necessary, from one to an entire backup cast. New York's Union Square Theatre and San Francisco's California Theatre exchanged plays and companies on a regular basis. The luxury of grand opera gave way to more popular opera buffa and musicales, both better money-makers. Tivoli Gardens, which opened in 1875 as an inexpensive beer garden offering musical entertainment, soon became the most popular setting for comic opera.

Maguire continued his dominance in theatrical affairs throughout the seventies, even though the depression caused him to lose such houses as the Alhambra (which later reopened as the Bush Street Theatre). Among Maguire's protégés, James A. Herne, outstanding as stage manager and player, was all the while acquiring proficiency as a playwright. Like so many others who founded their careers in San Francisco, he eventually moved east. Herne's assistant, a young man named David Belasco, coauthored a number of his early plays. Belasco had the distinction of being a native Californian, born in San Francisco a year after his English-Jewish parents had joined the Gold Rush. He launched his theatrical career at a very early age by running off from the monastery where he was being educated, to join a passing circus. His father had been a circus clown in the old country. For a number of years Belasco acted in the Baldwin Theatre's stock company, where his fellow performers included a child actress named Maude Adams and an Irish tragedian named James O'Neill, father of the playwright Eugene. When Belasco turned to producing and directing, his career took on new dimensions, and he became known for his daring innovations. Although his writing for the stage was prolific, his plays never achieved much distinction. In 1882, when Maguire lost his lease on the Baldwin because of financial difficulties, the not yet thirty-year-old Belasco left the West to become stage manager for New York's Madison Square Theatre. Maguire also went east within two years and lived there to an indigent old age.

The depression of the seventies cut short the career of a second brilliant impresario, John McCullough. During his nine-year reign as stage manager, as well as actor, for the California Theatre, the most celebrated international figures graced its stage. Perhaps the most startling production was a performance of *Hamlet* in which Helena Modjeska, one of Poland's leading actresses, played Ophelia in her native tongue. The rest of the cast delivered their lines in English. When the financial crisis and Ralston's death brought about a change of hands at the California, McCullough likewise moved east, where he died in the mid-eighties in an institution for the insane.

The most controversial episode up to that date in the city's theatrical history occurred in March, 1879, with the announcement of a play called *The Passion*. Written by the Jewish author Salmi Morse and directed by Belasco, it starred the Catholic James O'Neill in the role of Christ. Although the story was presented with total respect, the idea of the impersonation of Jesus shocked the community, in particular the clergy, and the city council threatened to prevent the opening. The theater outwitted them by opening several days ahead of schedule, but the victory was short-lived. Some members of the audience became emotional to the point of weeping and kneeling in prayer during the performances. The production closed within a week. Undaunted, its ecumenical producers waited briefly and tried again, this time reaping fines as well as public castigation. When anti-Semitic feelings surfaced and rioting occurred, Jewish citizens feared for their safety. By late in April Morse decided to take the play to New York, but the reception there was equally depressing; within months the morose playwright was a suicide.

Music was a natural part of the atmosphere in the gambling houses, the dance halls, and the melodeons that lined the Barbary Coast and clustered around the square. There was almost as much variety among the musicians as among the polyglot audience for whom they performed. For more than sixty years the most popular resort, the Bella Union, presented virtually all the forms of light music, starting in the spring of 1850 with a Spanish repertoire provided by a Mexican flautist, two harpists, and two guitarists. As early as 1849 an all-black choral group sang spirituals at the Aquila de Oro. Full orchestras often accompanied by celebrated soloists entertained at the El Dorado and several similarly elegant gambling houses. The music kept mostly to light classics, waltzes, quadrilles, and polkas. The Verandah competed with a single performer to whom were attached a variety of instruments by which he could create melody and timpani simultaneously as an accompaniment to his tap dance.

Many early concerts, often classical and popular music combined, took place on cabaret stages, the most notable being the Promenade Concerts in the spring of 1852 at the Arcade Saloon. Minstrels performed on the same circuit and became such favorites in San Francisco that for two decades the city reigned as the principal producer of minstrel troupes for a world market. The most famous was the Original San Francisco Minstrels, organized in 1864. Audiences particularly enjoyed soirees, which combined concerts, balls, and participatory singing into one grand evening's entertainment. In the gambling houses along Dupont Street, Chinese orchestras played music dissonant to the Western ear. Serious music also had its share of dedicated supporters from the earliest days. The city welcomed vocalists and instrumentalists in solo concerts and applauded ballet and opera troupes from Europe and Mexico.

Oddly enough, the fire fighters, who numbered twenty-three separate companies before the end of the decade, ranked among the leading patrons of early San Francisco music. The highly competitive volunteer brigades vied also in the excellence of their musical bands. After one of Elisa Biscaccianti's concerts, fire companies in full dress uniform showed their enthusiasm by unhitching the horses from the prima donna's carriage and towing it themselves back to her lodgings.

Coming from a long association in craft guilds which featured musical competitions, the large German population in San Francisco influenced the city's musical development from the start. A German musician, Dr. Augustus Malech, started San Francisco's first singing society in 1851, and within two years there were four choral groups in full voice. By 1854 the Turner Gesang Verein, an association of clubs devoted to liberal politics, gymnastics, and singing, boasted 6,000 members. Both the San Francisco Harmonie, organized in 1854, and the Germania Philharmonic Society, dating from 1855, were German groups.

George Loder, an Englishman, was the director of the first San Francisco Philharmonic Society, which he organized in collaboration with Henry Meiggs late in 1852. It achieved a great success in a series of concerts with the Pacific Musical Troupe, a quartet of singers, presented in the new 1,200-seat Musical Hall. Small orchestral groups played concerts of chamber music, and out of one of these, the Verandah Concert Society, a string group, grew the Germania Philharmonic Society.

The leading force behind the development of classical music in

San Francisco was Rudolph Herold, who came to San Francisco on concert tour in 1852 as accompanist to Catherine Hayes and chose to remain behind. Born in a village near Leipzig, he was a graduate of its conservatory and had embarked on his musical career after a favorable audition with Felix Mendelssohn. In San Francisco his musical contributions included conducting the Germania Philharmonic Society and the Turnverein Choral Society, as well as practically all of the other prominent singing groups in the community, Italian operas at the Metropolitan, the symphony orchestra, and the Handel and Haydn Society in concert; offering music lessons; playing the organ at St. Mary's Cathedral, the First Unitarian Church, and the Church of the Advent; and fostering popular music festivals, May Day festivals, and jubilees, which brought together various German musical groups from all over the state.

Many prominent artists, attracted by the extravagance of Gold Rush fees, and some by the mines themselves, came west to make their fortunes. Among those who performed for California audiences, the Viennese pianist Henri Herz was one who also tried gold mining. The celebrated Hungarian violinist Miska Hauser began his American career under the auspices of P. T. Barnum in the East. Within the first three months of his stay in San Francisco he had given twenty-six concerts. During his six-year sojourn in San Francisco, Christian Koppitz, a German flautist of international recognition, became one of the Germania Society's outstanding performers. Although the audiences in 1854 enjoyed the performances of the violinist Ole Bull, a Norwegian follower of Paganini, the critics did not hesitate to distinguish his mechanical legerdermain from real virtuoso playing.

One of the most accomplished musicians to perform in San Francisco, the French harpist Robert Nicolas Bochsa, never played in the West except in concert with, and overshadowed by, his paramour, the renowned singer Anna Bishop, although he directed at the Metropolitan with great local success. Bochsa, the illegitimate son of a musician, had shown early promise of musical genius. By twenty-four he was court harpist to the Emperor Napoleon and after that to King Louis XVIII. Involvement in a series of forgeries had caused him to flee France at the height of his career there and head across the Channel. His later elopement with Anna, the British wife of Sir Henry Bishop, had shocked the world and inspired George du Maurier to write the best-seller *Trilby*.

Grand opera, in spite of the costliness of its presentation, continuously captivated San Francisco audiences. The French Opera Troupe was among the earliest arrivals, followed shortly by the

Spanish Opera Company. As early as February, 1851, San Franciscans were enthusiastically attending the Pellegrini Italian Opera Troupe's chorusless performances of *La Sonnambula, Norma,* and *Ernani.* The following year the coloratura Elisa Biscaccianti and P. T. Barnum's protégée Catherine Hayes gave triumphant concert series. The Planel French Opera Company appeared throughout the 1853 season. In 1854 a series of operatic concerts established the Metropolitan Theatre, under actress Catherine Sinclair's management, as a serious music house. Among the stars that year was the famous Mrs. Bishop. During the next eighteen months, Mrs. Sinclair offered a full repertoire of grand opera, employing the glittering Madame Anna Thillon's English Company, which sang some of the classics in English translation and aroused the displeasure of the local critics, who found Madame less than scintillating; and the Barili-Thorn Italian Opera Company, which featured stars of international renown and introduced fifteen-year-old Carlotta Patti in her first public appearance. The soprano Caterina Barili and her second husband, Salvatore Patti, a tenor, were the parents of Carlotta and her younger sister, Adelina.

When the opera suffered the consequences of the mid-fifties depression equally with the theater, the Barili-Thorn company economically joined forces on occasion with others: Anna Bishop's opera troupe, the dancers of the Montplaisir Ballet, and various resident performers, members of touring groups who had chosen to remain in San Francisco, whom it assimilated. Such perseverance "developed in the people the habit of going to the opera; and . . . also, the musical talent of the city became concentrated into a musical stock company, and thus laid the foundation that made it possible later for the great productions to come."[24] A local supporting company eased the difficulties and expense of transporting to the coast an entire opera company with its accompanying musical entourage, sets, costumes, baggage, and general paraphernalia. In the summer of 1855, after a feisty public exchange over profits and salaries, the Barili-Thorn group withdrew from the Metropolitan, Mrs. Sinclair retired as manager, and the theater shifted to variety acts.

At the end of the fifties, the city's major impresario, the ubiquitous Thomas Maguire, assembled another classic opera company to perform at popular prices in his Opera House. Bolstered by imported companies—the Bianchi Italian Opera Company, the William Lyster English Opera Company, the Howison Opera Company, the Adelaide Phillipps Italian Company, and the Caroline Ritchings Opera Troupe—he continued to sponsor opera at both Maguire's Opera House and the Academy of Music well into the seventies. Financially, the opera was never a success. As production costs grew, Maguire's losses were proportionately devastating; he reputedly lost $30,000 on the Adelaide Phillipps Troupe alone. Yet such stubborn persistence was one of the ironies in the basically gold-oriented city. The patronage of the uneducated Maguire, in spite of his continuing financial losses, was instrumental in establishing opera as a permanent art in San Francisco. For many among the nouveau riche, the grandness of opera stood as another symbol of cultural success. But there were also real music lovers, like the Germans and Italians in the balconies, for whom opera was a natural continuation of their heritage.

Because church choirs included many professional musicians, the caliber of church music was exceptionally high. Musical benefits attracted large audiences who paid admission to hear a Mozart mass sung by St. Mary's Choir or Rossini's *Stabat Mater* sung by Signora Biscaccianti for Grace Episcopal Church. In another irony of the times, the adored Biscaccianti, one of the city's major influences on the appreciation of fine music during its formative years, returned to San Francisco in 1859 besieged by personal problems and drink and was soon reduced to performing at the Bella Union. After three years she left the city and never returned.

The fifties had also already established San Francisco as a manufacturing center for musical instruments, although it never developed into a prime industry. The great demand for musical instruments, too cumbersome for the immigrants to the Gold Rush to include among their baggage, was partly filled by less expensive steamer shipments of famous European brands and East Coast products. The first San Francisco instrument factory, established in 1849 on Jackson Street by J. H. Falkenberg, manufactured badly needed pianos. By 1855 there was competition: Jacob Zech began turning out pianos of a superior quality, winning a prize for his skill at the 1857 Mechanics' Institute Fair. Within the decade there were several piano makers, flute makers, organ builders, clarinet makers, an accordion manufacturer, a harp maker, and a number of violin, guitar, and banjo makers. At least half a dozen music companies opened during the fifties, some selling jewelry or perfume along with the pianofortes, others specializing in a particular instrument such as the reed organ, in demand for the melodeons. The first music store opened in 1850, stocked with a variety of instruments along with a miscellaneous supply of groceries that Andrew Kohler had arranged to ship with him when he came to the Gold Rush. Business was so successful that Kohler expanded into larger quarters, replaced foodstuffs with fancy goods, children's clothing, and toys, took on the wholesale end of the music trade, and, with the addition of two branches, became the largest music house in the West. By the end of the decade he was also publishing music and importing the finest makes of instruments, with his own European agencies set up to assist him. Now known as Kohler and Chase, the firm is still doing business on O'Farrell Street.

A number of early publications attested to the importance of music in the first decades of San Francisco's development. *Figaro,* for thirty years after its first issue in 1865, was a guide to all of the city's popular entertainments, including music. The *Pacific Musical Gazette,* the *Musical Monthly,* and *Walter S. Pierce's Musical Circular,* all published in 1867, and *Sherman and Hyde's Musical Review,* published in 1874, devoted themselves entirely to music. By 1877 the *Footlight,* a journal concerned with music, drama, and the fine arts, appeared on a daily basis.

Typical of the excesses that marked the early years, the 1870 Urso Festival to benefit the San Francisco Mercantile Library rated as one of the most spectacular of early musical events. A grand four-day extravaganza staged on the afternoons of February 22 to 25, it employed Rudolph Herold conducting 1,200 vocalists, 200 instrumentalists, and the festival's director, the celebrated soloist Camilla Urso, who performed a Beethoven violin concerto.

Before the Gold Rush, expeditions from abroad frequently employed such diarists and artists as Louis Choris of the *Rurik,* to record the details of their adventures. During the Gold Rush, numerous lithographers, engravers, and artists—Charles Nahl, Alonzo Delano, and J. W. Audubon prominently among them—made their fortunes dashing off sketches of the forty-niners and their activities. It was a graphic age. Hundreds of illustrations for letter sheets, book pages, journals, and wall hangings documented for the rest of the world every event connected with the Gold Rush, from the way a miner washed his clothes every Sunday to the latest hanging. Portraits and landscapes completed the description. Although Charles Nahl, perhaps the best of the early artists, painted traditional subjects in the romantic style popular at the moment, his hundreds of skillfully drafted genre drawings, woodcuts, engravings, and canvases rank him as one of the leading historians of the period. The community appreciated his artistry, the Board of Delegates commissioning him in 1855 to design a lavish $4,500 scroll, which was sent to New York for fine engraving, as a certificate of membership for the fire department.

While the art of the sixties remained largely provincial, two trends emerged: oil painting, sumptuous and thoroughly imitative, which flourished in the decades after the Gold Rush as a symbol of nouveau riche arrival; and landscape painting, exemplified by the California school, whose participants often seemed to believe that they could better capture the vastness of the geography by recording it on a canvas of like scope. The paintings of Albert Bierstadt, Thomas Ayres, and Thomas Hill, who liked to reproduce entire mountain ranges on a single canvas, made the wonders of Yosemite familiar landmarks to the whole world. Another painter, Thomas Moran, who had studied with Turner and therefore exhibited superior craftsmanship, was less popular because he was less spectacular. William Keith, the most respected of the group, who painted prolifically during the eighties, played with light and shade on a more intimate scale than his colleagues, replacing mountain peaks with diaphanous nooks, forest glades, and views of the university in Berkeley. Tony Rosenthal's painting "Elaine," based on a Tennyson poem, came to San Francisco from Munich by way of Boston, gathering highly favorable reviews en route. Once in San Francisco, it was promptly stolen. After a local cloak-and-dagger investigation, city detectives jailed the thieves and installed the portrait once again in the frame from which it had been slashed. The circumstances enticed thousands of curious, who focused more attention on Rosenthal's painting than most artists attract in a lifetime.

The San Francisco Art Association, organized in 1871 by about two dozen practicing artists, opened a school of design three years later under the direction of Virgil Williams, a landscapist and figure painter. A four-month session cost $32; $40, if instruction in oils was included. Public contributions and private donations supported the school; the French government, for example, through the urging of Monsieur Breuil, its consul in San Francisco, donated fifty-five casts of antique sculptures. The greatest gift of all was the palatial family mansion of Mark Hopkins, turned over to the school in 1893 by Edward Searles, the husband of Hopkins' widow.

In 1861 a group of seventy resident architects founded a San Francisco architectural fraternity. By 1869 the city also had a chartered branch of the American Institute of Architects.

Printing, a fine art in modern San Francisco, had its local beginnings in the early days of the Gold Rush. Printers and presses had arrived even before the gold discovery—the *Brooklyn* carried both in 1846—and a power press was in operation by April, 1850. The early efforts, hindered by lack of supplies, piecemeal fonts, and odd paper, managed nevertheless to supply the community with innumerable rudimentary journals and broadsides. The printing industry burgeoned along with the city, but it took several decades for the rise of the state's first fine printers, Edward Bosqui and Charles A. Murdock, who among their other work produced the *Lark,* a popular magazine of the 1890's. Edward Taylor, later a member of the renowned San Francisco printing firm of Taylor

and Taylor, was one of several young boys who dabbled in printing in the early decades. By the age of eleven he was putting out a
magazine on his own press. Home printing in San Francisco, a
popular occupation by the early seventies, was responsible for sev-
en amateur journals. Its advocates had their own club, the California Amateur Press Association.

Women printers, often beginning as helpmates to their husbands, worked in several early San Francisco plants. By 1868, under the direction of Mrs. Agnes Peterson, they formed the San
Francisco Women's Cooperative Printing Union. According to the
incorporation papers in the state archives, the WCPU's purpose
was "to give employment to women as type-setters and thereby
enable them to earn an independent and honest living and to conduct and carry on a general printing business."[25]

In April, 1972, a Los Angeles collector and graphics designer,
Michael Kessler, paid $18 in a Bay Area flea market for a group of
six old daguerreotypes. Two among the half dozen views of mid-
nineteenth-century public buildings turned out to be the earliest
photographs ever discovered of the White House and the United
States Capitol, the latter photographed under an earlier dome.
Historians at the Library of Congress, which paid $12,000 for the
collection, announced that the daguerreotypes, all views of federal buildings in Washington, D.C., taken by the firm of John
Plumbe, Jr., date back to 1846. Plumbe, who developed the first
United States chain of photography studios, moved from Washington to San Francisco in 1850, lured by the Gold Rush and plans
for a transcontinental railroad.

William Shew, the first practicing daguerreotypist in San Francisco, did a thriving business in 1851 from a wagon set up in the
square. The daguerreotype, which had come from France to the
eastern United States in 1839, helped, along with sketches and engravings, to fill the tremendous need for pictures to send back
home. It was particularly well suited to portraits. One of the oldest
photography firms, Bradley and Rulofson, which started business
in the first days of the Gold Rush, had within a few years mounted
a gallery that included most of the celebrities and visiting royalty
who had ever set foot in the city. By the mid-seventies the firm
had acquired a number of awards: the Mechanics' Institute gold
medal for the best photographs in the city; the city of Philadelphia's gold medal for the best photographs in the country; and
the bronze medal from the World Exposition in Vienna for the
best photographs in the world. Another of the earliest photographers, C. E. Watkins, did with his camera what the California
school did with its brushes, providing for the world views of Western landscape, in particular of Yosemite.

X

Letters and Education

LETTERS, among the earliest writings of Gold Rush California, conveyed an immediate sense of excitement to the people back home, while diaries preserved the dimensions of the event for the future. One of the most popular vehicles of correspondence was the letter sheet, a single fold-up page usually illustrated with timely graphics—the destruction caused by the latest fire, or the tribulations, often humorously drawn, of life at the mines—which served for sending news in brief, while incidentally providing employment for a number of printers and artists. More detailed letters, like those of Dame Shirley, often found their way into print. The reading audience was large. The rest of the world, its appetite for adventure already whetted by earlier travel reports, including Dana's, now gobbled up each word issuing from the West. Reciprocally, the uprooted forty-niners, playing out their roles in a context of total, isolated unreality, hungered for news of home, and gladly paid exorbitant prices for outdated Eastern newspapers.

In this climate, journalism was soon a thriving enterprise, with a legion of professionals to call on—reportedly there were more than 1,000 during the ten years after the gold discovery, and fifty printers working the first year alone.[26] The Gold Rush attracted a very large number of educated men, including a percentage of college graduates, according to some historians, greater than in any other American city of the time. The human resource was there. The demand for news was there. The fascination of events was there. With the joining of leisure, money, and stamina unique to the Gold Rush, they shortly produced an outpouring of journalism so great that early San Francisco could claim more published newspapers than London and a per capita circulation greater than New York.

One hundred and thirty-two papers, including all six of California's literary journals, appeared in San Francisco during the fifties. Although readership was certainly no problem, lack of type and newsprint was; early editions often came out with substitutions for missing letters and printed on wrapping paper in any one of a variety of colors, depending on what was available. Proofreading was sometimes so bad that articles were lamentably distorted, a tradition not currently much improved. Most newspapers had a life span of no more than a year, often less, subject as they were to the vagaries of advertisers, to changing political loyalties, to enthusiastic but unsustained special interest groups, to shortages of material, and to fluctuating financial backing. Fire destroyed a number of publishing plants. Job turnover was brisk; mining sometimes claimed whole staffs in one sweep. The *Bon Ton Critic,* for example, expired completely when its editor was sent off to San Quentin, convicted of grand larceny. Yet in general there were always people who could fill the masthead or run the press.

Its isolation contributed to San Francisco's distinction as the center of a dynamic area, a character it retained until the arrival of the telegraph in 1861 imposed on all the city's institutions, including its journals, nationwide standards and a form of dialogue where before there had been uninhibited individuality and self-expression.

The early quality of the journals left a great deal to be desired. When they were not promoting vested interests, they reported California events, stale news from abroad, and editorial opinion in an equally unrestrained, walloping journalese, sometimes substituting prose essays and other pieces of a more literary nature. Yet in this way they served as a training ground and exhibit case for the developing crop of California literati, nurturing the Western literary evolution from its beginning. That there was an interest in the perpetuation of cultural forms, no matter how cloaked in frontier roughness, is illustrated by William B. Ide's Proclamation on the occasion of the 1846 Bear Flag Rebellion, of which he was one of the leaders. The republic he envisioned listed among its other advantages the encouragement of "virtue and literature."

San Francisco's first newspaper, the *California Star,* was a 13- by 18-inch sheet, three columns wide, published weekly at a subscription price of $6 a year, payable in advance. The idea of a journal "devoted to the liberties and interests of the people of California," as well as the material to equip a press and office, had come with Brannan from New York in 1846. He did not delay in putting the hand press to work printing odd jobs as soon as it was installed in temporary offices above Nathan Spear's Clay Street gristmill. Brannan also put out two advance extras of the newspaper: the first related war news; the other gave his account of the Mormons' adventures and dalliances. Besides turning out moneymaking circulars, mostly legal proclamations and regulations of the port, the press produced such furbelows as a set of blue silk programs and badges, which along with San Francisco's first parade honored the arrival of Commodore Robert F. Stockton when he replaced Commodore John D. Sloat as the official in charge of United States forces on the Pacific coast. Full-scale production began on January 9, 1847, under a masthead engraved in New York before departure.

The first editor, Elbert P. Jones, an intemperate Southerner, had migrated overland from Kentucky in 1846, was, besides being the second proprietor of the Portsmouth House, a practicing attorney, a large property holder, a politician, and at one time secretary of the town council. Jones Street was named in his honor. Although he announced in the first issue his intent to pursue a policy of high-minded objectivity, it took him only a few installments to unleash a storm of invective. In reply to some chiding remarks by the Monterey journal the *Californian*, the short-tempered editor commented:

> We have received two late numbers of the *Californian,* a dim, dirty little paper printed at Monterey, on the worn out material of one of the old California war presses. It is published and edited by Walter Colton and Robt. Semple, the one a lying sychophant [*sic*] and the other an overgrown lickspittle. . . .

The second editor, Edward Cleveland Kemble, assumed office by bodily throwing Jones off the premises in a dispute over a hotheaded editorial. Jones, beaten, gave up editing for real estate and made a fortune. Kemble had arrived at the age of seventeen aboard the *Brooklyn* with the Mormon group, although he himself was not a member of the sect. His father, a New York state senator, had edited the Troy *Northern Budget;* through his mother he was great-grandson of a signer of the Declaration of Independence. Although Kemble was not of the Mormon faith, Brannan had employed him in New York as a printer in the Spruce Street offices of the church's publications, the *Prophet* and the *New York Messenger*. Once the press was set up above the gristmill, Kemble again took up his work for Brannan and built a small adobe structure in which to house the journal. In November he joined Frémont's forces and served until his discharge the following April. When the Kemble-Jones fisticuffs occurred, Brannan was out of town on a fruitless mission to persuade the Utah contingent of Saints to continue farther west. However, he clearly approved of—perhaps even authorized—the editorial changeover, which had simply been announced as Jones' "withdrawal"; the masthead after his return acknowledged Kemble as editor. In spite of his youth, which earned him at eighteen the understandable sobriquet of "Boy Editor," Kemble's high standards made him "the greatest of very early California journalists."[27]

Another prominent journalist, Edward C. Gilbert, who had joined Kemble as part owner and senior editor of the *Alta,* the merger of the *Star* and *Californian,* had, like Kemble, come from upstate New York, where he had also been a printer. He had arrived in California in 1846 as a member of Stevenson's regiment of New York volunteers. In 1849 he was elected delegate to the state's first constitutional convention, an excellent vantage point for reporting the proceedings for the *Alta.* The following fall, when Gilbert was elected to the United States Congress, the paper wisely preserved its neutrality.

Gilbert could not resist a few political gibes at some of his peers on occasion and in one instance got himself more heavily involved than he intended with an attack on the state's governor, John Bigler. When the governor rode at the head of a relief train on its way to a group of emigrants stranded in Nevada, Gilbert took issue, claiming that Bigler was using the affair to enhance his own popularity. Gilbert's attack brought a printed rejoinder from the governor's loyal supporters, including State Senator General James W. Denver, after whom that city was later named. The further exchange of diatribes aroused Gilbert's temper to such a pitch that he challenged Denver to a duel. The first exchange of rifle fire left both men sound, Gilbert through Denver's deliberate miss, it is believed. Everyone except Gilbert was at that point willing to concede that honor had been served and it was time to call the whole thing off, but the stubborn challenger refused; a few minutes later he lay dead, at age thirty-three. Because dueling was widely accepted at that time, the contest at first proved no obstacle to Denver in his further quest for political office. Within a year he was the California secretary of state; he later served in the United States Congress, then as governor of the Kansas Territory and as a brigadier general during the Civil War. A good thirty years after the Gilbert event, he lost the Democratic nomination for President to Grover Cleveland, the duel in his past finally having caught up with him.

The *Alta* began triweekly publication in the fall of 1849. When Washington Bartlett's not yet published *Daily Journal of Commerce* announced a January date for its first issue, the competitive *Alta* instantly turned into a daily and rushed into print a whole day before its new rival. A few months later in the great fire of May, 1850, the *Alta* offices burned, and it had to start afresh. A year later, in spite of its new brick building, the *Alta* burned down again.

Down and up, the newspaper continued on an obstacle course until 1856, when its popular pro-vigilante position spurred a shift of advertising and an influx of subscribers. Its financial success thus secured, the *Alta* continued as a significant influence in the community until it ceased publication in 1891.

The *Pacific News,* which appeared in the summer of 1849, voiced the official line of the Democratic Party, but suffered so many losses through successive fires that it did not survive beyond 1851. The *Daily Journal of Commerce* met the same fate. The *Herald,* also a daily, started publication in the summer of 1850 and engaged at once in a vigorous criticism of local politics. Its boldness resulted in the imprisonment of one of its editors by a judge whom he had criticized roundly and in a pair of duels fought between another editor and two city aldermen. (The first editor was released by a higher court; the second man was each time badly wounded.) Just as the revenue from transferred advertising had assured the *Alta* of a sound financial footing, so an exclusive block of advertising placed by the city's auctioneers kept the *Herald* solvent over the years.

James King of William had founded the *Bulletin* ostensibly as a crusade against the political corruption rampant in the city in 1855. It was no coincidence, however, that the paper appeared during the financial crisis of the mid-fifties, in which King, in the banking business most of the time since his arrival in 1848, had lost a fortune. Embittered, he had entered publishing to expose the manipulations of some of his former colleagues and their political brethren generally. In the spring of 1856 his printed attack on James P. Casey, a city supervisor, editor of the rival *Sunday Times,* and New York ex-convict, resulted in King's assassination and a full-blown resurgence of vigilantism. Feeling ran so high throughout the city that when the *Morning Herald* came out in print opposing the new Vigilance Committee's work, mobs sacked the offices, advertisers and subscribers queued up to cancel their business, and roving street gangs burned all the copies they could lay their hands on. The *Daily California Chronicle* had taken a similar stand and promptly lost many of its subscribers to the *Alta,* which had instantly championed the course of the 1856 committee.

The *Bulletin,* which had backed the committee all along, continued unbowed under the direction of James King's brother, Thomas Sim King. After three years C. K. Fitch and Loring Pickering took ownership and a short time later also bought the *Morning Call.* They published the two papers jointly, yet maintained strict editorial independence. Pickering edited the *Call* on fairly neutral ground politically; Fitch, on the other hand, continued the *Bulletin* in the same crusading spirit in which it had originated. When new management took over at the end of the century, it installed Fremont Older as editor, a career that was to make him famous.

In 1865 two teenaged brothers, Charles and Michael Harry De Young, started the publication of the *Daily Dramatic Chronicle* as a theater guide, distributed free and financed by its advertisers. The unrestrained satiric commentary which ran through the program attracted a large following. By 1868, boosted to prominence by a scoop on the news of Lincoln's assassination, the brothers shifted the publication to a regular daily journal, the *Morning Chronicle.* Editor Charles' use of personal invective flourished unabated in the new pages and led to attacks, both by him and on him, which were often physical as well as verbal. During the seventies, with the emergence of labor and the organization of the Workingmen's Party, De Young's *Chronicle* became bitterly involved, culminating in the editor's wounding of Isaac Kalloch, a Baptist minister, who was the Workingmen's Party's candidate for mayor—an event which probably helped Kalloch win the election. But De Young's belligerence had dire consequences. Kalloch's son revenged his father's shooting by murdering the editor. The *Chronicle* continued under M. H. De Young's direction and has remained in the family up to present times, one of two major dailies in the city.

The current rival, the San Francisco *Examiner,* has merged plant operations with the *Chronicle.* They now put out independent dailies and a joint Sunday edition. Both papers began the same year, emerging during the aftermath of the Civil War, but aligned at the beginning with opposite political factions. Lincoln's assassination had incensed San Francisco's antislavery partisans, a majority of the city's population; the most aroused took to violence against the proslavery advocates, including the *Democratic Press,* a copperhead newspaper and the *Examiner*'s predecessor. The mob reduced the plant to a shambles. What was left, including the staff and the Southern point of view, became the *Daily Examiner.* In 1880 George Hearst assumed ownership, using some of the fortune he had accumulated in the mines, and within a few years turned it over completely to William Randolph, his young son, who wanted to try his hand at the newspaper business. It was the start of a monumental domain, a new era in journalism surpassing any previous attempts at news management, the creation of an empire which did not shy away from manipulation and sensationalism to make its point. Since money was no problem, the young William Randolph Hearst assembled a staff that incorporated the best talent available, including Ambrose Bierce and Jack London, among whose assignments was coverage of the Russo-Japanese War.

Thirty-seven of the 132 journals published during the 1850's were in print at the end of the decade. Nine ethnic groups supported their own papers, several English-language journals printed foreign-language sections, and from the beginning of the decade San Franciscans had French, German, Spanish, Italian, Chinese, and Jewish newspapers; eight religious and political party organs; and medical and law journals, including the *Water Fount,* which advocated the use of hydropathy and which was published in New York—although, like the *Uncle Sam* published in Boston, it purported to be a San Francisco product. There were literary, humorous, and illustrated reviews and journals devoted to agriculture, commerce, whaling, mercantile price lists, and shipping information. Mechanics and firemen had periodicals, there was a *Police Gazette,* and a monthly publication reported the decisions of the district courts. Land squatters had a short-lived journal championing their cause. There were official temperance organs. *Hutching's Illustrated California Magazine,* founded in 1856 by the English writer J. M. Hutchings, focused on the scenic wonders of California, a successful departure from the standard formats which were more imitative of Eastern periodicals and depended less on local emphasis. And the *Hesperian,* a moralistic semimonthly literary paper founded by two women editors in 1858, included illustrations of Paris fashions and other tidbits aimed at the female reader.[28]

The weekly *Pacific,* the first of several literary journals to emerge in the fifties, printed poems and essays along with primarily religious materials in 1851. The *Golden Era,* which was perhaps the "most important journal ever published on the Pacific slope,"[29] began printing a mixture of news, chitchat, commentary, and belles lettres in 1852. It was as popular at the mines as it was in San Francisco. Two years later a literary monthly, the *Pioneer,* attracted a large reading public and managed to survive, even though it took no advertising, for a full two years before the depression put it out of business.

Most of the embryo literary efforts had energetic young editors, such as John MacDonough Foard, Rollin Mallory Daggett, and Ferdinand C. Ewer, and equally young contributors. Twenty-one-year-old Foard, who had arrived in San Francisco in 1849, joined with nineteen-year-old Daggett, who had come overland in 1851, to found and co-edit the *Golden Era.* Ewer, the *Pioneer*'s originator, was a thirty-year-old Harvard-trained civil engineer, who, after his journalistic endeavors, became an ordained Episcopalian minister and later still a rebellious Anglo-Catholic preacher.

Among the youthful corps of journalists was John Rollin Ridge, whose father and grandfather had been respected Cherokee chieftains and whose white mother was the daughter of the principal of the Connecticut school where his father was educated. Ridge wrote under the name of Yellow Bird. When he was only twelve, he saw his father stabbed to death in a tribal dispute that also claimed his grandfather. In 1850, a New England college education by then behind him, he joined the Gold Rush, where his success came through writing rather than mining. He contributed articles and poetry to a New Orleans newspaper, as well as to the local *Golden Era* and the *Hesperian.* His most significant work, a book on the bandit Joaquín Murrieta, was distorted by his own intense desire to see Mexican—and Indian—justice done. The traumatic events of Murrieta's life, including the rape of his fiancée before his eyes, paralleled in intensity the outrages to which Ridge had been witness. In Murrieta's case, revenge came through criminal pursuits; Ridge sought vengeance within the law through his writings. In spite of the factual liberties Ridge had taken and his romanticization of the hero, *The Life and Adventures of Joaquín Murrieta, the Celebrated California Bandit* became the source for the many subsequent accounts of Murrieta's adventures.

Twenty-six-year-old Lieutenant George Horatio Derby, United States Army, arrived in California from Massachusetts in 1849. A West Point graduate with an audacious sense of humor, he was soon writing voluminously for the newspapers and literary journals using the by-lines of John P. Squibob and John Phoenix. Under these names, two books of his collected works later appeared, one published by his friend Judge John Judson Ames, who apparently had forgiven the outrageous jest Derby once played on him: Judge Ames, taking leave as editor of the San Diego *Herald* to seek funds for his journal from the coffers of the Democratic Party, left Derby in charge. Derby thereupon put out issues endorsing the Whig candidate, Waldo, although the Democratically allied paper had been supporting the party nominee, Bigler, all along. Derby likely owed his continuing friendship with Ames, if not his very life, to the fact that Bigler managed to win the governorship without his backing, and the paper managed to remain solvent.

Alonzo Delano, under the pseudonym of Old Block, became noted for his portrayals of Gold Rush scenes and personalities. An educated Midwesterner, he was assimilating the material for his writing even as he came overland. A not always prosperous businessman, a much better banker than merchant, he eventually established his own banking firm and wrote solely for pleasure. Some of his collected works appeared as *Chips from the Old Block* and later, in collaboration with the artist Charles Nahl, as *Old Block's Sketch Book.*

Several early historians also began their careers in the fifties. In

1854 two Gold Rush journalists, Frank Soulé and James Nesbit, joined with Dr. John Gihon to publish the *Annals of San Francisco,* an exhaustive history of the city's first years of life. However, an unschooled bookdealer, Hubert Howe Bancroft, emerged as the state's most prolific chronicler with the later publication of his Western histories, seven volumes alone devoted to the development of California. Twenty years old when he came to California to mine in 1852, he quickly switched to selling books. By the midfifties he had established a sizable bookshop in San Francisco and begun a book collection which later was to make him famous. By 1869 his business, now incorporating publishing and such sidelines as the retailing of musical instruments, required a five-story brick building on lower Market Street and a staff of 200. Within thirty years the "factory" for historical research—Bancroft and a corps of several dozen indefatigable assistants installed on the top floor—had completed all thirty-nine volumes of the history. Although Bancroft claimed authorship, he actually wrote no more than a tenth of the total. His real contributions were his conception and organization of so vast a project, his perseverance, made the more effective by his wealth, his foresight in collecting the papers and interviews of all the important pioneers he could pin down, and his business skill, often criticized for such methods as engineering favorable reviews and testimonials to use in marketing the books.[30] Founded with the purchase of Bancroft's 50,000 volumes of Western source books, the Bancroft Library at the University of California is built around a prestigious collection of rare Western and California materials.

While the events of the fifties served as inspiration for the whole contingent of San Francisco writers already in residence, the effects were even more far-reaching on a number of young and impressionable arrivals, who were to emerge, in the decade following, as among the West's most important literary figures: Ina Coolbrith, who came to California as a child of ten in 1851; Charles Warren Stoddard, only twelve, in 1855; seventeen-year-old Bret Harte in 1854; Prentice Mulford, at twenty-two in 1856; nineteen-year-old Henry George in 1858; and Joaquin Miller, seventeen, in 1854, after an eleven-year family migration westward. Together with Mark Twain, aged twenty-six when he traveled west in the early sixties, and the twenty-four-year-old Ambrose Bierce, who arrived in 1866, they turned the decade of silver into a golden age of literature.

When the 1859 silver discoveries in Nevada proved to be an authentic new bonanza, the mining centers there and the Virginia City headquarters, almost entirely created, maintained, and exploited by San Franciscans, became in effect outposts of San Francisco. Many of the city's writers shifted their bases temporarily.

Among them were two staff members of San Francisco's *Golden Era,* Joseph T. Goodman and Denis McCarthy, who bought and revamped the *Territorial Enterprise.* They employed Rollin Daggett, one of the *Era's* founders, who had also followed the excitement to Virginia City, the humorist William Wright (Dan de Quille), and Samuel Clemens, who took on the job of reporter with only halfhearted enthusiasm.

The Civil War had blockaded the Mississippi and Clemens' career as a river pilot along with it. After a try at soldiering, which he found to be a miserable lot, he had migrated west to escape the conflict. His efforts at mining were so disappointing that he frequently resorted to sending pseudonymous articles to the *Enterprise* to earn some money; when De Quille took a leave of absence, the newspaper turned to Clemens to replace him. Reluctance turned to zeal a few months after his acceptance; within a year, under the pen name Mark Twain, Clemens was the most widely read writer in the area. Like De Quille before him, he was a regular contributor to San Francisco's *Golden Era,* and several journals reprinted his Nevada stories.

During his residence in Nevada, he made numerous trips to San Francisco. By the time he moved there in the spring of 1864 he felt very much at home, in fact, found it paradise in comparison to his former haunts, as he later wrote in *Roughing It.*

He enjoyed a brief period of living in high style until the silver market came down in a disastrous crash. Twain along with every other living being had speculated heavily. Forced again to earn his keep, he took on a lackluster job as staff reporter for the San Francisco *Morning Call.* His unsigned articles gave him no editorial leeway or even turning space for humor, and the sheer physical exertion involved in covering all the events in a city of 115,000 people was exhausting to a man whose natural pace was all drawl and dawdle. However, his short tenure on the *Call* was fortuitous in its way. He became acquainted with the already well-known writer Bret Harte, who worked as secretary to the director of the mint in the same building that housed the newspaper. From him Twain learned much about literary craftsmanship, form, and style, lessons he later acknowledged with gratitude, even when the friendship floundered. His firing was also fortuitous, for it allowed him to go back to writing full time and uninhibitedly under his pen name. His keen eye for detail coupled with his wit created a series of lively vignettes of San Francisco in the sixties, published widely in many of the leading journals, particularly the *Golden Era,* the *Californian,* and later the *Daily Dramatic Chronicle.*[31] For a man of his sharp observation, the life-style, the anecdotes, the speech, the lilt became permanently etched in his mind.

His first exodus was sudden and brief. Twain had posted bail

after his friend Steve Gillis became involved in a barroom brawl.
When the consequences looked sticky, the two quickly decided to
accept the invitation of Steve's brother for a three-month trip to
the Mother Lode. There Twain's ready ear took in all of the tall
tales for which the Angel's Camp area was famous. The story in
authentic lingo of a stranger betting an old-timer $40 on whose
frog could jump farther, then winning by stuffing the old fellow's
entry with quail shot, became Twain's first formal short story.
When "The Celebrated Jumping Frog of Calaveras County" was
published in the *Saturday Press* in New York, it created a sensation,
and Twain became instantly famous. He continued to turn out
humorous articles and reportage for the San Francisco press and
a series of daily commentaries both satirical and crusading for the
Territorial Enterprise. He also began lecturing in 1866 with tremendous success, starting with the accounts of his travels to the
Sandwich Islands. By 1867 the *Alta California* advanced him
$12,000—with another $2,000 to follow—for a series of travel letters describing his adventures abroad with an excursion of ministers. The perpetual fondness of Westerners for the Old World assured him an avid readership; the commentary on events and
places by a spokesman who was witty, irreverent, not bound by the
old traditions or burdened by a thorough education, yet a skilled
observer, a willing sentimentalist when the occasion required, and
an honest reporter with a healthy American bias, produced for his
readers a remarkable travelogue that is still read and reread. On
his return west, Twain worked the letters into book form for a
publisher on the East Coast, under the title of *The Innocents
Abroad.*[32]

After seven years, two and a half of them as a continuous San
Francisco resident, Twain ended his Western tenure. He took
back with him the stamp of the West, a permanent influence
throughout the rest of his career. And it was in San Francisco, in a
Montgomery Street Turkish bath, that Twain had met a real-life
cardplaying companion named Tom Sawyer.

In general, readers of the sixties enjoyed broad humor, spiritualism and the macabre, tall tales and hoaxes, and, conversely,
strict realism. They demanded vigor in writing as in everything
else. It was the custom to use pen names—a continuation of the
practice of the decade earlier, when Cadiz-Orion, Vide Poche,
Yellow Bird, Old Block, John Phoenix, Dame Shirley, and Jeems
Pipes of Pipesville all wrote pseudonymously. Some writers had
whole rosters of noms de plume. Since individual differences were
commonplace, the population respected originality, or at least
easily tolerated it, and warmly embraced all eccentrics, alive and
fictitious. To writers drawing on the local scene for color, there

were plenty of real characters to set off their imaginations: Emperor Norton ruled the public's fancy for years. The Great Unknown, probably William Frohm, a retired German tailor or upholsterer, a mysterious, elegantly dressed gentleman, paraded silently along Montgomery Street every afternoon for so many years that the preoccupation over his identity faded into boredom. Old Rosie got his name from the daily fresh flower in the lapel of his threadbare suit; Money King used his real last name as part of his title, engraved on a gold pin attached to a disheveled collar, and did a curbside money-lending business in the vicinity of the stock exchange. Professor Frederick Coombs, the city's leading practitioner of phrenology, who strongly resembled George Washington, took to stationing himself about the streets wearing a powdered wig and colonial costume and carrying a banner proclaiming himself "Washington the Second." The city had such a fondness for the antics of the socially prominent Lillie Hitchcock Coit that they enclosed her picture in the cornerstone of the new 1872 City Hall: her fascination with fires had propelled her to all of them, and she wore the pin of honorary member of Knickerbocker Engine Company Number Five, even into her grave.

Roistering and exaggerated humor, so prevalent as a source of release for early Californians, became the basic motivation for a whole organization known as E Clampus Vitus. Started by a Missouri argonaut named Joe Zumwalt, the Ancient and Honorable Order of ECV spread in the early fifties from chapters in all the mining communities to San Francisco and, by the time of its rejuvenation in the 1930's, as far as San Diego and Nevada. A parody of the serious fraternal organizations of the day, E Clampus Vitus was based on a constitution devoted to the principle that all members were officers and all officers were of equal indignity and on a ritual replete with nonsense terminology and oversized props. It named its chief officer Noble Grand Humbug, and other officers accordingly; it called its meeting house the Hall of Comparative Ovations; it made every member a chairman of the Most Important Committee; and it stood firmly, if drunkenly, behind its motto, *Credo Quia Absurdum* ("I believe because it is absurd"). If there is a dearth of written records from the early days, it is because no one was ever reportedly in condition to keep them during the meetings or to remember anything afterward. The present body of printed ECV lore includes a treatise on the discovery and colonization of California by the Chinese, a compleate historie of Drake's plate of brasse (Drake is of course claimed as an early Clamper), and a book of hewgagiana, or balladry. During the early days, when it wasn't cavorting, the organization reputedly devoted itself to the relief of orphans and widows, particularly the latter. In more modern times, its philanthropic thrust takes the form of preserving historical monuments, as a number of plaques throughout the Gold Country attest, and to researching such worthy projects as the verification of the spelling of Snowshoe Thompson's family name.

Oddballs, hoaxes, burlesques, and satires tickled the community spirit and kindled the imagination of its midcentury writers. When Lazarus, one of the two stray dogs that had attached themselves to Emperor Norton, died under the wheels of a fire engine, the city put on a grand public funeral for him. The council had already passed an ordinance exempting Lazarus and his even more highly esteemed companion, Bummer, from the new law expelling strays from city streets, with death the alternative. The two dogs had continued their well-behaved daily rounds of the restaurant and cocktail circuits. When Bummer died two years after Lazarus, the local press carried his obituary, even though he had lately neglected his manners and fallen into some disfavor. Among the writers who mourned his passing, Mark Twain wrote in the *Enterprise:*

> The old vagrant, Bummer, is really dead at last, and although he was always more respected than his obsequious vassal, the dog Lazarus, his exit has not made half as much stir in the newspaper world as signalized the departure of the latter. I think it is because he died a natural death, died with friends around him to smooth his pillow and wipe the death damps from his brow and receive his last words of love and resignation; because he died full of years and honor and disease and fleas.

Spoofing in deed, burlesquing in prose, and spinning tall tales were part of the same trend. As the decade passed, the satire became less slapstick and the critical attacks more sardonic. Most writers followed the style. Twain's writing developed certainly in this direction, and Bierce, as the Town Crier, used his column to launch attacks on victims related only by his invective. A particularly easy target was the oratory of the Civil War which was often guilty of gaudy excesses of rhetoric.

At its best Civil War oratory was silver-tongued and eloquent and, in published form, the basis of a literary genre descriptive of the blossoming Western culture. Aided by the support of much of the press, it was persuasive, politically, in pushing California firmly onto the Union side, as well as in arousing the citizens to contribute more than a million dollars, half of it from San Francisco, to the nation's total of four million for the Sanitary Commission, the mid-nineteenth-century forerunner of the Red Cross. Unfortunately, the partisanship of the city's newspapers also

aroused the citizens to other than philanthropic gestures. The period is marked by a number of altercations between rival editors,
newsmen, and politicians, such as the disagreement between the
proslavery *Times and Transcript* and the antislavery *Alta* over support of David Broderick's campaign for the State Senate, which
ended in a duel between two of the editors.

Both Eastern and foreign writers had an effect on the emerging
literature of the frontier. It was common, for instance, to pad out
an edition by reprinting, without due credit, selections not under
copyright from European and English publications. More important, prestigious visiting writers often contributed to the local
journals, most particularly to the *Era,* whose editor, Joe Lawrence, deliberately set out to entice them. No doubt the manicured East Coast-European style had some refining influence on
the unrestrained local prose, but the more that Western writing
emulated the refinements of the East, the more it lost its original
vigor. Uninhibited frontier realism was, fortunately for the style
of many a more placid Eastern author, happily contagious. The
offices of the *Era* became the principal literary hangout, where
newcomers congregated with the resident writing corps. A group
of the visitors were émigrés from New York's Pfaff's Tavern, the
gathering place for the East's thriving colony of bohemians. Led
by Charles Henry Webb, they exerted a substantial influence in
San Francisco, and by the mid-sixties bohemianism flourished
there as it did in Paris and New York. After Webb came west in
1862, he had joined Harte in founding the sophisticated literary
weekly, the *Californian.* Between 1864 and 1867 the best writing
appeared in its columns, but it was perhaps too high-toned to succeed. Although almost all of the Western writers got their start
through, or at least spent some time writing for, the *Golden Era,*
which gave it a singular historical importance, its quality was generally pedestrian, a fact to which some critics attribute its continuous popularity over a period of thirty years.

The Lick House, the Occidental, and Barry and Patten's,
though never reaching the eminence of Pfaff's, served as congenial enough local meeting grounds. By 1872, after most of the
grand figures of the preceding two decades had packed their
bohemian bags and moved on, the group remaining formally organized as the Bohemian Club in rooms on Pine Street and later
in a building on Post and Taylor. Now more conservative than
bohemian, the club is famous for the posh tone that pervades
even its summer campsite in the redwoods. But it still carries on
the tradition of offering its hospitality to the most prominent celebrities of the day.

At the end of the century, with the emergence of the new cult of
Western writers, the Montgomery Block, the grand old 1853

office building more familiarly known as the Monkey Block, housed the studios of such literati as Frank Norris, George Sterling, and Kathleen and Charles Norris. Their homes, however, clustered on Russian Hill, which attracted bohemian colonists over a considerable period. Besides the various Norrises and Sterling, Bierce and Joaquin Miller lived there, and Ina Coolbrith's cottage, nestled on its eastern heights, became the center of the San Francisco literary group. Will Irwin and Wallace Irwin, Charles Caldwell Dobie, John Dewey, and Gelett Burgess all settled on the hill at one time or another, side by side with the resident colony of artists and sculptors.

Although women were not numerous among the population, they contributed more than their share of poetry, novels, and journalism to the growing Western literature. Most of their work was pedestrian—some of Ina Coolbrith's writing is an exception—but their themes made them popular with readers. Women were responsible for most of the sentimental verse that glorified remembered domestic bliss in gushy romantic couplets and for crusades supporting social reforms.

In contrast with the saccharine school, there were writers who got their clout from shock. Adah Isaacs Menken's writing, often free verse after the daring style of her old friend Whitman, aroused the public as much as did her role in *Mazeppa,* where strapped seemingly naked to a lively horse, she rode precariously up a stage mountainside. Adah Isaacs Menken and Ada Clare combined careers in theater and literature, wrote prolifically for the *Era,* and conducted their private lives largely in public. Numerous liaisons with and marriages to illustrious partners, an illegitimate son born during Clare's Latin Quarter youth in Paris, assured them an avid following.

Women, cosmopolites or sentimentalists, were not the only poets. During the sixties there was an outpouring of verse by men as well, most of it equally mediocre, amateurish, imitative, and seldom concerned with local themes. In 1865 Bret Harte edited *Outcroppings,* the first published anthology of California poetry. It drew on newspaper files and, without her consent, a portfolio of clippings submitted to the publisher Anton Roman three years earlier by Miss Mary V. Tingley. Including the work of only nineteen poets, it was neither representative nor very good; its exclusions, however, started such controversies that everyone bought a copy. In the disputatious setting created by Harte's chaste volume, Sam Brannan, himself no man of letters, philanthropically lent financial support to another book, May (Mary Richardson Newman Doliver) Wentworth's *The Poetry of the Pacific,* which appeared within the year, including seventy-five writers. The quantity, unfortunately, had no salutary effect on the contents, a fact the com-

piler recognized in her preface. Remembering that California was
still an infant state, "a Hercules in the cradle," Mrs. Wentworth intended her anthology as a reference book of early California poetry, a poetry she hoped would improve and prosper in the future.
It had a long way to go, as these random samplings indicate:

> The air is chill, and the day grows late,
> And the clouds come in through the Golden Gate . . .
> > —From "Evening" by Edward Pollack in *Outcroppings*

> Perhaps the Sun is an egg of gold
> > In a nest of cloud, and Night must be
> A fidgety hen—for, look! she has rolled
> Out of the nest the egg of gold,
> And spilled the yelk [*sic*] in the sea!
> > —From "A Fancy" by C. W. Stoddard in *Outcroppings*

> Shadows of the summer-cloud
> > Fell on near and far land,
> Fragrantly the branches bowed
> > Every leafy garland;
> While, with shining head at rest,
> > Next my heart reclining,
> Love's white arms with soft caress,
> > Round my neck were twining;
> Till—ah, well! ah, well-a-day!
> > Love, who *can* resist thee?—
> On the river-banks that day,
> Cupid kissed me.
> > —From "Cupid Kissed Me" by Ina D. Coolbrith in
> > > *Outcroppings*

Both anthologies printed this poem, of which two stanzas follow:

> His father was an austere man—
> > An oyster-man was he,
> Who opened life by opening
> > The shell-fish of the sea;

> For though a mining minor, Tom
> > Was never known to shirk;
> And while with zeal he worked his claim,
> > His father claimed his work.
> > > —From "Tom Darling" by L. F. Wells in
> > > *Outcroppings* and *Poetry of the Pacific*

Better writing appeared in numerous essays and books where the expository prose was a reflection of real experience. Clarence King, a Yale-trained geologist, caught the public's interest with an excellent book on mountaineering in the West. John Muir, also a geologist, self-trained, turned out volumes of intriguing commentary for magazines on both coasts, in particular for the *Overland Monthly.* Josiah Royce's philosophical writings directly drew on man's experiences, including his own on the California frontier. Henry George's growing disillusion as he saw Everyman's Gold Rush take on more and more the characteristics of a Panacea for the Chosen Few resulted in his crusade in journals, magazines, and in his book *Progress and Poverty* for a new economics favorable to the common man.

The *Overland Monthly,* which began publication in 1868, the year after the *Californian's* demise, succeeded at least for a time where the *Californian* had failed, maintaining high editorial standards without sacrificing circulation. Its quality accounted, in fact, for a fair Eastern readership. Anton Roman, forty-niner, bookseller, and pioneer publisher, who had earlier hired Harte to edit *Outcroppings,* envisioned the new magazine and provided the freedom necessary to allow editor Harte's genius to flourish properly. In its coverage, its dedication to Western development, its lively style, and its dependence on only original writings, the *Overland* took on a much more Western character than any previous publication. Its fortunes diminished, however, after Harte's resignation and floundered during the depression that followed the completion of the transcontinental railroad. In 1875 it ceased publication altogether for eight years and then, resurrected, never again reached the success it had achieved in its heyday.

If the *Overland* owed much of its original quality to Harte, he in return could—but did not—thank it for the opportunity to publish what turned out to be the most persuasive of his writings. When Harte and Roman had started working together, Roman had intentionally regaled his editor with tales of his own adventures as a miner until Harte was properly steeped in Western lore and mining anecdotes, a background which became the basis of his literary success. In its second issue the *Overland* had carried "The Luck of Roaring Camp," a sensation then and long to remain a favorite among Harte's stories. In subsequent issues his tales followed the same successful pattern, unfolding sentimental themes on a solid base of craftsmanship. Although Harte's audience acclaimed him, and Roman and later his successor John H. Carmony were strenuous in their support, the cantankerous Harte felt unappreciated, even abused by the West. When the Eastern *Atlantic Monthly* offered him a fantastic salary, the *Overland* could not persuade him to stay, even with a counter-offer that included a percentage of the magazine and that coincided with an offer of a professorship in literature at the University of California. It was 1871 when Harte left, a date which marked the beginning of a decline in his writing. Even when exploiting Western themes, his later work seems to have lost its authentic Gold Rush punch, and consequently much of its appeal, and his reputation much of its grandeur.

During the peak of the *Overland*'s success, Harte had two principal literary allies, the poet Ina Coolbrith, and the neurotic, oversensitive Charles Warren Stoddard, whose major contributions were a series of South Sea island sketches. Joaquin Miller, whom Harte had never appreciated, had to wait until Harte's resignation before the journal would publish him, by which time he had acquired a considerable reputation on his own in literary circles abroad. The *Overland* published the first of Ambrose Bierce's short stories, a horror tale with a mining background, as well as a number of the loner Prentice Mulford's pieces which also drew on his experiences at the mines.

Ina Coolbrith, born Josephine D. Smith, led a life marked by hardships and little glamor. Her father, Don Carlos Smith, an elder of the Mormon church and brother of Joseph, the prophet of the Latter-Day Saints, died several months after his third daughter's birth. The family's lot was never easy, before or after her mother separated from the Mormon community. A few years after Don Carlos' death the widow remarried, and the family migrated to California in 1851 to try mining, then life in San Francisco and Los Angeles. Their journey westward was filled with the usual hair-raising adventures, and there were times when they came close to perishing.

By the age of eleven Ina had already had some of her poetry printed in the Los Angeles *Star*. In 1858, at the age of seventeen, she married, and at twenty divorced, a paranoidal, violent-tempered man named Robert B. Carsley. She moved back to San Francisco, taking the name Coolbrith, her mother's maiden name, wrote poetry continuously, achieving considerable recognition by the mid-sixties, taught school, and kept house for her parents when they needed her. The handsome woman never remarried, but family responsibilities nonetheless prevented her from exercising much freedom of movement. She reared her sister's two orphaned children, cared for Joaquin Miller's Indian daughter for a considerable period of time, and nursed her mother through ill health. She supported herself and her clan for thirty years as a librarian in the Oakland Public Library and later in the Bohemian Club. Jack London, one of the youngsters using the Oakland Library, first came under her influence there.

The literary set orbited around Ina Coolbrith. Her friendship, variously described as everything from sisterly to romantic, embraced at one time or another all the literati: Harte, Stoddard, Mulford, Clemens, Bierce, Miller, and all the later figures, residents and visitors alike, from Robert Louis Stevenson to Frank Norris and Gelett Burgess. As Ina grew older, the local literary world, bringing along any visiting writers, gathered regularly in her parlor and formally organized themselves into the California Literary Society. In 1915 the state of California officially recognized her as poet laureate, a title she retained until her death thirteen years later.

Joaquin Miller, born Cincinnatus Heine Miller, the eldest son of a poor, God-fearing, schoolteaching father and overworked mother, came from Indiana. The struggling family's eleven-year trek west in search of a livelihood ended in 1852 on an Oregon homestead. Two years later Miller, in a blaze of fantasy, fled to the mines of California, there intending to make his family's fortune. He spent four years with little success, but like several of his contemporaries, he was absorbing a background that would serve him for his future writing career. His own version of his life makes good reading, but as in all his work, fact is so intermingled with fiction that the real events are difficult to discern.

By the time he was twenty he had taken on an Indian mistress, and become the father of Cali-Shasta, the daughter he left in Ina Coolbrith's care in later years. In 1859, according to court records, he was involved in horse stealing, possibly innocently as he claims, and he did live amicably among the Indians for a considerable time, although not the tribe he later wrote about in his autobiographical novel. Mainly he gathered experiences and met a group of unforgettable characters on whom he would draw for his writings. In 1858, before he took up the pen on a full-time basis, he returned to Oregon, was graduated from the local college, taught school, studied law, rode for the Pony Express in Idaho, and edited the Eugene City, Oregon, *Democratic Register,* where he took such a strong anti-Union stance that the government intervened and stopped the paper's publication.

During this period Miller read the poetry of a young Oregonian named Minnie Myrtle, published in a San Francisco journal. Miller wrote, encouraging her. An exchange of letters followed. In the spring of 1863 the romantic Miller sought out Minnie in person and married her five days later. Off they went to San Francisco, where Miller hoped they could make their way by writing. Although their work was of generally poor quality, several publications, including the *Golden Era,* printed it, but remuneration was at best small and usually lacking altogether. After several months the temporarily deflated Miller pulled up stakes, took Minnie back to her parents, and set off by himself for more remote regions of Oregon. During the next six years he earned admission to the bar, in spite of his lack of formal training, and later became a judge. He reconciled with his wife, after which Minnie bore them three children. All the while he continued to write. By 1869 he published *Joaquin et al,* a book of poems, the principal one based on the Joaquín Murrieta adventures. He sent copies to San Francisco for review by the *Overland* and became so enamored with his own portrayal of the legend that he forthwith dropped the name of Cincinnatus Heine in favor of the bandit's Christian name. From then until his death in 1913 he was known as Joaquin Miller.

By the following year his career had reached a point of decision, since he was seriously in the running for a seat on the Oregon Supreme Court. When he failed in this appointment, he turned his back on Oregon, this time leaving his family definitively behind him, and headed for San Francisco again. There he spent a month hobnobbing with the resident literati and making arrangements for a European jaunt. He left with an agreement from the *Bulletin* to buy his travel letters from abroad and with a wreath of California laurel that he had gathered with Ina Coolbrith in Sausalito to place on Byron's English grave.

It was certainly to his advantage to follow in the successful wake of Mark Twain. The English seemed receptive to American writers and particularly responsive to eccentricity. Miller determined to capitalize on their open-mindedness and made himself the epitome of a swashbuckling Westerner. First he visited the shrines of all his heroes and became known to London literary society. In his role as the rough-hewn American frontiersman, he costumed himself, no matter how formal the occasion, in boots, red flannel shirt, and wide-brimmed hat over shoulder-length tresses. His tales of life in the West, exaggerated if not downright apochryphal, depicted one thrilling exploit after another. Not only did Miller's fecund imagination produce a body of Western lore, but his behavior embraced such antics as smoking several cigars simultaneously, whooping like an Indian, and paying attendance on the females present by nibbling and fondling them and dousing them in flowery poetics or real rose petals, depending on his mood. Although some of his broader excesses caused an adverse comment here and there, in general the British enjoyed the gyrations of such a startling character. One of them, a charming young woman named Iza Hardy, the daughter of a baronet, even became engaged to him for a time.

Long before he achieved notoriety, he had published at his own expense a modest number of copies of his verses under the title

Pacific Poems. Although the Americans had not found the rough-ness of his style admirable, the London circle of pre-Raphaelite artists to whom he showed the book—Dante, Christina and William Michael Rossetti, the editor Tom Hood, Swinburne, William Morris, Frederick Locke-Lampson, and Ford Madox Brown, among them—responded favorably; to them the writing fit the character Miller presented. In an attempt to gain the wider audi-ence they felt he deserved, his new friends offered criticism which helped him to rework the most awkward passages without losing the virility of the writing. After he had added material, they con-vinced the very good firm of Longmans to undertake the publica-tion. When the enlarged and rechristened *Songs of the Sierras* was released, their favorable reviews catapulted Miller into the fore-front of the English literary scene. He met Browning, Tennyson, and Carlyle and was invited to tea with the dean of Westminster Abbey.

In the midst of his conquests Miller had to return to the United States because of serious illness in his family. His American recep-tion was not nearly so cordial. Furthermore, when, in 1872, he re-turned to London after the interval, ready to take up where he had been forced to leave off, he found that the enthusiasm of his friends had waned. Without their help his next volume received harsh reviews for its repetitiveness instead of accolades for its vig-or, and Miller felt cast off like last year's bonnet. With a novel, *My Life Among the Modocs,* published in 1873, he successfully shifted from crude poetry, which was no longer intriguing, to romantic prose based on tales of the Western frontier. During the eighties Miller found himself again in California, this time installed on "The Hights," a vast acreage in Oakland. There he continued to write, to host literary figures and curious sightseers, and to play the role of daredevil Westerner and guru to all who would be his audience.

Like Miller, Ambrose Bierce came from Indiana, where his farming family was large and poor. Bierce left home at an early age to fight with the Union Army. He was severely wounded, but the inhumanity of the war scarred him more deeply. In 1866, when he was employed by the United States Mint in San Francis-co, his writing began to appear in the local journals. Unlike his friends Ina Coolbrith, Bret Harte, and Charles W. Stoddard, he was a latecomer to the California scene, experiencing mainly the aftermath rather than the original stimulus of the Gold Rush. His satirical style, which found abundant subject matter, developed fully when he took over the chief editorial position of Town Crier on the San Francisco *News Letter and Commercial Advertiser,* a journal devoted to shocking exposés and supported by voluminous advertising. Its format combined unbridled satire with a delight in violence and the macabre. As satirist in chief for four years, Bierce outdid his most irreverent contemporaries.

Early in the seventies Bierce joined the Western exodus on his honeymoon with Mollie Day and headed for London. He adored England instantly and would have happily stayed there forever. On a practical level he sold just enough articles to make his way; his spirit, however, was generously nourished by the patrician company he had become a part of. His wife did not fare so well and after some time departed with the children for America. When the reluctant Bierce followed, he may have returned physically to San Francisco, but his soul was forever bound to England. An irreversible Anglophile, he had become utterly snobbish: he championed the conservatism, the elegance, the formality, the superiority of the British, completely uncritically. His negative pen reflected his bitterness in America, and his classical satire led many a critic to liken him to Swift. He contributed the first of his "Prattle" columns in 1881 to the *Wasp* and wrote venomously for the *Argonaut.* He continued "Prattle" in Hearst's *Examiner,* with which he was associated from 1887 to 1913. Typical of his satirical insights are these excerpts from the best known of his work, *The Devil's Dictionary,* which began as a series of definitions for his column in the *Wasp:*

Abasement, n. A decent and customary mental attitude in the presence of wealth or power. Peculiarly appropriate in an employee when addressing an employer.

Clarionet, n. An instrument of torture operated by a person with cotton in his ears. There are two instruments that are worse than a clarionet—two clarionets.

Barometer, n. An ingenious instrument which indicates what kind of weather we are having.

Politics, n. A strife of interests masquerading as a contest of principles. The conduct of public affairs for private advantage.

Radicalism, n. The conservatism of to-morrow injected into the affairs of today.

Positive, adj. Mistaken at the top of one's voice.

Pray, v. To ask that the laws of the universe be annulled in behalf of a single petitioner confessedly unworthy.

Debauchée, n. One who has so earnestly pursued pleasure that he has had the misfortune to overtake it.

Virtues, n. pl. Certain abstentions.

Dentist, n. A prestidigitator who, putting metal into your mouth, pulls coins out of your pocket.

Once, adv. Enough.

Twice, adv. Once too often.

Déjeuner, n. The breakfast of an American who has been in Paris. Variously pronounced.

Hebrew, n. A male Jew, as distinguished from the Shebrew, an altogether superior creation.

Hand, n. A singular instrument worn at the end of a human arm and commonly thrust into somebody's pocket.

Happiness, n. An agreeable sensation arising from contemplating the misery of another.

Dead, adj.

> Done with the work of breathing; done
> With all the world; the mad race run
> Through to the end; the golden goal
> Attained and found to be a hole!
>
> *Squatol Johnes*

Throughout his work, Bierce hammered away at corruption in politics, hypocrisy in religion, inanity in war, and pretense wherever he found it. He was preoccupied with mystery, horror, and death, especially by suicide, themes repeated in his suspense stories. When two of his protégés, George Sterling and the poet Herman Scheffauer, ended their lives by suicide, many critics felt that Bierce's morbid influence was a factor.

His personal life reinforced his unhappiness. Both his sons died tragically, his marriage was unsuccessful, and he and his wife parted. In bitterness he lived, and in solitude he wrote, until at seventy he vanished in a mystery that has never been solved, last seen crossing the border into Mexico, supposed by some to be joining forces with the outlaw Pancho Villa. It was the eerie end of a twenty-five-year reign over the San Francisco literary scene, from which Bierce's influence had spread through the land.

During the fifties San Francisco had spawned the foundations of Western journalism and the early development of a literary cult. During the flourishing sixties Western writing had come into full bloom. As with so many things, the era of productivity ended with the arrival of the railroad, after which the nature of the West changed completely. The seventies became a decade when San Francisco, no longer isolated, lost that part of its uniqueness derived from unconventionality. It was a period of social aggrandizement and social questioning, a juxtaposition of workingman and tycoon, of excessive wealth and economic depression. Imitation and cultural borrowing layered a veneer of instant civilization over rugged frontier institutions. The excesses of wealth more often coincided with conventionality than good taste, no context for artistic creativity. Most of the writers showed signs of discontent, and by the early seventies the movement east and to Europe had begun. Not until the end of the century, with the emergence of such social critics as London and Norris, did San Francisco again inspire a flourishing literary congregation.

Among the traditional values that the forty-niners felt strongly about was education. Although in San Francisco's early days the dual role of pastor and teacher was not uncommon, nor were private schools an exception, differences arose over the issues of religious affiliation, government support, and vocational versus academic emphasis. The authors of the state constitution in 1849, concerned that the citizens recognize their traditional responsibility in support of education, required a public school for each of the districts currently established and made provisions for a state university. The state's first institution of higher learning was, however, sectarian: California Wesleyan University, founded in San Jose in 1851 (later University, now College, of the Pacific).

The first normal school in San Francisco began training teachers in 1862 (it later moved and became San Jose State College, now University). In 1863 San Francisco established its first kindergarten, a recent importation from Europe. In 1868 the embryo University of California took over the College of California, which had been operating as a private liberal arts school since 1855 under the direction of two ministers, Henry Durant, a Greek scholar, Yale graduate, and Congregationalist, and S. H. Willey, trained at Dartmouth and Union Theological Seminary. Before the college deeded its land to the state, a controversy developed over the academic commitment of its curriculum, a secular faction urging more vocational and practical training. Fortunately for the university, the widely aired debate that followed assured it a broader program from the start. The university received its charter in 1868, admitted its first class in 1869 and its first women, who heretofore had attended religious institutions, in 1870. Henry Durant became the first president. The campus, which lay across the bay in Oakland, later moved to Berkeley, a site that was to become famous. The university now has nine campuses and upwards of 105,000 students.

By the seventies San Francisco also had a Catholic college, St. Ignatius (now San Francisco University), one of six in the state, and by 1871 Dr. Cyrus Mills had opened Mills Seminary, a private nonsectarian college, in Oakland. Since the California schools modeled themselves largely on New England standards, it was not surprising that John Swett, San Francisco's Father of Education, saw schooling as a means of "Americanizing" the polyglot Californians. As state superintendent he crusaded for the far-reaching public school system which the 1866 legislature provided.

The West's outstanding private university, Stanford, was not founded until 1891. In the mid-eighties the Leland Stanfords had donated the equivalent of $30,000,000, at least six or seven times the capitalization of the leading Eastern schools, to establish the university in memory of their son.

During the Gold Rush years the hard-drinking, fast-gambling miners were also avid readers. In 1854 the men at Hawkings' Bar up in Tuolumne County pooled their resources to set up a circulating library, abundantly stocked with fiction, technical books, scientific treatises, and magazines brought in from San Francisco. Morgan Davis, the librarian, instituted a replacement policy that kept the materials current and in good supply until the library closed in 1870.

A number of San Francisco institutions such as the Society of California Pioneers, the Young Men's Christian Association, the Mercantile Library, the Mechanics' Institute, and the Odd Fellows' Society set up libraries during the fifties as viable alternatives to the more capricious outlets available in the Gold Rush city. They attracted dues-paying members with comfortable lounges, stocks of books and newspapers, and often programs of readings, lectures, and debates.

A group of merchants established the Mercantile Library in quarters in the California Exchange on Kearny and Clay streets in February, 1853, with the purchase of a private collection of about 2,500 volumes and an assortment of local and foreign journals, reviews, and magazines. Users paid $10 to join, $1 a month dues, and $25 to hold shares. The daily hours, from nine in the morning to ten in the evening, reserved two hours after noon for women, with or without escorts. The 1855 site in the Excelsior Building on Montgomery Street, one of several moves to larger quarters, is the current locale of the Playboy Club. Although its collection prospered, the library's financing was erratic, and in 1906 it consolidated with the more stable Mechanics' Institute.

A group of men interested in advancing the mechanical arts and sciences had met in the tax collector's office in December, 1854, and planned the Mechanics' Institute. By March they had enrolled a sufficient number of members, including many who were apprentice tradesmen, adopted a constitution, and elected officers for a proposed library. By June a rented fourth-floor room in the Wells, Fargo Express Building (owned by Sam Brannan), on California and Montgomery, served as the first headquarters. One of the popular money-raising devices of the times, the benefit performance, on this occasion of Julia Dean in *Madeleine, the Belle of Faubourg,* swelled the treasury by more than $1,000. However, the annual Mechanics' and Manufacturers' Fair supported almost entirely the early work of the institute and indirectly assured its later fortunes. The first fair, held on September 7, 1857, took place on Montgomery Street between Post and Sutter in a canvas-domed pavilion in the shape of a Greek cross; it made a profit of $2,784. The 1864 fair, the institute's fourth, took place in a newly constructed $22,000 building on the site of what is now Union Square. After expenses, including that year's hefty construction costs, the profit came to $3,413. A huge new pavilion on a $175,000 parcel of land housed the fairs from 1891 until their discontinuance in 1899. In 1912 the city chose this block, bounded by Polk, Hayes, Larkin, and Grove, as part of its proposed Civic Center complex and paid the institute $700,000 for it. The transaction erased the institute's debts, still leaving more than $350,000 in the treasury, and provided San Francisco with the site of its present Civic Auditorium. Although the primary purpose was from the first educational, the expositions acquired great social prestige.

In 1866 the institute bought the present Post Street site, but its first building there was a victim of the 1906 earthquake and fire. In 1869 Andrew Hallidie, more often recognized as the inventor of the cable car than as the president of the Mechanics' Institute, led a successful campaign to reorganize the library; since then all profits have reverted to the institution rather than to individual shareholders.

From the day that the founders defined the institute's objectives as "the establishment of a library, reading room, the collection of a cabinet, scientific apparatus, works of art, and for other literary and scientific purposes," there had been a strong emphasis on education. The institute soon offered a chess club, now counted as the oldest on the continent, lectures on science and technology, and instruction in mechanical and freehand drawing at a time when most of the state's formal educational institutions were nonexistent. When the University of California drew up its charter, it recognized the institute's importance in the formative years of California education by specifying that its president serve as an ex-officio member of the Board of Regents, a law which stood until an amendment to the state constitution, approved in the November, 1974 election, eliminated the position. An institute amendment in 1972 increased the entrance fee to $10 from the $1 it had been since 1855, and in January, 1975, the directors reluctantly raised the yearly dues, $6 since 1857, likewise to $10.

In 1861 R. B. Woodward, the proprietor of the What Cheer House, installed a library in his fashionable hotel, a facility reportedly not to be found in any comparable public lodging in the United States or Europe. The large room, the best patronized and most crowded of any in the establishment, also held files of newspapers from all California as well as the principal journals of the eastern United States and Europe. Its approximately 3,000 volumes covered every interest from bee raising to poetry. The What Cheer House further established a free museum for its guests.

In December, 1876, the Sonoma *Democrat* printed excerpts from a document on public libraries in the United States prepared by the Bureau of Education in Washington, D. C. The bureau listed 86 libraries in California, providing a total of 305,395 volumes, of which the following, along with their date of founding and the number of volumes in circulation, were operating in San Francisco: Notre Dame (1866) 1,000 volumes; Bancroft (1859) 12,000 volumes; Française (1875) 6,000 volumes; Almshouse (1870) 672 volumes; Industrial School (n.d.) 800 volumes; Turn Verein (1866) 470 volumes; Home Institute (1866) 500 volumes; San Francisco Law (n.d.) 12,500 volumes; Zeitska's (1870) 300 volumes; Mechanics' (1855) 24,108 volumes; Medical University (1864) 1,600 volumes; Mercantile (1853) 41,563 volumes; Military (1873) 900 volumes; Swedenborgian (1866) 610 volumes; Odd Fellows' (1854) 26,883 volumes; St. Ignatius' (1855) 5,000 volumes; San Francisco Sodality (n.d.) 3,000 volumes; San Francisco Sodality (n.d.) 1,500 volumes; Students' (n.d.) 1,500 volumes; St. Mary's (1863) 3,500 volumes; St. Mary's (1867) 800 volumes; S. F. Art Association (1872) 2,809 volumes; Verein (1853) 5,000 volumes; Pioneers' (1850) 2,500 volumes; Red Men (1875) 500 volumes; Territorial Pioneers' (1874) 530 volumes; Theological (1871) 5,000 volumes; U.S. Mint (n.d.) 300 volumes; and Young Men's Christian Association (1853) 5,000 volumes.

The University of California library across the Bay had, in comparison, 12,000 volumes, Mills 2,000, San Quentin State Prison 3,103, the State Supreme Court 5,600, and the State Library in Sacramento, in existence since 1850, 37,000 volumes.

Because all these institutions required some sort of affiliation to permit the reader the use of the facilities, State Senator George H. Rogers began during the seventies to push for a free public library. He corresponded with the directors of the most prominent prototypes in Europe and the United States and worked out a plan for a San Francisco collection. A notice in the August 2, 1877, San Francisco *Chronicle* called the citizens to an open meeting, where they drafted a bill to establish a public library. On June 7, 1879, the doors finally opened with a scant 5,000 volumes, to be read on the premises. By July, 1880, with better financing and acquisitions now numbering 25,000, the collection became circulating.

XI

Business and Professions

AFTER the gold discovery, business in San Francisco flourished, and professional men multiplied in a frantic attempt to supply the total needs of the bursting community. It was the day of the entrepreneur; inventiveness rewarded the alert with fortunes. Men who had never in their lives engaged in commerce became street criers, shop owners, open-air marketeers. Doctors and lawyers practiced sometimes with the benefit of academic degrees, and sometimes without. In the general confusion, chance determined whether the liquor store might this week also supply the customer's butter, and the hardware dealer his stockings and boots. In a half dozen years stable commercial patterns emerged; although very few of the original Gold Rush merchants were then still doing business, a number of firms with Gold Rush origins have prospered into modern times.

Campbell and Hoog's San Francisco Directory, issued in March, 1850, listed 177 businesses and professional offices. Since the street and numbering system was still rudimentary, addresses were often given in descriptive form: Nickerson and Adams, groceries and provisions, Sansome Street, second door west of Pine; Plume and Company, commission merchants, basement room, corner of Montgomery and Washington; C. C. Richmond and Company, wholesale and retail dealers in drugs, medicines, paints, oils, etc., foot of Jackson opposite the Canton Hotel; Steamboat Hotel, Clark's Point, first house on the hill.

The listings included express agents, commission merchants, importers and retailers, warehouses, bankers, refiners, assayers and gold dust brokers, music stores, jewelers, real estate brokers and land agents, auctioneers, lawyers and doctors, apothecaries, hotels and restaurants, carpenters, builders, painters, blacksmiths and tinsmiths, stove and boilermakers, and undertakers. E. P. Jones specialized in the sale of lots on Yerba Buena Island. I. P. H. Gildemeester combined his duties as consul of the Netherlands with his business as a commission merchant and Montgomery

185

Street banking partner in the firm of Gildemeester, de Fremery and Company. J. W. Palmer, MD, who had formerly served as city physician, advertised his services as a competent chemist in the accurate testing of minerals. H. K. Warren, recently of New York, offered for sale from his offices on the Niantic Dock, "the oriental or sovereign balm pills and extract of wild strawberry for the dysentery and fever and ague." Attorney John Bispham made his counsel available in English, French, and Spanish.

In May, Bogardus' Business Directory, its publication delayed by several days in order to give "the present location of those who were burnt out by the late fire," listed subscribers who had paid a $2 monthly fee in advance. In addition to the range of essential services covered by Campbell and Hoog, the new directory included firms offering China goods and curiosities, fresh teas, wines and liquors, Salamander safes and money vaults, and prefabricated houses in sizes from 12 by 15 feet, to 25 by 50 feet, to 30 by 35 feet, and ranging in price from $300 to $3,000. The Pacific Baths at 273 Montgomery Street opened at eight in the morning and closed at ten in the evening; the Kearny Street druggist and apothecary William Curehill provided soda water on draft and perfumes for sale; Charles Gary, who sold wines and liquors, also advertised sardines; John Conner, a joiner and cabinetmaker, tuned pianos on the side; and James King of William, a Montgomery Street money broker, offered exchange on London and principal cities of the United States.

The first firms were practical, developed to meet immediate needs of the Gold Rush community. What creature comforts they supplied were of the minimum, with few embellishments, although occasional luxuries such as the sardines and perfumes appeared with increasing frequency. Necessity, coupled with the pragmatic mentality of the time, produced profitable answers to unique business questions. To meet the almost complete lack of chicken eggs, a thriving business developed in wild seabird eggs from the Farallones, the rocky offshore islands just outside the Gate. The Washington Market and the Farallones Egg Depot on Front Street sold the eggs, collected fresh daily, for as high as $1 apiece. Business was so good that it endangered the bird population. In 1853, 12,000 eggs were collected in one two-day period. Only protective legislation prevented the birds' final extinction. To cope with muddy streets and slippery walkways, entrepreneurs hastily imported hip boots, cavalry footgear, and waterproof suiting in such quantities that they soon glutted the market. To accommodate traffic between the Mission and town, developers installed a plank road over the old trail, charging tolls of up to $1 while along the route purveyors provided oases for refreshments, as well as hotels and entertainments. Taking advantage of a laundry situation so bad that many forty-niners were sending their linens to Canton, four enterprising washerwomen retired after a short career, each with reserves of $15,000 to $20,000. Benjamin R. Buckelew, the proprietor of the town's best jewelry shop and famous for his skill in repairing precious heirlooms, began by making scales for the miners. When gold was the sole medium of exchange, and before the days of an official agency, private mints stamped out $20 double eagles and octagonal $30 gold pieces. An early street crier, who developed a thriving business sharpening knives and razors for restaurants and butchers, used a makeshift machine whose grinding stone connected to a drive wheel powered by two large dogs running inside it. One of his customers was likely the San Francisco butcher Henry Miller, who in later partnership with Charles Lux became famous as a California cattle baron. The German-born Miller, whose real name was Heinrich Alfred Kreiser, acquired his new name in 1849 along with a friend's nontransferable ticket to California. After his arrival in San Francisco, he opened a meat shop. To supply it, he was soon raising his own cattle and buying up the ranchlands to graze them on.

By 1852, although the emphasis was still on products of necessity, commerce had expanded considerably. More than twenty retailers supplied clothing and accessories of every conceivable degree of luxury; more than a dozen mills ground flour and sawed lumber; there were 19 banks, and over 160 hotels and restaurants, aided by 43 markets and 63 bakeries. Some two dozen bathhouses took care of the hygienic and tonsorial needs of a largely transient population. Happy Valley and Clark's Point housed iron manufactories, while the Davis Street area, built up over pilings at the Bay's edge, outfitted ships and the men who sailed them. On Kearny Street the City Hall, the Post Office, the customhouse, numerous cigar stores and fancy shops, livery stables, and harness-makers were neighbors of the town's swankier drinking parlors.

Serious businessmen, the bankers, the assayers, the gold buyers, and the jewelers, settled on Montgomery Street along with book-stores and newspaper offices. Auction houses, warehouses, and wholesalers crowded together on the recently.filled land at the edge of the Bay. Smaller businesses and gambling halls predominated on Dupont Street and stayed open late into the night. The Chilean washerwomen from the Washington, Kearny, Pacific, Montgomery area scrubbed and pounded great piles of linen in the coves along the Bay. Herds of goats grazed on the slopes of Telegraph Hill, a familiar sight until 1928, when an ordinance banned their presence. Italian women, milking their goats at the buyer's doorstep, became the Hill's milkmen.

Gradually during the fifties the makeshift and spontaneous enterprises of the first years turned into a solid industrial structure. As the decade progressed, the community produced more of its own necessities and developed as the marketplace and manufactory for many of the agricultural products introduced in the state. Its tanneries turned cattle hides into leather, its foundries changed ships' ballast into heavy equipment and machinery, its mills converted wool into textiles, wheat into flour, and redwood into lumber. By February, 1854, the city had converted to gaslighting. In celebration of the installation of three miles of municipal gas lines and eighty-four streetlamps, 300 citizens gathered at the Oriental Hotel in an illuminated banquet hall ablaze as with tropical sunshine. As Mayor Cornelius Garrison began his speech, a prankster pulled the switch and temporarily plunged the room into darkness. In 1855 a Los Angeles newspaper recognized San Francisco's business prominence when it carried four columns of advertising for firms in the city. In 1856 the pages of Heckendorn and Wilson's Miners' and Business Men's Directory chronicled the change that was taking place from mining community to metropolis: for buyers no longer satisfied with plain groceries and pedestrian hardware, Toomy and O'Keeffe's San Francisco Stores offered "epiceries, liqueurs, quincaillerie, verroterie, toujours un assortiment des mieux choisi," while to a growing upper-class clientele the coast's largest importer of jewelry, J. W. Tucker, announced the arrival of $300,000 of choice articles including thirty large single diamonds "of the first water," fine diamond necklaces worth from $400 to $2,400 each, an unusual assortment of watches with values up to $3,000, silverware, silver tea sets with or without salvers, silver trumpets, card cases, cake baskets, castors, etc. By 1854 Tucker's firm had already made the first solid gold service in the United States, commissioned by the city for $10,000, in gratitude to the retiring mayor Cornelius Garrison for such gestures as turning over his entire salary to charity. San Francisco was beginning to take itself seriously as a city.

By the end of the fifties the California State Agricultural Society's *Transactions,* published by resolution of the eleventh session of the state legislature, singled out almost two dozen San Francisco businesses among the 175 visited by the examining committee as the most prominent in the thriving city. (The report, made partly in an attempt to interest the community's proprietors in the annual Agricultural Society Fair, contained no numbers printed in arabic: with typical Gold Rush logic, when the printers learned that their pay was by the word, they spelled everything out.) Among the firms on which the committee lavished praise were manufacturers of wooden tubs and buckets, ornamental paraphernalia for uniforms, stoves and sheet metal products, oils, bedding materials, wagons and carriages, agricultural implements, condiments, glass, brooms, rope, chemicals, and paper products.*

The report singled out the extraordinary growth of three iron foundries: the Union, the Vulcan, and the Pacific Machine Shop. Peter Donahue's Union Iron Works, launched in 1849 with a sim-

*In its résumé, the committee noted that the tubs, buckets, and pails manufactured by Parish and Company from redwood, cedar, and mahogany compared favorably to the best imported receptacles. A "truly astonishing" production of fancy regalia for military and official clothing—embroidery with gold and silver, laces, gimps, fringes, cords, and tassels, all resembling the finest imports—were sold by the Norcross firm from a store at 144 Sacramento Street, the rooms above which were used for their manufacture. At the corner of Front and Washington streets, Gordon, Brooks, and Company made superior stoves, tin, and sheet iron ware. A successful Front Street neighbor, Stanford Brothers, processed crude oils brought in by ship and refined various fluids, oils, and camphenes for illumination. Jacob Schreiber, a Jackson Street importer, turned the raw Sandwich Island material known as pulu into cushions, pillows, beds, and mattresses, and J. A. Collins made bedding materials in a Sansome Street factory. H. Casebolt, at 157 California Street, produced every variety of wagon, buggy, carriage, and dray. The committee found the size of his plant, the number of employees, and the volume of work comparable to that of several better-known Eastern firms.

The report cited several other companies engaged in manufacturing. The agricultural implements company of Thomas Ogg Shaw on Sacramento Street, employing between 50 and 75 men and encompassing foundries, forges, planing machines, and huge presses, made every part in its own shops. Its daily output was 300 moldboards and a greater number of shovels and other light implements. It kept on hand a complete inventory for immediate duplication of worn or damaged pieces. Two Sacramento firms, Baker and Cutting and Erzgraber and Goetzen, put up pickles, catsup, vinegar, and other condiments. Baker and Cutting, the larger company, planted 30 acres of cucumbers to bottle $10,000 worth of pickles yearly. It also preserved 10,000 gallons a year of tomato catsup and made 500 gallons a day of champagne cider, "a very pleasant and innocent beverage," created by a secret process out of dried apples. To supply itself as well as others with bottles, a very expensive item, it established nearby the first glass factory on the West Coast. The output of C. W. and G. W. Armes of Sacramento Street reached 120,000 brooms a year selling for $3.50 to $6 a dozen. Coupled with the supplies from similar concerns, it eliminated almost completely the need to import brooms to San Francisco.

The Cordage Manufactory near the San Bruno Road, directed by Tubbs and Company, employed 54 machines, of which the greater part were of California invention and often improvements on existing patents. The company's daily production came to about 6,000 pounds of rope of all sizes, for which the firm imported Manila grass at six or seven cents a pound. The San Francisco Chemical Works near the Mission Dolores processed $100,000 worth of muriatic, nitric, and sulfuric acids yearly, reaching "a scale and magnificence" that the committee found "truly surprising." Besides the standard leaden tanks, the chemists made use of retorts and pots from the Sacramento Pottery and found them superior to the imported article. The Pioneer Paper Mill on Taylor and Jones employed 100 workers and used as much as $500 worth of rags a day, excluding wool, to produce 1,200 pounds of paper. The woolen fragments went by ship to New York for conversion into felt and carpeting.

ple forge and $100 worth of tools, had increased its assets in ten years to over $150,000 in machinery, several engines, and a force of 120 men. Its latest contract, for two oscillating steam engines of 125 horsepower and all other machinery for the USS *Saginaw,* came to $75,000.*

Two wine merchants drew the committee's praises, Sainsevain Brothers and Kohler, Froehling and Bauk. The Sainsevains, nephews of Jean-Louis Vignes, who came to California from Cadillac near Bordeaux in 1831, acquired Vignes' small Los Angeles vineyard and winery in 1855. Vignes, who was also the first to grow oranges in Los Angeles, made respectable wines with the help of imported French cuttings—probably the first in California—and aging in casks of local oak. The Sainsevains apparently stuck to the formula, for the committee noted that the quality of their products, which included table wines, dessert wines, a sparkling wine, and brandy, was so superior that "but little is now wanting to complete the triumph of California wine manufacture over any other portion of the world."

The large firm of Kohler and Froehling rented the entire basement of the Montgomery Block and divided it into ten large cellars for the making and storage of wine. It mixed the crush from its own Los Angeles vineyards with that from grapes grown in the north. By blending varieties and adding heavier wine to lighter or lighter to more robust, it achieved a uniform product which was so successful that by 1860 it had a New York agent dealing exclusively in its label.†

Kohler produced more for San Francisco than good wine. A German violinist who had continued to play professionally until

---

*The Vulcan Iron Works on First Street, with a capital and work force only slightly smaller than Donahue's, recorded annual sales of more than $500,000. Among current orders, one came from Mexico to provide machinery for the manufacture of sugar. A third firm, the Pacific Machine Shop, under the direction of Goddard, Hanscom, and Rankin, compared to the best in the country, according to the report; its blast furnace was capable of melting 13,000 pounds at a firing, its crews often numbering 90 men, and its inventory of patterns in excess of $50,000.

†The Sainsevain brothers expanded their acreage—at one time they had a vineyard and winery in Santa Clara County—put up 100 dozen bottles daily, and kept their San Francisco establishment stocked with between 25,000 and 75,000 gallons of great variety. Kohler and Froehling's annual output ranged from 120,000 to 175,000 gallons of wine, of which the Monkey Block cellars stored 120,000 gallons, along with 50,000 gallons of brandy from the vintage of "one thousand eight hundred and fifty nine." In the following decades the firm owned extensive vineyards in Sonoma, most of which were later destroyed by the phylloxera. At the end of the century the company merged into the California Wine Association.

the wine firm was securely established, he was also a founder and director of the San Francisco (later California) Insurance Company and the German Savings Bank Society of San Francisco, helped found and incorporate the cable car system, was a director of the public library for seventeen years, attended the San Francisco Charter conventions, and was a member of the vigilantes.

Artists also numbered among the top firms cited by the committee. By locating far out on Broadway, the Nahl Brothers hoped to be interrupted by "few if any calls except on business," while their elevated and open situation afforded a "landscape view seldom equalled [and] in every way calculated to give constant vigor to genius." The committee found their works, in both design and execution, second to no other drawing, painting, or lithography in California.

During the sixties the San Francisco economy developed erratically. The Civil War, to the extent that it had cut off the major transport of goods and supplies to the West, had spurred on the development of local industries. Although the railroad had glutted the market with cheap Eastern products, the quality and freshness of Western manufacture nevertheless kept the local markets in competition, and by 1872 Langley's San Francisco Directory listed "eight hundred and odd factories of different kinds which pulsate and throb within the precincts of this metropolis. . . ." If commerce, mining, and agriculture were still foremost in California's development in the 1870's, the variety of other, often related enterprises that had reached respectability gave San Francisco a well-rounded economy.

By the early seventies sixteen foundries, among them the Pacific, the Neptune, the Union, the Risdon, and the Vulcan Iron Works, were casting the implements and machinery for town use, for the mines, for the farms, and for such foreign customers as China and Japan. Their products included iron riverboats and even locomotives. Windmills, buggies, and agricultural equipment that evolved uniquely to meet the California scale of oversized ranches—horse-drawn plows, steam-powered threshers, machines which combined harvesting and threshing in one operation—often found markets beyond the original area.[33]

By 1870 farming employed more men than mining. Such California phenomena as the predictable lack of rain during the harvest season allowed wheat farmers to gather, thresh, and ship grain with little risk of spoilage. Ranches evolved to such enormous size that by 1870 the value of agricultural production passed that of mining. Isaac Friedlander dominated the industry. With other brokers and entrepreneurs, he developed the wheat business and such affiliated enterprises as the California Canal and Irrigation Company, until the San Joaquin Valley became known as the granary of the Pacific. By the mid-seventies California wheat was supplying a considerable part of the world market. The vast amount of shipping through the port of San Francisco made grain transportation easy: wheat and barley replaced ballast in an increasing number of ships, and it was customary to use them to fill the holds of all the vessels bringing ore to the smelters.

Reduction plants and smelters now treated lead, Comstock silver, gold, zinc, copper, and iron ore. The primary company, Selby Silver and Lead Smelting and Reduction Works, carried on its operations, perhaps the most complete in the country, at the foot of Hyde Street, where there was water deep enough to accommodate the ore-laden ships. San Francisco refined almost one-half of the state's total silver and gold production and kept six brass foundries, the largest of them Garrett's, in constant operation.

Mills and factories expanded the variety of manufactured goods during the seventies. The Pioneer Woolen Mills, the Pacific Woolen Mills, and the Mission Woolen Mills, the latter two of which eventually merged, loomed everything from blankets to "cassimeres." Twelve tanneries cured enough leather beyond local needs to export in quantity. In addition to two standard glass factories, one firm silvered only French plate glass for mirrors. The city now supported two candle factories; thirteen soap factories; a glue factory; a number of match factories; several oil refineries; marble works turning out gravestones and billiard tables; potteries; cement pipe plants; boot and shoe manufacturers; eight flour mills; several sugar refineries; meat-packers, smokers and curers; and canners and preservers of fruit and produce.

Even with such an abundance of local merchandise, S. Koshland and Company, on California Street, supplemented it with imported bags, twines, wools, and furs. Chin Lee on Kearny Street supplied exotic items from the Orient. There was also a sizable increase in businesses that catered to personal needs. Although primarily druggists, Justin and Gates also offered their clients Turkish and Russian steam baths, and the neighboring Montgomery Baths staffed a hairdressing salon. An American Agency on California Street placed Chinese and Japanese servants; a marriage bureau operated out of 607 Washington Street, and M. H. Lickenstein, a moneylender, occupied offices down the street. The U.S. General Business and Protective Bureau, a collection agency, pursued debtors from the same Kearny Street address used by the Pacific Coast Detective Agency, whose bonded agents operated in Arizona, Mexico, Texas, Oregon, Nevada, Washington Territory, and California.

Also by the seventies, two telegraph offices and their branches connected San Francisco with the rest of the country: the Atlantic and Pacific Telegraph Company, Leland Stanford, president, and the Western Union Telegraph Company, Frank Jaynes, manager. The first telephone exchange, the American Speaking Telephone Company, opened at 222 Sansome Street on February 17, 1878, with eighteen subscribers. The Gold and Stock Telegraph Company, a subsidiary of Western Union, ran it. The National Bell Telephone Company's Exchange, competing very soon on Montgomery Street, incorporated in 1906 as the Pacific Telephone and Telegraph. The first transcontinental telephone call in 1915 between Alexander Graham Bell and Thomas Watson went from New York to San Francisco. John Mackay's Commercial Pacific Cable Company, in which he became involved long after he had made his fortune as one of the silver kings, laid the first trans-Pacific cable from San Francisco in 1902.

The San Francisco Gas Company, which had been illuminating San Francisco since 1854 with gas manufactured largely from Australian coal, also made great strides in the seventies. Joseph Crockett, employed there in 1873 as an engineer and by 1885 the firm's president, developed a modern gasworks unequaled in its time. The fire of 1906 destroyed all of the Gas House Cove buildings and equipment save for Crockett's brick office headquarters, which now shelter the Merryvale Antique Showrooms under the original coffered ceiling.

Ferry traffic had increased steadily, and by 1877 the Central Pacific, Atlantic and Pacific, and Southern Pacific Coast Railways had erected a large Central Terminal Building to house their connecting ferry slips. The present Ferry Building, with its clock tower inspired by the Spanish Giralda, replaced the old wooden terminal in 1898.

With wood available and foundries in operation, home factories could meet almost the entire local demand for vehicles by the early seventies. John Studebaker, who started as a wagon builder in Placerville during the Gold Rush and later made his fortune in Indiana as a wagon and automobile manufacturer, ran a shop for carriages, buggies, and farm spring wagons in San Francisco at 201 Market Street. Studebaker Brothers Manufacturing Company was a neighbor of Hallidie's wire rope, Spreckels' sugar and shipping businesses and Vigilante leader William T. Coleman's merchandising firm.

Transportation itself had changed in many ways. The first regular city transit, established in 1852, was by omnibus, a horse-drawn stagecoachlike vehicle for eighteen passengers. Its resemblance to a coach was the more pronounced because several of the passengers had to ride on top. The Yellow Line ran from the Post Office at Clay and Kearny to Mission Dolores, at a cost of 50 cents on weekdays and $1 on Sundays. With the entry of the People's or Red Line into competition, fares went down to 10 cents. Henry Casebolt's plump little balloon horsecars, designed for the Sutter Street line, also charged 10 cents. They followed Pacific Avenue between Fillmore and Van Ness, turning at the end of the line on their own carriage beds by means of a swiveling mechanism designed by Mr. Casebolt, thus saving the need for cumbersome and expensive turntables.

The horse-drawn San Francisco Market Street Railroad Company carried passengers by 1857; four similar companies were running by 1870. The San Francisco-San Jose Railroad Company, an 1863 steam line connecting the two cities, took over the Market Street line, and both later became consolidated within the Southern Pacific empire. By 1875 eight rail lines, including a Clay Street Cable, were servicing the city. During this period the city granted a franchise to Abner Doble, who never exercised it, to tunnel from Broadway through Russian Hill; the passage was finally excavated some eighty years later. Horsecars, which at their peak harnessed 1,700 animals, survived until 1906, although many lines converted to cable. Steam lines generally connected the central city to the beach and other suburban resorts. Electric trolleys entered downtown service in 1891, delayed by popular sentiment against overhead installations. Feelings ran so high that the Market Street line did not put up its wires until 1906. When cable car tracks were installed on Market Street in 1883, the term "South of the Slot" came into general use for the district below the line.

Gertrude Stein's brother Michael engineered the second consolidation of street railways into the Market Street Railway Company in 1893. The Stein family, originally from Germany, had spent some time on the East Coast before settling in Oakland in 1888. Gertrude's father had become vice-president of the Omnibus Cable Company in San Francisco soon after their arrival, and when Michael returned from studies at Johns Hopkins, he joined the firm. After his father's death in 1891, Michael worked as the line's assistant superintendent, then as vice-president of the Market Street Railway Company after the 1893 consolidation, and within two years as superintendent of the division. During the 1902 cable car strike he championed the cause of the union, no doubt a decisive factor in his retirement the next year from what turned out to be a miscast role in business to a preferred life in Europe devoted to the art world. Loss of the Market Street line balanced the Steins' gain of an incredible and foresighted collection of art; their support helped foster the career of Matisse and a number of his most famous contemporaries.

Andrew S. Hallidie, owner of the California Wire Rope and Cable Company on Market Street, had been mulling over the problems of cable-run conveyances in connection with mining. In 1872 he had invented an inexpensive device for carrying ore to the mill. Using buckets and cars suspended from wire ropes, the system could cross mountainous terrain that was normally inaccessible. The steep grades of San Francisco hills, unreachable by horsecars, might be opened up as well by a cable traction system, and Hallidie succeeded in working out an adaptation of engineer Benjamin H. Brook's cable plan for street transportation. The basic invention combined a grip that would function efficiently without damaging the traveling cable, with a slotted run adapted to the irregularities of the San Francisco terrain. Although cables had been used generally before, it was Brook's and Hallidie's insight that perfected their application to the street system in San Francisco. Working in the sixties with W. H. Hepburn, a civil engineer, Brooks, the son of a pioneer attorney of 1849, planned the first San Francisco cable line. Together with C. S. Bushnell, A. Doubleday, and E. W. Steele, he formed the Clay Street Hill Railroad and in 1870 obtained the first city franchise for a street cable transportation system, "an endless wire cable, laid under the surface of the street and operated by a stationary engine." Unfortunately, he was not as successful in obtaining the necessary financial backing and, unable to proceed without it, sold the franchise and the plans to Hallidie in 1872. His successor, apparently a more convincing salesman, obtained the backing of at least three San Francisco businessmen.

Under the original name, the Clay Street Hill Railroad, the city's first line opened on August 1, 1873. It ran up Clay Street from Kearny to Jones. The California Street Cable Railroad to Nob Hill, described as "the crowning achievement of its class" by the 1880 San Francisco Directory, began service in 1878. It was headed by Leland Stanford and a number of millionaire cronies, among them Mark Hopkins, Charles Crocker, Louis Sloss, and David Colton, all of whom had houses on Nob Hill. By 1890 ten cable companies were clanging their way through San Francisco streets, making its hilltops accessible to settlement and encouraging expansion into areas beyond. The 1898 charter of the city and county of San Francisco authorized the ultimate municipalization of the street railway lines, but it was not until 1913 that the city actually proceeded to take over operation. Hallidie, the man most responsible for the cable car, also served twelve years as president of the Mechanics' Institute, was a founding trustee of the San Francisco Public Library, and a regent of the University of California.

In 1884 a cable railway installed by the contractor Joseph Fazackerley scaled Telegraph Hill. One of the company's backers, Gustav Sutro, also founded the Sutro Brothers investment firm which is operating today. The brainchild of Frederick Layman, the cable line climbed Greenwich Street from Powell beyond Kearny to the summit, where Layman just happened to have put up the Telegraph Hill Observatory, Restaurant, and Concert Hall, a sixty-two-foot-high two-story turreted octagonal German castle. Neither venture was much of a success. The railroad closed down within two years; the observatory went through a series of proprietors, including Duncan Ross, who installed an arena below its walls where he staged weekly broadsword contests. The castle finally succumbed to neglect and, no longer in use, burned down in 1903.

Not everyone attempted to make money from Telegraph Hill through improvements. From the early sixties until 1914 several firms quarried the slopes to provide rock for ballast, seawalls, concrete, and paving. The blasting and gouging that scarred the hill for almost a mile on the north and east sides, are still evident from the Embarcadero below, and landslides there are not uncommon. During the height of the activity some houses were blasted from their foundations, several slid down the cliffs, others were so undermined that they were rendered useless. Alexander Houston first burrowed along Battery Street to obtain rock for the portion of the seawall he had contracted to build, and somewhat later other builders employed the same destructive techniques to obtain material. By the nineties six firms were busy chewing into the hillside.

The largest enterprise of all, operated by Harry and George Gray, did irreparable damage. Besides attacking the east face of the hill, the Grays worked on Diamond Heights and Twin Peaks to supply the Gray Brothers Artificial Stone and Paving Company, the firm that put in a good portion of the city's curbs and sidewalks. In 1899 they purchased Layman's German Castle, but never got around to making whatever use of it they had in mind. Their operations caused continuous alarm among the residents who had the misfortune to be their neighbors. On several occasions enraged citizens stoned the workers and came close to riot. When illegal blasting on Diamond Heights damaged a school and injured several students, the city pressed suit against the Grays. Although the assistant city attorney, Jesse Steinhart, did not succeed in obtaining a sentence, the court issued strong orders to stop the blasting. In spite of such dodges as setting off blasts under the booming shield of Fourth of July cannons, the firm got into trouble financially, neglecting to pay its bills or its employees, one of whom, Joseph Lococo, finally shot and killed George Gray.

Lococo was acquitted, and the firm went into bankruptcy. As late as 1925 the city arrested and fined Harry Gray for illegal blasting on Diamond Heights.[34]

It followed naturally from San Francisco's geographical position that local shipping should burgeon into one of the city's most important industries. Starting in the early 1830's, when William Richardson was running launches on the Bay, it continued during the mid-forties with Leidesdorff's steamer plying the rivers up to Sacramento. When that boat sank in a storm, the salvaged engine found use turning a coffee grinder, and the hull, fitted with sails, again navigated the Bay. Later steamers often exploded. When Millen Griffith arrived in 1849, his lighter business grew so rapidly that he soon owned a fleet of tugs in addition. Until the seventies, when San Francisco firms turned out boats specifically designed for towing, the tugs were largely converted steamers. Goodall and Perkins' *Water Witch,* the first San Francisco-built tug, went into service in 1866 and became the West's most important coastal steamship line. Years later, when Captain Griffith's firm merged with Goodall, Nelson and Perkins' Red Stack Tugs, he also became a partner in the Pacific Whaling Company. The Ship Owners and Merchants' Tug Boat Company subsequently took over Red Stack Tugs, which today is launching towboats from Pier 3.

Beginning in September, 1849, the *Sacramento* introduced regular shipping service between San Francisco and Sacramento; river transportation of passengers and freight continued as the principal means of traffic well into the sixties. The California Steam Navigation Company, which sold out to the Central Pacific in 1871, dominated the trade from the early fifties. Local and international transportation of people, merchandise, and supplies by water had already become big business by the spring of 1851. Numerous dependent enterprises grew up around the port of San Francisco: warehouses, customs brokers, merchants' exchanges, sailmakers, chronometer and watchmaking shops, marine suppliers, shipbuilders, hotels, groggeries and eateries, schools of navigation, houses of prostitution, dance halls, dens, and dives of notorious character, and the highly profitable Barbary Coast commerce of supplying ships' crews by shanghaiing.

The semaphore which had been installed atop Telegraph Hill, to signal the type of vessel that was approaching the harbor was a boon to the homesick, the merchants, the hotelkeepers, the small boatsmen, and others who awaited news from home or might otherwise profit from a ship's arrival. In "The Man at the Semaphore," Bret Harte describes the telegraph system and the joy in the streets when the arms, at right angles, signaled a mail-carrying side-wheel steamer. By the time of Harte's description the system had been improved. The original owners had lived on the premises and turned a small profit from a refreshment stand installed downstairs. The new operators, who also ran the Merchants' Exchange, immediately installed a lookout station at Point Lobos, and the new service, by speeding up the time it took to get the news to contracting parties, produced good profits. By the fall of 1853 they had replaced the manual semaphore with one of the first electric telegraphs in California. Signals flashed over lines from Point Lobos to the Merchants' Exchange, where subscribers could now obtain the earliest possible shipping information. Until 1870, when it toppled over in a fierce gale, the old semaphore building, with its telescope and refreshment service, was a favorite place for an outing. The original semaphore arms continued in use, however, when two San Francisco watchmakers, Samuel Barrett and Robert Sherwood, devised a profitable scheme for the necessary adjustment of ships' chronometers—set for Greenwich time—against the local hour—signaled by semaphore. The precise time of the daily signal was known only to Barrett and Sherwood. For a fee, subscribing ships' masters could check the time recorded by their instruments against a key to the watchmakers' signals and adjust their chronometers accordingly.

Sailmakers and ships' chandlers were another spin-off from the city's maritime activities. One of the earliest firms in the 1850's, run by Andrew Crawford, continued in production until the San Francisco Weeks Company bought it out in the nineties; as the Howe-Emerson-Weeks Company, it is located today on Howard Street.

Bay traffic was so brisk that private entrepreneurs petitioned the city to erect new piers and a seawall. The state assumed responsibility instead and in 1863 delegated the port development to a new board of harbor commissioners. During the seventies, when the construction of the seawall began, the harbor's facilities increased to meet the expected demand. East Street, the roadway over the seawall, is today's Embarcadero. Construction of the barricade went by sections, the last of which was in place in 1914. The state-owned Belt Line Railroad, circulating north of Market Street in 1890, expanded in 1912 to connect the waterfront to the south and west and to public terminals and major railroads.

Until the advent of gasoline launches in 1905 the Bay was abob with a fleet of Whitehall boats, named after their New York counterparts that docked at the foot of Whitehall Street. Manned by enterprising oarsmen, they carried runners from every conceivable business that a ship's company might need ashore. As the scramble for customers became more aggressive, the Whitehall

boats rowed farther into the Bay, finally going out beyond the
Gate and many times waiting the night through for a vessel due
on the morrow. Henry C. Peterson, one of the most successful
Whitehall boatmen, switched in the eighties to towing and
launches and developed one of the most important businesses
along the waterfront. Another Whitehaller, "Hook-on" Crowley,
earned his name for the tenacity with which he hung onto a moving vessel. His sons, Tom and Dave, managed a launch service
from the Vallejo Street Wharf, and Tom later became one of the
Red Stack owners. Still functioning, Crowley's Launch and Tug-
boat Company works out of Pier 50. However, many of the boatsmen worked for crimps transporting entrapped sailors to waiting
ships; some resorted to robbery and occasionally to murder to eke
out a living.

John Spreckels launched the Black Stack Tug Boat Company to
save his shipping firm the costly rates of the Red Stack monopoly.
Spreckels entered the competition at twenty-four by making the
low bid for his father's account in sugar transport. After he established the Black Tugs, the two companies battled so fiercely for
trade, often heading out in Whitehall-like droves to capture incoming vessels, that a truce had to be called; the rivals underlined
alternately in red and black the arriving vessels published in the
daily lists and did business only with those who fell under their
colors.[35]

Spreckels' shipping empire eventually extended throughout
the Pacific, and he became one of the most important figures in
the trade. A competitor, the Swedish Captain William Matson,
had once worked for John's father Claus Spreckels after his arrival in San Francisco in 1867. It was the senior Spreckels who later
lent him enough to establish himself in the Hawaiian merchant
trade. Matson's successful firm exchanged sails for steam in the
nineties and eventually encompassed a large fleet of passenger
liners. His focus on Hawaii as the center of Pacific trade, together
with the Spreckels' vast sugar and shipping interests there, helped
shape the national policy that by 1898 led to acquisition. Matson's
daughter, Lurline, for whom a number of vessels were named,
married William P. Roth. After his father-in-law's death Roth
took over the Matson Navigation Company, purchased the
Spreckels' Oceanic Shipping Company, and built a thriving South
Seas tourist business with the introduction of giant luxury liners.

Robert Dollar, another of the shipping barons, came to the Bay
Area in 1888 seeking to improve his health. Engaged in lumbering in Mendocino, he entered the shipping business primarily to
provide transportation for his cargoes of wood. His greatest successes came when he entered trade with the Orient.

William T. Shorey, one of the most remarkable seamen connected with San Francisco, overcame many obstacles to follow a career in whaling from the 1880's well into the first decade of the new century. Captain Shorey's importance increased in the face of a decline in the whaling industry brought on by the competition of petroleum and other products. An even more difficult obstacle was William Shorey's color. A native of Barbados, British West Indies, Shorey grew up on a sugar plantation, which he left as a very young man. He reached Boston as a cabin boy with an aptitude for navigation and was soon crewing on a whaler. The partial destruction of the Eastern whaling fleet by Confederate vessels during the Civil War forced the industry to shift to a West Coast base; Shorey, by then wearing the uniform of an officer, sailed along with the whalers. With the decline of whaling, many white American seamen had taken up more remunerative pursuits; crews were of largely mixed ethnic backgrounds and therefore of weaker racial bias. Shorey rose quickly through the ranks; within ten years he was rewarded for his outstanding seamanship with the command of his own vessel. The only black captain on the West Coast, he continued until 1908, increasingly taking over more demanding posts. Along the way he married Julia Ann Shelton, the daughter of one of San Francisco's leading black families. Their descendants live in Oakland.

The volume of San Francisco shipping stimulated the construction of shipbuilding firms, dry-dock facilities for repairs, and assembly plants for putting together larger vessels from the East that had come in sections like prefabricated housing. The work centered on South Beach, including Hunters Point and Steamboat Point, the latter the subsequent site of the Southern Pacific terminal. Henry Tichenor's first dry dock at the foot of Second Street was ready for business in 1851. From the seventies on, two Scottish brothers, John and James Dickie, led the wooden shipbuilding trade. The largest of the builders, Matthew Turner, launched his career in San Francisco in 1868 and moved to Benicia fifteen years later. In the eighties Peter Donahue's Union Iron Works expanded, building iron and steel ships for commercial use and warships for the United States and other navies. Bethlehem Steel Corporation bought the plant in 1905, as well as the Risdon Iron Works in 1911. The Dickies' brother, George, worked for both, and James Dickie spent twenty years at the Union plant, in addition to his affiliation with the family business. Founded in 1893 at Hunters Point, Hans Anderson's firm, now producing under the name of Anderson and Cristofani, dominated the industry for many years. In 1939, anticipating the outbreak of war, Congress bought up most of the privately owned dry docks in the Hunters Point area and created the Hunters Point

Naval Shipyard, a major installation. The yard, which eventually included 454 buildings and 17 miles of railroad, closed down in June, 1974.

To cope with the problems of bulk transport around the San Francisco Bay region, local shipbuilders designed a unique scow-schooner. The scow's normally boxy construction, adapted to the San Francisco waterways, allowed a 60-ton craft to lift "as much as a hundred tons of hay, brick, grain, sand, or lumber—to mention some of the more common goods they carried. Their broad and unobstructed decks and great stability allowed stowage of most of their load topside, facilitating loading and unloading, while their flat bottoms allowed them to lie conveniently on the mud at low tide in the tiny estuaries among their ports of call. Scows were cheap to build and to operate."[36] They also handled well and could get up enough sail to win occasional regattas during the seventies and eighties. The highly specialized San Francisco version probably evolved directly out of the practical, if somewhat make-shift, boats of the Gold Rush era. By the sixties they were in general use throughout the area; by the end of the century several hundred sailed the Bay, most of them built in the Hunters Point docks.

From the days before the waterfront extended beyond Broadway and Pacific, the shorefront alleys had housed the Sydney Ducks. Judging from the scope and violence of their criminal activities, these ticket-of-leave men were not the usual pathetic English debtors that often made up the prison population of the Van Diemen's Land penal colony, but murderers and thieves of marked cunning and ferocity. The ex-convicts set the tone for the neighborhood. From the East Street waterfront inland to Chinatown and from Clay and Commercial up to Broadway, crime thrived with such virulence that by the sixties its victims had christened the neighborhood the Barbary Coast. Dedicated primarily to the exploitation of seamen, although anyone naïve enough to venture into its precincts was fair game, Coast business clustered largely around slop shops, cheap clothing stores, pawnshops, gambling dens, crimping joints, booze parlors, lewd entertainments, and bawdy houses.

Even before a sailor debarked in port, he had to run the gamut of Whitehall boatmen, many of them sinister characters in league with the boardinghouse crimps. The crimp, by whatever means he found expedient, supplied crews to ship's masters; from the Barbary Coast there were few who shipped out voluntarily. Dangling before his victim the bait of free women, board, and whiskey or plying him outright with doped cigars or jazzed-up gin, the crimp or his runner herded his catch back to the boardinghouse, where the real troubles began. There he was robbed, his gear seized, and his bills outrageously padded with invented charges until he was hopelessly in debt. Ship's masters in search of a crew had little difficulty signing them on in the boardinghouses. Those who were neither drunk nor drugged enough were more forcefully persuaded to put their names to the contract. The innkeeper, having already pocketed the advance on his wages, had no further use for his boarder and delivered him up to the ship's master to whom the sailor already owed the proceeds of the next voyage. The recalcitrant again received help in the form of an overdose of whiskey, often bolstered by a Mickey Finn or a convincing blow to the head from a bung starter.

If a man got through the Whitehallers and the boardinghouse gang still standing, he had ahead the entrapments of the gin mills, the bordellos, the dance halls, and the melodeons. To the tune of the reed organ, these fancy establishments treated carousers, sailors, and other comers alike to rotgut laced with laudanum, opium, or chloral hydrate, to clobberings with belaying pins, billy clubs, slingshots, or the ubiquitous bung starters, to fleecings, and sometimes even to murder if enough profit was in it. The trapdoor in the barroom floor sent many an unsuspecting reveler, drink still in hand, hurtling into the black hole beneath it, thence to be lugged, anesthetized, to some hell ship gathering a crew. No matter his former profession. The practice became so predominant in San Francisco that by 1852, with the heavy demands created by the Australian gold rush, there were two dozen teams of crimps wielding their truncheons. Since the unwitting seaman's destination was often as remote a port as Shanghai, "shanghaiing" became another term for crimping in Embarcadero language.

The most enterprising operator along the beach, Shanghai Kelly, ran a three-story house on stilts at the foot of Pacific; its yield of victims could be lowered directly into boats bobbing on the waves below the floor. Among the crimps, there developed specialists in dealing with ethnic groups, greenhorn farmers, whalers, and other such distinguishing categories. Two of the most villainous crimps were women. The Amazonian Mother Bronson, who ran a boardinghouse on Steuart Street, could convince a prospective crewman with her bare hands, saving her a good deal of money in knockout drops and slugging devices. Her sister-in-trade, the toothless Miss Piggott, being of a more diminutive stature, employed whatever help she could get. To her Davis Street premises her runner, a Laplander named Nikko, steered unsuspecting recruits, who then got the full treatment: spiked liquor, clubbed pate, and a one-way taxi-boat ride to the waiting ship in the harbor.

A versatile thug with a sharp iron hook where his left arm used to be, Johnny Devine made his reputation as a crimp, a burglar, a pimp, a demon fighter, and a runner for Shanghai Kelly. Before he was finally hanged for murder, the Shanghai Chicken, a name to which he also answered, had a stable of seven streetwalkers soliciting Barbary Coast business along alleys crammed with customers from the Boar's Head, the Nymphia, the So Different—also known as "Nigger" Purcell's—the Fierce Grizzly, Parenti's, Cowboy Mag's, the Thalia, the Bella Union, the Midway Plaisance, Fat Daugherty's, the O.K., the Hippodrome (where Ferde Grofé at one time played piano), the Crutch, Spider Kelly's, or any one of the more than 500 dives or concert saloons where alcoholic beverages were served. Bribery and protection money kept both the politicians and the Coast's proprietors in gold dust, and the shady doings, faithfully exaggerated in the columns of the *California Police Gazette*, kept that paper prosperous. They also served as the inspiration for the Pacific coast's first branch of the Salvation Army. Launched at 809 Montgomery Street by the indefatigable Major Alfred Wells in July, 1883, the office centered in the worst area of depravity. And they were certainly the basis of the open-air sermons that made the Methodist minister the Reverend William Taylor the most famous orator in Portsmouth Square.

A contingent of barhopping lawyers snared unhappy crewmen whom they convinced to bring suits against shipowners responsible for the harsh treatment they had received. When the court awarded a judgment in a sailor's favor, his attorney pocketed the cash, which always managed to coincide exactly with the amount of his fee. From 1851 a force of water police under the command of Captain Edgar Wakeman patrolled the Embarcadero, but their efforts had little effect. After the completion of the railroad, with the increase of coastal shipping and of shorter voyages, sailors were at least not as continuously long-suffering.

Throughout the sixties and seventies many sailors attempted to organize into unions, but they faced formidable adversaries. Finally, in 1885, responding simultaneously to a drastic wage cut and to the militant oratory of Sigismund Danielwicz, a professional organizer and member of the International Workmen's Association, about 200 men formed the Coast Seamen's Union. The Steamshipman's Union followed. The Sailors' Union of the Pacific, an 1891 amalgamation of the two, settled the unproductive rivalry between them. The result, a 4,000-member local, was the most powerful in the country. A bloody battle ensued between the Sailors' Union and the Shipowner's Association, weakening the seamen's party and depleting its funds. Out of the fray emerged Andrew Furuseth, an energetic Norwegian sailor and loner to the point of eccentricity, who steered the embattled sailors through the storm, became a successful Washington lobbyist on their behalf, and finally engineered both the International Seamen's Union and, with the help of Senator Robert La Follette, the 1915 Seamen's Act, which guaranteed the rights of all men at sea. During the 1890's one of his disciples, a Scots sailor named Walter MacArthur, edited the *Coast Seaman's Journal,* into which he incorporated true accounts of the cruelties suffered by sailors on shipboard. Publication of the entire collection of sixty-three cases, put out between shocking-crimson covers, startled the nation and helped rally theretofore unsuccessful efforts for relief legislation.

As in any port, the waterfront in San Francisco supported a lively business in prostitution, but in a city short of females from its beginning that neighborhood held no monopoly. Not until after the turn of the century was there a nearly equal division between the sexes; in the earlier days, even the sight of a woman would draw a crowd. The first prostitutes to arrive in any significant number came largely from south of the border in 1849 and 1850. They included several representatives of South American French colonies, their passage paid by waiting pimps to whom they became indentured. Their destination was the tent settlement of Little Chile or the mining camps. Before the year was out, reinforcements had come from the States, as well as a generous regiment from France, minor companies from England and Germany, and a single recruit from China. The French prostitutes who congregated around the Jackson-Commercial Street area, thereafter known as Frenchtown, added a certain tone to the profession no matter how low the circumstances from which most of them had emigrated. They often worked individually instead of in the lower-class cribs, or staffed parlor houses of a more elegant nature, such as the Parisian Mansion on Commercial Street, which stayed in business until 1917. The town's fascination with everything foreign, especially if it bore a French label, extended to these courtesans, their Gallic appeal, and the high price tag that went along with it. There was one exception to the widespread preference for matters French: girls who arrived in 1852 and 1853 or who were unintelligent enough to admit it were considered the dregs of France. A phony French lottery, its profits designed ostensibly to pay the passage of some 5,000 indigent Parisians who would get a new start in California, was in actuality a monarchist scheme to bankroll an imminent takeover of the Republic, simultaneously exporting a number of political enemies among the other preselected emigrants. A large contingent of underworld characters was substituted for the unemployed hopefuls who had signed for the voyage in good faith. The prizes, gold bars of varying denominations, lured thousands of buyers, but the winning tickets were rigged, and the proceeds went largely to fatten the treasury of the monarchists. The several thousand French who arrived in consequence of the lottery did include some reputable people among the prostitutes and derelicts, but it was better not to admit having entered the country from France at that time.

The lone Chinese courtesan who arrived in 1849, a stunning twenty-two-year-old, set up business in a Chinatown alleyway. A dozen variations on her name, the most common of which were Ah Toy and Ah Choy, appeared in print since she was often involved in litigation. When several other Chinese ladies of joy arrived soon after, Ah Toy set herself up as madam in a house in Waverly Place. The total number of Chinese women immigrants, which was extremely small, included by 1851 a corps of seven prostitutes. During the year following, several hundred girls arrived, most to be forced into prostitution; before long there was a heavy slave traffic in young Chinese women to supply the San Francisco cribs. In 1874 the Chinese Presbyterian Mission began attempts to aid the downtrodden and victimized Chinese women, but not until Donaldina Cameron took over the management of the new home at 900 Sacramento Street did rescue operations go forward in full gear. Her efforts to rehabilitate enslaved Chinese females earned her a worldwide reputation as a missionary.

By 1855 a government committee counted more than 100 houses of prostitution just in the few blocks inland from Kearny around the area of Portsmouth Square. The fancy parlor houses often entertained leading citizens at balls and soirees. In 1854 an attempt to put some restraints on the trade had resulted in the first antiprostitution law on the city's books. In practice, however, that measure, and others that followed, proved to be more racist than moralistic, being enforced mostly against nonwhites—the Mexicans, the South Americans of color, and particularly the Chinese; no one wanted to pursue the measure equally against Caucasians, especially, one may presume, if they spoke with a French accent. Prostitutes were barred from the Mechanics' Fair in 1857 and from various balls given by the gentry, but they could sneak into the popular masked balls, and there were curtained booths reserved at the theaters for those who chose to attend without exposing themselves to the stares of the public. One observer comments, after a careful study of the prevalence of prostitution that the scandal newspapers seemed to suggest:

> In brief, it was everywhere. The heaviest concentration of houses and cribs was in the area that stretched from Chinatown's Dupont Street to the Bay on the East. But there were also brothels on Sutter, Geary, and Stockton, even

though these streets had some of the city's finest residences. The business district had its share, along with the discreet French restaurants. To the north, there were rooms for assignation on the upper floor of the bathhouse on Meigg's [sic] Wharf. To the south and west there were assignation houses, brothels, and hog ranches aplenty on Mission Road, most of the way to the ocean.[37]

The *Varieties* and the *Phoenix,* the latter published by ex-San Francisco Judge Ed McGowan in Sacramento, dominated the scandal-sheet side of publishing for a decade beginning in the mid-fifties. Hawked noisily in the streets, the one-bit sheets supplied a good amount of gossip, sometimes inaccurate, an equal amount of snide conjecture, and, by the mere inclusion of so many featured articles on prostitution, a fairly reliable directory of the city's houses of ill repute. Copies of the *Phoenix* were impounded in 1858 under San Francisco's first obscenity law, designed, as a matter of fact, particularly with that paper in mind. Like everything else, prostitution and its allied trades were coming under scrutiny. San Francisco's attitude in such matters has actually remained fairly open over the years with only occasional splashes of morality.

From the first a procession of colorful proprietresses has kept up the city's standards for generous hospitality. Although a good deal of the elegance which history attributes to the early "Countess"—among other grand gestures, she was reported to have sent engraved invitations for the full-dress opening of her house on Portsmouth Square to all the leading citizens, including the clergy—may well have been more fancy than reality, two other madams of the 1850's did, without question, provide parlor houses of considerable *haut ton.* One of them was Irene McCready, the mistress and sometimes partner of James McCabe, proprietor of the El Dorado Saloon. The other was Belle Cora, the mistress and later wife of Charles Cora, who started her San Francisco career in 1852, still in her early twenties, running a house on Dupont Street. In the mid-fifties, she moved to far more elegant quarters on Waverly Place, then known as Pike Street, and no one challenged her role as the leading madam of the fifties. Her real fame came, perhaps vicariously, through her relationship with Cora, whom the Vigilance Committee convicted of murder. Belle married him just before the committee hanged him.

In contrast with the waterfront dives and Chinatown cribs which catered to the lower classes, the parlor houses vied with each other for the uptown clientele. A visit to one of the better establishments in the seventies or eighties would cost between $10 and $20, plus tips. Champagne was extra. By way of advertisement the inhabitants of the swankier houses had extensive wardrobes of the latest fashions which they displayed to advantage during Saturday promenades and Sunday night theater parties. One commentator of the times noted that "in Eastern cities the prostitutes tried to imitate in manner and dress the fashionable respectable ladies, but in San Francisco the rule was reversed—the latter copying after the former."[38] To keep their wardrobes up to date, the leading madams and their girls had accounts in the best shops. Many of the houses sent out for their food, but the most lavish kept their own chefs on the premises. Accessory services in Jessie Hayman's abodes brought in more revenue at the inflated prices she asked for them than did prostitution. Jessie promptly invested the profits in real estate and diamonds. She had been a member of Nina Hayman's troupe operating at 225 Ellis Street and took over the business and the name at the end of the century, when the first proprietress married into Peninsula society. Jessie's own career lasted until 1917, when she retired. After she died during a visit to London six years later, her estate amounted to $100,000 worth of baubles and downtown real estate.

Before either Nina or Jessie's tenure at the Ellis Street address, Dolly Adams ran the house, having opened it in the seventies. Dolly embarked on her career at the age of eleven when she appeared, in all her prematurely developed femininity, at the Bella Union, popping out of a skintight bathing costume, which enabled her to demonstrate her pulchritude along with various techniques of swimming in a large glass water tank. Dolly led a rich full life until the age of twenty-six, when she died of venereal disease and an addiction to opium.

Nina Hayman's marriage into a wealthy San Francisco family was by no means unique. Enduring affairs often existed between prominent courtesans and representatives of some of the richest and most powerful families in the city. Jessie Hayman managed to keep her alliance with Allen St. John Bowie, a Burlingame socialite and capitalist, a secret for many years. Maud Nelson was not so lucky: her match caught the full glare of publicity. She did well enough as the madam of a nineties bawdy house on Stockton Street, but, to the delight of every journalist, much better as the bride of ex-Senator James Fair's alcoholic son Charley. Although the marriage provided San Francisco with the best scandal of the age, the couple actually seemed to be highly compatible, Maud managing to be the most steadying influence ever exerted on her young groom's behalf. In 1902, living on Charley's inheritance from his multimillionaire parents, the young Fairs summered in Europe. During their visit in France with Charley's sister and her husband, the William K. Vanderbilts, with whom they had an affectionate relationship, Charley killed both Maud and himself speeding in his splendid new Mercedes racing car near Paris.

In spite of the congeniality of their backgrounds, the marriage of Tessie Wall, one of the most famous of San Francisco madams and Jessie Hayman's toughest competition, and Frank Daroux, a big-time gambler and local political boss, ended in disaster. Tessie had started out by running an O'Farrell Street lodging house in the Gay Nineties, lodging and boardinghouses being by that time almost universal San Francisco euphemisms for houses of prostitution. Like seamstresses, another of the city's polite coinages for *femmes de joie*, they could advertise openly in the directories. Only occasionally did someone turn up to have a dress fitted. Tessie's greatest feat in a career rich in spectaculars, and one attested to under oath in court, was to down twenty-two bottles of champagne on the night she met Frank, never once leaving the upstairs room of the French restaurant in which they were supping. After their marriage, Frank had the bad taste to allow his affections to stray seriously enough to bring divorce proceedings against Tessie, who forgave him the error by pumping several bullets into him on the corner of Anna Lane.

By the nineties the Barbary Coast and Chinatown cribs suffered some competition from the cubicles crammed into Morton Street, now Maiden Lane. An influx of European prostitutes at the turn of the century gave rise to conglomerates run on the scale of corporate business. The biggest house, the Nymphia, jammed 450 cribs into a three-story tenement and used a two-shift system of occupancy. In some of the larger cribs, fees increased as the girls' skin color decreased. Although a smaller operation than the Nymphia, the business at 620 Jackson Street was perhaps the most notorious in the city. Nicknamed the Municipal Crib because of the prevalent suspicion that city officials shared its profits, it remained in operation for some time even after political boss Abe Ruef confirmed the *Bulletin*'s accusations and confessed that he and the mayor had indeed been splitting one-quarter of the revenue from it.

The enormous consumption of champagne in the parlor houses, combined with the generally high level of imbibing throughout the city, assured the prosperity of the California wine industry. The early Kohler and Froehling and the Sainsevain wine depots in San Francisco were only the beginnings of what turned out to be one of the state's major business undertakings.

The missionaries had been the earliest California vineyardists, planting the first fields in 1770 in San Diego. The grapevine, cultivated as far north as Sonoma, followed the Mission trail as it had the route of the Roman legions centuries before. In 1824 Joseph Chapman had become the first American winegrower in the state when he put in 4,000 vines in the Los Angeles area; Jean-Louis Vignes' southern plantings bore fruit soon after. By the 1830's Los Angeles was producing about half the total grape crop in California. San Francisco, especially with the impetus from the Gold Rush, evolved as the market for the state, and the wine industry, taking advantage of the port facilities and the booming population, centered there. By 1859 twenty-three Los Angeles winemakers stocked commercial depots in San Francisco.

California's modern wine industry traces its growth from the early efforts of the 1850's. Its course was not entirely free of obstacles: in an attempt to fill the Gold Rush demand, many amateurs turned out wines of questionable character. It was common practice to bottle the juice well before it had a chance to age, to adulterate it, and to falsify labels. Grape growing was big business, and many of the new viticulturists, knowing little of the conditions of soil and climate, in their haste frequently planted in the wrong location. Further, the Mission grape, the principal variety in use for more than eighty years, although a hearty producer, was rough and of generally poor quality, often made worse by the blunders of amateur horticulturists. The European immigrants, many experienced in grape culture and winemaking, became the nucleus of the industry, at first preserving it from disaster and eventually bringing it into full quality production. In 1850 California bottled 58,055 gallons of wine. In 1887 the state exported 7,000,000 gallons to the East and foreign countries. By 1890 the California production came to well over 14,500,000 gallons, including champagne, and more than 1,000,000 gallons of brandy. After 1900, and until the devastating effects of Prohibition, the state put out well over 40,000,000 gallons of wine a year. Several California producers won prizes in competitions in Europe. The demand for barrels and bottles spurred the development of the cooperage and glass industries, particularly in San Francisco.

General Mariano Guadalupe Vallejo, the first commerical vintner of Sonoma County, took over the secularized Mission vineyards in the 1830's. By 1850 he made a profit of $6,000; by 1854, with the increased demand, his grapes brought in $20,000. His friend Colonel Agoston Haraszthy, the leading figure in the development of the California wine industry, introduced Vallejo to European stock better than the Mission grape with which he started. Meanwhile, Haraszthy's sons Arpad and Atilla married two of the general's daughters. The close connection may have helped Vallejo produce wine good enough to win prizes at the 1861 state fair.

In 1841 an English doctor, Edward Bale, put in a vineyard as part of an extensive ranch in the St. Helena area. Bale and his wife, a niece of General Vallejo, had two daughters, one of whom, Catherine, married Charles Krug in 1860. Krug had made wine for General Vallejo, as well as other early vineyardists, including his brother-in-law and St. Helena neighbor, Louis Bruck. He cultivated European grapes, among them zinfandel, on 30 acres in Sonoma purchased from Haraszthy and used the superior European varietals when he planted his St. Helena vineyard. By 1862 he had established the still-flourishing Charles Krug Winery.

Almadén and Paul Masson Vineyards, among the most profitable in California today, also had their beginnings during the Gold Rush. Almadén, near San José, was the original property of a native Frenchman, Charles Lefranc, who began harvesting good varietals there in 1857. His daughter married Paul Masson, a Burgundian vintner who became a partner in the winery with his brother-in-law, Henry. In the nineties Masson established the vineyard under his own name near Saratoga.

Jacob Gundlach, whose father had been a vintner and hotelman in Bavaria, set up the Bavarian Brewery in San Francisco in 1850 and a few years later began making German-type white varietal wines in Vineburg. In the mid-seventies Gundlach and his son-in-law, Charles Bundschu, shipped their wines by boat to San Francisco for aging and bottling under the Bacchus label.

A number of prominent Gold Rush and pre-Gold Rush figures engaged incidentally in the wine business, among them Captain Sutter, who, when he retreated to Hock Farm, put in 30 acres of vines there. Ernest Rufus, a former member of the Swiss guards who had helped Sutter organize his military crew of Indians and Kanakas when he migrated to California, planted a vineyard in Sonoma in the early fifties. John Bidwell, a Californian since 1841, had cultivated vines on his extensive rancho in Butte County and by 1860 had a production of 2,000 gallons of wine a year. (His marriage to a teetotaler eight years later not only changed his drinking habits, but cast him as the Prohibitionist Party's 1892 candidate for the United States Presidency.) James Lick, a part of whose fortune came from San Francisco real estate, also had about 75 acres planted to grapes in Santa Clara. Leland Stanford, searching for country property, bought the extensive Colombet vineyard, winery, and resort hotel at Warm Springs near San José in 1868, converting the earthquake-damaged hotel into a second winery. The production centered largely on bulk wines, but one of its superior reds, bottled in San Francisco by Lachman and Jacobi, became a standard at the Hotel Del Monte. Stanford later turned over the entire property to a brother who had nearby holdings and bought an extensive spread in Tehama County. Some years ago the Weibel Champagne Vineyards purchased a large portion of the old vineyard, as well as several of the original buildings. Stanford's second property, consisting of more than 10,000 acres, was a thriving vineyard and winery at the time of its acquisition in 1881. He expanded it under the name of Vina Vineyard to more than 3,500 planted acres, constructed warehouses, distilleries for brandy, a building for sherry production, and an additional brick winery of such dimensions that it, like the vineyard, was proclaimed the largest in the world. As part of the Stanford estate, the vineyard passed into the possession of Stanford University, which continued its operation until 1915.[39]

Colonel Agoston Haraszthy, the Hungarian émigré nobleman who had the greatest impact of any individual on the development of California wine, arrived in New York in 1840, spent some time in Illinois and Wisconsin (where he founded Sauk City), and moved on to San Diego, California, in 1849. While in Wisconsin, he made major contributions to that state's development, among them the introduction of hops, the basis of the now-flourishing beer industry. His career in public service originated there as state director of emigration and flourished in California as mayor, then sheriff, of San Diego and as a member of the 1851 California legislature. President Pierce, apparently impressed by Haraszthy's outstanding reputation for innovative public service, appointed him assayer of the United States Mint in San Francisco; within a short time he was also in charge of melting and refining.

During 1854 the U.S. Treasury Department dispatched J. Ross Browne as a confidential agent to begin an investigation into the cumulative losses at the San Francisco office. At best, Browne suspected, Haraszthy's inattention had allowed approximately $130,000 of gold to go up the flue, but taking into account his extensive landholdings, properties entirely out of proportion to his means, Browne was forced to conclude that Haraszthy was not altogether honest. In 1857, after careful scrutiny of the suspect and the records, Browne finally prepared to bring charges. At the end of April Haraszthy resigned; in June Browne lodged his formal complaint. Unable to post bond, Haraszthy deeded all his holdings to the government. In 1859 the United States grand jury indicted him; almost a year and a half later it acquitted him, although a final settlement and a clear title to his lands involved several more years of litigation and legal expenses. Even before his resignation, Haraszthy had undertaken a full-scale agricultural operation in Sonoma, beginning in February with the transplantation of 13,000 vines from his other holdings to the Buena Vista Ranch. Undaunted by the loss of title to the property, he had also contracted for a palatial manor house, to be constructed with classical Grecian columns and porticoes and decorated with draped statuary.

Despite all his personal problems, Haraszthy expanded his position as California's leading vintner. He also became the vineyardists' principal spokesman, gaining a foothold on both the State Board of Agriculture and the legislature's Committee on Vines. In 1861, in his capacity as one of three state commissioners of viticulture, he spent five months traveling through Spain, Portugal, Hungary, Italy, Germany, and France, gathering root stock and 200,000 cuttings representing hundreds of varieties. He kept copious notes on European methods of vine growing and winemaking, writing reports on his findings for the *Alta California.* In 1862 he published *Grape Culture, Wines and Wine-Making: With Notes upon Agriculture and Horticulture,* the vintners' bible for years to come. Although his European trek had been undertaken with the blessings of the legislature, its enthusiasm dimmed completely when it came to defraying the $12,000 expenses. Its members further refused to finance the distribution of the vines Haraszthy had so painstakingly collected and transported. After holding the vines for a year in case of a change of mind, he sold them to other vineyardists, but the difficulty of distribution and the inexperience of some of the buyers resulted in mixups and considerable losses. Haraszthy's troubles with the Republican-dominated legislature no doubt stemmed from his position as chairman of the State Democratic Committee and his unpopular position during the Civil War in favor of secession.

Haraszthy was meanwhile continuing his own extensive plantings at Buena Vista with the help of Chinese laborers, whom he also employed in a yearlong project of tunneling a cellar out of stone. The Chinese earned $8 a month plus board, in contrast with Anglo wages of $30 and board. Chinese workers also chiseled out the two tremendous limestone tunnels at Schramsberg Winery, the Beringer tunnels, completed in 1877, and the three tunnels in Livermore at Cresta Blanca, in the eighties. Schramsberg's founder, Jacob Schram, a San Francisco barber, continued during the sixties and seventies to shave and shear his neighbors on a house call basis until the vineyard matured and the winery went into production. Jack and Jamie Davies, the present owners, inhabit the handsome house which a team of New England carpenters built for Schram in 1875. It was Schramsberg champagne made by the Davies that Richard Nixon served the Chinese during his historic 1972 visit to Peking. In 1880, when Robert Louis Stevenson and Fanny Osbourne were encamped in a humble Silverado cabin on nearby Mount St. Helena, they called frequently on the Schrams. Stevenson described the vineyard and the tastings that he indulged in there in *Silverado Squatters*. Of Schramsberg he wrote: ". . . the stirring sunlight, and the growing vines, and the vats and bottles in the caverns, made a pleasant music for the mind." The frail young author went on to taste eighteen Schramsberg wines that day.

Haraszthy's liberal employment of the Chinese enabled him to expand his Sonoma vineyard until its large-scale production of wine and brandy brought general prosperity to the surrounding area. Land values increased twenty-five times over. Further, Haraszthy's methods and his writings on viticulture favorably affected the whole industry. He demonstrated by his prizewinning wines that irrigation was not necessary to produce superior grapes; he showed that hillside cultivation was practical and gave good results; he substituted redwood for oak casks when oak was in short supply; his lobbying efforts on behalf of the industry for years avoided prohibitive taxation; in 1862 he was instrumental in establishing the first California Wine Growers' Association in San Francisco; his importation of foreign root stock and cuttings constituted the foundation of the modern vineyard; and he made the first zinfandel, in casks, in 1862, introducing that variety to the West, although its origins are uncertain.

In 1863 Haraszthy sold Buena Vista to the Buena Vista Vinicultural Society, a corporation largely underwritten by W. C. Ralston, the San Francisco millionaire, but Haraszthy ran the show as general supervisor. Various difficulties set in, including a punitive $2.50-a-month tax on Chinese laborers, a disastrous failure of his French-trained son Arpad's first efforts at producing champagne—subsequent vintages turned out better—the explosion of a distillery, and a falling out with Ralston. The colonel decided it was time for a change of scene and resigned his position. By 1868 he was installed on a large plantation in Nicaragua. His wife succumbed to yellow fever only months after their arrival, and within a year Haraszthy disappeared, last seen in the vicinity of a crocodile-infested stream.

The robust drinking habits of the forty-niners also led directly to the development of a unique San Francisco industry, the brewing of steam beer. Ice in quantity, an essential element in the standard manufacture of beer, was unavailable in San Francisco until it could be transported after the completion of the railroad, forcing the local beer drinkers to invent a product that could be brewed without refrigeration. Made of barley, malt, and hops—no rice or corn or other lighteners—steam mash is naturally carbonated by the krausening method, rather than by artificial injections of carbon dioxide: after the first fermentation the aging beer turns flat; the krausen, a second, active brew, is added to the still beer, and the barrels are sealed; after three weeks the second fermentation produces pressure or steam, as much as 60 pounds to the square inch. To prevent the containers from blowing up, steam makers used an extra barrel hoop and special glass jugs with porcelain stoppers that anchored or screwed. A secondary industry grew up in San Francisco to provide the proper equipment, while several firms began to manufacture malt, one of beer's necessary ingredients. Francis Tilgner founded the Pioneer Malt House in the fifties, and Charles Bach, who succeeded him, ran it for the next fifty years until, still at the same Stockton Street location, it merged with the Bauer-Schweitzer Malt Company, which is still operating.

Steam, the only native American beer, was the sole brew available in San Francisco and the Pacific Northwest throughout the 1860's. With hundreds of breweries operating in the mining districts and San Francisco alone supporting twenty-seven plants, the words "steam" and "beer" became synonymous. After the importation of lager to San Francisco in the late seventies, the home-brewed steam became by contrast the rougher brew, and the import gained in popularity. In the 1870's William Lemp's Western Brewery offered only keg and bottled beer from St. Louis, Philip Frauenhalz's Bavaria Brewery advertised both lager and steam, "the best on the coast," and the Fredericksburg Brewing Company touted its product, steam or lager not specified, as a "first prize-winner." The North Beach area numbered at least ten breweries at the foot of Telegraph Hill, among them the North Beach Brewery, which shared the present site of the Francisco Junior High School with the San Francisco Stock Brewery. The Telegraph Hill delivery system for barreled beer was perhaps unique: climbing with his wagon beyond the delivery point, the driver could more easily roll the barrels downhill to their destination. In exchange for free beer, a crew of young men from the neighborhood steered the empties all the way to the bottom of the hill for pickup.

Traditionalists remained loyal to steam over the years, and in 1902 one of them, San Francisco District Attorney Billy Barnes, even wrote the "Ballad of Steam Beer" in its honor. There were still a dozen steam beer plants in San Francisco when Prohibition closed them. Only the Anchor Steam Brewery, dating back to 1851, reopened on Eighth Street, where it is still in operation, supplying about fifty Bay Area restaurants and bars, half of them in San Francisco.

The huge demand for lumber made sawmills one of the principal industries of the early days. Wood had uses everywhere: in building, in fencing, in timbering shafts and tunnels and constructing dams, flumes, and sluices at the mines, in planking city sidewalks, wharves, and roadways. Boatloads of redwood from northern coastal counties and Santa Cruz supplemented supplies of imported lumber for San Francisco mills. Henry Meiggs, an experienced, although at the time of the Gold Rush insolvent, New York lumberman, came around the Horn in January, 1849, with a ship full of lumber. With the proceeds from its sale, he established the California Lumber Manufacturing Company; by 1853 his schooners, loaded with wood from his mill in Mendocino, could dock at his own wharf in San Francisco. Meiggs' Wharf, a 2,000-foot projection from the area of Powell and Mason streets into the Bay, occupied the Embarcadero area now developed near Fisherman's Wharf and Pier 45. Under the new name of the Mendocino Lumber Company, the business prospered.

Meiggs, a former Brooklyn councilman, combined civic spirit, business bravado, and political savvy with a hefty dash of dishonesty. With Rudolph Herold he founded the San Francisco Philharmonic Society, the city's first orchestral and choral ensemble, personally donating the hall. He was on a back-slapping, first-name basis with half the city's voters and early won election as a San Francisco councilman. From that vantage point, he pushed through improvements to bolster his plans for the city's expansion from the North Beach area, where his original holdings lay, to the north and west, where he had invested heavily in coastal properties. Improved city grading and a new roadway, partly financed by Meiggs, made both sections of real estate more easily accessible, but the mercurial city economy failed to support a boom in that direction, and Meiggs and other substantial investors got no return on their money. Using stolen city warrants as security, he borrowed recklessly to cover his mounting pile of debts, while the shaky city economy, now verging on disaster, still refused to cooperate.

In October, 1854, "Honest Harry" Meiggs, one of the city's most popular citizens, bought the ship *American*. Under the pretext of preparing for a pleasure cruise on the Bay, he stocked it to the bulkheads with fancy provisions and casually set sail through the Gate with his family, including brother John, the city's newly elected comptroller. He left behind a large number of beachfront properties, the city's longest wharf, all his other business assets, a handsome house on Telegraph Hill with canaries still warbling in their cages, hundreds of ruined investors, and $1,000,000 in personal debts, $800,000 of it in embezzled city funds. By February the crisis had turned into panic, with twenty of the city's forty-two banks closing forever. Meanwhile, Meiggs had headed for Chile, where he was to make another fortune, this time retained, by building a railroad through the Andes to Peru. Over the years he repaid most of his San Francisco debts and increased his own wealth and fame well beyond South America. Although the California legislature passed a bill allowing him to return without prosecution, the governor vetoed it, and Meiggs died in Lima in 1877.

The businesses of a number of Gold Rush merchants survived to contemporary times, making their names familiar to most San Franciscans and in some cases to the nation. When Félix Verdier arrived in San Francisco in 1850 on the brig *Ville de Paris,* he sold the merchandise he had brought from Paris while it was still on the deck, the customers arriving and departing by lighter. The goods disappeared with such speed that Monsieur Verdier went back to France for a shipment large enough to stock a shop on Clay Street near Kearny. His laces and silks, bonnets, gowns, wines, liqueurs, and other Gallic niceties brought in fabulous profits. The store expanded and several times changed locations before it settled on Union Square in 1896. The 1906 fire destroyed the building; the 1909 structure which replaced it very much resembled the Galeries Lafayette in Paris. Until the new building was ready, the business operated like many others out of temporary quarters on Van Ness. In 1972 after 122 years of continuous direction by the Verdier family, the City of Paris closed its doors, unable to compete with the phenomenon of chain department stores. When the Liberty House group acquired the name and the premises, they were at first careful to preserve much of the original architecture, including the Eiffel Tower sign on the roof, to offer the same croissants and brioches which the city was accustomed to find on its breakfast tables, and to perpetuate such traditions as the forty-foot revolving Christmas tree, its branches soaring from the first floor all the way up to the rotunda. By the spring of 1974 Neiman-Marcus, the building's newest owner, announced plans to demolish it in favor of a newer design. Aroused citizens initiated procedures to have it placed under "landmark" status, which would have forestalled its destruction. It is now State Historical Landmark Number 876 and listed in the National Registry of Historic Places, designations which do not prevent its destruction or rebuilding, but ensure review procedures should state or federal funds be involved.

Many Gold Rush Frenchmen set up shops or staffed them, among them the Belloc Frères and Raphael Weill, who clerked at and later bought Davidson and Lane's and founded the White House Department Store. Like the City of Paris, it became a San Francisco institution and, like it, succumbed to the chain store competition, going down in bankruptcy in 1965. Weill, one of the city's greatest chefs, prepared gastronomic marvels for fellow members of the Bohemian Club, arranging memorable banquets for such visitors as the prima donna Nellie Melba, Sarah Bernhardt, Modjeska, Coquelin, and Paderewski.

H. Liebes, a women's specialty shop that also recently closed because of financial difficulties, did a thriving business in the 1870's in fur goods, especially apparel made of sealskin. O'Connor and Moffatt, dry goods merchants, another long-lived firm, traced its beginnings to 1851. Livingston Brothers, a department store that is still in business, dealt in notions and fabrics in 1876 at a Polk and Pine street address. In the nineties the management introduced ready-to-wear to a San Francisco clientele that had previously been entirely dependent on dressmakers. The New York establishment of W. and J. Sloane, located in the seventies on Market Street next to Gump's, created a still-thriving San Francisco branch to supply those of the Palace Hotel's rugs that were not on commission from French weavers. Sterling Furniture Company traded in the seventies on Sutter Street, while both the White Sewing Machine Company and the Singer Manufacturing Company had early outlets on Post Street.

Robert S. Atkins, at the corner of Clay and Montgomery streets in 1860, improved the town's sartorial splendor with imported men's furnishings. Roos Brothers, also men's clothiers, set up shop on Leidesdorff Street in 1860 and later moved to 33 Kearny Street, a three-story building on the Post Street corner across from the White House. The fashion plates of the time went there for "cassimere," Shaker flannel, merino wool, silk and serge suits; knickers and "breezy" sailor outfits for the boys; headgear, including top hats; morning coats and smoking jackets; and to put underneath it all, lamb's wool underwear. The modern firm of Roos-Atkins incorporates the two old-timers. Bullock and Jones, still dealing under the original name, dispensed imported men's clothing of similar class during the seventies from the 100 block of Montgomery Street between Sutter and Bush. The Hart Brothers, W. and I. Steinhart, and S. Fleishhacker, all prominent family names today, then ran tailoring shops and sold men's furnishings, while Louis Sloss, a name also currently well known, dealt in hides, wool, and furs during the same decade.

Whittier, Fuller and Company, which manufactured white lead and Pacific rubber paint, also stocked oils, window glass, and artists' materials on Front Street. Huntington and Hopkins, names that later dominated the railroad era, traded in iron products, hardware, and steel and barbed-wire fencing at the corner of Market and Front. For years A. S. Hallidie's California Wire

Works, established in 1857 at 329 Market Street, remained the only wire, cable, and rope manufacturer on the West Coast. The Curry Brothers bartered in imported shotguns, rifles, and pistols on Sansome Street. For those who became victims of Curry products, Nathaniel Gray, undertaker, provided "very stylish funerals," complete with Barstow's patent metallic burial cases and caskets. In business since 1850, the firm still makes final arrangements for San Franciscans under the management of its founder's descendants.

Anthony Zellerbach, the grandfather of James D. and Harold Zellerbach, sold books, newspapers, and writing paper from a shop at 509 Clay Street. In 1870 he embarked on a one-man paper distribution scheme with headquarters in the corner basement of Remington and Company, then the city's largest paper dealer. Within six years jobbing paid enough to make a move to his own store at Commercial and Sansome streets possible. In 1925, under the leadership of his son Isadore, the business converted to the Zellerbach (now Crown Zellerbach) Corporation, a holding company with $27,000,000 in assets. James D. Zellerbach, who served eighteen years as its president, also represented the United States as ambassador to Italy during the 1960's.

R. H. Macy's founder, twenty-seven-year-old Rowland Hussey Macy, came to California with his older brothers, Charles and Andrew, as a forty-niner. After a brief and unsuccessful fling at mining, they set up a general store in Marysville, modeled on Rowland's previous venture into merchandising, the R. H. Macy Needle and Thread Company of Boston. Retailing proved no more profitable than mining; within sixty days they sold the faltering clothing and dry goods emporium. In spite of early reverses, however, the Gold Rush did provide Rowland with the beginnings of his fortune: an investment in real estate netted several thousand dollars which enabled him to return east and launch the New York department store.

Another Gold Rush family that didn't stay long in California, the Michael Goldwassers, although they later became successful department store owners, acquired more fame through their grandson, Barry Goldwater. Grandfather Mike left Poland in his teens, learning tailoring in Paris and merchandising in London, and there married into a wealthy family and simplified his name. His unsuccessful efforts in 1852 to make a fortune in the California Gold Rush included a stint of itinerant peddling, which eventually took him to Arizona. There he settled as a clerk in a local store and later made a handsome success in merchandising. Michael and his wife, Sarah, formalized their early connection to San Francisco by dedicating to their parents, the Senator's great-grandparents, one of the stained glass windows now ornamenting the Sherith Israel Synagogue on Webster and California streets.

A number of pioneer California firms changed their emphasis through natural evolution. David Robison, on his way from New York to San Francisco in 1849, bought a load of green bananas in Panama which sold so readily when he arrived that he became a greengrocer rather than a miner. Within a short time he had produce stores on Washington Street and on Kearny. In obtaining his stock of tropical fruits from incoming vessels and in supplying fresh fruits, limes in particular, to outgoing voyagers, Robison was in constant contact with seagoing crews. His sailor friends amused him with gifts of gibbering monkeys, exotic birds, and the first goldfish to be seen in this country. Robison enjoyed the animals as curiosities, but when his customers wanted to buy them, he began to take his menagerie seriously and phased out fruits and vegetables altogether. Robison's son Ansel followed his father into the firm, which by the end of the century had a reputation as the leading dealer in rare and wondrous species of birds and animals. Robison's maintained agents all over the world to fill orders from private customers and zoos, both local and foreign. Frank Buck was one of Robison's men in the field, the start of his long career dedicated to wild animals. Robison's heirs, down to his great-great-grandson, have retained their connection with the firm. Now located on Maiden Lane, the House of Pets attracts crowds of shoppers who like to dawdle over the pedigreed cats, the talking mynas, the collection of brilliantly hued birds and parrots, and the latest look in rain boots for the family poodle.

One of the city's most prominent modern-day jewelry firms, Shreve and Company, had become well established by the early 1850's. Its Bostonian director, George C. Shreve, originally stocked fancy bric-a-brac, *objets d'art,* art goods, fine china and glassware, mostly of European pedigree. No longer family-owned, the store is now part of a syndicate. From its opening in April, 1852, Tobin and Duncan's Chinese Sales Room specialized in Oriental goods, although the proprietors also filled showrooms with European oils, Sèvres porcelains, antiques, and curiosities, many of which had once graced the palaces of European royalty. Joseph Duncan, one of the owners, was the father of the dancer Isadora. Another Orientalist, the Australian George Marsh, furnished a splendid shop on the Market Street side of the Palace Hotel in 1876, when trade with Japan opened. He stocked elegant Eastern goods and fine artwork, the same specialty for which Marsh's Oriental Art Company on Sutter Street is known today.

Gump's, the most famous among the city's dealers in Asian objects, did not develop that interest until after the turn of the century. Solomon Gump, the son of a cultured Jewish dealer in linens from Heidelberg, arrived in San Francisco in 1863. He joined the firm of his sister and brother-in-law, Gertrude and David Hausmann, who had preceded him by two years and prospered by making mirrors for saloons and cornices for the elaborate mansions that were then being built in the swankier sections of the city. Within a year, when the Hausmanns returned east, Solomon inherited the business. He later added a partner, younger brother Gustave, to the letterhead. As the firm grew, he made buying excursions to Europe, purchasing marble for pedestals and mantels, and collecting *objets d'art* for his own enjoyment. When his personal acquisitions grew too numerous for home display, Solomon moved them to the shop, where they immediately attracted buyers. Now launched into the sale of fine porcelains, vases, and figurines, he also incorporated a firm of art dealers, Jones, Wool and Sutherland, so that he could provide the pictures to fill the frames that he had begun to manufacture. As his collection of canvases multiplied, he furnished the saloons with oils, at first largely fleshy Parisian nudes, but then, as the drinking places displayed more elegance, with a whole range of subjects painted in the grand manner. Business was good. By the mid-seventies the firm transferred to larger quarters, a four-story gallery on Market and Second streets, and hired an assistant framer, a young Dutchman by the name of I. Magnin, who had arrived in the United States from England before the Civil War. By the turn of the century Gump's was the city's outstanding dealer in European and American art, imported antiques and furnishings, French figurines and other fine *objets,* onyx and Italian marbles, altars, mantels, frames, and related accessories. After the 1906 disaster, which destroyed the store and all its prized collections, the firm rebuilt in its present location on Post Street. Its stocks for the first time included the best in statuary, figurines, furniture, vases, carvings, scrolls, carpets, woodcuts, brocades and silks, jade and other jewelry from the Orient, a specialty which has grown over the years and made the store world-famous.

After a brief start in Gump's framing department, Isaac Magnin tried his own small shop on San Pablo Avenue near Fifteenth Street in Oakland. However, when it became clear that San Francisco offered rosier business prospects, he shifted back across the Bay to a Fifth Street address. His wife, Mary Ann, an excellent needlewoman, shared the premises with him. She stitched up elegant garments for women and children and sold notions, thread, buttons, needles, and the like. Prompted by the unexpected volume of dressmaking business and the desire to provide the elite clientele with fancier surroundings, the Magnins moved to larger

quarters in a grander neighborhood. The little sewing parlor
went on to become the exclusive I. Magnin chain of fine apparel
shops. Isaac's interest shifted accordingly from art frames to
women's clothing, and two sons, Emanuel John and Grover Arnold, joined the firm while it was still in its formative days. A
grandson later established a competitive business, the Joseph
Magnin apparel shops.

Levi Strauss joined the Gold Rush as a dry goods dealer rather
than as a prospector. Reared and educated in Bavaria, he had
kept the town records in Bad Ocheim before emigrating to New
York. When he docked in San Francisco in 1850, he unpacked
yards of heavy drill, needles, thread, and scissors, possibly destined to make tents, but used instead to sew up durable clothing
for the miners. When Strauss' sister married David Stern, he
joined the business, a tradition followed by in-laws in all the suc-
ceeding generations. The use of riveting distinguished Strauss'
work clothes, made them long-lasting and extremely popular. Today Levi's is a household word. In the 1960's the company, long
known for its compassion and civic concern, rebuilt an obsolete in-
ner-city plant rather than disrupt the lives of 350 employees, most
of whom wanted to continue working in their Mission District
neighborhood. As part of the refurbishing, the company installed
a mini-park, a basketball court, and chess tables for the use of its
neighbors and turned the building's corridors into a sales gallery
for minority artists. Current company policy also pays Spanish-
and Chinese-speaking employees to attend English language
classes and provides instruction to workers preparing for citizenship.

The manufacture of silk ribbons and spools of sewing silk during the sixties and seventies in San Francisco followed the agricultural introduction of the silkworm. The California Silk Manufacturing Company, the Union Pacific Silk Manufacturing Company,
and Belding Brothers and Company marketed silk products well
into the seventies, when business declined. Although the mulber-
ry trees had prospered and the legislature had subsidized the
growers to get them started, the American wages could not compete with the levels in countries where the industry was already
cheaply organized. Belding Corticelli Thread Company, although
no longer limited to silk, is still manufacturing thread in South
San Francisco.

Books, Inc., a chain of Western bookshops with a San Francisco
headquarters on Geary Street, has been dealing in printed matter,
albeit under other names, since 1851. The original retailer and
later publisher Anton Roman peddled books to the miners, carrying his stock by muleback. He had earned enough by 1859 to

equip a more traditional outlet in the Montgomery Block, which he sold to one of his clerks, Alexander Robertson, in 1881. As Robertson's on Maiden Lane, the company engaged in both retailing and publishing. In 1925 Leon Gelber and Harry Wyckoff bought it and added a third partner, Theodore Lilienthal, in 1926. In 1947 Books, Inc. bought it. Concentrating on the retail side, it merged in 1970 with Newbegin's, old-time book dealers who trace their origins as a subscription agency to 1891.

A large contingent of the German immigrants turned to merchandising, among them, Frederick William Dohrmann, the son of a Hamburg doctor, who arrived in 1862. He clerked for a time in a grocery, then manufactured breakfast foods. In 1868 he and Bernard Nathan, also of German origin, started selling household essentials, crockery, kitchenware, and the like. Until several years ago the Nathan-Dohrmann firm, the city's fanciest dealer in housewares, fronted on Union Square in the location taken over by Macy's, with branches and outlets throughout the state.

A number of early groceries survived into modern times. In 1850 Bowen Brothers sold food at 428 Pine near Kearny. Jacob Goldberg bought them out, along with Kroenig's on Sacramento and Kearny, in 1868. As Goldberg-Bowen, grocers and tea merchants, the company grew into a five-branched million-dollar enterprise, supplying imported delicacies to an ardent number of gourmets, many from outside the city, until a few years ago. In the Pine Street location, the management had installed one of the city's first telephones, telephone number: 1.

Another early settler, Domingo Ghirardelli, left Rapallo, Italy, well before the California Gold Rush had started. In Guatemala he discovered chocolate. In Lima, Peru, he manufactured it in a little shop next door to an American cabinetmaker named James Lick. Early in 1848 Lick left Peru for California, toting along several hundred pounds of Domingo's chocolate. Ghirardelli followed soon after the news of the gold discovery. In California he erected tent stores, first in Stockton, then in San Francisco, finally branching into several mining communities, where he traded in imported foodstuffs. In San Francisco he at first processed coffee, spices, mustard, and chocolate in a factory at 472, later moved to 415, Jackson Street. The elegantly reconstructed red-brick cluster of shops and restaurants known as Ghirardelli Square housed the San Francisco Woolen Factory before Ghirardelli blended chocolate there.

In the same neighborhood, Domenico de Domenico, an Italian immigrant of the eighties, opened the Golden Grain Macaroni Factory, which from its single pasta-making machine expanded into an empire that by 1962 had swallowed up the Ghirardelli Chocolate Company.

Joseph Brandenstein, who came from Germany to California as a teenager in 1850, made a success in tobacco rather than gold ore. His son Manfred, one of six, founded the still-thriving MJB Coffee Company in 1881. In the 1870's, Siegfried and Brandenstein on California Street advertised as tea importers, and Hart and Brandenstein, at 417 Market Street, as manufacturers and importers of saddlery, harnesses, Van Deusen whips and Spooner patented horse collars, a calling that has faded with the times. However, other coffee, tea, and spice dealers of the seventies did survive along with MJB: Hills Brothers, who were coffee merchants at 400 Sansome Street; A. Schilling and Company, at 7 California Street; and J. A. Folger and Company, at 104 California Street. An earlier firm, F. B. Folger and Hill, had conducted auctions on Montgomery Street. The Hass Brothers, California Street wholesale grocers in the seventies, now import green coffee on California Street.

As early as 1856 sugar production interested George Gordon, the versatile Englishman who had built South Park as well as San Francisco's first refinery. When the Pacific Sugar Company offered brief competition in 1861, the situation was immediately allayed by a merger. Gordon assumed the presidency, William T. Coleman went east temporarily as New York agent, and William C. Ralston served as a director of the new San Francisco and Pacific Sugar Company. Coleman later rose to prominence as one of the industry's leaders. Another early industrialist, Robert Oxnard, who headed the American Sugar Refining Company on Battery and Union streets, was a member of the family for whom the California town was named. The greatest of the tycoons was Claus Spreckels. His California Sugar factory, on Eighth and Brannan in 1865, later shared quarters and interests with his son John's Oceanic Steamship Company at 327 Market Street. In 1868 Spreckels tried a number of experiments utilizing domestic sugar beets instead of the commonly used raw cane sugar from Hawaii and China.

Spreckels came to the United States from Hanover as a penniless teenager. Stopping briefly in New York, he supported himself as a grocery clerk, then moved south. During the Gold Rush he migrated to California from North Carolina, where he had managed his own food business. As a purveyor in San Francisco he was doing what he knew best. Quick profits enabled him to branch out, first into beermaking, and then, with the founding of the Bay Sugar Refining Company, into the career that assured his fortune. Before he ventured into sugar processing, he spent a solid term of study and apprenticeship in the leading production centers all over the world. His Hawaiian connections helped develop the islands into one of the major sources of raw sugar. During the

nineties, when the Southern Pacific interests completely dominated the state, he and his son John joined James D. Phelan and
Adolph Sutro in building a competing rail line through the
agricultural center of the San Joaquin Valley. Pressures from the
Santa Fe, which had inaugurated its own line to Los Angeles in
the eighties, forced them into selling to the larger firm, in effect to
the Southern Pacific, which through rate agreements and stock
ownership dominated the Santa Fe. At the turn of the century,
during the height of the worst political conniving in the city's
already-spotted history, Spreckels' son Rudolph contributed a
quarter of a million dollars to aid the reform campaign spear-
headed by Fremont Older and District Attorney William Langdon.

The state's fishing industry, like its cattle industry and agricultural development, responded to the heavy demands of the Gold
Rush. J. Sposito, Gabriele Cuneo, I. Trapaui, A. Inguglia, A. Sil-
vestri, and A. Paladini, the last a familiar name on Fisherman's
Wharf until March, 1974, when it went out of business, ran thriving markets in fresh fish by the seventies; E. Antoni and Philip
Seibel dealt in fresh, smoked, and salted fish; Bertin and Lepari
and Charles Norris in oysters. Italian fishermen, who predominated, joined Dalmatians to fish in the bay and rivers and in ocean
grounds south of the Gate. They sold their catch largely from
stands in the San Francisco, Clay Street, and Washington markets.
Trawlers and feluccas, boats rigged with brightly colored lateen
sails characteristic of the Mediterranean, joined by an occasional
Chinese junk, formed the sizable fleet until the gasoline engine
replaced the sail in the early 1900's. By the mid-sixties the shrimp
beds in the bay attracted a large number of Chinese and Italian
fishermen, among whom Paladini worked one of the earliest
fisheries devoted to the tiny bay variety. He had outlets in all three
major markets.

In 1864 the city passed an ordinance that had obliquely anti-
Chinese sentiments. Requiring a $25-per-quarter license fee for
fishmongers, the measure drove many Chinese out of the business
and depleted the ranks of fishermen camped at China Beach. By
the eighties a large contingent of Chinese shrimpers settled in
China Camp near San Rafael across the Bay. The 1864 ordinance
left vacant many jobs for fish dealers, and when the men who replaced the Chinese altered prices to the suppliers, the industry rebelled. The fishermen, mostly Italians and some Dalmatians,
unionized, went out on strike, then finally solved the matter by
successfully organizing their own cooperative fish market. Many
fishing vessels are still painted blue and white in honor of Santa

Mission Dolores, 1856. *The Bancroft Library.*

"Dance of the Californians" (translation), the Indians at Mission Dolores, 1816, a watercolor by Louis Choris. *The Bancroft Library.*

Daguerreotype made circa 1850; reputedly the oldest photograph of San Francisco. Looking east from Clay and Kearny. *The Bancroft Library*.

Broadside published in Boston, M
sachusetts, in the 1850's. *The B
croft Library*.

"The Way to California," a Currier allegory, typical of the numerous cartoons published in response to the Gold Rush. *The Bancroft Library*.

THE WAY THEY GO TO CALIFORNIA.

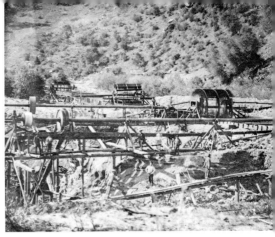

Six typical miners, 1850 (?). *The Bancroft Library.*

Mining in the riverbed. *The Bancroft Library.*

Northeast corner of Portsmouth Square, the original Plaza of the Spanish-Mexican era, in 1856. *The Bancroft Library.*

Stranded ships converted to land use; the *Niantic* as hotel on right. *The Bancroft Library.*

San Francisco street scene on a rainy night. *The Bancroft Library.*

FIRE IN SAN FRANCISCO.

In the Night from the 3ᵈ–4ᵗʰ May, 1851.

Loss $ 20,000,000.

Lith. Justh & Cᵒ. Broadway between Dupo...

Illustration for a letter sheet showing the San Francisco fire of May 3 and 4, 1851. *The Bancroft Library.*

Horse-drawn steamer of the early San Francisco fire department (no date). *California Historical Society.*

EXECUTION OF JAMES P. CASEY AND CHARLES CORA,
BY THE VIGILANCE COMMITTEE, OF SAN FRANCISCO,
On Thursday, May 22d, 1856, from the Windows of their Rooms, in Sacramento Street, between Front and Davis Streets.

JAMES P. CASEY AND CHARLES CORA.

hung by the Vigilance Committee at precisely twenty minutes after one o'clock—the for the murder of JAMES KING OF WM., and the latter for the murder of Gen. WILLIAM RICHARDSON. Both persons had been tried before the Committee, and found guilty. mise had been made to Casey that he should have a fair trial, and be permitted to ten minutes. These conditions had doubtlessly been observed. Casey was informed dnesday afternoon that he had been condemned to be hung. While under the charge Vigilance Committee his spirit appeared to be unbroken. Cora attracted less attention, nducted himself more quietly.

ight o'clock on Thursday morning, the General Committee was notified that Casey a would be executed at half-past one, and ordered to appear under arms. During rning preparations were made for the execution. Beams were run out over two of ndows of the Committee Room, and platforms about three feet square extending out each beam. These platforms were supported next the house by hinges, and outside es, extending up to the beams. Along the streets, for a considerable distance on each

side of the place of execution, were ranged the Committee—more than three thousand in number—some on foot with muskets, and others on horseback with sabers.

At a quarter past one o'clock Casey and Cora were brought out upon the platforms. The former was attended by the Rev. Father Gallagher. The arms of both were pinioned at the elbows. The noose was placed around Cora's neck, when he stepped upon the platform and stood firm as a statue, a white handkerchief being wrapped around his head. The noose was placed around Casey's neck, but at his request removed, while he had some three or four minutes' conversation with his priest. He then came forward and addressed the people.

After he had concluded, the noose was again adjusted, his eyes bandaged, and, as he was about to step forward, he faltered, and was about to sink, when the arms of two men were extended and supported him to the fatal spot.

Both prisoners being prepared, the signal was given, and at the same moment, the souls of James P. Casey and Charles Cora were launched into eternity, and their bodies became an inanimate mass of corruption. Neither of them struggled much, Casey showing the most physical suffering.

JAMES P. CASEY,	CHARLES CORA	YANKEE SULLIVAN,	EDW. M'COWAN,

ng to his own account, was born in rk City, in 1827, and at the time of h was twenty-nine years old; but by g Sing Prison certificate and descrip- his person, he is said to be at that time thirty-two years of age, which would m thirty-nine at the time of his death; his description is very accurate in espects, we are inclined to believe it liable in this.

Was born in Genoa, in the year 1813, and was forty-three years old at the time of his death. Of his early history little is known—the first we hear of him was at Natchez, Mississippi, about the year 1835. He was then quite a young man, leading a dissolute life, associat- ing with abandoned characters, and gambling for a livelihood. From there he went to New Orleans, where he took up with Belle Cora, with whom, in 1849 or '50, he came to Cali- fornia.

The subject of this sketch was born in Ireland, and at the time of his death was about forty-nine years of age. His vocation is too well known to require mention here. He came to California in 1856, and soon left for New York, from which place he returned to San Francisco in 1854. He was arrested by the Vigilance Committee, and terminated his career by suicide, for fear of being sent to Sydney, where he had been transported for felony, and escaped to the United States in 1849.

Who was indicted as an accomplice of Casey in the murder of JAMES KING OF WM., and who is now a fugitive from justice, has been a prominent politician in San Francisco, and held a responsible office under Gov. Bigler. He has been more or less connected with the leading political events of this city for the last four years. He has thus far eluded the vigilance of the Committee.

Letter sheet of 1856, showing the May 22 hanging of James P. Casey and Charles Cora by the Second Vigilance Committee. *The Bancroft Library.*

Above: North Beach in 1865. *The Bancroft Library.*

Left: Telegraph Hill. *The Bancroft Library.*

Below: an 1863 view of San Francisco and the Golden Gate seen from Telegraph Hill. *The Bancroft Library.*

Telegraph Hill steps in the 1880's. *The Bancroft Library.*

The Grand Hotel, 1870.
The Bancroft Library.

1870's cable car of the Clay Street Hill Railroad Company leaving Portsmouth Square from the Clay and Kearny Street corner. *The Bancroft Library.*

Cutting through Second Street in 1869. *The Bancroft Library.*

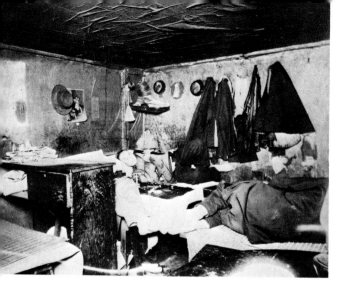

Interior of an opium den in San Francisco Chinatown, 1890. *The Bancroft Library.*

Tunneling in the Sierra to build the Central Pacific Railroad. *The Bancroft Library.*

The Chinatown squad of the San Francisco police department. *The Bancroft Library.*

Above: Cliff House from the beach at the turn of the century. *The Bancroft Library.*

Right: the Palace Hotel; the North Montgomery Street entrance to the Central Court in the 1880's. *The Bancroft Library.*

Above: Woodward's Gardens, a favorite San Francisco amusement park. *The Bancroft Library.*

Right: the Victoria Regina, the world's largest lilies, in Golden Gate Park in the 1880's. *The Bancroft Library.*

ct's rendering of the
evation of the Crocker
ce on Nob Hill. *The*
ft Library.

r of a stable of the
era. *The Bancroft Li-*

g north on Powell
in the 1890's, showing
ars and Nob Hill man-
The Bancroft Library.

Building the railroad, a work train in 1865. *The Bancroft Library.*

harles Crocker. *The Bancroft Library.*

Leland Stanford as governor of California. *The Bancroft Library.*

ollis P. Huntington. *The Bancroft Library.*

Mark Hopkins. *The Bancroft Library.*

William C. Ralston in fancy garb. *The Bancroft Library.*

Joshua A. Norton, Emperor of the United States and protector of Mexico. *The Bancroft Library.*

M. H. De Young of the *Chroni* at his desk. *California State Libra.*

Edward Blanquie, an early own of Jack's Restaurant, in 1896. *California State Library.*

Looking southeast from Nob Hill, the Claus Spreckels building, the tallest in sight, is on the corner of Market and Third streets. *The Bancroft Library.*

San Francisco street kitchen in use after the 1906 earthquake. *The Bancroft Library.*

Aftermath of the earthquake: the Crocker Restaurant in Union Square. *The Bancroft Library.*

Valencia Street Hotel after the 1906 earthquake. *The Bancroft Library.*

View down Sacramento Street from Powell. *The Bancroft Library.*

Relief camp on Nob Hill. *The Bancroft Library.*

Maria del Lume, the patron saint of the Latin fishermen, and there is annually a city ceremony with heavy Italian-Catholic overtones blessing the entire fleet.

The salmon industry developed earlier than the shrimp fisheries, before the Sacramento and San Joaquin rivers became contaminated with the debris of hydraulic mining. Salmon canneries, the first in the country, accommodated the catch. The Sacramento yield alone amounted to 200,000 salmon in 1857. The oyster beds which thrived in the Bay from the fifties until almost the end of the century also declined, as we have seen, because of silting and pollution from the mines.[40]

The market area centered in the Montgomery, Sansome, Commercial, Washington neighborhood and its fringes. In the adjacent 800 block of Kearny, John G. Ils sold French cooking ranges, a comment on the city's culinary leanings. By 1875 the bustling California Market was foremost among a dozen located downtown. It fronted on Pine and ran to California between Montgomery and Kearny. In 1876 B. E. Lloyd bragged to his readers:

> A visit to either the California or Centre Market is an interesting pastime, and never fails to astonish those who dwell in that part of the country where the year is but the alternating seasons of heat and frost. The abundance of tropical fruits would be remarked, and the great variety of California products would excite surprise and admiration as well. They would perhaps note the characteristic difference in the style of doing business from what they were accustomed. Almost everything is sold by the pound. A pound of apples is an incomprehensible quantity to those who have only bought and sold them by the bushel or dozen. The nearest approach to measurement that is had is "basket," "box" and "bag." . . . Thus the buying and selling of fruits and vegetables is attended almost unconsciously by a considerable traffic in lumber and jute fabrics, for all of which the consumer must certainly pay.[41]

A. P. Hotaling, the distiller and wholesale liquor dealer at 429 Jackson Street, furnished such bustling Montgomery Street restaurants as Collins and Wheeland, across the street from the Mining Exchange, with an average of fifty-five full barrels of whiskey a week. The firm also did a thriving business with the Barbary Coast resorts, which accounted in part for Charley Field's snide comment in verse, when in 1906 Hotaling's remained unscathed while all its neighbors crumbled in disaster:

> If, as they say, God spanked the town
> For being over-friskey—
> Why did he burn all the churches down
> And spare Hotaling's whiskey?

Many prominent San Francisco names figured in early wine and liquor sales: Eugene Verdier, with his partner Jean Marie Gales, sold spirits and cigars on Merchant Street; Wilmerding and Company, Front Street agents, represented Peruvian bitters and Delmonico's champagne; Hellman Brothers, also on Front Street, specialized in Krug Sec champagne; another neighbor, Lilienthal and Company, acted as wine, spirit and general commission merchants; and Sam Lachman advertised his wine vaults at 409 Market Street.

Because the quantity of champagne dispensed in the city's fancier houses of prostitution brought in such enormous profits, it was often the champagne dealer who backed a parlor house financially, lending and sometimes donating everything from rent to bail money, and paying protection insurance as often as it was needed. It was a small investment for the returns it brought.[42]

Excellent eating places were crammed into the bazaarlike atmosphere of the market area much in the manner of the Paris bistros in the original Les Halles. In 1854 a Parisian-style rotisserie on Kearny Street roasted to order poultry, meats, fish, and game bought on the premises or in the nearby stalls. Attached to the prongs of a three-rod iron grill, the succulent roasts turned slowly over a bed of coals filling a six-foot-wide fireplace. The charge for cooking a duck or chicken came to 50 cents, and all items had to be taken elsewhere for eating. The New Era German Bakery, run by Lautermilch and Durr on Montgomery Street, tempted its patrons with "pambernickel," rye, German, milk, and graham flour breads, as well as all sorts of confections. It later served meals and branched out to twenty-six locations. Sam Collins' and Jim Wheeland's venerable Montgomery Street resort, a landmark from the early 1860's until just before World War II, drew on the neighboring California Market for its supplies and some of its customers; other regulars flocked across the street from the Mining Exchange. Famous for its free lunch and hefty drinks, it admitted only males until the mid-thirties.

The California Market was one of the best places to obtain seafood, housing under its giant canopy such emporiums as Darbee and Immel's, M. B. Moraghan, the Pearl Oyster House, and Morgan's, where a typical two-bit meal consisted of a great mound of shellfish, a good small steak, and a mug of steaming coffee. Mayes Oyster House, still run by a crew of Yugoslavs, keeps on the current menu, besides Hangtown Fry, another early specialty, the oyster loaf. Consisting of a hollowed loaf of toasted French bread filled with plump fried oysters, the loaf earned an early reputation for being so good that it could calm the wrath of any spouse when brought home by an erring husband. Sam's Grill, also established in 1867 as a seafood restaurant in the California Market, specializes in cooking fish in its present location on Bush Street. In the early days its most popular dishes were breaded turtle steak and green turtle soup, and the proprietors continued to import live deep-sea turtles well into the 1930's.

Besides Mayes, Sam's, and Giuseppe Bazzuro with his famous cioppino, several restaurants built reputations on special dishes: Gobey's "Ladies and Gents Oyster Parlor" on Sutter Street on its boiled terrapin and its crab stew; the Buon Gusto on its dish of cioppino and polenta; Goodfellow's Grotto near the City Hall on its oysters; and Delmonico's on O'Farrell Street on its memorable lobsters. The Vesuvius, a modest Italian place next to the Clay Street Market, dispatched the cook's helper to the fish stands next door to fill each order as it was taken. The fish often arrived in the kitchen still flapping. Tadich Grill, known as the Wigwam when it opened on Pine Street in 1849, is among the state's 100 oldest enterprises. John Tadich, a Dalmatian immigrant, changed only the name when he became owner in 1882, but not the emphasis on fish and shellfish which it still retains.

Abe Warner's Cobweb Palace began to take shape in 1856 at the foot of Meiggs' Wharf not far from Three-Fingered Jack's and John Denny's bar and grocery store. For forty years he presided over an increasing clutter of bric-a-brac, assorted exotic animals purchased from incoming sailors, a collection of carved sperm whale teeth and walrus tusks that now resides in the De Young Museum, and a profusion of dust-laden spider webs which cloaked everything and eventually gave the place its name. The tavern became celebrated for its hot toddies and its excellent clam and crab dishes which the proprietor had learned to cook in Maine. His customary working attire was a respectful black suit, white apron, and high silk opera hat. The Waterfront area bustled with fish buyers, boardinghouse keepers, restaurateurs, and bargain-seeking poor folk, who threaded their way through garlands of drying mesh and islands of Sicilian fishermen sprawled in the sun, mending their nets with crude wooden shuttles. The customers dealt directly with the boatmen for their purchases or bought from wharfside stalls. The returning fishermen customarily breakfasted on deck, filling the dockside with the aroma of fresh fish grilling over charcoal.

Numerous boardinghouses dotted the streets running inland from the waterfront. Their tradition of simple home-style cooking is characteristic of the upper Broadway and North Beach neighborhood today, where several bistros and trattorias still serve family-style, and a few places continue to keep a regular table for boarders. Basques on the way to jobs as shepherds have always made the neighborhood their headquarters, and there are in particular several hotels and family-style eating places in the vicinity where the emphasis is on abundant but inexpensive Basque food. In the early days the usual meal, shared at a long common table, started with a steaming tureen of soup, a pasta or a risotto, on through salad, fish, roast, vegetables, cheese, dessert, fresh fruit, coffee, and a hearty vin ordinaire; it cost 25 cents. More elaborate eight-course meals with a full bottle of wine cost half a dollar. The fanciest meals came from the Fior d'Italia, opened on Broadway in 1886, and still a favorite place for special celebrations among the Italian community. Because Italians congregate today in large numbers in the North Beach area, it is as common to hear Italian as English spoken in the shops and on the streets; the upper Columbus Avenue shopping baskets bulge with fresh-made pasta, local salami, wheels of gorgonzola and imported parmesan, wild mushrooms, cardoons and fennel, bunches of fresh basil and dandelion shoots, sumptuous pastries, and rich brown coffee beans roasted darkly pungent for espresso.

The robust neighborhood cooking of the Italians, French, Mexicans, and Basques attracted a large clientele of bohemian writers and artists, who made the Washington-Jackson-Montgomery area the center of their social activities. They thronged to the Tour Eiffel, the Old Grotto, the Brooklyn Hotel, Luchetti's, the Fly Trap, Steve Sanguinetti's, Jules, and the St. Germaine. Luna's on Vallejo Street, a favorite evening hangout of Joaquin Miller, Frank Norris, and the literary crowd in general, prided itself on its spicy enchiladas, chili, and sausages and on its famous waiter, Ricardo, one-eyed, his waist entwined in a flaming red sash, his face adorned with a luxuriant mustache.

Coppa's, in the Monkey Block, the most famous of all the bohemian rendezvous, offered food above the general average, thanks to the considerable time Giuseppe Coppa, the Turinese chef, had spent cooking in some of the city's better restaurants. His specialty, chicken Portola, combined disjointed chicken, browned bacon, peppers, onions, corn, tomatoes, coconut shreds, and a spicy sauce, sealed inside a coconut, where the mélange stewed and bubbled for an hour, kept to a gentle simmer in a bain-marie. Coppa's generosity to down-and-out patrons was legendary. A contingent of his clients, including almost the entire roster of Bay Area artists, showed their appreciation at the turn of the century by repainting his place gratis after a hired worker had botched the job. The group fresco they produced after three months' labor covered three walls completely. The north wall, the first started, displayed a fierce five-foot-high lobster, which artist Porter Garnett set atop an island named Bohemia, along with two friendly nudes by the sculptor Robert Aitkin. A decorative border, bearing the names of all the bohemian cronies, circled the top of the wall below a parade of black cats. The artists generously endowed the work with caricatures, self-portraits, and a liberal sprinkling of musings printed in "English, Latin, Hebrew, and medieval French." The large clock mounted on one wall merged into the composition balanced on the legs of a supine Father Time, whose hourglass in one hand balanced his wine bottle in the other.[43]

Besides gathering for their country outings and socializing in a number of friendly city restaurants, the German singing societies and gymnastic groups made Deutsches Hall their headquarters. Now called California Hall, it became a meeting place for nearly 100 societies. Still a German center, it houses a large rathskeller-style restaurant. The Mission District, perhaps spurred on by the numerous German group expeditions to the early resorts in its vicinity, developed a resident German population which has continued to collect there into modern times. Among the first popular German restaurants of the early days, Zinkand's and the Louvre became the most famous, attracting a citywide clientele. During the nineties theatergoers flocked to Zinkand's following a performance, for the late suppers that had become a favorite pastime of that decade. At the turn of the century German family groups preferred the Heidelberg Inn for its Bavarian dishes and typical rathskeller atmosphere: clanking steins of beer, boisterous camaraderie, and the noisy orchestration of a German band.

The California Chinese population, which within a few years of the Gold Rush numbered well over 20,000, steadily increased. Ten thousand laborers alone came to work on the Southern Pacific Railroad, and thousands more to farm, to reclaim marshland, to tunnel out the vineyard cellars, and to work as domestics, laundry workers, and factory hands. By the 1880's the dozen or so blocks that made up San Francisco's Chinatown housed more than 30,000, hundreds crammed together in two enormous cellars running under Bartlett Alley and Washington Street. Entrance was secured by ladder. Although there was a wide variety of Western fare available in early San Francisco, its cooking was at a fairly crude level, and many Occidentals continued to prefer Chinese meals.

The city developed its vigorous interest in food and its vigorous tradition of eating out during Gold Rush days. However, good cooks were originally so scarce that a modestly talented cuisinière could make more money than a reasonably lucky miner. According to several early accounts of the 1850's, when the newly arrived Mammy Pleasant auctioned her services as a cook, the winning bid was $500 monthly. The millionaire François Pioche, a San Francisco resident from 1847, reportedly brought forty chefs from Paris to boost the city's feverish interest in French cuisine, the popularity of which increased with the age of the century. The Poodle Dog, the Maison Dorée, Jack's Rotisserie, Marchand's, the Maison Riche, the Maison Tortoni, the Pup, Delmonico's, the splendid dining room of the Palace Hotel—all served up extraordinary French cooking in banquets that lasted for hours.

Jack's has been serving meals in its original Sacramento Street location, except for a brief period in temporary quarters on Golden Gate Avenue after the earthquake, since 1864. When Jacques Monique, the proprietor from 1884, sold the place at the end of the century to Edward Blanquie, the new owner retained the name of Jack's Rotisserie, a name most likely selected for the frieze of jackrabbits that made up part of the early decor. Michel Redinger, who began working there in 1889, became a part owner after the 1906 earthquake. His brother Paul, an associate since 1903 and later a partner, rummaged through the ashes after the fire and found a menu dated April 17, 1906. The customers on the eve of the fateful catastrophe paid 75 cents to dine on tripe à la mode de Caen, green turtle steaks, pickled calf's heads, ragout of spring duck, and all the proper accompaniments, including a half bottle of wine. Kirsch or cognac added 12½ cents, or one bit, to the bill. Jack Redinger, Paul's son and the current owner, continues to run the place in much the same manner that it has always been.

Henry Bruen introduced into French restaurants Parisian cabinets particuliers in 1851, and a number of places accordingly had two entrances, one for the family, the other for private clients. Women, their identities shielded by heavy veiling, descended from shaded carriages to slip upstairs to the private rooms for intimate suppers and whatever romantic intrigues good food and drink might inspire. At the end of one of the typical repasts consumed in those days—as many as twelve to eighteen courses and taking a good six hours to eat—it was a wonder if any participant could do anything more dangerous than fall into a long, heavy stupor. In any case, the restaurants provided the appropriate accessories for dalliance: couches, locks on the doors, a system of buzzers and velvet pulls, and a corps of most discreet waiters. It was not unusual for clients to stay the night. Delmonico's and the Poodle Dog had elevators to the upstairs rooms. The latter was started by a New Orleans French family in 1849 as the Poulet d'Or or Poule d'Or, but the name soon became transformed by the usual miner's pronunciation. In its heyday it filled five entire floors: family groups on the ground level; banqueters on the second; and private clientele on the top three floors, which the management had thoughtfully fitted out with elegant parlors, bedrooms, and baths. In the nineties the Poodle Dog had one of the rare telephones in San Francisco, most frequently used by lonely male diners to call for female companionship. Such a volume of traffic existed to upstairs dining rooms that by the turn of the century San Francisco rivaled Paris as the naughtiest city in the world. As in Paris, such a state of existence was taken in stride; if anything, the citizenry was then, and is now, more pleased by its tradition of laissez-faire than bothered by it.

In the seventies Eastern nabobs, traveling west in private railcars to look into their investments, brought along their French chefs to sustain them in the wilderness. A great number of good cooks stayed on. Several restaurants soon began to call themselves Fashion restaurants, the modern Henry's Fashion being the sole survivor of the lot, signifying to the public at large that their cooking was in the individual style of Henri, Charles, Louis, or whomever. There was also the connotation of "fashionable" in the title, a characteristic that applied to more and more of the city's dining places, the French restaurants certainly included.

Bolstering its general image of naughtiness, San Francisco counted 3,117 establishments licensed to dispense liquor in the nineties, plus an additional 2,000 or more illegal pubs known as blind tigers. From the earliest days an epic promenade took place daily along the cocktail route from the Bank Exchange to Ernest Haquette's Palace of Art, to the Grand Hotel's Hoffman Café, the Palace Bar, the Reception, the Cardinal, and the Yellowstone. Besides buckets of champagne, imbibers downed Gold Rush Sazeracs (a shot of rye mixed with ice, bitters, absinthe, and anisette), typical of the new-styled iced cocktails served up by Johnny Farley's Peerless Saloon. Pisco Punch, a Peruvian brandy concoction that proved to be the most popular drink of the seventies, was invented by Duncan Nichols, the presiding figure in the Bank Exchange Bar. The regal marble-floored saloon, its walls hung with expensive oils, its ceiling ablaze with crystal chandeliers, outdid most of the competition in the nineties. Along with their drinks the strollers habitually partook of the free lunch along the route, a gargantuan spread set out between four in the afternoon and midnight. A typical day's buffet offered clams and oysters, fried or on the half shell, chili con carne, assorted sausages, headcheese, sliced ham, turkey, and corned beef, veal croquettes, crab salad, pigs' heads, sardines, pork and beans, stew, herring, jellied shrimp, venison, crab legs in a creamed sherry sauce, Saratoga chips, tongue, caviar, terrapin stew, smoked salmon, sweetbreads, assorted cheese, fruits, nuts, and all sorts of garnishes, and on oc-

casion a crisp whole suckling pig, juicy morsels of which each patron hacked off as his appetite dictated. Although some participants got carried away and ate more than a decent share, it was a
point of honor to exercise reasonable restraint. Fifty or sixty proprietors of the more stylish saloons once tried to abolish the institution of the free lunch; although a committee of their
representatives agreed that it should go, the tradition was too
firmly entrenched to be dismissed by fiat.

San Franciscans' sybaritic habits, which supported the food and
restaurant industries, the fancy resorts, and the wine and liquor
businesses, naturally supported another huge industry, the manufacture of cigars. Dozens of factories employing large numbers of
Chinese workers clustered along Battery, Front, and Market
streets. Among them, A. Ramon and Company, Meyer, Mish and
Company, Mercado Cohen, Charles Poppe, and Tisnado and
Verdugo, all of whom dealt in imported Havana tobaccos, advertised that their products were made by "white labor exclusively."

As a diversion, rides out to the Mission area and its several
amusement parks had always been highly popular. After the first
decade, a variety of excursions to resorts on the outskirts of town
and sometimes farther afield, began to catch the public fancy. San
Quentin, 12 miles north by ferry and the site of the state prison,
was a "noted summer and winter resort." Sumptuous Sunday
breakfasts at Dickey's Road House across from Golden Gate Park
or at the Cliff House overlooking Seal Rocks became a local institution. By the sixties the Point Lobos Toll Road provided a direct ride by horse car from Portsmouth Square to the shore for
half a dollar. Oceanside House, built of planking from a disabled
schooner, was probably the earliest beach resort to offer refreshments to the public. At about the same time Junius R. Foster, a
retired captain, operated the Seal Rock House on the beach, a
structural hodgepodge that he abandoned when he assumed
management of the Cliff House above it. The first Cliff House, if
Seal Rock House is not counted, was built around 1863 and managed by a team of Frenchmen before Foster took over the lease.
During his tenure the resort became variously the city's most
modish meeting place, a favorite hangout for local political types,
and a trysting place for gentlemen and their paramours. In 1887
the foundations suffered severe undermining when an 80,000-
pound cargo of dynamite blew up offshore. In 1894 a Christmas
Day fire demolished the building altogether. Within two years of
its destruction Adolph Sutro, who had purchased the property
along with all the surrounding acreage in 1879, built the most imposing of the several structures to rise on the site. The spires of
his Sutro Castle Cliff House ruled majestically over the rocks from

the same perch overlooking the Pacific that is enjoyed by its contemporary tenant. Under Sutro's ownership the Cliff House again became one of the city's fashionable rendezvous. By 1901 the Palace Hotel was offering its guests a daily round-trip excursion by horse-drawn coach between the city and the famous resort.

Roberts-at-the-Beach, another ocean gathering place that took on legendary character, started out as the Seabreeze Resort in 1897, catering primarily to the numerous horseback riders who galloped over the dunes of Ocean Beach. The Maltese proprietor, Dominic "Shorty" Roberts, and his descendants kept the rollicking establishment open to the public until 1955.

The Palace coach route to the Cliff House, which varied in each direction to afford its guests a scenic tour of the city, meandered through Golden Gate Park on the way out to the beach. The 1,000-acre expanse of greenery in the city's middle miraculously reclaimed a wind-torn patch of shifting sand dunes in the 1870's. William Hammond Hall, the first superintendent to attack the wasteland, designed and engineered the park much on the outlines that it fills today. Unfortunately the legislature, under whose jurisdiction it first fell, cut funds for the project in 1876 and the next decade therefore saw little progress. One exception was Avenue Park, now referred to as the Panhandle, developed in 1872 as a carriage entrance. Its narrowness was not part of the original design, but when determined landholders along the way refused to sell, a skimpy corridor resulted.

John McLaren, a young Scots gardener, became assistant superintendent in 1887, when only a small portion of the difficult terrain had been developed. With the political backing that Hall had lacked, he was very shortly named director, enabling him to develop Hall's schemes with his own elaborations. McLaren had learned a considerable amount about local conditions during his previous fifteen years as a landscape gardener for the wealthy residents on the Peninsula, where he had created the vast George Howard estate and tended the showplaces of Darius Mills, Alfred Poett, and William Ralston, among others. In his lifetime—he died in 1943 at the age of ninety-six—he planted an estimated 2,000,000 trees in the San Francisco area, including the avenues of eucalyptus that line El Camino Real. By his expert selection of grasses, trees, and shrubs to contain the shifting sands and by his development of underground sources of water, he transformed the desert into gardens, walkways, lakes, and playing fields. McLaren's stubborn nature helped him push through many of his projects and, perhaps more important, to prevent some to which he was opposed. He allowed no smoking on the job, no gloves worn by his workmen, no horseless carriages when they first appeared, no "Do Not Walk on the Grass " signs anywhere in his park. He demonstrated his hatred of statues by screening off any that appeared within his confines by artful plantings and natural camouflage. He was an inveterate blocker of trolley lines and paving projects.

During the nineties the park furnished a lively setting for recreational activities, its paths filled with cyclists, dog-cartists, and stylish gentry in fashionable carriages. Cycling during the eighties and nineties became all the rage, with the Bay City Wheelman and other clubs of bikers conducting extensive outings and formal competitions. The city's beaches drew enough two-wheel traffic to support the Wheelman's Rest, a café that by 1897 even had its own telephone. Men bikers increased the sale of knickerbockers in the local haberdasheries, while women cyclists, often roundly criticized, took to the paths in split skirts and, worse yet, sometimes even bloomers. Such costumes helped avoid entanglement in the normal cycle wheel as well as in the huge spokes of the high cartwheelers, a favorite exaggeration during the eighties, and the much-in-vogue cycles built for two, four, or more.

The Midwinter International Fair in 1894, set on 200 acres of the park, attracted more than 2,500,000 people. M. H. De Young, the publisher of the San Francisco *Chronicle* and a vice-president of Chicago's 1893 Columbian Exposition, envisioned a similar San Francisco world's fair to dispel the economic doldrums then gripping the community. By importing features wholesale from Chicago, De Young had the exposition ready to open at the beginning of January, 1894. The winter date was an intentional advertisement of the mild California climate.

The fair site centered on the present Music Concourse. John Philip Sousa's band and the Viennese orchestra of Fritz Scheel, both attractions at the Chicago Exposition, inaugurated the band shell, where open-air Sunday concerts still entertain crowds of music lovers every season. During the 1894 event the groups played a joint concert, perhaps the loudest feature of the fair. The De Young Memorial Museum dates back to the Midwinter Fair, although in those days its exhibits were housed near the present location in a brick building no longer part of the museum. The Academy of Sciences also began with the fair, as did the Japanese Tea Garden, then part of an authentic Japanese village. The Japanese, so infrequently seen beyond their own shores, had been something of a curiosity ever since Woodward's Gardens presented a troupe of native acrobats in the sixties. At the fair the exotically landscaped Oriental village was so popular that San Francisco decided to incorporate it as a permanent feature of the park. The directors appointed Makoto Hagiwara, a San Francisco restaurant owner, as manager.

Hagiwara, whose family arrived in San Francisco in 1870, had started his career washing dishes and cooking in local restaurants. Except for a few years early in the century when he and city officials could not see eye to eye on the area's development, three generations of his family had charge of the garden, expanding the ponds and plantings, bringing over bonsai from Japan, and constructing additional architectural features in keeping with a typical Japanese landscape. The income from the teahouse hardly compensated. With the United States entry into World War II, the entire Hagiwara family, of whom all except Makoto's widow had been born in this country, became involuntary inmates of detention camps. The board of park commissioners, who issued the "Notice to Quit," gave them three days to "deliver up" the tea garden. On the eve of their uprooting, and much to the concern of a number of citizens who felt that all of the Hagiwaras' personal improvements to the gardens should belong to the park, they transferred as many of their plants as could be transported to the Mill Valley nursery of a Caucasian friend. After their release, unable to negotiate successfully for their old position at the tea garden, the Hagiwaras sold their collection to the Fraser family, who eventually willed it back to the gardens in Golden Gate Park. In March, 1974, George Hagiwara, Makoto's seventy-year-old son, watched through a spring drizzle as his grandchildren, Michike Dawkins and Eric Nagata, unveiled a plaque set into a large rock near the entrance to the garden. The sculptress Ruth Asawa cast the lettering in Kanji and English with likenesses of a frog here, a salamander there. The inscription reads: "To Honor Makoto Hagiwara and His Family Who Nurtured and Shared This Garden from 1895 to 1942."

The Victoria Regina, a giant pond lily, was brought some time before from the tropics to the park's Crocker Conservatory, an addition of 1879 modeled on Kew Gardens. Acknowledged to be the world's largest flower, it was one of the fair's most talked-about attractions:

> . . . its blooming is one of the high lights of the eighteen-eighties. Every one talked of it. "Have you seen the Victoria Regia?" [*sic*] served to open conversation at dinner-parties, or to change the subject. Every one went to the Park to look at it. In single file the citizenry passed around the pond to marvel at the great flare of petals. It really was a remarkable flower. The green leaf of its foliage measured several feet across and lay like the top of a pool table on the water.[44]

The plethora of roadhouses, beach resorts, observatories, and entertainment gardens supplied the city's need to gallivant as continuously as possible. There were dozens of establishments in town devoted to keeping the population scrubbed, medicated, steamed, and well exercised, among them John D. Spreckels' Olympic Water Company, which supplied ocean water to the Lurline Baths and Plunge at Bush and Larkin streets. Besides the usual dressing-room accommodations, a few such places had private hospital connections, while others specialized in private rooms that could be rented for days or even weeks at a time. By the nineties public baths were a thriving institution; even the Occidental, the Grand, and the elegant Palace hotels had them. The most elaborate of all the city's bathing establishments, Sutro Baths, could accommodate 1,000 bathers in six enormous glass-enclosed swimming tanks, each at a different temperature ranging between 50 and 110 degrees. Three thousand spectators could observe from the galleries overlooking the pools and from the adjacent palm-studded decks and promenades. If they got tired of watching the splashers, they could stroll outside and enjoy the view over the Pacific Ocean. For the swimmers, a full day's exercise cost only 10 cents.

Establishments farther distant drew crowds who wanted more extended adventures. The continued fascination with country elegance helped assure the success of the extravagant Hotel del Monte from its opening in 1880. In what has become a tradition, more recently centered on annual golf and tennis tournaments and concourses dedicated to prize automobiles, the elite of San Francisco packed up their best clothes and traipsed down for a few days on the Monterey Peninsula. They put up in the luxurious lodge, enjoyed yachting, walks and drives, swimming, and soaking in the splendid scenery. When the fog rolled in, they chased the chill by settling in front of a good fire, went on to a dinner of epicurean proportions, and danced through half the night. The hotel's warmed bathing tanks, set in a handsome pavilion, attracted more swimmers than the cooler ocean waters. For several years a train jammed with guests from San Francisco made the daily run to Monterey in under four hours, a time that the automobile has reduced by half. The resort attracted San Franciscans as well as visitors, among them Lily Langtry, who during a theater engagement in San Francisco in 1884 that became part of the city's legend, made her way south to try out the favorite retreat.

Some of the city's less pleasurable aspects also gave rise to the development of local business. In 1863 the continued frequency of fire in San Francisco prompted a number of businessmen to organize a local insurance company, the Fireman's Fund. Until the termination of the volunteer fire department the management shared a percentage of the profits with the fire fighters, providing them an even greater incentive to put out the flames. Fireman's

Fund earned a national reputation as one of the few companies to settle its obligations in full after the Chicago fire of 1871. J. B. Levison, the director most instrumental in bringing the company to international prominence, was among the city's most active philanthropists. A flautist of professional abilities, he founded and presided over both the San Francisco Symphony Association and the San Francisco Opera Association and was a director of Mount Zion Hospital for thirty years, its president for twenty. He married Alice Gerstle, whose parents came to San Francisco in 1850 to found the Alaska Commercial Company and whose younger sister married Mortimer Fleishhacker, a member of another prominent San Francisco family. When San Francisco burned in 1906, the company's records along with it, the firm nevertheless paid its customers' losses, partly in cash and partly in stock. In the mid-1960's the group merged into the Fund America holding company.

If fire was a continuous San Francisco problem, so was water. At first drinking water was practically nonexistent, and problems of contamination were overwhelming. A brisk traffic developed in shipping pure water in tanks brought in by small steamers from Sausalito. In May, 1850, the city council authorized the digging of artesian wells and the construction of reservoirs throughout the city and at the same meeting voted that every household must keep at the ready six water buckets in case of fire. A year later, the earlier measures having proved inadequate, the council granted Arzo Merrifield a contract to pipe fresh springwater to the city, and the Mountain Lake Water Company came into being, although it took another year before there were sufficient funds to start work on the project.

William Ralston, more generally known for his prowess in banking, his control of early Comstock silver, his development of San Francisco industries, and his construction of such landmarks as the Belmont estate and the $7,000,000 Palace Hotel, also had a hand in furnishing the city's water supply. Ralston had been instrumental in developing the Spring Valley Water Company, which started in 1860, into the city's main supplier. Finding himself faced with increasingly difficult financial problems, he formulated a scheme to corner the water company's stock, enlarge the plant's facilities, and sell the entire package, at a handsome profit, to the city. In 1874 the 80,000 Spring Valley shares had a market value of $6,400,000. By the summer Ralston owned 49,608 of them, with control over a great number more belonging to his cronies. To guarantee the city's purchase, Ralston engineered legislation enabling the city council, rather than the people, to vote the issue. That accomplished, he entered the political arena to assure the election of candidates who would vote his way. Before the election, Ralston offered the enlarged company to the city at a purchase price of $15,500,000. The *Bulletin* and the *Call,* later joined by the Associated Press, exploded in editorial indignation, which increased as the September election grew nearer. The mayor announced that he would veto the water purchase if it passed the council. Ralston's supporters—and there were many who looked upon him as the town's first citizen—withdrew their advertising from the offending papers, while mobs of angry partisans attacked Fitch and Pickering, the respective editors. By August Ralston's empire had collapsed around him, and he was dead of drowning. The city, after many abortive attempts to acquire Spring Valley as a municipal system, finally purchased the company in 1930.

The lack of safe drinking water, together with the generally unsanitary conditions of the early Gold Rush community, accounted for an appalling number of deaths; a large contingent of phony doctors added to the tally. Those who escaped death en route to California still had to face the statistics of early San Francisco and the mining camps. The physician J. D. B. Stillman estimated that one out of every five persons died within six months of reaching California.

Of the approximately 1,500 practicing doctors who came in the first rush, perhaps only half had ever been inside a medical school. Since there was little knowledge about basic medical training even in the accredited schools, treatment generally resolved the symptoms rather than the underlying causes. Bleeding was prescribed for everything except childbirth; the pioneer Anchor Drug Company in North Beach stocked leeches until the late 1950's, and the nearby Lovotti-Rossi Pharmacy was still selling them in 1974 at $2.50 each. Those who did not respond favorably to the loss of blood—and they were the majority—faced cure by purging, cauterizing, or blistering. The widespread belief that emanations from the earth produced cholera delayed the development of a hygienic approach to the handling of the disease, with resulting epidemics in 1850, 1852, and 1854. There were few attempts to correct the universally unsanitary conditions that prevailed since their connection to illness was little understood. Beyond that, there were no specific statutes governing medical practice.

Unregulated fees varied so greatly that by October, 1850, the new Medical Society of San Francisco adopted a formal schedule: single visit or consultation, $32; additional visits for the same illness, or short office visits, $16 ($32 for an hour); night visits, $100;

postmortem, $200; cataract removal, correction of hernia, or skull surgery, $1,000; simple obstetrical delivery, $200 ($500 if breech); and vaccination, $32. There was no charge for anesthetic since there wasn't any. The newspapers felt that such exorbitant rates could hardly be excused, even taking into account that fees reflected generally high running expenses and included medications for which the doctors themselves paid dearly: as much as $1 a drop for laudanum and $1 a grain, or $64 an ounce, for quinine, the universal nostrum. Several of the doctors present at the Medical Society's fee-setting meeting, the second gathering since its inception on June 22, 1850, felt disgust at the suggested charges and withdrew. Dissension reigned not only over fee setting; as elsewhere in the nation, there were rivalries among homeopaths, advocates of hydropathy, eclectics, and standard practitioners. The medical fraternity itself disbanded within a few months. The city's doctors launched four successive local societies, as well as a state organization, but none of them prospered until the association of 1868, which is still in existence.

The opportunity to make a fortune in medical practice without enduring the hardships of mining attracted a legion of quacks. Diploma mills flourished, as did a market in falsified credentials. Attempts at reform often met editorial opposition because of the profit made on the extensive medical advertising. Pharmacists and doctors publicized cures for everything. Samuels and Company, a Battery Street apothecary, advertised itself as the city's sole agents for "Chewalla," a specific against rheumatism and gout, both widespread diseases among the mining population. A. E. Mintie, MD, a Kearny Street physician, announced his specialty in "nervous, private, and chronic diseases, lost manhood, seminal weakness, and all legitimate female complaints." And Dr. Robert Proby's ads modestly proclaimed:

Cancers cured. Sympathetic Warts and Ulcers cured. Read testimonials. We have hundreds at Office. Moles and Warts of every variety, which disfigure the face, hands and other portions of the body. Removed in 10 minutes by Dr. Robert Proby's vegetable system of treatment, which destroys the growth without pain or loss of blood, and in a few days not even a scar remains. Mother marks and cancers removed without pain or loss of blood. Catarrh permanently cured! Every form of ulceration successfully treated. Read testimonials from this city.

The patients flocked to the drugstores and the doctors' offices like pilgrims to Lourdes.

Diaries and journals of the time report on a doctor who ran a joint clinic and bar, doling out over the same counter aconite, opodeldoc, and quinine, or whiskey, rum, and brandy, depending on the circumstances; on a Dr. Thomas from Missouri, an ox driver before he took up medicine, who, seated on a white mule, dispensed variously colored liquids from his doctor's bag with no qualms of conscience since they wouldn't actually do anybody any harm; on a genuinely qualified physician, Dr. Palmer, who kept a gambling patient alive all night by infusions of beef tea, simultaneously determining the fee by playing cards with him; on a "King of Pain," who somehow earned his doctor's credentials during his former work as an upholsterer and who drove grandly through the community distributing remedies from a carriage pulled by a team of six white horses; on a German "chirurgeon," formerly a hairdresser-barber, whose universal treatment consisted of bark tea and bleeding.

The flood of practitioners, real and otherwise, made the profession less attractive to many of the authentically qualified physicians, a number of whom dropped their practice to try something else or worked at several callings simultaneously. Many of them entered politics: one was William Gwin, who joined in framing the California constitution and became one of the state's first Senators; another was Dr. J. Townsend, who opened the first doctor's office in San Francisco in 1846, carrying out most of his duties on horseback covering a 500-mile territory, while serving simultaneously as alcalde of San Francisco and as one of the first five public school trustees. Victor Fourgeaud was likewise a school trustee; T. M. Leavenworth was elected mayor in 1848; and Dr. Stephen Harris, the third mayor, a New York State commissioner of health for six years before he joined the Gold Rush, and San Francisco comptroller in 1853, ran a pharmacy along with his medical practice.

Li Po Tai, a Gold Rush doctor from China, the first so recorded, prescribed herb teas from his office facing the square but never entered politics. He agreed medically with the French and Italians that the liver was the seat of most medical problems, but whether he practiced acupuncture is not recorded. Dr. Berryman Bryant, who came to the Gold Rush with the actual intention of practicing medicine, brought along five trunkfuls of medications, in contrast with the four other physicians in his company, also from Alabama; they filled their cases with mining equipment. In his *Reminiscences of California 1849–52,* Dr. Bryant recounted that after a few days in San Francisco he hired a sailboat for Sacramento, a journey that took him five days. Once there he could find no proper place to store his medicines, so he shoveled out five large holes beyond the limits of the city, where he buried them. Covering the trunks with earth, he added stakes at each end of the mound so that they resembled gravesites. He then could be assured of supplies whenever he needed them.

When San Francisco's first public health officer, John Williamson Palmer, a Baltimore physician, arrived in August, 1849, he had to sleep on the sand dunes without shelter. Besides the general lack of facilities and the overwhelming task of treating the entire ill population of the city, there was at first little pay. When Dr. Palmer set up his own office, which he financed with his winnings at monte, he took in many vagrant charges, assigning them beds made of packing cases and having their meals brought in from a nearby restaurant. He wrote in later years that he came to San Francisco penniless, and left penniless, but that he experienced more than any man the entire sordid adventure of the formation of the community. Part of it was his early discovery that it was physically impossible for him as city physician to handle the throngs of indigent sick who were his responsibility. In a few years, when he left California, he turned to professional writing, serving on the staff of the New York *Times,* among other publications, and never returned to the practice of medicine.

During the Gold Rush the ill and the poor of San Francisco organized a sickman's march on the municipal council to inspire measures for their care. In response to their indignation, the board contracted with a Dr. Melhado to operate a private hospital for the care of public wards. Melhado's own patients, though hardly surrounded by luxury, were considerably better off than the public charges, forty or fifty of whom were jammed into each half of a small shed, with one nonmedical assistant in attendance. Street preacher William Taylor's ministry to the patients revealed to him the inhumane conditions that prevailed; his public denouncements served as the basis for a crusade for improvement. The council canceled its arrangements with Dr. Melhado and awarded the contract instead to Dr. Peter Smith, who agreed to care for each patient in his private hospital for $5 a day, none of which he could subsequently manage to collect in cash. Dr. Melhado declined to accept the arrangements and refused to release the patients; they in turn declined Dr. Melhado's further hospitality and hobbled and limped as best they could to the newly designated facilities. The unfortunate thirty who were too ill to go along found themselves the further victims of Dr. Melhado's methods when he refused to provide either care or food until the city paid him what it owed him. Another dozen invalids made their way with great difficulty to Dr. Smith's, while the Strangers' Friends Society, shepherded by the Reverend Mr. Taylor, carried the rest.

Dr. Smith's payments in scrip soon mounted to a noncashable

$64,431. When the hospital burned in an October, 1850, fire, destroying his investment of $40,000, he resigned his official post and sued the city for his pay. The court's favorable judgment forced the city to auction off real estate to raise the cash, inspiring other scrip holders to press similar suits; further difficulties arose when some citizens challenged the legality of the auction sales. The resulting mess kept some of the property titles clouded for as long as twenty years.

In May, 1850, the well-endowed State Marine Hospital opened a San Francisco infirmary for indigent sailors. A year later the city hospital merged with it, making it the community's first large-scale public health facility. It operated for five years, the last three in a federally built four-story brick building. The City and County Hospital on Stockton Street began service in 1855.

Cholera, which had not been a problem before October, 1850, when it was brought in on the *Carolina* out of Panama, became epidemic by November of the same year. At the peak of the attack a dozen persons died daily, and according to the *Alta,* within two months more than 500 people had succumbed to the disease. To meet the crisis, the city council convened a board of health which met in daily sessions; empowered a jury to investigate the polluted streets and generally unsanitary conditions throughout the city, assigning a tough fine to those who contributed to the problem; and set up a hospital on Broadway between Stockton and Dupont devoted entirely to cholera patients.

The French and German benevolent societies sponsored early day hospitals and, like the State Marine group, which pioneered the idea, offered low-cost prepaid health care to subscribing members. The Sisters of Mercy, a Catholic order, directed the city's most successful charity hospital after their arrival from Ireland in 1854. In spite of attacks against them, mostly political, they earned the community's allegiance, and by 1857 the nuns had taken over the old State Marine facilities. By the early sixties, under the new name of St. Mary's Hospital, they had installed a plumbing system featuring hot and cold running water to every floor that was a model of its kind and made St. Mary's the city's finest medical facility.

In 1859 a thirty-seven-year-old Gold Rush surgeon, Elias Samuel Cooper, enrolled ten students in the state's first medical school in his fourth-floor offices on Mission Street. In spite of its connections with the University of the Pacific, the school survived only two years after Cooper's untimely death in 1862 of a brain tumor. Hugh Huger Toland, a South Carolina physician who in 1852 had retreated from mining to medicine, took over most of the Cooper faculty and founded the Toland Medical College on

Stockton Street opposite the City and County Hospital and reasonably close to his Montgomery Street offices. In 1870 Toland became involved in a dispute over policy with Dr. Levi Cooper Lane, Elias Cooper's nephew; Lane resurrected the old medical school, seriously depleting Toland College's staff and student body. Both institutions managed to survive their differences, the Cooper medical group moving to a fine new brick building in 1882 and becoming a part of the Stanford Medical School in 1908. Meanwhile, in 1870 Toland deeded his property to the University of California; the actual transfer was not completed until 1873, when the school named a chair after him. In 1898, on a site donated by Adolph Sutro, the medical school moved to Parnassus Heights, along with the university's schools of dentistry and pharmacology.

When Toland's associate, Dr. Richard Beverly "King" Cole, succeeded him, he pushed forward a plan for the affiliation of the professional schools with the rest of the university in a unified campus. Part of his scheme, which was unsuccessful, centered on moving the headquarters to a site in the western end of the city. Among other difficulties, the law school balked at the move. Mayor Sutro, besides donating large parcels of land to the university, began to assemble a first-rate library on its behalf. The books, stored in a Mission District warehouse, managed to survive the 1906 disaster, but the city authorities mistakenly gave out a number of them to the victims of the earthquake and fire. Some wanted them solely for their paper content. Although Cole's dreams for a centralized university in San Francisco never materialized, his administrative talents found an outlet in the presidency of the American Medical Association. Robert Armistead McLean, the medical school's first native-born graduate, received his degree in 1874 and went on to become dean of the medical school faculty. His father, Dr. Samuel Merryweather McLean, had ministered to Gold Rush miners, and Robert was born in the Mother Lode country.

Another forty-niner, Dr. Henry Daniel Cogswell, practiced dentistry in an office on Portsmouth Square, but became better known for the dozens of drinking fountains he bestowed on San Francisco and other communities. The millionaire dentist, a teetotaler, hoped to encourage abstemiousness in the population, but it was a losing battle. The good doctor also founded the West's first tuition-free technical school, Cogswell Polytechnical College, in 1887, endowing the Folsom Street campus with one and a half million dollars earned from speculation in stocks and real estate, which paid even better than dentistry.

Although the introduction of medical training in San Francisco assured some improvement over the early practice of medicine, there was still much dispute over philosophical affiliations and educational theory generally. The average doctor's training consisted of less than a year of instruction coupled with a program of practical apprenticeship, and for several decades there was no procedure for licensing whatsoever. The first real spur to the profession came with the completion of the railroad, making San Francisco possible as the site of the 1871 national convention of the American Medical Society. The local doctors had to be on their best behavior, and the exchange of ideas, although it did little to further an understanding of antiseptic procedures or to ameliorate the differences between the eclectics and the regulars, stimulated the professionalism of Western medical practice. On the other hand, the 214 delegates also heard their august president proclaim that women were not fit by nature to be physicians. San Francisco had a woman doctor as far back as 1853, when a Dr. Kammel opened her office on Dupont Street and advertised the successful treatment of cancer, dropsy, scrofula, and female disorders.

In 1874 the state finally introduced the first statutes governing the licensing of doctors. By 1876, with the passage of the Medical Practice Act, licensing became obligatory. Since several schools of medical theory still persisted, a separate board had to be set up to regulate the homeopaths, the eclectics, and the standard practitioners. As late as 1910 one-quarter of California's 4,500 physicians still divided their allegiance between eclecticism and homeopathy.

From the opening of the Marine Hospital, reliable records of the city's health problems became more easily available. The leading cause of admissions during the latter eight months of 1850 was diarrhea. Coupled with dysentery, it accounted for one-third of the hospital's patients and killed more than fifty of them. Hepatitus, typhoid fever, cholera, and malaria were prevalent, while venereal diseases and delirium tremens claimed their share of victims. Scurvy, rheumatism, pneumonia, and bronchitis took a heavy toll, especially of travelers and miners, who suffered prolonged exposure to dank weather and other unhealthy surroundings. In San Francisco deaths for the year ending in July, 1851, amounted to 1,475; from 1851 through 1853, 4,000 died, most of them males, and most of them young.

The rudimentary state of medical knowledge certainly contributed to the large number of fatalities, along with the lack of sanitation, the absence of antiseptic precautions, the deficiency of anesthetics, and the prevalence of dubious remedies. T. D. Borthwick, an English national who recorded his Gold Rush adventures, remarked on the peculiar American phenomenon of "imbibing quack remedies in huge quantities." Every argonaut was "a walking apothecary, laden with boxes of pills and bottles of vile liquids for every known disease. The moment they imagined that there was anything wrong with them, they dosed themselves with all the medicines they could get hold of, so that when they really were taken ill, they were already half poisoned with the stuff they had been swallowing. Many killed themselves by excessive drinking of the wretched liquor which was sold under the name of brandy."[45]

Many of those on the death rolls set out deliberately to take their own lives. In 1874 B. E. Lloyd reported fifty-eight suicides in San Francisco with sixty-four the year following—more than one per week. There was no pattern attributable to race, health, or sex, but swift changes of economic status and overwhelming personal difficulties, the fickleness of fate, seemed most likely to derange judgment and admit depression. Half the suicides shot themselves, a good proportion took their lives by hanging, drowning, or slitting their throats, and the rest did themselves in by gulping down opium, strychnine, or other poisons. Another large San Francisco group succumbed to the pressures of the California adventure by losing their sanity. The proportion of San Franciscans adjudged insane exceeded that in more settled communities by an unusually large degree. Their tolerance by the city sometimes reached such extremes as led to the entire populace's entering into the fantasies of Emperor Norton.

XII

Fire

SAN FRANCISCO suffered six devastating fires in the eighteen months between December, 1849, and June, 1851, most of them clearly set by incendiaries as a screen for plundering and robbery. The blame usually fell on the Sydney Ducks. The first huge conflagration started on Christmas Eve in Denison's Exchange and counted for a loss of $1,250,000. On May 4, 1850, a blaze in the same general area swept away several blocks with more than 300 buildings in seven hours. The loss came to more than $4,000,000. The firm belief that the fire had been set by arsonists led to an offer of a $5,000 reward for information leading to their arrest. Since the deliberateness of the fire's origin could not be proved, however, the suspects escaped without difficulty. Several contemporary accounts remark that appeals for assistance from the large crowds that had gathered went coldly unheeded until accompanied by payment. The price was $3 an hour for fire fighting, $60 for a cartload or $1 for a bucket of water. When confronted with demands for payment by a group who had lent their services gratis, the city council, with some indignation, passed an ordinance instead that made the giving of such aid obligatory, with penalties for noncompliance. As an aftermath of the May fire San Francisco also framed the first California building ordinance, one that prohibited the construction of any building made of cotton cloth.

The fire of June 14, which erupted before the rebuilding had been completed from the previous holocaust, raged for three days, consumed several hundred houses, and accounted for a loss of just under $5,000,000. On September 17 a smaller fire, confined mostly to one-story frame dwellings, resulted in a loss of no more than $500,000. A minor blaze on the Clay Street Hill destroyed the City Hospital owned by Dr. Peter Smith on October 31 and severely injured a number of patients. Although in monetary terms it was relatively inconsequential and the amount of destruction did not qualify it as among the half dozen major disasters of

246

the period, the suffering that it caused made it significant in the minds of the citizens.

The next million-dollar blaze in December was notable for the fact that several of the new and supposedly fireproof iron buildings were total disasters. On May 3 and 4, 1851, a strong wind fanned a bad fire into a flaming horror: it consumed a large part of the business district—22 blocks in all—between 1,000 and 2,000 houses, some by blasting to thwart the progress of the flames, and a number of storeships, the *Niantic* among them. De-Witt and Harrison saved their building by pouring 83,000 gallons of vinegar on it. Many people were killed and many more injured. This time the loss totaled $12,000,000. The merchants stored what goods they could rescue on board ships in the harbor, but robber gangs nonetheless made off with enormous quantities.

The increasing destruction by fire was recognized officially as early as 1850, when the design for the city seal incorporated a phoenix. The May holocaust, followed by another blaze on June 3, 1851, finally aroused the city to action: the authorities arrested the suspected arsonist but had to release him again on a technicality. The citizens, their patience exhausted, began to think seriously about taking matters into their own hands. Incendiarism was a major force behind the formation of the Vigilance Committee of 1851.

Robert S. La Motte, in a letter to a friend in Pennsylvania written in March, 1851, some three months before that committee was an actuality, described the atmosphere created by the continuously troubling blazes. At 4 A.M. on March 4 the cry of fire aroused him, and donning his appropriate blue shirt, belt, and glazed cap, he rushed to Central Wharf to help contain the flames that were consuming two fine steamboats and threatening several others. The following evening, anticipating a good, quiet sleep to make up for the hours missed the night before, he dozed soundly until midnight, when the alarm again aroused him. A blaze had been set in some stores within a block of his office, and a strong wind augured considerable danger. Cinders fell steadily on the building and once or twice ignited it. A group of friends helped him remove his iron chest, books, papers, and other valuables and extinguish the fire. Although his "little habitation" came through safely, eight or ten others burned to the ground.

La Motte wrote at length of his enthusiasm for the fire companies, whose vigorous participation was in marked contrast with the behavior of the earlier reluctant volunteers:

Almost without exception the firemen here are gentlemen & al-

most every gentleman in the town is a fireman. I never saw any men
work as well and as hard as they do here at a fire, fearing nothing &
caring for nothing but stopping the destruction. And then after it is
over instead of stopping a while to have a fight—as they file past
one another on their way home—you hear such cries as—Hurrah
for the "Howard"!—She's always the first in service!—Three cheers
for the "California"—She is *some* [sic] at a fire!—Here comes the
"Monumental"! good for the Baltimorians—&etc. [sic] but nothing
unkind or tending to interrupt the universal harmony and good
feeling between the different companies. The only difficulty is that
the City is so *flat broke* that the companies cannot get good engines,
or even have the old ones repaired.[46]

Before the disastrous Christmas Eve fire of 1849, San Francisco
had had no fire department. The day after that great blaze, an
alarmed citizenry, in spite of the fact it was Christmas Day, had
called a mass meeting to organize into proper volunteer companies. The town then had only two inefficient engines: one, a well-
worn veteran in disrepair, belonged to an importing firm; the other, an 1820 model originally used to wet down the gardens on
President Martin Van Buren's New York estates, had been
brought around the Horn to pump water at the mines. Mayor
John Geary supplemented them as quickly as possible with an order for two sidestrokers from New York for Engine Companies
Number One and Two, and William D. Howard bought the engine for Company Number Three. Yet these first companies
could not keep up with the ever-increasing outbreaks of fire. After the city's sixth major conflagration, of June, 1851, the community took more formal measures for its protection, looking, for
example, to the volunteer system so successful in New York. New
companies formed, and the council allocated funds to pay a chief
and his assistants, to contribute to the construction of engine
houses, and to aid in the placement of water tanks and cisterns.
Before there were reservoirs, the critical lack of water had dictated a fire-fighting technique which depended largely on blasting
buildings with gunpowder or plastering them with mud, which
was usually in abundant supply. Although blasting was destructive, it at least helped block the advance of the flames.

For the first years the companies themselves raised the money
to complete and furnish their houses, to buy their uniforms, to
purchase their engines and equipment, and to host the extravagant social events for which they became famous. The spirited volunteers quickly won the city's affection. Participating in all the
balls, parades, and other festivities, they provided one of the principal sources of social life; it was a mark of distinction to be a volunteer. Many men had served as volunteers in their home com-

munities, and the new companies drew from a cross section of the population, members often enlisting on the basis of geographic origins or common work experiences. The fierce competition which developed among the companies was eventually a factor in their dissolution. They contrived to outdo each other in the elegance of their quarters, the splendor of their engines, their prowess at fisticuffs, the accuracy of their target shooting, the lavishness of their entertainments, the sweetness of their singing voices, the stylishness of their parade uniforms, and, above all, the speed with which they arrived at and conquered a fire. The citizens attached themselves with partisan passion to favorite companies, cheering them on, often running along with them, lending a hand with the rope towing the engine.

The volunteer fire department consisted of fourteen engine companies, three hook and ladder companies, and a contingent of boys who, when darkness fell, ran ahead of the engines, bearing flaming torches to light the way over the hazardously pitted roadways. By the sixties there were half a dozen hose companies in addition, and steam engines, at first scoffed at, began to replace the old hand-drawn machines. Lookouts and alarm bells in each of the company houses supplemented a twenty-four-hour fire watch in City Hall for all eight districts. At the sound of the bell the entire town turned out, the volunteers to fight the blaze and the rest to cheer on their favorites.

Engine Company Number One with members drawn mostly from New York, came to be known variously as Empire One; as Independent One, referring to its origin as one of the first three companies; and as Broderick One, after its first foreman, Senator David C. Broderick, who had been instrumental in the establishment of the original department. Another member, Frederick Kohler, a business associate of Broderick's in Moffat and Company (an early manufacturer of coinage) was the city's first fire chief. The most colorful chief, David Scannell, previously a foreman of Engine Number One, was elected through the political push of the New York faction. Scannell came west with Stevenson's Regiment in 1847 and distinguished himself some time after as the sheriff who almost fell afoul of the Vigilance Committee for refusing to turn over to them the prisoners James Casey and Charles Cora. His other considerable achievement was as a gourmet, a quality admired in San Francisco from the beginning. It is said that people came to the Occidental Restaurant on Washington Street just to watch Scannell and his five regular companions dine. The proprietor kept a permanent round table for them, all of them trenchermen of enormous physique and all of them volunteer firemen. They sometimes spent as much as five or six hours at a meal, which would always include the finest delicacies available. Another of Empire One's distinguishing features was its crack target company. After the fashion in New York, Empire One organized 125 rifle-bearing members into the Empire Guards, with annual public competitions.

Also comprised largely of New Yorkers, Engine Company Number Two, the old Protection Company, reorganized and adopted the name Manhattan Two. Its foreman, Con Mooney, owned the Pony Express Saloon, where he ran cock and dogfights, at that time legal. A burly man treated therefore with respect, he once had a finger shot off in a barroom duel. Mooney rose to assistant chief but to his disappointment never won the top post. Years later, in the early eighties, when San Franciscans could ride from town out to the Pacific beaches on the new Ocean Railroad, Mooney led a group of entrepreneurs in providing them with amusements and provisions. Unfortunately, he also sold them real estate, none of it his to sell, and some of it several feet under the Pacific Ocean. When his activities came to light, the authorities tore down the shantytown in which he had housed himself, his cronies, and all their illegal enterprises.

The third New York company was Knickerbocker Engine Company Number Five, one of whose members, Curly Jack Carroll, earned a place in history by dashing off to a fire instead of to his wedding, dressed in the $100 suit bought for the ceremony. The New York company's most famous member, however, was a woman, Eliza Wychie Hitchcock, always called Lillie, the daughter of a well-to-do Southern family. Her father, Charles, added considerably to the family fortunes when he gave up his commission as an Army surgeon and took up private practice in Gold Rush San Francisco. Her mother, Martha, reared in the strictest traditions of the Southern belle, never gave up her ties to the soil of the South. Wherever she was, she relentlessly pursued the society of Southerners, with the exception of occasional worthwhile celebrities. She could not bear to see the decay setting in at Huntington plantation in North Carolina where she had grown up and placed the high bid when it was finally auctioned off after her parents' deaths. Such was her zeal that when she could not beat the taxes, she burned the mansion by her own hand rather than allow it to fall to the squatters who had encamped there. Seven-year-old Lillie presumably witnessed the act.

The Hitchcocks came to San Francisco in 1851, when Lillie was eight, and settled into the life of uprooted Southern aristocrats. Seven months later Lillie had a second traumatic brush with fire and to it owed her unflagging allegiance to Engine Company Number Five. John Boynton, a volunteer with that company, saved her from a blaze in the unfinished hulk of the Fitzmaurice Hotel, which she was exploring with several of her playmates. When her escape was blocked, Boynton cut through the roof, lowered himself on a rope, and hauled her to safety on his shoulders. Two of her companions didn't make it. After that, whenever Lillie saw Number Five racing to a fire, she ran along with them, helping them pull their engine up the hills. Her parents were horrified. When their exhortations failed, they sent her off to school in the country. Although she declined to the point of illness, they remained adamant.

An accident which threatened the sight of her eye finally forced them to retrieve her. After a lengthy confinement in the family's suite in the Occidental Hotel, during which the fire companies reportedly spread tanbark in the nearby streets to stifle the noise of traffic and the neighboring ironworks temporarily ceased their clamorous production, Lillie recovered. Her parents, realizing how much the attentions of the firemen during her illness had helped restore her health, reluctantly gave in. Lillie, in red blouse and black skirt, wearing the gold pin, a miniature helmet, that Number Five had given her during her convalescence, again answered every alarm as the mascot of the company.

The whole city adored her. She rode next to the driver on Engine Five in all the parades and festivities, a personification of San Francisco's devotion to the fire department. By sixteen she was the belle of San Francisco, surrounded by a circle of suitors, who forgave her, as did the rest of the city, her wild escapades and flouting of conventions. Secreted in back rooms, she played poker with her male friends, drank bourbon and smoked cigars. A photograph exists showing her posed daringly with a bottle of liquor. She reportedly entered all-male precincts, including the sacrosanct High Jinks of the Bohemian Club, by disguising herself in masculine attire. She drove a team with abandon and skill, taught by some of the best drivers in the territory. Alternately, in her elegant Paris gowns, she attended the balls, instantly filled her program card, danced with grace, and fluttered her lace fan prettily, revealing to the discerning eye an embroidered "five" among the ruffles. Her undergarments bore the same needlework insignia.

Lillie's political sympathies were entirely with the secessionists. Yet when the war between North and South erupted, her loyalty to the New York engine company never waivered, in spite of the enmity between them and Monumental Company Number Six, made up largely of Baltimoreans. Lillie had on occasion accompanied her mother on long sojourns to the South to rescue other declining family plantations in Maryland and Sea Islands, Georgia. She made no secret of her allegiances. However, when her father discovered that she had gone so far as to help smuggle a rebel aboard a Navy ship, he feared trouble. Added to both women's outspoken partisanship, the offer of the post of surgeon general of the Confederate Army, made to the doctor personally by his old friend Jefferson Davis, although refused, left the family's loyalties even more suspect. Hoping to prevent the confiscation of their properties if the South should lose the war, the doctor sent Lillie and her mother off to Paris for the duration. Martha, undaunted, rerouted them through the South to check up on her plantations. Lillie, in character, managed to smuggle through secret documents for the rebel cause.

Once in Paris, the Hitchcocks were in the thick of the social whirl and became habitués of the court, where Lillie, at their request, translated war communiqués for Napoleon III and Empress Eugénie. Both Lillie and, more prolifically, her mother engaged in professional writing, Martha's forte being scandal and gossip. As Paris correspondent for the San Francisco *Evening Bulletin*, Lillie penned a long series of letters containing her observations on life abroad.

When Lillie promised beseechingly to be on her good behavior, Dr. Hitchcock allowed the women to come home. Martha again detoured them through the South. With forged documents and bribes they made their way through the blockade and behind the lines. Unbelieving, they saw for themselves the devastation that now overwhelmed the land. When they finally reached San Francisco, a tremendous reception welcomed them. Engine Company Number Five presented Lillie, now a mature twenty-year-old, with a certificate of full-fledged membership, making her the only honorary woman member of a fire department in the United States. Along with it came a second pin, a gold fire helmet with a diamond set in its Number Five shield. Lillie once again engaged the city's full-scale attention.

She never lacked for squires, some ardent enough to propose marriage, but her only romantic interest, according to her confessions, was Howard Coit. Howard's father, Benjamin Coit, a prominent surgeon from Buffalo, New York, had arrived in San Francisco alone in 1849. His wife and daughter had refused to accompany him and Howard remained east until he finished his schooling. Then traveling west, he stopped in Arizona, where he became part owner of a profitable mine. He often visited his father and eventually settled in San Francisco, where he became the caller, and in the eighties chairman of the board, of the old Stock Exchange on Pine Street and where he acquired the reputation of a bon vivant. In 1869, when his friendship with Lillie turned into romance, they eloped. The Hitchcocks considered their Yankee son-in-law distinctly their inferior and disowned Lillie. They later made partial amends, and in 1875 both Martha, now living apart from the doctor, and the young couple took up neighboring residences in the new Palace Hotel.

Between constant undermining by Martha and Howard's naturally roving eye, the young couple's marriage was not altogether happy; after several tearful separations and joyous reconciliations, the Coits also separated. Lillie's father, although in poor health, took Lillie abroad to console her. When they returned, he built her a country house in Calistoga, to which she gave the name Larkmead, a happier choice than Lonely, the doctor's country retreat. During her days at Larkmead, Lillie met Robert Louis Stevenson, then living in a Silverado miner's cabin. Their friendship lasted through the remainder of his stay in the Napa Valley.

In the spring of 1855, shortly after the death of Lillie's father, Coit died unexpectedly at the age of forty-seven. He left his entire fortune to Lillie. The shock of the two deaths and the evidence of Howard's everlasting affection overwhelmed her, and she sank into a morbid depression. When she finally began the climb back from despair, her behavior became more and more erratic. She entertained her friends in droves and ran her life at manic pitch. Tired of being in the country, she took off for Paris; bored with recovery from an illness, she joined a pleasure cruise to Hawaii. At fifty-seven she settled in again at the Palace Hotel and scandalized the entire country by arranging a private exhibition bout in her apartments between two middleweight boxing champions. It drew comments from the press as far afield as Boston and New York. Aghast at her daring, yet admiring the freedom of spirit that allowed San Franciscans to take her in stride, the writers wondered if her independence did not augur a new era for woman.

When she was sixty, a dramatic incident changed the course of Lillie's life. A distant cousin from the South, a ne'er-do-well named Alexander Garnett, drunkenly unhappy with the handouts from Lillie, attempted to shoot her. At the moment that he barged into her suite at the Palace, Lillie was in conference with Major Joseph McClung, her financial adviser and an old friend of her father's. When McClung interceded, Garnett shot him and would have shot Lillie, too, but for the prompt arrival of help alerted by a neighbor. McClung died; Garnett was arrested, and Lillie refused to provide him with a false alibi. He vowed from his cell to kill her on his release. She fled San Francisco and spent the next two dozen years as a citizen of the world. When travels tired her, she established herself again in Paris, surrounded as she always had been by a devoted coterie, many of them the grandsons of her old admirers. In 1923, when Garnett died in a Virginia mental institution, Lillie went home to San Francisco, where she set up residence in the St. Francis Hotel.

Her health and her age began to catch up with her. In the winter of 1929 the Superior Court put her and her vast estate into the hands of guardians. On Monday, July 22, 1929, at the age of eighty-eight, Lillie died in Dante Sanitarium. Among the crowds that gathered at Grace Cathedral two days later for her funeral, a detail of twenty-two men in spanking blue uniforms officially represented the San Francisco fire department. Three white-haired gentlemen, all of whom had known Lillie in her heyday, led the procession: Captain J. H. McMenomy, who had been a member of the old Empire Company Number Eleven; Samuel Baker, the past president of the Veteran Firemen's Association; and Richard Cox, from Monumental Number Six, an organizer of the present-day fire department. Behind them came the coffin draped in a profusion of lilies. When she was cremated, as she had requested, she was wearing as usual the beloved gold pin of Number Five.

In her will, Lillie left $100,000 to be used for the beautification of San Francisco. City officials, along with her heirs, decided on two memorials: the monument to the firemen in North Beach's Washington Square and the 170-foot Lillie Hitchcock Coit white granite tower on Telegraph Hill. In 1876, when the California Society of Pioneers had owned the site they named it Pioneer Park. Now, on October 8, 1933, the Pioneers joined the throngs that gathered on the hill for the dedication. The crowd was so large that down below in Washington Square the overflow followed the proceedings by loudspeaker. George Barron, representing the old volunteers, pointed out that "Organizers of the Volunteer Fire Department gave their city the first real gentlemen's club of its history. Bankers, butchers, doctors, clerks, lawyers, grocery men, laborers—met in the common purpose of preserving the city and remaining together as comrades and friends. In those stern pioneering days, a man was a man—and a fireman."

Three companies, Three, Six and Twelve, led the rest in social éclat. They built sumptuous quarters and fitted out rooms for public receptions as elegant as any in the city. They were famous for their dances and fancy dress balls, for which the public preened with outrageous care, overflowing the town's bathhouses and driving the town's barbers to distraction getting them shaved and puffing and curling up their hair. Social Three, as the Howard company became known, drew its members largely from Boston. It boasted a piano and a glee club in its stone-fronted brick house on Merchant Street, and its members ranked as the best singers among all the companies. Its foreman, Frank Whitney, who originated the temperance theme of the Dashaway Society, later became the first chief of the paid fire department. In the parades, Three's members decked themselves out in gold capes, and their silver-plated $20,000 engine outshone all the rest. Although the city's fire chief carried a silver trumpet, Engine Three's foreman bore a gold one, the gift of Samuel Brannan, one of its members.

The Baltimore company, Monumental Six, put on the first full dress ball of the volunteers, with tickets going for $20 apiece. Big Six, as they were commonly called, also held the record for the farthest throw for a hand engine, a stream of water 229 feet and 8 inches high, as measured in a Sacramento competition. The company's great bell rang out as the public signal for all fire alarms, for all festive celebrations, for all meetings of the 1851 Vigilance Committee, and for all deaths of the community, whether through natural causes or via the hangman. Although it had the biggest hand engine, the company, led by its foreman, George Hossefross, outmaneuvered the others in tight competition to become the first in town to use steam. Their joy turned to tragedy in the Niantic Hotel Fire when they rushed the brakeless machine from its housing on Brenham Place down the Washington Street hill. Careening out of control, the steamer threw Walter Bohen and James Washington under the boiler, killing them.

When Pennsylvania Engine Company Number Twelve, the other member of the social triumvirate, lost $500 to Number Six by coming in a close second in a steam engine competition, they made up for it by being the first to use a team of horses to pull their equipment. Largely Philadelphians, many of them members of first families, Number Twelve paraded in frock coats, patent-leather boots, and stovepipe hats, which their rivals often accused them of wearing even to a fire to maintain their dignity at all costs. They earned the name of High-toned Twelve. The company ordered an elaborate engine from Philadelphia, sending an advance which more than covered the cost, followed by a second equally generous one. When the puzzled manufacturer asked how to apply the money they had sent, the company instructed him to spend it on abundant silver and gold ornamentation laid on as lavishly as possible.

California Engine Company Number Four and Tiger Engine Company Number Fourteen, as well as Two and Ten, prided themselves on their lack of ostentation and the simplicity of their dress, although an 1855 bill for $1,300 indicates that Number Four still preferred to send for its uniforms all the way to New York. Four Company, on Market between Sansome and Montgomery, drew most of its members from the residents of Happy

Valley, who worked in the foundries and mills located there. William S. O'Brien, later famous as one of the Big Four who controlled the Comstock bonanza, was at one time its' foreman. Another member, Isaiah Lees, served as San Francisco's chief of police and earned a national reputation as a detective. William T. Coleman, who piloted the Second Vigilance Committee, was a member of Number Four.

Tiger Fourteen, located on Second Street near Howard, was the last of the engine companies to organize in 1855. Primarily Happy Valley butchers and grocers, its members focused their social activities on the fire hall. Claus Spreckels, whose sugar-based fortune later made him one of the richest men in the West, owned a small neighborhood grocery when he joined Tiger Fourteen. Like Spreckels, several of Fourteen's members became millionaires.

Removed by distance from the site of most fires, both Four and Fourteen were consequently less active companies. Another, the Young America Company Number Thirteen, also called the Rough Diamond Company, was organized in 1854 by residents of the Mission Dolores neighborhood primarily to provide local protection. Although the community acknowledged the fire-fighting capabilities of Volunteer Company Number Seven, Viligant Company Number Nine, and Columbian Company Number Eleven, companies geographically in the thick of things, those brigades never developed the individuality which so readily distinguished the others.

Near Pacific Wharf on Front Street between Jackson and Pacific, Pacific Engine Company Number Eight became dubbed Sailor Eight because of the large number of seamen in its ranks. It was certainly due to them that the sea chantey rose to such popularity among the firemen, although the practice of singing actually originated when Number Five's Curly Jack Carrol calmed the victims of the Sarsfield Hall fire with "Oh, We'll Hunt the Buffalo." Each company had its favorites and sang their songs at fires and banquets with equal passion. When Number Six lost two men in the Niantic fire, composer Charles Rhoades dedicated "Our Engine on the Hill" to the Company.

Crescent Engine Company Number Ten, whose members migrated largely from New Orleans, inadvertently started the most vigorous of the fire companies' competitions. Arriving first at a fire one day, they mounted a broom atop the engine to indicate their clean sweep over the other companies. Because the broom proved too cumbersome a trophy, they replaced it with a foxtail, and a proud tradition soon developed ruling its possession. The contest to be first on the scene, and therefore entitled to the foxtail, changed from vigorous to fierce. Before long, companies were staging fake fires in order to have on hand a big crew drawn from a deliberately full bunkhouse and which could gallop over a predetermined route, supplied by fresh relief runners all along the way. The most intense rivalry of all developed between Two and Ten, the first company to flaunt the trophy. By special vote, the city council designated May 4 official Firemen's Day, to be marked by an annual parade for which, year after year, the companies polished their equipment to a high gloss and decked it out with ribbons and flowers and special wreaths. The most cherished decoration of all was the foxtail. The plots and counterplots for its possession unfolded with unrelenting vengeance the closer the day of the parade. The contest continued for years, until the foxtail mysteriously disappeared, perhaps by intention to put an end to the fierceness of the rivalry.

St. Francis Hook and Ladder Number One was comprised mostly of Germans. Its foreman, Charles Schultz, an excellent violinist and conductor, composed the official "Fireman's March" and always donned his helmet when he directed it. The French membership of Lafayette Company Number Two organized their hook and ladder brigade on the principles of the Parisian fire companies, which included a rigorous daily drill. Sansome Hook and Ladder Company Number Three filled its roster from the residents of the Sansome Street neighborhood, although its $44,000 headquarters was actually on Montgomery Street. The company had charge of the powder magazine when explosive devices were called for and maintained a truck which carried 50-foot ladders, the largest in California. Tom Sawyer, whom Sam Clemens met during his days as a San Francisco journalist and later immortalized, was among the organizers and a foreman of Liberty Hose Company Number Two. Also a volunteer fireman in his home state of New York, he came to the Gold Rush early in 1850. Not successful at mining, he went to sea on a steamer, heroically rescued a number of passengers when the vessel burned and sank on a reef, became a patrolman on shore, served twenty-one years as a customs inspector, and finally, in the eighties, became the proprietor of a saloon on Mission Street.

On March 25, 1853, the California legislature enacted a bill exempting from jury duty and military service all volunteer firemen with five years' active participation. In 1860 the large number of firemen thus qualified formed the Exempt Fire Company; within two years the legislature voted them a house and their own fire apparatus. But the days of the volunteers were coming to a close. The use of the steam engine instead of the hand pumper, the horse instead of the human conveyor, and the telegraphic alarm instead of the manual bell had rendered many of the volunteers' functions obsolete. In the East, which set the trend for such things, more efficient paid departments had begun to replace outmoded volunteer organizations. In 1863 the California legislature began a two-year debate over a bill to set up a paid fire brigade. An unhappy event stemming from the rivalry among the volunteers settled the issue. The chauvinism of Number Five's New Yorkers and Social Three's Bostonians had always made for a strain between them; the natural enmity between the Yankees and the Southerners of Monumental Six was even more pronounced. During the war years the tensions had mounted. A few days before Christmas of 1865 bad feelings erupted into bloody violence. During the usually competitive race to a fire, the three companies became embroiled, attacking each other physically with every implement at hand from blunderbuss to pistol. Several dozen men suffered gunshots, bruises, wounds, and broken bones. It was the final contest, providing the legislature with the thrust it needed to pass the measure immediately. By December 3, 1866, San Francisco had a paid fire department.

XIII

"Priez pour Eux"

DOLORES Street, not far from downtown San Francisco, is a quiet boulevard divided by an island of grass studded with palms. Just beyond Sixteenth, it passes an ocher building topped by two embossed towers, the work of some pastry chef of basilican architecture. In spite of the borrowed ornamentation, it is the kind of modern church that remains heavy and anonymous. To the left of the entrance, a smaller, older church faces the avenue. It is simplicity itself: whitewashed adobe walls, arched central portal atop five steps, spare columns flanking the doors and echoed among the few windows set above. About two-thirds of the way up, an open balcony, posts set on end under a narrow rail, runs the 22 feet across. Clay tiles on timbers of redwood lashed with rawhide come to a moderate peak where a single cross rises. An office-souvenir stand wedges like a lean-to between the old church and a low abode wall which continues south some distance along the sidewalk. In summer a splash of purple bougainvillea rambles across the side and spills onto the balcony. It shocks the eye like neon against the naked adobe.

Inside four-foot-thick walls, the old church of the Mission of San Francisco de Asís, more lately known as the Mission Dolores, is decorated with eighteenth-century altars carved in Mexico, hand-whittled statues, and ceiling designs painted in the soft vegetable colors that the Indians used. Back toward the altar, to the west, a door opens into the cemetery. A botanical extravaganza tumbles among tilting headstones and leaning statuary. Pampas grass, pines, holly, and juniper bush out along the walls and fondle paths flanked by violas and hydrangeas. Green spikes of yew jut upright. Cascades of fuchias hang in baskets under the protecting arms of a toyon tree. The ground is a profusion of alyssum, ivies, mosses, grasses; weeds mix uninvited patterns with the lacework of ferns and poinsettias. Cactus hens and chickens scamper past the rose bushes, and here and there a purple hibiscus ranges like an ungainly child among the orderly azaleas and ca-

259

mellias. Except for the occasional squeal of a tire, the honking of an impatient horn, or, bursting with the recess in the schoolyard next door, a clap of parochial laughter, it is peaceful here, very much like a small country churchyard.

Over on the southern side, toward the front of the site, the tranquility is broken by a sobering marker: *"Ici reposent Athalie Baudichon avec Charles et Blanche ses deux Enfants trois victimes de l'horrible explosion du Steamboat Jenny Lind le 11 Avril 1853. Priez pour eux."* The churchyard is full of other such reminders of San Francisco's early internationalism. In the shade of a tree, alongside a broken segment of path, a flat marble marker set with an oval of carved flowers, reads: *"Aqui reposan los restos mortales de Dona Francisca Granados, natural de Sonora (Mejico) fallecida el dia 28 de Julio de 1858 los 33 anos de edad."* Near a little circular fountain edged in moss, one can make out: *"Qui riposano Le Ceneri Di Lorenzo Fagioni Mori in Età di 30 anni, Nativo di Ragusa."* Here rises the headstone of Marie Ruiz from Santiago de Chile, departed in 1857; there rests Catherine Stewart of Ayrshire, who lived two decades longer. Under an old fruit tree near the front wall lie the remains of Eliza Grover, who was born in New Orleans and died, in 1856, in San Francisco. A little farther on rests Henry Valley, born in Verchère, Lower Canada, 1812, and Mary Reagan of Dublin, who died in 1869. Near the door to the old church is the grave of a native-born San Franciscan, Patrick Kelly: born in 1853, died in 1856, aged two years, eight months, nine days.

There are other monuments. A large statue of Fra Junipero Serra salutes the founder of the missions. Over some round stepping-stones, past poplars and oxalis, a grotto of Lourdes—1920 version—a misshapen hulk of stone, with statuary and cactus tucked among its craggy features, memorializes those in the churchyard who remain "Neglected and Forgotten." Another modern pedestal, this one marble, supports the figure of an Indian woman. Wearing laced boots, a fringed apron over her skirt, a shawl over her shoulders, she clutches the prayer beads of her conversion. Except for her size, Tekakwitha looks like a piece of cheap souvenir statuary from a curio shop. Her presence commemorates "In Prayerful Memory, Our Faithful Indians." She is identified as "the Lily of the Mohawks," an Eastern tribe whose habitat lay between the St. Lawrence and the Catskills. No California Indians are buried in the main churchyard. Most of their graves are now covered over by Dolores Street.

Over against the wall, under the shock of bougainvillea, another monument tops the huge concrete tomb of Don Luis Antonio Argüello, an American-born Spaniard who became governor of California after the 1822 Mexican revolution. Alongside him, in a plot marked off by a rusty iron fence, lies one James Sullivan, a native of Ireland, "who died by the hands of the V.C., May 31st, 1856, aged 45 years." It is no coincidence that two others lying here also died at the end of May, 1856. In the shadow of a large square monument, full of cracks and peelings, and trimmed with four fireman's bonnets, symbols of the "respect and esteem" of the members of the old Engine Company Number Ten, lies James P. Casey, "who departed this life May 22, 1856, aged 27 years, 'May God forgive my persecutors,' Requiescat in pace." On the very same day death claimed Charles Cora. His remains lie at the other end of the cemetery, between the grave of the infant Patrick Kelly and the family plot of John Rodgers, encircled by the iron curlicues, rococo columns, flutings and crossed obelisks of a fence that is giving way to rust and corrosion. A monument distinguishes the Cora site with a stone couple in deepest mourning: she with bouquet, he with hat grasped, each raising a free hand to a plaintive brow, each inclined toward an urn raised up on a pediment, from which cascade the weeping tresses of a sorrowful tree. Through a profusion of bluest lilies of the Nile, fuchsias, and the crimson fruits of a heavily pruned berry bush, these words stand out: "Sacred to the memory of CHARLES CORA, a native of Italy, who died May 22, 1856; aged 40 years. Also his wife ARABELLA CORA, a native of Baltimore, Maryland, Died Feb. 18, 1862; aged 35 years." Sullivan committed suicide while in custody; Casey and Cora were each hanged by the neck by the vigilantes.

What terrible circumstances twice moved San Franciscans to take the law into their own hands as vigilantes? By 1851 the increasing deterioration of orderly institutions had brought the city to the brink of anarchy: a lawlessness that terrorized its inhabitants by fire and physical violence, a breakdown of justice, and a gross political inefficiency which, by the time of the Second Committee of Vigilance, had turned the municipal government into an agency of corruption. More than 180 citizens actively rebelled, convinced that their only recourse, if they were to preserve the system under which they existed, was to go beyond it. The committee grew to more than 700 members. The city's population was 30,000. By 1856, when the same set of circumstances again proved unyielding to normal measures, the reconstituted second committee resorted as before to corrective actions outside the law. This time the tribunal attracted thousands.

San Francisco had been established under the law: Spanish and Mexican law in the early days and an orderly American form of city government by the beginning of 1850. The initial Gold Rush

accounts remark on the honesty that prevailed in the new settlement, on the fact that no one needed arms, that great stores of
goods could be left confidently unattended on the beach. When
the city began to overflow with the hordes of would-be gold miners, the moral cast of the community shifted, and the law-abiding majority found itself burdened by a host of predatory and dis-
honest men.

In the winter of 1849–50, when the severity of the weather
forced all but the hardiest individuals back from the diggings to
the city, San Francisco began to experience the ambivalent attitudes toward the law learned in the mining camps. These settlements, populated by people from diverse communities, far from
the constituted authorities, the jails, the courts, and the people to
manage them properly, had depended at first on the most primitive frontier codes, which later evolved into miners' courts, and on
a system of self-government. It took some time before the formal
organization of courts and legal officers achieved any authority.
The body of mining camp laws—at first largely verbal agreements
accepted at mass meetings and only later recorded in writing—
encompassed with great exactness the size of land claims, the de-
terminations for ownership and forfeiture, the mechanisms for
settling differences, and the measures, both civil and criminal, under which the community could function. Severe crimes such as
stealing or murder sometimes called for punishments that were
far more serious than banishment or flogging, the common remedy imposed for claim jumping or other infractions of mining
conduct. Cropping a thief's ears before sending him away was
common, and hanging became increasingly frequent. As early as
January, 1849, three men had been hanged on the verdict of a
self-constituted jury in Dry Diggings near Coloma. From then on
the place was called Hangtown. That name should better have
been given to Downieville, where mob anger demanded the life of
a twenty-three-year-old Mexican woman known only as Juanita. A
drunken Scotsman named Cannon had either blundered into or
purposely entered the house she shared with a Mexican gambler.
The accounts are not clear. At some point, whether assuming he
could buy her favors or simply in the heat of the altercation that
followed, he called her a whore; she responded by stabbing him in
the heart. For her pains, the community hanged her.

In most cases, however, the citizens who lived in settlements
without normal legal machinery attempted to create fair rules, to
be heard in trials before juries, and to employ orderly, if simplified, procedures that resembled the legal structures of their
home communities. It was a credit to the majority of miners that
their spontaneous attempts at self-government followed legal

courses, even when forced by circumstances into extralegal procedures. Yet such a system invited abuse from the hotheaded,
vengeful, and unprincipled rogues who joined the Gold Rush in
considerable numbers. Mob rule and lynch law were the worst of
the public consequences, but there was also a considerable internal effect on the average forty-niner. In dealing with deviant
conduct he accepted going beyond the law, he had an ambiva-
lence toward authority, and he existed in an atmosphere of dehu-
manization that disposed the population to vigilantism.

When Dame Shirley wrote her letters to her sister, she described the rude justice and lack of order that frequently prevailed in the mining communities: legal decisions based on who
could best defray the costs of the improvised court or most handsomely line the amateur judge's pocket; the hasty trial and hanging of a man whose crime was stealing gold; the three-week period at Indian Bar when so little order existed that the toll of violence included a number of murders and other bloody deaths,
several fearful accidents, whippings, mob uprisings, one hanging,
one unsuccessful suicide, and one duel which ended in a fatality.

Another commentator, a discouraged miner who had lost his all
on the Stanislaus River, writing home to Albany in a letter dated
San Francisco, December 9, 1850, and signed only "Sam," described the funeral of one Jack Smith, a sporting man: first in the
procession came a band of music followed by about eighty men,
then the hearse and three carriages, and last eighteen horsemen.
"His death," wrote Sam, "was caused by being shot about three
weeks since by Judge Jones of Stockton a man who has murdered
10 or 12 others but who [is] always found guiltless as his pocket is
long."

Under the illustration on another letter sheet of a man mounted backward on a horse, the caption reads: "What: Jim! . . .
Come home tight again?—No, I ant tight; I'v been knocket of my
horse and robbed, and after robbing me, they put me on my horse
again and cut his head of! . . ."

And in a letter from Sacramento City, Jack Smith, a bricklayer
and no relation to the sporting man, wrote that "the Legislatur is
in session a making laws for us—duling is lawful here. Hardy a
week pases but what one is fought and one of the party falls to rise
no more and stabbing the same." He adds that he witnessed the
court scene disposing of the cases of thirty-six Chinese whom the
police had arrested for disturbing the peace: "it was the greatest
site i ever saw you couldn't understand a word they said. The
judges fined them $10 a piece."[47]

Writing on native Californians, T. T. Waterman describes an
old pioneer—a prospector, miner, and trapper by trade—whose

bedding included a blanket lined with Indian scalps, all of which he had personally taken a number of years previously. He had not been an official government scout, soldier, or officer of the law, whose duties might have put him in confrontation with the Indians; he had killed them entirely for his own motives and had never been called to account for his acts.[48]

Social disorganization began in San Francisco with a breakdown of moral codes that the authorities could not deal with. Unlike Colonel J. D. Stevenson, who became a land speculator and very well-to-do businessman after his New York regiment disbanded, the remnants of the company who remained in San Francisco—many of them toughs who had been members of such New York gangs as the Bowery Boys—began to foment trouble under the banner of creating order. They had come to California originally in 1847 to fight the Mexicans and to provide a permanent United States settlement. With the war ended, they constituted themselves into a volunteer police force under Lieutenant Sam Roberts, working for captains and shipowners to bring back sailors who had deserted, at $25 a head.

Soon they left off tracking down runaways and turned their attention to the sizable group of defenseless settlers of Latin origin who inhabited an area of North Beach and Telegraph Hill. From their headquarters in a large tent commonly known as Tammany Hall, the Regulators or Hounds, as they called themselves, planned to cleanse the city of such undesirables as Chileños, Peruvians, and Mexicans, whose main fault seemed to be that they were not proper Americans. Under the guise of municipal housecleaning, the Hounds confiscated whatever goods they could lay their hands on, claiming them in lieu of the Latins' share of payments for keeping the town in good order. At first they went on forays into the Latin quarter, pillaging, threatening, and generally terrorizing the inhabitants until they could boldly extract the tributes they demanded for protection. In time their focus widened to include all foreigners, whom they considered equally to be intruders. They took to wearing exaggerated uniforms and staged their raids heralded by drum and fife. Their bullying became more violent as they became more daring. They stalked the city at any hour, drinking and eating their fill and gathering up such merchandise as appealed to them without ever paying, extending their harassment well beyond the original quarters. They committed vandalism on the least provocation, and merchants felt themselves lucky if all they lost was merchandise. On the night of July 15, 1849, they staged a shooting raid on Little Chile, ripping down the tents and shanties, raping some women, and bludgeoning the men. One woman was murdered.

Under Sam Brannan's leadership, the outraged citizenry assembled the next afternoon in the square and, calling themselves the Law and Order Party, organized a counterattack. By sunset they had raised money to help in the Chileños' rehabilitation and, with the sanction of Mayor Thaddeus Leavenworth, had run down nineteen of the rowdies, including Lieutenant Sam. A large segment of the gang fled the community. The mayor, assisted by two judges elected by the populace for the purpose, convened the grand jury and proceeded to try the culprits. The convicted men received sentences from banishment to imprisonment, but without a police force to guard them or proper jail to house them, most escaped their punishment. Although the Hounds no longer functioned as a gang, a number of their members drifted down to the waterfront to join the depredations launched by the Sydney Ducks.

Fire was one problem, vandalism and robbery another, and a poor government a third major factor behind the final formation of a people's tribunal. However, besides feeling the more immediate effects of frontier law, mining community ethics, and the corruption set in motion by such types as the Sydney Ducks, San Francisco Gold Rush morality derived in part from events of even earlier times. The period of Drake and other respectable pirates had not only accepted buccaneering against the Spanish as honorable, but sanctioned it by official license. Later in California, numerous squatters, taking advantage of the uncertainty of land titles derived from Mexican land grants, had ended up with possession of the real estate in question, as well as with voting rights obtained through politicans who traded help on a claim for a yes at the polls. When the early Californians got no action from Congress in setting up a government, they took matters into their own hands, setting a precedent for conduct that bypassed inadequate official authority. After all, America itself had been a product of revolution; it was no surprise that seventy-five years later its citizens still accepted the idea of rebellion if the cause seemed right.

Peter Burnett, who was to become the state's first elected governor, described dealing with the political ambiguity he found when he came to San Francisco in March, 1849. A Tennessean by birth, he had grown up on the Missouri frontier, had been admitted to the bar there, had emigrated to Oregon in 1843, and had come to California early in the Gold Rush. Among his earliest activities in California was a stint as Sutter's attorney. Chronicling his Western career, Burnett wrote that he had not been more than ten days in San Francisco when he realized the unsatisfactory condition of its government. Still living under the military regime inherited from Governor Mason of Mexican War days, the dissatisfied Californians had petitioned Congress to set up a state government. Congress, locked into the question over slavery and its effect on California and other new territories, seemed unable to provide any governmental structure at all but did manage to implement its program of taxation.

The disgruntled citizens decided to take up the problem themselves. In a number of towns, meetings took place to coordinate steps for a California provisional government. In San Francisco the citizens elected Burnett and a number of others to a legislative assembly, but the government under the military command of General Persifor Smith refused to recognize its authority, and General Bennett Riley, the civil commander, proclaimed that the San Francisco Assembly had "usurped powers which are vested only in the Congress of the United States." Riley then proceeded to set up his own machinery for a constitutional convention. The settlers, whose aim this had been in the first place, went along with little protest. The convention took place on September 1, 1849, in Monterey. On November 13, 1849, a month after the convention had finished its business, Burnett was elected the first governor of California. The voters also ratified the constitution by a vote of 12,061 to 811. In December the new legislature elected William Gwin and John Charles Frémont the state's first Senators.[49] On September 9, 1850, California was admitted to the Union—but only after the citizens had acted on their own behalf.

Unfortunately the new legal structure did not ensure decent government, and soon San Francisco was again feeling troubled. The letters and diaries of the day recorded what was coming to pass. Letter sheets bore such illustrations as the one showing "Honest Voters Trying to Elect Their Officers" by accepted procedures in front of a house, while behind it the ballot-box stuffers assure the results for their own shady candidate. Since it was possible to rig a jury, many a guilty man bought his innocence. There were so many quack lawyers around that the courts were bogged down with questionable suits. Attorneys would even prey on arriving ships' passengers, many of whom had undergone very trying voyages, to stir them up to the point of bringing suit against the steamship companies.

In the fall of 1849 the governor authorized a San Francisco civil court with jurisdiction in cases involving more than $100. The judge, a Missourian named William B. Almond, became famous during his seven-month tenure for the originality of his courtroom demeanor. He thought nothing of puffing on a large cigar while court was in session, passing the butt to anyone who needed a light. An English observer described the scene as so chummy that a man felt as much at home there as he did in a tavern. The judge was prone to early adjournments when he felt the need for a drink and often took his whiskey in company with members of the jury. The court doubly earned its name of the Court of First Instance by generally deciding the case after hearing only one witness, without bothering with the usual arguments by counsel.

Such politically ambitious men as David C. Broderick, a New York Irishman and former Tammany ward heeler, recruited many of their henchmen from among the strong-arm types inhabiting Sydney Town. Broderick's crew included Yankee Sullivan, an ex-prizefighter, now taken to heavy drink and the practice of blackmail and credited with perfecting a false-bottomed ballot box which saw active service in particular precincts of San Francisco; after being ordered deported, he ended up slashing his wrists in his cell in the 1856 Vigilance Committee headquarters. Dutch Charlie Duane, a notorious ruffian, blackmailer, and right-hand man of Broderick, fled to Panama in 1851 at the invitation of the vigilantes.

Billy Mulligan, another Sydney Town tough, later became a deputy sheriff and the official county jailkeeper. Ned McGowan and James P. Casey, both of whom ran afoul of the 1856 Vigilance Committee, held positions of judge and member of the board of supervisors, respectively. Before coming to San Francisco, McGowan had risen through the ranks of Philadelphia policemen and graduated a bank robber. Casey had put in time at Sing Sing on a charge of grand larceny. T. Belcher Kay, an escapee from the worst of the Australian prisoners' colonies at Van Diemen's Land, Tasmania, held the office of Warden of the Port of San Francisco, on appointment by California Governor John McDougal, who thought he was respectable. The position gave Kay complete knowledge of cargo movements, invaluable for planning future larceny.

Even before the bad fires in May and June, 1851, another incident had aroused the town to an action which anticipated vigilantism. On February 19 two members of a gang of hoodlums beat and robbed Charles Jansen, one of the town's well-established dry-goods merchants. Several newspapers gave extensive coverage to the crime, the *Courier* going so far as to suggest hanging the culprits when they were caught. The authorities, under heavy community pressure, hastily apprehended William Windred, who fitted one of the descriptions Jansen had managed to give them. Later in the day an out-of-town officer apprehended a person thought to be James Stuart, an escaped Marysville prisoner wanted for an assortment of crimes, including more than one murder, and who seemed to fit the description of Jansen's second assailant. However, the man gave his name as Thomas Berdue (sometimes spelled Burdue).

Both prisoners had come from Australia, and both vehemently denied the accusations heaped upon them. Jansen, still suffering gravely from his injuries, identified the men on three different occasions, mistakenly, as it later turned out. Popular feeling ran high against the suspects, who now symbolized all the ills perpetrated upon the community. Aroused townspeople jammed the City Hall and crowded the streets in minor skirmishes with the authorities. The mayor, several judges, and the normally hotheaded Sam Brannan addressed the crowd. Those assembled agreed to the appointment of a committee of twelve men to work with the authorities and to the establishment of a guard over the prisoners to prevent a lynching, a recourse that was now being bandied about. Most people felt that the official police could not handle the situation without help.

The following day a second gathering attracted almost 6,000 citizens, who adopted the proposal of William Coleman, a young merchant still in his twenties, that a people's court be appointed. John F. Spence accepted the position of judge, and D. D. Shattuck, a bona fide associate justice of the Superior Court, gave the group legal sanction of a sort by acting as one of the attorneys for the defense. Hall McAllister became Windred's counsel. Coleman's nomination as prosecutor received the crowd's overwhelming approval. The court tried Stuart first. The jury voted nine to three for conviction and, much to the disgust of the majority of citizens, turned the undecided case back to the legally constituted authorities, who held both men for later trial on bail of $10,000 each.

A few days later a San Francisco mob unmercifully beat a robber but stopped short of using the rope they had brought along. In May a group in nearby Napa seized Hamilton McCauley, a prisoner whose death sentence Governor McDougal had commuted, and hanged him in the darkness of the night. Anger and violence were in the air. The press emotionally urged drastic measures, in one instance stating that proved criminals should forthwith be shot, hanged or burned alive. The *Alta* carried an article urging the formation of committees to deny entry to arriving Australians of undesirable character, as well as to search out hardened criminals already resident in the city in order to banish them.

Early in June Judge Levi Parsons abolished the acting grand jury, the only body before which criminal charges could be filed, and dismissed before trial the case of Benjamin Lewis, a suspected arsonist against whom there had been strong evidence of guilt. On June 9, just a few days after the last attempted arson and Judge Parsons' actions, a group of about forty men assembled at the instigation of Sam Brannan, George Oakes, and James Neall to take positive action. They formed a committee with the authority to handle the situation. By the next night they had 103 signatures on the constitution they had composed the day before; a president, Sam Brannan; a secretary, Isaac Bluxome; a password, "Lewis," the name of the suspected arsonist; and a name, the San Francisco Committee of Vigilance.

Besides Oakes, Neall, Brannan, and Secretary Bluxome (who had been the leader of the group previously mounted against the Hounds, the organizer of the Washington Guards, and a member of the merchants' volunteer police force), the original signers included Selim Woodworth, the first to affix his name; Robert La Motte, the author of a series of informative letters to his family back in Pennsylvania; Colonel Stevenson, a great number of whose ex-troops had started much of the trouble to begin with; G. E. Schenck, one of the three jurors who had held for Berdue's acquittal; and William Tell Coleman, who went on to become the leader of the Vigilance Committee of 1856, as well as the head of the Committee of Safety in 1877. The majority of the men who had been invited to join the organization, although young, were well-established merchants or held other positions of reasonable importance in the community; most had suffered physical attacks or losses by theft or fire. They intended to keep the group respectable by limiting future membership to those approved by a committee on admissions.

A logbook contained the handwritten constitution and the members' signatures. Penned on finely lined pale-blue paper, the preamble and first article clearly established the purposes and confines of the committee:

> Whereas it has become apparent to the Citizens of San Francisco that there is no security for life and property either under the regulations of Society as it at present exists or under the laws as now administered, therefore, the Citizens whose names are hereunto attached do unite themselves into an association for the maintenance of the peace and good order of Society and the preservation of the lives and property of the Citizens of San Francisco and do bind ourselves each unto the other to do and perform every lawful act for the maintenance of law and order and to sustain the laws when faithfully and properly administered but we are determined that no thief burglar incendiary or assassin shall escape punishment,

either by the quibbles of the law the insecurity of prisons the care-
lessness or corruption of the Police or a laxity of those who pretend
to administer justice.

And to secure the objects of this association we do hereby agree;

First,—that, the name and style of the association shall be the
Committee of Vigilance for the protection of the lives and property
of the Citizens and residents of the City of San Francisco[50]

The very night of its formation, the designated signal of four
strokes of the fire bell called the committee to its first business:
George Virgin, a shipping agent, had surprised a thief in his
office, who was captured after a wild boat chase halfway to Sydney
Town. Instead of being marched off to the regular authorities, he
was turned over to the Viligance Committee, which immediately
tried him and, finding him guilty, unanimously voted to hang
him. By ten minutes past two, the body of John Jenkins swung
from the Old Adobe in the square. When the coroner's inquest
into Jenkins' death implicated nine members of the vigilantes, the
committee published the entire list of its members, now grown to
183 individuals, and divided the responsibility among them all, an
act which won wide community support. The coroner's jury,
forced to name all the participants as parties to the hanging, now
had no practical power over any of them.

The sixth great fire on June 22, which caused $3,000,000 in
damages and was clearly of incendiary origin, only strengthened
the city's belief in the need for a committee of vigilance. By the
end of June the committee had grown to 500 members, and the
city had heard the Reverend Timothy Dwight Hunt preach a
rousing sermon in its support.

During the first days of July, while the committee was interro-
gating an Englishman who identified himself as William Stephens
about a recent robbery, one of the members made a startling discovery. The suspect, whom he had known well over a period of
several months at Foster's Bar, was really James Stuart, who had
been wanted for the murder of the sheriff of Auburn and assorted other serious crimes. Under further questioning, the real
Stuart confessed to almost twenty-five misdeeds, including the
robbery of Jansen, and named a number of his associates in crime,
thereby vindicating the three people's court jurors who had voted
against Berdue's conviction. After unhurried deliberation, the
Vigilance Committee condemned Stuart to death and, on July 11
in midafternoon, hanged him from a derrick far out on the Market Street Wharf. Released from the charge of murder, Berdue
faced a still-extant San Francisco charge of assault; he was quickly
acquitted. The committee was instrumental in helping raise a subscription for him. Windred, the other man originally accused of

the attack on Jansen, had long since escaped from jail and taken refuge on a ship headed for Panama.

Following Stuart's hanging, while membership of the committee increased to nearly 600, two official denunciations appeared: a mayoral proclamation condemning acts that went beyond the law; and a charge to the grand jury by Judge Alexander Campbell that declared every party to the hanging guilty of murder. Since eight of the jurors were members of the Vigilance Committee, no indictments followed. Operating from a position of strength, the committee entered a period of cooperation with the authorities, turning over a number of prisoners, supplying the grand jury with evidence when requested, and raising money for a new jail. The grand jury twice and the governor once visited the committee headquarters. Calm turned to chaos when the committee, sitting in judgment on the cases of Sam Whittaker and Robert McKenzie, found the men guilty of the most flagrant crimes and sentenced them to hanging. On the eve of the scheduled execution, the governor, the mayor, and the sheriff, with the backup of a court warrant, seized the prisoners in a daring raid on the committee's rooms and whisked them off to the jail. On Sunday, August 24, the committee, in an equally daring counterattack, broke into the jailhouse and spirited them to vigilante headquarters, where their hanging took place immediately from two beams projecting above the committee rooms.

This was the last serious business that the committee conducted. After disposing of a few minor cases, it turned its attentions to backing an independent slate of nonpartisan office seekers, most of whom won positions in the city election of September 1. Two committee members also gained seats in the state legislature. On September 15, just 100 days after it had begun, the by now 700-member Committee of Vigilance voted to disband its activities.

For a short time, San Francisco suffered few crimes. But in a year or two local politics sank to a new low. By 1855 the peppery editor James King of William was using the pages of the *Bulletin* as the platform for his sustained attack on the morals of San Francisco. One of King's particular targets was David Broderick and his henchmen. Another was prostitution and gambling; the professional gambler he considered as much a criminal as the thief or blackmailer. Therefore, when Charles Cora shot and killed United States Marshal William H. Richardson and the jury failed to agree on a verdict, King lashed out at them all, in effect accusing the wealthy gambler and the madam Arabella Ryan, who at that time was still his mistress, of buying the verdict. Belle Ryan had innocently been the cause of the murder in the first place. At the elegant opening of the American Theatre, she and Cora had tak-

en seats in a box directly behind the Richardsons; that such a
tainted woman should be allowed socially to impose her presence
on his upright wife drove Richardson into an uncontrollable anger, and the Richardsons stormed out. The following evening,
still simmering, Richardson, who witnesses say had also been
drinking heavily, abused Cora in the street. He drew a pistol, but
Cora proved the quicker hand, and Richardson lay dead on the
spot. After the first indecisive trial Cora languished in the county
jail, awaiting a second hearing. The fact that the jailer was his
friend Billy Mulligan brought King to further inflammatory
prose, vigorously proposing that hanging would be the proper
end for Mulligan, as well as for his superior, Sheriff David Scannell, should Cora escape.

On May 14, 1856, King revealed Casey's prison record and accused him of having won election to the board by stuffing the ballot box. The short-tempered Casey had no column for a reply;
when he attempted satisfaction through a duel, King refused the
challenge. Casey stomped from the *Bulletin* offices. An hour later,
when the editor left his office, Casey surprised and shot him down
in full daylight in front of the Bank Exchange Saloon. There was
divided opinion on whether the severely wounded King had been
armed and whether Casey had warned him before the lethal shot
rang out. It made little difference to popular sentiment: King was
immediately the community's hero, and Casey its villain.

That evening a number of 1851 Committee members, including Coleman, inserted a newspaper notice calling a meeting at
105½ Sacramento Street at nine o'clock in the morning. The revitalized tribunal which emerged under the leadership of William
Tell Coleman had a more military stance and a far greater air of
secrecy. In three days it had organized into companies of 100 men
each, put in a store of arms, and was drilling a force of 2,500. Ten
companies formed a regiment. A good deal of the military effi-
ciency came through the large enrollment of militiamen from
William T. Sherman's company. The French formed their own divisions, with French-speaking officers. The organization included
units of artillery and cavalry alongside the infantry detachments.
The committee mounted cannons on the rooftops of its permanent headquarters at 41 Sacramento Street, as well as on the rooftops of neighboring buildings, and stationed armed sentinels at
frequent posts about the premises. They erected a barricade of
sandbags of such dimensions that the building became known as
Fort Gunnybags. Highly disciplined and serious men, they were
clearly prepared for the worst. Their ultimate membership
reached nearly 8,000.

On May 18, the army of vigilantes marched on the jail and one hour apart removed Casey and Cora to their headquarters. One hundred and fifty deputies watched without aiming a musket. As the men's trials proceeded before the tribunal King barely hung to life. His battery of doctors could not agree on the best course to save him, and after his death there was considerable division of the learned testimony given on whether it should be attributed to the assassin's bullet or to the complications inflicted by those doctors who packed the wound with a sponge. Dr. Beverly Cole, King's physician, early removed himself from the case because of his complete disagreement with the procedures being followed. In any case, King died on the twentieth, just as the committee was trying Cora. Sentiment was so strong that both he and Casey received sentences of hanging. The execution and the funeral took place at the same time on the twenty-second. As the statue over their grave bears witness, Cora married Belle before he died.

Although the committee had reorganized specifically to deal with Casey and Cora, it continued in session after the hanging in order to eliminate the general corruption that again beset the city. One result was that instead of appealing the already-inadequate sentences that had been imposed by friendly courts, such criminals as the murderer Rodman Backus obediently served them out (two and a half years and a $3,000 fine for killing in cold blood in Backus' case) rather than come under the committee's jurisdiction. In July the committee tried Philander Brace and Joseph Hetherington, both of whom they found guilty of murder and hanged on the twenty-ninth. They set out to arrest Peter Wightman and Judge Edward McGowan, whom they suspected of complicity in the death of James King of William, but both fled before them. After almost a year, a good part of it apparently spent hiding out in the wilds, an unkempt McGowan surfaced to face trial in Napa, a friendly jurisdiction, and, as he had expected, to obtain acquittal. Even before the advent of vigilantism, the San Francisco grand jury, a reasonably responsible group of citizens at that point, had issued a denunciation of McGowan and two other justices for their dereliction of duty. McGowan continued to protest his innocence on all counts and wrote, in rebuttal to the committee's charges, an entire volume: *The Narrative of Edward McGowan, including a full account of the Author's Adventures and Perils, while persecuted by the San Francisco Vigilance Committee of 1856.*

Besides its greater size and more military bearing, the second committee differed from its predecessor in several ways. One was in regard to punishment: although the second committee employed hanging, it reserved such a sentence for murderers, in spite of the fact that even a state law condoned it as a discretionary alternative for lesser crimes. It gave up flogging altogether. Its

greatest weapon was deportation, a sentence it meted out to thirty
of the city's worst culprits, generally speeding them on their way
by booking and paying for the passage. It kept a rogue's gallery of
daguerreotypes of the banished and furnished these portraits to
the authorities of other countries as an aid to law enforcement
generally. Thus the committee ordered Billy Mulligan, Yankee
Sullivan, and Martin Gallagher deported as "disturbers of the
peace of our city, destroyers of the purity of our elections, active
members and leaders of the organized gang who have invaded
the sanctity of our ballot-boxes, and perfect pests to
Society. . . ."[51] Sullivan, as has been noted, committed suicide before he could be deported.

In similar manner, the committee dispatched Billy Carr, the
"king of the wharf rats" and, as inspector of the first ward, a ballot-box stuffer unparalleled in the city (he elected his candidates
by a third more votes than there were voters in the district). Edward Bulger, Charles Duane, and Woolly Kearny likewise sailed
out through the Gate by the committee's express arrangement,
Bulger along with Carr and Gallagher on the *Yankee* to the Sandwich Islands, Duane, Mulligan, and Kearny on the *Golden Age* to
Panama. The *Sonora* carried a sole deportee, John Crowe. In the
same month the vigilantes shipped off Terrence Kelly, Bill Lewis,
Alexander Purple, Jack McGuire, John Lawler, James Hennessey,
T. B. Cunningham, Tom Mulloy, William Hamilton, and Frank
Murray on the *Sierra Nevada*. Subsequently a number of others
suffered sentences of exile: Mike Brannagan, a bad character and
known ballot-box tamperer; Abraham Craft, a card cheat and
troublemaker; the tough Christian Lilly; and William McLean,
who had had the ingenuity to use his post as precinct election
judge to alter the returns, making himself a supervisor.The committee concentrated on the corrupt politicians and their henchmen, the crooks and robbers and murderers of the town. Those
who committed other offenses did not come into their self-defined
province but were promptly turned over to the regular authorities.

The 1856 Committee differed from the first organization in a
second major respect: its open confrontation of the constituted
authorities. Conceived under the Law and Order banner, but having little else in common with the original Brannan group, the opposition to the second committee included John McDougal, who
had been governor of California in 1851, James Van Ness, the
current mayor, David Scannell, the sheriff, General Sherman, the
commandant of the San Francisco detachment of the state militia,
and David S. Terry, a justice of the State Supreme Court, along
with most of the other of the town's attorneys, authorities, and

officials; the *Herald,* then the town's largest newspaper; and a number of citizens to whom resorting to measures outside the law seemed reprehensible no matter how great the provocation. A large contingent of Southerners, who had become known as the Chivalry or Chiv Democrats under the leadership of William Gwin, as well as the New York Tammany machine led by Broderick, belonged to the Law and Order faction of the community. So, ironically, did the Sydney Ducks, the ruffians, cheats, blackmailers, hoodlums—all the contemptible rogues who would suffer most at the hands of the vigilantes.

Early in June the committee was holding Billy Mulligan, the infamous jailkeeper and deputy sheriff, in its custody. Justice Terry, a stanch Chiv Democrat, issued a writ of habeas corpus for his release. When the committee refused service, Sheriff Scannell sought help from higher officials. As the ultimate state authority, the twenty-eight-year-old governor, J. Neely Johnson, issued orders to General Sherman to call up the necessary state militia; two days later Johnson declared San Francisco in open insurrection. Commander Sherman, in full military glory, formulated plans that, had he been able to carry them out, might well have brought the city and state into civil warfare. He ordered all nonexempt men under forty-five to enlist immediately in the California guard, a directive reinforced by the governor's proclamation. He called on General John Wool, in charge of the federal troops and arsenal at Benicia, for a supply of arms, and on Captain Farragut, of the naval yard at Mare Island, for the use of a ship. His plan was to force the vigilantes to yield their authority and disband or be placed under armed siege, the rest of the city apparently along with them. The governor, meanwhile, appealed to President Pierce for arms and ammunition.

There were few recruits, at most perhaps 700 or 800. Many of these represented the worst element in the city. The *Alta* wondered critically why Sherman was about to direct the community's criminals in an attack on its most respectable citizens. General Wool refused to turn over any federal arms. The President, finding no evidence to support Johnson's claims of insurrection by the committee, refused his request for arms to subdue it. These disappointments, coupled with the damaging boycott of his bank by pro-vigilante clients, convinced Sherman to withdraw from the fray, and he promptly resigned. A former Texas attorney general, Volney Howard, took his place, inspiring a fellow Texan, Terry, to even greater endeavors on behalf of the Law and Order forces. His first contribution was some strenuous research which turned up a law requiring the national garrison to furnish a quota of weapons to the state militia. When Wool, in compliance, shipped 100 muskets, the wily vigilantes promptly boarded the vessel and seized them.

J. R. Maloney, the militiaman in whose charge the arms had been entrusted, salved his anger by broadcasting diatribes against the committee. More important, in accounting for the piratical incident to Terry and other Law and Order colleagues, he brought the committee to realize the seriousness with which the authorities might indeed view its actions. To forestall his giving any further evidence, the committee decided to place Maloney and his assistant, John Phillips, under arrest. They promptly dispatched a party led by Sterling Hopkins, whose past service had included acting as executioner in the hanging of Casey and Cora. Hopkins found his prey with a whole nest of Law and Order leaders. A chase and scuffle ensued, during which a vigilante's pistol accidentally discharged, driving the volatile Terry to plunge a bowie knife, presumably in self-defense, deep into Hopkins' neck. In the confusion that followed, Terry escaped to the armory of the San Francisco Blues but, realizing the futility of resisting the large body of armed vigilantes that had quickly surrounded the building, exchanged surrender for safe conduct. The vigilantes, for good measure, took along Maloney and Phillips and the whole stash of arms on the premises. In addition, they marched in full force on all the Law and Order depositories, confiscating whatever arms remained in the possession of the opposition and arresting 200 men in the bargain. Having shown their strength, they released the prisoners shortly thereafter, with a warning of the dire consequences that would follow should they ever again enlist against the committee.

Meanwhile, the committee's forebodings about the consequence of seizing government arms proved accurate: the government brought charges of piracy against John Durkee, a former San Francisco police officer and leader of the boarding party, and Charles Rand, another of the principals. Given the tension of the times, it is fortunate that the court acquitted them.

The committee, having captured Terry, suddenly found itself sitting in judgment on a Supreme Court justice. The trial, which took twenty-five days, included four additional charges of assault committed on previous occasions. Fortunately for the entire community, Hopkins recovered, but on July 22 the committee nevertheless found Terry guilty of assault. Agreement on a sentence proved considerably harder to reach, and finally, on August 7, the committee released him. The town was in an uproar at the news, most people voicing complete disagreement with the verdict, some even threatening mob action. Terry, afraid for his life, refused the refuge offered by the secretary of the committee and

shielded himself instead on the *John Adams,* a United States naval
vessel that had been anchored menacingly off Sacramento Street
with its guns trained on Fort Gunnybags. Terry's persistently violent behavior—the stabbing of Hopkins as well as the preceding
assaults on Messrs. Purdy, King, Broadhurst, and Evans—did
much to bolster the community view that the Law and Order party was neither lawful nor orderly.

On August 18, after nearly three months of activities, the last of
which nearly threw the city and state into armed conflict, the Second Committee of Vigilance, having concluded its work, voluntarily disbanded. More than 6,000 armed men, accompanied by
bands, cavalry, and mounted artillery, paraded through flag-
decked streets in a final show of strength.

The first committee had discharged forty-one of the ninety-one
suspects it arrested, and turned over another fifteen individuals to
the regular authorities. Both committees hanged four men. The
1851 group flogged one person, a punishment the 1856 vigilantes
disdained. Both groups actively deported scores of wrongdoers:
the first shipped off fourteen men directly to Australia and ordered as many more to leave the state; the second dispatched
twenty-five troublemakers to a variety of places, often paying
their way, sometimes first-class, and ordered the banishment of
five more. However, after 1857, when the committee rescinded its
sentence of exile, many of the deported returned to the city.
Along with other former recipients of vigilante justice, several
deportees brought individual lawsuits—mostly for damages, but
occasionally on criminal charges—against principal committee
leaders. Almost invariably, although the suits were legally unsuccessful, they involved considerable cost and nuisance. Sometimes,
before he could get the charges against him straightened out, a
man had to raise huge sums of bail money, particularly bothersome if he happened to be picked up by authorities while away
from home. Several members reported physical attacks, which
usually occurred when, during their travels, they had the bad luck
to encounter one or another of their former targets.

The men who became vigilantes were not all free of sin themselves. Sam Brannan, whose impatient oratory most conspicuous-
ly urged the formation of the committee, built the first great California fortune, as Walton Bean points out, "on money that he had
diverted from church property and tithes to his personal use and
profit, a practice not far from robbing of alms boxes."[52] Among
the general membership were twenty-two shipmasters, thirteen
physicians, two dentists, ten bankers, ten clerks, five journalists,
two customs officers, two blacksmiths, two naval officers, one pilot,
one undertaker, one saloonkeeper, one insurance agent, five di-

rectors of the Pacific Marine Insurance Company, a number of small shopkeepers, a drayman, a carriagemaker, two watchmakers, two carpenter-builders, one porter, and although no laborers, a variety of representatives of the working classes. Bean suggests that among the last group a large contingent had joined for the sole purpose of saving themselves from hanging. The committee, over the course of its life, expelled several members.[53] In general, however, the membership by its nature excluded men without a business or property that gave them some purpose in preserving the roots they had established in the community and included many of the city's most prominent men. The largest representation, the merchants, controlled the committee by making up the majority of its executive body. Although the roster listed men of various political persuasions, both Christians and Jews, and a small number of foreign born, they were all white and predominantly American.

> The philosphy of the vigilante leadership clearly reflected a set of attitudes characteristic of most early California businessmen and some later ones—their dislike and distrust of government and of public officeholders, their resentment of taxation, and their contempt for politicians as an inferior class. These feelings were peculiarly accentuated in a new community in which all business was highly speculative, and in which so many men—businessmen and politicians alike—were hoping to make large fortunes quickly.[54]

Although there was within the community some division of opinion regarding the propriety of a popular tribunal, certainly a majority of the citizens gave the movement their fullest sympathy. Having allowed the city to degenerate through neglect of their own civic responsibilities, the troubled populace was now only too happy to support those among them inclined to remedy the situation. Almost all the newspapers and a goodly number of the clergy supported the committee. The boycott of businesses that sided with the opposition was telling enough, as when Sherman's bank became a target, influencing his decision to resign as commander of the militia, and when an 1856 boycott almost drove the *Herald* from the scene: when the paper, which had wholeheartedly backed the earlier committee, came out adamantly against the second, the volume of public indignation, canceled advertising, and dropped subscriptions nearly forced it out of existence. As it was, it never regained the leadership of its precommittee days.

Although officially the established authorities arrayed themselves against the committee, several officials privately expressed their agreement with its principles, and such officers as General John E. Wool refused to turn over arms, until legally forced to do so, to the Law and Order opposition. Part of Wool's hesitation was no doubt a fear of the ultrareactionary element which largely controlled the official camp, part a negative response to the numbers of Law and Order judges, lawyers, politicians, and officeholders, who had obtained their positions only through the worst violations of the system. In the eyes of the general public, the fact that the Broderick political machine, with its false ballot boxes and sleazy assemblage of scofflaws, had also aligned itself against the committee, only served to strengthen the need for extralegal procedures.

Not only did the committees' contemporaries support them in large numbers, but most historians, including Bancroft, Eldredge, Royce, Dana, and Hittell, found sufficient rationale to approve of their action. So did the ladies of Trinity Parish, who felt strongly enough to present the 1851 Committee with a testimonial blue satin banner lettered and decorated in gilt and shaded in hues of darker red and blue. The five-foot-two by seven-foot-eight-inch standard, bearing a legend which came from the first article of the committee's constitution, entwined three motifs: oak, symbolic of the committee's strength; fig, representing the homes under the committee's protection; and olive, symbolic of the peace and safety that followed after crime was controlled by the committee's exertions. The reverse side, all pink satin, pink roses, and blue morning glories, denoted the delicate character of the ladies of Trinity Parish.

Even though General Sherman vilified the committee, in his correspondence and memoirs he stated that he was convinced that nine-tenths of the people of the state ratified the acts of the vigilantes, although many did think they had gone far enough. When he later noted that all resistance to the committee had ceased and that the committee held absolute sway over the city, he admitted that "all men hurrahed and applauded" the wisdom of the vigilantes.

In a sermon suggested by the June 10 execution of Jenkins, the Reverend Timothy Dwight Hunt, pastor of the First Congregational Church in San Francisco, stated:

> Actual *incapacity*, or *gross corruption*, on the part of rulers, may sometimes justify, and even require, a people to overthrow and change the administration, or, during the exigency of the times, to take the power into their own hands. . . .
> I believe that when notorious offenders go unpunished by the constituted authorities, and there is no time to be lost in a new election, and no hope of a better government if one be chosen, then I cannot censure a people, if having been long and needlessly outraged by a gang of villains, they rise in their sovereign majesty, and

quietly, and by orderly procedure, seize upon, try, condemn, and execute one, even though they have to set aside the authority they dare not trust with the culprit. It is sometimes necessary to the existence of society thus to be its own lawgiver, judge, and executioner.[55]

The Reverend Mr. Hunt and many of the other supporters of the committees were willing to understand vigilantism beyond the original sense of the word which embodied the idea of wakefulness, alertness, watchfulness in the face of danger. The concept had grown in San Francisco to include the far more dangerous idea of revolution and in this sense alarmed the opposition to the point of a nearly disastrous armed confrontation. The governor's nervous proclamation of June 3, 1856, shrouded in officialese that bristled with military implications, did nothing but heighten the resentment against the authorities that was already festering in the city:

Whereas satisfactory information has been received by me that Combinations to resist the execution of legal process by force exist in the County of San Francisco in this State, and that an unlawful organization styling themselves the Vigilance Committee, have resisted by force the execution of Criminal process and that the power of said County has been exerted and has not been sufficient to enable the sheriff of said County to execute such process—Now therefore, I, J. Neely Johnson, Governor of the State of California, by virtue of the powers vested in me, by the Constitution and Laws thereof, do hereby declare said County of San Francisco in a state of insurrection, and I hereby order and direct all of the Volunteer Military Companies of the County of San Francisco, also all persons subject to Military duty within said County to report themselves for duty, immediately to Major General Wm. T. Sherman, Commanding Second Division California Militia, to serve for such term in the performance of Military duty under the Command of said Sherman until discharged from service by his orders—also that all Volunteer Military Companies now organized or which may be organized within the Third, Fourth, and Fifth Military Divisions of this State—also all persons subject to the performance of Military duty in said Military divisions, hold themselves in readiness to respond to and obey the orders of the Governor of this State or said Sherman for the performance of Military duty in such manner and at such time and place as may be directed by the Governor of this State.

Not only was the response of the volunteers laggard, but feeling against the authorities ran so high that the National Guard, rather than allow itself to be called in arms against the committee, voluntarily disbanded. Instead of obeying the governor's directive, the group furthermore reconstituted itself as the Independent National Guard and foreswore its allegiance to the state authorities altogether.

Did the vigilantes do any good? In the long run, probably not. If there was a lessening of crime, an exodus of criminals, an improvement in the political process, these were temporary. Yet, by resorting to remedies that lay beyond the law, the committees, themselves symptomatic of the social illness that beset the community, contributed in the final analysis to a diminished respect for the law. The circumstances of the West gave rise to such an attitude in any case and went far beyond local boundaries, as evidenced by the numerous filibustering expeditions originating during the fifties in San Francisco. In attempting to seize foreign land, private citizens brashly ignored United States laws, extending the Western readiness to disregard the law, or make its own, even to international matters. In the case of the vigilantes' extralegal activities, it is still debated whether there was justified provocation.

Unlike lynch mobs acting outside the law entirely and miners' courts employing legal forms arbitrarily, if at all, the San Francisco committees did establish a concrete body of rules which were generally based on existing criminal statutes. They openly published the lists of their members, restricted their main focus to criminal justice, and turned other infractions over to the regular authorities. They restricted their own province to the city and county of San Francisco and, by terminating their activities voluntarily at the end of their mission, clearly forsook any suggestions of permanent revolution. Yet they did not hold their trials in open court, although they carefully preserved all their records, as incriminating as they might have been. Although they treated all their prisoners humanely and allowed them counsel, the defender had to be chosen from among the vigilantes. In several instances they acted in anger and in haste. They did not consider motions for a change of venue. Witnesses for the defendants were usually afraid to testify or even to appear, and the sentence of hanging was eight times the committees' recourse because they had no way to enforce a sentence of long-term imprisonment. There was no way that a man could appeal his sentence or ask for clemency.[56]

The San Francisco committee inspired many other troubled communities who in short order established vigilance committees of their own; several of them fraternally offered their help when the city group found itself in confrontation with the authorities. Unfortunately, the majority of rustic committees, acting more in accordance with mob rule and frontier justice than the more sophisticated urban original, chalked up far more sullied histories than the San Francisco groups. Forty-seven hangings took place by vigilantes in 1855, only nineteen of them for murder; none of them occurred in San Francisco. Besides the California committees, at one point or another there was some form of popular tribunal in Utah, Nevada, Oregon, Washington, British Columbia, Alaska, Idaho, Montana, Arizona, New Mexico, and Mexico. They did little to further the basic cause of good government.

In contrast with the bodies that had convened before it, the Safety Committee of 1877 was formed in San Francisco at the request of and in full cooperation with the authorities. In July of that year labor agitations, often supported by socialist ideology, erupted on a national scale. Discontent, inflamed by the poor state of the economy, led to violent confrontations between workingmen and employers, especially in the railroad industry and in manufacturing. Within a week there were outbreaks in Baltimore, Pittsburgh, Buffalo, Cincinnati, and New York. In San Francisco the agitation took on the racist-socialistic line, focused on the Chinese and the Irish. When the combined force of 150 police and 1,200 members of the militia appeared inadequate to cope with the threatened disorders, the military, in the person of Brigadier General McComb, called for citizens to take action.

William T. Coleman by popular request chaired the July 23 meeting of San Francisco businessmen and property owners; by the end of the day he had been unanimously appointed chairman and architect of a committee of safety to assist the civil and military authorities in protecting the lives and property of San Francisco citizens. The city's supply of arms being considered too meager, Coleman petitioned the Secretary of War for the loan of several thousand weapons, which the government made available within twenty-four hours. Within another day, more than 5,000 men had organized into drill companies of 100. Coleman's prescribed powers were almost dictatorial in scope. The governor personally assured him that the responsibility for the city lay entirely on his shoulders, and in consequence he had the authority, including the ultimate command of the military units, to enforce whatever measures he saw necessary.

The enrollment quickly mounted to 9,500 volunteers, including a division of Civil War veterans, who in spite of past differences united in the face of the new threat to the city. Within two days after the formation of the Safety Committee, the community raised $48,000 in its support. During this period there were minor skirmishes between workingmen and the Chinese, resulting in the burning of several laundries and the murders of two men. The first real violence of a large-scale nature erupted on the twenty-eighth, when incendiaries set fire to the lumberyards neighboring the Pacific Mail docks, where the *City of Tokio* [*sic*], just arrived from China, lay at anchor with 138 Chinese migrants aboard. A fierce battle followed. The toll came to several dead and many more wounded. Fighting broke out in other areas; Coleman described it as a night of terror, with alarms of fire sounding in several quarters and stray bullets flying in every direction.

Within a few days the committee's prompt efforts at quelling the violence had relieved the situation considerably, and the group adjourned. Several bankers offered $100,000 to the municipal government to pay the salaries of an additional police force that would double the size of the existing body and stipulated that its members be chosen by the Safety Committee. Coleman commented: "God forbid we should ever again need vigilance or safety committees. The people of California do not want them. Those who organized and controlled these movements appreciate the undesirability of all such proceedings as fully as any one can, and would never have recourse to them except in extreme necessity."[57] Coleman's part in the San Francisco movements gained him such stature on a national basis that his admirers advanced him as an 1884 Presidential candidate. It is also descriptive of the man that when his firm failed in 1886, he took it upon himself to pay off his debts rather than accept bankruptcy.

Although the improved circumstances which made it possible for the 1877 Committee to work in cooperation with the authorities were largely a reflection of a later time, and certainly a sign of the community's growth away from the frontier and toward maturity, the earlier committees must receive some of the credit for the improved climate. Their backing assured the election of people's reform candidates across the slate in the 1856 contest, with the consequent reduction of government operating costs and taxes. They aided in seeking out candidates of higher caliber and saw to it that one respected person in each ward oversaw the election process. For the next several years the representatives of the People's Party captured most of the municipal offices, and the community experienced an interval of upright government so peaceful that it brought accolades where only a short time before there had been denunciation. However, the partisan differences generated by the election of Lincoln, the crises leading to and the problems following the Civil War, and the political machinations of the railroad crowd destroyed the People's Party and with it the era of good government. San Francisco descended into the political mire from which it all too briefly had emerged, but with attention diverted by the national scene, the problems of local government did not again become a serious consideration until the seventies. The temporary improvement in the late fifties and early sixties did perhaps restore some measure of faith in the long-range ability of the flagging system to correct itself.

A latter-day vigilante committee received very little backing and a good deal of editorial castigation. In 1966 a number of the citizens of the unincorporated town of Clyde in California's Contra Costa County decided to take up arms, ostensibly to guard against thieves, but actually to "get" demonstrators who were legally picketing the Naval Weapons Station in Port Chicago. The self-appointed patrol refused to disband when ordered to do so by the local authorities and resorted to violence, including shooting, against the corps of press and photographers who were attempting to report their activities. On September 22, the San Francisco *Chronicle* summed up editorially the area's feelings about the Citizens Patrol for the Protection of Clyde:

> Thus far, these bully boys have kept generally within the law while doing inestimable violence to its spirit and basic principles, and local authorities plead inability to act against them. But their very existence as an organized body forebodes mischief and bloodshed, and the organization should be promptly dispersed as a clear and present danger.
> Northern California has been thankfully free of self-appointed storm troopers and has no sympathy for or patience with this Contra Costa county chapter. If action of any kind is warranted against anti-Vietnam demonstrators or any persons who interfere with military activities, existing laws and established authorities are quite adequate. They need no help from overzealous volunteer enforcers. There is no need and no demand for Vigilantes in California in 1966.

SECTION FOUR
Big Money

XIV

The Bankers, the Silver Kings, and the Era of Finance

Remember that money is of a prolific generating nature. Money can beget money, and its offspring can beget more.
—BENJAMIN FRANKLIN

DURING the first days of the Gold Rush only the most primitive facilities existed to handle the steady production of gold. Safe-keeping was a major problem. The early miners made use of any-thing suitable for storage: chests, bottles, bins, the bottom of an old duffel bag. Often the saloonkeeper acted as safekeeper. As long as honesty prevailed, such a system was adequate, but soon the need for more secure facilities was clearly indicated. Weighing gold in order to evaluate it turned a number of merchants into bankers. Several express agencies which had entered the field as mail carriers making gold deliveries followed suit. Because there was no common currency and coin was extremely scarce, gold was the universal medium of exchange until well into the sixties, by which time most of the rest of the country was dealing largely in paper.

In 1848 Dr. Stephen A. Wright opened the city's first bona fide bank with a capital of $200,000. By September, 1849, he was pay-ing $6,000-a-month rent for offices in a simple frame cottage on the Kearny-Washington corner of Portsmouth Square. Among its other functions, Wright and Company issued its own $10 gold pieces. Before long, fourteen separate assay offices were operat-ing in San Francisco as private mints whose gold coins shifted in value so erratically that what was in use at full value one day was being discounted at 20 percent the next. To cope with the prob-lem, the legislature, in 1851, passed a law making it mandatory that all new coinage have its true value stamped upon it and that the processors redeem such when requested. Nonetheless, more drastic regulation was needed and a local branch of the official United States Mint started production in 1854.

Early firms included Kohler and Company, the express agents

287

Palmer, Cook and Company, Wells, Fargo, Adams and Company, Henry M. Naglee, and Lucas Turner and Company. The London house of Rothschild had a local representative to whom Heinrich Schliemann sent most of his purchases of gold dust during his brief tenure as a banker in Sacramento. Daniel Wadsworth Coit had come to California specifically as an agent for a firm connected with the Rothschilds.

Representatives of another banking family, the Jewish brothers Joseph and Jesse Seligman, came to the Gold Rush as merchants selling supplies to the miners. They made a fortune when the fire of May, 1851, destroyed a good part of San Francisco but left their brick building on Sansome and California streets whole and in full operation. The resulting windfall helped them when they shifted to banking. In the spring of 1873 the Anglo-Californian Bank Limited, an organization of London bankers, took over Seligman and Company.

Banking in the early days remained unregulated and fairly rudimentary, leaving the community's financial structure unable to cope with any fiscal crisis. On February 22, 1855, Page, Bacon and Company, a branch of a St. Louis banking and express company, shut down. The next day, the historical Black Friday, the Miners' Exchange, Robinson and Company, Adams and Company, Wells, Fargo and others closed. Half of the city's forty-two banking firms never recovered. When William C. Ralston opened the Bank of California in July, 1864 with $2,000,000, he controlled the largest capital structure of any bank in the country. Its failure in 1875 plunged San Francisco into another financial crisis.

Under the impact of the Gold Rush and of the Silver Bonanza a decade later, regulatory measures were difficult to impose and therefore slow to come. The First National Gold Bank of San Francisco, opened by James Phelan and James Moffitt, received the state's first national bank charter in 1870, placing it under federal supervision and regulation. First National later introduced gold-backed paper currency to California. Within months of its debut in 1875 the state's first clearinghouse did enough business to be considered among the leading houses in the nation. But not until 1897 did the state finally set up a badly needed Board of Bank Commissioners.

In 1876 the international firm of Lazard Frères established a San Francisco agency, which was absorbed in 1884 by the London, Paris and American Bank Limited, a British institution. The bank continued functioning under British laws until 1908, when Herbert Fleishhacker and a group of California investors reorganized it as the London Paris National Bank.

The current San Francisco Stock Exchange opened in 1882, followed a year later by the Crocker-Woolworth Bank, one of whose founders was Charles Crocker, the railroad tycoon, and another his son William. In later years it merged successively with three of the state's earliest banks: in 1934, with the former First National Gold Bank, to become the Crocker First National Bank; in 1956, with the Anglo-California National Bank, to become the Crocker-Anglo National Bank; and still later, with the Southern California Citizens' National Bank, to become the present-day Crocker National Bank.

If the requirements of the Gold Rush had given the banking industry its impetus, the erratic silver market formed the basis for the tremendous expansion in the field. Ten years after its discovery, gold also brought about the discovery of Nevada silver. Argonauts, continuously expanding their search, reached into the neighboring state. There was enough gold at first to keep them interested, but extraction of the Washoe ore became complicated by the persistence of an unidentified bluish substance. When it was finally assayed, the ubiquitous presence proved to be silver in heavy concentrations.

Henry Comstock, a cantankerous old gold miner, muscled his way in on, and gave his name to, the most famous of all the silver-bearing lodes, then a gold-bearing claim worked by a team of his buddies. Up to that point, his two principal connections with silver had been the annoyance that he and his partners had suffered when the bothersome stuff mixed into their gold and his earlier acquaintance with two prospectors named Grosch, who had turned up the first hint of the great lode of silver but kept the location secret and died before they could do anything more about it.

Once identified publicly, silver started a new rush, this time to Nevada. By the fall of 1859 miners were swamping the area of Mount Davidson and Virginia City. In effect, Nevada became a branch of California. "In the first season some thirty-seven companies were organized with a stock issue exceeding $30,000,000 and in 1861 an additional forty-nine companies incorporated, all clustered on the slopes of Mt. Davidson, though some had no footage on the Comstock Lode."[1] Meanwhile, Comstock and his three partners sold out their claims one by one for what history later proved to have been a mere pittance. Mount Davidson produced the richest vieins of silver in the world. Together with the gold with which it was mixed, the Nevada yield came to $400,000,000.

Getting to the rich deposits presented almost insuperable problems. The depths of the silver called for new techniques in mining, new ways of tunneling to prevent cave-ins, and new standards of endurance and stamina in the face of boiling temperatures, sometimes as high as 120 degrees, and the disastrous flooding at the lower levels.

The complex machinery needed for the development of the mines required vast resources of capital, much of it raised through the selling of shares on the San Francisco market. Speculation in mining stocks soon overshadowed every other San Francisco activity; the fluctuations were so erratic that they kept the town's gambling appetite continuously whetted. The boom in silver did not last five years before a number of serious difficulties set in. In many mines the flooding and heat had halted operations. In others the silver had given way to borrasca.* By the end of 1864 the only mine not in difficulties was the Gould and Curry, which was itself flooded within a year. To remain solvent, several mines were forced to assess their shareholders and to borrow capital. The San Francisco market in silver stocks slipped depressingly downward.

At this point the banker William C. Ralston entered the scene through his Nevada branch manager, William Sharon. Gambling on the experts' opinions that the lode was a true fissure vein and that the troubled mines all held richer strikes under the current 500-foot barrier, they offered loans to the mine- and millowners, at 1 to 3 percent lower than the prevailing rate. The Bank of California captured the loan market to the amount of a $3,500,000 investment. When the mining situation did not improve and the owners could not pay off their borrowings, Ralston cracked down, the inevitable foreclosures followed, and the Bank of California controlled almost the entire Nevada silver enterprise in one neat sweep.

To avoid sharing the profits with the entire group of the bank's stockholders, Ralston's Ring, a small clique consisting of Ralston, Sharon, Darius Odgen Mills, and several other officials, assured itself of most of the Nevada returns by diverting a good portion of the mining business to its own company, the Union Mill and Mining Company. The combine even went so far as to mix rock with the ore; this prolonged the milling process and increased the company's gains at the expense of the mineowners, who often lost their dividends and, worse, were sometimes assessed to pay the milling costs.

*Miners commonly used the term *borrasca*, the Spanish word for tempest, storm, or obstruction, when they struck an unprofitable lead, or for barren rock or an unproductive mine itself. The term developed as an antithesis to the Spanish word *bonanza*, literally calm, fair weather.

Ralston intended to make San Francisco into one of the world's greatest financial centers, a jewel among cities, with himself the benevolent ruler of the kingdom. To this end he invested in every facet of the city's development; the range of his support gave the city a proper amount of industry and added to its cultural enterprise. Besides the Bank of California, he founded or controlled the Kimball Carriage Factory, which manufactured rolling stock and equipment for the railroads; the Pacific and Mission Woolen Mills, which employed well over 800 workers, 456 of them Chinese; the San Francisco and Pacific Sugar Refinery; the California Theatre, and its stock company under the direction of the leading Shakespeareans John McCullough and Lawrence Barrett; the West Coast Furniture Factory, which, like a number of his enterprises, was built to supply the needs of the Palace Hotel; the Buena Vista Vini-cultural Society, a partnership that owned 400 producing acres in Sonoma and southern California; the Cornell Watch Factory; the Union Pacific Silk Manufacturing Company, for which he imported silkworms from China and Japan; the Culp Consolidated Tobacco Company, which grew Havana tobacco in the Santa Clara Valley; and the $2,000,000 New Montgomery Real Estate Company. He put money into wheat farming and orchards, into reclaiming land for agricultural and industrial use, into importing Hereford cattle. He backed the Central Pacific railroad when it needed help in the early days of construction and was instrumental in the development of other lines, including the San Francisco, Oakland, and Alameda and the San Francisco and San Jose. He was behind the building of the first huge dry dock at Hunters Point. He lent generously to Peter Donahue's foundry and the Vulcan Iron Works, which supplied the equipment and machinery needed for the Comstock mines. He held the controlling interest in the Spring Valley Water Company, although he failed in his ultimate scheme to sell it to the city at an enormous profit.

He expanded his suburban Belmont estate from the Corsican Count Cipriani's original villa to a showplace that was famous the world over. He entertained royally, inviting every San Francisco visitor of prominence to share in its splendors. For the elite traveler, a trip to the city became synonymous with a visit to the mansion at Belmont. Ralston thought nothing of sending down a message that he was bringing home an unexpected entourage of 50 or 100 for lunch or dinner. On one occasion his guest, the United States Ambassador Anson Burlingame, stopping off en route to China, became so enamored of the landscape that he purchased a Peninsula homesite from among Ralston's properties. Ralston in turn named the area Burlingame.

Ralston invested with Asbury Harpending in the 400-room half-million-dollar Grand Hotel, a deluxe structure on Market and Montgomery streets, considered the best in the West when it was completed in 1870. At the same time and with the same flamboyance with which he had directed his other projects, Ralston planned the Palace Hotel on a scale that was imperial from the start. He sent the architect, John P. Gaynor, to study the most splendid Eastern hostelries and the great palaces of Vienna before he made a single drawing. The resulting $7,000,000 building, its proportions from foundations to dome designed on a noble scale, filled two and a half acres and took five years to build. Every room had a fireplace, a clothes closet, and a private toilet, and every two rooms shared a bath. Seven hundred bay windows brightened the outer rooms and lightened the massive facade. The decoration matched the architecture in luxurious abandon: rare woods and European marbles, imported Irish linens, chinaware from Bavaria and porcelain from France, French rugs woven to order or made in the specially opened San Francisco shop of W. and J. Sloane.

The plans called for all sorts of electrical novelties, including clocks; the latest devices for fire protection—a thermostatic bulb in every room and hallway that would indicate in the central office the location of any excessive rise in heat; an annunciator for each floor; a "tube receptacle" for mail leading to a letter box in the main office; an intramural pneumatic dispatch tube for messages and packages, connecting to all floors; 2,042 ventilating tubes running from all rooms to the roof; an electrical indicator registering the watchman's rounds in the main office; and to supplement the seven staircases, five hydraulic elevators. The hotel had its own 630,000-gallon reservoir, four artesian wells, and its own steam engines and pumps for use in case of fire. Other accommodations included a drawing room for ladies and separate dining rooms for children and private parties.

The entire seven-story structure centered in tiers around the Grand Court, one of three interior courts, into which carriages drove directly from Montgomery Street through an arched entryway. When the clatter over the circular driveway proved too disturbing to guests whose rooms surrounded the great courtyard, carriage traffic was abandoned. Hundreds of gas-fueled flares lit the marble-columned enclosure, domed over in glass and surrounded by a marble-tiled promenade and a tropical garden, playing fountains, and classic statuary. The effect was spectacular. An orchestra in its own music pavilion adjoined the Grand Court. After the carriage traffic halted, the court became famous for its gargantuan receptions, the best known of which honored General

Ulysses S. Grant with a serenading choir of 500 voices descending from one of the balconies. When Alexander Sharon, the hotel's third manager, took over, he introduced an all-black orchestra costumed in brightly hued uniforms. Putting up the court's yearly Christmas tree, a fir of enormous proportions interlaced with hundreds of dazzling electric lights, remained an honored tradition until the 1906 fire destroyed the structure that had housed it.

The hotel's dinner service included 9,000 Haviland plates and a corresponding number of matching pieces. The gold service, still used for special celebrations, serves 100. Besides Bavarian china, it includes flatware, glassware, and every conceivable accessory from horseradish holders and cigar lighters to stands for quill toothpicks and Bar-le-Duc containers, none of which sees much service today.

The staff to run the gigantic enterprise outnumbered any like congregation in the country and at one time consisted mostly of black workers. Thirty men were employed to tend bar. By the turn of the century the Palace Grill Room outshone any restaurant in the territory, and lawmakers conducted more state business unofficially over its bar than at the capital. The restaurant's mirrored walls reflected an extravaganza of French cooking elaborate enough to match the heavily draped decor and to please the most sophisticated of its diners. Under Jules Harder, who came from Delmonico's and was the first to wear the Palace toque, and Fred Mergenthaler, Parisian-trained and former chef to European royalty, the nouveau riche Californians received a classic gastronomic education. While some of the diners, Leland Stanford for one, responded with enthusiasm, others retained their earthy preferences, which no amount of virtuosity at the saucepot could elevate. In keeping with his finicky health, Sharon ate sparingly, and what he did consume was overwhelmingly dull; the silver king James G. Fair attacked his food with no discrimination whatsoever; and his partner John W. Mackay's tastes remained stubbornly commonplace throughout his well-heeled career. However, winning the admiration of sophisticated localites and high-living visitors, among them members of royalty, and gentlemen such as J. P. Morgan, who sometimes brought along their own chefs, wines, and supplies, saved the San Francisco chefs' sanity and allowed their creativity to flourish unabated. Within a few decades of the Gold Rush, San Francisco's cuisine ranked among its prime attractions, and its residents were as wise in the ways of the table as any people anywhere. The city's chefs, headed by the men at the Palace, astounded foreign visitors with their presentation of native foods. Everyone enthused over grizzly bear steaks, California venison, sand dabs grilled or bathed in French sauces, abalone, and a variety of Western game birds. Chef Ernest Arbogast made the name of John C. Kirkpatrick, the hotel's $30,000-a-year gourmet manager, even more famous for the oyster dish created in his honor: Pacific oysters laced with bacon and catsup served bubbling on the half shell, directly from under the broiler. The Palace was the first San Francisco dining room to feature artichokes on its menu, and its kitchen created the creamy tarragon dressing called Green Goddess.

Ralston never enjoyed any of these accomplishments or even saw the hotel completed; he was dead two months before it opened in October, 1875.

He had acquired a taste for luxury in his youth. Both his father and his maternal grandfather had run highly profitable ferries on the Ohio River, near which he was born. Life there was extremely comfortable until the well-to-do family's fortune went down with his father's boat. For several years after that Ralston worked at carpentry and shipped up and down the Mississippi, admiring the colorful existence, particularly of the moneyed gentry, in the towns along the way. New Orleans, a mixture of bawdy houses and opera houses, of French, Indian, and Spanish cultures, particularly appealed to him. Its underlying similarities to San Francisco spurred him on in his later attempts to develop that city into an even greater metropolis.

In 1849, at the age of twenty-three, he was off to the California Gold Rush. En route he met two old friends, captains he had known well on the river, who had gone into the banking and shipping business on the Isthmus. For two years he worked with them in Panama. As a reward for his skillful captaining of a stranded steamer back to San Francisco, he was made a member of the firm. The business brought him into contact with the leading shipping figures of New York and almost into the family of Cornelius Vanderbilt, to whose granddaughter he became engaged. She died before the marriage could take place. When he did marry Elizabeth Fry in the spring of 1858, he grandly invited the entire fourteen-member wedding party along on the honeymoon to Yosemite Valley.

Ralston had finally settled in San Francisco in March, 1854, in charge of the Panama company's California headquarters. Shortly after the disastrous loss of the *Yankee Blade*, its crack steamship, the firm went out of business. Ralston then embarked on a new banking enterprise, with himself and Joseph Donohoe in the Western office and Eugene Kelly taking care of the New York business. The firm prospered over the next several years, largely through the handling of silver shipments, and the Ralstons, installed in princely fashion on Rincon Hill, were considered among the leading citizens of San Francisco.

Disagreements over business policies convinced Ralston to break with his partners, but not before he had clandestinely organized the Bank of California around the best of the old firm's clients, most of them silver accounts. Ralston took the position of cashier. The presidency went to forty-year-old Darius Ogden Mills, a wealthy Sacramento banker, who agreed to the figurehead position if Ralston would tend to the real responsibilities.

Mills, a forty-niner, and his two brothers had run a Sacramento store before he set up a highly successful banking business there. He was by nature a conservative, humorless man, in noticeable contrast to the flamboyant, dandified, exhilarating Ralston. But he displayed the same Renaissance character of many of the early California entrepreneurs, conducting business simultaneously in iron foundries, real estate, building construction, as a partner in the Union Mill and Mining Company, oilfield development, quicksilver mines, and railroad building, the last of which led him to the presidency of the Virginia and Truckee Railroad.

When the silver market suffered a severe crisis in 1864 and Ralston had dispatched William Sharon to Virginia City, the new Bank of California's resulting control over most of the Comstock made it more urgent than ever that a solution be found to the technical problems of mining. The flooding and heating now threatened the entire financial structure of the bank and called forth the same inventiveness that characteristically dealt with problems unique to the Western frontier. Artificial systems of ventilation lowered the 120-degree temperatures and cleansed the poisonous air. Pumps rid the shafts of the scalding bursts of water entrapped in underground chambers. Devices for hauling the ore to the surface speeded the laborious mining operations. The more ingenious the new methods, however, the more costly their construction; the more complicated the mechanisms, the more frequent their breakdowns. The serious problems remained far from being conquered.

At this point Adolph Sutro, a young millowner and engineer of Jewish-Prussian origin, proposed a scheme that was so eminently sensible that everyone, including the Bank of California, was at first enthusiastic about it. On closer analysis it threatened to usurp all of Ralston and Sharon's Comstock business; they dropped their support to become its prime opponents. Sutro's revolutionary plan involved building a 1,650-foot-deep tunnel under Mount Davidson directly to the silver vein. The 4-mile passageway would simultaneously drain the flooded portions of the lode, allow natural air to ventilate it, lower the excessive temperatures, and provide immediate downhill transporation of the ore to the mills on the Carson River at the tunnel's entrance. Besides resolving all the most difficult problems at once, Sutro's proposal was a far less expensive solution than the cumbersome and only occasionally effective machinery that was in current use. By making many of the bank's operations obsolete, the tunnel would have shifted the dependency of the mines to Sutro, who, even if he charged the most nominal fees for the benefits the tunnel would provide, would clearly make a fortune. In terms of lives lost and injuries sustained, there was no question that Sutro's scheme was overwhelmingly safer.

Its supremacy threatened, the bank and all those beholden to it blocked Sutro's efforts on every level from obtaining private financing to getting approval of a Congressional loan. Ralston and Sharon were nervous enough to build their own 21-mile railroad between Virginia City and Carson City, thus obviating one of the tunnel's greatest attractions, the low cost of transporting ore to the mills. County funds went into the railroad, as did investments of several companies indebted to the bank, but the controlling interests were subscribed by Mills, Ralston, and Sharon. The Virginia and Truckee was in operation by November, 1869, only a short time after limited construction had finally begun on Sutro's tunnel.

For years Sutro had fought steadfastly against the giant opponent, obtaining a Nevada franchise here, a 1,280-acre federal grant there, but never the capital sufficient to start construction. Funds finally came from the miners themselves, in the wake of a horrendous fire in the Yellow Jacket Mine. Forty-two men perished who would certainly have escaped had Sutro's tunnel been in operation. Once the union's investment enabled Sutro to start building, a number of Scots bankers added their backing. However, Sutro had to do battle for another ten years against the unrelenting opposition of the Bank of California and its successor as ruler of the Comstock, the combine of Irishmen known as the Silver Kings, before his tunnel was finally completed. By then the bonanza days of the Comstock were just about over.

When Sutro had finally succeeded in burrowing under the Comstock, he used the million-dollar profit that the sale of the tunnel had netted him to invest in San Francisco real estate. He bought great parcels of land when prices were low and ended up, according to various estimates, owning something between one-twelfth and one-sixth of the city's total acreage. Sutro eventually held much of the reclaimed land of the Richmond and Sunset districts, several acres surrounding Fort Miley and the area that is Lincoln Park, and some 12,000 acres of Rancho San Miguel, which incorporated the Twin Peaks, Sutro Forest, Mount Davidson, and Mount Sutro areas.

Among his purchases was the vast property that he turned into the Sutro Heights estate; its romantic setting overlooking the sea had appealed to him the moment he first saw it. Over the years he spent more than $1,000,000 on its improvement. Towering above the beach, it commanded an expansive view of the Pacific. Its gardens and promenades, generously ornamented with statues and urns, wandered beneath a forest of rare flora collected from around the world. Serpentine paths meandered through the trees, fountains splashed, wells assured ample water, and the mansion, perched majestically on the cliff, overlooked it all. At the height of his success, Sutro kept a crew of eighteen caretakers and gardeners beyond the normal complement of domestic servants. He owned about 21 acres adjoining the Heights, on which stood the Cliff House and the gigantic glass-domed public baths built in 1896. The National Park Service plans to include that property in the Golden Gate National Recreation Area. Sutro was known for his numerous philanthropies and for his generous hospitality to the public, who were always welcome to share the enjoyment of his gardens and his view. Enraged by the railroad's refusal to grant a 5-cent fare on the subsidiary steam line that ran to the oceanside estate, Sutro built his own electric rail line, running along Clement to Thirty-third Avenue, then over to Point Lobos, to his gardens, and to the great baths erected on the bluff below.

Among his legacies are a system of boulevards that lead to the ocean areas of the city, and the Sutro Library, a large collection of rare books and incunabula. Sutro's daughter, Dr. Emma Merritt, deeded the estate to the city before her death. She was one of the University of California's first women medical students and lived on the Heights until her death in 1938 at the age of eighty-two.

By the end of the sixties Sharon, as prime overseer of the Comstock, had under his and the Bank of California's control the major mines and mills and most of the dependent enterprises supplying them with water, fuel, lumber, and machinery. The building of the Virginia and Truckee Railroad extended that influence over transportation, and all that prevented a complete monopoly were the few independents that had managed to hold out. In 1875, with Ralston's demise, Sharon, who assumed Ralston's debts but cagily settled with the creditors for a pittance, ended up owner of the West Coast Furniture Company, the Grand Hotel, and the Palace Hotel and became the new resident of the Belmont estate. That he should emerge so handsomely from Ralston's destruction solidified the city's belief that he had had a hand in creating the disaster. Although a number of Ralston's creditors, feeling they had been misled about the resources left with which to pay them, sued Sharon for a fairer share, the Senator still came out worth something between $20,000,000 and $30,000,000.

Sharon, from Carrollton, Illinois, and a graduate of Athens College, had studied law with Edward Stanton, the Secretary of War under President Lincoln. During his first dozen years in San Francisco he had amassed a fortune of a quarter of a million dollars as a merchant and real estate entrepreneur. Election to the city council was the nearest application he ever made of his legal training. When Sharon lost his original fortune, Ralston had come to his rescue lending him funds and sending him to Nevada in the important post of manager of the branch office of the Bank of California. In 1875, with the full backing of the *Territorial Enterprise*, one of Virginia City's leading newspapers, which he had bought the year before, Sharon won a six-year term as United States Senator from Nevada, defeating Adolph Sutro. Sharon's election added the final touch to his position as King of the Comstock. His Senate career was most notable for his absence.

After his wife's death in 1875, Sharon supported a series of mistresses, although he was never indiscreet enough to set them up in his Palace apartment. After eight years of widowhood, the Senator, now sixty-five, and to all appearances still unmarried, made national headlines by being arrested on charges of adultery. His accuser, a beautiful young-thirtyish charmer named Sarah Althea Hill, alleged that the Senator had married her in 1880 and that she had a contract to prove it, as well as a note in which she had pledged to keep the liaison secret for a number of years. Her complaint at first named Gertie Dietz, who had shortly before borne the Senator a child, but later specified eight other corespondents. The Senator countered with a civil suit in the federal courts denying her any of the claims of marriage on the basis that the contract was a forgery. That the Senator had set Sarah up in a lavish apartment in the Grand Hotel from which she could cross to his Palace Hotel apartment by the connecting bridge over Market Street, neither one denied. Nor was there any dispute over whether Sarah had received $500 monthly for expenses. The question was rather whether she had behaved in this manner in her capacity as a wife or as a mistress. The legal battle lasted almost ten years, dragging through a series of criminal and civil charges in both state and federal courts. In 1884 the original state court granted a divorce in Sarah's favor and awarded her $2,500 monthly alimony. A year later the federal court found in the Senator's favor and declared the marriage contract and a number of connubial letters to be forgeries.

During the course of these two major court battles the Senator employed an army of ten attorneys, while Sarah had half a dozen. The roster of witnesses included fortune-tellers, occultists, and a mysterious and powerful black woman, Mary Ellen, or Mammy Pleasant. At a time when spiritualism, astrology, and fortune-telling ran high, the testimony about casting spells, doling out love potions, employing charms, and most especially burying a packet of the Senator's clothing under a casket in the Masonic Cemetery, kept the audience enthralled. In response to a number of black witnesses from New Orleans who testified to Sarah's belief in occult sciences, the *Wasp* commented on April 19, 1884:

> The testimony this week in the Sharon trial must be of intense interest to the colored population. If the dusky children of the South have not lied, Sarah Althea should be crowned a Voudoo [sic] queen. It presents a most singular mess of superstition, which would form a grand basis for a dime-novel story. But its colossal nastiness is its most impressive feature.

Secondary skirmishes involved several of the participants in trials for perjury, obscenity, embezzlement, disbarment, battery, unpaid bills, procuring false affidavits, desecration of a gravesite to obtain pertinent evidence, contempt of court, and criminal libel. When a witness and her son both drew pistols during the primary court battle, the judge ruled that everyone in attendance had to be searched before entering the courtroom.

The State Supreme Court upheld the divorce ruling when it was appealed. The Senator had meanwhile fallen ill. In November, 1885, he died, leaving his estate almost entirely in trust for his children, with only the most meager sum bequeathed to a few charitable causes. Although he specifically excluded Sarah Althea Hill, a court decision that certified her marriage to the Senator would have entitled her to her share of community property. A year later Sarah married sixty-two-year-old David Terry, who had been one of her lawyers and whose wife had died during the course of the trial. The federal suit over the validity of the Sharon-Hill marriage documents, settled in the Senator's favor one month after he died, excluded Sarah's claims to any part of the estate. The judge's opinion found that the Senator's position and material success conclusively made him the more credible witness.

In 1888 the United States Supreme Court Justice Stephen Field, sitting with the two other justices of the California circuit court, upheld the federal judgment on appeal. When he ordered Sarah to remand the illegal marriage contract to the court, she was furious. She accused the judge of being bought; she shouted that he was a social intimate of Sharon's son-in-law and a welcome freeloader at the Palace Hotel whenever he was in town. Both the accusations were true. Violence erupted, producing knives, guns, and bared fists. The altercation earned Sarah one month and Terry six months in jail. Ironically, Judge Field had succeeded Terry in 1859, when the latter had resigned as chief justice of the California Supreme Court. Terry had, furthermore, administered the oath to Field when he had first joined the court as an associate justice. Now Field had launched a merciless denunciation of Terry's behavior before a court of law. His disapproval extended to the rigid denial of any reduction of sentence, even for the good behavior credited to Terry. In the past Field himself had compiled quite a record of violence and questionable conduct: he had the distinction of being the first person ever held in contempt of a California court, as well as being the first attorney to be disbarred in the state. He had participated in several duels, for one of which, canceled at the last moment by his opponent's apology, David Broderick had engaged as his second. Terry, smarting under the humiliations heaped on him by Field, made public threats against the justice.

Field returned to California from Washington a year ahead of schedule to serve his biennial stint on the circuit bench, very likely to force a confrontation. The United States attorney, responding to the tense atmosphere, assigned David Neagle, a San Francisco deputy sheriff, as Field's bodyguard. By chance, Terry and Sarah boarded the San Francisco-bound train on which Field was traveling. The antagonists met at a breakfast stop in the Southern Pacific's Lathrop station dining room. Sarah marched back to the train; the impetuous Terry, perhaps intending to precipitate a duel, slapped the seated Field on the face with the back of his hand. Field's bodyguard jumped to his feet and shot the unarmed Terry twice. He died instantly. The distraught Sarah filed a murder complaint against Neagle, naming Field as his accomplice. The same federal court that had ruled against her in her dealings with Sharon took jurisdiction, in spite of a heated controversy over the priority of states' rights. The court dismissed the charges against Field and exonerated Neagle. This was hardly a surprise to the gallery of spectators; they had witnessed Field frequently emerging from the presiding judge's chambers and had otherwise observed irregularities so flagrant that they were indignantly reported in the national press. An appeal to the United States Supreme Court upheld the decision.

Through 1890 new appeals and retrials of the Sharon-Hill litigations continued to come before the courts, always ending in Sarah's defeat. Although she tried to pursue the legal contests as vigorously as before, after Terry's death she was a defeated and exhausted petitioner. Now sadly aged and disheveled, she remained almost entirely in seclusion on the Stockton ranch she had shared with Terry. On her infrequent visits to San Francisco friends, it became more and more evident that she was losing her mind. Her hallucinations and generally bizarre behavior, although injurious to no one but herself, finally persuaded Mrs. Pleasant, one of the several acquaintances who had been attempting to look after her, to have her brought before the court for a sanity hearing. In March, 1892, Judge Walter H. Levy, who had once served among Sarah's attorneys, committed her to the Stockton State Hospital for the Insane. For the next forty-five years she charmed her fellow patients and the staff and died there in 1937.

During the long series of litigations between Sarah and Sharon, Mrs. Pleasant had been a constant presence in the courtroom, usually sitting directly behind Sarah. Her connections to the case drew suspicious comments from the press, spurred on by her reputation as a voodoo queen, a procuress, her mysterious influence over a number of powerful and wealthy San Franciscans, and her suspected dealings in blackmail, matchmaking, sorcery and the buying and selling of babies. Her caricatured likeness appeared in several cartoons reporting the progress of the trial, and she even rated a drawing all to herself on the cover of the August 9, 1884, *Wasp:* shown carrying a large basket of babies slung over her arm and captioned "Little Buttercup in Judge Sullivan's Court," Mammy says, "When I was young and charming, I practised baby farming."

At the age of eighty-seven, ill and poor, Mrs. Pleasant decided to break the silence which had made her activities a matter of conjecture and fascination. She called to her bedside Samuel Davis, an old friend and journalist, and gave him an account of her life, along with a letter certifying its authenticity and declaring it her official autobiography. Davis found some of the statements in startling variance with previously accepted stories. Her alleged connections to leading San Francisco families were astonishing. He asked for, and claims to have received, corroborative evidence. Backed by such items as a diary covering fifty years of Mrs. Pleasant's life, Davis sold the verbatim narrative, interspersed with his own commentary and such tidbits as the report that Mrs. Pleasant had "made and checked out" through local banks more than $1,000,000. The buyer was the *Pandex of the Press,* a new journal which planned to print the revelations in serial form during the course of the first year's publication and on that basis built up a sizable list of subscribers before the first issue came out. However, only one installment appeared, a note in the second issue explaining that through an unfortunate misunderstanding between author and editor, the journal found it necessary to discontinue their publication. Generally believed to have been born a Georgia slave, to have gained her freedom and early education through the kindness of a wealthy Missouri planter who bought her when she was still a child, and to have spent some time in New Orleans, to which several biographers attribute her knowledge of voodoo, Mary Ellen Pleasant told quite a different story in her official account. Her birth on August 19, 1814, took place at 9 Barley Street in Philadelphia. She was not born in slavery to a quadroon mother and white plantation-owner father, but in freedom, the daughter of a full-blooded Louisiana black woman and a native Kanaka commercial man named Louis Alexander Williams. Claiming to have been separated from her at six, she knew little of her mother except that she was without education and therefore incapable of the contact through letters that kept the young girl for a time in touch with her father. From the latter writings young Mary Ellen judged him to be of fair education and of great intelligence and learned something of his silk importing business. She made no mention of a maternal genealogy of voodoo queens to which it was commonly conceded she was a successor, or of the episode with the wealthy Missouri planter, but instead described being sent at the age of six to Nantucket to live with a Quaker woman named Hussey. Because she proved a magnetic attraction as a clerk in the Hussey's store, she remained behind the counter, the money her father had provided for her education never being applied for that purpose. She apologized for revealing her misgivings on that account, something she would not have done, she explained, had the Husseys still been alive, for she was very fond of them. At that point the authorized facts that Davis published left off.

It is known that she stayed some years in the Nantucket-Boston area. She was married twice, first to a Cuban tobacco planter, Boston contractor, and fervent abolitionist named Smith and, after his death, to a Virginian, James Plaissance, or Pleasants, or Pleasant. She came to San Francisco early in the Gold Rush, her fame as a cook having preceded her, and received immediate offers of employment at outrageously inflated wages. She cooked and kept house for several bachelors' clubs, including the Case-Heiser Commission House, and served in the same capacity for Fred and Selim Woodworth and the former Governor and United States Senator Milton Latham. She made excellent use of her position with influential families, listening astutely to all conversations among them and their guests, be they scandals that might later serve to pressure individuals or tips on the market that would help build a considerable pyramid of investments.

She herself hired, or placed strategically in the employment of others, numbers of black workers, whose loyalty to her was a mixture of gratitude for her efforts in behalf of abolition and awe of her powers as a voodoo chief. She made money running three laundries on the side and opened a series of boarding and parlor houses which included the most elegant in the city. One of them, at 920 Washington Street, attracted such stellar lodgers in 1870 as William B. Hughes, a United States quartermaster; Charles Marshall, of the tax collector's office; William E. McArthur, a clerk for the United States Revenue Service; Thomas Wright, a master mariner whose holdings in real estate and personal property exceeded $45,000; George Wright, a businessman, whose assets came to $5,000 more; and Newton Booth, who became the governor of California within a few months of his stay at Mrs. Pleasant's.[2]

The assignations she arranged strengthened her hold over several of the town's leading citizens. She gathered further useful information from her guests via the reporting of her corps of faithful servants. She set up a number of protégées, young, white, and beautiful, in handsome homes and married them off to men of position. She supplied or took away babies as the situations warranted.

For years she lived in the great Octavia Street mansion of Thomas Bell, a close associate of Ralston's and a financier who had early served as her investment counselor. Ostensibly his housekeeper, she completely dominated the family. Having introduced him to his wife, Theresa, one of her protégées, she apparently then succeeded in turning her against him. Having access to Bell's fortunes, she invested much of them in extravagant projects, held the deeds to his property in her name, and kept him and his children virtually enslaved in their own household. Bell died when he fell three stories into the courtyard of what had become known as the House of Mystery; popular belief had it that his fall had not been accidental. Mrs. Pleasant and the family for years carried on a court battle over the estate.

Before the Civil War and after several years in San Francisco, Mrs. Pleasant had traveled east to deliver personally to John Brown a draft for $30,000, partly her inheritance from Smith, to be used in the cause of abolition. When Brown was arrested at Harpers Ferry, a note initialed "M.P." found on his person was widely attributed to Mammy Pleasant. In 1864, in an era of bigotry that prevented free California blacks from homesteading, from joining the militia, from giving testimony in court, or from riding the municipal street cars, Mrs. Pleasant brought suit against the omnibus company, and won it. She also interceded in the case, and helped obtain the freedom, of Archy Lee, an ex-slave, whom the pro-Southern California Supreme Court had ruled technically "free," but to be returned in slavery to his Southern master. Although her detractors conclude that Mrs. Pleasant's efforts in furthering civil rights were performed to ensure her the allegiance of the black community, her victories, no matter the motives, did much to further the goal of equality.

During Sharon's supremacy in silver at the end of the sixties, two challenges besides Sutro's had threatened his and Ralston's hold over the Comstock. Members of their own bank ring, Alvinza Hayward and John P. Jones, when they discovered promising new deposits in the Crown Point Mine, secretly bought up the controlling stock through their own Nevada Mill and Mining Company. Their profits were enormous. More significantly, the emergence of the Consolidated Virginia, a mining enterprise designed by James Flood, William O'Brien, James Fair, and John Mackay, coincided with the first rumblings of overextension in Ralston's financial empire. Out of the ensuing battle for control, the four Irishmen emerged as the undisputed kings of the Comstock, the wealthiest representatives of San Francisco's colony of multimillionaires.

James Flood's carriage repair shop on the corner of Ellis and Mason stood neighbor to O'Brien's chandlery business. When both failed in the mid-decade depression, the two friends decided to switch to saloonkeeping as a guarantee against the erratic business conditions that had affected them so adversely. They presided over the Auction Lunch, which did a thriving business with clients from the Washington Market, the nearby auction houses, and, more important, the neighboring Mining Exchange. The leading brokers who frequented their place handed them market tips with the same generosity with which Flood and O'Brien doled out the free lunch. By the mid-sixties the partners had accumulated a considerable fortune in mining stocks, sold their saloon, and set themselves up as Montgomery Street stockbrokers.

Mackay and Fair, both of whom had had considerable experience in California gold mining, by the mid-1860's had shifted their interests to Nevada silver. Mackay had become a major owner of the small Kentuck mine, and Fair had put in a term as a superintendent of the Hale and Norcross.

After Sharon had cornered the market and gained control over the Hale and Norcross, its production and share values had declined sharply. Fair and Mackay, confident that the mine held rich deposits yet to be uncovered, allied themselves with the stockbrokers Flood and O'Brien, who quietly went about buying up shares. Having aroused no suspicions whatsoever, the four suddenly emerged the new owners. Sharon and the bank crowd united against the newcomers. However, nature was on the Irishmen's side: when the mine produced a series of rich deposits, the four were clearly on their way to success. With their profits they bought up other properties, many of them fallen into neglect when production had slackened, and plowed funds into exploration. By 1873, now incorporated as the Consolidated Virginia, they had mined into the heart of the Comstock vein, directly into the big bonanza.

At this point Ralston's investments in beginning San Francisco industries had begun to suffer from the competitive Eastern manufactures that inundated the market on the completion of the railroad. The diamond swindle, for which he felt much personal responsibility, and his commitments for the construction of the Palace Hotel had cost him heavily. He attempted to recoup by cornering the stock of the Ophir mine, convinced that it would share in the bonanza of the neighboring Consolidated Virginia properties. He succeeded in buying up the stock by paying outrageously inflated prices; Elias Baldwin, from whom he got the major portion of shares at an immense profit to Baldwin, was thereafer known as Lucky.* Ralston, however, was not so well looked on by the gods. No bonanza developed, and the value of the Ophir stock, a good part of Ralston's fortune along with it, plummeted perilously. Ralston's final bid to regain his losses, which had centered on his unsuccessful efforts to capture the Spring Valley water supply and sell it to the city, cost him only further inroads into his fortune and gained him the animosity of a good part of the press and the population.

San Francisco had meanwhile responded to the improved mining situation by speculating more crazily than ever in Comstock shares. The bonanza kings, by the spread of rumors and false information, manipulated the market to reap enormous profits. In the summer of 1875 the market again spiraled downward. A run on the Bank of California forced it to close on August 26. The next day Ralston resigned as cashier. He left the building on foot and followed his customary route from Montgomery Street down Columbus past Northpoint and Beach Street to the area that is now Aquatic Park. A strong swimmer since his boyhood days on the river, he enjoyed a daily swim off North Beach. This day, whether by intention or by accident, he drowned. He left debts amounting to almost $5,000,000.

The new Comstock kings swept up a number of the Bank of California's Nevada properties and dominated the San Francisco banking scene with their Bank of Nevada, opened just a few months before as a direct challenge to the Sharon-Ralston inter-

*Baldwin's luck did not hold. In 1898 fire destroyed his hotel and theater on the corner of Powell and Market streets. It was uninsured, and the resulting $3,000,000 loss spelled his ruin.

ests. To show that they were serious, they had endowed the bank with a capitalization said to be in the neighborhood of $10,000,000, the largest in the world, and installed such princely accessories as overmantels of gold-bearing quartz dug out of the Comstock. The quartet now had under their control a much vaster empire than the Bank of California had ever amassed. Mills and several other members of the Bank of California's directorate who had not invested in Ralston's more daring enterprises did not suffer severe financial losses and were able to reopen the bank shortly under their own more conservative direction.

James C. Flood, a twenty-two-year-old carriagemaker and carpenter of some skill, came to California as a forty-niner from New York, his birthplace. His first Western stay was brief; by 1851 he had returned to the East Coast and subsequently bought a farm in Illinois with the several thousand dollars' profit realized from his California mining adventure. However, the hardships of a frontier farm existence coupled with the promise of the West lured him back to San Francisco within a year. There he set up in business but failed in the economic slump of the mid-fifties, along with so many of the town's other entrepreneurs.

William S. O'Brien's background paralleled Flood's in several instances. He, too, was a forty-niner, although his Irish heritage was first generation: he hailed from Dublin, from which he emigrated to New York while still a youngster. There he worked as a grocery clerk until he headed west in his twenty-third year. In contrast with Flood's stern and unyielding personality, O'Brien's manner was marked by geniality. From the position of their own firm, the new brokerage partners were in the most advantageous spot to enter the field of silver mining in company with Mackay and Fair. When the alliance had control of the Kentuck, the Hale and Norcross, the Bullion, and the Savage mines, the profit enabled them to purchase the Virginia and the California. Then they struck the heavy veins in the heart of the lode.

When the fortune began to flow into the Consolidated Virginia, Flood indulged himself extravagantly in the luxuries to which he had already grown accustomed as a highly successful stockbroker. Successively grand mansions followed one on the other. Most notable among them was his 1877 Menlo Park estate, Linden Towers, an architectural fantasy so adorned with turrets and crenellations that it was locally dubbed the Wedding Cake; it remained Flood's favorite, the spot to which he withdrew when failing health forced him into semiretirement. His one-and-a-half-million-dollar San Francisco residence, the forty-odd-room brownstone edifice atop Nob Hill that now houses the Pacific Union

Club, vied with its elysian neighbors in the splendor and dimensions of its appointments, and in its encircling bronze fence, famous for the fact that it cost $30,000 and that the sole task of one of Flood's employees was to keep its rails polished. The assortment of carriages in which Flood and his family paraded through town dazzled the populace, as they were intended to do. The Floods' entertainments, remarked on for their magnificence, hospitably included most visitors to the city, among them Ulysses S. Grant during his 1879 sojourn in San Francisco. The general's son, who was accompanying him at the time, became engaged to the young Jennie Flood, a relationship that never reached the stage of marriage.

Flood, in spite of his generous attentions to charitable causes, vied with Fair as the least liked of the four silver kings, and was the brunt of many of the journalistic attacks which abounded in the latter part of the seventies, as the full machinations of the group came to light. When the Bank of California failed and Ralston drowned in the North Beach surf, many believed that the Bank of Nevada, and Flood, deserved a good deal of the responsibility. Although Louis McLane, the principal shareholder in the Wells, Fargo Company, filled the presidency at the time, it was generally acknowledged that Flood and his three partners conceived, owned, and directed the enterprise. When Flood succeeded McLane in office, it further bolstered the theory. After O'Brien's death, Fair, never an enthusiastic participant and at odds with his partners, sold out, forced into that position by Flood, who wanted control. In the late eighties, with MacKay off on a European jaunt, the ailing Flood hired George L. Brander as an executive assistant. The young Scotsman, on bad advice, tried unsuccessfully to corner the wheat market, diminishing rather than augmenting the capital of the Bank of Nevada in the process. By the time the partners got wind of the deal Brander had already borrowed heavily in the bank's name and dipped into the partners' own private cash reserves, secured in the bank's vaults. The reorganized Bank of California and a number of financiers, Fair among them, saved the situation by providing large loans. Fair's price was the presidency of the Bank of Nevada. In 1891 I. W. Hellman of Wells, Fargo bought the bank and merged the two institutions. Two years before, at the age of sixty-two, while attempting to recover his failing health, Flood died in Germany. The date was February 21, 1889.

O'Brien never married, but maintained close ties to his family, particularly to his handsome sisters, Kate McDonough and Marie Coleman. He helped the McDonoughs financially when they moved west and took in Marie Coleman and her children when she was widowed in 1877. When he died in 1878 at the modest age of fifty-two, all his nieces and nephews received generous bequests, and the sisters shared millions. He also divided $50,000 between two orphanages and left deliberately uncollected several hundred thousand dollars in loans made to less fortunate friends. O'Brien's estate did not escape challenge, however, in this case from a long-lost brother, supposedly dead, whose widow and daughter O'Brien had taken into his home and provided for with generosity. Rather than go through a lengthy court test of the will, the heirs settled with brother Patrick for more than half a million dollars.

O'Brien's tastes and preferences changed little with the acquisition of a fortune. What luxuries he most enjoyed were those lavished on his sisters and their families. His Sutter Street mansion served as home for several of them; he provided them extravagantly the accommodations that he himself shunned; they moved through the circles of high society gowned in elegance, bejeweled, waited upon by liveried servants, fetched to and fro in splendid carriages. Meanwhile, O'Brien preferred his old cronies, the tested drinking houses, the back room card games. Although he participated in the activities of the partnership, he was very much less involved and, in consequence, much less responsible for the conduct of their business. Since he offered comparatively little threat to his partners, he never fought with any of them, in contrast with the growing animosities in which the other three became embroiled. He seldom used his seat on the Stock Exchange or his proper office in the Bank of Nevada, and he entered the halls of society only when the occasion demanded an escort for his widowed sister. By generally accepting his fortune as the result of his lucky association with his more aggressive partners, in particular Flood, he was happy to give them the credit and to lead his life much as he had before the windfall. He was more elated with election to the position of foreman of Engine Company Number Four than with any of his subsequent material successes. His most elaborate architectural contribution, in contrast with the monuments constructed by his colleagues, was the mausoleum he had built for himself before his death.

James G. Fair was born in 1831 in Dublin, the birthplace of three of the four bonanza partners. He was, however, the only Protestant among them. He spent the first dozen years of his boyhood in Ireland and the next several between a farm in Illinois and a machine shop in Chicago. He was eighteen when he joined the Gold Rush. Life as a California miner, although for a number of years at least as difficult and no more successful than that of most of his peers, challenged him sufficiently to make him stick to it. Quartz mining and the whole aspect of the engineering and machinery necessary to it turned out to be his element, and his successes mounted quickly. By the time of his association with Mackay, Flood, and O'Brien, Fair was thoroughly experienced in the field and had the income to prove it. He sold out his California gold mine in 1865 to try his luck at Comstock silver, moving in on the scene just at the moment when the first wave of miners, discouraged by the failing productivity of the lode, were moving out. After a year he left the superintendency of the Ophir mine to take a position with the weakening Hale and Norcross, which during his tenure resumed its once profitable production. When he teamed up with the brokers Flood and O'Brien and the miner Mackay, whom he had met and become friends with early in his Nevada days, he brought to the combination an insider's educated knowledge of the Hale and Norcross and a firm belief, which proved to be right, that there was a great deal of unplumbed silver in the lower depths of the Nevada hills.

The incredible successes of the four silver kings owed as much to Fair's prowess, greed, and total lack of conscience as to his expertise in mining technology. His enormous ego needed constant feeding, and to this end he generally claimed all the credit for success, whether due him or not. The scale on which the four men manipulated the San Francisco market by concealments of failure or achievement, false rumors, and exploitation of the press enabled them to gain wholesale control over the Comstock and to milk it unmercifully. As their power grew out of all proportion even to the fantastic coups which they achieved, resentment against them mounted. At first the unsuspecting public looked on the silver explosion as a universal bonanza, speculating heavily in the reasonable expectation that everyone could reap a share. Increasingly, however, they found that the great profits were going directly into the pockets of a few, while the average man had little chance for gain. Indignation mounted as the four swept in further profits from the major companies on which the mines depended for milling and supplies, all of which they themselves owned. Of the store of ill feeling directed toward them, Fair, who so badly needed and always sought the limelight, the applause, and the recognition of his fellows, could claim the greatest part. The distinction was one which may have troubled him, in spite of his stonewall façade.

In his public poses, Fair presented himself as an innocent, though not naïve, good-natured, forthright businessman, whose intentions were always of the highest, along with those of his partners; to them he frequently, although not in the least way unkindly, attributed less talent and consequently more blame for the team's devious enterprises.

His biography in Bancroft's *Chronicles of the Builders,* a seven-volume production in which the portraits were generally paid for and largely dictated by the subjects, reads: "In person he is of medium height, being five feet eight inches, weight about two hundred pounds, strongly and compactly built, with an easy carriage, alert manner, bright, clear, deep-set eyes, high forehead, full whiskers, and altogether strikingly fine and handsome features. He looks younger than he is, though in ability and intelligence he has been always far in advance of his years." And in another instance: "His manner is always courteous; he has a kind heart and most benevolent disposition."

Commenting on his Comstock fortune, the writer pays further tribute: "And if wit and pertinacity were essential to the securing of a fortune even on scientific principles, amidst fortune's rapidly revolving wheels on the Comstock, how much more wisdom and circumspection were necessary to keep it." Dismissing his lack of education, the result of a boyhood spent in a schoolless Irish community that could at best share one hired teacher with several neighboring districts, the biographer asserts that "nature, without education, has oftener raised man to glory and virtue than education without natural abilities." On describing his arrival at eighteen in California, the *Chronicle* comments: "Here was a young giant, with head uplifted, with sleeves unrolled, come hither to command men and money, and to this end ready to uproot nature, turn streams from their channels, and disembowel the hill." Concerning his subsequent success, the text humbly admits that "merit is not the true and invariable measure of success; the gods do not always help those who help themselves; but he who, by intellectual force and skill, can carve fortune out of the mountains and the desert may command even the gods." The price Fair reportedly paid for this encomium was $15,000.

Fair's self-appraisal as the intellect and savior of the group derived in large part from his real feeling that only he could handle most facets of the firm's business with sufficient capability, be it the signing of checks that numbered into the thousands or the supervision to the last detail of the intricate operations of the mines. Such a heavy obligation, although self-imposed, periodically drained Fair's health, and he had several serious bouts of undefined illness and frequent resort to the bottle.

As the Comstock production began to decline, Fair, like his partners, devoted more and more attention to other interests. In 1879 he ran as a Democrat for the United States Senate from Nevada and beat the incumbent, William Sharon, in a campaign that cost hundreds of thousands of dollars. His winning strategy, aside from the fact that he was perspicaciously part of a general Democratic sweep, consisted largely of being one of the boys, convincing the mining constituency on a man-to-man basis that he could better represent them. After an interlude of faithful, if silent, attendance, however, he spent little of the next six years occupying his seat on the Senate floor and a great deal of time attending to his affairs in California. His most noteworthy expression as a Senator was a rare speech to his colleagues in support of the Chinese Exclusion Act of 1881. He did not run again for office.

His business interests throughout the eighties centered on acquiring San Francisco real estate, until his California income properties rivaled in relative extent his domain of Comstock holdings. Pleading the extravagant city tax rate, he steadfastly refused to provide even the nominal upkeep that less shrewd landlords made their own responsibility. From this vast and unkempt empire he collected an enormous income, reported to have been as much as a quarter of a million dollars monthly.

The eighties brought many significant changes to Fair's life beyond his business interests. After twenty-one years of marriage, his wife, Theresa Rooney Fair, a devout Catholic widow whom he had married when she ran a Nevada boardinghouse, sued him for divorce on the grounds of habitual adultery. The court awarded her the decision, the custody of their daughters, Birdie (Virginia) and Theresa, their San Francisco home, a settlement of almost $5,000,000, and another $200,000 in fees for her attorney. Fair got custody of the two boys, Jimmy and Charley. His losses, however, were more than domestic and financial: during the marital difficulties, his two still-living partners, Flood and Mackay, had come to Mrs. Fair's aid, and it was partly through their astute counsel that she won such a handsome settlement. Fair could never begin to forgive them, and only their unalterable business connections prevented a complete break in the relationship. However, he was permanently disaffected with Nevada, where the divorce proceedings had taken place, and turned his back on it. His single consolation, aside from the custody of his sons, was the enormous amount of publicity, negative though it might have been, that the affair focused on him. Only the beginning of a voluminous reportage that went on for years, it covered the wills of one deceased member of the family after the next and the several attempts to break them by the family itself and by a number of miscellaneous claimants. Various accounts described supposed marriage documents, later wills, mysterious disappearances, and enough instruments of questionable veracity to keep newspaper readers endlessly enthralled.

Both sons followed the paternal drinking pattern, but neither handled it as well. Jimmy was an acknowledged alcoholic, dead by the beginning of the nineties, reportedly from either overindulgence or more direct suicide. His mother had died only a few months before. Charley's alcoholism was not as bad, in his father's eyes, as his marriage to Maud Nelson, the onetime proprietress of a parlor house, which promptly brought Fair to disinherit him. The union, however, proved happy, and a blessing for Charley, for Maud took excellent care of her erring spouse. Fair finally relented and put the young heir back in his will. Theresa made an excellent marriage to Herman Oelrichs, a wealthy New Yorker, and several years later Birdie married William K. Vanderbilt, Jr.

Fair continued to live in the two rooms he had occupied for years in the Lick House, one of his San Francisco properties, and to trundle back and forth to his crowded office just down the way on Montgomery Street. Weakened by increasingly poor health and extremely debilitating attacks of asthma and consumed by more frequent and stupifying bouts of intoxication, Fair died on December 29, 1894, at the age of sixty-three. His estate, although the true value was never exactly known, was estimated to be about $45,000,000; in spite of the low assessments on his real estate, he had managed to be the largest taxpayer in San Francisco.

John W. Mackay was born in the same year, 1831, and the same place, Dublin, as his friend Fair and, like him, spent the first years of his boyhood in poor circumstances in Ireland. The family pushed on to New York when Mackay was just nine; by the age of eleven and for the five years following, he had to shoulder much of the responsibility for his recently widowed mother and his young sister. After a miscellany of jobs, he apprenticed for four years to a shipbuilder and sailed in 1851 on one of the firm's vessels to try his fortunes in California. He was by then twenty.

For the next eight years he led the rigorous life of a miner, never with much success, but with apparent enjoyment. Like Fair, he thrived on hard labor and physical accomplishment. When he moved on to the silver mines of Nevada, he became involved in the construction end of mining and took his pay, as was often the custom, partly in stocks. These first small stakes enabled him to expand his shares, and he eventually held the controlling interest in the Kentuck mine. After a fruitless period which drained his financial limits to the breaking point, his luck changed; a rich vein yielded more than $5,000,000.

During those early years in Virginia City, Fair and his wife had befriended Mackay and in fact introduced him to the woman he was to marry. They often invited Mackay to dinner and a social evening, and just as often asked in Marie Louise Hungerford Bryant, a neighbor widow of extremely modest circumstances. The plain daughter of a man who, although once a colonel in the armed forces, now barely made a living at barbering, she was some dozen years Mackay's junior. A bride at sixteen, she had married a young and promising physician, who died a few years later, having deserted her and their two children. By then a broken and ill man, he was addicted both to alcohol and to the drugs easily available to him in his profession. The nineteen-year-old Mrs. Bryant had supported her small family, soon made smaller by the death of baby Marie, by sewing and teaching French, a language she had learned from her French grandmother and her mother. After their marriage, Mackay adopted her surviving child, Eva, and in the years following the couple had two boys of their own. John, better known as Willie, was killed at twenty-five in a bizarre riding accident near Paris; Clarence ended up in a fifty-room French mansion on the shores of Long Island, a wedding present from Papa, from which vantage point he could preside over more and more of the business responsibilities which his father turned over to him.

Coming from a very poor Irish family, Mackay, like the others, had had little education. He was further handicapped by a stutter, which he largely managed to conquer by substituting deliberately measured speech. In spite of his limited cultural background, he enjoyed with immense enthusiasm all aspects of the theater and was an avid partisan of music, particularly opera. That his interest was genuine, unlike that of so many of his peers to whom attendance was purely a matter of earning prestige, is clear from the early dates at which he began to go to performances. He put in faithful attendance at Piper's Virginia City Opera House long before he could afford a decent seat. As his own wealth increased, he supported the house financially, enabling him to make lasting friendships with a number of the great artists of the day who played there. He also extended sizable loans to those actors whose luck was down and who meticulously repaid him when their own fortunes brightened. In his later years he was one of the founders of the New York Metropolitan Opera Company.

Mackay's custom to lend money or to dole it out directly extended to almost all small-scale borrowers. His gesture was as much in self-defense as through real generosity: plagued by hordes of people trying to make a touch, he found that one of the simplest ways to get rid of them was to give them money. Occasionally his liberality caught up with him and provoked sudden and ill-tempered demands for repayment. His real charities were numerous, his gifts always strictly anonymous, often paid in cash so that the source would not be identifiable. He picked up the tab for all the groceries charged by miners during serious periods of slack or supplied fuel to the homeless camping in makeshift quarters after the devastating fire that razed a good part of Virginia City in

1875. He pensioned a number of old-time miners on a monthly basis for as long as they lived. His unrepaid bounties totaled almost $5,000,000.

Unlike his wife, he disliked ostentation and display of any kind and found, in fact, that the life-style of a very rich man was distasteful to him. Display he could shun, but the phony society folk, the hangers-on, the unknown seekers of money he found harder to pry off when they attached themselves, leechlike, to his privacy. A great many of his tastes he preserved because they were the simple pleasures he had always enjoyed: he loved physical workouts and boxed with enthusiasm; he liked plain cooking and whiskey, but consumed both only in moderation; he enjoyed a good hand at poker. It gave him double satisfaction that these preferences countered his wife's fascination with everything foreign, with lavish entertainments, extravagant clothes, fabulous jewels, of which she acquired a million-dollar collection, with haute cuisine accompanied by priceless vintages, with homes abroad, and with a coterie of internationally recognized society people whom she gathered about her like a queen bee.

After their first trip to Europe, taken in the early seventies, Mrs. Mackay could not remain content with life in Virginia City. Her parents, who had accompanied the Mackays on the European excursion and who felt much the same way, had, in fact, stayed on in Paris, supported in style by their wealthy son-in-law. Mackay increasingly had to spend time on business in Nevada; Mrs. Mackay and the children preferred to set up housekeeping in San Francisco. Only a few years passed, however, before the glamor of a European sojourn beckoned again, and Mrs. Mackay persuaded her overly busy husband that she and the rest of the family would be better off in Paris. After that the marriage was conducted on a commuting basis: Mrs. Mackay did not revisit the United States for years, and then her trips, generally sparked by some enormous event such as the attempted assassination of her husband, were infrequent. Mackay did almost all the traveling, on a once-a-year schedule. After his wife's departure his lodgings were an assortment of hotel rooms; Madame, on the other hand, established herself on the swanky Rue Tilsit, off the Champs-Élysées, in an extravagantly expensive château that she furnished with ostentatious abandon. From this perch she launched her campaign to enter French society.

Her first grand coup, which elevated her immediately to the top rank, was to capture General Grant for a banquet and soiree in his honor. In preparation, she redid the entire mansion, even to reupholstering the furniture in the U.S. colors and importing by the dozens flowers and shrubs from southern France. The curious gathered on the sidewalks to watch the conversion of the house into a full-scale stage set appropriate to the entertainment of the former President. Eventually the crowds grew so numerous that police guards had to be stationed to keep order. From then on all of Mrs. Mackay's doings became world news.

She engaged the members of the Opéra and the actors from the Comédie Française to entertain privately at her galas. Among her good friends was Queen Isabella. Her dinner service of Comstock silver dazzled the Paris Exposition of 1878. The 1,500 pieces exhibited, only a part of the eventual total, represented more than two years' work by Tiffany craftsmen. The novelist Ludovic Halévy produced a best-seller, *L'Abbé Constantin*, clearly modeled on the life of Louise Mackay. The book went into more than fifty editions and, in French, was used widely as a school text in America. When the coronation of Alexander III took place in Moscow in May, 1881, the Mackays were there in full regalia, John Mackay having been appointed special ambassador of the United States by President Chester Arthur.

The Mackays' numerous encounters with royalty were always faithfully reported, but two family marriages drew particular attention, the 1879 union of Mrs. Mackay's sister Ada to a wealthy Austro-Italian nobleman, the Count Joseph Telfener, and the wedding of the Mackays' daughter, Eva, to an Italian prince, Ferdinando Galatro-Colonna. Several years later Eva's presumably blissful match ended unhappily in scandal and, after a handsome payoff arranged by Mackay, in divorce.

The adverse publicity attending Mrs. Mackay's disagreement over her portrait with its painter Jean Meissonier, at the time the most celebrated artist in Paris, was a primary factor in her move to London. On the pretext of being near her sons, whom she had enrolled in the fashionable Beaumont School in England, she gave up her French residency for the less hostile setting across the Channel. The argument stemmed from her suggestions for several flattering changes in the Meissonier painting, which the artist, with some indignation, refused to make. Rather than have him sell the portrait publicly, which he threatened to do, she bought it unchanged and, according to some accounts, burned it with great ceremony before a group of fascinated friends. Her granddaughter, Ellin Berlin, the daughter of Clarie and the wife of Irving Berlin, denies the story in the biographical account of the family, *Silver Platter*.

Once in London, Mrs. Mackay bought the former home of the Duke of Leinster, a mansion rivaling in its grandeur the château now shuttered in Paris. Settled into 6 Carlton House Terrace, she continued to provide the lavish entertainments for which she was

world-famous, the most extravagant of which honored the Prince
of Wales.

As Mrs. Mackay pursued her increasingly prominent career in
society, her husband, on the other side of the Atlantic, sought out
new business ventures to replace the declining activities of mining. By 1883 he had sold his Comstock holdings and launched a
new career aimed at breaking the monopoly held by Jay Gould on
transatlantic cables. Mackay's partner in the Commercial Cable
Company, James Gordon Bennett, owned the New York *Herald,*
which stood to benefit handsomely by any improvement in cable
rates. When it became clear that the trans-American lines were as
essential to control as the transocean cables, Mackay proceeded to
buy up the Postal Telegraph Company and as many of the independents as he needed to compete nationally with Western
Union. By the turn of the century the Mackay company forged
another link in its competitive chain by laying a transpacific line.
All along, however, the venture had been fraught with such difficulties as crippling rate wars and almost-fatal deficits. These problems added considerable strain to the normal burdens of aging
that were beginning to make inroads on Mackay's once-robust
constitution. In July, 1902, he became seriously ill in London and
died there on the twentieth, of heart disease complicated by pneumonia. The last survivor of the silver kings, he had lived eight
years longer than Fair. After her daughter Eva's death a few years
later, Mrs. Mackay, herself suffering a heart condition, no longer
felt a strong tie to the continent. She returned to the United States
to reside with her divorced son Clarie and his children in the
Long Island showplace. There she died of a heart attack in September, 1928, at the age of eighty-four.

In the forty years after their discovery, the silver mines of Nevada had poured into San Francisco more than $500,000,000
worth of precious metals, creating in the process multimillionaires
of almost unparalleled dimension. Under normal circumstances,
the wealth of the real estate baron Michael Reese or the czar of Panama transportation, Trenor Park, would have seemed the ultimate aspiration to the multitudes, but the deluge of silver overwhelmed their feats and pushed their millions into comparative
oblivion.

The new lords of the kingdom had risen so rapidly from the
ranks of the poor that they had neither the time nor the inclination to acquire much in the way of critical education. They tried to
acquire instant culture, but their mansions, their entertainments,
their wholesale collections of jewels, paintings, sculptures, and libraries largely followed a course of taste based on ability to pay
rather than discrimination. Theaters became at least as important

as a setting for the audience as for the performance. Ralston alone among them also had the desire to make San Francisco a metropolis that the world would admire, and his efforts, never mind how much he could bask in the reflected glory, did much to build the city's industries, increase its commerce, and add such gems to its beauty as the Palace Hotel.

Although the wealth of the Comstock originally spurred California industry, its principal beneficiaries never numbered beyond the handful of giants, and its eventual effects on the masses were devastating. Solving the mechanics of mining and providing machinery for the Silver Bonanza meant that foundries prospered, inventiveness became profitable, and ingenuity commanded some rewards. And watching a common, uneducated man rise to the mastery of men, to become an in-law of royalty and an entertainer of Presidents, kept hope eternal in a population that believed fervently in gambling for the long shot. But more and more it became clear that the odds were largely in favor of the men already in power. When Mrs. Huntington forgot her purse in the showroom of a New York art dealer with $3,500,000 worth of pearl necklaces tossed casually inside, the average spectator, although certainly impressed, must also have been overwhelmed with the lack of proportion it suggested. Such examples of the concentration of power fed a rising social consciousness. Political reform was in the air.

Early in the seventies San Francisco responded to the enormous wealth of the decade by maturing physically into the metropolitan center that the Gold Rush had merely suggested. Palaces arose on the hills, cable cars clanged up to meet them, the shops took on new elegance, and the hotels and dining rooms rivaled the finest in the world. The Southerners, who had always been the leaders of society, suddenly found the Peninsula retreats to which they had moved from the South Park neighborhood challenged by such newcomers as Flood and his ornate Menlo Park estate. Yet the city preserved much of its original flavor: the miscellany of style and population and the continuous shift of power and position resisted the onslaught of conformity which the new wealth tried to impose. And although in the end a small number reaped all the profits, everyone had at least at one time or another been caught up in the mania of speculation and in this sense had had a common share in the adventure. The feeling prevailed that anyone of them could have, with a shift of luck, been one of the "race of bonanza kings" whom Bancroft described as having "silver souls": "silver were their friends, and silver were their enemies, for to be worthy of consideration at all, they must be of silver; silver was their meat and meditations; their doors where barred with silver, and silver paved their way to the final abode of souls."[3]

XV

The Railroad and the Big Four-and-a-Half

THE increasing demands of the Gold Rush for transportation of passengers, mail, gold, and supplies, had pushed the advance of the stage companies, inspired the Pony Express, and spurred the development of riverboats and ocean shipping. By 1854 the various river companies had merged into the California Steam Navigation Company and the stage lines had consolidated into the California Stage Company, but commerce with the rest of the world continued slow and cumbersome. With each run, the Panama steamers set new records, yet their best time was still unsatisfactory, and the public attributed the unfortunate number of explosions to the breakneck speed forced on racing skippers. The overland stages and the financially unsuccessful Pony Express, although glamorous, brought little improvement to transcontinental transportation.

> Their true significance is that they gave practical demonstration of the possibility of through service on the overland routes, that by their very shortcomings they helped to evoke the railroad, and that by the boldness of their design they commanded attention to the problem of western communications.[4]

A transcontinental railroad, first proposed by Asa Whitney in 1845, had again been bandied about as the solution to cross-country transportation since the early days of the Gold Rush; advocates for continental unity urged the idea on Congress from both sides of the nation. The opening of commerce with the Pacific focused further attention on a link to the Western gateway. Californians exaggerated its imagined virtues until they saw it as the answer to all of the state's problems, especially its economic ones. Ironically, by the seventies they were blaming it for all of the state's economic ills. In 1853 the national government appropriated funds for a survey of possible western routes, but partisan disagreements prevented any decision until the secession of the

318

South forced the issue in 1862 to a north-central conclusion. The North had feared a southern route for its possible benefits to the cause of slavery, while the South just as vehemently had opposed a northern artery for its potential in developing antislave states.

Theodore Judah, the real father of the Pacific railroad, combined a young visionary's enthusiasm with a thorough expertise in engineering and a professional's skill at lobbying. His genius had enabled him, still in his twenties, to build the Sacramento Valley Railroad, the West Coast's first line, among a number of engineering feats. During the later fifties he alternated between successfully mapping the Sierras to choose a national railroad route and unsuccessfully arguing the railroad's cause before Congress. Dutch Flat, the most promising choice for the railroad's passage through the Sierras, allowed the 7,000-foot climb from the valley to the summit along a 70-mile slope that was gradual enough to be workable. Official support, although only partial, finally came when the state convened the Pacific Railroad Convention in the fall of 1859 and selected Judah to present its case in Washington.

Still unable to obtain national commitment, although he won a great many officials to the cause, Judah determined to set up the machinery himself and formulated plans for the Central Pacific Railroad of California. He, the Dutch Flat dentist Daniel Strong, and several local residents put up the starting finances, but the big San Francisco moneymen on whom they had counted for the rest failed to come through, preferring the high returns on their current investments to speculation on some grandiose scheme for the future. Judah then successfully turned to a number of small-time but by then reasonably well-to-do Sacramento businessmen, among them Collis P. Huntington and Mark Hopkins, over whose hardware store the group first met, Leland Stanford, a grocer, Charles Crocker, a dry-goods seller, James Bailey, a jeweler, and Lucius A. Booth, a merchant. Their original interest was in controlling the sale of goods to the mining communities beyond the mountains. That the railroad would be a link to the transcontinental line was at first only incidental. To protect their investments, they became the first officers and directors of the company after its incorporation; ironically, Huntington at first declined to purchase stock, but Judah finally persuaded him. Stanford became president, Huntington vice-president, Hopkins treasurer, and chief engineer Judah a director.

Although he had envisioned the railroad, had done the planning, selected and mapped the routing, and laid the groundwork in Washington, Judah, although he didn't know it, was no longer a controlling factor in the development of the Central Pacific. Stanford, Huntington, Crocker, and Hopkins, with the idea of making as much money in as short a time as possible, dominated the company from the first. Less aggressive directors resigned, and the Big Four tolerated Judah's participation in direct proportion to his usefulness in pushing through the railroad.

With the incorporation of the company and Judah's appointment through Senatorial influence as a member of the railroad committees of both houses of Congress, Washington's backing became much more accessible. Impressed by the wartime urgency of keeping the West and its gold and silver assets a functioning part of the Union, in 1862 Congress passed and President Lincoln signed the Pacific Railroad Act, granting two companies, the Central Pacific and the Union Pacific, generous land grants and subsidies to build the road. Central Pacific's route was to go east from Sacramento; Union Pacific, chartered by Congress, was to build west from Omaha, Nebraska.

In 1861 Stanford, a Republican, having tried unsuccessfully once before, had run for and won election, in the predominantly pro-Northern atmosphere of the state, as governor of California. From this position he could influence the state's contributions to the railroad's well-being, ensuring their dubious legality by such moves as filling a Supreme Court vacancy with the Central Pacific's practicing legal counsel, Edwin Crocker, who happened, incidentally, to be Charles' brother. Edwin found that it was no trouble to hold down both jobs simultaneously. In the same spirit, the railroad awarded construction contracts to the Charles Crocker Company, a phony corporation owned equally by Crocker, Huntington, Hopkins, and Stanford. Judah was beside himself. Ever since the passage of the Pacific Railroad Act, with its enticements of federal grants and bountiful subsidies, the fundamental differences between him and the Big Four had become each day startlingly clearer. Judah's grand concept of a transcontinental railroad had little in common with the Big Four's totally exploitative view of the project. They would reap the most business with the least outlay—the completion of the system be damned— meanwhile grabbing up the government subsidy as quickly and as minimally as they could meet the requirements. The total railroad was of little interest to them except as it contributed to their profits. They viewed the costly link to the rest of the country, once it left their bailiwick, as an encroachment on their earnings and an investment to be avoided as vigorously as possible. However, with the sudden advent of larger subsidies from both federal and state governments, their reluctance turned to greed. Such was their appetite that when Judah refused to go along with an inflated claim for mountain trackage, which would have brought them a higher federal increment based on the more difficult terrain, they enlisted the testimony of the state geologist, who by means of soil analysis magnanimously created 20 miles of mountains where there was in reality only valley, netting the combine an additional $640,000.

After considerable internal feuding, Judah sold out for $100,-000 and sailed for New York to obtain Eastern capital to buy up the options he had obtained on his partners' shares and to reorganize the company. He never had the chance to pursue his plan; by November, 1863, not quite thirty-eight, he was struck down by yellow fever contracted during his passage through Panama one month earlier. His colleagues neither memorialized his considerable connection to the railroad by naming any part of it after him nor saw that his widow received as much as a penny in remuneration. Without Judah's hindrance, in fact, the Big Four set out to develop a scheme for self-enrichment on a scale that before that, even in the context of those times, was unimaginable. When Judah had first persuaded them to incorporate, the state law had required subscriptions of $1,000 for each mile of track, or $115,000 in shares initially, to finance the 115 miles of proposed track. Other buyers brought the original total to 1,580 shares. Since only 10 percent of the whole had to be paid down, the actual cash investment came to $15,800. The Big Four and Judah took 150 shares each at $100 a share, on which they needed to make only a 10 percent payment. From this investment all but the unfortunate Judah went on to become multimillionaires.

Stanford, Hopkins, and Huntington took over Judah's lobbying tasks on both local and national levels, as well as the actual running of the company. Crocker's job was superintendent of construction, a position from which he could let inflated contracts to companies fronting for the Big Four. (The Union Pacific, it should be said, did the same thing through the offices of the Crédit Mobilier.) Thanks to other lofty connections, the Central Pacific solved a seriously mounting financial problem by persuading the legislature to supplement federal subsidies with state funds and the state and several counties to purchase $1,500,000 of Central Pacific stock, as well as to assume the interest on a like amount of bonds. A generous amendment to the national Railroad Act allowed advance payments of some subsidies, doubled the original land grants, and eased the security required for the extensive loan already made to the company.

The railroad faced one further major difficulty: labor. Besides the constant turnover of the corps of white workers, most of whom used their employment as a free ride to the mines, the feisty Irish, in spite of the fact that the railroad thought their wages excessive, threatened to strike. Crocker persuaded his colleagues, including Stanford, whose inaugural address had contained heated words against Chinese immigration, to allow him to experiment with fifty coolie laborers. The Chinese workman more than made up for his small physical stature by his willingness to toil long hours under distressing conditions at a very small rate of pay. Crocker's pilot crew, more successful than even he had imagined, inspired a recruiting drive that brought in thousands of Chinese laborers, at first from California and then from China, until by 1869 there were between 10,000 and 15,000 Asian immigrants at work on the Central Pacific line. During the sixties mounting antagonism to Oriental competition stayed just short of violence largely because the railroad work, continuous throughout the most severe weather, became more backbreaking, more dangerous, and thoroughly unattractive to white labor. However, the white rhetoric flowed unabated, setting the emotional groundwork for the gigantic labor problems of the following decade, when the flood of Chinese railroad workers was released onto the general market.

Meanwhile, the tireless southern Chinese performed astonishing feats of construction without much more mechanical assistance than wheelbarrows and picks and loads of black powder. When the management disdained the use of a newfangled steam drill and gave up nitroglycerine after several untoward explosions, the Chinese workmen spent well over a year chiseling out one-quarter of a mile of solid granite, by hand, to complete the Summit Tunnel; for protection against the heavy Sierra snows they constructed almost 40 miles of snowsheds; and most spectacularly, they conquered the 1,000-foot sheer verticality of the Cape Horn cliff by harrowing and chiseling a shelf for the railbed out of the solid rock face while hanging from above in wicker baskets. Perhaps their ultimate achievement was the laying of 10 miles of track in a single day.

There was now tremendous competition between the Central Pacific and the Union Pacific to build as much road as possible, since the federal government doled out its subsidies on the basis of miles of completed track. The Union Pacific crew, headed by General Grenville M. Dodge, employed 5,000 Irish laborers and large numbers of recently discharged soldiers, whose trials across the plains of Nebraska and Wyoming were hardly comparable to the challenges posed by the Sierras. The feats of the Chinese coolies seemed even more remarkable.

As the Chinese chiseled eastward with their hand tools, the Union Pacific crews, aided by every device they could employ, pushed westward. The farther the competing teams advanced, the larger the subsidies the companies collected from the government. Had not Congress suddenly realized, as the advance parties of the two groups raced past each other, that no meeting point had been established, the railroads would no doubt have continued in parallel lines, the directors pocketing the augmenting federal funds, until the oceans alone stopped them. In haste, Congress named Promontory, Utah, as the junction, and on May 10, 1869, the last spike driven, the rails united, the Pacific railroad was a reality. It marked the end of California's geographic provincialism.

Even before the line's completion San Franciscans had begun to have misgivings. Partly based on the realization that Sacramento businessmen controlled the operation—even though San Francisco financiers had had first crack at it but had turned it down—the city's animosity mounted as it became clear that the railroad's purposes and the city's interests were contrary. The city found it difficult to approve the state legislative act, railroad-inspired, enabling it to subscribe to railroad stock, while the railroad crowd, faced with mounting San Francisco opposition at a time when they badly needed the city's money, openly bought the municipal election. When local authorities still refused to comply, the matter was in and out of the courts for years before San Francisco finally had to give over its funds.

In order to complete its control over traffic and freight rates, the Central Pacific had to eliminate all significant competition on land and water. Its attack was so effective that it finally dominated virtually all Western business enterprises and political forces and earned its well-deserved image of an octopus, along with the undying hatred of the populace. "Big business today is multiple; . . . in the late nineteenth century all other enterprises were so overshadowed by the railroad as to be reduced to the stature of small businesses."[5]

The Big Four built their monopoly first by extending the major Central Pacific lines westward from Sacramento to San Francisco. They bought up existing interior lines and built others: their new California and Oregon line to the north and San Joaquin Valley road to the south were the beginnings of the Southern Pacific Railroad, a name that soon became synonymous with Central Pacific and the Big Four. It was made official in 1884 when the whole system incorporated as the Southern Pacific in the state of Kentucky, where the relevant laws were the most relaxed. As predicted, the completed transcontinental link speeded commerce between Europe and the Orient; this made the control of shipping a highly important cog in the operation. To this end, the Central Pacific took over as much of the Oakland and San Francisco waterfronts as they could and set up barriers to the development of

any facilities other than their own. A controlling interest in the
Oakland Waterfront Company assured them virtually complete
dominance over the Oakland port by 1868. Stanford became a
principal stockholder in an agreement that made Oakland the
railroad's main East Bay terminus. At the same time the scrappy
San Franciscans battled the takeover and forced the railroad into
two major retreats: the abandonment of a state bill which would
have given them a huge stretch of city waterfront and virtual monopoly of the port and the abandonment of federal legislation
which would have given them control over Yerba Buena Island
and its facilities.

Despite these setbacks, the railroad got 60 acres of San Francisco waterfront, enough for a terminal. Through its authority over
the state harbor commission, the company controlled almost all
water transportation around San Francisco Bay: the bay ferries,
the California Steam Navigation Company, the river traffic to inland areas, and the Pacific Mail Steamship Company, its trans-
pacific and Panama traffic. With such a monopoly they could fix
rates on any scale they chose; they chose the most exorbitant fees
they could get away with. Before the Pacific Steamship Company
would comply to setting competitive rates, the railroad had had to
start its own shipping line, the Occidental and Oriental. It under-
cut charges to force Pacific Mail out of competition, leaving it no
choice but to enter into a rate-fixing agreement. The rate was generally flexible, based entirely on the customer's success at any giv-
en moment. The railroad never allowed the businessman more
than a small margin of profit, absorbing any excesses by hoisting
the freight rates and preventing failure by temporarily lowering
them until conditions were again favorable.

> It was perhaps the nation's choicest example of a complete
> and sustained monopoly, an almost ideal demonstration of the
> power of a corporation to control for its own profit the economic
> resources of a region comprising one-sixth of the area of the na-
> tion. . . . The result was that from the middle '70's to 1910 the
> major share of the profit of virtually every business and industry
> on the Coast was diverted from its normal channel into the
> hands of the railroad and its controlling group.[6]

To set up revenues for the Southern Pacific lines in lower California, the railroad let out for development great parcels of land
that the federal government had reserved for it. The easy terms
advertised by the railroad enticed many Eastern settlers; the sale
price, to be fixed at a later date, would be moderate. Through a
Sacramento-based land office, the railroad trumpeted the glories
of the area in circulars, guidebooks, travel accounts, and a miscel-

lany of inflated writings. The settlers nearly starved to death before they engineered a viable system for water distribution and managed to reap the resulting harvest. The railroad, to avoid property taxes, had meanwhile delayed picking up title to the holdings it had conditionally sold to the farmers. In 1877, however, with the well-irrigated land now producing bountiful crops, the settlers found that the railroad had suddenly taken title and, in complete disregard of the terms originally agreed upon, offered it up at public sale for highly advanced prices.

A series of legal battles, evictions, and repossessions followed. When the settlers forcibly ejected one family of recent buyers and set fire to their house, the railroad retaliated by sending in a pair of toughs to whom they promised free land if they could hold off the settlers. The result was the Battle of Mussel Slough, immortalized twenty years later in Frank Norris' novel *The Octopus* and in Josiah Royce's *The Feud of Oakfield Creek*. The tally was seven dead, five of them farmers, two the railroad's sharpshooters. The railroad took measures to censor the news, inhibit investigation, and disseminate false information, but shaken public opinion rallied once again behind the opponents of the railroad. The victimized farmers, their lands and improvements lost, dropped the court battle for lack of funds. Several years later the Supreme Court, in an equivalent case, finally ruled in favor of a group of settlers.

When passenger traffic flagged, as it did on the service to the Monterey Peninsula, the Southern Pacific lent its financial backing to an anticipated new drawing card, the swanky Del Monte Hotel. At the debut the strategically arranged presence of the proper newspaper reporters and society editors assured its instant appeal as an excursion resort for well-to-do socialites and social climbers and significantly bolstered the railroad's passenger receipts from the 1880's on. In 1898 the Southern Pacific started its own promotional magazine with a heavy emphasis on the history of California and the glories of the West. It was named *Sunset* after the Sunset Limited, one of the crack trains on the transcontinental run. In 1914 the railroad sold the journal to a number of employees; in 1928 a new owner, L. W. Lane, revamped it into one of the country's leading regional publications.

When opposition surfaced, the railroad barons would generally crush it. If the opponent proved to be formidable, the railroad declared open warfare, and actual battles often followed. John L. Davie, an Oakland coal dealer, proved to be one of the most upsetting adversaries. His simple attempt to build a warehouse on the Oakland estuary challenged the railroad's sovereignty. The confrontation took on such proportions that the two sides launched armed forces in battle. During the course of their litigations Davie managed to build a storehouse on tidelands belonging to the Morgan Oyster Company and thereby exempt from government control and from railroad domination. He recruited and supplied arms to a gang of oyster pirates whose shanty stood on the same property, among them a young roustabout named Jack London. The fight went all the way to the Supreme Court, where the railroad lost the case. Davie, with substantial popular backing, challenged the railroad on a second issue, their monopoly of bay ferry service at ridiculously high rates. The gauntlet here took the form of a line of nickel ferries, and again the challenge resulted in warfare. Davie lost this battle by attrition: the cost of running nickel ferries soon put him out of business.

During the prosperous decade of the eighties the railroads maintained their political power, keeping local control through the machinery of the blind San Francisco boss Chris Buckley. The city suffered along with the rest of the country in the depression of 1893, when eighteen of San Francisco's banks closed their doors and several hundred unemployed formed a delegation to march on Washington. One indication of the growing feeling against domination by big business was the election in 1894 of Adolph Sutro as mayor on a Populist, anti-Southern Pacific ticket.

After enduring twenty years of railroad control over the shipping business, the trampled owners finally revolted. By a complicated arrangement of transshipping by sea under foreign colors and later, when that had been declared illegal, by operating such new American lines as the Atlantic and Pacific Steamship Company, the Traffic Association, the new organization of shippers, forced the railroad to come to terms. But where there was no threat of competition, the railroad extracted the usual high fees. The only relief from monopoly clearly lay in an alternate rail line. To this end, and with the full force and financial backing of an aroused public, the Traffic Association shepherded the building of the California Valley Road. In December, 1898, the Atchison, Topeka, and Santa Fe Railroad, having incorporated the Atlantic and Pacific line and the successful California Valley system, operated a second complete transcontinental railroad.

During the last decade of the century the railroad and the government engaged in a battle over the amount and terms of payment of the Central Pacific's accumulated $59,000,000 federal debt. A powerful group led by San Francisco's Mayor Adolph Sutro and William Randolph Hearst helped to focus opposition to the "Octopus" and to bring about the defeat of the railroad and its funding bill. The most persistent attacks came from Hearst's team, Ambrose Bierce and Homer Davenport, on the scene in

Washington. With all the vitriolic force of prose and cartoon at their talented commands, they flayed Huntington and the railroad until defeat was assured.

In 1901, all members of the Big Four now dead, Edward H. Harriman, a stockbroker and the reorganizer of the Union Pacific Railroad, bought out the Southern Pacific heirs and used the majority interest to create an even more gigantic entity by merging the two systems. The new corporation controlled more than 15,000 miles of track and lasted until the government dissolved it in 1913.

Ironically the men who had created one of the world's largest business empires came from essentially poor backgrounds and were of limited experience. Their control of vast amounts of wealth and such power as derived from it heavily influenced the development of San Francisco and the West and permeated every feature of life from politics and justice to architecture and social custom. They were much more different from each other than the deliberately unified picture they at first presented to the public; as the railroad grew more successful, their differences loomed larger and in the end erupted into feuds and open animosities. A January 4, 1878, accounting of the amounts each drew from the railroad treasury for his personal use during the four months since August 1, 1877, is descriptive: Huntington $57,000, Crocker $31,000, Hopkins $800, and Stanford $276,000.[7]

From the first, the Big Four went into the railroad venture with but one goal, to make a profit. They left to visionaries like Judah the grander notions of ending Western isolation, uniting the country, and even pulling off the engineering feat of the century. Their interests lay in the immediate advantages: the government subsidies and the land grants. To them the most direct route meant the least subsidies; the more difficult the terrain, invented or otherwise, the higher the increments. In many cases their devious meanderings had to be corrected when the road actually went into operation. Once the subsidies were collected, it was time to get out, especially since general economic difficulties were becoming more intrusive by the day. The Union Pacific directorate disposed of that road as speedily as possible once it was completed and the government payments ceased. Of the Central Pacific crowd, Crocker made the first move, selling his interest to the other partners, but he returned to the fold a short time later only because the worsening economic situation caught him with no real alternative. Huntington for years mumbled and complained in his written correspondence about his desire to get out from under the tremendous burdens the railroad imposed on him, but he never acted unilaterally. Hopkins, who took his cues largely from

Huntington, was agreeable to the idea of selling, but Stanford, the inveterate office seeker, enjoyed the prestige of the presidency too much to want to give it up. At one point the group entered into serious negotiations to sell out to Darius Ogden Mills, the banker, and a number of his colleagues, but nothing came of it in the end, and the panic of 1873 completely wiped out all further chances to sell. The Four, having no choice, stuck it out, unaware during that time of doldrums that the Central Pacific was on its way to becoming unprecedentedly profitable.

At first the direction rested in Sacramento, the western terminus. In 1871, when the company incorporated the California Pacific from Sacramento to San Francisco, the latter city became the railroad's headquarters. Within a few years three of the partners, Hopkins, Stanford, and Crocker, had started to build their famous Nob Hill mansions, but Huntington did not move to the Hill until the early nineties. The company's assets came into full play even on Nob Hill: once company engineers had solved the problems of hillside construction, the Stanford and Hopkins homes rose above a granite battlement, a retaining wall of enormous proportions, built by the company's masons out of rock from the company's quarries.

Among the four, Hopkins had two distinctions: he was the best liked and also the oldest. Born in Henderson, New York, in 1813, he clerked in a store at the age of fifteen and continued a storekeeper, basically, the rest of his life. He was a man of simple tastes, by preference a vegetarian—he continued to grow his own vegetables in his own garden plot long after he came into the millions—and presented a lank figure next to his colleagues, who each weighed in at well over 200 pounds, Crocker topping them all at over 250. By nature he was compulsive, ascetic, almost miserly in his avoidance of complications. He lived contentedly in a rented cottage for five years after he was well able to afford the Nob Hill mansion he finally consented to build for his wife. She was his cousin, Mary Sherwood, twenty years younger, whose boredom with the lackluster life pushed him out of his simple habits, at least to the extent of purchasing land on the Hill and starting construction. Mary worked out most of the ideas for the huge mansion, much to Hopkins' relief, since the proliferation of towers and gingerbread curlicues would hardly have been to his taste. The Hopkinses had one adopted child, Timothy Nolan, the son of a widow who worked in the household. Although he was accepted for years as their own offspring, his legal adoption actually proceeded under Mary's auspices after her husband's death. Timothy, who had learned the railroad business well under his surrogate father, took over as treasurer with enthusiasm. He had one further tie to the family, his marriage to Mrs. Hopkins' niece, Clara Crittenden.

Mark Hopkins died in March, 1878, weakened and in pain from a persistent rheumatism. He left his widow an immense fortune, including the unfinished palace on Nob Hill, a legacy so spectacular that she was lifted immediately into the public eye. She did not enjoy the publicity. Printed speculations and inaccuracies about her private life increasingly troubled her until she fled, half in anger, half in despair, to Massachusetts. She seemed hardly able to manage. She built a $2,000,000 château, and peevishly fired, one after the other, two sets of architects who must have had some question about fitting an overpowering mass of French grandeur into the simple Great Barrington landscape. Edward T. Searles, a young decorator she befriended in San Francisco, supervised the final construction. Her behavior became increasingly arrogant, her eccentricities bordering on illness. She collected houses as if they were trinkets on a bracelet: two in Massachusetts, one in New York City, a summer place on Block Island, and the completed castle on Nob Hill.

Now fifty, she became infatuated with the twenty-eight-year-old Searles, whom she had met when he called on her with the hopes of seeing from a decorator's point of view the famous contents of her Nob Hill mansion. Over the increasing objections of her adopted son, Timothy, she and Searles married in the East. Angered by Timothy's suspicions and mounting protestations, she broke contact with him, to resume her relations on a business basis only when her efforts to replace him as her financial manager failed. When she died in the summer of 1891, she had disinherited him totally, leaving her entire estate to Searles. Timothy sued successfully, obtaining several millions in an out-of-court settlement. Searles, however, retained the shares in the Southern Pacific. He voted them in Huntington's favor, a fact for which the foresighted Huntington had prepared by befriending Searles at an earlier date. As the feuding between partners or their heirs became more energetic, Searles' votes became more important.

In 1893, perhaps as a means of easing the public indignation over the terms of Mary Hopkins Searles' will—not one philanthropic clause did it contain—Searles donated the crenellated Nob Hill structure to the San Francisco Art Association. Its gilded salons and turreted chambers were quite an improvement over the previous quarters, the loft above the butcher shops and fish stalls of the California Market. In gratitude, the Art Association changed its name to the Mark Hopkins Institute of Art and enjoyed the plush headquarters until they were destroyed in the

1906 fire. As the California School of Fine Arts the group occupied the present Chestnut Street site a number of years later and made a further name change in the early 1960's to the San Francisco Institute of Art, its present title. In the 1920's the Mark Hopkins Hotel rose on the gutted Nob Hill site.

Charles Crocker was also a New Yorker, born in Troy in 1822. He was a wage earner from the age of twelve, buying and running his own newspaper agency. At fourteen he joined the rest of the family on a farm in Indiana and, among his other skills, was a good blacksmith. He arrived in California early in 1850, drawn by the Gold Rush, but did not stay long at mining, preferring the dry goods business. He was making a comfortable profit as a shopkeeper when Judah tapped him for the railroad.

He enjoyed the activity of superintending the construction; and the prospect of a merely administrative existence after the railroad's completion motivated his aborted effort to sell out to his partners. During his period of severance he traveled extensively in Europe, financed in high style by the chunk of Central Pacific stock he had received as payment to the construction companies owned by him and his partners. When he rejoined the directorate, he began to acquire property, made a second European excursion exclusively to buy furnishings and art goods for his Nob Hill showplace, founded a landholding company and developed an irrigation network in the San Joaquin Valley, entered into coal mining, and set up his sons in banking and cattle ranching by acquiring the majority stocks in a banking concern and large tracts of Nevada grazing land.

He had no trouble extending his domain to any corner of the country that he set his sights on, except one: a small property adjacent to his Nob Hill mansion, an acquisition he needed to complete his ownership of the block surrounding him. He had bought up the whole parcel, with that one notable exception, bordered by Jones, Sacramento, California, and Taylor streets, and to him it was insupportable that an insignificant undertaker named Yung should thwart his grand schemes by hanging onto his modest property. Yung was adamant. He refused all of Crocker's offers. The enraged tycoon tried another tactic, the building of a 40-foot-high fence that completely surrounded the Yung cottage. Yung suffered a number of sunless years before he finally yielded. Meanwhile, the spite fence took on large significance as a symbol of the insolence of the rich in a city that was becoming more openly critical of its economic inequalities. Denis Kearney's Workingmen's Party used the Crocker fence as a starting point for demonstrations against the wealthy, especially singling out the Big Four. There already existed animosity between them because the railroad had had the audacity to employ Chinese workers on the construction crews, and the Chinese were increasingly the focus of labor's attacks. Invective flew, mobs milled menacingly about the Hill, and finally a group of ruffians down below sacked several Chinese businesses, attacked Chinese residents, and set fire to a good part of the Chinese district. The wealthy escaped without harm.

In the eighties Crocker added to his residences a new quarter-million-dollar New York mansion on Fifty-eighth Street. However, to them all he much preferred the surroundings of the Del Monte Lodge, the construction of which he had so much enjoyed supervising. It was there that he died of the complications of diabetes in August, 1888.

Like Crocker, Leland Stanford was born in the area of Troy, New York, in 1824, one of eight children. His father made his living concurrently as a farmer and as the proprietor of the Bull's Head Tavern. Leland attended a seminary near Syracuse, from which he was never graduated, followed by a three-year apprenticeship in a law firm. His admission to the bar took place the year before the Gold Rush. He joined the march to California in 1852 to enter the grocery business his brothers had already set up. While managing the Sacramento branch, he accepted the major shares in a customer's quartz mine in lieu of payment. When the mine subsequently produced, he made several hundred thousand dollars' profit.

From the first he was interested in politics, starting out as a justice of the peace, but losing contests for alderman and state treasurer. By 1862 he was the governor of California. In 1885, when he decided that a seat in the United States Senate would be an appropriate addition to his career, he had unfortunately already promised his endorsement, and consequently that of the railroad, to Aaron Sargent. Sargent, who had served for years as a California representative in both the House and the Senate, was reentering politics after a ten-year retirement. A good friend of both Stanford and Huntington, he had the election in his pocket until Stanford's last-minute announcement. Stanford's victory was the beginning of total and open animosity between Huntington and himself. Huntington's distaste for Stanford's grandiose style was only one facet of their long-standing hostility. Until the Sargent affair, the differences among the partners had more or less remained concealed for the sake of presenting a harmonious front to the public.

As a person Stanford seemed slow and plodding and a poor conversationalist. Although Huntington completely overshadowed him in actual dominance over the company, Stanford was content with the title of president of the Central Pacific. The personal dynasty which he created hardly accorded with any lesser office. His Nob Hill mansion stood on a plot covering 2 acres. His Palo Alto farm and horse-breeding ranch comprised 9,000 acres. His Vina property contained 55,000 acres, 3,500 of them in grapes, the 2,800,000 vines making it the world's largest vineyard. He spared no expense in anything he did or on anything he acquired. When he traveled about, he luxuriated in a private railway car, done up as befitted the president of the company, and wallowed in the staged salutes and planned receptions at all the whistle-stops along his route. His fervid interest in mechanics extended beyond the mines, where most of his technical suggestions and his purchases of the latest machines were stoutly vetoed by the foreman. At home no one had a veto, and the various abodes, in particular the Nob Hill mansion, brimmed with mechanical marvels. It was Stanford who financed the photographic sequence of "The Horse in Motion," successive shots of a racing Stanford thoroughbred that prophesied the motion picture and brought fame to the photographer Eadweard Muybridge.

Stanford's son Leland, Jr., born after twenty years of a childless marriage to Jane Lathrop Stanford, died before he was sixteen of typhoid fever in Florence, Italy. During his short life he had received a fine education, traveled widely, and developed a lively intellectual curiosity. His mania for collecting had filled three rooms of the Nob Hill house. As a suitable memorial, the Stanfords planned to add a technical school to the University of California, but when the state legislature turned down Stanford's proposed appointment as a regent of the university, he founded Stanford University instead.

Stanford died suddenly in June, 1893, leaving a tremendous accumulation of debts. The estate had the further obligation of paying its share of the government bonds which were coming to maturity just at that point. Creditors demanded that the university be closed until the debts were cleared. Huntington stood forcefully behind such a move, having thought of the institution as another extension of Stanford's flamboyant style, and nothing more than an extravagance of the worst sort. Mrs. Stanford behaved in a remarkable fashion, cutting back on her own manner of living, paring her expenses, selling off some of the stock from the breeding farm, stopping operations on the nonprofitable vineyard, and reluctantly placing a tuition charge on the heretofore-free university. Her generosity and devotion to the university helped see it through the crisis, though her overbearing, officious concern with all aspects of its functions almost brought it to a close.

She lived until 1905, having survived an unsolved episode of possible poisoning by strychnine a short time before her death of old age in Honolulu.

Collis P. Huntington shouldered the major responsibility for running the railroad and constantly reminded his colleagues of the fact. Although he thoroughly dominated the Big Four, he disliked being conspicuous, and his command received no deliberate publicity. He would not put up with any frills, and the austerity of the company's stations and offices was entirely his doing. He was the exact opposite of Stanford, and it was the latter's need for show and self-adornment that rankled Huntington from the first.

He was born in Harwinton, Connecticut, in 1821, and no doubt inherited much of the severity of his nature from his father, a tightfisted, hard-driving tinker. His schooling, at first part time, did not continue beyond the age of thirteen. By fifteen he had left home to open a store in New York with an older brother. When he crossed the Isthmus en route to the Gold Rush in 1850, he made use of the time to do a little trading and ended up several thousand dollars richer.

He married twice. The first union, to Elizabeth Stoddard, was childless, but the couple brought up Clara Prentice, a niece, orphaned before she was a year old. She was among the San Francisco girls who later married into royalty, taking as her husband the German Prince von Hatzfeldt-Wildenberg. At age sixty-three, now a widower, Huntington married Mrs. Arabella Duval Yarrington Worsham, of New York by way of Alabama. She had a softening influence on him, and for the first time he expanded his style of living and even made a benefaction or two. His concern for his fellowman had never before been evidenced, and he was known actively to disapprove of philanthropy. It therefore came as a surprise to those who knew him that he built a chapel to his mother's memory in his hometown in Connecticut, that he donated a small library to Westchester, New York, and that he backed the Hampton Industrial School in the South, a trade school for blacks based on the premise that they were unsuited for a more formal education. He built a $2,000,000 town house in New York and spent more and more of his time there. He had a box at the Metropolitan Opera and began buying paintings, books, and appropriate furnishings. When he was in San Francisco, and business required his presence at least several times a year, he stayed in the Palace Hotel. His aversion to the city and the state grew as the aroused feelings of the public against the railroad barons became more vocal. Yet in the nineties he mellowed enough to purchase the Colton home on Nob Hill and from that time on spent at least half his time in San Francisco.

A complete businessman in all his functions, he was pitiless in his dealings with others, rigid in his goals, calculating and deceptive, and capable of total dishonesty when that got him what he wanted. The only hint of feeling this obdurate man allowed concerned his increasing baldness: he disliked it so much that he was never seen without his hat or a skullcap. His differences with Stanford came to a peak after the Stanford-Sargent affair, and with all the guile of which he was capable, he used it to take over the presidency of the railroad. He spent five years coldly trapping his prey. With a promise to destroy all the evidence of the shady maneuverings in the former contest for the Senate and the pledge of support for Stanford's reelection to that office, Huntington engineered Stanford's resignation. Once he had taken over the chair himself, he publicly announced that railroad money had bought Stanford the election—a piece of news the community had long suspected. The feud raged in the public press and did not add to the railroad's image, but Stanford managed to win reelection in spite of it.

Huntington, who admired his nephew Henry Edwards Huntington as much as he disapproved of Stanford, coached him as his personal assistant and made him one of his heirs. The young man, with his uncle's blessing, took over more and more of the important responsibilities of the railroad and at the time of his uncle's death was also manager of that part of San Francisco's streetcar system that was controlled by the railroad. After Collis' death, Henry became vice-president of the Southern Pacific, but when it became clear that he would not gain the presidency, he sold his shares to Harriman of the Union Pacific. The nephew's marriage to Clara's older sister, Mary Alice Prentice, ended in divorce in 1906, but the family fortune stayed intact in any case: Collis died in the Adirondacks in August, 1900, and seven years later Henry married his widow. They both were then in their sixties and richer than Collis had ever been. Henry had himself amassed a fortune of several millions in southern California by developing interurban rail lines over properties he had foresightedly bought up. By the early 1900's, settled on their San Marino estate, they turned to improving their collection of manuscripts, rare books, and paintings. Huntington could outbid any competitor, and he did. He gathered whole libraries at a scoop. The acquisitions formed the basis of the great Huntington Library, which opened after his death in 1927, housed in the family mansion.

For a period of time the Big Four became known as the Big Four-and-a-Half. General David Douty Colton, represented by the fraction, was a crafty, ambitious, egocentric resident of Maine who first came to California during the Gold Rush. He never saw active military service; his title represented only his affiliation with the state militia. He thrust himself on men who were leaders in the hopes of acquiring power through reflected glory. In the late fifties he had served as an aide to Senator David C. Broderick and, as his second, witnessed his assassination in the duel with Chief Justice David S. Terry. He made a handsome sum of money on some of Broderick's real estate after his death, not without arousing widespread suspicions that he had come by the property deviously. He returned east to study law and by the end of the Civil War was in practice in San Francisco.

In 1871 he was victimized along with about two dozen financial geniuses of the West in the Great Diamond Hoax. The bilking of the century came about when two leathery old prospectors ostentatiously deposited several sacks of rough diamonds and other precious stones in Ralston's bank. Their gesture alerted Ralston immediately, and after several interviews it was agreed that the men would sell a half interest in their fabulous desert stake if two of Ralston's representatives, blindfolded both coming and going, authenticated the find. Ralston chose Colton as one of them. When Colton returned, overwhelmed by the acres of gems he had seen, Ralston immediately cabled for his old friend Asbury Harpending, who had made a fortune in the California gold mines and was now in London on business. Harpending received the request with the gravest doubts but returned from London reluctantly to aid his friend in this strange venture.

Meanwhile, Ralston checked into the prospectors' backgrounds: every source—and they were known by a number of local people—found them reputable. The miners, to show their good faith, offered to collect more than $1,000,000 worth of gems to keep on deposit with Ralston while the final negotiations were worked out. The potential buyers dispatched Harpending to New York with a sampling of the stones to get the expert appraisal of Tiffany and Company; they found them genuine and of exceptional quality. Based on the sample, the lot in Ralston's safekeeping was worth at least $1,500,000.

The Ralston group then lobbied a bill through Congress making it possible to take title to gem fields, something which had not theretofore been covered by the law. When they dispatched one of the country's leading engineers to the fields, he turned in an enthusiastic report. The yield might be a million a month. Twenty-five San Francisco financiers then incorporated the San Francisco and New York Mining and Commercial Company. The London Rothschilds bought in through their local representatives. Besides the considerable amounts expended on preliminary investigations, lobbying, and incorporation, and the $300,000 already paid to the miners for a one-half interest in the gem fields, the company invested a further $300,000 to buy out the prospectors altogether.

A government scientist, sent to make an official examination of the new national wonder, discovered, after his initial response of unbounded enthusiasm, that whereas some gems were lodged where they would not naturally occur, none could be found in layers where they should have been. After more extensive examination, he sadly wired Ralston that the fields were without a doubt salted, a total fraud. The company, in a state of shock, reviewed all the official testimonials of the experts and concluded that appraisers, financiers, and engineers alike had been most skillfully duped. The fields were predominantly low-grade gems, bought largely for the purpose in European markets.

To his partners' and the public's satisfaction, Ralston personally repaid the $2,000,000 that the financial backers had so far advanced and completely shouldered the other half million dollars of accumulated expenses. The public had long eyed Harpending, however, as a devious character, based largely on his part in a Civil War conspiracy. Although he had originally joined the diamond group against his better judgment, now Harpending took the brunt of the blame in the public view. Colton, in good company, got off with an extreme case of embarrassment.

When Colton established himself in San Francisco, he aimed to circle as close to the important men as possible; one way of suggesting his own prestige was to construct a substantial home on Nob Hill. When Crocker built across from him, the opportunity for a friendship presented itself. They exchanged business favors. Through Crocker's efforts the general invested in and was made manager of a railroad subsidiary, the Rocky Mountain Coal and Iron Company. Although his character failed to appeal to Stanford or Hopkins, Huntington thought his qualifications perfect: he had the political connections, the drive, and the savvy to serve the railroad well. The general was admitted to the group as a limited partner and financial director, with the other four retaining the right to cancel the arrangement within two years. In 1876 they did decide to terminate the connection but reversed themselves.

Colton, whose attachment to the Big Four meant that, if only by association, he had reached the top of the heap, embroidered his role, inflated his ties to the partnership, and generally convinced the public, the journalists, and especially the leaders of society that he was on an equal footing with the Big Four. Although, in keeping with his posture, he referred to the partnership in editorial terms as the "five of us," some of the less friendly newspapers preferred the "Big Four-and-a-Half."

Early in October, 1878, Colton's carriage arrived at his door, and the general, in a state of total collapse, was carried into the house. Doctors rushed to the scene. Two days later he died at the age of forty-seven, rumored to have been brutally stabbed but officially injured in a fall from a horse on his ranch. After his death the Big Four forced on his widow a very unsatisfactory settlement, based on their claims that the estate owed the railroad a sizable debt, $1,000,000 on a note soon due for Colton's original purchase into the corporation, plus all the subsequent assessments and obligations, as well as a number of considerably valuable dividends from a subsidiary, which they were recalling. To help persuade the widow that she must pay off all of the general's heavy obligations to the railroad, they claimed to have uncovered evidence that Colton had manipulated company funds, a fact they threatened to make public if she didn't agree to their terms. When the Hopkins estate was being settled at about the same time, Mrs. Colton discovered that the very securities that she was concerned with had in that case been given a much different value, that, in effect, she had been roundly cheated. She went to court, hoping to have the agreement she had signed annulled. The trial took eight years, and the widow lost, but during the course of the procedure it was at least proved that the general had embezzled no company funds.

The importance of the trial, however, had little to do with who won or lost. In the course of her appeal, Mrs. Colton made public more than 600 letters exchanged between Colton and Huntington, proving, as they were introduced to do, that Colton was a thoroughly trusted member of the directorate. More important, they revealed that the railroad had controlled legislation and legislators beyond the wildest suppositions, that it had brought its full force to manipulate California elections to obtain officials who were completely prorailroad. Although the railroad's political maneuvering had never been altogether successful, the antirailroad forces generally winning in San Francisco, the revelations gave impetus to a growing movement to curb the railroad's monopolistic control, particularly in politics.

XVI

Society

IF the Gold Rush, the discovery of silver, and the railroad had invigorating, though not always beneficial, influences on the course of San Francisco's cultural awakening, they were equal forces in shaping the city's social organization. People doing well do not ordinarily seek new frontiers, but the gold discovery, the promise of land, and the Silver Bonanza managed to lure, besides the expected numbers of restless fortune seekers, respectable poor, malcontents, derelicts, and exiles, a large segment of established gentlemen and professionals from all over the world.

To many the Gold Rush represented a way to make a fortune without having to have money to begin with. From New England came acquisitive businessmen, strong believers in piety, schooling, community, English law and traditions, the bastions of civilization; from the South, blacks, who saw a possible escape from slavery, and whites, followers of the British agrarian tradition, proud, stubbornly aristocratic, given to a life-style defined by grand mansions, devoted servants, gently cultivated women, leisure bordering on indolence, courtly manners, and a tradition of oratory, arrogance, politics, and military competence; from the frontier, homesteaders, families accustomed to hardships, deprivations, and a simple existence, suspicious of foreign elements and given easily to violence.

From Europe came political exiles and adventurers; from China, most often through misrepresentation or coercion, hordes of coolies; from Australia's prisons, delinquents whose crimes were often more serious than economic.

Most who came were men; of the women a goodly number were not considered proper by the community that richly supported them. With normal gauges of male respectability cast aside and the common reversal of status, a pragmatic equality prospered. "A man on coming to California could no more expect to retain his old nature unchanged than he could retain in his lungs the air he had inhaled on the Atlantic shore."[8]

The same adaptability with which the population dealt with the physical rigors of the city prevailed in the emergence of the new social order. To cope with the mud, men tucked their trousers into their boot tops, women stitched up their hems and affected high-topped boots. To resolve the great need for social community, society in a fundamental sense, the populace formed itself into geographical cliques, military groups, ethnic clubs, service and charitable organizations, branches of established orders, and, peculiar to the West, societies of pioneers and a social network of fire fighters.

Out of this maelstrom emerged a unique community that had to accommodate its various sets of civilized manners to the destructive forces of the frontier, which urged abandonment of traditional values as insistently as the populace tried to re-create them. Just as a poor man could become wealthy with profits from gold or silver, so could he change his social expectations and climb the ladder of high society. Even with the closing of the frontier, with the influx of a new class of immigrant whose greatest hardship was a railroad journey from the Atlantic coast, Western metropolitanism, no matter how faithfully patterned after established Eastern and European models, never shook free either from its anarchism or its ingenuousness.

Increasing prosperity influenced the San Franciscan's life-style from his clothing to his social habits. As the community took shape, it abandoned the fixtures of its early days; dress, which at first was no clue to achievement, began to recapture some of its former meaning. The favored wide-brimmed slouch hats, nondescript black pants, and flannel shirts of the miner gave way to frilled linen, frock coats, and beaver headgear. The sombrero, a popular link with the past, remained high in favor, and the boot was an absolute necessity. For a ball, predominantly masculine, the gentlemen paid as much as $50 for stylish patent-leather boots to match the elegance of their dress shirts and white kid gloves. Ethnic groups delighted in turning out in full costume for their various festivities—the German gymnasts in their tunics and pantaloons, the Chinese paraders in embroidered ceremonial garb. Even the gambling resorts, eminently sociable, had established modes of dress: the typical costume, showing a heavy Mexican influence, consisted of fancy dark trousers, white linen shirts with real diamond studs, ornate vests sashed in red, and the inevitable sombrero. Dress again reflected a person's economic well-being as the affluent strove to take up the social forms that perpetuated class distinctions.

By 1850 extremes of American patriotism were forcing ethnic groups into closer social ties and dependence on their own traditions. Under a chauvinistic act passed by the legislature, foreigners paid $20 a month for a license to mine. To the extent that American provincialism died down and economic competition leveled off, at least some of the foreign traits disappeared into the general social pattern. Although such national events as Bastille Day and St. Patrick's Day, the German May Day and Singing Society outings, and the Spanish fiestas remained entirely partisan, the whole community attended festivities celebrating statehood or American nationalism such as Admission Day and the Fourth of July. The Willows, the garden and amusement park on the road past the Mission, was a favorite Sunday outing place for an ethnic cross section of San Francisco; another was Russ Gardens, where most of the national celebrations took place.

More fashionable, but requiring a full day's journey in each direction, was an early fifties' resort above Napa named White Sulphur Springs after the stylish Virginia watering spot. The Spanish had enjoyed the beneficial effects of the warm mineral waters long before Gold Rush society excursioned there.

In 1866, when R. B. Woodward threw open his Mission Street estate to the public, it became the most popular of all the outdoor resorts. Visitors to Woodward's Gardens found a constant choice of entertainments: boating, skating, meandering through the lushly planted landscape. There was a playground, a bandstand, and a concert stage. But the primary attraction set among the artificial lakes and manicured gardens was the private zoo and its seal tank, where the daily feeding attracted an audience that filled an entire grandstand. Woodward's hospitality included access to his art gallery, occupying one section of the house. There viewers could gaze on a collection of more than 100 copies of old European masters, painted for Woodward on commission by the San Francisco artist Virgil Williams.

The pastime of strolling provided diversion closer to home, but even here class distinctions became apparent. The weekday strollers along the fashionable promenades were stylish, their Sunday counterparts considered common folk. Shops and places of entertainment did a thriving Sunday business, drawing reproofs from a minority of citizens who blamed such Sabbath recklessness on the "Parisian" influence. Later, and more seriously, the prominence of Jewish merchants who engaged in Sunday business because their Sabbath fell on Saturday attracted a series of anti-Semitic attacks and proposals for corrective legislation, but the latter never amounted to much.

A series of subscription balls, among the most fashionable social events of the early fifties, drew a cosmopolitan crowd from the ranks of the wealthy to Apollo Hall on Pacific Street. Lucy Gwin,

the Senator's daughter, danced with Billy Botts, whose father was
a governor of Virginia. Romano Bernardo Sanches, a Spaniard
from Florida, Robert Johnson, son of the consul from Sweden,
Henri Tricou from France, Emil Justh from Hungary, Alfred
Goddefroy from Germany, and Willy Sillem from England were
notable among the participants.[9]

Among the ballgoers in 1851 was Talbot H. Green, a wealthy
San Franciscan, whose eminence was such that the city had named
Green Street in his honor and who was accordingly about to run
for mayor. While engaged in the dance, this gentleman found
himself confronted by a lady who addressed him as Paul Geddes,
which was indeed his name. He had shed his former identity
when he fled to the West with the loot from a bank he had robbed
in Philadelphia. The dance ended Mr. Geddes' San Francisco career, but the street still bears his alias.

Some of the early attempts at social organization met unusual
problems. In 1849 one club, which acquired its new members by
majority vote, took daily meals together along with a dozen or so
invited guests. The group weekly elected a new president, who on
assuming office stood the entire company to dinner with wine and
all the trimmings. Such gentlemanly largess soon became an enormous burden, owing to the high Gold Rush prices and the short-
ness of provisions.

On other occasions, the spirit of Western camaraderie got completely out of hand, and one such bout of overindulgence by the
Howard Engine Company resulted in the formation of the Dashaway Society, the city's first temperance league. More familiarly
known as Social Three, the entire volunteer fire company, undoubtedly well hung over, pledged itself to total abstinence, ce-
menting the vow by smashing all remaining supplies of alcoholic
beverages. One verse of a subsequent company song set forth
their feelings to the tune of "America":

> Pure may our spirit be,
> As the wild currents, free,
> Happy and gay.
> With manly self-control
> We'll *dash away* the bowl,
> That would ensnare the soul
> To wine's dark sway.[10]

The Dashaway Society represented the minority viewpoint in
early San Francisco. Because the saloon provided companionship
and a jovial atmosphere, it was the most thriving early social institution. According to the *Christian Advocate*, there were 537
drinking houses by 1853. The fellowship was, however, informal,

lacking in ceremony, organization, and causes to rally around. The Masons and the Odd Fellows, both with San Francisco chapters by 1849, organized almost as a counterbalance to the predominant saloon culture. In 1852 the city directory listed twenty-five benevolent and social fraternities, including Bible and tract groups; a Philharmonic Society; a Hibernian Society; several German singing groups; Hebrew and French benevolent societies; a New England club; a cricket club; three temperance groups besides Engine Three's Dashaway Society; five Masonic chapters (thirteen within a year including a French group, La Parfaite Union Lodge, No. 17); two Odd Fellows' lodges (three more by 1853); and the Pacific Club. *The Elite Directory of 1879,* the city's first social handbook, added the Bar Association, the Art Association, the Loring Club, a choral group, the Berkeley Club, the Chit-Chat Club, the Union Club, the Bohemian Club, the Concordia Club, the Spanish-American Club, and the Olympic Club. *The Social Manual of San Francisco and Oakland,* which followed in 1884, listed in addition the Cosmos Club and Le Cercle Français.

Often social occasions combined entertainment with fund raising for charitable purposes; both the Masons and Odd Fellows dispensed camaraderie and relief funds on an equal basis. The Authors' Carnival Association, a club that was going strong by the eighties, had as its sole objective raising funds for worthy public causes by appropriate entertainments. The association aided the Ladies' Protective and Relief Society, the YWCA, the Old Ladies' Home, the San Francisco Female Hospital, the Pacific Dispensary-Hospital for Women and Children, and the Little Sisters' Infant Shelter. The latter, founded by eight teenaged girls in 1871, provided care for children of working mothers and infants from broken homes. By March, 1874, the teenagers, now numbering twelve, had raised enough money to open a nursery in rented Bush Street quarters, to staff it with a full-time housekeeper, and to purchase for themselves navy blue uniforms, starched white bonnets, and high-topped boots. In later years the shelter moved to larger facilities and broadened its scope to include the care of handicapped children. In the 1940's costs ran so high that the directors reluctantly sold the home, keeping the Infant Shelter name, however, and investing its funds. The proceeds enabled them to contribute to orphanages and other Bay Area charities. In 1970 the shelter merged with and turned over all its funds to the San Francisco Hearing and Speech Center.

James Hutchinson, whose humanitarian ire was raised when he witnessed the cruel treatment of an escaped pig, started San Francisco's Society for the Prevention of Cruelty to Animals in 1868.

The large population of horses drew most of the society's attention for the first years, but in 1877 one of its crews put a stop to a
then-illegal bullfight, arresting a number of spectators. Such
crackdowns forced aficionados to hold their contests beyond the
city's limits, where, although the SPCA no longer had legal jurisdiction, its influence had humanizing effects. However, the society
campaigned until 1905 to get legislation against cock and dog
fighting. Another group of animal lovers organized a Kennel
Club in 1897 and thereafter held annual showings.

In 1850 the Jewish community formed one of the earliest charitable groups, the Eureka Benevolent Association, which established a fund for widows and orphans and a relief committee for
sheltering the dependent poor. After the 1906 earthquake the society spent $5,000 for a 75- by 120-foot lot on First Avenue, where
it moved twenty-one cottages, obtained through the San Francisco
Rehabilitation Committee, to house aged couples. It also maintained a permanent liaison with the Hebrew Board of Relief.
Many among its members became leaders and benefactors of San
Francisco: Brandenstein, Blum, Boas, Dinkelspiel, Ehrman, Haas,
Roos, Salz, Schwabacher, Sloss, Steinhart, Sutro, Weill, Fleishhacker, Gump, Heller, Hellman, Koshland, Roth, Liebes, Lilienthal, Livingston, Magnin, Norton, Ruef, Stern, Rosenshine, Levi,
Strauss, Toklas, and Zellerbach. Almost all were members by the
seventies.

Writing in 1887, Mary Watson remarked that no community in
the city was so wide and unbounded in its charities as the Jewish
community; that no matter the cause, be it Jewish or otherwise,
the Jew in San Francisco was seldom appealed to in vain; that
there were few Christian charitable societies whose managers
would not freely admit the extent of Jewish liberality that had
helped them over financial hurdles; and that beyond their generosity to orphans and churches, the Jewish community also contributed a number of leaders to the patronage of the arts.[11]

Because the Jews joined in the Gold Rush as early as everybody
else and suffered the same hardships and successes, their position
in society, their opportunities, and their acceptance more nearly
than usual paralleled those of the rest of the white population. Although, as the number of graves in the 1850's Jewish Cemetery in
Grass Valley bears witness, the Jews joined the trek to the Mother
Lode, their role at the mines was principally as merchants, not
prospectors. With an inheritance of persecution, the Jews came
with an interest in settling, principally in San Francisco, in building their homes there, and in contributing to the cultural and economic foundations of a new city. Their cultural heritage, dedication to learning, and general economic success were stabilizing

influences on the community. They gained admiration for their
temperate habits of drink and for the fact that fewer of their
number in those lawless days appeared before the San Francisco
criminal courts than any other group. The role gained them, in
the most part, a genuine acceptance by their fellow citizens, to
which they responded by dropping their traditional exclusivity:

> The Jews are numerous in San Francisco. . . . As citizens, they
> are very valuable to the community. There is not that hard line of
> distinction between them and the Christian population that is so
> generally apparent elsewhere. In California, Catholic and Protes-
> tant, Jew and Gentile, all seem to have united in the one effort of es-
> tablishing a civilization on a broad and liberal foundation, the rules
> of which would not restrict in any way the liberties of any, so long
> as they observed the acknowledged principles of right. There is a
> more liberal religious sentiment among all sects in San Francisco
> than obtains in most American cities. The Jews, who have, since the
> foundation of their faith was first laid, been characterized by their
> retired isolation from those holding different beliefs, are conform-
> ing more to modern thought, and, in San Francisco, mingle to a
> considerable extent with the Christian sects.[12]

Even so, the *Elite Directory of 1879* segregated their names under the title "Jewish Address List"; three other groups received
similar recognition: there was an "Oakland Address List," an
"Army Calling and Address List," and a "Navy Calling and Address List." By 1884 the *Social Manual of San Francisco and Oakland*
changed the heading for the Jewish listing to the "Supplemental
Address List." The city's first *Blue Book,* issued in December,
1888, listed all of San Francisco's elite alphabetically, with no further distinctions other than could be drawn from the inclusion of
reception days and country residences.

Over the years, numerous groups organized along benevolent
lines, among them the California Club of 1897.* Women members could participate in everything from music, art, literature,
and drama to French, whist, and social science. The last section

---

*Others included the Ladies' Union Beneficial Society, established in Septem-
ber, 1860, to take care of its own members (provided, of course, that they were in
good standing) in case of illness and to appropriate $40 for funeral expenses in
case of death. Another, the San Francisco branch of the Needlework Guild of
America, dating from 1892, made and distributed free garments to the community's unemployed. The Association for the Improvement and Adornment of
San Francisco began just a year before the city was devastated by earthquake and
fire to promote "in every practical way" the beautification of the streets, the public buildings, and the squares; to institute "artistic municipal betterments"; to
stimulate civic pride in private property; and to suggest appropriate civic philan-
thropies.

spent considerable time visiting prisons and hospitals. A turn-of-the-century report by its Insane Hospital Division of the Legislative Committee focused not on the problems of the patients but on the injustices to women physicians: administrators at Stockton and Napa hospitals ignored a state law empowering women to act as fourth assistant physicians in hospitals for the insane by employing men instead. The club petitioned Governor Henry Gage, and by 1900 two club candidates, Margaret H. Smyth, MD, and Dr. Myrtle Ap Lynne, were victoriously installed at Stockton and Napa. Within five years after this breakthrough, the legislature validated the employment of women doctors whose ranks would be determined by ability rather than by arbitrary fiat. The club's beneficial effects on the community extended even to holiday shopping. Under the aegis of the Christmas Shopping Section, the club printed up 500 placards in the fall of 1906, urging the women of San Francisco to do their Christmas shopping no later than the week before and never after 5 P.M. The club's signs, posted liberally in streetcars and in the principal stores on Van Ness, Fillmore, Divisadero, in the Mission and in Presidio Heights, brought in much favorable comment from the community.

Mrs. L. Manson-Buckmaster founded the first full-fledged social club for women, the Laurel Hall Club, in February, 1886, drawing largely on the graduates of the fashionable Peninsula boarding school of the same name. The ladies engaged in intellectual pursuits, musicales, and merrymaking. The club also invited a number of distinguished guests, whose talks, to judge from the report of the recording secretary in 1899, titillated the audience: "General Shafter thrilled us with the experiences of the Army in Cuba"; Professor Fryer lectured on "The Women of China"; Mr. [sic] Waage described the personal experiences of a Red Cross nurse; the Honorable Julius Kahn spoke on "Expansion,"whose or which not further explained; Miss Lillie Martin told of her observations in a psychological laboratory; and Mrs. Purnell, from Sacramento, drew a parallel between "the highest class nineteenth-century woman and the woman of Solomon's time."

At about the same date the mother of Frank and Charles Norris gathered together a number of ladies interested in literature and formed the Browning Circle. The Literary and Musical Club, another group with an intellectual bent that prospered during the eighties, was coeducational, while the Addisonian Literary Society, founded in 1865, specifically excluded women. The coeducational Sadik Club, named after the Persian word for truth and devoted to social and literary interests, had not always had a mixed membership. The 1887 *Annual* revealed: "In our earlier years, we organized a society from which the girls were rigorously excluded. We saw our error. We corrected our fault. Now we have poetry, music, flowers, grace and beauty."

On the other hand, the founders of the turn-of-the-century California Writers Club included Ina Coolbrith, along with Jack London, George Sterling, John Muir, and Edwin Markham. The San Francisco Press Club, however, active since 1888 in bringing the newspaper and other professions together on a social basis, did not succumb to female wiles until the fall of 1973. Dedicated to promoting good fellowship among male artists, journalists, publishers, magistrates, doctors, lawyers, professors, architects, painters, musicians, actors, and others deemed acceptable as participants, it specifically barred women from its inception, as Section 9 of its bylaws made forcefully clear: "No woman shall be eligible to active or associate membership in this club." The group did see fit, however, to vote in Lillian Russell on an honorary basis. In the early 1970's some of the more enlightened constituents tried, unsuccessfully, to change the rules. After the second attempt, a number of newswomen joined with the American Civil Liberties Union to bring suit in Superior Court on the grounds that exclusion denied them the peer contacts necessary to reach their full professional potential in San Francisco, as well as in the eighty-seven other press clubs around the country with exchange privileges. The club's limited compromise still denied women journalists entry to the bar before 5 P.M., kept them out of the pool altogether, and did not allow them to vote. Although in January, 1973, the litigants lost their suit in court, the club had a change of heart and formally voted women full participation the following October.

San Francisco's women gained a great deal of inspiration in 1888 during the Memorial Day visit of Julia Ward Howe, who gave several talks on women's suffrage in general and the women's clubs of Boston in particular and crowned her stay by preaching a sermon to the congregation of the Unitarian Church. On the heels of her visit, Sarah D. Hamlin founded what was to become one of the most distinguished women's associations of San Francisco, the Century Club. Under the leadership of its first president, Mrs. George Hearst, the group discussed art and literature in the sociable confines of its Sutter Street clubhouse.

The early stirring of women's liberation spreading across the country made possible broader opportunities in education and increased social flexibility. During the nineties San Francisco's women could dine respectably in the French restaurants, could pursue a wider range of education, enter previously limited professions, and follow their interests, including intellectual ones, in formal groups that managed more than quilting bees and death benefits for members in good standing. The Women's Council of San Francisco embarked in 1892 on the study of literature, history, and the discussion of civic and current topics "that are inviting the attention of the progressive minds of the age." In the 1897 annual report to the women of the literary and social Forum Club founded two years earlier, Clare J. Whitney, the president, remarked:

In this age of progress in art, science, and invention, it will not do for a woman to stand still, she must with quick step and active brain keep abreast with the age. Susan B. Anthony in her visit to us last year, gave us some statements in regard to women, only a hundred years ago, that would seem almost incredible in the light of to-day. At that time no woman was admitted to any college, and now in our own State a woman has been made regent of a university, a prominent factor in the education of the State. I do not think a century ago such a thing as a woman's club was ever even dreamed of, and if it had been, would have been promptly frowned down by the lords of Creation, who deemed the home the only sphere for women. When approached in regard to those matters they have been quoted as saying, they did not approve the idea of women in general becoming cultivated, advanced, or even to their belonging to a club, but their objections were confined to their own particular wives. When they discovered that a woman could be a good wife and mother, and yet belong to an intellectual organization, they lost their prejudice in that respect, and now seem to be much interested in the particular club to which that particular little woman belongs.

Men's clubs, not hampered by the same artificial restraints that had inhibited women, formed around every possible interest. National affiliations often had a military cast, elaborate uniforms, drills, and annual fresh-air outings where, to the accompaniment of spirited brass bands, the members could strut, and show off their skills in sporting competitions. The Compagnia Bersaglieri Italiani Indipendenti, founded under that name in 1873 (although based on an earlier group), had two purposes: to aid its members in case of illness and, when the former proved fatal, to provide decent burials; and to engage in military exercises, gymnastics, and the art of fencing. The Irish Montgomery Guards turned out their members in splendid scarlet jackets and enormous bearskin headgear. The Fenian Brotherhood and the Ancient Order of Hibernians, Irish pseudomilitary groups, both thrived during the seventies. A Celtic compatriot, the Irish Fine Arts Aid Society, however, established in 1860, had no military aspect.

The American Legion of Honor's San Francisco chapter, which met in Red Men's Hall by 1880, and the San Francisco Fusileers, a

California order of the National Guard, actually allowed ladies to try their skills at target shooting during the annual outings. Active and honorary former members made up the roster of the City Guard Club in 1872. Functioning since 1854, the guards had affiliated with the California Infantry, First Regiment, Second Brigade of the National Guard in 1861. The San Francisco Cadets dazzled the city when they paraded in bright-blue coats and tasseled red Moroccan fezzes. And three secret societies, the Committee of Thirty, the Far West Knights of the Golden Circle, and the Knights of the Columbian Star, had more serious purposes in mind than parades and outings. Southerners, they were clandestinely promoting the cause of secession.

The Caledonian Club, founded in 1866, was limited to native-born Scotsmen, their sons, or their grandsons and within ten years numbered 500. Their annual outings centered on popular competitions in Scottish games. Not all the sporting groups had ethnic ties: the Sportsman's Club of California, popular during the seventies, was based on a common interest in hunting and offered a standing $50 reward for the arrest and conviction of any person violating the game laws of the state, a copy of which they printed for each member.

Ever since the Indians traveled about the Bay in tule boats, water has influenced the life-style of San Francisco and its economic development. Over the oceans came the early traders, the hide and tallow men, the whalers, the fur seekers, the explorers, and a goodly number of the participants in the Gold Rush, along with the imports to sustain them. San Franciscans have always been accustomed to the life of a port, to being surrounded by sea and bay. It followed naturally that they also made use of the water for recreational activities. Informal groups delighted in chartering boats for excursions on the water. Many of the early clubs held their outings on other shores, partly for the fun of boating there. By September, 1852, San Francisco even had a yacht club of sorts. About thirty ardent sailors bought the pleasure craft *Belle* for an excursion group called the Pioneer Yacht Club, but it was apparently a short-lived venture.

Sailing enthusiasts had to wait until 1869 for the West Coast's first real association, the San Francisco Yacht Club. Many of its sailors, contrary to the common custom of hiring crews, took pride in hoisting their own mainsails and jibs. They built a small clubhouse on Long Bridge spanning Mission Bay and arranged the first regattas. During a period of financial instability they sold their site to the Central Pacific Railroad but reorganized in 1873 in New Sausalito near enough to the ferry landing to accommodate the majority of its San Francisco membership. A dissident group which did not like the site chose to build farther up the shore at Shelter Cove, under the banner of the Pacific Yacht Club. Most of the splinter faction preferred hiring professional crews to doing their own sailing.

Small boats became increasingly popular, partly in response to annual Mosquito Regattas, and in 1886 several of those dedicated to promoting the interests of smaller craft formed the Corinthian Yacht Club in Tiburon. No one was admitted who owned a boat whose deck spanned more than 45 feet. The Encinal Yacht Club became active at about the same time. By 1896 the sport was so popular that a Pacific Inter-Club Yacht Association of Northern California was inaugurated.

In 1897 the San Francisco Club lost its records, its collections of models, paintings, and photographs, and most of its property through fire. Within a year a new clubhouse rose on the same location. Meanwhile, the Pacific Club was losing momentum, and in 1905, when it ceased operations, most of the rebels returned to the parent association. In the 1920's, when increased ferry traffic between San Francisco and Sausalito caused such turbulence in the adjacent yacht harbor that it damaged boats at anchor, the club purchased land on Richardson Bay in Tiburon, behind Belvedere Island. Again several dissenters, owners of larger yachts who wanted deeper moorings, split off and created the St. Francis Yacht Club on the San Francisco Marina, where an excellent harbor had been developed for the 1915 Panama-Pacific International Exposition. Since they included many of the most affluent yachtsmen, their withdrawal caused the Tiburon club financial embarrassment. The 1929 stock market crash and subsequent depression made matters considerably worse. When the construction of a clubhouse became economically impossible, the undaunted members took on the project themselves. The club has greatly expanded since the modest quarters were dedicated in 1934, with a current roster of 700 and a waiting list for admission. Although the club's boats have won their share of racing trophies, the most famous, the 94-foot schooner *Casco,* found a place in history when its millionaire owner, Dr. Samuel Merritt of Oakland, chartered it to Robert Louis Stevenson for his South Sea Islands' cruises.

The Olympic Club, the city's most prominent athletic organization and the oldest such club in the country, has existed continuously since May 6, 1860. Its forerunner, an informal association of athletes, many of them volunteer firemen, had been exercising together since 1855 in a backyard gymnasium built by Charles and Arthur Nahl. At a meeting in the Lafayette Hook and Ladder Company, 16 men formed a gymnastic club which proved so popular that it soon numbered 75. Their monthly performances for public benefits were among the fashionable entertainments of the city for many years. In expanded quarters, the membership grew to 500. A faction more interested in the social than the athletic aspects split off in 1871 and formed the California Olympic Club, but within two years there was a reconciliation. The roster grew to more than 6,000 members, including a goodly number of the city's business, professional, and industrial leaders, and the enlarged facilities provided golf courses, saltwater plunges, elegant clubhouses, tennis courts, track and field equipment, solariums, billiard rooms, target ranges, and bowling alleys.

From the earliest days Olympic Club athletes have won local, national, and international honors in every sport from football to fencing. Gentleman Jim Corbett, a Wells, Fargo bank clerk when he introduced boxing to the Olympic Club, later turned professional and in 1892 won the world heavyweight championship from John L. Sullivan. By 1906 the AAU American Boxing Championships were being staged at the club. Syd Cavill, who introduced the Australian crawl to the United States, was an associate. By the time of the Olympic Games of 1924 the club placed twenty-two athletes on United States teams, more than any other organization. In 1936 Don Budge, Gene Mako, Helen Wills Moody, and Alice Marble played a series of exhibition matches to launch the newest tennis courts, the choice a year later for the first Davis Cup matches ever held in the western United States. The difficult Lakeside golf course provided a challenge for the 1955 USGA National Open and in 1958 for the America's Cup and National Amateur matches.

In the 1870's women associates had an exercise class. Currently both the city and the country facilities accommodate wives and women friends, but golf is the major sport in which they participate actively. Their usual contributions are social: theatrical productions, aquacade swimming exhibitions, fashion shows, grand balls, and the like. In the earlier days women also helped with the entertainment: the twentieth annual exhibition program, in 1880, for example, featured Mrs. Tobin's popular opera company in *The Chimes of Normandy,* followed by male members in a display of gymnastic feats and acrobatic daring. The demonstration on the horizontal bars, Indian clubs, and Japanese rope preceded a violin solo, "Fantasie Caprice," rendered by Master Henry Larsen, and the program concluded with the double trapeze, ladders, boxing, and "The Great London Illusion! Dissolving Statues! Ancient and Modern," depicting Canover's Boxers dissolving into Rebecca at the Well, the Disk Thrower in Repose turning into a Tambourine Girl, and the Dying Gladiator fading into the Rock of Ages. The members loved it.

A German brewmaster, John Wieland, donated a barge to a group of fellow German gymnasts who in 1877 had started a rowing club at Taylor and Bay. The brewery's gift enabled the Dolphin Swimming and Boating Club to become officially chartered and presumably earned the loyalty of the large beer-drinking membership. It swimmers still startle onlookers at Aquatic Park when they plunge into the chill Bay waters for their daily dip.

San Franciscans joined local chapters of such national organizations as the American Geographic Society, which had a branch by 1881. The local Harvard Club was the second in the country. Horace Davis, a graduate who came west in 1849, was struck by the number of Harvard men among the San Francisco population of the early fifties. Inspired when the New York alumni established a formal fraternity, he followed suit. Forty members joined in 1873, the first year, fifty-four the second. The Yale alumni did not wait long to follow. By their second annual dinner they were well enough established to meet in the Palace Hotel for a fourteen-course banquet. The program notes that the assembly sang not only "Alma Mater" and "Eli Yale," but also "Fair Harvard."

Although most clubs, no matter their primary purpose, had a social aspect, for some their main reason for being was to have a good time. The Merchants' Club grew out of a business outing given by the William T. Coleman Company, the leading import-export firm and largest handler of canned goods in the West. The wholesale merchants who assembled on the Coleman tract in 1887 in San Rafael enjoyed themselves so much that they decided to keep up their association. In 1910, with 800 members, the Merchants' Club changed its name to the Commercial Club, and is still functioning on California Street.

The Occidental Convivial Club, formed in 1863 "to cultivate social, convivial intercourse between its members," barred married men from its roster. Its colors were red, white, and blue; its motto was *Vita sine voluptas, mors est (sic)*. Also dedicated to the promotion of social niceties, the Cosmos Club in 1881 provided club-rooms, lodgings, a restaurant, a library, and wine, billiard, and card rooms for its members. Profane and vulgar conversation, especially *ad alta voce*, was discouraged under threat of fine, with suspension for multiple offenders, and whistling and singing in the halls were strictly forbidden.

The Chit-Chat Club, inspired by ten young lawyers in 1874, met monthly for dinner followed by a member's essay and a discussion of literary or political-economic merit. Josiah Royce, one of the group's most distinguished speakers, joined in 1879. The only officers were a treasurer and a secretary to announce the next meeting, the reader of the last meeting presiding at the next. For several years the dinners took place at Frank's Montgomery Street Restaurant; later the group moved about sampling fine hotel dining rooms and French restaurants. In a speech to the 1910 members Charles Murdock suggested that, in fact, the repasts were entirely too good; should they be cut by at least two courses, the participants would be "in better train for appreciating and discussing an essay, and might save, say, 25 cents."

Four years before that, on April 8, 1906, the three hundred and seventy-eighth meeting had taken place amid the pomp and splendors of the Palace Hotel. In spite of the fact that the most devastating earthquake and fire razed most of the city in mid-April, the three hundred and seventy-ninth meeting took place on schedule in May in the surviving front room of a two-story frame structure at 2437 California Street. In announcing the meeting, Secretary Wheelan commented: "We see no reason why geology should be permitted to interfere with literature and the pursuit of truth." The caterer, and owner of the house, a Mrs. Polastri, did her cooking on a sidewalk range temporarily sheltered under a lean-to. Promptly at 6:30 P.M. twelve members arrived with two guests, one from Liverpool, the other from Japan. Mrs. Polastri, assisted by a crew of waitresses named Skelly, Lea, and London, provided them for $1.50 with a seven-course dinner of oysters on the half shell, bouillon, crab à la poulette, an entrée, a Roman punch, chops and peas, a dessert, and coffee. The essayist Louis Hengstler confessed that even had his paper for the evening, "Uncle Sam as a Policeman," not gone up in flames along with the rest of his library, he would have chosen to speak on a more spiritual matter, the effects of the shattering experience they had just shared. Whereas before he would have addressed his colleagues as "Gentlemen," now they were "Gentlemen and Brothers." "We used to live in different houses, on different streets, in different sections of a somewhat cosmopolitan and divided community, but now, *our* common homestead has been shaken by a powerful arm; we have gone through the blazing furnace, hand in hand. . . . We have all lost much in worldly goods; but, I think, we have also gained much in effects of a more durable nature."

Several of the early clubs, many of them bastions of male society and gathering places of the city's emerging aristocracy, are still functioning in San Francisco: the California Society of Pioneers, the California Historical Society, the now combined Pacific-Union Club, the merged Concordia-Argonaut Club, the Bohemian and its splinter group the Family Club, the University Club, and the

Commonwealth Club. For most, their male exclusivity and their elitism remain largely unchanged.

Any man who had arrived in California before January 1, 1850, became eligible for the California Society of Pioneers, organized in August of the same year to perpetuate the memory of Gold Rush events. To this end, the society currently maintains a museum in its McAllister Street headquarters. The roster lists direct male descendants who can establish their lineage through either maternal or paternal linkage to the original pioneers. Some can trace their ancestry to the Spanish members of the 1769 Portolá expedition which discovered San Francisco Bay.

Open to men and women alike, association in the more democratic California Historical Society requires only an interest in Western history. Founded in 1852, it maintains extensive collections of books, pictures, and memorabilia and publishes journals and books relevant to the field. The Territorial Pioneers of California, launched in 1874 and defunct some twenty-one years later, required its members to have been California residents before September 9, 1850; to have served in the Mexican War of 1846–47; or to have rendered distinguished service either to the Pioneers or to the state. Among those who qualified were General John C. Frémont, James Marshall, John Sutter, Miss E. A. Rockwell, an artist, and Theresa Corlett, an author.

The Pacific Club, the first gentlemen's club in the city, grew out of a congregation of men who drank and gambled together during the early fifties in Steve Whipple's Commercial Street Saloon. By 1852, under the influence of such Eastern social stylists as Cutler McAllister, the habitués excluded flannels and slouch hats in preference to tailcoats, ruffled shirts, and the jeweled accessories of the full-dress uniform; converted Whipple's old rooms into stylish quarters of considerable luxury; and relegated gambling, which still flourished unabated, to the status of entertainment in a private casino. They could hardly recognize each other. Cutler's nephew, Ward, the son and namesake of New York's society leader and a perennial bachelor, became a permanent Pacific Club resident when he settled in the West. The new bylaws forbade dogs on the premises, pipe smoking in the clubrooms, and wagers of more than $10 anywhere, while ensuring a first-class billiard room, wine cellar, and cigar supply to make up for the deprivations.

During the early decades the Pacific Club, the Union Club, and later the California Club on Sutter Street remained the select territory of the wealthy, maintaining exclusivity by charging healthy fees. The Pacific Club outgrew Steve Whipple's accommodations and found grander quarters in the Parrott Building above the offices of the Wells, Fargo Express. When a shipment of nitro-glycerine exploded one noon below the crowded dining room, the club and the city lost several of its elite. In 1889 the Pacific and the rival Union Club consolidated their rosters; the total membership represented the wealthiest and highest ranking white Christian members of the community. In 1911 the club, known more famili-iarly as the P.U., moved again, to the ornate Flood mansion on Nob Hill, more in keeping with its millionaire status. The massive Connecticut brownstone palace with French and Italian Renais-sance overtones was the only structure in the neighborhood to withstand the 1906 earthquake and fire. Thus securely but-tressed, the Pacific-Union remains a fortress of male chauvinism and prides itself on its record of having admitted women only twice into the California Street sanctum sanctorum. Its atmo-sphere is apparently soothing to gentlemen in the process of sepa-rating from their spouses since they often take up residence there.

The 2,000-member Bohemian Club, no longer remotely bohe-mian, represents another citadel of maleness. Although it has a long waiting list, it often awards membership to personages such as the late President Herbert Hoover, whose sculptured bust graces the lounge, and, before his troubles, to Richard Nixon.

The club began in 1871, when local artists and writers, Henry George among them, congregated for Sunday breakfasts at the home of *Chronicle* editorial writer James Bowan. To ensure the continued enjoyment of intellectual exchanges in an amenable so-cial setting, they organized on a formal basis, limited membership to artists, actors, writers, and musicians, and scheduled regular meetings in rooms over the California Market, shared with a drinking club called the Jolly Corks. When they began to admit those who were interested in the arts but not practicing artists themselves, their number increased to 750. By 1877, the Bohemi-ans had moved out of their meager quarters into rooms of their own on Pine Street. As the company took on a more and more elitist stamp, the accommodations took on a more appropriately luxurious character. Because the arty originators and their kin added color, the club continued to seek their participation, but their kind soon decreased to a small minority. The club offered one of them, George Sterling, a particular favorite for his author-ship of verse and plays for club programs, private rooms on the premises. In these lodgings, in 1926, Sterling drank a fatal dose of potassium cyanide.

The High Jinks, monthly supper meetings featuring entertain-ing debates, often rose to high levels of creativity. The Midsum-mer Jinks, theatrical pageants performed during the annual two-week encampments in the Russian River redwoods, became

famous for their professional character, while the civilized amenities of the permanent campsite drew praise for their infinite sophistication. The boyish release that many men experience in
fraternal congregations accounts for the Bohemian Club's share
of sophomoric pranks, drinking bouts, and off-color stories. One
camp is proud of its collection of pornography, another of its annual feast on bulls' testicles supplied by one of its members, a big-
time rancher, from newly castrated cattle.

Women have always been strictly forbidden at the encampments but during the rest of the season may join picnics in the
Bohemian Grove. On the other side of the river, however, a few
miles from camp, the populations of Healdsburg, Guerneville,
and Monte Rio, resort towns of normally around 1,000 residents
each, swell during the encampment with an influx of high-class
prostitutes. In 1971 a new law and order sheriff suddenly thrust
the town's small but thriving off-limits prostitution business, the
Bohemian Club along with it, into the public consciousness by his
investigation and indictment of a number of the principals. When
the chief witness turned out to be a former prostitute, the court
declared a mistrial, sparing a number of Bohemian Club politicians who had not yet been named, and several prominent business leaders, some of whom had, considerable embarrassment.
President Nixon, scheduled as one of the major 1971 Bohemian
camp speakers, canceled his rendezvous, not, it was said, as a result of the prostitution scandal, but at the request of club officials
who were becoming increasingly alarmed by the news media's
outcry over another matter: the President, in the best club tradition, was about to give an off-the-record speech secreted in a
grove of redwood trees to a number of the most "influential powers" in the country.

In 1902, in a division of allegiances over President McKinley's
assassination, a faction split off to form the Family Club. Like its
parent, the Family Club remains strictly a men's social organization, its name intended to suggest no more than a family of good
fellows.

German Jewish citizens formed three clubs: the Argonaut in
1853, the Concordia Society in 1864, and the Alemanian, which
changed its name to the House of Concord in 1865. It is likely but
not certain that the Concordia Club of 1868 was an amalgamation
of the latter two; all the records burned in 1906. The Argonaut
and the Concordia merged in 1939, shedding both the Germanic
influence and the purely sectarian character, as the membership
of Willie Mays bears witness. However, it remains a male bastion,
allowing women guests only during the evening.

The University Club, located atop Nob Hill on the site of Leland Stanford's 1876 stables, has followed the same policy toward women. Organized in 1890 by Harvard graduates, it still draws heavily on Eastern schools, most of which, including Harvard, are now thoroughly coeducational. If it has decided to cope with women except as occasional evening guests, it prefers to remain silent about it. In an attempt to avoid all publicity, possibly in the wake of a local news item which reminded readers of the club's equine origins, the board of directors, according to the secretary, passed a resolution late in 1972 forbidding any further release of information.

The Commonwealth Club, dedicated to "getting the facts" concerning public issues, has maintained an open forum for the debate of current problems since 1903. The founding fathers, marshaled by *Chronicle* editorial writer Edward Adams, included John P. Young, the newspaper's managing editor, Dr. Benjamin Ide Wheeler, the president of the University of California, Dr. Frederic Burk, the president of the San Francisco Normal School, and Attorney William P. Lawlor, who later became a justice of the California Supreme Court. Distinguished and often highly controversial Friday luncheon speakers have included women, such as Queen Juliana and Clare Boothe Luce. The club publishes the reports of its study sections on timely issues; backs legislative matters of state and national consequence; maintains a sizable open-stack library; and awards two gold and five silver medals annually to California's best writers. Sara Bard Field Wood, the poet, and authors William Saroyan, John Steinbeck, and Eric Hoffer are among the many Commonwealth medalists.

One of the most exclusive San Francisco congregations, the Burlingame Country Club, has been located since 1893 in a fashionable suburban setting "down the Peninsula." The club first modeled itself on the aristocratic Chevy Chase Club, complete (except for the local use of artificial prey) to the red-jacketed fox hunts and star-spangled membership list.

Although the Southern influence represented by the tone of Chevy Chase often merged with social traditions brought from Philadelphia, New York, New England, and Europe, it was the most important formative influence by far on emerging San Francisco society. The more prosperous the community became, the more it abandoned the easy, egalitarian standards of its early days in favor of stereotyped criteria of wealth and class distinction, as most readily defined by the Southern contingent. However, there were always fundamental differences between society in San Francisco and society elsewhere. With exceptions, San Francisco has never taken itself so seriously, has always been more tolerant of individualists and more receptive to newcomers. Although such customary hallmarks of acceptability as elite neighborhoods and palatial dwellings distinguished many early residents, fashionable San Franciscans also lived permanently in hotels, the number and elegance of which increased in about equal proportions. After the railroad, when the arts and the theater had lost much of their spontaneity and imported standards were conquering innovation, there was still room for social mobility in a town where fortunes rose and fell on the tidal waves of the economy. In this setting elitists tried to impose the standards that were the yardsticks of social exclusion back home, while the nouveaux riches, like recent converts to a new religion, espoused the dogma with predictable rigidity.

The Southerners were the natural vanguard in imposing aristocratic standards on the rest of the community. The number of leading Southern families that participated in the Gold Rush is large:

> From Virginia came the very "flower": the Harrison Randolphs; Mrs. George Hearst, whose mother was a Whitmire related to the Randolphs; Mrs. Charles McPhail Hitchcock, of the Virginia Hunters; William Botts, son of Governor Botts of Virginia; Harry Wise, nephew of another Governor of Virginia; Charles Fairfax of Virginia and of British nobility; Octavia Benson Boggs, related to the Fitzhughs and Lees; Mrs. General John Wilson, a Tennessee belle, cousin of President James K. Polk; Enoch Peyton, whose grandfather was the surgeon of Virginia in the Revolution and married a relative of George Washington; Mrs. James R. Keene, a Daingerfield of Virginia; the Louis McLanes of Baltimore; the Sanderses and Thorntons and Crittendens of Kentucky; the Hush family; Dr. Richard Ashe, for whose family Asheville, North Carolina, was named. . . .[13]

There were also the Blandings, the Parrotts, the Tod Robinsons, the Albert Sidney Johnstons, the Friedlanders, and above all others, the Gwins and the McAllisters, who became the undisputed leaders of San Francisco society.

Although many of the Southerners, like other participants in the Gold Rush, came west primarily to improve their financial standing, a large number of men, Gwin included, came to get in on the ground level of politics. Among the educated gentlemen of the South for whom politics was a tradition, the new California, unlike the established South, offered endless opportunities for involvement and consequently for power. William Gwin and John C. Frémont became the first United States Senators from California. The Gwins' dividing their time between a Washington mansion and one of the fashionable South Park residences, radiated social respectability and became famous for lavish entertainments. They built the first ballroom in South Park, a distinction even in what was for years the most fashionable place to live. The Gwins' South Park neighbors, chiefly Southern aristocrats, set the city's social tone with their receptions, grand dress balls, musicales, and theatricals. In the seventies the Southern contingent introduced the highly popular "kettledrum," a less than formal social gathering featuring dancing and refreshments, the name derived from the military officer's practice of using a kettledrum as a dining table for lack of something better. Diners sometimes ate to the beat of a drum and flower-decked kettledrums often appeared as accessories at the soirees.

As befitted their role as social leaders, the Matthew Hall McAllisters lived variously in palatial homes on the Hill and on Stockton Street, another of the prestigious early neighborhoods. A Georgia politician, Matthew was the great-grandson of Archibald, who came to the Cumberland Valley from Scotland in 1730, acquired land, and set up a gristmill and smithy. Matthew's grandfather, a 1779 graduate of the College of New Jersey, was an eminent lawyer. In 1850 Matthew Hall and his wife, Louisa Charlotte Cutler of New York, came to San Francisco. They brought three of their five offspring, Cutler, Frances Marion, and Harriet Hanah. McAllister began to practice law with Hall and Ward, two sons who had preceded them. When he received a Presidential appointment to a federal judgeship in the First Circuit Court of California, he promptly installed his son Cutler as court clerk.

Before his father's arrival, Ward and a partner, Adolphe Mailliard, kept busy converting the beached ship *Niantic* to a hotel and warehouse. Back in New York in 1852 with a comfortable accumulation of Gold Rush profits, he married Sarah T. Gibbons, the daughter of a Georgia millionaire. They made their home in Newport, Rhode Island, and wintered in New York and Savannah, except for several years abroad devoted to polishing their social attributes and forming connections of the right social distinction. By the late sixties Ward McAllister was the undisputed arbiter of New York society, while his brother Hall's family filled the same role in San Francisco. In 1872, in defiance of a small New York clique whose enormous wealth gave them the power of social exclusion, Ward formalized the heads of New York's oldest families, the Patriarchs, as the final judges of position: an invitation to their subscription ball was a passport to high society. Ward single-handedly created New York's Four Hundred by pruning Mrs. William Astor's unwieldy guest list for a grand ball in the 1890's.

Brother Hall, actually Matthew Hall after his father, but shortened when he left Yale, was barely twenty when he, Ward, and
their cousin Samuel came to San Francisco in 1849. Cousin Sam, a
descendant of the governor of Rhode Island and brother of Julia
Ward Howe, later achieved considerable fame as a Washington
lobbyist. The three young men at first set themselves up as merchants. However, Hall, a recent member of the Georgia bar,
found his professional services in great demand and thus embarked on a legal career which lasted for forty years. According to
the San Francisco Bar Association, he tried and won more cases
than any other California barrister of his time, incidentally collecting the largest fees then on record.

His most famous defense was of Adolph Spreckels in the shooting of M. H. De Young of the *Chronicle*. Young Spreckels, his ire
having been aroused for three consecutive years by more than
120 San Francisco *Chronicle* attacks on his family, finally reacted
with outrage. On Sunday, November 16, 1884, an article, pur-
portedly based on reports of the annual meeting, alleged that his
father, Claus, had defrauded fellow stockholders of the Hawaiian
Commercial and Sugar Company of more than $1,000,000. An
editorial the day following, suggesting that the conduct of Spreckels and the board of directors made them liable to criminal action,
provoked Adolph beyond endurance. On Wednesday he followed
De Young into the newspaper offices. During the confrontation
that followed, he shot the editor twice, wounding him severely,
and was himself shot by George Emerson, an assistant bookkeep-
er. Spreckels' jury trial on charges of assault with intent to commit
murder began on January 31, 1885, one month after Emerson's
case had been dismissed for lack of prosecution. It ended on July
2 in an acquittal. The prosecuting attorney's warning to the jury
that they not be swayed by McAllister's "melodious and persuasive
eloquence" apparently went unheeded.

Hall McAllister's wife, variously described as brilliant, charming, talented, dynamic, fascinating, and possessing the voice of a
nightingale, was the reigning queen of San Francisco society
throughout the sixties and seventies.

Just as the Civil War affected San Francisco's politics, it could
not help influencing the city's social deportment. Although most
of the Southern families, by that date a minority, preserved their
cordial relations with the Northerners, they made no secret of
their partisanship, applauding Southern victories, singing Southern songs, raising relief funds for Confederate prisoners, and
supporting the secret military societies. After Lincoln's assassina-

tion, although black bunting draped San Francisco in deepest mourning, there were small gatherings of Southern celebrants partying behind their somber shutters.

During the fighting the enlisted men, volunteers, and officers of both armies who went east to the battlefields, brought the war closer to the far-removed San Franciscans. Resident army officers and their wives saw to it that the Presidio continued to be a primary scene of social entertainments. The military influence became a prominent theme for social decor, the popularity of the kettledrums being one example. Many of the city's social events, besides benefiting the Sanitary Commission, provided for soldiers' supplies and raised funds for prisoners' relief and other war-related charities. One of the major social events of the period was a civil and military ball honoring the officers of a Russian fleet at anchor in San Francisco Bay as a Russian gesture of support for the Northern cause. Women's clothing blossomed in hues of red, white, and blue, and the same patriotic colors appeared in the flower arrangements, buntings, and banners of the balls and other entertainments. When the war ended, a goodly number of Southern fortunes ended with it. In San Francisco it was not unusual for a respected Southern woman to take in boarders with no loss of her social standing. Many years passed before the Southern influence on society lost its dominance. By the time that former President Grant arrived in San Francisco, the entire city, Southerners, Northerners, laborers, and millionaires alike, could turn out to honor him with warmth and spontaneity. Even he was overwhelmed by the reception.

If the South prescribed the form of social function, the Continent provided the setting. During the days of the Silver Bonanza, San Francisco's plutocrats went wild with an ostentation remarkable for both its dimension and its lack of taste. In a mistaken notion that substituted conspicuous consumption for true class, the very rich, vying with each other like the tower builders of old Italy in putting up the biggest monument, borrowed ideas and furnishings that they associated with aristocratic success. In the hope that by some magical osmosis they could absorb the culture they were not trained to, they imported most heavily from the urban East and Europe. Architecture, painting, furniture, sculpture, bibelots, tapestries all became the more valuable by importation. Women ordered their ball gowns from Paris and adorned themselves with French cosmetics and perfumes. In November, 1878, the entire Baldwin Theatre was filled with a French scent, prepared especially for the occasion by the Parisian firm of Berranger. French bals masqués were favored forms of entertainment,

French restaurants emulated Parisian models in naughtiness and chic, and the nobility of style and service that the Palace and other grand hotels took on suggested the finest hostelries in Europe. Society happily accepted patrician members of the French colony: Baron Blanc, Paul Verdier, the Weills, Jules Tavernier, Antoine Borel, the Maillairds, the Le Bretons, and Picot de Moras, of the family of the Vicomte de Chifflet, who sold newspapers in the streets of San Francisco when he first arrived. The French Ransom Fair, to raise funds to be exchanged for the removal of German troops from France, was a highpoint of the 1872 social season and netted $30,000 for the cause. Travel to Europe was an absolute necessity, and often the travelers took up extended residence abroad. Since the fifties, stylish daughters had to acquire at least a part of their education through foreign travel, or, better still, through attendance in a European school. By the seventies the traffic in persons, ideas, styles, and *objets* set records between San Francisco and the Continent.

San Francisco's transition from a frontier society to a bluebook society took place, along with most of the other manifestations of urbanization, over an extremely short period of time. No matter how much it attempted to ape New York, Paris, or Savannah, the new metropolis turned out its own breed of social creature. From the beginning there were those whose espousal of the arts derived from genuine appreciation, whose philanthropy arose from true generosity, whose power and high position followed from personal endowments. This group, more wary of public attention than seeking it, was only a nucleus about which spiraled the power seekers, the ostentatious spenders, the publicity hounds, the nouveaux riches. In San Francisco the railroad and the silver era produced numbers of such gaudy parvenus, who shaped the imitative society of the seventies, a society which, because its basic values were material, proclaimed itself by excessive displays of wealth, which in turn affected the arts and influenced the politics of the community. William Randolph Hearst's later accumulation, through worldwide agents, of paintings, furnishings, tapestries, statues, whole ceilings, walls, rooms, chapels, even sections of castles, most of them never uncrated, pushed the same trait to the extreme. Like his predecessors in the silver era, no matter how much he spent, he could not buy taste. The collector, installed at San Simeon, surrounded by his stupendous acquisitions, still kept the catsup bottle and paper napkins on the refectory table.

In 1851, when the booksellers Cooke and LeCount published *A "Pile," or, A Glance at the Wealth of the Monied Men of San Francisco and Sacramento City,* they listed 431 San Francisco firms and individuals with assets of more than $5,000. The Pacific Mail Steamship Company, with $1,500,000, headed the tally, followed by James Lick, with $750,000. F. Argenti had $500,000; Joseph Folsom, who had arrived in 1847 with Stevenson's regiment, $400,000; the merchants W. D. M. Howard and Henry Mellus, $375,000 and $325,000, respectively; the jeweler Buckelew, $250,000; Sam Brannan, $275,000; Jonathan D. Stevenson, $350,000; James King of William, $125,000; Elizabeth Sullivan, $300,000; the surveyor Vioget, $50,000; John C. Frémont, $75,000; John Parrott, $60,000; David C. Broderick, $30,000; John Geary, $125,000; Hall McAllister, $30,000; and James Phelan, $25,000. Twenty-three individuals and a dozen firms, including Wells and Company, Laws' Line, and Macondray and Company, had more than $100,000. Crocker and Martin were worth only $30,000, and the booksellers who published the information, Cooke and LeCount, $15,000.

Twenty years later, when the San Francisco *Morning Call* ran a similar breakdown, only four of the original names remained among the city's wealthiest: Lick, now worth $3,000,000; Parrott, $4,000,000; Phelan, $2,500,000; and Brannan, whom the *Call* actually neglected to mention, $1,000,000. By this time 122 individuals controlled $146,000,000. Leland Stanford was now the wealthiest man in town, a millionaire ten times over. Only a few million behind him came Ben Holladay of the Stage Coach Company, and Stanford's partners Collis Huntington, Charles Crocker, and Mark Hopkins. Michael Reese, Darius Ogden Mills, Miller and Lux, James Ben Ali Haggin, Lloyd Tevis, Nicolas Luning, George Howard, Alvinza Hayward, W. C. Ralston, William Bourne, and Andrew Pope were all worth between $1,000,000 and $4,000,000. Well before the end of the seventies even these fortunes were outdistanced. The Irish quartet who had masterminded the Nevada Comstock Lode and who dominated the silver era, John Mackay, uneducated laborer, James Fair, mechanic and farmer, and James Flood and William O'Brien, proprietors of the Auction Lunch Saloon, became the undisputed giants of the community.

Until the time of the railroad the Southern-dominated neighborhood of Rincon Hill and South Park had become the most elite residential area, the veritable social center of the city. As the new crop of millionaires emerged, and the end of the Civil War weakened the influence of the Southern contingent, two further developments, the Second Street cut and the cable car, contributed to the reshuffling of the social-residential pattern. At the same time, with the filling of the bay in the Montgomery area cut back by

state control, the city's entrepreneurs began to look seriously at
the swampy land south of Rincon Hill as a possibility for a level
area for industrial expansion.

The elegant mound of real estate rising up 100 feet in the middle of a major industrial area hindered commerce between the
newly constructed Pacific Mail docks at Second and Brannan
Streets and the mills, foundries, refineries, docks, and wharves
that already existed in the flatlands below Market Street, First
Street, and along the Embarcadero. The residential hill also
blocked future traffic to the proposed Central Pacific Railroad terminal and its connections to the East. John Middleton, a single-
minded real estate developer, with a scheme ostensibly designed
to improve the transportation of wagon freight, proposed access
by cutting Second Street down to grade directly through Rincon
Hill, meanwhile reclaiming the muddy flatlands by using the excavated earth for fill. To attain this end, he ran for, and was elected to, the 1867 state legislature, where he pushed through a bill
that legalized a Second Street cut. Bolstered by a tremendous protest from Rincon Hill residents, the city government at first chose
to ignore the legislation, but Middleton obtained a Supreme
Court order compelling compliance. Most of the city, keyed to expansion, profit, and commercial progress, actually agreed with
the scheme. Within a year 500 workers had gouged out a chasm
bisecting the hill to depths of from 60 to 75 feet, while heavy rains
added to its ultimate destruction. The cleavage and the subsequent bridging cost more than $90,000; they also ruined the char-
acter of the neighborhood, spurring an affluent retreat from the
fine mansions and manicured gardens to newer neighborhoods
such as Nob Hill. The ellipse of South Park still stands, although
the original houses were lost through fire, but the remains of Rincon Hill have disappeared under the approaches to the Bay
Bridge.

Just as the new millionaires were ready to move into the territory of the social elite, the most fashionable neighborhood had lost
its distinction. At first the rich retreated to Stockton Street, spread
out to Van Ness, nestled at the foot of Russian and Nob hills. With
the installation of cable car lines on Clay Street by 1873 and California Street by 1878, the very summits of the once-inaccessible
hillsides came within reach, and the era of mansion building began in earnest with James Ben Ali Haggin's sixty-room spread on
Taylor Street, complete with its own stables. Not long after, the
$2,000,000 Crocker mansion on the site of the present Grace
Cathedral had joined General David Colton's Italianate palace to
crown Nob Hill. In 1874, the Stanford mansion, also in the
$2,000,000 class, had gone up one block below on California and

Powell streets, neighbor to Mark Hopkins' $3,000,000 showplace. The 1885 Flood mansion stood between the Crockers and the Huntingtons. James G. Fair's splendid site on the top of California Street between Powell and Mason displayed no more than an encircling wall of granite when he died, still a resident of more humble quarters below on Pine and Jones. The luxurious Fairmont Hotel, erected on the property by his daughter, Tessie Fair Oelrichs, as a monument to his success, almost fell victim to the earthquake and fire, its interior entirely gutted by the flames. But the building itself remained sound enough to refurbish in even grander fashion than the original. William T. Coleman later built a white Roman villa surrounded by walled gardens across from the Haggin mansion, and the George Hearsts' stucco palacio added a Spanish touch on Jackson Street.

While the city's ballrooms seemed never to dim their lights, palatial country estates had begun to rival them as the scene of extravagant entertainments as early as the sixties. The Black Hawk Estate, a 1,500-acre 1860 spread in Millbrae, outdid all competition at that time. Created by Ansel Easton of the Pacific Mail Steamship Company, it included its own track, Shell Park, to accommodate the thoroughbred racing stock he imported from Kentucky. James Ben Ali Haggin had a horse-breeding ranch near Sacramento and in later years owned a 3,000-acre Kentucky spread with tracks and stables for the stock and a $350,000 summerhouse for the family. Alvinza Hayward's San Mateo home also included its own racetrack. Senator Latham, who had been among the early Rincon Hill aristocrats, rebuilt the W. E. Barrons' lordly country mansion at Menlo Park, where the Floods, the Edward Eyers, the Edgar Millses and the Faxon Dean Athertons all had splendid estates. Darius Ogden Mills constructed a lavishly landscaped French-style villa in the midst of a 1,500-acre Spanish ranch site at Millbrae, while the William Colemans located their Ross Valley estate on the old Spanish land grant of Don Timoteo Murphy. William Ralston drove his teams the 20 miles to Belmont every evening, where the enormous château could, and frequently did, accommodate hundreds of banqueting guests at a sitting. Ralston had a private telegraph installed so that he could communicate directly from his San Francisco office to Belmont. The Stanfords' substantial country estate in Palo Alto is the site of the present university, including their Palo Alto Stock Farm for racehorses, which comprised more than 7,500 acres in Santa Clara Valley and for which the university became known as The Farm.

The interest in thoroughbreds that Western society acquired from the South and Europe went beyond all reasonable preoccupation with breeding, racing, or even such elegant forms of personal transportation as the English coach-and-four, and the horse-drawn broughams, phaetons, and barouches that filled the city. In the stables that adjoined every mansion, crystal chandeliers glinted over mahogany stalls and harness rooms hung with silver trappings. Alvinza Hayward's stables even boasted mosaic-tile flooring.

With such elegant decor lavished on the stables, the nabobs went about furnishing their own habitations with unrestrained splendor. In most cases the feudal castles, Venetian palazzos, and French châteaux, staffed with retinues of Chinese servants, managed to cram in architectural details borrowed from all over the world, as well as turrets, towers, marbles, colonnades, carved fittings, rare inlays, imported woods and mosaics of generous catholicity. The painted wooden exteriors simulated marble, an unfortunate substitution which resulted in their destruction during the 1906 fire. The interiors surrounded courtyards filled with statuary, scented blossoms, and bubbling fountains. Murals, oils, bronzes, and marbles filled the galleries to overflowing; sets of books, in many cases bought by the yard rather than by the title, crammed the shelves of the new libraries, and paintings, such as the landscapes of Thomas Hill that Ralston bought for Belmont, were purchased by the studioful. There was an increasing use of glass areas, and windows bowing out to take advantage of the view often provided Nob Hill guests with displays of fireworks set off below for their diversion.

Typical of the Nob Hill mansions, the Stanford house combined mechanical wizardry with luxurious decor designed to astonish the visitor. The picture gallery surrounded a round crimson couch behind the cushions of which rose plants filled with mechanical birds that burst into song at the press of a button. One wall of the gallery housed a ceiling-high orchestrion that could be activated to swell the house with music. The entry hall rose three stories to an amber-domed skylight that reflected the signs of the zodiac set in black mosaic in the white stone floor. The paintings mounted on the ceilings by the artists who made them were all the work of Italians. The elaborately carved furniture and silk brocades of the Chinese Room came as a gift of the Chinese government, after Stanford saw and tried to buy them during the 1876 Centennial Exposition in Philadelphia. One reception room with upholsteries in heavy black satin inset with embroideries, carried out an Indian effect, while the Pompeiian reception room which adjoined the gallery displayed a table of onyx that had been cut from a faulty pillar in St. Peter's in Rome. The frescoed walls made a fine backdrop for the embroidered cream-satin furnishings. All the rooms on the main floor opened by large sliding doors onto the hallway, where marble statues nestled beneath giant columns of granite set among illuminated shrubs and flowers. Besides the gallery and reception rooms, the first floor housed a leather-upholstered billard room, an informal purple and gold velvet family parlor, a conservatory with a gurgling fountain surrounded by choice plants from the hothouse, and a dining room which could seat thirty-six with ease. The family bedrooms were on the second floor, above that the rooms devoted to collections of antiquities. The grand ballroom, the wardrobe, an adjacent supper room, and living quarters for the staff occupied the space below the main floor.[14] The Stanford mansion was a far cry from earlier Nob Hill housing, when inaccessibility guaranteed privacy but precluded the use of elaborate materials. In 1856, when Dr. Arthur Hayne and his bride, the actress Julia Dean, built a wood and adobe cottage on the land Fair later purchased, the workmen had to hack their way through thick underbrush just to reach the site.

During the seventies the wild speculation in silver stocks jammed the old Stock Exchange with so many traders that it proved almost instantly inadequate; by January, 1872, the new exchange was in full operation. The *Elite Directory* of 1879 listed an upper crust of 6,000 families, in spite of the inroads that resulted from the 1875 depression. Those few at the very top shared the greater part of the excesses created by the bonanza and accordingly set the style for the rest of the community.

Besides surrounding themselves with newly acquired symbols of culture, elegant residences, and personal adornments and indulging in frequent travels abroad, the new plutocrats astonished themselves and the world by the extravagance of their entertainments. Their continued preoccupation with celebrities, especially of royal blood, assured anyone of fame who chanced through San Francisco the most lavish hospitality: a party of Japanese ambassadors and princesses, the Crown Prince of Siam, the Emperor of Brazil, the Earl and Countess of Dufferin, General Sherman, Admiral Farragut, the English Princess Louise, daughter of Queen Victoria, and the Hawaiians, Queen Kapiolani, Princess Liliuokalani, and King Kalakaua, who, on the last of several visits, died in his suite at the Palace Hotel. The elite turned out at balls, banquets, theater parties, and receptions to rub shoulders with the distinguished visitors and hosted entertainments of such dimensions that the press the world over commented on their extravagance. Details of the architectural settings, the richness of the furnishings, the lushness of the gardens, the brilliance of the lighting, the profusion of floral displays, the perfection and abundance of the French cuisine, the character of the wines and liquors, the stylishness of the costumes, the opulence of the jewels, the charm of the music, and the spirit of the dancing bolstered journalistic comparisons of San Francisco entertainments with the most elegant in the world.

The most notable spectacular honoring the Grants, who sailed into San Francisco on September 20, 1879, for an extended stay, was the Sharons' reception at Belmont for 2,000 guests who were transported to the Peninsula estate by private railroad car. It even outdid the lavish debuts a few years earlier of Elizabeth Mills at Millbrae and of Flora Sharon at Belmont, at which likewise sizable entourages of guests arrived by private train, and the 1874 wedding reception for Clara Sharon and Francis Newlands at the family house in town. On that occasion 800 guests gathered in the drawing room at 511 Sutter Street before gold satin draperies which cost more than $2,000 for each window. The standards set by the private entertainments assured the success of such public festivities as the February 22, 1876, Grand Centennial subscription ball, one of the high points of the decade, and the Young Gentleman's Ball two years later, which honored the ladies of San Francisco while reciprocating their hospitality. The latter proved so popular that it became an annual event.

The fascination with royalty did not stop at entertainment. By the eighties a number of young San Francisco women besides Clara Huntington and Eva Mackay had managed to pick up titles of their own: Flora Sharon by marrying the Baronet Thomas George Fermor-Hesketh; Mary Ellen Donahue, the Baron Henry von Schroeder; Virginia Bonynge, the Viscount Deerhurst; her sister Louise, the English Lord John Maxwell; and the two Holladay daughters, by marrying the Baron de Boussière and the Comte de Pourtalès. Other marriages, such as Virginia Fair Vanderbilt's, made up for their lack of title by the brilliance of the match. Elizabeth Mills married Whitelaw Reid. Margaret Hamilton lived a long, happy life as the wife of Sir Sydney Hedley Waterlow, the ex-lord mayor of London.

Theatergoing was becoming a major social event, the theater a place for the new rich to parade in all their finery, to see and be seen. Bulwer-Lytton's play *Money*, which launched Ralston's splendid California Theatre on January 18, 1869, was an augury of the principal influence on San Francisco over the next several decades. It was a fortunate coincidence that as the productions had to revamp under the impact of the mid-seventies depression, the unformed tastes of a large portion of the audience in any case preferred melodrama to serious drama and musical comedy to Italian opera.

Economic prosperity meant good box office, and after the doldrums of the mid-seventies, the economy again prospered until depression hit in 1893. The country, the theater along with it, began to respond to the monopolistic forces of nineteenth-century industrialization. The popular taste for lighter entertainment persisted as the commercialization of the theater and a new group of entrepreneurs took over. Michael B. Leavitt, the first to make innovations that brought in profits with little thought to quality, filled his own string of theaters from coast to coast with traveling troups of vaudevillians. Not only did he put together his own companies with entertainers gleaned from all over the world, but he also established a central booking agency which handled artists and theaters by the hundreds. His large-scale efforts shaped vaudeville more than any other factor. In 1886 one of his assistants, Al Hayman, joined Charles Frohman to set up an aggressive plan, concentrating on Western bookings. By 1896 its success led to a broader-based combine, the Theatrical Syndicate. Hayman, now operating out of New York, assured them potential nationwide control by including among the six partners key representatives from such cities as Philadelphia and New York. With their own stable of performers and a large network of important houses, they completely dominated the theatrical scene. They dictated to everyone connected with the industry, from theater manager to playwright. No one performed, wrote, produced, or booked without turning over a fee to the combine. Those who took exception—the Fishes, Belasco, and Sarah Bernhardt among them—often found themselves with no place to put on a performance or with a full-scale obstacle course between them and success. Thanks to the high caliber of many who did perform, happily or otherwise, under the syndicate's auspices, some good theater survived alongside the melodrama and the vaudeville. The syndicate's control, which lasted well beyond the turn of the century, finally diminished through the persistence of such impresarios as David Belasco and through competition from the growing Shubert agency.

Escapist entertainment in the theater appealed to an audience that found equal diversion in playing at billiards and practicing archery (nearly as great a craze in San Francisco as roller skating and bicycling), in dawdling over many-coursed banquets in French restaurants, in decking themselves out in costumes for masked balls on Nob Hill, or galloping off to Sunday breakfast at the Cliff House or to a weekend in Monterey. These audiences thrived on romantic acting, melodrama, musical comedy, farce, and burlesque, plays that treated familiar themes rather than pushed messages of reform or social significance. Experiment and serious drama had limited appeal.

Although numbers of conversions were made, at least half the audience that jammed the Turk Street Tabernacle to hear the preachings of the evangelists Dwight Moody and Ira Sankey came for entertainment rather than religion. One of the big hits of the eighties was Buffalo Bill Cody and his troop of Indians. By the nineties the interest in minstrelsy had declined, but the community responded enthusiastically to Madame Jones and her troup of Colored Troubadours. Victor Herbert operettas had a tremendous vogue, as did the more sophisticated Gilbert and Sullivan, along with various forms of exotic dancing performed in old Barbary Coast melodeons.

During this era vaudeville was supreme: it made the Bush Street Theatre prosperous, and by 1887 Gustav Walter had built and dedicated the Orpheum Theatre entirely to its performance. Among the budding vaudevillians appearing there were Marie Dressler, famous in the early days for her buck and wing, George M. Cohan, and Houdini. Years later, Houdini's assistant, Larry Lewis, took a job at the age of eighty as a waiter at the St. Francis Hotel, where he worked until he was a hundred and five. He retired then to do promotion work for the Western Girl employment agency. He continued to jog more than six miles through Golden Gate Park every morning until he was hospitalized with pneumonia at the age of a hundred and six. In bad times, big-name legitimate actors often made ends meet by performing skits at the Orpheum. In good times, however, San Francisco and New York were the only cities that guaranteed valuable players lengthy and prosperous engagements.

Grand opera was not dead, but in spite of numerous successful performances, the art could not single-handedly sustain a theater for a complete season. The Grand Opera House interspersed its serious musical productions with variety acts, light comedies, plays featuring celebrated actors, and concert performances by such artists as Madame Scalchi and Adelina Patti. The audiences applauded them wildly and in return heard an encore, the favorite being "Home Sweet Home." When Ellen Terry and Henry Irving played the Grand with the London Lyceum Company, there was standing room only. In 1894 Walter Morosco assumed the management and shifted to melodrama at popular prices. In 1899, at the crest of an interest in serious music, he attempted to return entirely to opera. Although there was a high degree of enthusiasm, it was not sufficient to sustain the hall solely as an opera house for more than a year.

While the old Mission Street Opera House presented serious operatic companies and celebrated singers—the New York Metropolitan Opera Company, Schumann-Heink, and Caruso, for example—the Tivoli Opera House filled the seasons mostly with Gilbert and Sullivan and other musical drama. Built on Eddy Street in 1879 by the Kreling family that owned Tivoli Gardens on Sutter, the new Tivoli appealed to popular audiences with local performers and low prices that included between-acts refreshments. When the hall was condemned, the family replaced it in 1904 with a building that was consumed only two years later in the earthquake and fire.

The silver generation at first frequented the elegant California Theatre on Bush Street, but it was not far enough uptown to retain its popularity beyond 1888. By the time it reopened in a better location, it no longer attracted quality productions. The elite flocked instead to the Baldwin, which soon underwent major refurbishings befitting its position as the foremost theater in San Francisco. It prospered until its destruction by fire in 1898, presenting first-run attractions from the East.

In contrast, a number of lesser theaters carried on the stock company tradition. The Alcazar, built by Michael De Young in 1885, depended largely on a local company, with visiting firemen taking over starring roles. Its popular prices and varied programs attracted a family audience until its demise in the 1906 earthquake. Another minor house, Stockwell's Theatre, opened in 1892 with a resident company playing light comedies and popular melodramas. Within three years the syndicate had taken it into the fold. By 1900, refitted and renamed the Columbia, it was the city's principal playhouse. At the turn of the century the California Theatre played melodrama and burlesque; Fischer's, musicals; the Tivoli, Central, and Alcazar, melodramas; and the Grand Opera House, varied productions of serious music, drama, and occasional lighter entertainment. On April 17, 1906, a tony audience at the Third and Mission Opera House applauded Enrico Caruso singing Don José in the Metropolitan Opera Company's production of *Carmen*. A few hours after the last fancy dress swept out of the hall, the building trembled, the chandelier crashed into the empty seats below, and the theater joined the ruins of the earthquake-shattered city. The shaken Caruso vowed never to return to San Francisco. All the city's theaters perished but three: the Chutes, a Haight Street amusement park that included a playhouse; the Colonial Playhouse on McAllister Street; and the old South San Francisco Opera House.

Such popular entertainers of the seventies as Lotta Crabtree, James O'Neill, Edwin Booth, and Modjeska, now speaking better English, returned to San Francisco frequently in the decades that followed. They played beside John Drew, Otis Skinner, James Lewis, Lillie Langtry, Weber and Fields, Kolb and Dill, Ada Rehan, Ann Hartley Gilbert, Adelina Patti, and Emma Nevada, a successful opera star from the West, who emerged as the big names of the eighties. Adelina Patti's concert performance at the Grand in March, 1884, an event that created a furor even before it took place, was the most memorable attraction of the decade. Speculators made minor fortunes filling the demand for tickets, while such crowds mobbed the box office that they caused considerable damage to the theater. Flowers overflowed Madame Patti's suite at the Palace. Entertainments in her honor preempted all other social events in a sociable city. Breathless accounts of the concert filled columns of local newsprint, devoting equal space to the brilliance of her voice and the brilliance of her diamonds. In the years following, when she returned in a series of "farewell" appearances, the city bestowed its unrestrained admiration, but the fever never matched the pitch of the 1884 reception. Prima donnas of the eighties such as Patti and Langtry traveled about the country in luxurious private railroad cars and felt very much at home among the ostentatious silver gentry of San Francisco.

Tomasso Salvini's Italian reading of Shakespeare in the midst of a company that otherwise was playing in English was one of the high points of the 1886 season. In 1887, before the California Theatre lost its glitter, Lillie Langtry appeared there and at the Baldwin to a very favorable response. During her stay she purchased a Lake County ranch for breeding horses but after one enjoyable season never used it again. During the nineties Sarah Bernhardt, sometimes costarring with Coquelin the Elder, did a number of productions at the Grand entirely in French: *Camille, Cyrano de Bergerac,* and several works of Molière. In 1899, when the house established its serious opera policy, Melba's *Faust* launched the season. During the same decade the fighters Jim Corbett and John L. Sullivan also trod the boards in San Francisco, alongside such stars as Richard Mansfield, Maude Adams, Anna Held, Maurice Barrymore and Georgiana Drew (the parents of Lionel, Ethel, and John); by 1895 the young Ethel had a minor role in Henry Arthur Jones' *The Bauble Shop.* Eleanor Robson, the daughter of a prominent English acting family, made her theatrical debut at the age of seventeen in San Francisco. A few years later as an international star she attracted the attentions of George Bernard Shaw, who showered her, as he did Ellen Terry, with a profusion of letters proclaiming his eternal affection. After much soul-searching she gave up her career and entered into a happy and lasting marriage with August Belmont, a millionaire, twenty-six years her senior. By the new century De Wolf Hopper, Lillian Russell, Eddie Cantor, Al Jolson, Sophie Tucker, and Luisa Tetrazzini were beginning to capture the headlines. When

William "Doc" Leahy, the impresario of the Tivoli Opera House, had discovered Tetrazzini singing in a second-string company in Mexico City, he had rushed her to San Francisco. She made her local debut in 1905, in a performance that heralded a triumphant career.

From the silver decades through the turn of the century playgoers saw such respectable offerings as *A School for Scandal, She Stoops to Conquer, The Admirable Crichton, The Devil's Disciple, Tartuffe,* Tennyson's *Becket,* and a goodly sampling of Shakespeare: *The Taming of the Shrew, As You Like It, Much Ado About Nothing, A Midsummer Night's Dream, Romeo and Juliet, Macbeth,* and *The Merchant of Venice.* In 1895 *Trilby* opened at the Baldwin to wildly enthusiastic audiences conditioned in their mode of dress and every affect by a craze brought on by *Harper's* serialization of the novel. Interspersed among the dramas and comedies, and equally popular, were often bad productions by American playwrights on American themes, such melodramas as *The Money Spinner, The Curse of Cain, Drifting Apart, The Wages of Sin, The Pace That Kills, Stolen Kisses, His Japanese Wife, Lover on Crutches,* and *Horrors,* a musical comedy which introduced Lillian Russell to San Francisco.

By the last years of the century millionaires as glittering as any in the country clustered at the theater and in the diamond horseshoe of the San Francisco Opera, as much a spectacle in their boxes and loges as the official production taking place on the stage. Among the new society, some of the changes on a personal level were as dramatic as the circumstances which produced them. Dr. and Mrs. Hugh Toland's retired Irish cook, a millionairess from the proceeds of silver stocks, now presided over her own guests from the vantage point of a raised dais in the middle of her drawing room. The head gardener for Woodward, Charles Bonynge, returning to his native England after making a million in the Comstock, installed himself and his Southern wife in a fashionable London estate, entertained the aristocracy there and at his equally posh country establishment, and married off two daughters into the nobility. A fair number of women who started their San Francisco careers as courtesans ended up as respectable matrons, many of them in positions of wealth and social esteem.

The man who had the most profound influence on San Francisco society, who vigorously passed judgment on those who could belong, not surprisingly came to the city in the mid-seventies as a mere salesman for Mumm's champagne. Edward Greenway, only twenty-two when he arrived from Baltimore, tagged along with the socially prominent young people until, by osmosis, he had made himself inseparable from them. His subsequent success as the city's social arbiter followed partly from the changes that were taking place in the nature of society itself as it tried to divest itself of the rough aspects of its early days. Greenway was part of the pattern. During the winter of 1887 he introduced the Bachelors' Cotillion, a series of subscription dances, which the city embraced with such enthusiasm that within a few years it was one of the major institutions defining society itself. Its hold was so tenacious that it prospered until 1914, and its present-day counterpart has a sober importance for many of the participants, as well as those who are left out.

In Greenway's day he and his assistant, Mrs. Eleanor Martin, arbitrarily decided which debutantes might join the Friday night dancing assemblies, their acceptability rising in direct proportion to their family's wealth, social prestige, and visible accomplishments. In making his judgments, Greenway never discarded such biases as petty revenge or personal aversion to some member of the family. Nevertheless, San Franciscans acknowledged an invitation to the "Greenways" as a badge of membership in high society. Inez Shore's Cotillion Club, which formed shortly after, accommodated the Greenway rejects, but was also competitive on its own merits. The Lunts' Polk Street dancing school, *de rigueur* for the younger generations of the eighties and nineties, prepared the aspirants.

Ned Greenway's closest competition as social arbiter came from William Chambliss, who gave up a career at sea for a social life in San Francisco in 1890. He entered the arena by starting a Monday Evening Club in direct opposition to Greenway's Friday night cotillions. To counter the power Greenway derived from his position as one of the *Chronicle*'s social scribes, Chambliss wrote for the *Examiner*. Basing his attack on the thesis that San Francisco "aristocracy" was comprised largely of vulgarians who had lately come into a lot of money, he decided to publish his own "blue book," a volume devoted to praise of himself and to a venomous account of the San Francisco social hierarchy.

Claiming to be writing for the good of society, Chambliss coined the word "Parvenucracy (pronouced Par'-ven-ŏoc-'ra-cy)" to distinguish the real society from its vulgar imitation: "Parvenucracy means those arch-parvenus, and their followers, who imagine that the mere acquisition of a few thousand dollars, coupled with an unlimited supply of insolence and arrogance, is all that they require in order to gain admission to the homes of persons of culture and refinement." In a further preamble to the actual diatribe, he excused the slander to follow: if it should be wrong to point out corruptions, to criticize so-called gentlemen for ignoring their marriage vows, or to say that "the negro ex-slave—the very lowest of all creation resembling man—is unfit to become the husband of the American gentleman's daughter, the flower of our nation," then he would hope that his reminiscences might never reach the "intelligent public."

The text itself wastes no time in getting down to specifics. It advocates passage of a federal exclusion act specifically to keep out of this country "penniless princes, lords, barons, counts, and all other cheap-titled adventurers who, like Prince André Poniatowski and Count de Castellane, are likely to be sent over here in the future, by the same board of matrimonial brokers that sent these two sweet-scented 'noblemen' (?), to marry rich parvenuesses on percentage." Besides keeping out undesirable fortune seekers, the act should ban the return to America of all the "soulless women" who go abroad and marry titled paupers, a class morally worse than the unfortunate Oriental dancing girls who end up in houses of prostitution "similar to the house kept by Maud Nelson, the daughter-in-law of the millionaire ex-senator, James C. Fair of Nevada and California." Further, "not one of Mr. Fair's daughters has succeeded in marrying a prince as yet, but the up-to-date 'Magdalen' that his son Charlie married has a part record that, from a moral point of view, would compare favorably, as far as the income from her peculiar business permitted her to go, with that of any prince who has lived since the days of Charles II; not excepting even Prince Hatzfeldt, who married the 'adopted' (?) daughter of the C.P.R.R. octopus, surnamed Huntington; Prince Colonna, who married the daughter of Bonanza Mackay's 'wife'; of Prince Poniatowski, whom William H. Crocker, the 'king' of Snob Hill, is said to have purchased for a Fourth of July present for his 'true American' sister-in-law, Miss Beth Sperry, soon after old man Carpentier, of Oakland, refused to buy it for his little niece, Miss Maude Burke, before the latter became Lady Bache-Cunard." Altogether the book estimates that the seventy "shabby, shop-worn, out of date" titles acquired by American girls cost an accumulated $200,000,000, a figure happily verified by the *Examiner;* the seven titles picked up by Californians depleted the state's economy by an estimated $20,000,000.

Chambliss' performance outdid in vulgarity anything even he had dredged up or imagined about his victims. He lashed out against blacks on many pages, referring to them as odorous, two-legged animals; he questioned the femininity of the clique of professional workingwomen ("What! Kiss a hand which had filed charges, counter charges, demurrers, and other vulgar type-written documents in murder cases, bigamy cases, divorce cases, and other hideous litigation!"); he vented equally angry feelings against "effeminate supposed-to-be-men," of whom Oscar Wilde was his most depraved example; he described a crying baby that had the misfortune to disturb his sleep aboard a Pullman as a "noisy brat"; he referred to a Jewish artist and his attorney with whom he had unhappy business dealings as "sheenies and shysters"; and he unleashed diatribes against everyone who crossed him, who disagreed with him, or of whom he did not approve. Included prominently among them was his rival Ned Greenway, depicted in a cartoon as a bediamonded, Semitically hawk-nosed individual to whom Chambliss attributed ten sacrilegious "Commandments of E. Moses Greenway," one of which admonished: "Honor thy father and thy mother as long as they honoreth thy check." Chambliss' own character, amply described in the autobiography which threads through the book, was, of course, exemplary.[15]

Not able to produce the *Diary* locally, likely because of clandestine interference from such families as the Huntingtons and Crockers, he had it published by a firm which shared the New York address of the Hearst headquarters. When the 10,000 scurrilous volumes of *Chambliss' Diary; or, Society as It Really Is* appeared in 1895, San Franciscans did all they could to buy them up or destroy them.

During the nineties, although there now remained a few traces of the rowdy culture so characteristic of Gold Rush days, the extravagances of the Silver Bonanza carried over. Society by then had generally accepted the cosmopolitan graces introduced by the Southern and Eastern aristocracies, the disciplined formality of the cotillions, the fashionable promenades, the elegant balls, the splendid carriages, the mansions and country estates. With pioneer defiance they also accepted the honky-tonk dives of the Barbary Coast and risked possible muggings and fleecings by the habitués of the quarter in order to take in every facet of local color. The traffic to the upstairs rooms of the city's French restaurants was brisk enough to gain San Francisco a worldwide reputation for naughtiness. In spite of the Spanish-American War, which barely touched San Francisco, and the more serious depression of 1893, the city even more than the rest of the country enjoyed an era of gaiety and abandon, the justly named Gay Nineties. With the introduction of the automobile and the telephone, the world seemed a vastly different sphere, and in full gear San Franciscans raced into the first years of the new century.

SECTION FIVE
Politics and Labor

XVII

North versus South

BESIDES the early problems of crime, inefficiency of government, and corruption of office to which vigilantism of the 1850's was the reply, there were three major influences on San Francisco politics during the fifties, sixties, and seventies: the North-South issue that culminated nationally in the Civil War, the problem of labor and the Chinese, and the continuing maneuvers of the silver lords and the railroad kings to ensure their retention of power.

From its beginnings until the start of the Civil War, San Francisco, along with the rest of the state, was principally Democratic. Very early the party had split into two camps: the followers of Senator Gwin and those of David Broderick. Gwin, a well-educated doctor from Tennessee with the advantage of formal legal training besides, embodied the habitual charms and courtesy of a Southern gentleman; his allegiances were to Polk and Jackson, and he had come to California in 1849 deliberately to seek office. Broderick, feisty and Irish-tempered, a former New York saloonkeeper of little education but domineering drive, was only twenty-nine when he emigrated, also in 1849, with the intention of dominating California politics; he was a veteran of the Tammany machine and by 1857 Gwin's colleague in the Senate.

Their bitter rivalry caused such destruction within the Democratic Party that it resulted in losing the 1855 state election, the only one of the decade that the Democrats did not win, to Governor J. Neely Johnson and the superpatriotic, anti-Catholic, antiforeign Native American Party. Better known as the Know-Nothings, they grew out of such secret organizations as the Order of the Star-Spangled Banner, whose local founder was Lieutenant Sam Roberts of the Hounds.

Broderick and Gwin's battle, although basically concerned with political power, reflected the growing national bitterness over slavery. The Whig Party, badly split on the issue, had gone under altogether by 1854. Although both men represented California in the Senate, Broderick, through his political bossism, had won the

379

longer term, but not the affections of President Buchanan, who
had gained his own office on the proslavery program for Kansas
with which Gwin was also associated. The President consequently
doled out all the political patronage to Gwin's followers, contributing to a further breach between the Senators.

In 1859 David Terry, the chief justice of the State Supreme
Court, campaigned for his reelection on the Gwin proslavery
theme, enraging Broderick even further, especially since in 1856
he had supported Terry during his difficulties with the Vigilance
Committee. The animosity festered and produced scathing public
insults between them. When Terry lost the nomination for justice,
he resigned what was left of his short term and challenged Broderick to a duel. The encounter cost the Senator his life. Although
the Terry-Broderick duel was not basically fought over the issue
of the territorial expansion of slavery, it might as well have been,
considering the partisan sentiments it aroused and the high moral
tone attributed to it. What it did do was clarify and sharpen the
antislavery feeling that existed. Popular opinion loomed strongly
against Terry as well as against Gwin and the Chiv Democrats with
whom he was allied; in 1860 the state swung to Lincoln and the
Republican ticket.

The population of California was in any case heavily Northern
in its basic sympathies, although the Southern faction may have
been the more vociferous. In 1850 most of the native-born American residents of California—and they made up three-quarters of
the total population—were from the Northern states, Westerners
coming in a close second. By 1860, when Americans represented
only 61 percent of the total, 74,000 of them were Northerners,
and fewer than 29,000 Southerners. By 1870 the native-to-
foreign ratio having increased only 2 percent during the decade,
the Southerners made up 28,000 of the population, the Northerners 85,000.[1]

On such public celebrations as the Fourth of July, the pro-
Union sentiment was overwhelmingly clear. In 1863, when the
City Guard gave its civil and military ball in honor of the pro-
Union Russian fleet, the community attended in its most elegant
plumage, and tickets went for as high as $100. Masses of red,
white, and blue decorations lent a patriotic tone. The revelers
danced through the night and consumed a banquet of sixty-eight
dishes. It was one of the great social events of the decade.

During the fifties a southern California move for a north-south
division, arising from the inequality of taxation and representation, was interpreted in Washington as a symptom of the national
North-South dissension. The eleven southern California delegates to the 1849 constitutional convention had clearly foreseen

that the heavy representational bias would favor the northern communities, with thirty-seven votes. The southern attempt to make California a separate territory whose expenses would be borne by the federal exchequer was unsuccessful, but its logic was confirmed. In 1852, for example, six southern counties with 6,000 residents paid exactly twice the property tax of the northern counties with a population of 120,000.

As early as 1851 the southern part of the state had again campaigned for a convention to divide California, the residents proposing to reorganize as a territory until they had a large enough population for statehood. Although there was widespread support from the governor and the assembly, full legislative approval did not come until 1859. The proposal ultimately failed when Congress, preoccupied with the approaching Civil War, viewed the move as a means of establishing another proslavery territory, an erroneous charge that the *Alta* had much earlier laid. The issue of slavery had been prevalent since the founding of the state. During the Monterey convention the delegates had voted not only overwhelmingly for statehood, but unanimously for the exclusion of slavery. The vote, however, had been no more than a practical Northern solution to the attempts of several Southern forty-niners to take over an unfair share of mining claims because they had the slave labor to work them.

The scheme to form a Pacific republic, a movement that had been suggested during the Mexican Revolution of 1836 and again by the Bear Flag Rebellion, also came into sharp focus during the fifties and early sixties. California's physical distance from the rest of the country was one precipitating factor; its neglect by Washington, as evidenced, among many grievances, most prominently by the continuous failure to pass legislation for a transcontinental railroad, was perhaps even more important. Although they did not admit it publicly for fear of precipitating armed conflict, the Second Vigilance Committee seriously considered secession as one way of thwarting federal authorities. When the South actually did secede from the Union, the idea received new impetus in California as a means of avoiding a choice of allegiance between North and South, a choice which for some would inevitably have meant bearing arms against their brothers. Governor John Weller in his annual state message claimed that secession was the inevitable course that California would follow, and Congressman John Burch, reinforced by Senators Latham and Gwin, actively campaigned for the idea. However, owing to economic and other complicating factors, the loyalists prevailed.

Partly because the South had fired the first shot on Fort Sumter, partly because such orators as Colonel Edward Dickinson Baker and the Reverend Thomas Starr King had spoken so eloquently for the Union, and partly because of the large antislavery segment among the state's population, the combined legislature pledged California's allegiance to the North with only seventeen dissenting voices. Baker, a personal friend of Lincoln (the President named one of his sons Edward Dickinson Lincoln), a man of eminent forensic skill, tears running from his eyes, had delivered the funeral speech for Broderick. By attributing to him highly unlikely dying words on behalf of the antislavery cause, he had made Broderick a martyr and a rallying point for the Union cause.

In the 1861 state election Leland Stanford, profiting from a divided Democratic Party and pro-Unionist tide, became the first Republican governor. During his wartime tenure California's military involvement remained minimal, largely because the national government did not draft men or make great use of volunteers from California. The costs of transporting troops such a distance was one deterrent, the still-strong Southern sentiment in the state another. Several newspapers, mostly from small communities outside San Francisco, touted the Confederate cause. For three months the commanding West Coast general, George Wright, banned the Visalia *Equal Rights Expositor* and a half dozen other "secesh" papers from the mails. When he later arrested the *Expositor*'s editor, Lovick P. Hall, for printing treasonous remarks, Hall gained his release by expediently signing a loyalty oath to the United States Constitution. According to his interpretation, there was no conflict between his actions and beliefs and the written code. The *Expositor* came to an end four months later, however, when a group of thirty enraged soldiers physically reduced the offices and equipment to rubble.

The San Francisco *Newsletter and Commercial Advertiser,* founded as a satirical sheet in 1856 by the English advocate of aerial navigation, Frederick Marriott, had two main claims to fame: it gave Ambrose Bierce his start in San Francisco, and it became the city's leading pro-South journal. Although its open ridicule of the Northern cause somehow escaped the censure of General Wright, it did not go long unheeded by the run of Union sympathizers. On Lincoln's assassination an angry mob plundered the offices, destroying the press and flinging the type into the street. The paper survived the episode and some years afterward hired Bierce as Town Crier.

When the Reverend William Scott, a Confederate sympathizer, claimed from the pulpit of the Calvary Presbyterian Church that Jefferson Davis was as loyal as George Washington and as worthy of the blessings of the Lord as the other reigning President, Lincoln, demonstrators forced his resignation and his removal from

California. The climate also gave rise to a clamor for loyalty oaths; in 1863 the legislature passed, and the Supreme Court upheld, a law requiring oaths of all parties to court processes, a statute which remained on the books until 1872.

In February, 1861, two companies of artillery arrived in San Francisco to occupy Fort Point, the only Civil War battlement built in the West. Rumor had it that Senator Gwin and Brigadier General Albert Sidney Johnston, the West's chief commanding officer from late 1860 to April, 1861, were conspiring, in the event of hostilities, to deliver the state and the federal forces over to the South. Johnston, in truth, carried out his duties with exemplary loyalty until, having tendered his resignation, he was physically replaced by General Edwin Sumner. He lost his life on the Confederate side at the Battle of Shiloh. Sumner arrested Gwin on suspicion of treason some months later aboard a steamer carrying them both to Panama, the general to a new assignment, and the Senator to a new career after his defeat in the California election. Gwin spent some time in Northern detention. He later lived in Paris for several years and after his return was known as the Duke de Gwin.

The pro-Confederate secret societies helped give rise to prevalent rumors of Southern conspiracies by their clandestine military drills in the sand hills out of sight of the city. One rumor had it that General Johnston himself would lead the Golden Circle in an insurrection. The number of members in the groups turned out to be greatly exaggerated, and their efforts amounted to little more than fantasy and flourish. Authorities thwarted the one seditious plot that did materialize. Under the guise of conducting a commercial voyage to Manzanillo, a contingent of Southerners, including the adventurous twenty-three-year-old Kentuckian Asbury Harpending, furtively armed the 91-ton schooner *J. W. Chapman*. Loaded with 2 brass 12-pound cannons, a howitzer, 30 rifles, 150 Colt revolvers, 8 cases of shells and 5 of powder, and a generous assortment of similar paraphernalia including uniforms, most of them stashed away in boxes marked "machinery," the *Chapman* set forth from San Francisco Harbor for Mexico with the intention of intercepting a Pacific Mail steamer. This was to be the first of a fleet of vessels captured for the Confederacy. It would sail as a privateer under a letter of marque that Harpending, having run the blockade, had personally obtained, along with a Confederate naval commission, from Jefferson Davis. The *Chapman*'s immediate goal, to disrupt Union shipping and more particularly to lay hands on the large shipments of gold bullion leaving California for the East, was the first step in taking California out of the Union and establishing a Pacific republic. The plot included the eventual seizure of the arsenal at Benicia, the capture of emplacements on Alcatraz and Fort Point, and the mounting of an army of 1,000 men to capture California and force its break from the Union. The federal authorities, aware of the scheme almost from its inception, seized the *Chapman* before it was out of San Francisco Harbor. The leaders of the conspiracy, including Harpending, although convicted and sentenced to ten years in prison and $10,000 fines, escaped punishment when Lincoln signed a general amnesty.

Of the 16,000 Californians who served the Union cause, most had Western patrol duty, but some 500 saw action in the California Battalion, attached to the Second Massachusetts Cavalry. The state's real contribution was in helping finance the Union side through its mining bonanzas, in providing a refuge for families escaping the conflict—one San Francisco newspaper suggested that in the second year of the war nearly 100,000 refugees fled to California—and, largely through the humanitarian oratory of the Reverend Mr. King, in raising more than $1,000,000, one-fourth of the national total, for the Sanitary Commission.

XVIII

Social Change: The Chinese and Labor

They are among the most industrious, quiet, patient people among us. Perhaps the citizens of no nation except the Germans are more quiet and valuable. They seem to live under our laws as if born and bred under them, and already have commenced an expression of their preference by applying for citizenship, by filing their intention in our courts. What will be the extent of the movement now going on in China and here is not easily foreseen. We shall undoubtedly have a very large addition to our population, and it may not be many years before the Halls of Congress are graced by the presence of a long queued Mandarin sitting, voting, and speaking, beside a Don from Santa Fe, and a Kanaker [*sic*] from Hawaii.

—The *Alta,* May 12, 1851

THE CHINESE

THE early fur trade between Yankee traders and Canton had formed the basis for a traditional friendship between China and the United States. In the first years of the fifties, when the Chinese joined the worldwide migration to California, they participated in community activities along with everybody else. Fifty Chinese took part in the celebrations in honor of California's admission to the Union; they shared equally in the services to the memory of Zachary Taylor; their faithful cooperation in the parades and other ceremonies brought approving comments for their public spirit, for the exotic character of their costume, and for the quaintness of their manner. For a brief period their fellow adventurers in the Gold Rush looked on them with curiosity and with tolerance. But contrary to the optimistic predictions of the *Alta* writer, by the beginning of 1852 the Chinese had become the primary focus of antiforeign sentiment in the state.

For two centuries China had experienced internal difficulties which came to a peak between 1839 and 1842 in the Opium War, a defeating confrontation with the British, and in 1851 in the civil

385

war which erupted when the Taipings rebelled against the Manchu dynasty. Many Chinese nationals, already impoverished by a series of droughts, floods, and famines, found the promise of California irresistible. In 1852 more than 20,000 Chinese arrived in California, a few of them by sampan. Of the eight sampans that sailed for America that year, six were lost, one landed in Monterey, and one above Mendocino. They were part of the first significant Asian immigration, one which then made them the state's largest minority. Whereas most of the immigrants in 1849 had been of the merchant class, the majority of the later arrivals were laborers, "credit-ticket" men, whose passage, on credit, had to be repaid along with interim expenses out of future earnings. The host of contractors, many of them Chinese businessmen setting up industries in California, exercised so much financial control over the workers that they virtually enslaved them. Although the actual use of contract or indentured labor, which grew up to replace the slackening slave trade of the nineteenth century, never succeeded in California because of the antislavery attitudes there, shippers under British, Chinese, and American flags made fortunes transporting Chinese laborers, indentured or otherwise.

With the promise of a long civil war ahead in China—the Taiping Rebellion lasted thirteen years and the outbreak of district warfare in the Pearl Delta region in 1856 lasted another twelve— the voluntary interest in temporary emigration to California remained very much alive. The potential number of sojourners, however, greatly alarmed some Californians, while it delighted others:

> The enemy of the Asiatics elaborated the old arguments: they were competing unfairly with Yankees, draining wealth out of the country, dragging down morality, encouraging monopolies, and threatening the tranquility of the mines. Similarly, the exploitationist declared that the Chinese were necessary for the advancement of the economy but even invented new arguments: the Chinese were more docile than the Hispanos and their morality superior.[2]

Whether from the enemy or exploitationist point of view, the basic issue was economic: the Chinese threatened the status quo if by their presence they competed with the local workers and equally if by their absence they denied the economy a major source of cheap labor and steady consumers. That racism was only a tool to arouse the ugliest fears and partisan prejudices of the masses is clear from its ups and downs; it gained adherents when the Chinese appeared an economic threat, and opponents when they bestowed benefits. Some of the same people alternately championed both sides of the issue depending on the moment's expediency, most notably Charles Crocker, Leland Stanford, and State Senator George B. Tingley. Tingley switched from exclusion to exploitation by introducing the first bill to legalize Chinese labor at fixed rates on ten-year contracts. Governor Stanford's unfortunate proclamation that the presence of the Chinese, "degraded and distinct people" that they were, could not but exert a "deleterious influence upon the superior race" was repudiated a short time later, when he and his railroad became one of their major employers. Years later, when he ran for Senator, he took the popular stand of the moment and became anti-Chinese again.

The state's leaders had followed inconsistent policies that variously embraced measures to exclude immigration, to expel from the mines those foreigners who had already arrived, to exploit immigrants through special taxation, and even, as in the cases when Crocker and company needed unskilled builders for the railroad and the large mining combines needed laborers for construction, to solicit recruits from China. In 1850 the state began to pass a series of taxes on foreigners, the first of which, a $20-a-month mining fee, drove thousands of Mexicans, including many who had already become American citizens, south across the border. Again a practical economic consideration defeated the measure: when the storekeepers began to lose too much money for lack of customers, they forced its repeal. Bills which replaced the $20 license with a $3- and a $4-dollar-a-month fee passed in 1852 and 1853, remained in force through 1870, and produced the largest single source of California's income. The Chinese paid by far the greatest share, one-quarter of the state's total revenue. No wonder that the legislature appropriated $600 for printing 4,000 copies of the law in Chinese translation.

In the West the early antiforeign bias derived more from rural frontier traditions that dealt with the control of rebellious, troublesome, and presumedly inferior peoples than from the Eastern urban movements, expressions against radical working-class philosophy and against the Irish and Catholicism, that came to a head in the seventies. The authors of the *Annals of San Francisco* expressed a sentiment typical of the early 1850's when they wrote:

> Indians, Spaniards of many provinces, Hawaiians, Japanese, Chinese, Malays, Tartars and Russians, must all give place to the resistless flood of Anglo-Saxon or American progress. These peoples need not, and most of them probably cannot be swept from the face of the earth; but undoubtedly their national characteristics and opposing qualities and customs must be materially modified, and closely assimilated to those of the civilizing and dominant race.[3]

But this attitude had to be maintained in the face of positive evidence to the contrary. From the arrival of the first Chinese emigrants in the spring of 1848, two men and a woman, servants to

Charles Gillespie and his family who arrived aboard the clipper ship *Eagle,* California had become the beneficiary of Chinese industry and over the years—often unwittingly—assimilated a great deal of Far Eastern culture. The Chinese immediately filled the jobs so hastily vacated by fledgling miners. The early hotelman Brown wrote in his *Reminiscences* that it was so difficult during the early part of 1849 to find stewards and cooks that he nearly gave up the hotel's boarding department entirely. That he did not was due to the arrival of an Englishman from the Sandwich Islands with a dozen Chinese in tow; their services, along with the Englishman's as interpreter, cost Brown $1,200 a month, a sum which he willingly paid, reporting that during their three months' tenure the new help did very well, gave general satisfaction, and that he was very pleased.

The great swarm of Chinese arrivals in 1852 included only fourteen women. Chinese men took over without reluctance many of the jobs normally relegated in the community to women: laundering, cooking, household services. They did the meanest labor uncomplainingly, and took on the dirtiest assignments for little pay. When they went into mining, they did not preempt new grounds, but bought up old claims or took over abandoned tailings, managing by their thoroughness and unflagging industry to eke out several dollars a day from areas that their predecessors had already discarded as worthless. They were more often employed at low pay by American and Chinese mining companies. As the number of Chinese miners increased, their profitable labors brought increased resentment. Since a natural segregation existed in the mining communities—ethnic or geographic groups tending to set up camp together—the Chinese were an easy target. Chinese Camp, known also as Chinese Diggings, eight or ten miles south of Sonora, became one of the most prominent outposts and the labor distribution center for all the southern mines.

Beyond obvious differences of race, the Chinese did not readily learn English, inviting even more abuse than that which their white American neighbors unleashed on the French, the Chilean, and the Mexican "foreigners." What had at first appeared exotic (the difference in dress, the worship of pagan gods, the eating of strange food), coupled with the suspicions that the Chinese were carriers of unpleasant diseases and had a low sense of morality, turned popular sentiment strongly against them. At the mines they found the obstacles to filing a claim almost insurmountable and were consequently often driven away from profitable diggings by miners with no greater rights than their own. They were frequently the targets of mob attack and the principal victims of fictitious tax collectors, to whom they paid the taxes on foreign miners several times over. Even the California Indians showed their hostility by offering help to the officials to search out those Chinese miners who had gone into hiding to avoid paying taxes.

The Chinese, like so many of the Gold Rush participants, had come to make their fortunes and return home; that they assimilated less than any of the other groups was obviously due to their extremely close ties to homeland, family, and ancestors and the greater differences in their language, costume, and culture. The fact that they were the common enemy, surrounded by hostile and often brutal people, encouraged them to band together even more for the protection and comfort they could derive from familiar ways. But the more exclusive they became, the more threatening they loomed to their adversaries. "The sojourners' dominant concern in their new environment was survival, not liberty. 'Bitter strength,' the literal translation of the Chinese term *k'u-li* for these laborers, suggests the dimensions of the sojourners' experience."[4]

Taxes and exclusion from the mining districts represented only two of the oppressive measures directed against the Chinese. In 1855 the legislature extended to Asians an existing law which barred the testimony of Indians and blacks from court procedures involving whites. Through various confusions, the Chinese were considered part of the same race as American Indians and therefore subjected to all the same disadvantages. Thus classified, they were not eligible to become citizens, even had they wanted to, or to vote against any of the measures that were aimed distinctly to harass them. When charged with a crime, a Chinese found it almost impossible to obtain bail through any normal channel. In 1855 the legislature further imposed a $50 head tax on aliens who could not take up citizenship, an act later ruled unconstitutional by the State Supreme Court.

Later ordinances, many of them invalidated by their conflict with the federal Civil Rights Act of 1870, the due process and equal protection clauses of the Fourteenth Amendment, and the right of free immigration established by the 1868 Burlingame Treaty, badgered the Chinese almost beyond endurance. Taxes discriminated against "Mongolians" over eighteen years of age; against laundry owners, fishermen, and vegetable sellers—all occupations staffed largely by Chinese. A lodging house law, aimed at the overcrowded conditions in Chinatown, imposed penalties on occupants of premises which contained less than 500 cubic feet for each individual; the prime offender turned out to be the government, whose jails forced the Chinese violators into half the space required by the legislation. The queue statute demanded that each county jail prisoner be sheared of his hair to within one inch of his scalp, diminishing the Oriental's self-respect along with his prized pigtail. Chinese children were denied public education, a measure modified briefly in 1866 to allow them attendance in public schools if white parents raised no objection. Another act briefly in force required shipowners and captains to guarantee by bond that their passengers would not become public charges or engage in such illegal acts as prostitution. During the 1860's and 1870's Chinese were denied admission to the San Francisco County Hospital. The ubiquitous shoulder pole used by the worker to transport practically everything was banned by decree from use in the streets. An 1873 order taxed laundries $2 every quarter for using a vehicle drawn by one horse, $4 for using more than one vehicle, and $15 for using no vehicle at all, the prevalent Chinese custom. The expression "He hasn't got a Chinaman's chance" became more apt by the day. In 1866 the one-year-old black newspaper the *Elevator* editorially demanded a stop to Chinese immigration, although the black community remained divided in its opinion.

When the railroad on its completion released the thousands of coolies who had made up the bulk of its construction crews, the Chinese had no choice but to compete for jobs in agriculture and among the city's existing corps of unskilled laborers. When the railroad furthermore flooded the market with competitive manufactures brought in from the East and San Francisco felt the full effects of the national depression, community agitation against the Chinese mounted even higher.

By 1876, when the Chinese issue was reaching a peak, the Chinese Six Companies estimated that the state's Oriental population—mostly males of working age—was around 75,000, out of a national total of between 108,000 to 150,000.* At the same time there were at least 50,000 unemployed workers in the state, with some estimates going as high as 100,000. The results, again, were most unfortunate for the Chinese, on whom an emotional community heaped all the blame. Unsuspecting coolie laborers kept arriving in California, their immigration arranged cooperatively by the not entirely benevolent Chinese Six Companies, the large industries (several of them Chinese) seeking cheap labor, and the steamship companies, always happier for a full complement of passengers. Repressive measures convinced a good many Chinese to sail for home, but too often indebtedness prevented escape. Persecution erupted into violence, the most outrageous instance being the Los Angeles Massacre of 1871, when about twenty

*Figures are approximations because there are discrepancies among the records of the Six Companies, the United States Census, and the State and County Treasury Reports of Taxes on Foreigners.

Chinese died, most of them left hanging on the gallows for all to contemplate. In the state election of the same year Newton Booth became governor by advocating regulation of the railroad and exclusion of the Chinese.

Labor unions were on the rise alongside the growing anticoolie movements. Of the 152 delegates elected to the state constitutional convention of 1878, 51 represented Denis Kearney's brand-new western Workingmen's Party. Thirty of these were San Franciscans. The seventy-eight candidates who ran and were elected as nonpartisans were backed by both parties in an effort to stem the sudden rise of Kearneyites, whose radical philosophies attacked the rich as well as the Chinese. The California Workingmen's Party was made up largely of the neighborhood anticoolie clubs, which in most instances were the same as the old Democratic ward machines, and of Irish laborers, who formed almost as large a segment of the San Francisco population, about 20 percent, as the Chinese. The Irish, however, besides being white and English-speaking, also had the vote. Tallied with the farm bloc represented by the Grangers and their sympathizers, their ballots effected a number of modifications in the new state constitution. Ratified by a small majority in 1879, it included an elaborate anti-Chinese section, strictly limiting employment of the Chinese and generally protecting the state from their presence through measures later declared invalid.

Although national authorities generally looked on the problem as a state matter, the Chinese issue had caused such commotion that Congress, prodded by a California lobby, felt obliged to dispatch a Joint Committee of Investigation in 1876. Before politicians took up full-scale anti-Chinese platforms on a national level, however, they had to come to the realization that the anti-Chinese Western states now held the balance of electoral votes in Presidential contests and that their wishes were therefore of practical national significance. With Congress now ready to accede, federal legislation provided the Chinese Exclusion Act by 1882.

In 1888 a new act prohibited the reentry of any Chinese laborer who was temporarily away from the United States. This denied readmission to some 20,000 travelers, even though they had certificates of return. Six hundred Chinese, caught by its passage in midocean en route back to the United States, could not reenter on their arrival. In 1892 the Exclusion Act was extended for ten years. In April, 1902, Congress voted an indefinite extension of all laws excluding Chinese immigration, including those applying to Hawaii. The Exclusion Acts remained in force until their repeal in 1943 in the administration of President Franklin Delano Roosevelt.

As an aid to the immigrants coping with the new laws, a map later appeared in San Francisco Chinatown showing the major streets in that vicinity, indicating some of the prominent buildings, such as the Hall of Justice, the Daan Kwei Chinese Opera Theatre on Washington Street, and the Hang Far Low Restaurant on Grant, and giving such miscellaneous information as the routes of the cable cars and street trolleys. What was unusual about this map, and made clear the reason for its publication, was the inclusion of a series of questions and answers which, once mastered, would enable a Chinese to pose as a longtime resident not subject to investigation as an illegal immigrant. "When was the big fair held here, and where?" asks the imaginary inquisitor. "The fair was held here in the 5th and 6th months of the reign of Emperor Kwang Hsu 19th year and took place at the New Park," comes the answer, referring to the Midwinter Exposition of 1893–94 in Golden Gate Park. "What year did the doctors blockade Chinatown?" asks the question. "It was Kwang Hsu 26th year, 5th month and was done for about two weeks," replies the supposed old-timer, recalling an episode in 1900 when the city's physicians closed the quarter as the suspected source of the plague. To "Where is the Imperial House's post office?" and "Where is the 9-story house?" the Chinese reader learns that the government's post office is at Washington and Sansome streets in the custom house, while the Palace Hotel graces Market Street.[5]

From the eighties on, when the Chinese became less and less available as a source of cheap labor, a large-scale Japanese immigration began to fill the gap. Although many of the Japanese intended to settle in America, to establish families, and to invest in their adopted land, their racial kinship to the Chinese and their similar role in the state's economy lay them open to the same basic abuses and the same racist prejudices, which culminated in their wholesale internment in relocation camps during the Second World War.

Meanwhile, the early Chinese community of San Francisco, much in self-defense, had developed into a unique subculture. Like other newcomers, the Chinese had to adapt to a completely new social structure, in their case without the help of the elders and village leaders, the scholars, educators, and artists who did not in general participate in the early exodus to America. The first who arrived, merchants and businessmen, became the *de facto* leaders and oftentimes the exploiters of the working-class Chinese. Although not ranked high on the scale of accomplishment in their homeland, in California the merchants not only set the tone for the community; they became the mandarins. The formal structure of the new world settlement depended on groupings by kinship, by geographical origin, and by other self-defining institutions. Such arrangements allowed the Chinese to tend their own house, gave them comfort during the long exile from home, and helped keep the majority of the poor dependent on those who controlled the agencies.

When the Chinese immigrants debarked in San Francisco, representatives of merchandise stores and later members of the Chinese Six Companies met them at the dock and offered lodging, board, and whatever other necessities were called for until more permanent arrangements could be made. Forerunners of the family associations, the merchandise stores, each run by a family unit, served the community as the basic seat of social control and the center of economic activities. The importance of the family group, the traditional unit of control in a mainland community, persisted in Chinatown until about the time of World War II. Certain families or people from particular districts controlled one type of business or occupation: the Dear family (with many alternate spellings) ran the San Francisco fruit and candy business; the Yee and Lee families provided the majority of cooks and owned many of the finer restaurants; the people of the Yeong Wo district did most of the tenant farming and controlled the fruit industry of the Sacramento Valley. Since families tended to congregate heavily in one location, a particular name often dominated a whole town.

The family associations, larger organizations with formal headquarters, brought together whole clans and arose with the need for broader authority. Structured like a family village in which the elders had control, the associations gave over responsibility for their mutual welfare and the adjudication of differences to the family seniors. In later years, if threatened difficulties seemed likely to cause a serious break between groups, the elders would call in their peers from other sections of the country for advice, much as a doctor calls in consultants on a difficult case. When problems occurred between single families, the yet higher authority of the district association handled the matter. These groups combined families from the same district in China. In San Francisco most of the immigrants came from some twenty-four of the ninety-odd Canton districts.

The need for concerted action in the face of America's anti-Chinese attitudes, as well as the call for a more equitable rendering of justice than the Chinese could obtain before American courts, gave rise to the Chinese Consolidated Benevolent Association. Put together well after the establishment of traditional family and district organizations, it was a uniquely American manifestation of Chinese culture, with no counterpart in China. Its membership was representative of and elected by the most powerful district forces: the Kong Chow, Ning Yeung, Sam Yup, Yeong Wo, Hop Wo, and Yan Wo. The association served the Chinese settlement as its spokesman, its highest court, and, until there was an official consulate in the late seventies, its representative of the Manchu government. Known commonly as the Chinese Six Companies, although at one time the number of member groups came to eight, the association also kept an official census; instituted Chinese educational and medical services (it still operates one of the largest language schools in Chinatown, the Chinese High School, with quarters on the top floor of the Six Companies' headquarters); mounted legal battles against all the government legislation of an anti-Chinese nature; ran a home for indigent males; and was instrumental in assisting the Chinese business community. The latter role brought frequent criticism that the Six Companies were helping to perpetuate the credit-ticket business for the benefit of commercial interests. The Six Companies were in effect the governing body of Chinatown, with complete understanding that all Chinese activities, be they fund raising, participating in public celebrations, or welcoming visiting dignitaries, needed their stamp of approval.[6]

The tongs were originally merely associations of groups with common interests, the word "tong" meaning simply "association," as in Sunday tongs (churches) or medicine tongs (drugstores). But the term was early taken over by the formal criminal element in the community in a sordid history that revolved around gangsters, hatchet men, and extortionists. From the 1860's the big tongs controlled both legitimate and more frequently illegitimate enterprises and attracted many otherwise unwilling members through fear of reprisals or as a means of protecting a place in the business community. After a time there remained little connection between the purposeful-sounding names of the tongs and the illicit trades in which they were involved. "The traffickers in slave girls, On Leong Society, meant the 'Chamber of Tranquil Conscientiousness.' Another society founded for the same purpose, the Kwong Dak Tong, was the 'Chamber of Far-Reaching Virtue.' The gambling fraternity, the Hip Shing Tong, was synonymous with the 'Hall of Victorious Union.' "[7]

Often called highbinders, the new tong members came to power almost mysteriously, the exact circumstances of their rise still uncertain. One explanation is that these all-male groups were dissenting members of a legitimate association known as the Chee Kung Tong. A second theory holds that the tongs grew out of the ranks of the Taiping rebels who had fled China and sought refuge among their sympathizers in San Francisco. When the generosity of local sponsors began to slacken, the rebels resorted to blackmail and shakedowns to keep the contributors in line, sometimes even "trying" reticent business leaders before mock courts. Certainly one factor was the loss of power by the Six Companies over government-required registration documents. Having told the people not to sign such papers, the Six leadership was humiliated by a Supreme Court decision that declared them legal. With the Six Companies' power thus diminished, the tongs found an opportunity to move in. Whatever the case, they often fought openly with each other; their use of all types of weapons—knives, cleavers, guns (often concealed in the billowy sleeves of their costumes)—gave rise to their designation as hatchet men. They controlled the prolific gambling and slave girl rackets, the opium dens, and Chinatown labor racketeering.

The gangsterism of the tongs repelled a large part of the Chinese community as well as wide-eyed American observers from coast to coast. However, the fear of physical violence and economic sanctions made the Chinese leaders extremely cautious about initiating or even aiding any attempts to break the tongs' hold over Chinatown. Since the Chinese traditionally believed that the individual had to forgo his own rights in deference to the honor of the larger community, groups tended to exert a policing effect on their members, and the higher fraternities tended to obtain obedience from the associations within their jurisdiction. The Peace Association, a kind of tong court, apparently established with the blessings of the regular judiciary and the city police, arbitrated differences between tong adversaries. By tong agreement, warring factions had to submit their grievances to the final authority of the Peace group before resorting to open warfare. This self-regulating device eventually helped cut down the bloody wars, but it had little effect in diminishing tong power, which thrived unabated until the earthquake finally broke its hold.

Another dominant force in the Chinese society was its temples. In a small settlement the principal district association would build one temple which would serve for all. A number of them still exist, nestled incongruously among Western buildings in the old mining towns. In a city the size of San Francisco, the residents congregated in seven temples, of which the Kong Chow Temple, rebuilt on Pine Street after the 1906 earthquake, is probably the oldest. Since religious belief among the Chinese is spread among many deities and is a rather personal expression, the temples, although each was dedicated to one principal deity, often permitted simultaneous worship of several. The temples performed a number of functions that had no religious connection, in particular providing quarters for the sick and indigent and classrooms for the Chinese language schools. Early in the fifties the American

Missionary Association attempted to bring the Chinese into the Christian faith, especially through the teaching of English, but Presbyterian Minister William Speer, the principal Chinatown missionary, never reported overwhelming success with his flock. Speer, who had done missionary service in Canton and who was in San Francisco specifically to continue his work with the Chinese, championed their cause and fought the harsh measures against them until he had literally drained away his health.[8]

The Chinese, with their strong belief in preserving traditional cultural ties, placed much emphasis on maintaining Chinese schools in the community, whether or not they were permitted other educational resources. With the exception of a short-lived Oriental day school and an evening school for Chinese which was legislated out of existence by 1871, the general exclusion of Chinese students from public schools prevailed in San Francisco until 1885. Then the first of several State Supreme Court decisions held that any Chinese child aged six to twenty-one who had been born and continuously resided in San Francisco could obtain admission. In practice, however, the Chinese students were still refused entry into existing schools in favor of an Oriental school newly established for the purpose of continuing their segregation; with few exceptions the policy persisted until 1906 in spite of the court's rulings. After the earthquake and a brief period of camaraderie and integration, the school board, citing "overcrowded conditions" in white schools, managed to shift twenty-three Chinese, ninety-three Japanese, three Korean, and one Eskimo student to a new school on the old Chinatown site. California laws in effect permitted segregation in separate public Oriental schools to continue until 1946.

Before the end of the century Chinatown was supporting a dozen or more private schools, as well as its own community school administered by the district associations. The same reverence for Chinese culture led to the formation of the Wên-hua She, or the Society of the Splendors of Literature. Every home in Chinatown had a special box for discarded writings, and the entire community meticulously saved its newspapers, old books, letters, and other written materials, which were collected and turned over to the society. The Wên-hua She headquarters contained the brick Furnace of Mon War, the Furnace of Beautiful Writing, to which the writings were ceremoniously committed amid the vapors of incense and the incantations of the faithful. After the burning, the ashes, properly wrapped in burlap, were flung far out to sea. Today the same respect for preserving Chinese ways and transmitting Chinese culture is behind the anti-integration position held by the many Cantonese residents of Chinatown who are among the principal opponents of the modern issue of busing. It also explains why many of the younger generation still attend both city schools and Chinese-language institutions on a daily basis.

When the coolie laborers were released after the completion of the railroad, they settled in such numbers in San Francisco that the city's Chinatown became and still remains the largest Chinese settlement outside the homeland. Their part in developing California went far beyond the vision of the Russian Count Rezanov, who suggested during his visit in 1806 in a letter to his government that Chinese should be used in California to replace Indian labor.

By the turn of the century Chinese made up practically the entire force working the canneries and constituted a large part of the manpower in the laundries, the garment, cigar, match, boot, and broom factories, and the fishing and fish-packing industries. Their overwhelming presence in the packing plants gave rise to the term "iron Chink," for a mechanical gadget necessary to the preparation of fish for canning. The 150 Chinese fishermen who inhabited the community south of Rincon Point fished from two dozen junks and sampans until their use was later restricted. Using sweepseining in deep water and hook and line along the shores, the fishermen, in spite of prohibitions against their employment of more efficient drift and fyke nets, brought in a daily catch in the neighborhood of 3,000 pounds, largely sturgeon, shark, herring, some salmon, and a variety of rock and bottom fish. They dried the herring, as they did much of the shrimp they gathered, for use in Chinese communities elsewhere. As the principal shrimpers in California, they brought in such quantities that by 1880 the state led the nation in shrimp production. Hundreds of fishermen established camps, principally on San Francisco and Tomales bays. By 1897 twenty-six shrimp camps existed, of which fourteen were still in working operation as late as 1930. China Camp, a settlement of more than 1,000 inhabitants on the small rented cove of the McNear Ranch in Marin, was the most notable of the shrimp villages. It thrived until 1910, when the state turned San Pablo Bay into a bass nursery for sport fishing and consequently banned netting operations. The white fishermen's union further limited Chinese participation in fishing for the general market, and legislation enacted in 1901 designated a closed season for shrimp from May through August. A statute passed in 1905 banned the exportation of dried shrimp, which additionally curtailed the Chinese operations. By the mid-1940's the shrimp had virtually disappeared from the Bay, largely done in by pollution, the same fate which now seems to be facing the Dungeness crab in the San Francisco area. In the early days the Chinese fished for crab from the city wharves and sold about $75,000 worth a year; they went for 75 cents a dozen. The Chinese popularized another California favorite, abalone, although it was the iridescence of the shell rather than the delicacy of the meat that at first attracted Californians.

The designation of the term "Chinaman's Room" for a tiny servant's quarter still tucked away in many old San Francisco houses came into use as the Chinese houseboy took over the role of domestic employee. Even at the height of anti-Chinese feeling in San Francisco, employers of Chinese houseworkers and cooks so revered their services that they paid them well above the going wage for other servants, and sometimes even double. Chinese waiters, dishwashers, busboys, and chefs began to staff the city's restaurants, a tradition that manifests itself in modern times: The best Neapolitan cooking in the city has been prepared for the last twenty-five years by a Chinese chef and pizza maker named Tom, who fittingly named his restaurant Tommaso's.

During the seventies when the Chinese made up between 70 and 80 percent of the work force, they were a constant source of controversy. In 1877, for example, the prison managers publicly complained that Chinese laborers, working for 25 cents or less a day, were ruining the penitentiaries. The law at the time permitted convicts to be hired out at 50 cents a day, a wage which no contractor who could get Chinese workers at half the price would willingly pay.

A decline in numbers of Chinese workers in San Francisco industries followed the exclusion of newcomers and the discriminatory practices against those already employed. Many laborers left the area altogether, going as far afield as New England and the South. The Chinese who went to the Napa Valley were responsible for many of the stone barricades, the concrete work, and some of the construction of the Inglenook Winery, the tunnels at Beringer Brothers and Schramsburg wineries, and a stone fence which runs along the Silverado Trail from Napa to Calistoga. Quicksilver mining became the valley's second-largest industry to employ Chinese.

Chinese workers completed the excavation of the hill and the filling of the Bay for the Pacific Mail Steamship Company wharves, the erection of the Parrott Building out of huge blocks of imported granite, and the building of numerous stone bridges, fences, and mountain roads. During the construction of the Parrott Building, an architect had to come from China to help decipher the hieroglyphics on the granite which told the American contractor how to assemble the giant Chinese puzzle.

The Chinese entered factory work on a large scale for the first

time in 1859, when Englebricht and Levy hired Chinese workers
to manufacture cigars in their San Francisco plant. By 1864 San
Francisco was the center of the industry; within another four
years California was fourth in production among the states. By
1866, when the output was valued at $1,000,000, one-half of the
San Francisco factories were owned by Chinese. Having been
from the first the target of discriminatory hiring practices by the
Segar Makers' Association, the Chinese had set up their own businesses, often under such names as Ramirez and Company or Ca-
banes and Company, and marketed the same quality cigars at considerably lower prices. They also owned or staffed most of the factories manufacturing cigar boxes. Pressure from the white Cigar
Makers Union along with anti-Chinese legislation forced most of
them out of the industry by the mid-eighties, after which the cigar
business went into a considerable decline.

In 1859, when Heyneman, Pick and Company opened the Pioneer Woolen Mills, California's first, it employed a large number
of Chinese workers. Within ten years approximately 500 Chinese
had found jobs in the San Francisco knitting industry. In the seventies about 2,500 Chinese worked in the manufacture of clothing, sewing, doing piecework, lacemaking, and embroidery. During the same period, Chinese workers made about half the boots
and shoes manufactured in California. Although a Frenchman
had introduced the industry to the state, by 1870 eleven of the
dozen slipper factories were Chinese-owned. Fong Ching, or Little Pete, one of the most notorious of San Francisco's Chinese
gangsters, began as errand boy and ended as owner of the F. C.
Peters and Company shoe factory; unfortunately he did not stick
to that career.

Several miles south of San Francisco, Chinese flower growers
raised blooms for cutting. A rainbow of asters, sweet peas, and
chrysanthemums filled the enormous baskets in which the vendors transported their bouquets for sale to the city. The major as-
ter growers supplying today's market are still the Chinese.

Although by the 1880's they made up the bulk of migratory and
seasonal laborers, only a small number of Chinese took up full-
time farming. As with all the fields that they entered, as farmers,
full or part time, they excelled at the work. Most often the full-
time workers made land-leasing arrangements, often hiring their
countrymen to work the fields; many preferred truck gardening
on the perimeter of the city on small plots of their own. Their labors in the sand dunes encircling the city converted arid hillocks
into luscious' patches of greenery. To market their fruits and
vegetables, they used the shoulder pole until it was prohibited,
adding a great deal of color to the San Francisco marketplace.

The Chinese raised most of the peanuts and strawberries in the area, among a wide variety of produce; Chinese farmers were involved in hatching eggs by artificial means, in cleaning fields and cutting wood, and in odd jobs such as collecting the wild mustard of Monterey.

Growing produce was not the only connection the Chinese had with food. From the earliest days of the Gold Rush, Chinese restaurants offered the city an entirely new cuisine, and as the many testimonials bear witness, the Westerners enjoyed it thoroughly. Quantities of imported ingredients made it possible for the chefs to produce authentic Cantonese cooking. Until very recently, when the influx of immigrants from other provinces changed the San Francisco balance, the restaurants in San Francisco, as well as in the rest of country, specialized in the food from that province. San Francisco readily adopted the Cantonese custom of taking light meals and snacks in teahouses; today dim sum is almost as familiar to the Westerner as to the Cantonese immigrants who introduced it to the city. Another nicety, one that disappeared in the 1930's along with the bottomless pot of tea on every shop counter, was the pedi-catering service. "It was not unusual to see a Chinese wearing an Occidental cap, balancing a 30″ by 30″ wooden tray on top of his head, delivering a full course dinner complete with dinner ware, to a household. In wet weather, the tray would be covered over with a black oil cloth, fastened down with clothes pins. The soiled dishes would be left at the doorway to be picked up the next day."[9]

The cigar workers, the boot- and shoemakers, the sewing tradesmen, and the laundry workers banded together into a number of guilds to protect their interests. In several instances where wages were outrageously low and conditions almost unbearable, the men struck. About 2,000 stopped work on the Southern Pacific but, lacking the support of the other laborers, were unsuccessful. Farmhands likewise demonstrated unsuccessfully in Napa on numerous occasions, as did the cigar- and boot- and shoemakers in San Francisco. The latter group provided seventy-five men on three-year contracts to the Calvin Sampson Shoe Factory in North Adams, Massachusetts, when that firm's workers went on strike. The move did not help increase the popularity of the Chinese in New England. The sewing trades in San Francisco divided into three affiliated guilds: one for tailors and makers of men's clothing, one for shirtmakers, ladies' clothing and underwear, and the third for those making overalls and work clothes. At first the wage earners were almost entirely men; when women began to enter the trade, they were not permitted, even had they wanted it, to join the guilds. Not before the late 1930's did they have any labor representation at all.

The Chinese contributed more to the developing community than a large part of its labor force. Their influence on Western culture made its impression with everything from the simplest ceramic pot carried by the railroad worker to the game of Mah-Jongg and the flavors of Cantonese cooking. The Western interest in Oriental *objets d'art* accounted for the successful businesses of Gump's and George Marsh, both of which are now famous far beyond the confines of California. The abundance of handsomely lettered signs and banners in Chinese calligraphy did as much to acquaint the Western eye with the harmony and order of Oriental art forms as the contemplative watercolors and landscapes by Chinese painters. Several American artists, most notably Morris Graves, Mark Tobey, and more directly Dong Kingman, trace some of their technique to Chinese writing and painting. The high-fired ceramics and the subtlety of Chinese glazes likewise influenced California pottery making.

Because the Western ear did not appreciate the pentatonic scale to which the Chinese musicians tuned their instruments, nor Western patience endure the endless hours of Chinese theatre, these arts never much appealed to the non-Oriental audience except as a curiosity. But there is a trace of Chinese styling in Bay Area architecture. In most cases the Chinese did not attempt to re-create their national architecture in San Francisco but adopted instead American forms of construction; consequently there was little early influence in this field. The Oriental flavor which early Chinatown displayed came from the few joss houses and temples in the quarter and the profusion of lettered banners and signs, iron balconies, lanterns, and gaudy colors. Its Chinese character today in general derives from postquake construction. Such traditional buildings as the Chinese Telephone Company on Washington Street, rising under a three-pagodaed roof, painted in black lacquer with handsome red and gold trimming and intricate carvings, went up three years after the earthquake. The company, now defunct, employed only Chinese operators from its founding in 1894 until 1949, when the exchange converted from manual to dial service. In the old days the operators, who were fluent in English and all the dialects spoken in Chinatown, knew the names, street numbers, and telephone listings of the entire directory of 2,477 subscribers.

A number of California architects, most notably Bernard Maybeck, incorporated both Chinese and Japanese motifs in their designs. Maybeck adapted the Chinese system of controlling inside temperature by raising the house on a stone foundation and extending the roof eaves to much greater widths. The Chinese custom of staining the underside of temple eaves suggested a similar use of colored stains to Maybeck. The unity of house and garden, of rooms which open to the outdoors, and the concept of the garden as an extension of the house—all are visible influences of Chinese as well as later Japanese architecture on California.

The Chinese love of gambling and games proved equally appealing to their Caucasian neighbors. Chinatown gambling dens became a major nineteenth-century tourist attraction, although Westerners could only participate, and then but for a brief period, in betting on the lottery.

As the Western community gradually responded to Chinese ways, the Chinese residents, still sticking to their traditions, began little by little to become more flexible about their stay on foreign soil. Although many Americans continued their harassment, they observed the Orientals' qualities of loyalty, obedience, and tireless endeavor and their capacity to persevere in the face of the most overwhelming obstacles; the Chinese, in their turn, began to settle in, to view their stay no longer entirely as sojourners but with the possiblity of permanence.

LABOR

IN 1849 the first San Francisco strike on record netted thirty protesting carpenters $13 a day, $3 short of their demands, but with a guaranteed future increase. As wages vacillated wildly along with the rest of the economy, unions at first organized around short-range goals: raises in pay, shorter days, and other immediate improvements in working conditions. By 1850 the printers were unionized, followed shortly by construction workers, stevedores, teamsters, musicians, and sailors. In 1853 about 400 carpenters, not satisfied with the $8-a-day level for which most of their peers had settled, met in the square and, to draw attention to their cause, paraded grandly through the city streets with flags and music. In the same year some 300 longshoremen successfully demonstrated on the docks, obtaining $6 daily pay instead of $5, and reducing their workload from ten to nine hours. Ship's calkers and carpenters by like demands raised their daily wages to $10, masons to $12 and firemen and coal haulers to $25 a month more. Perhaps more important than the immediate benefits that organization achieved, it called attention to the inequalities of pay rates and working hours and other unfavorable practices. Although workers were later instrumental in getting through laws granting mechanics' liens and a uniform working day and in helping create a state bureau of labor statistics, unfortunately, there were few provisions to ensure proper enforcement; their action did give impetus, however, to a growing concern for the workingman.

Although looked on as a major crisis, the labor agitations of the seventies—already mentioned in connection with the demonstrations against the Pacific Mail Steamship Company, the Chinese, and the rise of Coleman's Safety Committee—had little to do with genuine trade unionism. The emphasis was instead on political action, and the leaders such as Kearney had few cohorts from organized labor. Many, unemployed altogether, became involved on the practical grounds of finding a job. The growing racial antagonism gave focus and direction to the Kearneyites and for a time through them to the entire labor movement, for which the Chinese became "the indispensable enemy."[10]

The California Workingmen's Party, developed in the sandlots of San Francisco rather than in the official chambers of the labor hierarchy, differed in a number of respects from the national socialist Workingmen's Party. With a large Irish membership, the Western organization concentrated on the labor issue as a Chinese issue; its socialist line, although it frightened a good segment of the community, never went much beyond slogan and bluster. The Eastern organization, German in the majority and Marxist in orientation, later changed its name to the Socialist Labor Party.

On July 23, 1877, before there was any official California organization, the national party called the original San Francisco sandlot meeting to express sympathy with the Eastern strike against the railroads; it also served as a platform for social grievances against business monopolies and political demagoguery in general. Interrupted and dominated by rowdies and anticoolie groups, however, it turned into a brazen attack on the "Yellow Peril." The belligerents sacked the Chinese quarter and fomented several days of riots, resulting in severe damage with many dead and injured, before the intervention of Coleman's Safety Committee and its pickhandle brigade of thousands of volunteers.

Kearney, whose slogan, "The Chinese Must Go!," once got him arrested for the provocation of his language, was born in Ireland two years before the start of the Gold Rush. Orphaned as a boy, he went to sea, eventually arriving in San Francisco at the age of twenty-one as mate of the clipper *Shooting Star*. After a few years working out of San Francisco Harbor, he became the owner of a small draying business. Shortly after the action of Coleman's committee, on which Kearney served as a member of the brigade through his allegiance as a small businessman, he began to champion the cause he had just fought against. He spoke out publicly against big business and political corruption and for reform that would benefit the common man. Because of his talents at bombastic oratory, he found himself the hero of the little man, especially within the power struggle developing in the Workingmen's Party itself; he became its first secretary. Later, after a turn at the presidency, he took on the title of Lieutenant General; even such anti-Chinese journals as the *Wasp* could not resist caricaturing him as an ass in a general's uniform.

By the fall elections of 1879 the Workingmen's Party had gained enough statewide support to elect sixteen assemblymen, eleven senators, and the chief justice and five associate justices of the State Supreme Court. The Reverend Isaac Kalloch, whose son later killed the *Chronicle*'s Charles De Young, was the party's successful candidate for mayor of San Francisco.

As the force of depression weakened, the dissension within the party—particularly between Kearney and the avid trade unionist Frank Roney—grew stronger. The Workingmen's chief distinction having been its dubious contribution to the passage of the Chinese Exclusion Acts, it had within a few years eliminated its own usefulness. By 1880 it disappeared into the general prosperity. The great agitator Kearney retreated to the anonymity of his horse and cart, and the *Wasp* cartoonist retired his portrait of the masquerading ass.

During the eighties San Francisco labor developed more or less along national patterns, divided by both political differences and organizational preferences. In San Francisco, as in much of the rest of the country, most workers who joined unions were adherents of the American Federation of Labor. Founded in Pittsburgh in 1881, it organized around individual craft unions. The Noble Order of the Knights of Labor, a national catchall union with socialistic ideals, gained some followers, while a number of anarchists whose ideas were much more revolutionary and sometimes violent were less in favor. Most of the more vocal leaders advocated socialist principles at least in moderation. In 1881 Frank Roney, Kearney's former adversary, emerged as one of the principal radical reformers, becoming president of the San Francisco Trade Assembly, and in 1891, a major organizer of the Coast Seamen's Union. Burnette Haskell, whose founding role in the same union was of equal importance, came from a moneyed family of pioneers but forsook a lucrative legal practice to enter radical labor politics. Most influential of all was Andrew Furuseth, whose crusading Sailors' Union of the Pacific was behind many of the most significant improvements in the lives of seamen. Ship's crews had experienced by far the worst conditions of all workers, making their unionization, especially in a major port like San Francisco, a virtual necessity for survival. Until the turn of the century corporal punishment at sea was justifiable for the flimsiest of excuses, and as late as 1915 sailors who quit their jobs were legally punishable as deserters.[11]

In general, however, unionism exerted only a modest force in San Francisco until the end of the nineteenth century, when a strong and pervasive swell of interest finally pushed the city into a position of national leadership.

In July, 1901, the sailors and dockworkers went out on a strike; hundreds were injured, and five dead, before it ended three months later. The use of the city police by Mayor James Phelan, who succeeded Sutro, to aid as strikebreakers, rekindled some of labor's interest in obtaining power through politics. It also lost Mayor Phelan, whose administration had been marked by many innovative measures, much of the respect that his reforms had gained him. A millionaire, socially elite Irish Catholic banker, Phelan was a patron of the arts and a founding father of the Association for the Improvement and Adornment of San Francisco. He won office in 1898 as a reform Democrat. Along with Claus and John Spreckels and Adolph Sutro, he had been one of the group that built the San Joaquin Valley Railroad—which they soon sold to the Santa Fe—in competition to the Southern Pacific. Although he generally followed liberal principles, Phelan made notorious use of anti-Oriental statements throughout his career to gain advantage for his party. During his three terms as mayor, he initiated many improvements: granting city ownership over municipal utilities, democratizing procedures for giving franchises, setting up a control board over public services with legislative authority, and getting voter approval of a generous $18,000,000 program to beautify the city with parks and playgrounds. The labor issue destroyed his chances of reelection. His use of city police as strikebreakers angered the workers, while his refusal to involve the state guard damned him with the conservatives. Out of the battle rose the Union Labor Party, which three times successively elected the musicians' union's Eugene E. Schmitz, a fashionable, good-looking, and for a brief moment reasonably honest orchestra leader, to the mayor's chair.

In spite of its name, the party contained no single important functionary of any of San Francisco's major unions, whose aims were not in accord with the direct kind of political participation that the new party had in mind. Trade unionism, in any case, was not yet an important force in San Francisco, the power of the workers still more of a potential than an actuality. Abraham Ruef, the political boss who saw the Union Labor Party as a vehicle for his personal success, brilliantly directed its victory and became the virtual dictator of city politics. He was a highly intelligent, well-educated French Jew, a graduate at eighteen, and valedictorian of the class of 1883 of the University of California, and a product of its law school. As a student at the university, although he majored in classical languages, he wrote a senior thesis on "Purity in Politics." However, a few disappointing excursions as a political liberal convinced him to adopt an uncompromisingly practical style of operation. Ruef's opportunistic regime staggered even San Francisco; his role as the shakedown king of California finally did more to spark a genuine effort at political reform than the combined efforts of a dozen zealous patriots.

By 1905 the Ruef machine, having elected not only the mayor but the full board of eighteen supervisors, was unabashedly collecting payoffs from French restaurateurs, pimps and prostitutes, gambling halls and dance houses, saloons which needed license renewals, corporations and respectable businessmen, the prize-fight trust, two telephone companies, the Parkside Transit Company, the Pacific Gas and Electric Company, the United Railroads and other municipal utilities and streetcar lines dependent on city franchises. In Chinatown, Ruef's henchman, Fong Ching, or Little Pete, paraded about surrounded by a company of armed white bodyguards, diverting the profits from tong-controlled vice rings to the city machine and, by the simple expedient of doping the right race horse at the right moment, conducting an enormously profitable betting business. One blatant mistake, attempted bribery on behalf of one of his gang who had committed murder, earned Fong Ching a five-year sentence in San Quentin. After his release he made a second error, this time fatal. He went unattended to a barbershop in Waverly Place, where he was shot down from his chair before the barber had finished braiding his queue.

In true gangster tradition, Little Pete's cohorts attempted to give him a magnificent funeral. After two hours of intricate last rites, performed by four priests from his favorite joss house, his casket was placed in a resplendent hearse drawn by six black-draped white horses. Hired mourners preceded the hearse, burning joss sticks and wildly beating the air with uplifted arms. From a carriage, four Chinese busily tossed out bits of paper punched with square holes—to confuse the devils seeking to make off with the spirit of the departed. The fantastic cortege, led by a popular orchestra playing the funeral march from *Saul*, proceeded through streets lined with spectators to the Chinese Cemetery down the Peninsula. Here a mob of onlookers—not hoodlums, but respectable San Franciscans indignant over losing bets on race horses doped by Pete's henchmen—greeted priests and mourners with hoots and clods of earth. The Chinese were compelled to haul the coffin back to the city where, at the old Chinese cemetery, Little Pete's remains were interred pending arrangements for shipment to China. The wagonloads of roast pig, duck, cakes, tea, and gin left beside the grave were guzzled by the crowd of white onlookers.[12]

The municipal situation in San Francisco, although not unique in turn-of-the-century politics, had grown so outrageous by 1905 that three reformers decided to take steps to stop the abuses. They were Fremont Older, the editor of the San Francisco *Bulletin,* and leader of the group; Rudolph Spreckels, one of the millionaire heirs of the sugar kingdom, who contributed a quarter of a million dollars to ensure that a thorough investigation could proceed; and James Phelan, who contributed both his moral and his financial support. The trio found that the district attorney, William Langdon, a former school superintendent who had somehow slipped into office unnoticed in the midst of the Ruef machine, was completely in agreement with their plans and willing to use his office to investigate and prosecute the wrongdoers to the fullest. Convinced by Older's persuasive ardor, President Theodore Roosevelt lent the reformers two federal agents, William J. Burns, a brilliant detective and chief of the Treasury Department's Secret Service Division, and Francis J. Heney, one of the federal government's leading prosecutors; they had already achieved some fame for their investigation of a timber fraud in Oregon. Langdon promptly appointed Heney an official district attorney of San Francisco. Before the investigation got much beyond the planning stage, the great earthquake and fire of 1906 threw the city into a state of complete turmoil. The graft prosecutions, along with so many other things, had to be put aside for a later time, while the city coped with even more urgent matters.

SECTION SIX
San Francisco at the
Turn of the Century

XIX

The City Comes of Age

IN the midst of the pleasures of the Gay Nineties, the state's politics, then still dominated by the railroad, inspired among the crusades for reform a new style of socially oriented literature and an aggressive journalism.

At the turn of the century two writers, Jack London and Frank Norris, expressed the typical new attitudes in their novels. London, who knew first hand the drudgery of cannery work, the danger of oyster pirating, the wildness of the Klondike, and the hardships behind the mast, converted his personal experience into some of the most popular literature ever to come from the West. His success lay in a vigorous style, a combination of forthright adventure stories and radical interpretations of social injustices as seen through a romantic eye. *The Call of the Wild* and *The Sea-Wolf* demonstrate his keen observation of character and setting: the collision of the two ferryboats in *The Sea-Wolf* was drawn from his own view of the run-in on November 30, 1901, of the *Sausalito* and the *San Rafael* off Alcatraz Island. *The Iron Heel* expounds his radical allegiances, while *John Barleycorn* and *Martin Eden* describe his narrowly disguised personal life. A University of California dropout after one semester, he was one of the founders of the Intercollegiate Socialist Society, which matured into the League for Industrial Democracy. Hard-living, hard-drinking, socially outraged but paradoxically a racist and in his later years a reactionary, London had a drive for money that pushed him into tremendous schedules of overwork; he died an ill man on his large estate in Glen Ellen, California, in 1916, at the age of forty.

London's contemporary, Frank Norris, was, in his brief thirty-two-year life span, the more sophisticated writer of the two. He treated social ills in his early San Francisco-based novels, of which *McTeague*, written in 1899, best sets forth his analysis of man's destruction by greed. In his later books, he applied his ideas more broadly. *The Octopus*, in 1901, and *The Pit*, in 1903, two parts of an uncompleted trilogy, extend the analysis to a whole popula-

411

tion. The books treat the devastations felt by the California wheat farmers, the economic pressures of the railroad, and the Chicago marketplace. Although his works are particularly noteworthy in the writing of the Far West for their naturalistic style, it was the underlying plea for social reform that gave them their impetus.

Having dropped the notion of becoming a painter, Norris spent four years at the university in Berkeley. Deliberately pursuing a course which would prepare him for a career as a writer of fiction, he chose to ignore the requirements for graduation. In his sophomore year he had petitioned the president and faculty to allow him to follow a special program instead of the Latin and mathematics and other normal prerequisites leading to a degree, even though he knew that it would mean forgoing his diploma. His evidence was a long narrative poem in the chivalric tradition, *Yvernelle,* already published by Lippincott, but the authorities turned him down. Perhaps it was his poor spelling, perhaps his thoroughly mediocre record; in any case, after four unsanctioned years following his own prescribed program, Norris received an "honorary dismissal."

During the nineties the new magazine the *Lark* attracted national attention, aiming barbs at society's revered institutions, sometimes so subtly that the reader missed their thrust. For its entire life of two years, Gelett Burgess, along with the cofounders, Willis Polk, Porter Garnett, and Bruce Porter, led a staff of talented contributors, dubbed "Les Jeunes" by the New York *Times,* through an exercise in journalism based on witticisms, absurdities, and social criticism. The small monthly—it measured only six by eight inches—was printed on a thin paper made of Chinese bamboo. The artists Maynard Dixon, Florence Lundborg, and Ernest C. Peixotto contributed regularly as did the writer Juliet Wilbor Tompkins and the poet Carolyn Wells, both much in favor at the time. Consistent with the youthful enthusiasm of the enterprise and with its commitment to total unconventionality, Burgess ceased publication in the full bloom of success, to spare the magazine any of the indignities of aging. Although a good deal of delightful joshing appeared in the *Lark's* pages, it is best remembered for Burgess' nonsense verse on the "Purple Cow" and the two words he added to the English vocabulary, "bromide," and "blurb." When the *Lark* ceased publication, the entire staff, save one, moved to New York.

Hearst's *Examiner* also employed a large number of cartoonists, many of whom subsequently became famous, notably Rube Goldberg, James Swinnerton, Homer Davenport, and Bud Fisher, among whose productions were the "Katzenjammer Kids" and "Mutt and Jeff," the first contemporary comics.

Perhaps the most prominent journalists late in the century were Henry George and Fremont Older. George, onetime managing editor of the *Chronicle*, a founder and editor of the *Post*, and a founder of the city's public library, made his reputation with the publication of *Progress and Poverty* in 1879, a book which advocates a single tax on land as the solution to society's economic ills and which has, since its publication, sold well over 3,000,000 copies. Fremont Older's reputation as a turn-of-the-century hellfire newspaper crusader increased with his dedication to reform and contributed handsomely to the subscription rate of the *Bulletin*. His journalistic techniques were flamboyant, and under his direction the paper augmented its attacks on city corruption. Besides unmasking the Ruef-Schmitz machine and the worst graft scandal in city history, Older later investigated the Preparedness Day Bombing case. His disgust with the lack of impartiality in the prosecution of Tom Mooney and Warren Billings, the accused, led him to the discovery of a number of letters in evidence of perjured testimony. Their publication in the *Bulletin*, in the prejudiced atmosphere of the day, brought criticism rather than gratitude, and Older, rather than relent, resigned. He took over again when the *Bulletin* merged, ten years later, with the *Call*. In the interval he had edited the *Call and Post*.

Another of the early editors, first of the old *Evening Bulletin* and later of the *Post*, was William Prescott Frost, the adventure-loving father of the poet Robert Lee Frost. William came to San Francisco after graduation from Harvard and took immediately to the hard-living style of the West. Before his death of tuberculosis at thirty-five, he had switched to the *Post* to work as Henry George's assistant. Robert Frost was born in San Francisco in 1874, and the many descriptions of the city and Western landscape that appear in his works, although not always identified as such, come from indelible impressions of his first ten years. One of his poems, "At Woodward's Gardens," recalls the delighted excitement he and his sister Jeannie shared as they wandered through one of the city's most popular attractions. In 1885 the widow Frost and her brood returned to live in Lawrence, Massachusetts; young Robert, who was to become a great "New England poet," took with him enduring images of the Western scene.

The West also had a profound influence on the subsequent writing of Robert Louis Stevenson, after his sojourn in California. Napa Valley scenery later made its way into all sorts of settings: Spy-Glass Hill in *Treasure Island* bears a strong resemblance, for example, to Mount St. Helena. Born of respectable, well-to-do Scots parents, Stevenson was by contrast a long-haired maverick, often barefoot, eccentric in his rumpled, soiled clothes, with no inclination to do proper work. His family considered it a disaster when he followed Fanny Osbourne from Grez, France, to California. Separated from but still married to a San Francisco court reporter, she was the mother of two children and eleven years Stevenson's senior. After her divorce and subsequently happy marriage to Stevenson, the family relented and even aided the desperately poor couple financially.

First arrived in California, Stevenson spent several months in the Monterey area and then, in 1879, moved to a cottage at 608 Bush Street, San Francisco, in the block that now crosses over the Stockton Street Tunnel. Mrs. Mary Carson, his landlady, rented him a large front room for $4 a month. He lived on Bush Street from Christmas until spring. The tubercular young writer's stay through the foggy winter was marked by bouts of serious illness that had already weakened him considerably during his rigorous 6,000-mile journey. On May 19, 1880, when he and Fanny were married, they took off for a honeymoon to Sam Brannan's health resort in Calistoga. Once in the neighborhood, the newlyweds heard of the abandoned Silverado Mine on the slopes of Mount St. Helena; for the next two months they resided there rent free. The result was a vast improvement in Stevenson's health and a detailed journal that provided the material for a book four years later, *Silverado Squatters.* Written after his return to Britain, it is rich in descriptions of the natural endowments of the Napa Valley: the old Bale gristmill, the petrified redwood forest, the surrounding mountains and vineyards, and Stevenson's enjoyable excursions in wine tasting. Although enchanted by the Mayacamas stone trees, Stevenson found Charley Evans, the forest's proprietor, a "far more delightful curiosity." In 1888 the Stevensons again stayed briefly in San Francisco, this time at the Occidental Hotel, as they made preparations for a voyage to the South Seas on Dr. Samuel Merritt's yacht *Casco.* Fanny later bought a house on Hyde Street, where she lived for a time after Stevenson's death in Samoa in 1894. A bronze sculptured galleon, erected in 1897 largely through the efforts of Bruce Porter and Willis Polk, stands as San Francisco's memorial to the writer in Portsmouth Square.

A number of visits by celebrated authors kept San Francisco titillated in the last decades of the century. At the end of March, 1882, Oscar Wilde descended on the city as part of a nationwide money-raising lecture tour, appropriately decked out in effete velvet breeches, hair flowing to the shoulders of his six-foot frame, and wearing ruffles, stockings of silk, pointed shoes, diamond jewelry, and yellow gloves. His visit was planned in collaboration with Rupert D'Oyly Carte, producer of Gilbert and Sullivan's comic opera *Patience,* the rage of the country at the moment. It caricatured the Aesthetes and their movement, which Wilde represented, and one of its characters, Bunthorne, bore a strong resemblance to him. Although his posturing was diverting, his lecture audiences found him a platitudinous bore, and in spite of several defenders, a good part of the local press took no pains to conceal their distaste. Amelia Neville wrote that Wilde's visit, anticipated with such expectations and so close on the heels of the successful tour of Charles Dickens, Jr., "created no furor"; she went to some lengths to describe his black velvet Fauntleroy get-up, but the only word she could remember of his lectures was "dado." Bierce was absolutely contemptuous of Wilde, and his *Wasp* columns flayed the twenty-eight-year-old British phenomenon for his foppish manners, bad elocution, and vapid commentaries. The visit seems to have ended, at least in San Francisco, the mad vogue of such affectations as the sunflowers, dahlias, calla lillies and other giant flora with which the Aesthetes surrounded themselves.[1]

A short time before, the young Dickens had read, and read well, from his father's works, had visited the local sights, dutifully exclaiming on the enormity of the Victoria Regina, "the world's largest pond lily," in Golden Gate Park, and in general had reacted with discreet and temperate enthusiasm to all that he was shown.

The art of fine printing developed naturally by the turn of the century alongside the San Francisco interest in reading. The first California printers of high quality were Taylor and Taylor; Edward Bosqui and Charles Murdock, the printers of the *Lark;* and John Henry Nash, an 1895 migrant from Canada. They set standards for a San Francisco profession that came into full maturity in the 1920's and that, with half a dozen celebrated presses going today, still attracts attention among world collectors. In 1901 Nash established the Tomoyé Press with Paul Elder, and subsequently spent some time printing with the Taylors before working entirely on his own. During his forty-three-year career in San Francisco, Nash employed a number of women as designers and compositors, following a San Francisco tradition that had supported a union of women printers from 1868 until after the turn of the century. Amateurs, who had taken up printing as a hobby in earlier decades, kept the interest in the field high. Among other efforts, Samuel Lloyd Osbourne printed the poetry of his stepfather, Robert Louis Stevenson.

San Francisco has never been notable among cities for its support or recognition of local painters, and few artists of enduring

distinction have been for long associated with the city. As early as
1876 B. E. Lloyd was writing:

> It is not an idle boast to assert that San Francisco has some excel-
> lent artists. . . . For a long time, however, they struggled in ob-
> scurity—the inhabitants of their own city patronizing the eastern
> and foreign professionals in preference to them. But thus it has
> ever been. Even in the remote past ages, a prophet was without
> honor in his own country. When we are in familiar intercourse with
> a person, we are quick to recognize his faults and imperfections;
> but slow to see his merit. So it was, until the local artists of San Fran-
> cisco had received favorable notice from distant cities, they were
> unappreciated at home.[2]

During the seventies *Harper's Weekly* had commissioned two
French artists to depict the West. During their stay in San
Francisco, Jules Tavernier and Paul Frenzeny became lively participants in the artists' colony, and both were elected to membership in the Bohemian Club. Their series of San Francisco
woodcuts, particularly showing the exotic character of Chinatown, fascinated thousands of Easterners.

William Keith, who was little known outside the state, remained
the most prolific San Francisco painter from the eighties through
the turn of the century, and landscapes the most popular California subject. Keith's work showed some start toward experiment-
ing with light and obtaining realistic effects without using camera-
like accuracy, but the results were even so fairly traditional.

During the late decades of the century a good amount of monumental sculpture decorated the city's streets, squares, and some of
its parks. Douglas Tilden's massive bronzes, the most familiar of
which is probably the Mechanics' Monument, occupied several
Market Street corners, while the work of a number of his protégés
filled other prominent spots, such as Robert Ingersoll's Victory
Monument in Union Square. Tilden, deaf from the age of five, attended the California School for the Deaf in Berkeley and with its
$500 scholarship-loan went on to study in Paris after his gradua-
tion in 1879. When he died, his daughter laid claim to a sculpture
depicting a struggle between two Indians and a bear—one of the
products of his Paris stay—but the courts awarded it to the school,
whose grounds it had been ornamenting since 1894.

Arthur Putnam, probably the most famous of the turn-of-the-
century sculptors, produced hundreds of pieces, bas-reliefs and
friezes, most of them likenesses of animals. His ability to re-create
down to the last rippling muscle impeccable images of beasts tame
and wild, grew out of an early familiarity with animals: he had
worked in a San Francisco slaughterhouse, ranched horses and

cattle herds, and made the forests familiar haunts. The vigor of his style reflected a rebellious and irreverent spirit, which, coupled with his disregard for money, often got him into serious difficulties. He and his painter wife, Grace, were not infrequently on the verge of starvation. As a vital part of the artistic crowd he benefited in a practical way from his friendship with Willis Polk, the architect, and Bruce Porter, both sculptor and architect. As decorative motifs were needed for some of the new buildings they were doing, they helped to steer the assignments to Putnam. Between those commissions and the patronage of Mrs. William H. Crocker, he and Grace could afford a study trip abroad. The Europeans were delighted by the realism and vitality of his work.

His prolific San Francisco production came after the 1906 quake and fire; the city therefore abounds with his bronze ornaments, his panels and his cast figures, among them the statue of Fra Junipero Serra in the Mission Cemetery. He designed the light standards that adorned Market Street for so many years, and carved the ceiling of the remodeled Pacific Union Club. The largest collection of his works, although now mostly kept in storage, belongs to the California Palace of the Legion of Honor. When the Spreckels family gave the museum to the city, Mrs. Adolph B. Spreckels bought for it many of Putnam's works in plaster, and sent them to Paris for casting. Examples of his sculpture also stand in many museums in the United States and Europe (including New York's Metropolitan).

In 1915 Putnam took on the post of Director of Sculpture for the huge Panama-Pacific Exposition. Four years earlier he had successfully undergone surgery for the removal of a brain tumor, but his left side never recovered from the paralysis that had been one of its major symptoms. He found it increasingly difficult to work. Although he lived to the age of fifty-seven, the frustration of his efforts caused him to explode in frequent rages; he and Grace were subsequently divorced. He later married again and continued to live for a number of years in the shack on the beach that he had called home since his return from Paris.

At the end of the century a San Francisco regional architecture began to take shape. It originated perhaps in rebellion against the Victorian exaggerations of European design that marked the mansions of the wealthy, and the equally imitative and fussy row houses that were beginning to clutter the city's residential quarters; it modified what would otherwise have been a wholly imitative and inappropriate revival of American Colonial.

The new style involved revitalization of the Spanish and Mission themes of California's past and adaptation of Colonial and

Oriental traits that lent themselves particularly well to the Bay Area setting. In public buildings, however, the dominance of Neoclassic style prevailed; the influence of the École des Beaux-Arts of Paris, where everyone trained, remained evident in the work of even the most energetic innovators.

Among the influential figures late in the century, European-trained A. Paige Brown moved his office from New York to San Francisco in 1889. He had submitted the winning design for the California pavilion which was put up for the 1893 Columbian Exposition in Chicago. Calling wide attention to the Mission style of the West, it adapted Mediterranean techniques of masonry to its adobe-esque cement walls, graceful arcades, and roof covered over in red clay tile. Brown was also one of the principal designers of the Ferry Building, which has marked the San Francisco skyline since its completion in 1898.

Willis Polk, a Kentuckian, came to San Francisco in 1886 to work as an assistant to Brown. Something of a child prodigy and a madcap, Polk had worked in a St. Louis architectual office from the age of thirteen; by fifteen he had submitted the winning entry in a contest to design an Arkansas schoolhouse. In San Francisco he helped plan the Ferry Building, but most of the structures for which he is known went up after the earthquake and contributed to his fame as the man who rebuilt San Francisco. Earlier he built his own home on Russian Hill, a neighborhood he grew strongly attached to during the remodeling of a Vallejo Street mansion. The influence of a neighbor, the Reverend Joseph Worcester from Massachusetts, attracted Polk's attention—and also that of another architect, Bernard Maybeck—to the unpainted shingle style of New England, derived from the North European techniques with wood, and in which Worcester had built three houses and a cottage on the hill in 1890. The simplicity it embodied proved so compatible to a Western setting that Polk and several colleagues began to adapt some of its features to their own designs. Polk, Brown, and a small group of associates led the trend away from the excesses of bonanza building, depending not only on the restrained elements adapted from the Mission and New England shingle styles, but returning to the purity of classic forms. Polk founded the *Architectural News* in 1890. It was a showcase for the new designs, particularly to illustrate his belief that Mission architecture should be a viable contemporary force.

The person who most seriously influenced the emerging Bay Area style of regional architecture was the innovative Bernard Maybeck. Born in New York in 1862, he followed his father's career as a woodcarver; then, still in his teens, he was off to Paris to study furniture design and the classic disciplines offered by the

École des Beaux-Arts. When he arrived in San Francisco in 1889, he worked for Ernest Coxhead, a Britisher who was interested in new things (and probably more influenced by than an influence on Maybeck), and for A. Paige Brown. Maybeck joined the faculty of the University of California in 1890, where he taught Julia Morgan, Arthur Brown, Jr., and John Bakewell, Jr. Miss Morgan was the first woman graduate of the university's Department of Engineering, the first woman master's graduate of the École des Beaux-Arts, and the state of California's first licensed woman architect. She owed much of the contemporary character of her style to her association with and admiraton for Maybeck. Her largest project, as the architect for William Randolph Hearst, was the vast seacoast estate at San Simeon. Brown and Bakewell followed their studies at the university with the traditional courses at the École des Beaux-Arts and in 1905 formed a partnership in San Francisco. Their firm designed the City Hall, the Opera House, Temple Emanu-El, and Coit Tower.

Maybeck and his coterie of pupils took from the past those simple elements that could best be applied to the present without losing a sense of the classic or dispensing with the romantic. Their architecture included an easy spaciousness, achieved in domestic designs by cathedral ceilings; they emphasized the natural quality of materials, particularly wood and in the BayArea especially redwood. They often used no paint, unless the light stains or colored tintings derived from the Orient. Their designs distinguished simplicity from starkness by incorporating rich materials and carefully rendered details such as carvings, leaded windows, repeated patterns, peaked gables. Maybeck's major departure from standard architecture grew out of his ability to relate building to setting, to connect indoors to outdoors, and, by controlling brightness with sweeping overhangs, to splash interiors with natural light admitted through great areas of glass and expanses of windows. Maybeck's influence on Western architecture, and in turn on contemporary architecture in general, is clearly in evidence in buildings that range from the sprawling ranch-style house to the most experimental contemporary building.

In 1904 James D. Phelan invited to San Francisco Daniel Burnham, the chief architect responsible for the recent Columbian Exposition in Chicago and a city planner noted for his redevelopment proposals for Manila, Cleveland, and Detroit. Burnham had previously designed a number of San Francisco buildings and had employed Willis Polk to help with the plans for the Chicago fair. A year before the catastrophe of 1906 Burnham and his staff completed a visionary master plan for the beautification of San Francisco. Drawn up on a magnificent scale, it emphasized the city's unique setting, preserving views, hills, and greenery and inter-spersing them with elaborate watercourses and a series of grand boulevards. Nothing of this dimension had even occurred to the city fathers. Overwhelmed by the grandeur of Burnham's propo-sals, they planned for the community an exhibition of his designs and had them printed up in book form. Before they could attend to the distribution of a single copy, the earthquake of 1906 re-duced the city to rubble; the Burnham plan took on a new dimen-sion as a ready-made blueprint for the reconstruction of what would be the world's most breathtaking metropolis.

Before the earthquake San Francisco enjoyed an unchallenged position as the financial and social center of the West. Its port was the major gateway to the Orient, its shores the terminus of the transcontinental railroad. Extra-fare Pullman cars brought in the wealthy, coddled in luxuries that the overlanders would never have believed: richly carpeted, paneled in mahogany, the hand-some carriages provided fine meals, libraries in which to while away the journey, and observation platforms over whose polished brass railings the interested could take in the scenery unimpeded. When they arrived, visitors marveled at the splendor of the ho-tels—three of the finest, the Grand, the Palace, and the Baldwin, lined the great width of Market Street just a short way up from the Southern Pacific ferry docks. The excellent reputation and va-riety of restaurants sharpened travelers' appetites long before they arrived. The mysteries of the Chinese quarter tempted sight-seers, who, like the local San Franciscans, found the neighbor-hood food a delicious revelation; the North Beach bohemian re-sorts offered abundant, tasty, inexpensive meals, along with gen-erous samplings of red wine and local color; the rotisseries and grills became the showplaces for the wealth of local products; and by 1905 the Spreckels Rotisserie, on top of the Call Building, boasted a view fifteen stories above the city.

The Palace dining room was world famous for the sophistica-tion of its French cooking, and other hotel kitchens by necessity provided strong competition. The Occidental typically offered its guests an 1895 Christmas dinner that went through oysters; con-sommé with quenelle de faisan à la Hubert; hors d'oeuvres; fish; a variety of joints including "Bershire" shoat with applesauce; an equal number of entrées, among them braised goose, saddle of bear, and grouse cooked with apricot compote au riz Richelieu; punch and champagne sherbet; peas, spinach, and a full garden of other vegetables; cold courses; game beyond that already offered; entremets; such desserts as cakes, petits fours, mixed can-dies, and puddings; chesse; sherry; café noir; and bonbons. In

1898 the same hotel's menu listed Château Yquem and Clos de Vougeot at $4 a bottle, Château Lafite at $3, and, among the eighteen California wines, a house cabernet or zinfandel for 50 cents a quart; the same quantity of Haraszthy's grand prize champagne cost $2.

In 1903 the San Francisco saloon tax then being $84 a year, the lowest license fee in the country, the city abounded in barrooms. A number of its drinks and its drinking places became widely famous, as much for their cosmopolitan company as for their crystal chandeliers, galleries of fine paintings, and tables heaped with the hundreds of succulent dishes that made up the free lunch. Perhaps the most famous mix of all was still Pisco Punch, the concoction served in Duncan Nichols' Bank Exchange in the Montgomery Block. Both the drink and the bar, which had been in existence since 1854, survived the temblor of 1906, but not Prohibition. When A. P. Giannini and his father-in-law founded the Bank of Italy in 1904, they chose for office space the premises next to the Bank Exchange's corner quarters. Oliver Perry Stidger, manager of the Montgomery Block and an habitué of the pioneer saloon, likened Pisco Punch "to the scimitar of Harroun whose edge was so fine that after a slash a man walked on unaware that his head had been severed from his body until his knees gave way and he fell to the ground dead."*

During the last decades of the century a number of developments, although in no way detractions from the dazzle of San Francisco, began to foretell a shift in importance to the southern

---

*After the demise of the Bank Exchange and subsequently of Duncan Nichols, who had gotten the secret formula from the original owners, the drink disappered from the local repertoire. Several versions claimed to be close approximations, but they either were bottled ready-mixes or introduced the licorice hints of absinthe, pernod, or herbsaint. Horrified drinkers of the original dismissed them without further notice. The closest to the real thing, and the case for its authenticity seems reasonably convincing, came from one John Lannes, a bartender from 1900 on, in the later years at the Bank Exchange. Although Nichols never wrote the formula down or mixed it in front of anyone, it is conceivable, because of the late date of their association, that in Lannes' case he either relented or prepared it unwittingly in his view. The old-timers attested to the fact that Lannes' instructions produced the drink that they remembered: to prepare Pisco Punch, cut a fresh pineapple in half-inch squares and soak overnight in a syrup of gum arabic. Mix 8 ounces of the marinating syrup in a bowl with 16 ounces of distilled water, 10 ounces of lemon juice, and one 24-ounce bottle of Peruvian Pisco brandy. Serve ice cold, taking care that the ice does not dilute, with a chunk of pineapple and additional syrup or lemon juice according to taste. (See William Bronson, "Secrets of Pisco Punch Revealed," *California Historical Society Quarterly*, Vol. LII, [Fall, 1973], pp. 229, 230–40.) In 1974 Transamerica Corporation recreated the Bank Exchange Saloon, featuring an exact replica of the original mahogany bar, in its new pryamidal office building.

part of the state. The growth of agriculture, especially of the citrus industry which centered in the south, was a large factor in attracting a new population. Doctors began to believe that the mild climate of southern California was a panacea for all kinds of illnesses, particularly tuberculosis, and on their advice great numbers of the halt and the lame headed for the sunshine. The trend died down, but never entirely died out, around the beginning of the new century. The completion of the Santa Fe Railroad as far as Los Angeles put it into competition with the Southern Pacific by 1885; the resulting cutthroat fares—at one point only $1 between Kansas City and Los Angeles—enticed many new Californians. An additional boost came from advertising, particularly by the Southern Pacific in an attempt to attract buyers to the more than 10,000,000 acres it owned, mostly in southern California. The railroad enlisted the aid of private agencies, newspapers, and a legion of writers, who in company with the other boosters, turned out guides, brochures, testimonials, pamphlets, and a deluge of books and articles, as well as the Southern Pacific's own magazine, *Sunset,* to extol the glories of the southland. In contrast with the palatial Pullman cars that carried the rich, the Southern Pacific put on special emigrant coaches, crowded facilities which offered cramped sleeping accommodations and cooking arrangements without extra charge. The railroad ran employment agencies with representatives abroad and provided foreign interpreters at home when that was necessary.

At the same time the development of hydroelectricity, introduced in the south early in the eighties, brought the promise of power to the entire state. The creation of a complex system of irrigation canals prepared the way for the huge plantings of orchards and a large-scale conversion from wheat to fruit. Another positive prospect was oil. The first modest strike of the sixties swelled to a flow of 4,000,000 barrels by 1900, still only a hint of the tremendous output to follow.

All these factors, plus the deluge of propaganda, produced an enormous land boom. By the eighties real estate promoters had created new towns, subdivided drought-ridden cattle ranches, deserts, mountains, and swamplands that were virtually uninhabitable, and sold farmlands by the orchardful, in some cases even hanging oranges on wasteland trees to dupe unsophisticated buyers. Among the earliest promoters, Sam Brannan and a company of San Francisco financiers made the first large sale of 200,000 subdivided acres, clearing an immediate $2,000,000 profit. The historian John Caughey estimates that real estate sales in 1887 could be put conservatively at $200,000,000, adding that promoters blueprinted sixty new towns totaling 80,000 acres within two years and that the population of Los Angeles alone increased from 11,000 in 1880 to 80,000 in the summer of 1887, just before the boom collapsed.[3]

The severe financial crisis which followed depleted Los Angeles' population to a mere 50,000 by 1890, but it turned people's attention to less speculative pursuits in industry and agriculture. By the turn of the century California farming amounted to a $130,000,000 industry. Although wheat from the Central Valley remained the state's largest agricultural product from the sixties until the panic of 1893, to which its decline was a contributing factor, a good deal of the total came from the southern California production of oranges, lemons, and cotton.

The development of Los Angeles got a further boost in 1902, when Henry Huntington consolidated the connecting interurban and municipal railways. Los Angeles' introduction to the motion picture, to loom so large in its future, took place in April, 1902, when the Electric Theater advertised a rudimentary type of cinema. The American pioneers in the field were still all working in the East, but in 1906 the independent producers began an exodus to southern California; it proved so superior a setting that within only a few years Hollywood had become the film capital of the world.

Although all these signs of expansion were to cause a significant shift in the patterns of the state's economy and the direction of its population growth, at the turn of the century they were only in their beginnings. The north was still supreme. By 1900, a million and a half people lived in California, and its economy had stabilized around mining, agriculture, lumbering, shipping, and a variety of manufactures. From this secure base the state made a good recovery from the panic of 1893 and such interruptions as the Pullman strike of 1894. The decade is remembered more for its opulence than its depressions. San Francisco, as the leading city in the West, was by 1900 also the ninth largest community in the country, with 342,000 inhabitants.

At the turn of the century, several events of national importance had an effect on the port of San Francisco largely because of its geographical position: the Klondike gold rush of 1898, the Spanish-American War and the sinking of the *Maine,* the annexation of the Philippines and Hawaii, and the construction of the Panama Canal. San Francisco served as the embarkation point for both Alaska and the Philippines, but neither the gold strike nor the war caused much serious excitement. San Francisco's contribution to the latter was largely a series of lighthearted fiestas for the soldiers temporarily camped on the Presidio hillside. As the transports which had filled the harbor sailed through the Gate, the strains of martial music faded in the streets behind, along with the farewell flowers that had wished the men cheer on their way. When San Franciscans did sentimental things, they did them well.

Expansion and maturity were not confined to the industrial side of the community. The railroad made it feasible for Western students to attend Eastern universities, which many of them did. "Notwithstanding these 'exports,' from the eighties to the teens, California far exceeded the rate of the nation in expanding and improving her colleges and universities."[4] Stanford University, endowed with the family's millions and directed by the eminent and farsighted David Starr Jordan, set a high standard for other Western schools. On the other shore of the bay, Benjamin Ide Wheeler served as president of the University of California from 1899 to 1919. His regime revitalized the campus, across which he often bounded on horseback. San Franciscans had begun to think seriously about their educational facilities in more permanent terms than did a transient population of Gold Rush inspiration. The purely academic was not the only side that received attention. The Wilmerding School of Industrial Arts started classes in 1900, financed by a bequest of $400,000 from J. Clute Wilmerding in 1894. Later merged with the nearby Lick School, it became one of the community's outstanding educational institutions, combining academic learning with training in practical skills.

Many Californians were becoming increasingly concerned with the preservation of the state's natural beauty and the conservation of its resources, an issue which is still one of the major preoccupations of a good portion of the population. The principal crusader in the early days was John Muir, a Scots immigrant who grew up in a fairly undeveloped area of Wisconsin. Raised with an almost religious fervor in regard to nature, Muir loved the Yosemite Valley of California from the first moment he saw it in 1868. He led an appeal to the legislature to return the valley to federal control so that it could receive better care than it was then getting under state auspices. One of Muir's admirers was Robert Underwood Johnson, through whose efforts as an editor of Century magazine the project aroused national attention. In response, the federal government created Yosemite National Park, comprised of the forest areas surrounding the valley, but the state reaction came more slowly. The Sierra Club, a conservationist group which Muir organized in 1892, aided his home campaign, which finally succeeded in 1905. Within a year after the state turned back the valley to federal control, Congress had approved its incorporation as part of Yosemite National Park.

Other lobbying efforts, such as those of the bicyclists, resulted in legislation for better roads. The city's twenty-year rage for cycling was still strong at the turn of the century, even though the horseless carriage was making frequent enough appearances to warrant the opening of the California State Automobile Association in San Francisco in 1900.

The town's sporting ardor was not confined to cycling. By the beginning of the new century San Francisco was the world capital of boxing. James J. Jeffries, the world's heavyweight titleholder, knocked out Bob Fitzsimmons in an eight-round bout in 1902; kayoed James J. Corbett in ten rounds one year later; and retained the world championship by downing Jack Munroe in two rounds the year following. The contests of the early 1900's were a great improvement over those of the 1860's, when matches tested endurance rather than skill, sometimes going as many as 106 rounds. The fighters of the early 1900's congregated in the Pup, a bistro that was also the favorite haunt of Abe Ruef, Mayor Schmitz, and their cronies.

Another entertainment of the time was the excursion up Mount Tamalpais. Since 1893 a steam engine had made the circuitous eight-mile climb. Those passengers who survived the 283 curves along the route could take refreshments at an inn on the way down.

The San Franciscans who faced the new century were a different breed from other Americans. Their traditions reflected strong Gold Rush influences of liberality, independence of thought, individuality, defiance of accepted standards, sentimentality, inventiveness. Their ingenuity had created cable cars to scale the hills, scow schooners to penetrate the shallow inland waters connecting to the Bay, agricultural machinery so successful that it provided models for the rest of the country, and bay windows to broaden the views and let in the western sunshine. Fred Marriott, the founder of the *News Letter,* started in journalism simply to raise money to build his flying machine. His inventiveness was evident in the newspaper field, too: he introduced the *News Letter* as a one-page letter-sized journal which, folded twice, turned into its own envelope and could be sent through the mails. When the letter-sheet format proved inadequate, the paper grew to sixteen pages, but not before the originality of the idea had given it a successful start. Now financially able, Marriott founded the Aerial Steam Navigation Company and perfected his machine, the *Aviator,* a 37-foot winged dirigible propelled at 5 miles an hour by a steam boiler. Two tests in the summer of 1869 were successful, the second, a flight on July 4, covering over a mile. Unfortunately a smoker approached too closely, igniting the large quantity of hydrogen gas that filled the body; the *Aviator* and Marriott's incentive were consumed by the tremendous explosion that followed.*

Another innovator, Hermann Wenzel, a deserter from the German Army who came to San Francisco in 1850, invented a clock that operated on compressed air. Almost all of the large number of air clocks in use in San Francisco were destroyed by the 1906 earthquake, along with the plans for their construction. However, ten clocks remained in good working order in the Holbrook mansion on Van Ness and Washington. The old Victorian, having escaped destruction in the quake by being on the other side of the Van Ness fire line, fell victim to the automobile in 1946, when commercial interests razed it in favor of a parking lot.

The early habits of a masculine society, freewheeling, free-drinking, hard-living, persevered, even though by the end of the century they were somewhat chastened by the more normal proportion of females in the population. The favorite ballad of the time was still "There'll Be a Hot Time in the Old Town Tonight." As a group, San Franciscans were never dowdy and enjoyed the fads and followed the latest fashions. Although they produced record numbers of alcoholics and resorted too frequently to suicide, they pursued life with equal intensity. They had a great sense of ceremony and a fine sense of humor. They were lively, enterprising people, eager for self-improvement, although improvement most often meant a higher social position, power, and money. At heart San Franciscans were gamblers; they believed that the odds could turn spectacularly in their favor. They had the examples of Gold Rush millionaires, Silver Bonanza kings, and railroad barons before them. There was, underlying all, California's "encouragement of small men to reach beyond themselves."[5]

San Franciscans were also charitable, a habit that grew out of taking care of the less fortunate among them in the early days. In 1893 the city had 204 agencies devoted specifically to charitable purposes, besides some seventy-five churches and a large number of private individuals who donated generously to worthy causes. In that year the Lick free baths provided sixty tubs daily to some

---

*The poor quality of transportation during the Gold Rush also inspired Rufus Porter, a Yankee writer, mural painter, and inventor, to push for the completion of an airship, a dirigiblelike transport he had designed some years before, to carry as many as 100 passengers from New York to California in three days. In order to raise funds, he, like Marriott, turned to journalism, publishing a sixteen-page pamphlet, *Aerial Navigation,* and founding America's oldest magazine, *Scientific American.* However, he never managed to build more than working models of his flying machine.

250 people who did not have their own facilities or the money to pay for private ablutions.

Although the cultural development of San Franciscans lacked the finesse of a more finished population—embrace too warm, applause too quick—they were ready participants, and many went on to genuine appreciation. At worst, they supported enough art, music, and theater for the entire community to grow on. Their style of life as exemplified by their outings, their sports, their regional architecture, their admiration and support of such men as John Muir, expressed a connection to nature that has remained a vital component of Western living.

Politically, although the smaller number of Southerners dominated the scene through the fifties, the majority of people reflected ideas that saw California enter the Union as a free state on the side of the North; become the first state to recognize women's property rights; several times rise in revolt against the corruption in their midst, even though in the case of the vigilantes it meant going beyond the law themselves; provide a sizable contribution to the development of trade unionism; mount a campaign against the Chinese that was so odious that it ended in the Chinese Exclusion Acts; yet set an atmosphere of tolerance that allowed Jewish residents a degree of acceptance not usually accorded elsewhere.

Perhaps the most distinctive characteristics of San Franciscans at the turn of the century came from their training: they could cope with the rigors of the unknown; they were accustomed to the swift changes of fortune; and they had the resilience to recover from a series of disasters. Fortified by a positive enjoyment of life and a drive to push ahead, they could unite and endure in the face of a common adversity. San Franciscans acted and reacted on a bold scale to match the enormity of events in their history. At the beginning of the new century little were they aware that this heritage would soon be called on to face the most enormous event of all.

XX

The Earthquake

WHERE the constantly shifting layers that form the earth's crust overlap, the resulting faults accumulate tensions that are released periodically in the violent upheavals we call earthquakes. The magnitude of the energy released is measured on a logarithmic scale devised by Charles F. Richter. The designation "1.0" on the Richter scale is the energy equivalent of 6 ounces of dynamite; "9.0" equates with 199,000,000 tons of TNT. The most dangerous areas when an earthquake strikes are the lands composed of fill, sand, silt, clay, mud, or other deposited matter; rock is by far more resistant to earthquake disturbance. In California there are ten major faults, some of them branches of the longest one, the San Andreas, which runs under the ocean floor outside the Golden Gate and which was responsible for the 1906 disaster.

Records at the Smithsonian Institution note 465 earthquakes, many of them minor, in San Francisco between 1850 and 1906. Two of them, the 1865 quake and the 1868 quake, caused considerable damage. During the nineteenth century three other earthquakes of major proportions occurred in California: the 1875 disturbance at Tejon Pass, also caused by the San Andreas Fault; the midcentury Bay Area rupture of the Hayward Fault, an eastern branch of the San Andreas; and the Owens Valley shock of 1872, which had the greatest magnitude of any recorded earthquake in the history of California.

Earthquakes are mentioned in the earliest accounts of the state. The explorer Portolá named Santa Ana de los Temblores because of the earthquake that occurred there. Robinson's *Life in California* includes an extensive account of an early San Francisco earthquake. A picture in the *Police Gazette* that came out just after the October, 1865, disturbance in San Francisco illustrates the event by showing a well-known but frightened senator fleeing a fancy Portsmouth Square bordello clad only in his long johns. William Chapman Ralston rushed to his bank to assure that business would go on as usual after the upheaval of 1868. It did, among broken cornices, cracked walls, and forty nervous clerks and tell-

428

ers. Commented one citizen, in the aftermath of the same earthquake: "The dem place seems shaky on her pins, but there's one consolation, anyhow, we've got the best climate in the world."[6] Writing on architecture, Samuel Williams commented on the elaborate cornices that were the terror of timid pedestrians during times of earthquakes. Bancroft, discussing the fashion for frame houses which prevailed in the several decades following the Gold Rush, remarked that it was the fear of temblors which had exercised the strongest influence against brick dwellings. Robert Louis Stevenson observed the same phenomenon during his stay in San Francisco, further pointing out the companion danger of fire:

> Earthquakes are not only common, they are sometimes threatening in their violence; the fear of them grows yearly on a resident; he begins with indifference, ends in sheer panic; and no one feels safe in any but a wooden house. Hence it comes that, in that rainless clime, the whole city is built of timber—a woodyard of unusual extent and complication; that fires spring up readily, and served by the unwearying trade wind, swiftly spread; that all over the city there are fire-signal boxes; that the sound of the bell, telling the number of the threatened ward, is soon familiar to the ear; and that nowhere else in the world is the art of the fireman carried to so nice a point.[7]

His mention of the city's incendiary possibilities forecast the horror that was to follow. On Wednesday, April 18, 1906, at five hours, twelve minutes, and forty-eight seconds after midnight, the earth under San Francisco shook violently for twenty-eight seconds. The earthquake's magnitude, as measured by today's Richter scale, was 8.3. The results, although devastating, were less severe in San Francisco, where the rift ran offshore under the sea bottom, than in San Jose, Palo Alto—particularly at Stanford University—and Santa Rosa. In San Francisco, according to the board of supervisors' Municipal Reports for the fiscal year of 1905–06, there was considerable damage to the areas built over fill; several buildings in poor condition suffered complete destruction, while others in better shape received severe punishment through breaks in the masonry or, in the case of frame buildings, through shifts from their foundations. The pipes which ran underground near the areas of the earth's displacement, including the conduits that brought the city's water supply from the reservoirs a good 20 miles away, ruptured in so many places that they were completely useless. Gas connections broke, electric wires fell, chimneys tumbled, stoves overturned, and broken vials released volatile and ignitable chemicals. Fifty-two recorded fires started. Although most of them could be controlled early, the loss of the city's water supply made it impossible to extinguish those that got beyond the first stages, and a number of them were soon completely out' of control. As the city, along with its fire department, watched horrified, the flames raged through almost five square miles. The fire burned continuously for three days, until on the fourth day it finally smoldered insignificantly. San Francisco, with 478 officially dead, 250,000 homeless, 28,000 structures destroyed, and a loss that amounted to well over $500,000,000, lay a mass of collapsed walls, torn streets, smoking ashes, and tangled rubble.

Fire consumed almost all of the 490-block area—with the exception of a few stretches—east of Van Ness as far south as Golden Gate, beyond Van Ness as far west as Octavia in the Hayes Valley area above Market Street, east from Dolores Street south of Market along Twentieth, Howard, Bryant, and Townsend streets, north and east all the way to the Bay. The greatest loss of live occurred in the south of Market working-class neighborhoods, where perhaps one-sixth of the city's population lived. The tinderbox dwellings and cheap rooming houses there trapped many inhabitants in jumbled wreckage which flames quickly consumed. Both the quake and the fire did tremendous damage north of Market, ravaging the wholesale district, the produce markets, the financial district, the entire business section including the retail shops around Union Square and almost three-quarters of the neighborhood's residences and lodging houses. Fifteen million gallons of wine stored in warehouses were a total loss. To the many who had considered Chinatown a blot on the city, its utter destruction seemed long overdue. Large areas of the Mission District, built on fill over Willow and Mission creeks, fared little better. Everywhere the tremor leveled chimneys, dislodged porticoes, and shook loose cornices and parapets. On Hayes Street near Gough, a woman cooking breakfast inadvertently set her house on fire when sparks escaped through an earthquake-damaged flue. The flames spread and turned into a major conflagration. The fires melted, twisted, and consumed everything in their path. At the peak, the temperature soared possibly as high as 2,000°F.

The newly completed $6,000,000 City Hall, twenty years in building, along with most of the municipal records, suffered almost total devastation.* The Post Office and United States Mint

*In August, 1974, however, while searching the basement of the present City Hall for old municipal bonds, the city archivist came upon a cache of records, treasury receipts, city council minutes, and other government documents covering the years 1849 to 1860. Long since assumed lost in the 1906 fire, they fill in many details such as the cost of street repairs, the licenses issued, the salaries

survived only through the efforts of employees, who tirelessly pumped water from storage tanks on the spot. The postal service claimed that it lost not one single piece of mail during the disaster. The Palace Hotel, for all its foresighted installation of reservoirs, had no water left when the flames actually engulfed it: the supply had been used to wet the building down when the fire was still a distant threat. Flames consumed seventeen engine houses and nine other fire department buildings, the Hall of Justice, numerous police stations and prisons, the Mechanics' Pavilion, thirty schools, the main library, and several of its branches. The damage sustained by other municipal buildings, vehicles, apparatus, tools, equipment, furnishings, fire hydrants, sewers, gas lines, water mains, electrical wiring, and police and fire alarm systems was incalculable. Flames destroyed 41,000 feet of fire hose alone.

One piece of good fortune when the city later came to rebuild, as well as a means of remaining continuously in contact with the rest of the world, was the small amount of damage to the waterfront. Crews with fireboats at their command and water from the Bay saved the wharves from ruin. With attention then diverted to other areas, however, the undefended grain wharves below Telegraph Hill burned to rubble. In the central area the three blocks bordered by Montgomery on the west, Battery on the east, Jackson on the north, and Washington and Merchant on the south, although encircled by fire, managed to survive it unscathed. A secret United States Navy report, released in April, 1975, discloses that a naval force under Lieutenant Frederick Newton saved the Jackson Square area by stretching a mile-long fire hose from Meiggs' Wharf over the top of Telegraph Hill. Kept so long under wraps because of the scandalous conduct to which it also testified, the government document revealed that a large contingent of San Franciscans had rendered themselves hopelessly drunk by looting saloons and liquor stores. They not only ignored the city's plight but refused to give assistance except for an outrageous rate of pay. Many of them perished in the flames. Stealing was so widespread and the mob behavior so dangerous that even the fire crews in the North Beach area had to carry arms against the raiders. Some portions of Green, Vallejo, Broadway, Jones, and Leavenworth streets on the crest of Russian Hill were high enough and solid enough to escape damage; several blocks on the crown of Telegraph Hill were saved by using burlap soaked in wine to protect the sides and roofs of buildings.

---

paid to city officials, the preoccupations of the mayor, and the actions of the supervisors, along with the revelation that in 1849 Sam Brannan refused to pay his share of the San Francisco business tax.

The disaster was a new experience only because of its dimensions. The city had managed to live through all its previous devastations by fire and to withstand the earlier temblors visited on it, and it had on several occasions taken measures to stave off the damage from such events. But its efforts had been half measures, carelessly enforced and certainly not sufficient when both events occurred simultaneously. In October, 1905, the National Board of Fire Underwriters had reported San Francisco's water system inadequate against any substantial fire, but nothing had been done about it. A perennial optimism was perhaps largely responsible.

> In theory the pessimists are right, but in practice the optimists are seldom wrong. There was one man in San Francisco who, long before it actually occurred, had been expecting and preparing for the San Francisco earthquake; he was the Chief of the Fire Brigade [Dennis T. Sullivan, a twenty-six-year veteran of the force], and he knew that when the expected calamity took place the greatest danger of all would be the cutting off of the water supply and a general conflagration. He was a pessimist, but he was right, and for weeks and weeks he worked night and day to perfect a plan which would have saved the great city from the horrors of fire and panic. The fatal day at last came, and the farseeing pessimist was the first man to be killed by the first chimney-pot that fell down! The others—the thousands of men, women, and children—unreasoning optimists all, most of them escaped unhurt and have rebuilt their destroyed homes as if nothing could ever happen again.[8]

The death of their chief left the force of 585 firemen, well trained and gallant as they may have been, facing a major catastrophe without a leader. With no chief, no water, and no system of communication except a makeshift relay of horsemen, pedestrian messengers, and commandeered automobiles, a master counterattack against the fire proved an impossibility. The firemen fought as best they could with water from the Bay, from storage tanks, bathtubs, and an inadequate number of cisterns. A large-scale attempt at creating fire breaks by dynamiting did no good, in fact, in many cases spreading the fire rather than containing it. An experienced explosives crew, brought in during the late stages of the blaze, dynamited the east side of Van Ness and finally stopped the flames. Under the direction of Brigadier General Frederick Funston, the local military forces, assisted by armed reinforcements from other areas, patrolled the city to prevent looting. In several cases they also kept authorized persons from rescuing records and removing items of considerable value. In one instance, their overzealous policing resulted in shooting to death H. C. Tilden, who was on an official Red Cross mission. Over and over again in their misguided confusion they refused willing citizens the chance to assist undermanned crews in fighting the holocaust. San Francisco, overwhelmed by the enormity of the disaster, could not defend itself.

During the first few days some 300,000 people found themselves homeless, some of them leaving their domiciles out of fear of being trapped by a strong aftershock or fire. Temporary shelters, mostly tents lent by the military, provided for 40,000 people in Golden Gate Park. Other camps filled Jefferson Square, Mission Park, parts of the Presidio, Union Square, Lobos Square (now Funsten Playground), the Harbor View area on the Marina, Alamo Square, Park Presidio Drive, and old Portsmouth Plaza. Steamers began ferrying people across the Bay and up the rivers to towns that had offered aid to the dislocated. By April 25 seven teams of workmen hauled city election booths to the parks to supplement the tents as housing for the refugees. The stables at Ingleside Racetrack, converted into living quarters, sheltered a large group of the elderly. More permanent cottages soon replaced the tents. In the fall about 17,000 mostly working-class campers still lived in wooden shacks for which they contributed $2 a month in rent, to be applied to ownership when it might be possible to relocate them. At the end of the summer of 1907, continuing on into 1908, several people moved their cottages to private lots, where many of them stand today, their dramatic origins forgotten. Another 12,000 people, who did not care for the military discipline imposed in the formal campsites or who could not pay the monthly fee, set up housekeeping in makeshift shanties. In September an outbreak of typhoid threatened the shantytown inhabitants but was brought under early control.

The municipal government had taken immediate steps to ensure order and to expedite recovery. Early on Wednesday morning, April 18, Mayor Schmitz issued a proclamation in which he announced that federal troops, policemen, and special officers had the authority to kill any persons found looting or involved in other criminal activity; that he had ordered all gas and electricity indefinitely cut off; that all citizens were to remain at home during the hours of darkness until order had been restored; and that the community was warned of the danger that existed of fire from damaged or destroyed chimneys and broken or leaking gas pipes. Further, the mayor and city commissioners, meeting on Wednesday afternoon, appointed a Citizen's Relief Committee of Fifty, former Mayor James D. Phelan effectively in charge.

By Thursday emergency regulations had permitted certified bakeries to begin making bread to sell at no more than 10 cents a loaf, with purchases limited to five loaves a customer. Distribution centers had started to dole out food supplies and reported that queues remained orderly throughout the program. All cooking had to be done outdoors, a situation which prevailed for months because of the time required for an inspection committee to make certain that chimneys, flues, and pipes were safe. The board of public works divided the city into districts, to each of which it supplied two sprinkler wagons filled with water from outlying reaches for cooking and drinking. The same department hauled and burned accumulating garbage in distant fields, meanwhile building chutes at the Mission Street Wharf through which on completion the collected refuse could be transferred to barges and towed out to sea for dumping. The department's wagons, which had already seen service removing household goods during the fire, transported bedding and hospital supplies and, under the direction of the board of health, hauled chloride of lime and other needed disinfectants. Public works teams inspected and repaired sewers and built hundreds of toilets. City inspectors ordered dangerously damaged walls and ruins to be removed, usually by dynamiting. The Brick Masons' Union, with a work force of 1,500, suspended the trade rules under which they normally operated and began the arduous task of restoring chimneys and fireplaces for domestic use.

The city's teachers, on enforced vacation, received their salaries nevertheless in the guise of vacation pay. Most of them volunteered to help in the restoration of the school system. They manned makeshift classes set up in tents in Golden Gate Park, largely to keep the children purposefully occupied in the midst of chaos. By the end of July sessions had resumed in 256 temporary classrooms. Children from all over the country contributed $31,000 toward the rebuilding of San Francisco schools, and the teachers of the city of New York raised just under $12,000 for the relief of their colleagues.

The congregation of the First Unitarian Church offered its premises to the Jewish members of Temple Emanu-El, whose synagogue had been lost to the flames. The fraternal gesture, extended in return for the hospitality of the Jewish worshipers twenty years before when the Unitarian church had been under construction, is still commemorated annually in joint Thanksgiving Day services.[9]

Help poured in from all over the world: foodstuffs, medicines, blankets, manpower, and supplies, and a total of $9,000,000, $475,000 of it from fourteen foreign countries. On April 30 the Red Cross served 313,000 meals. President Theodore Roosevelt channeled all incoming relief funds through a Red Cross committee under the national chairmanship of Dr. Edward T. Devine. Outside assistance notwithstanding, the municipal authorities, through their own citizens' committees, always kept control of the programs for relief and for the city's restoration.

There were sloganeering, pamphleteering, and mounting demonstrations against the relief committees by a vocal segment of agitators who charged the officials with financial hanky-panky and mismanagement of the funds in their own self-interest. The dissidents, although they gained national attention, did not achieve their goal of having the funds and supplies turned directly over to the people whom they were to benefit. Most of the community, in fact, approved of the way its officials were handling the situation.

With city authorization, the United Railroads almost immediately began construction of a Market Street overhead trolley line. General business had resumed within a week, turning Fillmore Street and later Van Ness, into the city's main shopping thoroughfares. Supplemented by temporary structures, former private residences became restaurants, stores, and markets. Several newspapers had begun to put out editions using the equipment of the Oakland *Tribune*.

The city was trying to return to normality as quickly as possible. In the ten days following the disaster, the proper government bureau issued from temporary quarters 220 marriage licenses, the first of them on the day following the fire. A vaudeville performance at the Chutes, the most prominent of the three theaters to survive, went on as scheduled and played to a packed house only eight days after the fire.

Insurance payments, already an overwhelming problem because of the scope of the destruction, became the more complicated by the losses of owners' policies and companies' records. Most underwriters tried nevertheless to compensate their clients. Several firms made up the staggering sums they paid out by assessing their stockholders. Others, including six German agencies, refused entirely to make any reimbursements. The Fireman's Fund repaid its policyholders part of their losses in company stock. Twelve American firms, unable to cope with the immensity of the problem, went out of business altogether.

One month after the catastrophe the city authorities, fortuitously armed with the existing Burnham plan for reconstruction, adopted it, but under overwhelming pressures to rebuild quickly the authorities never put it into operation. By the early spring of 1907 most of the major debris having been cleared away, the city proclaimed March 3 official cleaning day. Volunteers from all classes and interests labored to put things back into as good order as possible. Former Mayor Phelan, himself a million dollars poorer following the upheaval, emerged as one of the most powerful forces behind the community's survival. His own position, that a city so recently born had comparatively little to lose, explained a good deal about the positive outlook of the majority of San Franciscans. Material things could be restored. Buildings could be rebuilt. Fortunes could be earned again. The city had been witness to this on many occasions. Institutions, traditions, and attitudes did not yield to earthquakes or fire. With their customary energy and perseverance, its citizens began to put San Francisco back together again.

finis tomi primi

NOTES

SECTION ONE: BEFORE GOLD

Chapter I. The Beginnings
1. Soulé, et al., *Annals*, p. 22.
2. Powers, *Tribes of California*, p. 403.
3. Kroeber, *Handbook of the Indians*, p. 471.
4. Powers, *Tribes of California*, pp. 412–15.
5. Choris, *Voyage autour du monde*, Part III, p. 9
6. Nelson, "Shellmounds," pp. 340–43.
7. Kroeber, *Handbook of the Indians*, p. 930.
8. Cook, *Conflict*, p. 3.
9. Powers, *Tribes of California*, p. 400.

Chapter II. The Whale, the Otter, and the Empire
10. Vancouver, *Voyage Around the World*, Vol. 3, pp. 7–25.
11. Mahr, *Visit of the "Rurik,"* pp.77, 79.
12. Kemble, "West Through Salt Spray," p. 70.
13. Robinson, *Life in California*, pp. 230–31.

Chapter III. The Spanish and the Anglo-Saxons
14. Chapman, *History of California*, pp. 304–6.
15. Caughey, *California*, p. 167.
16. *Ibid.*, p. 159.
17. *Ibid.*, p. 159.
18. Atherton, *Rezánov*, p. 159.
19. Robinson, *Life in California*, p. 89.
20. Smith, *Virgin Land*, pp. 54–55.
21. Pearce, *Savages of America*, pp. 1–7.

Chapter IV. The Emigrants
22. Smith, *Virgin Land*, p. 18.
23. *Ibid.*, p. 165.
24. Van Orman, "Bard in the West," pp. 35–36.
25. Clark, *Frontier America*, p. 446.
26. Bancroft, *History of California*, Vol. V [*Works*, Vol. XXII], p.694.

SECTION TWO: THE GOLD ERA

Chapter V. Gold
 1. Caughey, *California,* p. 38.
 2. Larkin, "Larkin to His Sons," pp. 297–300.
 3. Dillon, *Fool's Gold,* p. 318.
 4. Monguio, "Lust for Riches," pp. 237–48.

Chapter VI. The Voyagers
 5. Johnson, *California, Sermon,* p. 3.
 6. Stillman, *Golden Fleece,* p. 180.
 7. *Ibid.,* p. 237.
 8. *Ibid.,* p. 202.
 9. *Ibid.,* p. 265.
 10. Groh, *Gold Fever,* pp. 59–60.
 11. Upham, *Notes of a Voyage,* p. 50.
 12. Barra, *Tale of Two Oceans,* p. 40.
 13. Swasey, *Early Days,* p. 13.
 14. Jackson, *Gold Rush Album,* pp. 24–25.
 15. "The Way to Go to California," lithograph in the Honeyman Collection, Bancroft Library, University of California, Berkeley.
 16. Caughey, *California,* p. 250.
 17. Anonymous, "Millions for a Cent," pp. 40–41.

Chapter VII. The Mines
 18. Clappe, *Shirley Letters,* pp. 120-21.
 19. Groh, *Gold Fever,* pp. 4–5.
 20. Clark, ed., *Gold Rush Diary, passim.*
 21. Haskins, *Argonauts, passim.*
 22. Quaife, *Pictures,* pp. 364–65, 370.
 23. Clappe, *Shirley Letters,* pp. 121–25.
 24. *Ibid.,* pp. 140–41, 102–03.
 25. Stewart, *Names on the Land,* p. 268.

SECTION THREE: FROM VILLAGE
TO METROPOLIS

Chapter VIII. Transformation
 1. Gardiner, *Golden Dream,* p. 310.
 2. Moerenhout, *Inside Story,* pp. 51–70.
 3. Soulé, et al., *Annals,* pp. 445–47.

4. Chinn, *History of Chinese, passim.*
5. Kirker, *Architectural Frontier,* p. 75.
6. *Ibid.,* p. 37.
7. *Ibid.,* pp. 53–54; Chap. 3 *passim.*
8. *Ibid.,* p. 60.
9. Peterson, "Pre-Fabs," pp. 318–24.
10. Kirker, *Architectural Frontier,* p. 85.
11. Olmstead and Watkins, *Here Today, passim.*
12. Clappe, *Shirley Letters,* pp. 7, 65–66, 114.
13. Gardiner, *Golden Dream,* pp. 164–65.
14. Barrett, *Oyster Industry,* pp. 5–98.
15. Soulé, et al., *Annals,* p. 640.
16. Huggins, *Continuation of Annals,* pp. 89–90.
17. Neville, *Fantastic City,* pp. 136–37.
18. Soulé, et al., *Annals,* p. 254.
19. *Ibid.,* p. 651.
20. La Motte family letters, in the manuscript collections of the Bancroft Library, University of California, Berkeley.
21. Lloyd, *Lights and Shades,* p. 185.
22. Will and Finck Company (Price List), (undated), *passim.*

Chapter IX. Entertainment and the Arts
23. Gagey, *San Francisco Stage,* pp. 96–97, Chaps. 1–3, *passim.*
24. Jacobson, *Golden 'Fifties,* pp. 257–58.
25. Rather, *Women Printers,* p. 23.

Chapter X. Letters and Education
26. Walker, *Literary Frontier,* pp. 22, 14.
27. Rogers, *California Star,* p. vii.
28. Kemble, *California Newspapers,* pp. 67–132, 272–97.
29. Walker, *Literary Frontier,* p. 24.
30. *Ibid.,* pp. 302–15.
31. Taper, *Twain's San Francisco,* p. xvi.
32. Walker, *Literary Frontier,* pp. 316–23.

Chapter XI. Business and Professions
33. Nash, "Economic Growth," p. 318.
34. Myrick, *Telegraph Hill,* pp. 52–67.
35. Riesenberg, *Golden Gate,* pp. 235–37.
36. Olmstead, "Packets," pp. 35–36.
37. Gentry, *Madams,* p. 115 *passim.*
38. Lloyd, *Lights and Shades,* p. 80.
39. Peninou and Greenleaf, *Directory of Wine Growers, passim.*
40. Kemble, *San Francisco Bay,* p. 99.
41. Lloyd, *Lights and Shades,* p. 378.

42. Gentry, *Madams,* p. 161.
43. Lewis, *Bohemia,* pp. 102–3.
44. Neville, *Fantastic City,* p. 240.
45. Groh, *Gold Fever,* p. 41.

Chapter XII. Fire
46. La Motte family letters, in the manuscript collections of the Bancroft Library, University of California, Berkeley.

Chapter XIII. "Priez Pour Eux"
47. Letter sheets from the Honeyman Collection, Bancroft Library, University of California, Berkeley.
48. Waterman, "Ishi, the Last Yahi," p. 483.
49. Bari, *Course of Empire,* pp. 209–11.
50. Original papers of the San Francisco Committee of Vigilance, 1851, from the Manuscript Collection, Bancroft Library, University of California, Berkeley.
51. Bancroft, *Popular Tribunals,* Vol. 2 [*Works,* Vol. XXXVII], p. 272.
52. Bean, *California,* p. 137.
53. Stewart, *Committee of Vigilance,* p. 332.
54. Bean, *California,* p. 148.
55. Hunt, *Sermon,* pp. 9, 14.
56. Bean, *California,* p. 137.
57. Bancroft, *Chronicles of the Builders,* Vol. 1, p. 378.

SECTION FOUR: BIG MONEY

Chapter XIV. The Bankers, the Silver Kings, and the Era of Finance
1. Caughey, *California,* p. 269.
2. Parker and Abajian, *Walking Tour,* p. 2.
3. Bancroft, *California Interpocula* [*Works,* Vol. XXXV], p. 316.

Chapter XV. The Railroad and the Big Four-and-a-Half
4. Caughey, *California,* p. 357.
5. *Ibid.,* p. 381.
6. Lewis, *Big Four,* p. 365.
7. *Ibid.,* p. 189.

Chapter XVI. Society
8. Taylor, *El Dorado,* p. 233.
9. Neville, *Fantastic City,* pp. 80–81.
10. Jacobson, *Golden 'Fifties,* p. 67.

11. Watson, "San Francisco Society," p. 27.
12. Lloyd, *Lights and Shades,* p. 401.
13. Altrocchi, *Spectacular San Franciscans,* p. 43.
14. Berner, *Mrs. Leland Stanford,* pp. 16–20.
15. Chambliss, *Diary, passim.*

SECTION FIVE: POLITICS AND LABOR

Chapter XVII. North Versus South
  1. Wright, "Cosmopolitan California," pp. 332–33.

Chapter XVIII. Social Change: The Chinese and Labor
  2. Pitt, "Beginnings of Nativism," p. 36.
  3. Soulé, et al., *Annals,* pp. 53–54.
  4. Barth, *Bitter Strength,* p. 3.
  5. Hoy, "Gold Mountain," pp. 256–58.
  6. Chinn, ed., *History of Chinese,* pp. 64–67.
  7. Dobie, *Chinatown,* pp. 138–39; Chinn, *History of Chinese,* pp. 67–68.
  8. San Francisco Chamber of Commerce, *Chinatown,* pp. 8–9.
  9. Chinn, *History of Chinese,* pp. 62, 49–63.
 10. Saxton, *Indispensable Enemy, passim.*
 11. Bean, *California,* pp. 287–89.
 12. Housen, ed., *San Francisco,* p. 215.

SECTION SIX: SAN FRANCISCO AT THE TURN OF THE CENTURY

Chapter XIX. The City Comes of Age
  1. Rodecape, "Gilding the Sunflower," pp. 97–112.
  2. Lloyd, *Lights and Shades,* p. 416.
  3. Caughey, *California,* p. 405.
  4. *Ibid.,* p. 444.
  5. Starr, *California Dream,* p. 119.

Chapter XX. The Earthquake
  6. Williams, *Golden Gate,* p. 30.
  7. Stevenson, "Pacific Capitals," in Hart, ed., *From Scotland to Silverado,* p. 182.
  8. Simon, *Wine and Spirits,* pp. 94–95.
  9. Bronson, *Earth Shook,* p. 186.

BIBLIOGRAPHY

AIDALA, THOMAS, AND CURT BRUCE. *The Great Houses of San Francisco.* New York: Alfred A. Knopf, 1974.

ALLEN, FREDERICK LEWIS. *Only Yesterday.* New York: Bantam Books, 1959.

ALTIMIRA, JOSÉ. "The First Exploration of the Bay of San Francisco, North," *Hutchings' Illustrated California Magazine,* Vol. 5 (July, 1860), pp. 28–30.

ALTROCCHI, JULIA COOLEY. *The Spectacular San Franciscans.* New York: E. P. Dutton & Co., 1949.

ANONYMOUS. "Millions for a Cent," *California Historical Society Quarterly,* Vol. 11, No. 1 (March, 1932), pp. 40–41.

ANSTED, DAVID THOMAS. *The Gold Seeker's Manual.* New York: D. Appleton & Co., 1849.

ANTIN, MARY. *The Promised Land.* Boston: Houghton Mifflin, 1912.

APTHEKER, HERBERT, ed. *A Documentary History of the Negro People in the U.S.* New York: The Citadel Press, 1951; rev. ed. 1965.

ASBURY, HERBERT. *The Barbary Coast: An Informal History of the San Francisco Underworld.* Garden City, N.Y.: Garden City Publishing Co., 1933.

ATHERTON, GERTRUDE F. *California: An Intimate History.* Rev. ed. New York: Blue Ribbon Books, 1936.

———. *My San Francisco.* New York: Bobbs-Merrill, 1946.

———. *Rezánov.* New York: F. A. Stokes Co., 1906.

BANCROFT, HUBERT HOWE. *California Inter Pocula,* Vol. XXXV of *Works.* San Francisco: The History Company, 1888.

———. *Chronicles of the Builders of the Commonwealth.* San Francisco: The History Company, 1892. 7 vols.

———. *History of California,* Vols. 18–24 of *Works.* San Francisco: The History Company, 1890. 7 vols.

———. "Pioneer Register," Appendices to Vols. 2–5 of the *History of California.*

———. *Popular Tribunals,* Vols. 36–37 of *Works.* San Francisco: The History Company, 1887. 2 Vols.

———. Scrapbook [Bancroft Scraps], covering the period 1887–1906. In Collections of the Bancroft Library, University of California, Berkeley. 1 vol. (unpaged).

———. *Why a World Centre of Industry at San Francisco Bay?* New York: Bancroft Company, 1916.

BARI, VALESKA, comp. *The Course of Empire.* New York: Coward-McCann, 1931.

BARRA, EZEKIEL I. *A Tale of Two Oceans: Philadelphia to San Francisco Around the Horn.* San Francisco: Eastman & Co., 1893.

BARRETT, ELINOR MAGEE. "The California Oyster Industry," *The Resources Agency of California,* Department of Fish and Game, Fish Bulletin #123, 1963.

BARRY, T. A., AND B. A. PATTEN. *Men and Memories of San Francisco in the Spring of 1850.* San Francisco: A. L. Bancroft & Co., 1873.

BARTH, GUNTHER. *Bitter Strength.* Cambridge, Mass.: Harvard University Press, 1964.

BEAN, WALTON. *Boss Ruef's San Francisco; The Story of the Union Labor Party, Big Business, and the Graft Prosecution.* Berkeley: University of California Press, 1952.

———. *California: An Interpretive History,* 2d ed. New York: McGraw-Hill Book Co., 1973.

BEASLEY, DELILAH. *The Negro Trail Blazers of California.* San Francisco: California Historical Society and San Francisco Negro Historical and Cultural Society, 1968.

BECKER, HOWARD S., ed. *Culture and Civility in San Francisco.* N.p.: Transaction Books, 1971.

BEEBE, LUCIUS, AND CHARLES CLEGG. *San Francisco's Golden Era.* Berkeley: Howell-North, 1960.

BERLIN, ELLIN. *Silver Platter.* New York: Doubleday, 1957.

BERNER, BERTHA. *Mrs. Leland Stanford: An Intimate Account.* Stanford: Stanford University Press, 1935.

BERRINGER, EDWIN JOHN. Preface to Calendar of Documents, 1849–1856 [Larkin Papers]. MS. thesis, 1907. In Bancroft Library, University of California, Berkeley.

BERWANGER, EUGENE H. *The Frontier Against Slavery: Western Anti-Negro Prejudice and the Slavery Extension Controversy.* Urbana: University of Illinois Press, 1967.

BIDWELL, JOHN. *A Journey to California.* Berkeley: The Friends of the Bancroft Library, 1964.

———. *Life in California Before the Gold Discovery.* Palo Alto: Lewis Osborne, 1966.

BIERCE, AMBROSE. *The Devil's Dictionary.* American Century Series. New York: Sagamore Press, 1957.

————. *The Sardonic Humor of Ambrose Bierce,* ed. George Barkin. New York: Dover Publications, 1963.

BLACK, ELEANORA, AND SIDNEY ROBERTSON. *The Gold Rush Song Book.* San Francisco: The Colt Press, 1940.

BLOCK, EUGENE B. *The Immortal San Franciscans: For Whom the Streets Were Named.* San Francisco: Chronicle Books, 1971.

BOGARDUS, J. P. *Bogardus' San Francisco, Sacramento City and Marysville Business Directory.* San Francisco, May, July, 1850.

BOHEMIAN CLUB. *The Annals.* San Francisco: The Bohemian Club, 1872–1972.

————. *A Chronicle of Our Years . . . Seventy-Fifth Anniversary.* San Francisco: Grabhorn Press, 1947.

BOLTON, HERBERT EUGENE. *Anza's California Expeditions,* Vol. 2. Berkeley: University of California Press, 1930.

————. "The Mission as a Frontier Institution in the Spanish-American Colonies." *The American Historical Review,* Vol. 23, No. 7 (October, 1917).

BONNET, THEODORE, ed. *Annals of the Olympic Club, San Francisco, 1914.* San Francisco, 1914.

BOSQUI, EDWARD. *Memoirs.* Oakland: Holmes Book Co., 1952.

BRANCH, EDGAR M. *Clemens of the Call: Mark Twain in San Francisco.* Berkeley: University of California Press, 1969.

BRONSON, WILLIAM. *The Earth Shook, The Sky Burned.* Garden City, N.Y.: Doubleday, 1959.

BRONSTRUP, G. A. *Club Men in Caricature.* San Francisco: G. A. Bronstrup, 1918.

BROOKS, J. TYRWHITT, M.D. [pseud. of Henry Vizetelly], *Four Months Among the Gold Finders in California.* New York: D. Appleton & Co., 1849.

BROWN, JOHN HENRY. *Reminiscences and Incidents of the Early Days of San Francisco (1845–50).* San Francisco: The Grabhorn Press, 1933.

BRUCE, JOHN. *Gaudy Century; The Story of San Francisco's Hundred Years of Robust Journalism.* New York: Random House, 1948.

BRUFF, J. GOLDSBOROUGH. *Gold Rush; The Journals and Other Papers of J. Goldsborough Bruff,* eds. Georgia Willis Read and Ruth Gaines. New York: Columbia University Press, 1944.

BRYANT, BERRYMAN, M.D. "Reminiscences of California 1849–1852," *California Historical Society Quarterly,* Vol. 11, No. 1 (March, 1932), pp. 35–39.

BRYANT, EDWIN. *What I Saw in California.* Palo Alto: Lewis Osborne, 1967.

Bulletin of the Sutro Library Project, No. 1, June, 1939. (Sutro Branch, California State Library, Sacramento.) San Francisco: Sutro Library Project, W.P.A., 1939.

CALIFORNIA, STATE OF, DEPARTMENT OF INDUSTRIAL RELATIONS, DIVISION OF FAIR EMPLOYMENT PRACTICES. *American Indians in California*. San Francisco, November, 1965.

———. *Californians of Japanese, Chinese, and Filipino Ancestry*. San Francisco, June, 1965.

———. *Californians of Spanish Surnames*. San Francisco, May, 1964.

———. *Negro Californians*. San Francisco, June, 1963.

California, Past, Present, Future. Lakewood, Calif.: Edward V. Salitore, 1973.

CAMP, WILLIAM MARTIN. *San Francisco: Port of Gold*. Garden City, N.Y. Doubleday, 1948.

CAMPBELL AND HOOGS. *Campbell and Hoogs' Business Directory for San Francisco and Sacramento City*. San Francisco, March, 1850.

CAMPBELL, CHARLES B. *The American Barkeeper*. San Francisco: Mullin, Mahon & Co., 1867.

CAROSSO, VINCENT PHILLIP. *The California Wine Industry 1830–1895; A Study of the Formative Years*. Berkeley: University of California Press, 1951.

———. Collection of photostats of miscellaneous articles on viticulture in California, with tables, 1873–74. In Collections of Bancroft Library, University of California, Berkeley.

———. The Commercial Development of California Viticulture, 1830–1890 (typewritten thesis). University of California, Berkeley, 1948.

CAUGHEY, JOHN WALTON. *California*, 2d ed. Englewood Cliffs, N.J.: Prentice-Hall, 1953.

CHAMBLISS, WILLIAM H. *Chambliss' Diary; or, Society As It Really Is*. New York: Chambliss & Co., 1895.

CHAMISSO, ADELBERT VON. *A Sojourn at San Francisco Bay*. San Francisco: The Book Club of California, 1936.

CHAPMAN, CHARLES EDWARD. "The Founding of San Francisco," In *The Pacific Ocean in History*. Eds. E. Morse Stephens and Herbert E. Bolton, New York: Macmillan, 1917.

———. *A History of California: The Spanish Period*. New York: Macmillan, 1930.

CHEVIGNY, HECTOR. *Lost Empire: The Life and Adventures of Nikolai Petrovich Rezánov*. New York: Macmillan, 1937.

China and California. Catalogue to an exhibition. Davis, California, University of California Library, May 15–July 1, 1966.

CHINN, THOMAS W., ed. *A History of the Chinese in California*. San Francisco: Chinese Historical Society of America, 1969.

CHIT-CHAT CLUB, *Sixteenth Annual Meeting of the Chit-Chat Club*, San Francisco, November 13, 1890.

———. *Thirty-Sixth Anniversary*. San Francisco, University Club,

November 14, 1910.

CHITTENDEN, HIRAM MARTIN. *The American Fur Trade of the Far West.* New York: The Press of the Pioneers, Inc., 1935. 2 vols.

CHIU, PING. *Chinese Labor in California, 1850–80.* Madison: State Historical Society of Wisconsin, 1963.

CHORIS, LOUIS. *San Francisco One Hundred Years Ago,* Tr. Porter Garnett. San Francisco: A. M. Robertson, 1913.

————. *Voyage Pittoresque Autour du Monde.* Paris: Didot, 1822.

Cities [twelve articles reprinted from *Scientific American,* September, 1965]. New York: Alfred A. Knopf, 1965.

CLAPPE, LOUISE AMELIA KNAPP (SMITH). *The Shirley Letters from the California Mines, 1851–1852,* ed. Carl I. Wheat. New York: Alfred A. Knopf, 1965.

CLARK, THOMAS D. *Frontier America: The Story of the Westward Movement.* New York: Charles Scribner's Sons, 1959.

————. *Gold Rush Diary.* Lexington: University of Kentucky Press, 1967.

CLELAND, ROBERT GLASS. *From Wilderness to Empire.* New York: Alfred A. Knopf, 1959.

COBLENTZ, STANTON A. *Villains and Vigilantes.* New York: Thomas Yoseloff, Inc., 1957.

COIT, DANIEL WADSWORTH. *Digging for Gold Without a Shovel.* San Francisco: Fred A. Rosenstock, Old West Publishing Co., 1967.

COLEMAN, WILLIAM TELL. The Vigilance Committee (a statement), 1856 (manuscript). In Collections of the Bancroft Library, University of California, Berkeley.

COLVILLE, SAMUEL. *San Francisco Gazetteer, 1856.* San Francisco: Commercial Steam Presses: Monson, Valentine and Co., 1856.

COMMERCIAL CLUB. *By-laws, House Rules, Officers and Members of the San Francisco Commercial Club.* San Francisco: N.p., 1888.

Commission to Enquire into City Property, Report of. Printed at the Office of the *Evening Picayune,* 1851.

COMMONWEALTH CLUB. *Constitution.* San Francisco: Phillips, Smyth & Van Orden, 1903.

COMPAGNIE FRANÇAISE DES SAPEURS-POMPIERS LAFAYETTE No. 2 DES ECHELLES ET CROCHETS. *Constitution et Reglement Interieur.* San Francisco *Daily Evening News,* 1854.

CONGREGATION EMANU-EL. *The Chronicles of Emanu-El* (July 1850–December 1900). San Francisco: G. Spaulding & Co. Press, 1900.

————. AND EUREKA BENEVOLENT SOCIETY. *Rules and Regulations of the Navo Shalom "Home of Peace" Cemetery.* San Francisco: Towne & Bacon, 1860.

COOK, SHERBURNE F. *The Conflict Between the California Indian and*

White Civilization. Berkeley: University of California Press, 1943. 4 vols.

COOKE AND LECOUNT. *A "Pile," or, a Glance at the Wealth of the Monied Men of San Francisco and Sacramento City.* San Francisco: Cooke and LeCount, Booksellers, 1851.

COOLIDGE, MARY ROBERTS. *Chinese Immigration.* New York: Henry Holt, 1909.

COSMOS CLUB. *The Constitution, By-Laws, House Rules and List of Members of the Cosmos Club of San Francisco.* April, 1907.

COULTER, EDITH. *An Artist in El Dorado: The Drawings and Letters of Daniel Wadsworth Coit.* San Francisco: Grabhorn Press, 1937.

COWAN, ROBERT ERNEST, ANNE BANCROFT, AND ADDIE L. BALLOU. *The Forgotten Characters of Old San Francisco.* San Francisco: Ward Ritchie Press, 1964.

CROMPTON, ARNOLD. *Apostle of Liberty: Starr King in California.* Boston: Beacon Press, 1950.

CROSS, IRA B. *Financing an Empire: History of Banking in California.* Chicago, S. S. Clarke Pub. Co., 1927. 4 vols.

———. *A History of the Labor Movement in California.* University of California Publications in Economics, Vol. 14. Berkeley: University of California Press, 1935.

CROSS, RALPH HERBERT. *The Early Inns of California, 1844–1869.* San Francisco: Lawton Kennedy, 1954.

CRUIKSHANK, PERCY. *Hints to Emigrants or Incidents in the Emigration of John Smith of Smith Town.* London: J. Harwood, 1849.

DANA, JULIAN. *A. P. Giannini: Giant in the West.* New York: Prentice-Hall, 1947.

DANA, RICHARD HENRY. *Two Years Before the Mast.* New York: Random House, 1936.

DAVIS, SAMUEL. "'Mammy' Pleasant Memoirs and Autobiography," *The Pandex of the Press* (San Francisco), Vol. 1, No. 1 (January, 1902), pp. 1–6.

DAVIS, WILLIAM HEATH. *Seventy-Five Years in California.* San Francisco: Howell Press, 1929.

DEFORD, MIRIAM. *They Were San Franciscans.* N.p.: The Caxton Printers, Ltd., 1941.

DICKSON, SAMUEL. *Tales of San Francisco.* Stanford: Stanford University Press, 1957.

DILLON, RICHARD HUGH. *Embarcadero.* New York: Coward-McCann, 1959.

———. *Fool's Gold: The Decline and Fall of Captain John Sutter of California.* New York; Coward-McCann, 1967.

———. *The Hatchet Men.* New York: Coward-McCann, 1962.

———. *Humbugs and Heroes.* New York: Doubleday, 1970.

————. *Shanghaiing Days.* New York: Coward-McCann, 1961.

Directory of Churches and Religious Organizations in San Francisco, California (mimeographed). Northern California Historical Records Survey, W.P.A. San Francisco, 1941.

DOBIE, CHARLES CALDWELL. *San Francisco: A Pageant.* New York: D. Appleton-Century Co., 1939.

————. *San Francisco's Chinatown.* New York: D. Appleton-Century Co., 1936.

DOBLE, JOHN. *John Doble's Journal and Letters from the Mines,* ed. Charles L. Camp. Denver: The Old West Publishing Co., 1962.

DOMHOFF, G. WILLIAM. *The Bohemian Grove and Other Retreats.* New York: Harper & Row, 1974.

DOSS, MARGOT PATTERSON. *Early California Trade Cards.* Keepsake Series. San Francisco: Book Club of California, 1966.

DOWNEY, JOSEPH T. *Filings from an Old Saw . . .* [series of eighteen articles originally printed in *Golden Era,* January 9 to July 3, 1853]. San Francisco: John Howell, 1956.

DRAKE, SIR FRANCIS. *The World Encompassed.* London: The Hakluyt Society, 1854.

DRESSLER, ALBERT, ed. *California's Pioneer Circus, Joseph Andrew Rowe, Founder.* San Francisco: H. S. Crocker Co., 1926.

DRIVER, HAROLD E. "Northwest California," from Culture Element Distribution Series, *University of California Publications in Anthropological Records,* Vol. 1, No. 6. Berkeley: University of California Press, 1939.

DUNLAP, DAVE. *The Story of E Clampus Vitus Then and Now 1852–1966.* Stockton, Calif.: Simard Printing Co. Press, 1966.

DURHAM, PHILIP, AND EVERETT L. JONES. *The Negro Cowboys.* New York: Dodd, Mead, 1965.

DWINELLE, JOHN WHIPPLE. "Address on Acquisition of California by the United States to Society of California Pioneers," *The California Miscellany,* Vol. 13, No. 3 (1866), p. 1.

————. *The Colonial History of the City of San Francisco.* San Francisco: Towne and Bacon, 1863.

DWYER, RICHARD A., AND RICHARD E. LINGENFELTER. *Songs of the Gold Rush.* Berkeley: University of California Press, 1964.

EAVES, LUCILLE. *A History of California Labor Legislation.* Berkeley: University of California Press, 1910.

ECKART, NELSON A. "The Water Supply System of San Francisco," *Journal of the American Water Works Association,* Vol. 32, No. 5 (May, 1940).

EGOIAN, BARBARA. *Faith in San Francisco: A Guide to San Francisco Churches and Synagogues.* San Francisco: Howard Edwards Co., 1961.

Elite Directory of San Francisco, 1879. San Francisco: Argonaut Publishing Co., 1879.

EMPIRE FIRE ENGINE COMPANY. *Code of Laws of the Empire Fire Engine Company No. 1.* San Francisco: Alta California Steam Presses, 1850.

ENGLEHARDT, ZEPHYRIN. *The Missions and Missionaries of California.* San Francisco: J. H. Barry Co., 1908–16. 4 vols.

ETEROVICH, ADAM S., ed. *Proceedings of the First State Convention of Colored Citizens of the State of California* (1855, 1856, 1865). Reprinted, San Francisco: R. & E. Research Associates, 1969.

EUREKA BENEVOLENT SOCIETY, SAN FRANCISCO. *Annual Reports.*

EVANS, ALBERT S. *À la California.* San Francisco: A. L. Bancroft & Co., 1873.

FAGES, PEDRO. "Expedition to S. F. Bay in 1770," *Publications of the Academy of Pacific Coast History,* Vol. 2, No. 3 (1911).

FERRIER, WILLIAM WARREN. *Ninety Years of Education in California.* Berkeley: Sather Gate Book Shop, 1937.

FORBES, JACK D. *Afro-Americans in the Far West.* Berkeley Far West Laboratory for Educational Research and Development, n.d.

FOREMAN, GRANT. *Marcy and the Gold Seekers.* Norman: University of Oklahoma Press, 1939.

FORUM CLUB. *Second Annual Report of the Forum Club of San Francisco.* 1897.

Four Americans in Paris: The Collections of Gertrude Stein and Her Family. New York: The Museum of Modern Art, 1970.

FURNAS, J. C. *The Americans.* New York: G. P. Putnam's Sons, 1969.

GAGEY, EDMOND M. *The San Francisco Stage.* New York: Columbia University Press, 1950.

GALVIN, JOHN, ed. *The Coming of Justice to California: Three Documents,* tr. Adelaide Smithers. San Francisco: John Howell Books, 1963.

GARDINER, HOWARD C. *In Pursuit of the Golden Dream: Reminiscences of San Francisco and the Northern and Southern Mines, 1849–1857,* ed. Dale L. Morgan. Stoughton, Mass.: Western Hemisphere, Inc., 1970.

GARNETT, PORTER. *The Green Knight* (play). San Francisco: The Bohemian Club, 1921.

———, AND MARY FLOYD WILLIAMS, eds. *Papers of the San Francisco Committee of Vigilance.* Berkeley: University of California Press, 1910.

GAY, THERESA. *James W. Marshall: The Discoverer of California Gold, A Biography.* Georgetown, California: Talisman Press, 1967.

GENTHE, ARNOLD. *Pictures of Old Chinatown.* Text by Will Irwin. New York: Moffat, Yard and Co., 1909.

GENTRY, CURT. *The Madams of San Francisco.* Garden City, N.Y.: Doubleday, 1964.

GERSTACHER, FRIEDRICH. *Scenes of Life in California,* tr. George Cosgrave. San Francisco: John Howell Books, 1942.

GILLIAM, HAROLD. *San Francisco Bay.* Garden City, N.Y.: Doubleday, 1957.

———, AND PHIL PALMER. *The Face of San Francisco.* Garden City, N.Y.: Doubleday, 1960.

GOMPERS, SAMUEL, AND HERMAN GUTSTADT. *Meat Vs. Rice: American Manhood Against Asiatic Coolieism* [1902]. Reprinted, San Francisco: Asiatic Exclusion League, 1908.

GOODRICH, MARY. *The Palace Hotel.* San Francisco: Dewitt, 1930.

GREEN, CONSTANCE McLAUGHLIN. *American Cities in the Growth of the Nation.* New York: Harper & Row, 1965.

GRINNELL, E. "Making Acorn Bread," *Records of University of California Archaelogical Survey.* Los Angeles: University of California, 1958.

GROH, GEORGE. *Gold Fever.* New York: William Morrow, 1966.

GRUBER, FERDINAND. *Illustrated Guide and Catalogue of Woodward's Gardens.* San Francisco: Francis, Valentine and Co., 1873, 1880.

GUDDE, ERWIN G. *California Place Names,* 3d rev. ed. Berkeley: University of California Press, 1969.

———. "Frémont-Preuss and Western Names," reprinted from *Names,* Vol. 5, No. 3 (September, 1957), pp. 169-81.

———. *German Pioneers in Early California.* Hoboken: The Concord Society, 1927.

A Guide to Church Vital Statistics Records in California. San Francisco: The Northern California Historical Records Survey Project, W.P.A., May, 1942.

HACKETT, FRED H., ed. *The Industries of San Francisco: Her Rank, Resources, Advantages, Trade, Commerce, and Manufactures.* San Francisco: Payot & Co., July, 1884.

HALL, JOHN LINVILLE. *Journal of the Hartford Union Mining and Trading Co.* San Francisco, printed by J. L. Hall on board the *Henry Lee,* 1849; reprinted as *Around the Horn in '49* by Reverend J. L. Hall, Wethersfield, Conn., 1898.

HAMMOND, GEORGE PETER, ed. *Digging for Gold Without a Shovel: The Letters of Daniel Wadsworth Coit.* Denver: Old West Publishing Co., 1967.

———. *The Larkin Papers.* Berkeley: University of California Press, 1951–64. 10 vols.

———. *Who Saw the Elephant?* San Francisco: California Historical Society, 1964.

HANDLIN, OSCAR. *The Uprooted.* New York: Grosset and Dunlap, 1951.

HANSEN, GLADYS, ed. *San Francisco, the Bay and Its Cities,* new rev. ed. New York: Hastings House (American Guide Series), 1973 [1947], comp. by Writers' Program, W.P.A.

————, AND WILLIAM F. HEINTZ, comps. *The Chinese in California: A Brief Bibliographic History.* Portland, Ore.: Richard Abel & Co., 1970.

HARRIS, BOGARDUS, AND LABATT, comps. *San Francisco City Directory.* San Francisco; Harris, Bogardus, and Labatt, 1856.

HART, JAMES D. *American Images of Spanish California.* Berkeley: The Friends of the Bancroft Library, University of California, 1960.

————. *Fine Printing in California.* Keepsake Series No. 1. Berkeley: California Library Association, 1960.

————, ed. *From Scotland to Silverado,* Cambridge, Mass.: The Belknap Press of Harvard University, 1966.

————. *The Oxford Companion to American Literature,* 4th ed. New York: Oxford University Press, 1965.

————, ed. *The Vine in Early California.* San Francisco: Book Club of California, 1955.

HARTE, FRANCIS BRET. *Bret Harte's Tales of the Gold Rush,* ed. Oscar Lewis. New York: Heritage Press, 1944.

————. *The Heathen Chinee* [facsimile of the original manuscript . . . for the *Overland Monthly* of September, 1870]. San Francisco: John H. Carmany and Co., n.d.

————. *Outcroppings.* San Francisco: A. Roman and Co., 1866.

————, AND MARK TWAIN. *Sketches of the Sixties.* San Francisco: Howell, 1927.

HASKINS, C. W. *The Argonauts of California.* New York: Fords, Howard and Hulbert, 1890.

HECKENDORN AND WILSON. *Miners and Businessmen's Directory.* Columbia: Printed at the Clipper Office, 1856.

HEIZER, ROBERT FLEMING. "California Gold Discovery," *California Historical Society Quarterly,* Vol. 26, No. 2 (1947).

————. "Indians of the San Francisco Bay Area," *Geologic Guidebook of the San Francisco Bay Counties.* San Francisco: Department of Natural Resources, Division of Mines, Bulletin 154, December, 1951.

————. *Languages, Territories, and Names of California Indian Tribes.* Berkeley: University of California Press, 1966.

HELPER, HINTON ROWAN. *Compendium of the Impending Crisis of the South.* New York: A. B. Burdick, 1860.

————. *Dreadful California,* eds. Charles Clegg and Lucius Beebe. Indianapolis: Bobbs-Merrill, 1948.

————. *The Land of Gold: Reality Versus Fiction.* Baltimore: H. Taylor, 1855.

HENSHAW, HENRY WETHERBEE. *The Mission Indian Vocabularies.* Berkeley: University of California Press, 1955.

"A Historic Document: A Contract for Transportation Across the Plains to California," *California Historical Society Quarterly,* Vol. 11, No. 1 (March, 1932), p. 34.

HITTEL, THEODORE H. *Brief History of California,* Book I. San Francisco: The Stone Educational Co., 1898.

HOLDREDGE, HELEN. *Mammy Pleasant.* New York: G. P. Putnam's Sons, 1953.

————. *The Woman in Black: The Life of Lola Montez.* New York: G. P. Putnam's Sons, 1955.

HOLLINGSWORTH, JOHN McHENRY. *The Journal of John McHenry Hollingsworth of the First New York Volunteers* (September, 1845–August, 1849). San Francisco: California Historical Society, 1923.

HOOVER, MILDRED BROOKE, HERO EUGENE RENSCH, AND ETHEL GRACE RENSCH. *Historic Spots in California,* 3d ed., rev. by William N. Abeloe. Stanford: Stanford University Press, 1966.

HOY, WILLIAM. "Gold Mountain, Big City, Chinese Map," *California Historical Society Quarterly,* Vol. 27 (September, 1948), pp. 256–58.

HUGGINS, DOROTHY H., comp. *Continuation of the Annals of San Francisco,* Part I (from June 1, 1854, to December 31, 1855). San Francisco: California Historical Society, 1939.

————, ed., " 'San Francisco Society' from *The Elite Directory* of 1879," *California Historical Society Quarterly,* Vol. 19 (1940), pp. 225–39.

HUNT, TIMOTHY DWIGHT. *Sermon Suggested by the Execution of Jenkins.* San Francisco: Marvin Hitchcock, 1851.

The Illustrated Directory. San Francisco, 1894–95.

IRWIN, WILL. *The City That Was: A Requiem of Old San Francisco.* New York: B. W. Huebsch, 1908.

JACKSON, JOSEPH HENRY, ed. *Gold Rush Album.* New York: Charles Scribner's Sons, 1949.

————. *San Francisco Murders.* New York: Duell, Sloan and Pearce, 1947.

JACOBSON, PAULINE. *City of the Golden 'Fifties.* Berkeley: University of California Press, 1941.

JAMES, MARQUIS, AND BESSIE ROWLAND. *Biography of a Bank: The Story of Bank of America.* New York: Harper & Brothers, 1954.

JENNESS, CHARLES KELLEY. *The Charities of San Francisco: A Directory.* San Francisco: Stanford University Press, 1894.

JOHNSON, KENNETH M. *San Francisco as It Is: "Gleanings from the Picayune."* Georgetown, California: Talisman Press, 1964.

JOHNSON, SAMUEL ROOSEVELT. *California: A Sermon in St. John's Church Brooklyn.* New York: Stanford and Swords, 1849.

JONES, EVAN ROWLAND. *The Emigrant's Friend,* rev. ed. London: Searle & Rivington, 1882.

JONES, IDWAL. *Ark of Empire: San Francisco's Montgomery Block.* Garden City, N.Y.: Doubleday, 1951.

KAHN, EDGAR MYRON. "Andrew Smith Hallidie," *California Historical Society Quarterly,* Vol. 19, No. 2 (June, 1940), pp. 144–56.

———. *Cable Car Days in San Francisco,* rev. ed. Stanford: Stanford University Press, 1948.

KELLER, GEORGE. *A Trip Across the Plains and Life in California.* Oakland: Biobooks, 1955.

KEMBLE, EDWARD CLEVELAND. *A History of California Newspapers 1846–1858,* ed. Helen H. Bretnor. Los Gatos, California: Talisman Press, 1962.

———. *A Kemble Reader: Stories of California, 1846–48, by an Early California Journalist,* ed. Fred Blackburn Rogers. San Francisco: The California Historical Society, 1963.

KEMBLE, JOHN HASKELL. *San Francisco Bay: A Pictorial Maritime History.* New York: Cornell Maritime Press, 1957.

———. "The West Through Salt Spray," *The American West,* Vol. 1, No. 4 (Fall, 1964).

KENNEDY, JOHN CASTILLO. *The Great Earthquake and Fire: San Francisco, 1906.* New York: William Morrow, 1963.

[KENWORTHY, C. W.]. *Amelia Sherwood; or, Bloody Scenes at the California Gold Mines; with a Narrative of the Tragic Incidents on a Voyage to San Francisco.* Richmond: Barclay and Co., 1850.

KIMBALL, CHARLES PROCTOR. *The San Francisco City Directory.* San Francisco: Journal of Commerce Press, 1850.

KIP, LEONARD. *California Sketches with Recollections of the Gold Mines.* Los Angeles: N. A. Kovach, 1946.

———. *The Volcano Diggings: A Tale of California Law.* New York: J. S. Redfield, 1851.

KIRKER, HAROLD. *California's Architectural Frontier.* San Marino, Calif.: Huntington Library, 1960.

KNOWER, DANIEL. *The Adventures of a Forty-Niner.* Albany, N.Y.: Weed-Parsons Printing Co., 1894.

KOCH, HARRY WALTER. *San Francisco: The Illustrated History.* San Francisco: Ken-Books, 1966.

KROEBER, A. L. "The Chumash and Costanoan Languages," *American Archaeology and Ethnology,* Vol. 9, No. 2 (November, 1910), pp. 237–71.

———. *Handbook of the Indians of California.* Smithsonian Institution, Bureau of American Ethnology Bulletin 78. Washington, D.C.: Government Printing Office, 1925.

———. "Tribes Surveyed," *Culture Element Distributions Series,*

University of California Publications in Anthropological Records, Vol. 1, No. 7. Berkeley: University of California Press, 1939.

KROEBER, THEODORA. *Ishi in Two Worlds: A Biography of the Last Wild Indian in North America.* Berkeley: University of California Press, 1968.

KRONINGER, ROBERT H. *Sarah and the Senator.* Berkeley: Howell-North, 1964.

LA FARGE, OLIVER. *The American Indian.* New York: Golden Press, 1960.

LA MOTTE, ROBERT SMITH. *La Motte Family Letters, 1849–1872.* In Collections of the Bancroft Library, University of California, Berkeley.

LANE, ALLEN STANLEY. *Emperor Norton: The Mad Monarch of America.* Caldwell, Idaho: The Caxton Printers, Ltd., 1939.

LANGDON, WILLIAM CHAUNCEY. *Everyday Things in American Life 1776–1876,* Vol. 2. New York: Charles Scribner's Sons, 1941.

LANGLEY, HENRY GRACE. *Guide to San Francisco.* San Francisco, 1875.

Langley's San Francisco Business Directory and Metropolitan Guide. San Francisco, 1867–78.

LANGSDORFF, GEORGE HEINRICH VON. *Narrative of Rezánov Voyage.* San Francisco: The Private Press of T. C. Russell, 1927.

LAPÉROUSE, JEAN FRANÇOIS DE GALUP, COMTE DE, "A Visit to Monterey in 1786 and a Description of the Indians of California," *California Historical Society Quarterly,* Vol. 15, No. 3 (1936), pp. 216–22.

LAPP, RUDOLPH M. "The Negro in Gold Rush California," *The Journal of Negro History,* Vol. 49, No. 2 (April, 1964).

———. "Negro Rights Activities in Gold Rush California," *California Historical Society Quarterly,* Vol. 45, No. 1 (March, 1966), p. 3.

LARKIN, THOMAS O. *Chapters in the Early Life of Thomas Oliver Larkin.* San Francisco: California Historical Society, 1939.

———. "Larkin to His Sons," ed. A. T. Leonard, Jr., M.D. *California Historical Society Quarterly,* Vol. 27, No. 4 (1948), pp. 297–300.

LAUREL HALL CLUB. *Laurel Hall Club Annual Report.* San Francisco, 1900.

———. *Laurel Hall Club of San Francisco Year Book,* 1907–08.

LeCount & Strong's San Francisco City Directory, 1854.

LEFLER, HUGH TALMADGE. *Hinton Rowan Helper, Advocate of a "White America."* Charlottesville: The Historical Publishing Co., 1935.

LENGYEL, CORNELL, ed. History of Music in San Francisco Series. (mimeographed) San Francisco, History of Music Project, W.P.A., 1939–1942. 7 vols.

LÉVY, DANIEL. *Les Français en Californie.* San Francisco: Grégoire, Tauzy et cie, 1884.

LEVY, HARRIET LANE. *920 O'Farrell Street.* Garden City, N.Y.: Doubleday, 1947.

LEWIS, OSCAR. *Bay Window Bohemia.* Garden City, N.Y.: Doubleday, 1956.

————. *The Big Four.* New York: Alfred A. Knopf, 1959.

————. *California in 1846.* San Francisco: Grabhorn Press, 1934.

————. *San Francisco: Mission to Metropolis.* Berkeley: Howell-North Books, 1966.

————. *Silver Kings.* New York: Alfred A. Knopf, 1959.

————. *Sutter's Fort: Gateway to the Gold Fields.* Englewood Cliffs, N.J.: Prentice-Hall, 1966.

————, ed. and comp. *This Was San Francisco: Being First Hand Accounts of the Evolution of One of America's Favorite Cities.* New York: David McKay, 1962.

————, AND CARROLL D. HALL. *Bonanza Inn.* New York: Alfred A. Knopf, 1939.

"Library of the What Cheer House." *Hutchings' California Magazine,* Vol. 5, No. 7 (January, 1861), pp. 294–95.

LINSENMEYER, HELEN WALKER. *From Fingers to Finger Bowls.* San Diego: Copley Books, Union-Tribune Publishing Co., 1972.

LITTLEJOHN, DAVID. "San Francisco Architecture," *KQED Focus* (August, 1968).

LIU, KWANG-CHING. *Americans and Chinese.* Cambridge, Mass.: Harvard University Press, 1963.

LLOYD, B. E. *Lights and Shades in San Francisco.* San Francisco: A. L. Bancroft and Co., 1876.

LOFTIS, ANNE. *California: Where the Twain Did Meet.* New York: Macmillan, 1973.

LONGSTREET, STEPHEN. *The Wilder Shore.* New York: Doubleday, 1968.

LOTCHIN, ROGER W. *San Francisco: 1846–1856, from Hamlet to City.* New York: Oxford University Press, 1974.

LYMAN, GEORGE D. *Ralston's Ring: California Plunders the Comstock Lode.* New York: Charles Scribner's Sons, 1945.

————. "The Scalpel Under Three Flags in California," *California Historical Society Quarterly,* Vol. 4, No. 2 (1925).

————. "Victor J. Fourgeaud, M.D.," *California Historical Society Quarterly,* Vol. 11, No. 2 (June, 1932), pp. 138–49.

LYNCH, JEREMIAH. *The Life of David C. Broderick: A Senator of the Fifties.* New York: The Baker & Taylor Co., 1911.

MACGREGOR, WILLIAM LAIRD. *Hotels and Hotel Life, at San Francisco, California, in 1876.* San Francisco: San Francisco News Co., 1877.

MAHR, AUGUST C. *The Visit of the "Rurik" to San Francisco in 1816.*

Stanford University History, Economics, and Political Science Series, Vol. 2, No. 2. Stanford: Stanford University Press, 1932.

MARBERRY, MARION M. *The Golden Voice: A Biography of Isaac Kalloch.* New York: Farrar, Straus and Co., 1947.

MARCY, RANDOLPH BARNES. *The Prairie Traveller: A Handbook for Overland Expeditions.* New York: Harper & Bros., 1859.

MARRYAT, FRANK. *Mountains and Molehills; or, Recollections of a Burnt Journal.* New York: Harper & Bros., 1855; rev. ed., J. B. Lippincott, 1962.

McCOLLUM, WILLIAM. *California as I Saw It,* ed. Dale Morgan. Los Gatos, California: Talisman Press, 1960.

McDOWELL, JACK, ed. *San Francisco.* Menlo Park: Lane Magazine and Book Co., 1969.

McELROY, WALTER, ed. *San Francisco: The Bay and Its Cities.* New York: Hastings House, 1947.

McGLOIN, JOHN BERNARD. *California's First Archbishop: The Life of Joseph Sadoc Alemany.* New York: Herder and Herder, 1966.

McGOWAN, EDWARD. *Narrative of Edward McGowan.* San Francisco: Thomas C. Russell, 1917.

McLEOD, ALEXANDER. *Pigtails and Gold Dust.* Caldwell, Idaho: Caxton Printers, Ltd., 1947.

McWILLIAMS, CAREY. *California: The Great Exception.* New York: Current Books, 1949.

——, ed. *The California Revolution.* New York: Grossman Publishers, 1968.

MECHANICS' INSTITUTE. *Constitution, By-Laws and Rules of Order.* San Francisco, 1855.

——. *One Hundred Years of the Mechanics' Institute in San Francisco.* San Francisco: The Mechanics' Institute, 1955.

Menus of Early San Francisco Hotels and Restaurants. In Collections of Bancroft Library, University of California, Berkeley.

MITCHELL, GRACE. *The Kingdom of Content.* San Francisco: Kohnke Printing Co., 1928.

MOERENHOUT, JACQUES ANTOINE. *The Inside Story of the Gold Rush,* tr. and ed. George Ezra Dane. San Francisco: California Historical Society, 1935.

MONAGHAN, JAMES. *Australians and the Gold Rush.* Berkeley: University of California Press, 1966.

MONGUIO, LUIS. "Lust for Riches," *California Historical Society Quarterly,* Vol. 27, No. 3 (September, 1948), pp. 237–48.

MOSES, BERNARD. *The Establishment of Municipal Government in San Francisco.* Baltimore: Johns Hopkins University Press, 1889.

MYERS MYERS, JOHN. *San Francisco's Reign of Terror.* Garden City, N.Y.: Doubleday, 1966.

MYRICK, DAVID F. *San Francisco's Telegraph Hill.* Berkeley: Howell-North Books, 1972.

NASH, GERALD D. "Stages of California's Economic Growth," *California Historical Quarterly*, Vol. 51, No. 4 (Winter, 1972). [Journal's title varies with date—ed.]

NELSON, N. C. "Shellmounds in the San Francisco Bay Region," *University of California Publications in American Archaeology and Ethnology*, Vol. 7, No. 4 (December, 1909).

NEVILLE, MRS. AMELIA RANSOME. *The Fantastic City: Memoirs of the Social and Romantic Life of Old San Francisco.* Boston: Houghton Mifflin, 1932.

NEWMARK, HARRIS. *Sixty Years in Southern California.* Los Angeles: Zeitlin and Ver Brugge, 1970.

OCCIDENTAL CONVIVIAL CLUB. *Constitution and By-Laws of the Occidental Convivial Club.* San Francisco: F. B. Sterett, Printer, 1863.

OLDER, CORA (MRS. FREMONT). *San Francisco: Magic City.* New York: Longmans, Green, 1961.

OLMSTEAD, ROGER. "The Square-Toed Packets of San Francisco Bay," *California Historical Society Quarterly*, Vol. 51, No. 1 (Spring, 1972), pp. 35–58.

OLMSTEAD, ROGER, AND T. H. WATKINS. *Here Today.* San Francisco: Chronicle Books, 1968.

OLYMPIC CLUB. *By-Laws and List of Members.* San Francisco, 1879.

―――. *One Hundred Years; the Olympic Club Centennial* [1860–1960]. San Francisco, 1960.

PACIFIC-UNION CLUB. *Constitution and By-Laws* (pamphlets). 1889–1968.

PALMER, JOHN WILLIAMSON. *The New and the Old.* New York: Rudd and Carleton, 1859.

PARKER, ELIZABETH L., and JAMES ABAJIAN. *A Walking Tour of the Black Presence in San Francisco during the Nineteenth Century.* San Francisco: African American Historical and Cultural Society, 1974.

PARKER, JAMES M. *The San Francisco Directory for the Year 1852–3.* San Francisco: J. M. Parker, 1852.

PARKER, ROBERT J. "The Great Potato Speculation at Yerba Buena in 1843," *The Quarterly of the Historical Society of Southern California*, Vol. 22 (1940), pp. 30–32.

PARRY, ALBERT. *Garrets and Pretenders.* New York: Dover Publications, 1960.

PAUL, RODMAN W., ed. *The California Gold Discovery.* Georgetown, Calif.: Talisman Press, 1966.

PAULEY, THOMAS H. "J. Ross Browne: Wine Lobbyist and Frontier Opportunist," *California Historical Society Quarterly*, Vol. 51, No. 2 (Summer, 1972), pp. 99–116.

PEARCE, ROY HARVEY. *The Savages of America.* Baltimore: The Johns Hopkins Press, 1953.

PENDLETON, HARRY C. *The Exempt Firemen of San Francisco, Their*

Unique and Gallant Record, Together with a Résumé of the San Francisco Fire Department and Its Personnel. San Francisco: Commercial Publishing Co., 1900.

PENINOU, ERNEST P., and SIDNEY S. GREENLEAF. *A Directory of California Wine Growers and Wine Makers in 1860.* Berkeley: Tamalpais Press, 1967.

PERKINS, ELISHA DOUGLASS. *Gold Rush Diary,* ed. Thomas D. Clark. Lexington: University of Kentucky Press, 1967.

PERKINS, WILLIAM, DALE L. MORGAN, AND JAMES R. SCOBIE, eds. *Three Years in California.* Berkeley: University of California Press, 1964.

PETERS, HARRY T. *California on Stone.* Garden City, N.Y.: Doubleday, Doran and Co., 1935.

PETERSON, CHARLES E. "Prefabs in the California Gold Rush, 1849," *Journal of the Society of Architectural Historians,* Vol. 24 (December, 1965).

PFIZER COMPANY. "An Informal History of San Francisco," Pfizer's *Spectrum,* Vol. 12, No. 2 (Summer, 1964).

PHILLIPS, CATHERINE COFFIN. *Portsmouth Plaza, The Cradle of San Francisco.* San Francisco: J. H. Nash, 1932.

PINART, ALPHONSE LOUIS, comp. *The Mission Indian Vocabularies.* Berkeley: University of California Press, 1952.

PITT, LEONARD. "The Beginnings of Nativism in California," *Pacific Historical Review,* Vol. 30 (February, 1961), pp. 23–38.

Polk's San Francisco City Directory. R. L. Polk & Co., 1858–1905.

POTTER, ELIZABETH GRAY. *The San Francisco Skyline.* New York: Dodd, Mead, 1939.

POWERS, STEPHEN. "Tribes of California," *Contributions to North American Ethnology,* Vol. 3. Washington, D.C.: Government Printing Office, Department of Interior, 1877.

PRENDERGAST, THOMAS F. *Forgotten Pioneers: Irish Leaders in Early California.* San Francisco: The Trade Pressroom, 1942.

PRICE, J., AND C. S. HALEY. *Buyers' Manual and Business Guide.* San Francisco: Francis and Valentine Steam Book and Job Printing Establishment, 1872.

QUAIFE, MILO MILTON, ed. *Pictures of Gold Rush California.* Lakeside Classics Series. Chicago: The Lakeside Press, R.R. Donnelly and Sons, 1949.

RASMUSSEN, LOUIS J. *San Francisco Ship Passenger Lists.* Colma: San Francisco Historic Record and Genealogy Bulletin, 1965–1970.

RATHER, LOIS. *San Francisco's First Printing Press.* Oakland: Rather Press, 1970.

———. *Women as Printers.* Oakland: Rather Press, 1970.

REVERE, JOSEPH WARREN. *Naval Duty in California* [first published 1849 under title *A Tour of Duty in California*]. Oakland: Biobooks, 1947.

RIESENBERG, FELIX, JR. *Golden Gate: The Story of San Francisco Harbor.* New York: Tudor Publishing Co., 1940.

RIORDAN, JOSEPH W. *The First Half Century of St. Ignatius Church and College.* San Francisco: H. S. Crocker Co., 1905.

ROBINSON, ALFRED. *Life in California.* San Francisco: William Doxey, 1891; reprinted, San Francisco: The Private Press of T. C. Russell, 1925.

RODECAPE, LOUIS FOSTER. "Gilding the Sunflower," *California Historical Society Quarterly*, Vol. 19 (June, 1940), pp. 97–112.

ROGERS, FRED BLACKBURN. *The California Star.* Berkeley: Howell-North Books, 1965.

ROOT, FRANK ALBERT, AND WILLIAM ELSEY CONNELLEY. *The Overland Stage to California.* Topeka: Published by the authors, 1901.

ROURKE, CONSTANCE. *Troupers of the Gold Coast: or The Rise of Lotta Crabtree.* New York: Harcourt, Brace, 1928.

ROYCE, JOSIAH. *California, from the Conquest in 1846 to the Second Vigilance Committee in San Francisco: A Study of American Character.* New York: Alfred A. Knopf, 1948.

———. *The Feud of Oakfield Creek.* Boston: Houghton Mifflin, 1887.

ST. ANDREWS SOCIETY OF SAN FRANCISCO. *Historical Report.* San Francisco: J. Wallace, 1871.

SANDMEYER, ELMER C. *The Anti-Chinese Movement in California.* Urbana: University of Illinois Press, 1939.

SAN FRANCISCO BAY CONSERVATION STUDY COMMISSION. *A Report to the California Legislature,* 1965.

San Francisco Blue Book. San Francisco: C. C. Hoag, 1888–1915.

San Francisco Business Firms (after 1885). San Francisco: Post Publishing Co.

SAN FRANCISCO CHAMBER OF COMMERCE. *Law and Order in San Francisco: A Beginning.* San Francisco, 1916.

———. San Francisco's Chinatown: History, Function and Importance of Social Organizations (mimeographed). San Francisco, 1953.

SAN FRANCISCO COMMITTEE OF VIGILANCE, 1851, Papers 1851–52. In Collections of Bancroft Library, University of California, Berkeley.

SAN FRANCISCO COMMITTEE OF VIGILANCE, 1856, Papers. In Collections of the Bancroft Library, University of California, Berkeley.

San Francisco Infant Shelter. (Bound pamphlet.) In the Phelan Collection, Bancroft Library, University of California, Berkeley. San Francisco, 1927.

The San Francisco, Oakland and Alameda Business Directory. N.p., 1880.

San Francisco, Pamphlets on Cemeteries, Chinese in California, Chinese Immigration (1855–93), Churches, Clubs, Courts, Libraries (1860–99), Negroes in California, Parks, Politics and Government, Streets, and Miscellaneous Topics. In Collections of the Bancroft Library, University of California, Berkeley.

SAN FRANCISCO PERMANENT FREE MARKET COMMITTEE. *The Free Public Market on the San Francisco Waterfront.* San Francisco, 1898.

SAN FRANCISCO SOCIETY FOR THE PREVENTION OF CRUELTY TO ANIMALS. *Thirty-Fourth Annual Report,* 1902.

SAN FRANCISCO YACHT CLUB. *The First One Hundred Years of the San Francisco Yacht Club* (yearbook). San Francisco, 1970.

SAUM, LEWIS O. "Frenchmen, Englishmen, and the Indian," *The American West,* Vol. 1, No. 4 (Fall, 1964).

SAXTON, ALEXANDER. *The Indispensable Enemy: Labor and the Anti-Chinese Movement in California.* Berkeley: University of California Press, 1971.

SCHAEFER, ANTON HENRY. Municipal Railroads of San Francisco. Unpublished manuscript (1920's), Bancroft Library, University of California, Berkeley.

SCHLIEMANN, HEINRICH. *Schliemann's First Visit to America 1850–51,* ed. Shirley H. Weber. Cambridge, Mass.: Harvard University Press, 1942.

SCHMÖLDER, B. *The Emigrant's Guide to California.* London: P. Richardson, [1849?].

SCHOCK, JIM. *San Francisco: A Time and Place for Everything.* San Francisco: Unicorn Publishing Co., 1959.

SCOTT, REVA. *Samuel Brannan and the Golden Fleece.* New York: Macmillan, 1944.

SELVIN, DAVID F. *The Other San Francisco.* New York: Seabury Press, 1969.

SHAW, WILLIAM. *Golden Dreams and Waking Realities: Being the Adventures of a Gold-seeker in California and the Pacific Islands.* London: Smith, Elder and Co., 1851.

SHINN, CHARLES HOWARD. *Graphic Description of Pacific Coast Outlaws, Thrilling Exploits of Their Arch-Enemy, Sheriff Harry N. Morse.* Los Angeles: Westernlore Press, 1958.

———."Land Laws of Mining Districts," *Johns Hopkins University Studies in Historical and Political Science,* 2d series, Vol. 12 (December, 1884).

———. *Mining Camps: A Study in American Frontier Government.* New York: Alfred A. Knopf, 1948.

SHUMATE, ALBERT. *A Visit to Rincon Hill and South Park.* San Francisco: Privately printed by Yerba Buena Chapter of E Clampus Vitus, 1963.

SIMON, ANDRÉ. *Wine and Spirits.* London: Duckworth, 1919.

SMITH, HENRY NASH. *Virgin Land: The American West as Symbol and Myth.* New York: Vintage Books, 1957.

A Social Manual for San Francisco and Oakland. San Francisco: The City Publishing Co., 1884.

SOULÉ, FRANK, JOHN H. GIHON, and JAMES NISBET. *The Annals of San Francisco.* New York: D. Appleton & Co., 1855.

The Sportsman's Club of California. *List of Members of the Sportsman's Club of California, and the Game Laws of the State of California.* San Francisco, 1878.

STANFORD, SALLY. *The Lady of the House.* New York: G. P. Putnam's Sons, 1966.

STARR, KEVIN. *Americans and the California Dream 1850–1915.* New York: Oxford University Press, 1973.

STELLMAN, LOUIS J. *Sam Brannan: Builder of San Francisco.* New York: Exposition Press, 1953.

STERN, MADELEINE B. "Anton Rowan," *California Historical Society Quarterly,* Vol. 28, No. 1 (March, 1949), pp. 1–18.

STEVENSON, ROBERT LOUIS. *San Francisco, A Modern Cosmopolis.* San Francisco: Book Club of California, 1963.

———. *The Silverado Squatters.* London: Chatto and Windus, 1883.

STEWART, GEORGE R. *Committee of Vigilance: Revolution in San Francisco, 1851.* Boston: Houghton Mifflin, 1964.

———. *Good Lives.* Boston: Houghton Mifflin, 1967.

———. *Names on the Land: A Historical Account of Place-naming in the United States,* rev. and enlarged ed. Boston: Houghton Mifflin, 1958.

STILLMAN, JACOB DAVIS BABCOCK. *Around the Horn to California in 1849.* Palo Alto: Lewis Osborne, 1967.

———. *The Gold Rush Letters of J. D. B. Stillman.* Palo Alto: Lewis Osborne, 1967.

———. *Seeking the Golden Fleece.* Palo Alto: Lewis Osborne, 1967.

STODDARD, CHARLES WARREN. *In Old Bohemia: Memories of San Francisco in the Sixties.* San Francisco: N.p., n.d.

The Stranger's Guide to the City of San Francisco. San Francisco: Bacon and Co., 1875.

SUGGS, ROBERT C. *The Archaeology of San Francisco.* New York: Thomas Y. Crowell, 1965.

SUTTER, JOHN AUGUSTUS. *The Diary of Johann August Sutter,* intro. by Douglas S. Watson. San Francisco: The Grabhorn Press, 1932.

———. Personal Reminiscences, 1876, recorded by H. H. Bancroft (typed transcript). In Collections of Bancroft Library, University of California, Berkeley.

———, with explanatory note by Charles L. Camp. "Sutter Writes of the Gold Discovery," *California Historical Society Quarterly,* Vol. 11, No. 1 (March, 1932), pp. 42–43.

SWANBERG, W. A. *Citizen Hearst: A Biography of William Randolph Hearst.* New York: Charles Scribner's Sons, 1961.

SWASEY, WILLIAM F. *The Early Days and Men of California.* Oakland: Pacific Press Publishing Co., 1891.

———. *New Helvetia Diary* (a record kept by John Sutter and his clerks, September, 1845, to May 25, 1848). San Francisco: Grabhorn Press and Society of California Pioneers, 1939.

TAPER, BERNARD, ed. *Mark Twain's San Francisco.* New York: McGraw-Hill, 1963.

TAYLOR, BAYARD. *Eldorado: or Adventures in the Path of Empire.* New York: Alfred A. Knopf, 1949.

TAYLOR, REVEREND WILLIAM. *California Life Illustrated.* New York: Carlton and Porter, 1858.

———. *Seven Years' Street Preaching in San Francisco.* New York: Carlton and Porter, 1856.

TAYS, GEORGE. Telegraph Hill (unpublished manuscript, 1936). In Bancroft Library, University of California, Berkeley.

THOMAS, GORDON, and MAY MORGAN WITTS. *San Francisco Earthquake.* New York: Dell Publishing Co., 1971.

THOMAS, LATELY. *A Debonair Scoundrel: An Episode in the Moral History of San Francisco.* New York: Holt, Rinehart and Winston, 1962.

———. *Sam Ward: King of the Lobby.* Boston: Houghton Mifflin, 1965.

THURMAN, SUE BAILEY. *Pioneers of Negro Origin in California.* San Francisco: Acme Publishing Co., 1952.

TODD, FRANK MORTON. *The Chamber of Commerce Handbook for San Francisco, 1914.* San Francisco: Chamber of Commerce, 1914.

———. *Eradicating Plague from San Francisco.* Report of the Citizen's Health Committee. San Francisco: C. A. Murdock & Co., 1909.

TOMPKINS, E. BERKELEY. "Black Ahab: William T. Shorey, Whaling Master," *California Historical Society Quarterly,* Vol. 51, No. 1 (Spring, 1972), pp. 75–83.

Transactions of the California State Agricultural Society, 1859. Published by resolution of the Legislature of the State of California, 11th session. Sacramento: C. T. Botts, State Printer, 1860.

TRANSPORTATION TECHNICAL COMMITTEE. *History of Public Transit in San Francisco, 1850–1948.* San Francisco: Department of Public Works, 1948.

TWAIN, MARK. *Roughing It,* from the *Complete Works of Mark Twain,* Vol. 6. New York: Harper Bros., 1913. 24 vols.

UNDERHILL, REUBEN LUKENS. *From Cowhides to Golden Fleece: A Narrative of California, 1832–1858.* Stanford: Stanford University Press, 1946.

UPHAM, SAMUEL CURTIS. *Notes of a Voyage to California via Cape Horn.* Philadelphia: Published by the author, 1878.

VAIL, WESLEY D. *Victorians.* San Francisco: W. D. Vail, 1964.

VANCOUVER, CAPTAIN GEORGE. *A Voyage of Discovery to the North Pacific Ocean and Round the World,* Vol. 3. London: John Stockdale, Piccadilly, 1801.

VAN DER ZEE, JOHN. *The Greatest Men's Party on Earth.* New York: Harcourt, Brace, Jovanovich, 1974.

VAN ORMAN, RICHARD A. "The Bard in the West," *Western Historical Quarterly,* Vol. 5, No. 1 (January, 1974).

WAGNER, HENRY R. *Sir Francis Drake's Voyage Around the World.* San Francisco: John Howell, 1926.

WALKER, FRANKLIN. *San Francisco's Literary Frontier.* New York: Alfred A. Knopf, 1939.

——. *The Seacoast of Bohemia.* San Francisco: Book Club of California, 1966.

WARD, JOHN WILLIAM. *Red, White, and Blue: Men, Books, and Ideas in American Culture.* New York: Oxford University Press, 1969.

WARE, JOSEPH E. *The Emigrants' Guide to California* (reprinted from 1849 edition), intro. and notes by John Caughey. Princeton: Princeton University Press, 1932.

WATERMAN, T. T. "Ishi, the Last Yahi," *California Indians: A Source Book,* eds. R. F. Heizer and A. Whipple. Berkeley: University of California Press, 1951.

WATSON, DOUGLAS S. "The Great Express Extra of the California Star of April 1, 1848," *California Historical Society Quarterly,* Vol. 11, No. 2 (June, 1932), pp. 129–37.

——, trans. "Millions for a Cent! Gold Mines of California," *California Historical Society Quarterly,* Vol. 11, No. 1 (March, 1932), pp. 40–41.

——. "Sam Brannan, Herald of the Gold Rush," *California Historical Society Quarterly,* Vol. 10, No. 3 (September, 1931).

——. "The San Francisco McAllisters," *California Historical Society Quarterly,* Vol. 11, No. 2 (June, 1932), pp. 124–28.

——. "Spurious Californiana. 'Four Months Among the Gold Finders.'" [Henry Vizetelly's Confession to an Astounding Literary Hoax], *California Historical Society Quarterly,* Vol. 11 (March, 1932), pp. 65–68.

——, George D. Lyman, and Helen T. Pratt; "Report on the First House in Yerba Buena," *California Historical Society Quarterly,* Vol. 11 (1932), pp. 73–78.

WATSON, MARY. "San Francisco Society; Its Characters and Its Characteristics." In Descriptive Pamphlets on San Francisco in Collections of Bancroft Library, University of California, Berkeley. San Francisco: Francis, Valentine & Co., 1887.

WECTER, DIXON. *The Saga of American Society: A Record of Social Aspiration 1807–1937.* New York: Charles Scribner's Sons, 1937.

WELLS, EVELYN. *Fremont Order.* New York: D. Appleton-Century Co., 1936.

WENTWORTH, MAY, ed. *Poetry of the Pacific.* San Francisco: Pacific Publishing Co., 1867.

Western Jewry. San Francisco: Published by Congregation Emanu-El, 1906.

WHEAT, CARL I. *Books of the California Gold Rush.* San Francisco: Colt Press, 1949.

————, ed. *Pictorial Humor of the Gold Rush.* Keepsake Series, Part 2. San Francisco: Book Club of California, 1953.

WHEELER, ALFRED. *Land Titles in San Francisco, and the Laws Affecting the Same.* N.p., 1852.

WHITNEY, JAMES AMAZIAH. *The Chinese and the Chinese Question.* New York: Thompson and Moreau, 1880.

WILL AND FINCK COMPANY. Price List. San Francisco, n.d.

WILLIAMS, JAMES. *Life and Adventures of James Williams.* San Francisco: Women's Union Printers, 1873.

WILLIAMS, MARY FLOYD. *History of the San Francisco Committee of Vigilance of 1851.* Berkeley: University of California Press, 1921.

————, ed. *Papers of the San Francisco Committee of Vigilance.* Berkeley: University of California Press, 1919.

WILLIAMS, SAMUEL. *The City of the Golden Gate: A Description of San Francisco in 1875.* San Francisco: The Book Club of California, 1921.

WILSON, CAROL GREEN. *Chinatown Quest: The Life and Adventures of Donaldina Cameron.* Stanford: Stanford University Press, 1931.

————. *Gump's Treasure Trade.* New York: Thomas Y. Crowell Co., 1949.

WILTSEE, ERNEST A. "Hawes and Company's San Francisco and New York Express," *California Historical Society Quarterly,* Vol. 11, No. 1 (March, 1932), pp. 30–32.

WOOD, JOHN H., comp. *Seventy-Five Years of History of the Mechanics' Institute of San Francisco.* San Francisco: Mechanics' Institute, 1930.

WOODBRIDGE, JOHN and SALLY. *Buildings of the Bay Area.* New York: Grove Press, 1960.

WRIGHT, DORIS MARION. "The Making of Cosmopolitan California," *California Historical Society Quarterly,* Vol. 19 (1940).

WRIGHT, LOUIS B. *Culture on the Moving Frontier.* Bloomington: Indiana University Press, 1955.

YOUNG, JOHN PHILIP. *Journalism in California, and Pacific Coast and Exposition Biographies.* San Francisco: Chronicle Publishing Co., 1915.

———. *San Francisco: A History of the Pacific Coast Metropolis.* San Francisco: The S. J. Clarke Publishing Co. [1912]. 2 vols.

ZARCHIN, MICHAEL M. *Glimpses of Jewish Life in San Francisco,* 2d rev. ed. Oakland: Judah L. Magnes Memorial Museum, 1964.

ZIEGLER, WILBUR GLEASON. *Story of the Earth Quake and Fire.* San Francisco: Leon C. Osteyer, Press of Morris and Blair, 1906.

Besides the specific references cited in the Notes, I used a number of newspapers and periodicals in the preparation of the work, among them:

Alta California, American West, California Historical Society Quarterly and *Notes, California Star, Call-Bulletin, Cry California, Daily Alta California* (see *Alta California*), *Daily Herald and Mirror, Elevator, Mirror of the Times,* Philadelphia *Public Ledger,* Sacramento *Bee,* San Francisco *Call,* San Francisco *Magazine,* San Francisco *Chronicle,* San Francisco *Examiner, Saturday Review, Society of California Pioneers Quarterly, Voice of Israel (Kol Yisra'el), Wassaja.*

I also found many useful materials—memorabilia, prints, pictures, letter sheets, and the like—among the Collections of the California State Library in Sacramento, the Judah L. Magnes Memorial Museum in Berkeley, the Special Collections Department of the San Francisco Public Library, the Chinese Historical Society in San Francisco, the Oakland Museum, the San Francisco Negro and Cultural Society in San Francisco, the Silverado Museum in St. Helena, California, the Wells Fargo History Room in San Francisco, the San Francisco Maritime Museum, the Society of California Pioneers in San Francisco, and in particular the Bancroft Library at the University of California in Berkeley.

INDEX

San Francisco
circa 1850's

(Golden Gate)
FORT POINT THE PRESIDIO FORT MASON
SEAL ROCKS
CLIFF HOUSE GOLDEN GATE PARK (AREA OF DETAIL MAP)
San Fra...

N

FORT POINT
THE PRESIDIO
FORT MASON

JEFFERSON STREET
Meig's Wharf (PROJECTED)
BEACH
PIONEER WOOLEN MILLS
NORTH PT (1849-'50)
Approximate, Extent of Bay Fill, after 1850
STREET
BAY
(Original Shore line)
FRANCISCO
STREET
CHESTNUT
329 DIVISADERO ST. (ABNER PHELPS HOUSE)
LOMBARD
STREET
GREENBUSH
North Beach
FILBERT
STREET
TELEGRAPH (SIGNAL)
Telegraph Hill
UNION STREET
OCTOGON HOUSE (1861)
Washington Square
Cowell's Wharf
GREEN
FEUSIER OCTOGON HOUSE
BULL FIGHT RING
ST. FRANCIS OF ASSISI CHURCH
Law's Wharf
VALLEJO
Russian Hill
TEMPLE EMANU-EL
Little Chile
Sydney Town
Buckelew's Wharf
Cunningham's Wharf
BROADWAY
SHERITH ISRAEL
The Barbary Coast
BANK OF LUCAS TURNER
FORT MONTGOMERY
Clark's Point
Broadway Wharf
GHIRARDELLI BLDG.
Pacific Street Wharf
PACIFIC
Chinatown
GOLDEN ERA
HOTALING BLDG. (1866)
"EUPHEMIA"
Jackson St. Wharf
1 CITY HALL, (JENNY LIND THEATRE)
2 PARKER HOUSE
3 ELDORADO
4 WASHINGTON HALL
5 ALTA
6 BELLA UNION
7 CALIFORNIA STAR
JACKSON
CHINESE THEATRES
CHINESE
OPERA HOUSE
Monky Block
POST OFFICE (1854)
MERCHANT'S EXCHANGE
Washington St. Wharf
WASHINGTON
Spring Valley
Portsmouth Square
WM RICHARDSON'S HOUSE
JACOB LEESE'S HOUSE (ST. FRANCIS HOTEL)
"APOLLO"
Clay Street Wharf
CLAY
Nob Hill (Fern Hill)
CITY HOTEL (BROWN'S)
FIRST PUBLIC SCHOOL
THE MINT (ORIG.)
"NIANTIC"
Central Wharf
SACRAMENTO
OLD ST. MARY'S
ENGINE CO. #1
ENGINE CO. #5
FORT GUNNYBAGS (1856)
Howison's Wharf
Market Stree... Wh...
CALIFORNIA
Wells Fargo
California St. Whf.
1 PACIFIC CLUB (1852)
2 UNION CLUB (1865)
3 BANK OF CALIFORNIA (18...
4 AMERICAN THEATRE
5 OVERLAND MONTHLY (18...
6 LEIDESDORFF'S WAREH...
7 LEIDESDORFF'S COTTA...
8 MAGUIRE'S ACADEMY OF MUSIC
PINE
CALIFORNIA MARKET
NEVADA BANK (1875)
RUSS HOUSE (1865)
ORIENTAL HOTEL
BUSH
CALLE DE LA FUNDACION (1835)
ENGINE CO. #2
MERCANTILE LIBRARY BLDG.
OCCIDENTAL HOTEL
TIVOLI GARDENS
SUTTER
OLYMPIC CLUB (ORIG. 1860)
MECHANIC'S LIBRARY (1866)
LICK HOUSE (1862)
TOLL HOUSE
POST
Union Sq.
GEARY
SEAL ROCKS CLIFF HOUSE GOLDEN GATE PARK
GRAND HOTEL (1869)
ORIGINAL ST. PATRICK'S CHURCH (PALACE HOTEL 1875)
(Original Shorel...
O'FARRELL
ELLIS
ST. PATRICK'S CHURCH (NEW 1872)
Happy Valley
Pleasant Valley
EDDY
BALDWIN HOTEL
TURK
TYLER
MISSION ROAD
Rincon Point
MAC ALLISTER STREET
YERBA BUENA CEMETERY
MISSION DOLORES
BATTLE MOUNTAIN
OLD RACE TRACKS
BULL-FIGHT RINGS
South Park
GROVE
MARKET
WOODWARD'S GARDENS (1866)
THE WILLOWS
HUNTERS POINT

Streets: JEFFERSON, BEACH, NORTH PT, BAY, FRANCISCO, CHESTNUT, LOMBARD, GREENBUSH, FILBERT, UNION, GREEN, VALLEJO, BROADWAY, PACIFIC, JACKSON, WASHINGTON, CLAY, SACRAMENTO, CALIFORNIA, PINE, BUSH, SUTTER, POST, GEARY, O'FARRELL, ELLIS, EDDY, TURK, TYLER, MAC ALLISTER, GROVE

COLUMBUS (now) AVENUE
LARKIN, HYDE, LEAVENWORTH, JONES, TAYLOR, MASON, POWELL, STOCKTON, DUPONT (GRANT), KEARNEY, MONTGOMERY, SANSOME, BATTERY, FRONT, DAVIS, FIRST, FREMONT, BEALE, MAIN, SPEAR, STEUART
FIRST, SECOND, THIRD, FOURTH, FIFTH, SIXTH, SEVENTH
MISSION, HOWARD, FOLSOM, HARRISON, BRYANT, BRANNON

A EVENING BULLETIN
B DRAMATIC CHRONICLE (186...)
C CALIFORNIA BANK (1864)
D BOHEMIAN CLUB (1872)
E CUSTOM HOUSE (1854)
F MEDICO-DENTAL BLDG. (186...)
G FLOOD & O'BRIEN'S AUCTION LUNCH
H SCENE, ASSASSINATION, JAMES KING OF WILLIAM
I BANK EXCHANGE SALOON